THE
SECOND
WYCLIFFE
OMNIBUS

THE SECOND WYCLIFFE OMNIBUS

Wycliffe and the Last Rites
Wycliffe and the Dead Flautist
Wycliffe and the Schoolgirls

W. J. BURLEY

VICTOR GOLLANCZ
LONDON

Wycliffe and the Last Rites first published in Great Britain 1992
by Victor Gollancz Ltd, © W. J. Burley 1992
Wycliffe and the Dead Flautist first published in Great Britain 1991
by Victor Gollancz Ltd, © W. J. Burley 1991
Wycliffe and the Schoolgirls first published in Great Britain 1976
by Victor Gollancz Ltd, © W. J. Burley 1976

The Second Wycliffe Omnibus published in Great Britain 1997
by Victor Gollancz
An imprint of the Cassell Group
Wellington House, 125 Strand, London WC2R 0BB

© W. J. Burley 1997

A catalogue record for this book is
available from the British Library.

ISBN 0 575 06481 1

Printed and bound in Finland by Werner Söderström Oy

97 98 99   5 4 3 2 1

Contents

Contents

WYCLIFFE
AND THE SCHOOLGIRLS

Prologue among the schoolgirls

ELAINE

'I can't eat all that, mum.'

'Of course you can, you need a decent breakfast inside you.'

'I shall be sick on the coach.'

Her mother, a little barrel of a woman in a spotless, white overall, stood over her.

'Be sensible, Elaine, you don't know when you'll get your next meal.'

'But I'm taking a picnic lunch to have on the trip.'

'I mean a proper meal.'

Elaine was fifteen, nearly sixteen, short like her mother but well proportioned. She was dark with large, soft eyes but a straight, determined mouth.

'I hope this Miss Russell isn't going to mind you coming dressed like that.'

'The letter said leisure clothes.'

'But jeans and a T-shirt . . .'

'Mother, I've told you, it's what the other girls are wearing.'

The Bennetts' dining room was little more than a wide passage between the bakery and the shop. At one end a glass door with a pattern of incised stars led into the shop; at the other a plank door, painted green, opened into a little yard which led to the bakehouse. There, with two assistants, her father baked the crusty bread and yeast cakes which were the mainstay of the business. A business prosperous enough to pay Elaine's fees at Bishop Fuller's, a rather exclusive day-school for girls.

The plank door was pushed open and Elaine's father came in carrying a wire tray of bread rolls.

'That makes fourteen dozen, do you think that'll be enough, Dot?'

'There's nine dozen ordered . . .'

The shop, the bakery, their house were all one. Elaine was used to it, she had been brought up in the all-pervading, warm, yeasty atmosphere and rarely noticed it. Her mother looked after the shop with the help of a girl who was not much older than Elaine.

Mr Bennett went through with the bread rolls, came back and lingered. He was as tall and thin as his wife was short and fat and he was dusted all over with flour.

'Well, girl, you'll soon be off. Willie will take you to the school in the van. I've told him to pick you up at twenty to nine.' He stooped and kissed his daughter on the forehead. 'Have a good time and look after yourself.' He slipped two one-pound notes into the waistband of her jeans.

'Thanks, dad.'

'You spoil her, Sidney!'

'And why not?'

'Well, she's got enough pocket money already.' But Mrs Bennett's plump features were smiling.

At twenty minutes to nine a curly headed youth of nineteen or twenty pushed open the door from the shop and put his head round, 'Your carriage awaits, madam.'

Elaine kissed her mother and went out to the van. Willie followed carrying an enormous hold-all which was almost bursting at the zip.

ROSALINE

Rosaline Parkin stood with a cup of tea in one hand and a piece of bread-and-jam in the other. She was wearing jeans and a brassiere while her aunt ironed her T-shirt to dry it after a last-minute washing.

'Have you got everything else you want?' Her aunt could not have been more than fifty but her features had long since set in a mould of sadness and resignation. She was pale and she moved with slow deliberation as though any effort taxed her to the limit.

'I packed last night.'

'I suppose you've got enough money?'

'I'll manage.'

The little kitchen was a lean-to, its tiny window looked out on a brick-walled yard and the backs of the houses in the next street. Every minute or two a heavy lorry rumbled down the front street causing the doors and windows to rattle.

Rosaline had the thin, wiry body of a ballet dancer and her skin was white in startling contrast with her mop of jet-black hair. She had high, broad cheek-bones though her face narrowed to a pointed chin giving her a mischievous, elfin look. But her eyes were sullen and her mouth was hard. She had passed the eleven-plus selection test for Cholsey Grammar and she had become friendly with Elaine Bennett through inter-schools hockey. Now they were going on a community holiday with girls from several of the city's schools.

Her aunt finished ironing the shirt and handed it to her; she slipped it on.

'That's it, then. I'll be off.' She picked up a suitcase then dropped it again. 'Christ, I've forgotten my camera!'

'I wish you wouldn't speak like that, Rosaline.'

She dashed upstairs and came down with the camera slung over her shoulder. Her aunt looked at it and shook her head.

'I wish I knew where you got the money to buy that.'

'I worked in the Easter holidays, didn't I?'

'When will you be back?'

'Three weeks, I told you.'

'You'll write?'

'I wouldn't count on it, you know what I am.'

'Have you got your tablets?'

'I haven't had a fit for months.'

'I know that but being away from home . . .'

'Oh, forget it!'

Her aunt followed her to the front door. 'Look after yourself.' She stood watching while her niece walked up the dismal little street to the bus stop on the corner.

JANE

The kitchen at 37 Oakshott Avenue glowed in the morning sunshine; primrose-yellow walls, white and chromium fittings. The Rendells were at breakfast, seated round a plastic-topped table.

'You'll telephone if there's anything you want, Jane?'

'Yes, mother.'

'Are you sure you've had enough breakfast?'

'I couldn't eat any more.'

'Another cup of coffee?'

'No, thanks.'

'You usually have two cups.'

Jane's father intervened. 'She might not want to, love, going on a long coach trip.'

Jane was small for her age, thin and underdeveloped. She had straight, dark hair and a sad little face which might have been used in an appeal on behalf of deprived children. But with Jane it was heredity, she was like her mother.

'You're sure you've got enough spending money?' Her father was a grave, anxious man, almost morbidly meticulous.

'Yes, thank you, daddy.'

Jane went to the School of the Sacred Heart, a Catholic school though the Rendells were not Catholics.

'All the girls come from good homes and the fees are reasonable.'

Jane wore her school uniform, a black blazer with the school badge and a blue and white summer dress.

'The sisters said it would be best to wear school uniform

on the trip but to take casual clothes to wear when we get there.'

'We shall miss you, Jane.' Mr Rendell's large hand closed over his daughter's and squeezed affectionately.

'I shall miss you, daddy.'

'Don't make her cry, Jim, she's going to enjoy herself. I've put a dozen postcards in your bag all stamped and addressed. If you haven't got time to write you can always pop one of those in the post.'

'Yes, mother.'

'You'll have Barbara Brooks for company.' Barbara was the only other girl from the School of the Sacred Heart who would be going on the holiday. 'You've always liked Barbara, haven't you?'

'I'll be all right, mother.'

'It's lucky it's a Saturday and that your father can take you to the school. If it had been a weekday we should have needed a taxi.'

It was a strange atmosphere. In the Rendell household nobody ever spoke a harsh word but all three of them seemed to be permanently tense. Harmony on taut strings.

Mr Rendell looked at his watch. 'Twenty-five to. We've got to pick up Barbara so it's time we were going.'

A pale-blue Cortina, six years old but looking like new, stood at the gate. Mr Rendell carried his daughter's case.

'Sure you've got everything?'

Mrs Rendell was crying. She hugged her daughter, clutching at her thin little body.

SHEILA

The Jukeses lived on a council estate—14 Stoke's Road, in the Cholsey district of the city. Sheila was the youngest of three, her two brothers worked as machinists in a factory where her father was a welder. To everybody's surprise and

13

tolerant amusement, Sheila had passed the eleven-plus test for Cholsey Grammar.

On Saturday mornings it was unusual for anybody to be up before ten or half-past so Sheila had the living room to herself. She was scraping butter on to slices of cut bread and slapping slivers of cooked ham between them. Sheila was plump with a large behind and a prominent bosom. Her jeans did not meet her blouse and a pink roll of flesh bridged the gap. She gathered her sandwiches into a polythene bag and put them in a haversack then she went to the bottom of the stairs.

'Mam!'

'What is it now?'

'I can't find my wedge heels.'

'They're in your wardrobe.'

'No, I've looked.'

Her mother muttered something inaudible.

Sheila went to the open dresser on which china was kept and took down a soup tureen from the top shelf. She lifted the lid and disclosed a number of crumpled one and five-pound notes. She slipped one of the fivers into the pocket of her jeans then, after a moment of hesitation, added three singles. Then she put the tureen back in its place.

There was a sound of footsteps on the stairs and her mother came in. She was Sheila thirty years on, her heavy breasts scarcely concealed by her nightgown, her features almost lost in fat. The first cigarette of the day hung from her lips. She dropped Sheila's wedge heels on the table.

'Where did you find 'em?'

'In the bloody wardrobe where I said. You don't look.' She glanced round the room and yawned. 'Any tea?'

'In the pot, it's not long made.'

Her mother poured herself a cup of tea. 'How you off for money?'

'I took eight quid out of the dish, is that all right?'

'Christ, your father gave you a fiver, you aren't going to the Costa del bloody Sol.'

'It's three weeks, mam.'

Mrs Jukes looked at the clock. 'You'll be late.'

'Tony said he'd take me on his bike.'

'Tony's still in bed.'

Sheila went to the bottom of the stairs and yelled. 'Tony!'

'What is it?'

'You got to take me to the school.'

Eventually Tony came downstairs, his eyes full of sleep, dressed in jeans and a shirt. 'O.K. Let's get it over with.'

Mrs Jukes stood in the doorway in her nightdress to see them off. The bike roared down the road with Sheila bouncing on the back, clinging to her brother with one hand and her haversack with the other.

The coach with twenty-four schoolgirls and a mistress on board sped along the A35. It was a hot, August afternoon but, because it was a Saturday, there was little traffic. Miss Dorothy Russell, thirty-nine years old, sat in front by the driver. She wore a light-blue dress patterned with huge white daisies which confused but did nothing to soften the aggressive angularity of her figure. She had light, brown hair, cut short and kinked at the ends to make it turn inwards; her features were small and sharp and she had a tiny mouth with thin lips.

'In a few minutes the old Roman road joins us, the one which led from Isca, that is Exeter, to Durnovaria which was their name for Dorchester.'

The girls looked out on the green landscape of subtle contours and unexpected shadows thinking their own thoughts. In the back seat Rosaline Parkin sat with Sheila Jukes and Elaine Bennett. Rosaline drew surreptitiously on a cigarette and let the smoke trickle slowly from her lips in a thin, grey spiral. Once she passed the cigarette to Elaine who almost gave the game away by a fit of violent coughing. Miss Russell turned round.

'Are you all right, Elaine?'

'Yes, thank you, Miss Russell.'

'She nearly swallowed the hole in her Polo mint,' Rosaline said.

There was a general laugh.

Miss Russell, who had not taught for seventeen years for ·nothing, remarked that she hoped it wouldn't prove carcinogenic.

'We are staying near Maiden Castle, a famous Iron Age fortress which fell to Vespasian in the first century A.D. Vespasian eventually became emperor.'

'Bully for him!' Rosaline muttered but only loud enough to be heard in the back seats.

Jane, with her friend, Barbara Brooks, sat primly in the seat behind Miss Russell, the only ones in more or less formal dress. Barbara was a complete contrast to Jane, she was pink skinned and she had kept a lot of her puppy fat though a figure was beginning to struggle through. Miss Russell turned to speak to them.

'Have you done the history of the Roman occupation at your school?'

Jane answered. 'No, Miss Russell, we did the eighteenth and nineteenth centuries for "O" level.'

'But when you were younger, surely ...'

'Oh, yes, I think we did about it in the third form but I've forgotten.' Jane blushed at the admission.

'You must read it up; Dorset is a most interesting county for that period.'

'Yes, Miss Russell.'

There was a derisive chuckle from further back.

The coach slowed down then turned off the main road into a narrow lane which had passing places at intervals. They jolted along for about half a mile then pulled into a gravelled drive which led to a gaunt, two-storeyed house with a pillared porch from which stucco was peeling.

'Well, girls, this is home for the next three weeks.'

The coach came to a standstill, the driver climbed down.

Miss Russell stood while the girls trooped past her and out of the coach to gather in chattering groups on the gravel.

'Looks a crummy joint to me,' Rosaline said. 'God help us if we can't get into Dorchester in the evenings.'

'Get your baggage from the boot of the coach and assemble in the front hall.'

'How far is it?' Elaine asked.

Rosaline's thoughts had moved on. 'How far is what?'

'Dorchester.'

'Three miles.'

'We could walk, I suppose.'

Rosaline opened her dark eyes wide. 'Listen to the girl! Walk, she says. You should see me. There must be some farm lout or somebody with a car or even a motor bike.' She looked round the deserted countryside with obvious misgivings. 'We shall have to get organised.'

The hall was bare with a floor made of stone flags which extended down a passage on each side of a rather impressive staircase. There was no carpet on the stairs and the treads were badly worn. Miss Russell stood on the third stair to talk to them.

'Well, this is it! I hope that we shall all enjoy the next three weeks. I want us all to get to know each other better and to learn to live together as a community. There are five of the city's schools represented in our party, all day-schools, and we shall probably find by the end of our stay that we have made new friends, had a few corners knocked off and learned something about ourselves.

'There are a few rules which I shall post on the notice board and I want you to keep strictly to them. They are not unreasonable and should not stop you enjoying yourselves.'

'Fat chance!' Sheila Jukes muttered. 'Stuck out here in the bloody wilds. She said it was near the town.'

'Are there any buses into town, Miss Russell?'

'Yes, quite a good service for a rural area. There is a bus stop about a hundred yards beyond the point where we turned off from the main road. But, and I must emphasise this as one

17

of our most important rules, no one goes into town without getting my permission first.'

There was a general groan and Miss Russell moved up another step to command her audience more effectively.

'Quiet, please, girls. I want to give you some more details.

'There are two dormitories and twelve girls will sleep in each. Pamela O'Brien and Rosaline Parkin, will you come here, please?'

A slim girl with red-gold hair and freckles joined Rosaline to stand demurely a step or two below Miss Russell.

'I have a list of girls who will sleep in each dormitory and there will be no changes without my approval. The girls in each dormitory will be answerable to Pamela and Rosaline respectively, not only in the dormitories but in all matters concerning discipline while we are here.' Miss Russell cleared her throat. 'I will post the lists with a copy of the rules on the notice board.'

Miss Russell looked slowly round the group. 'Are there any questions?'

No one spoke.

Miss Russell came down the stairs and went over to the notice board of moth-eaten green baize to pin up the sheets. The girls crowded round to read them.

The dormitories were in the front of the house, each with two tall sash-windows looking out over the Dorsetshire countryside. The ceilings were ornamented with plaster mouldings and the skirtings were almost two feet high.

'Lady Chatterley summons Mellors to her boudoir,' Rosaline said, glancing round at the evidence of former elegance.

'You don't have beds in boudoirs.' Sheila Jukes flopped down on one of the twelve black-iron bedsteads.

'No? You do things your way and I'll do things mine.'

The two girls who had sat so primly on the coach were standing near Rosaline, waiting to be noticed.

'What do you want?'

Once more Jane was the spokesman. 'We want to know which beds we are to have.'

18

Rosaline looked them over appraisingly. 'Are you the Sacred Heart lot?'

'That's right.'

'Did they tell you to dress like that?'

'They said we should wear school uniform on the trip.'

'Christ!' She glanced along the rows of beds. 'You'd better have the two beds at the end—not that end—by the door. What are you called?'

'I'm Jane Rendell and this is Barbara Brooks.'

Rosaline shrugged. 'Too much for me, I shall call you Buttercup and Daisy.'

They had a meal at six-thirty and when the meal was over Miss Russell said, 'Now you have the rest of the evening to settle in. Bed at ten, lights out a ten-thirty.' She smiled. 'I should like to see Rosaline and Pamela in my room for a few minutes. My room is upstairs on the main corridor and my name is on the door.' She paused for a moment, then added, 'There is a games room at the back of the ground floor next to the showers and toilets.'

'May we go into Dorchester this evening, Miss Russell?'

'Not tonight, Sheila, let's all use tonight to get really settled in.'

Rosaline Parkin, Elaine Bennett and Sheila Jukes had taken possession of beds at the far end of the dormitory. The two girls from the Sacred Heart were at the other end, by the door. They undressed demurely, careful not to expose their bodies while Sheila Jukes stormed about wearing only pyjama trousers and looking for the top.

'Which of you bastards nicked my top?'

At ten-thirty sharp, Rosaline called up the room, 'Put the lights out Buttercup.'

Jane got out of bed and flicked the two switches leaving the room in darkness except for the pale lights coming in through the tall windows. Five minutes later Miss Russell opened the door.

'That's splendid, all of you; good-night, girls.'

'Good-night, Miss Russell.'

They could hear her footsteps until they stopped at the door of her room.

'All right, Buttercup.'

'What?'

'Put the lights on, you fool, she's gone, hasn't she?'

The trio put a table between the rows of beds and settled down to pontoon.

'Penny points.'

'I haven't got any change.'

'Neither have I.'

'All right, we'll play for matches and settle up in the morning.'

It was the first time Jane and her friend had slept away from home except when they were on holiday with their parents. Jane lay in bed staring up at the elaborately moulded ceiling-rose from which a thin flex dangled absurdly.

Between hands Elaine Bennett said, 'What did she want you and O'Brien for?'

'Pep talk.'

Jukes said, 'And?'

'And nothing as far as I'm concerned. I left O'Brien there. I've had enough of that.' She studied her cards, 'Twist.' She took a card. 'And again.' She took another. 'And again —damn!' She threw her cards down. 'Bust!'

'Enough of what?' Elaine enquired.

'What do you think? Do you want me to draw a map? Our Rusty is one of those. Silly old cow, but I'll fix her.'

'Gosh, I don't think any of ours are like that.'

'Well, we've only got the one and that's enough.' She adopted a grotesque travesty of Miss Russell's speech. "I want you to think of me as the mother you lost, dear..." Hands like a randy billy goat.'

'Billy goats don't have hands.'

'No? Well, dear, you should know about such things.' Rosaline looked at her watch. 'Are we playing this silly game or going to bed?'

It was after midnight when the lights finally went out and

some time later when Jane went to sleep, troubled in her mind.

Next morning, after breakfast, she tapped on Miss Russell's door.

'Come in.'

Miss Russell was standing in front of the dressing table mirror, doing her hair.

'What is it, Jane?'

'There's something I think you should know, Miss Russell. Some of the girls were playing cards last night until twelve o'clock—for money.'

Miss Russell continued back-combing her skimpy hair. 'Rosaline Parkin is in charge of your dormitory, Jane, you should talk to her about it.'

'But she was one of the girls playing, Miss Russell.'

Miss Russell put down her comb and came over. 'Now listen to me, Jane. You are here to learn something about living in a community and one of the things you should learn is self-reliance, another is loyalty. If some of the girls were doing what you say they were doing it was very wrong of them. But it is also wrong of you to come tale-bearing to me. Do you understand?'

'Yes, Miss Russell.'

'Then run along.'

As she reached the door Miss Russell called her back. As a good Anglican she had deeply-rooted suspicions of Roman Catholic institutions. 'I expect you are encouraged to do this sort of thing at your school?'

'I don't know, Miss Russell.'

'Well, you certainly will not be popular if you do it here.'

That night when Jane sat on her bed to take off her shoes the head and foot collapsed and she thudded on the floor while the whole dormitory laughed. She realised that Miss Russell had not kept her confidence but she did not suspect that there was worse to come. The next night her bed was soaking wet and she had to double up with her friend, Barbara.

On the fourth day Jane went to see Miss Russell again, this time her lips and her voice were trembling.

'I wanted to ask you if I may change with one of the girls in the other dormitory, Miss Russell.'

'No, Jane, you may not. You started off in a very foolish way and brought on yourself whatever it is that is happening to you now. You must take it in good part and make the best of it. If you start running away from the consequences of your own actions there is no knowing where it will end.'

Miss Russell looked at the thin, anaemic girl with a distaste which she could barely conceal. 'It is for your own good, Jane.'

'Yes, Miss Russell.'

The days were not so bad. They tramped all over Maiden Castle, they made two trips into Dorchester and saw the room where Judge Jeffreys is supposed to have conducted his 'bloody assize', the Shire Hall where the Tolpuddle Martyrs were tried and the County museum.

'We shall come again and devote a whole day to Hardy,' Miss Russell promised.

Pamela O'Brien seemed to take pity on the two girls from the Sacred Heart and made it her business to see that they were included in all that went on. Jane, emboldened by her kindness, confided her troubles but Pamela's response was disappointing.

'Oh, you don't want to worry too much about our Rosie, her bark is worse than her bite. If you put up with it for a bit she'll soon get tired.'

'It's not only her, it's the three of them,' Jane complained.

'Yes, well, they do stick together.'

The remainder of the three weeks stretched ahead interminably. She considered ringing her parents but she knew how upset they would be.

'We've been selfish, Jane, dear. We've kept you too much to ourselves instead of letting you mix with girls of your own age.'

Miss Russell's exercise in communal living had seemed

22

like the answer to their particular need and they had paid the fifteen pounds, which they could ill afford, just as they paid Jane's school fees at the Sacred Heart, to give her the chance to grow up amongst 'nice' girls.

The climax came over the showers. Miss Russell's rules required that the girls should take a shower each morning, one dormitory between seven and seven-thirty and the other between seven-thirty and eight. They alternated on different days. Communal showers, after games, were common-place to the other girls but such things were unknown at the Sacred Heart and Jane planned with Barbara to get up at six-thirty and so secure their privacy. In fact, Barbara liked her bed too much and so, each morning, in her dressing gown, carrying towel and soap, Jane stole downstairs alone. She was always back in the dormitory by the time the other girls began to stir and it seemed that nobody had noticed.

One morning, a week after their arrival, Jane went down to the showers as usual. Although sunshine was already streaming through the front windows the back of the house was still dimly lit and the whole place was as silent as the grave so that even a creaking stair made a startling noise. She hung up her dressing gown and pyjamas, threw her towel on top, kicked off her slippers and made for the nearest shower. She had just turned the mixing valve when Elaine Bennett dashed through from the direction of the lavatories, snatched up all Jane's things and rushed out leaving the door swinging. Jane was left wet and naked without even a towel. She did not panic but began a systematic search to see if there was anything she could wear or use to dry herself. She found a face-towel which somebody had left behind, dried herself roughly and then used it to cover herself as well as she could. She crept along the passage and up the stairs without meeting anyone until she reached the door of the dormitory.

'Here she is!' Sheila Jukes's voice.

The door was slammed and locked in her face. She could hear them giggling. She was about to try the other dormitory,

23

to ask Pamela O'Brien for help, when Rosaline came sauntering down the corridor, hands in the pockets of her blue, quilted dressing gown, sponge-bag over her arm.

'Hullo, Butters, in trouble?'

She was too near to tears to answer and Rosaline stood, looking at her and smiling. 'Never mind, kid, it's only a joke. Your clothes are in Rusty's room, all you've got to do is to go in and get them.'

'But I can't go in Miss Russell's room like this!'

'Of course you can, she's not there, she's in the staff bathroom and you know how long she takes. Here, I'll come with you.'

A little way from Miss Russell's room Rosaline halted. 'In you go, I'll keep look-out.'

Jane had the door open and was about to go in when Rosaline called, 'Butters!'

She turned and in that instant the camera-flash went off. She gave a little cry and crumpled up where she was, sobbing hysterically.

Rosaline got her back to the dormitory, she was given her clothes and by breakfast time she had recovered sufficiently to go down with the others. In fact she was somewhat relieved, the trio had been nice to her and it seemed at last that she had been forgiven.

The following three days were the pleasantest she had spent since coming to the hostel. As far as she could tell Miss Russell had heard nothing of the incident and it was not referred to again in the dormitory or anywhere else in her hearing. They spent a day at Weymouth where they bathed and, though the weather broke, she enjoyed Miss Russell's conducted tour of the Hardy country. By the time she came down to breakfast on her third Sunday in the hostel she was beginning to feel relaxed and secure.

After breakfast she went, as usual, to look at the notice board and there, in the middle of the board, was an enlargement of the flash-light photograph Rosaline had taken. Standing, holding the knob of the door on which Miss

24

Russell's name was clearly visible, she had half turned to the camera, clutching at the absurd towel with her free hand.

She rushed up to the dormitory only to find another pinned to her locker. They were everywhere, all over the building.

Miss Russell was almost inarticulate with anger. The trio were summoned to her room and interviewed separately while the rest of the girls, including Jane, waited in the dormitories.

Rosaline came back from her interview unruffled.

'What happened?'

'Nothing happened. I said I'd fix her and I have, she's scared out of her tiny mind.'

Jane lay on her bed whimpering while the other girls maintained a deathly silence.

When Jane was called for interview she had a wild hope that she would now be vindicated, seen as the victim of a wicked persecution but the hope soon died. Miss Russell did not give her a chance to open her mouth.

'I do not want to hear anything from you, not one word! If I had the choice I would not have you near me but I have to tell you of the arrangements I have made. In an hour a taxi will arrive to take you to the station in Dorchester where you will be put on a train for home. I have telephoned your parents to expect you. Pamela O'Brien and Joan Simmonds will go with you to the station to see that you get on the train but apart from those two you are to have no contact with any of the girls. You will remain in this room until the taxi arrives and your things will be packed for you.'

CHAPTER ONE

THREE O'CLOCK ON a wet January afternoon. Wycliffe sat at his desk reading an article in an old research bulletin: *Electrostatic Detection of Footprints*. The floor is dusted with minute expanded-polystyrene beads then, provided the omens are favourable, the beads which have not fallen on a recent footprint may easily be blown away while those which are in contact with a print remain to tell their tale.

The truth was that he was bored. For several days after Christmas and into the New Year professional crooks seem to call a truce or, perhaps, they are exhausted by their exertions during the great bonanza. Chief Inspector Gill, his deputy, was taking advantage of the situation to have some time off. Wycliffe felt lethargic and disinclined to settle to the routine of paper-work of which there was plenty. For his lethargy he blamed the heating and ventilating system against which he waged constant war.

He got up and went over to the large window which looked out over a dismal landscaped garden to one of the main highways in and out of the city. Double glazing. The damned thing wouldn't even open and the room was very nearly sound proof. Like being in a padded cell.

Outside rain fell vertically out of a leaden sky, cars trooped nose to tail in ordered lanes, their screen-wipers beating time. . . .

'Futile!'

He would have found it difficult to say exactly what it was that struck him as futile; the cars following each other like sheep, his job, or just life.

He was addicted to staring out of windows but from this

one there was rarely anything to see but the endless streams of traffic. On a good day he might catch sight of the grounds-man clearing litter, weeding or cutting the grass. It was a poor exchange for his old office which had overlooked a small public park where there were mothers and children, lovers and tramps and old gentlemen who each had a special seat on which to sleep in the sunshine. It could not always have been sunny but, in retrospect, it seemed so.

The telephone rang. He sighed and turned back to his desk.

'Wycliffe.'

Sergeant Bourne, his administrative assistant, reported the finding of a body in a flat in one of the new blocks near the city centre.

'Grenville House, sixth floor, a woman dead in suspicious circumstances, sir. The caretaker phoned the local station and they are passing it to us. Inspector Scales is on his way there with D.C. Dixon.'

'What do they mean by "suspicious circumstances"? Why can't they say what they mean?' Wycliffe was irritable.

'Perhaps they're not sure what they mean yet, sir.'

Bourne was good at putting the sting in a soft answer. Anyway it was an excuse to get out of the office.

Grenville House was one of the first fruits of a 'new community policy' for the city centre. Translated, it meant that the council wanted people to go back to live in an area from which the developers had turned them out. Grenville House consisted of fairly expensive flats over shops.

Wycliffe drove slowly in the afternoon traffic. The street lamps were on and, despite the rain, there were crowds of pedestrians milling around between the big stores where the January sales were persuading people to part with the money they had held on to over Christmas.

The entrance to Grenville House was between a furniture shop and a hi-fi establishment. A uniformed constable stepped out of the shelter of the canopied doorway and saluted as Wycliffe parked on the yellow lines.

'Flat 602, sir. Inspector Scales is up there with the doctor.'

The entrance was blue-carpeted, the lift smooth and silent. He got out on the sixth; a carpeted landing with four doors and a corridor with a notice: To Emergency Stairs. The door of 602 was open and in the hall a constable tried to make himself small. A card in a metal frame secured to the door read: Miss Debbie Joyce.

Scales was in the living room, a large room on split levels; up three steps to the dining area and the kitchen beyond. A large window, going almost to the floor, looked out over the grey city which, for the most part, had not yet sprouted above three or four floors. Scales was talking to the doctor who was in shirt sleeves and they broke off as Wycliffe came in. Scales was elegant. Not only was he the best-dressed man in the squad but his manner and general bearing suggested a top-ranking executive rather than a policeman. Wycliffe always felt foolishly diffident about giving him orders.

'She's in the kitchen, sir.'

'The *kitchen*?'

Few murders are committed in kitchens so if this proved to be murder the case had got off to an unusual start.

Wycliffe shook hands with the doctor, a wizened little man with a swingeing cold. The doctor took out a white handkerchief and blew violently.

'This damned weather!' He rubbed his nose and put the handkerchief away. 'She was strangled but I fancy she was knocked on the head first. She certainly received a blow to the base of her skull. I haven't moved her, of course.'

'Could she have struck her head in falling?'

'Possible, but I don't think so. You'll have to ask Franks when he's taken a look at her.' He sneezed. 'You'll get it all from him.'

'How long has she been dead?'

The doctor shrugged. 'A week? Several days, certainly. There again you'll have to rely on your experts.' He sneezed again. 'You won't want me any more? I've got work to do.'

'No, thank you for your help, doctor. We know where to find you.'

The doctor put on his jacket, picked up his bag and bustled out.

Wycliffe turned to Scales. 'She's been lying in there for a week?'

'It looks like it. The caretaker says she's a singer in the cabaret at the Golden Cockerel—the place in Judson Street.'

'A young woman, then?'

'Early to middle twenties. It's like this, sir: a week ago yesterday she told the caretaker of the flats that the club was closing for ten days for a face-lift and that she was going to London. She said that there was something wrong with her electric cooker and that she had asked the Electricity Board to send a man while she was away. She wanted the caretaker to let the chap in with his pass key. The electrician arrived this afternoon, the caretaker let him in and, together, they found her body.'

Wycliffe went up the three steps to the dining alcove and opened the kitchen door. The nauseating stench of putrefaction halted him for a moment.

'I opened the kitchen window. There seemed no point . . .'

'No, of course not.'

The kitchen was small but well equipped. White fittings with green patterned tiles on floor and walls. The body was lying partly on its right side and partly on the face with the head near the window which had a low sill paved with tiles. Rain spattered on to the sill through the open window. The dead girl wore a snugly fitting black jumper and slacks. She had a mass of black hair which almost hid her face but what he could see of it was livid and becoming bloated. The body was facing an open refrigerator. Fragments of a jug with a floral pattern were scattered for some distance around the body and the floor was stained, presumably where milk had dried on the tiles.

An electric kettle was plugged in but switched off and a teapot with two cups and saucers of the same pattern as the broken jug stood on a tray near the kettle. On the face of it she had been killed while she was making tea.

Wycliffe went back to the living room. 'Where's Dixon?'

'I've sent him to take a statement from the woman next door—604. D.C. Fowler is here too, he's doing the other flats in the building.'

Scales had tipped the contents of the girl's handbag on to the table. A cigarette pack, lighter, compact, lipstick, tissues, thirty-seven pounds in notes and some coin, a cheque book and banker's card. Scales pointed to a key ring with a yellow cockerel on the tab.

Wycliffe knew the club, a canopied entrance with a garish cockerel in neon lights over the door. It had a limited gaming licence and it was a favourite rendezvous for the city's wide-boys. The place had been raided more than once but the proprietor, a Maltese called Bourg, was always a jump ahead. Ten to one the girl had got herself mixed up in some sordid intrigue and had tried to be too clever. He imagined a young face framed in that soft, fine, black hair.

'Futile!'

There was a commotion in the hall; Smith, the police photographer, had arrived with his equipment. Sergeant Smith was middle-aged, morose, and a martyr to indigestion. Lean and grey; his hair, his clothes, even his skin were grey. He acknowledged Wycliffe with the minimum of ceremony.

'Where is it?'

Soon he would be grumbling about the stench, the position of the body, the lighting, the space he had to work in and the inadequacy of his equipment but the grumbles were routine and only very new boys took any notice.

Debbie, he supposed, was short for Deborah though mothers are capable of anything. Well, Debbie had been murdered and the professionals, the specialists, were taking over, taking over her body, her flat and, as far as possible, they would take over her life as she had led it up to the moment of her dissolution. There were specialists for everything these days and it was getting worse.

A good witchdoctor could identify, convict and punish the guilty; in his spare time he could restore fertility to crops, cattle and women; treat the diseases of animals and men; drive out devils and make rain. What could he, Detective Chief Superintendent Wycliffe, do? Here at the scene of the crime he was redundant, waiting on his specialists. In fact, if he followed protocol, he would not be here at all, he would be sitting in his hermetically sealed office, sifting through reports, directing, co-ordinating and making more reports. . . . To hell with that!

Perhaps he was in for a bout of 'flu, there was a lot of it about.

There was little furniture in the living room, almost everything was built in. A studio couch which looked as though it could also serve as a bed had certainly seen better days. There were two battered easy chairs which did not match and a corner cupboard full of knick-knacks. Apart from a record player and a radio that was all. No pictures on the walls; only professional photographs of Debbie stuck on with sellotape. They were all signed in an affected scrawl, 'Debbie'. Seen full-faced she was broad across the forehead and between her high cheekbones but her face narrowed quickly to a small, pointed chin which gave her a puckish look, mischievous with more than a hint of malice. The photographs showed an evolutionary trend from the all-revealing to the almost total cover-up. Her most recent photographs (they were all dated) showed her in a white gown which swept the floor.

'Franks is taking his time, isn't he?'

'He was at a meeting in the hospital.'

Wycliffe looked round the flat.

In the bedroom there was a travelling case open on the floor by the wardrobe and partly packed. Other items, waiting to be packed, were laid out on the bed and these included a white evening gown in a polythene dust-cover. The bed was double and made up for two. In the wardrobe, hanging with her clothes, he found a man's dressing gown, soiled and shabby with a cigarette burn in the lapel. On the floor of the wardrobe, with a dozen pairs of her shoes, there was a pair of men's slippers, the soles worn through. They were on the small side, six-and-a-half or seven.

From the bedroom he went to the bathroom, the lavatory and he even snooped in a small closet used for storing junk. His impression was one of tattiness and neglect. What furniture there was could have been bought in the nearest sale room. Whatever else Debbie Joyce had been she was not house-proud.

He went back to the living room, lit his pipe and stood, staring out of the window. Night was closing over the city although it was still short of five o'clock. There was an office block not far away which looked like a layer cake—alternate bands of light and dark. He could see into one large office where rows of girls sat at typewriters, and on another floor men were working at drawing boards clamped in special stands like easels.

At about this time a week ago Debbie Joyce had been in her bedroom packing a case for her trip to London. Somebody had rung the doorbell and she had answered it. Either she knew her visitor or he had told a good enough tale to be invited in and offered a cup of tea. (Wycliffe was quite sure that it was not a woman's crime.) Surely they must have been acquainted, well enough acquainted for the man to have a motive for murder.

She had gone into the kitchen to make tea. Perhaps they continued to talk through the open door; then, quite naturally, he had joined her. . . .

Someone she trusted or someone who seemed harmless.

Wycliffe turned away from the window. 'I'll be back.'

Scales smiled. He had worked with Wycliffe for long enough to know his ways.

604 had a card on the door also. Mr and Mrs Gordon Clarke. As Wycliffe was about to ring, the door opened and he was confronted by D.C. Dixon, the youngest of his detectives. Dixon had fair hair and freckles and a seemingly incurable habit of blushing whenever he found himself in

any situation in the least degree embarrassing. He blushed now.

'I'm sorry, sir.'

'What for?'

A short, plump woman, fortyish, was seeing Dixon out.

'Mrs Clarke?' Wycliffe introduced himself.

'I've just told your young man all I know about it.'

'I'm sure you have but I'd like to ask you a few questions if I may.'

She was soft skinned and pink, inclined to wobble like a jelly and, Wycliffe suspected, as likely to laugh as cry. She was not really averse to telling her story again; she would certainly repeat it endlessly to her friends at the hairdresser's and elsewhere.

'My hubby's away a lot, he's a sales rep for Rabat Toiletries —sales manager, really—so I'm often here alone and it's nice to have someone handy who can . . .'

'You were a friend of Miss Joyce?'

'Not exactly a friend, more an acquaintance. Actually you couldn't say that she was a friendly sort of girl. In fact, at first, she was really stand-offish, quite rude, but she soon got over that.'

'Who pays for the flat?'

She chuckled, as though at a risqué joke. 'Oh, so you've tumbled to that already? Well, it's obvious somebody does, isn't it? But I don't know who he is. These flats aren't cheap.' Her baby face became solemn. 'I shouldn't laugh, should I? But it's difficult to realise . . . You think; I've been here all week imagining about her living it up in London and all the time she's been lying there.'

'Have you seen him?'

She looked vague, momentarily. 'Her man, you mean? Oh, yes, I've seen him several times. He's about your age, distinguished-looking.'

'Could be her father.'

'Not on your life! Debbie didn't come out of the top drawer and he did, you can always tell.'

34

'When have you seen him here?'

'Afternoons. I often go window shopping in the afternoons and twice he's come out of the lift while I've been waiting to go down. I've also passed him two or three times in the vestibule downstairs.'

'Five or six times—in how long?'

'Spread over the eight months since we moved in.'

'Can you describe him?'

She screwed up her face. 'He's tall, slim but putting it on a bit round the middle. He's got a big head with tiny features all close together. Funny looking.'

'How does he dress?'

'Very quiet and expensive. Grey; either mottled or with a fine stripe. No hat. Which reminds me, he's sandy haired, going thin.'

'She never mentioned him?'

'Never. She wasn't one for telling you her business.'

'Did she have many visitors?'

'Hardly any. Of course she was working every evening; she'd come home about three in the morning and she wouldn't be up until eleven or twelve . . . you know she worked at the club?'

'The Golden Cockerel, yes, I know. Did she ever bring anybody home with her?'

Mrs Clarke seemed amused. Her manner was arch. 'Well, no, I don't think anybody came home with her.'

Wycliffe almost expected her to pat his knee and say, 'You naughty boy!'

The husband must have done pretty well out of his toiletries. The living room was expensively furnished with a large settee and easy chairs covered with real hide. There was a stereo outfit which looked like something out of science fiction and a gigantic colour television. The colour scheme was old gold from the carpet to the wallpaper, cushions and curtains. Everything was 'to tone' as Mrs Clarke would almost certainly have said. The pictures on the wall were real

35

paintings but he was sure that she had bought them with a piece of curtain material in her hand.

'Tell me about when you last saw her.'

'Well, it was a week ago today, last Monday. She came to lunch as usual, about one . . .'

'You mean that she came in here for lunch?'

'Oh, yes, most days. That's how I came to know her as well as I do. As I said, I'm on my own most of the time and it's nice to have somebody coming in, there's no satisfaction in cooking for one. When I suggested it she wasn't keen but she came round and now she seems to look forward to it—I mean she did.' She was playing with the pendant stone which hung in the plunging V-neck of her woollen dress. 'I don't think the poor girl was very domesticated; if she hadn't come here she would have been eating out of tins.'

'What about the people in the other two flats on this floor?'

She shifted her position and pulled down her dress to within speaking distance of her plump knees. 'Well, there's nobody in 601 most of the time. It belongs to Pneumax Industries and they keep it for visiting executives. In 603 there's a couple with two boys, aged seven and eleven. It's a bigger flat than this. He's the manager of a building society; they're pleasant enough people but when you try to keep your place nice you don't want two boys romping all over it. To be honest, I haven't given Mrs Woodward—that's her name— much encouragement.'

'Did Debbie tell you anything about herself or her family?'

'Practically nothing. She didn't give much away. She did say once that she'd gone to school in the city and that she'd been brought up by a maiden aunt. I can't think of anything else.'

'You must have talked about something.'

She smiled. 'Perhaps I did most of the talking. When she said anything it was usually about the club. She had a way of telling a story—laugh! Yet she hardly fetched a smile.

36

What goes on in those places you'd never believe and Debbie had a wicked way of telling it.'

'You were going to tell me about the last time you saw her.'

'So I was. Well, as I said, she came here to lunch and by the time we'd washed up it must have been after two. She said, "I'd better be getting my skates on, I'm catching the night train and I haven't done a thing about getting ready." Of course, I knew the club was closed and that she was going to London for a week.'

'She was going for a week?'

'That's what she said. She told me to expect her back sometime on Monday, that's today. As a matter of fact, I took in extra milk and a loaf of bread for her this morning.'

She reached for a box of cigarettes, offered them to Wycliffe and, when he refused, lit one herself. She held the cigarette awkwardly and the smoke made her cough.

'I don't smoke very often but I need something to settle my nerves.'

'When did you first hear what had happened?'

'When Stebbings, the caretaker, came ringing my doorbell looking as though he was going to pass out. He phoned the doctor from here, nothing would have persuaded him to go back in that flat.'

The light was so dim that it was becoming difficult to see across the room. Her face, as she talked, was a pale blur. He would have liked to switch on the light but he had no reasonable excuse for doing so.

'What did you think of her as a person?'

A mild exclamation of protest. 'That's a question; I don't speak ill of the living let alone the dead.'

'Unless we find out all we can about Debbie Joyce we are unlikely to discover her murderer, Mrs Clarke.'

After a time she allowed herself to be persuaded. 'Well, I must admit that Debbie had a side to her that I didn't like. You got the impression sometimes that she took a delight in hurting people. I suppose you could say that she had a mischievous streak, like people who are always playing practical jokes, but I think there was more to it than that.' She looked at Wycliffe anxiously, fearful that her candour might shock him.

'I can't forget what she told me about the pianist at the club. That really upset me. All he did was to criticise the way she sang one of her songs and she fixed it so that he lost his job, a man with a wife and two children to support.'

'What did she do?'

'Well, they were losing cigarettes from the store and Bourg, the boss, was furious about it. Anyway, Debbie took four hundred cigarettes and hid them in the pianist's locker, then tipped off the boss that they were there.' She broke off, genuinely agitated. 'The worst of it was that she seemed proud of what she'd done. "Nobody treads on my neck", that was her favourite expression.'

She was silent for a while, waiting for him to speak, but then she went on, 'I don't want you to think she was always like that, she could be good company and I was glad to have her coming in but she had that other side to her.'

When Wycliffe still did not speak she said, 'Well, I suppose we've all got our faults and our funny ways, but you did ask . . .'

She could not know that Wycliffe was beginning to live in a new world, a world which she was helping to create for him, the world of Debbie Joyce.

'You really have been a great help, Mrs Clarke.'

'Have I really?' She seemed pleased and surprised.

Wycliffe returned to the dead girl's flat. The case was getting under way. Inspector Scales had been joined by two more detectives and they were making a thorough search of the flat. Dr Franks, the pathologist, was examining the body prior to its removal to the mortuary and Sergeant Smith was standing by to take more photographs. In an hour or two every detail of the flat and of its contents would have been recorded on film and on paper.

As Wycliffe entered the living room Franks came out of the kitchen.

'Well?' Wycliffe greeted him.

'You can have her moved when you like.'

Franks had worked with Wycliffe so often that they were like members of the same team. They no longer needed to spell out ideas and they could sense each other's doubts and reservations but physically and temperamentally they could hardly have been less alike. The pathologist was stout, pink and shining like a precocious baby fresh from his bath. He was invincibly cheerful, he accepted things as he found them and seemed utterly lacking in any desire to change either himself or his world. By comparison, Wycliffe seemed, to himself at least, tentative, often self-conscious and given to needless worry. He was certainly aware of his own defects and frequently discouraged by the world about him.

Franks made his preliminary report.

'She died of strangulation, there can be no doubt of that, but she had a nasty bump on her head—occipital region. It must have been a fairly heavy blow. She's got a good mop of hair but it wasn't enough to cushion the impact much.'

'But it didn't kill her—the blow, I mean?'

'No, in my opinion the blow knocked her unconscious and then she was strangled.'

'How?'

'From the marks on her neck I should say by a nylon cord.'

Wycliffe nodded. 'Try this: she was making tea and while she was stooping to get a jug of milk from the refrigerator her assailant struck her across the base of the skull and she collapsed on the floor, he then strangled her with a nylon cord.'

Franks agreed. 'That would fit. Now, as to the time of death, I'll try to do better after the autopsy but at the moment I can't get closer than a few days.'

'As far as we know she was last seen alive exactly a week ago.'

'I wouldn't quarrel with that.' Franks took his coat from a chair and put it on. 'Well, I'm off. Get her over to me as soon as you can and I'll let you have my report in the morning.'

The specialist at work, clear thinking, incisive. No bumbling there. Wycliffe envied him. He turned to find D.C. Dixon standing at his elbow and spoke brusquely, 'Nothing to do, Dixon? Do you know the Golden Cockerel?'

'Night club in Judson Street, sir. Limited gaming licence. Everybody calls it the Cock.'

'Indeed.' He was always a little moved as well as irritated by Dixon's anxiety to do and say the right thing. 'Well, the proprietor is a Maltese called Bourg. I want you to get hold of him and find out what you can about the girl. I think he lives in Palmerston Crescent.'

'I know the place, sir. A great Victorian barracks with about twenty rooms. He lives there with momma and eight kids. At least it was eight at the last count. They say he's devoted to them. Apparently his wife was a real doll when he married her, now she's as broad as she's long.'

'Really.'

Even Dixon was doing it.

'Just remember one thing, Dixon, Riccy Bourg may be the ideal husband and father but he's also a crook and a clever one so don't let him put anything over.'

'You can rely on me, sir.'

'I hope so. And Dixon—ask him what happened to his pianist.'

'Sir?'

Wycliffe explained.

Dixon went out and Wycliffe watched him go with a twinge of regret. When a case was on he wanted to be everywhere and to do everything; everything but what he was expected to do, to sit in his office and issue instructions.

'Have you been in the bedroom, sir?' Scales was going through the drawers of a built-in unit in the living room.

'Just glanced in, why?'

'She has a man who sleeps there pretty regularly.'

'I saw the dressing gown and slippers.'

40

Scales nodded. 'The bed linen too. She wasn't fussy about her laundry.'

Who had shared Debbie's bed? Surely not the tall, elegant gentleman Mrs Clarke had described; yet it would be surprising if Debbie had had a lover of whom her neighbour knew nothing.

'John!'

'Sir?'

'Get on to the ground landlords and find out who holds the lease on the flat and who pays the overheads.'

'I already have. The flat is in the girl's name and she paid all the bills herself.'

'Does this place have a back entrance?'

'And a service lift, sir. I told them to bring the mortuary van round the back; they're due any minute.'

Wycliffe decided that he might really be more use in his office. He went down in the lift without seeing a soul. Outside it was still raining and people were on their way home from work, the evening rush hour was beginning. Despite the rain a small crowd had gathered on the pavement though there was nothing to see but the fluted glass of the swing doors to the foyer. A reporter from the *News* accosted Wycliffe as he was getting into his car.

'Is it true that a girl has been murdered, Mr Wycliffe?'

'Quite true.' He was never needlessly coy with the press.

'Who was she?'

'A Miss Debbie Joyce; she was a singer at the Golden Cockerel. She was strangled.'

'When did it happen?'

'Her body was discovered this afternoon but she has been dead for several days.'

'Have you—?'

'I've told you all I know at the moment and I've got work to do.'

'Your man won't let me into the building.'

'There would be no point.'

41

CHAPTER TWO

WYCLIFFE'S HEADQUARTERS OCCUPIED the first floor of one wing of the new area police building. For almost a fortnight it had been a lifeless place. People arrived at nine in the morning and by five-fifteen most of the offices were in darkness. His staff went about with an air of listlessness as though what they were doing might just as well have been left until the next day or not done at all. It was, presumably, the same malaise which had led him to stand by his big window, watching the traffic and to murmur :

'Futile!'

But when he returned there at a little before six the change was dramatic. Lights were on everywhere, typewriters were clacking, telephones ringing and people were bustling around with a new sense of urgency and purpose. It was odd, because as yet very few of them were involved in any way with the new case. Even undertakers must get depressed when business is slack.

He had scarcely sat at his desk when W.P.C. Saxton, his clerical assistant, came in with a tray of tea.

'I thought you might be glad of that, sir.'

'Thank you, Diane.'

She was blonde, immaculate, always band-box fresh and very efficient, like a secretary in a TV commercial. She worried him : when she was near him he could not help wondering whether his collar was clean or if he had dandruff. He could not recall in what circumstances he had ever had the temerity to start calling her by her first name.

Reports were beginning to come in. First from D.C. Fowler who had questioned the caretaker and the occupants of the other flats. There were thirty-two flats in the building and he had spoken to someone in twenty-four of them. Only one person admitted to knowing anything about Debbie Joyce, a woman doctor on the seventh floor. Like most doctors she was prickly but Fowler was an old hand.

'Yes, I know the girl, at least I know of her.'

Fowler adopted a confidential manner and outlined what had happened in the flat below.

'Well, if, as you tell me, the girl is dead, I suppose there is no reason why I shouldn't tell you what happened. It was about three months ago, early October, between five and six in the morning, when I was awakened by someone ringing my doorbell. When I went to the door I found a young man in a dressing gown; he was distraught, barely coherent, but I gathered that there was someone ill in 602 and I went down with him.

'I found a young woman lying on the floor by the bed. She was recovering from an epileptic fit. I did what was necessary and got her back to bed. By that time she had completely recovered and she told me that she had been an epileptic since childhood but that in recent years her attacks had become less frequent and she had, rightly, given up taking the drugs which had been prescribed. I suggested, a little tartly, that if she had taken her husband into her confidence she could have avoided scaring him out of his wits. Of course, it emerged that the young man was not her husband.

'Anyway, I advised the girl to see her own doctor and left them to it. As far as I was concerned that was the end of the matter.'

'Could you describe the young man or would you recognise him again if you saw him?'

'I can describe him and I have seen him again.'

'When have you seen him?'

'Two or three times, the last time was a fortnight ago. On each occasion we met in the lift, going up around midnight. To be honest I doubt whether I would have noticed him had he not been looking at me with a somewhat guilty expression which drew my attention. Then he spoke.'

The description was professionally detailed:

'Short—five feet five or six. Twentyish, slim with fair, curly hair and heavy sideburns; broad features, fresh complexion and rather cow-like brown eyes. On each occasion he wore blue jeans and a leather jacket with a checked shirt. Oh, yes, I remember, he had an old scar over his left eye. He struck me as a bit dim.'

'Do you practise from here?'

'No, I'm attached to a group practice at the Horton Health Centre.'

'Then how would he know that you are a doctor?'

'He may be dim but I imagine that he can read. My name is on the board in the hall—Dr Mary Peskett.'

Wycliffe was pleased; with that sort of description it shouldn't be difficult to pick up Debbie's sleeping partner. He was also interested to learn that she was an epileptic. Would this lead Franks to change his mind about the cause of her skull injury? In a *grand mal* attack the subject often threshes about with great violence; was it possible that she had come by her injury in this way? That the killer had then taken advantage of the fact that she was unconscious to finish her off? It sounded and was, almost certainly, absurd.

The truth was that Wycliffe had been troubled about the blow on the head. It was outside the usual pattern. Stranglers generally fall into one of two categories. There are those who commit an unpremeditated crime in circumstances of un-endurable frustration or anger and there are others who deliberately strangle out of perverted lust. For them the act of strangulation is associated with or is a substitute for the act of sex and they will go on killing until they are caught. In neither case is the victim likely to be knocked on the head first nor attacked while in the kitchen making tea.

D.C. Dixon was back from his interview with Bourg, the proprietor of the Golden Cockerel. He had been welcomed like an honoured guest and had been introduced to all the children from Marco aged two to Elisa who was sixteen.

'Momma, you hear this terrible thing? Little Debbie who sing at the club. Such a thing to happen.'

And Momma too was deeply distressed.

'She was a good girl,' Ricky went on. 'She work for me seven—no, eight months and everybody like her. She sing songs that are a little naughty but she look so . . . what is the word? Pure? Chaste—that is it. All beautiful in a white dress like a little girl at her first communion in my village where I was born. People like that, men and women. They do not know whether to laugh a little or cry a little and that is good.'

He sighed. 'She was to do something special for when we open again on Wednesday. Tomorrow she would come for rehearsal.'

Mr Bourg absolutely refused to countenance the possibility that Debbie might have involved herself in anything discreditable. About the piano player he was contemptuous.

'He was a rogue that one. If Debbie set a little trap it was to help me; for proof of something I know already. In any case he was not good on the piano. That girl, she was as another daughter to me.'

After a pause for reflection he added : 'I tell you one thing and that is gossip only, you understand. It was said that Debbie is married and that she leave her husband. Who she marry I do not know but you will find out.'

Asked who passed on this gossip he professed, grandly, never to remember such details.

Another pause and Mr Bourg reached his great conclusion. 'You find that bastard, her husband, my friend, he is the one for sure. And tell Mr Wycliffe that Riccardo Bourg give you this tip for free—no strings.'

Poor Dixon had been swamped by magnanimity and Wycliffe was highly amused even by the edited version of the interview which reached him.

The pattern was growing more complex, the colours richer. Riccy Bourg, his club, his singer, his wronged piano player and Debbie's illicit lover. Now there was the suggestion of a husband in the background.

Scales came in to say that, so far, he had been unable to trace Debbie's relatives; there had been almost nothing of a strictly personal nature in the flat. There was a cheque book but few of the counterfoils had been filled in.

'In the morning you can have a word with her bank manager.'

The wheels were beginning to turn. The description of the young man was being circulated to every policeman in the city; the occupants of the flats in Grenville House were being questioned for the second time, partly because husbands would be home, partly because they could now be questioned about the young man.

'I suppose we should get out an identikit picture of him?'

Wycliffe shrugged. 'If we don't pull him in tonight we can try it.'

He gave instructions for a man to remain in the flat through the night. 'As she was expected back today he might turn up.'

'Unless he killed her.'

'There you are, Mr Norman.' His secretary helped him on with his overcoat, straightened his collar at the back and handed him his briefcase and gloves.

Norman glanced briefly round his office. 'You'll see that those files go back to registry, Miss Hopkins?'

'Right away, sir.'

He lingered in the doorway. 'They shouldn't be left here overnight.' A brief pause. 'Very well, nine-thirty in the morning.'

'Nine-thirty, Mr Norman. Good-night.'

Norman set off down the long corridor to the lift. He had to pass his surgical wards. The door of the television lounge was open and he could see several patients sitting round the set. The voice of a news reader reached him:

'... identified as Miss Debbie Joyce, a singer in one of the city's clubs. Detective Chief Superintendent Wycliffe stated that the police are treating her death as a case of murder.'

A domestic, pushing a trolley, steered round him and looked back with curiosity. A ward sister stopped, 'Are you all right, Mr Norman?'

He looked at her sharply. 'All right? Of course I'm all right.'

He walked on to the lift. A staff nurse, already in the lift on her way down, made herself as inconspicuous as possible. On the ground floor he stepped out of the lift and crossed the vast entrance hall. The porter on duty dashed to open one of the doors.

'Good-night, Mr Norman, sir.'

It was raining, a fine drizzle, but his car was drawn up under the canopy. A middle-aged man in a chauffeur's cap opened the car door for him.

'A nasty night, sir.'

Norman sank into the back seat and said nothing.

The telephone rang.

'Wycliffe.'

'A Mr Matthew Norman on the line for you, sir, senior consultant surgeon at Millfield General.'

'Put him through.'

A cultured voice, dry and tight. 'I understand that a Miss Debbie Joyce has been murdered.'

'That is so.'

A moment of silence, then, 'I must talk to you, perhaps I could come to your office. . . .'

'I would prefer to call on you.'

'As you wish. I live at twenty-four Conniston Gardens. What I have to tell you is important so the sooner you are able to come . . .'

'I'll be with you in half an hour.'

In the bottom flat at 14 Edgcumbe Close, Elaine Bennett was studying herself in the dressing table mirror. She was flushed, and she was feeling unwell. All day she had been conscious of a constriction in her throat, now it was painful and she had a headache.

Elaine was a nurse in private practice and her present job was nightnurse to a wealthy old lady who lived at Kemsley Rise, a bus trip across the city. For the past three weeks, each night, she had left the flat at half-past nine and walked to Godolphin Road where she boarded a 622 bus which took her to the bottom of Kemsley Rise. She had no day off for she preferred to work for short, intensive spells then take a week or two off between jobs. Her present job was something of a sinecure for she could sleep most of the night.

'I think I've got a temperature, Val.'

Valerie Hughes, her flat mate, was in the sitting room watching television but the door between was open.

'I told you.'

Elaine came through from the bedroom with a thermometer in her mouth. After a while she took it out and read it.

'A hundred and one.'

'I told you.'

'Can't you think of anything else to say?'

'Well, you can't go to work tonight, that's for sure.'

'But the old girl depends on me. If it gets round that I don't turn up at my cases I'm sunk.'

'She won't thank you for giving her the 'flu.'

'I suppose not. I'd better go out to the phone and ring the woman who does days. She might be willing to stop on.'

'I'll do it.'

'What? Ring?'

'No, look after the old woman. I suppose she would put up with me for one night.'

'But you're on six-till-two.'

'Tomorrow's my day off.' Valerie was a nurse at Millfield General.

'You're an angel! I do feel pretty bloody.'

'You look it.'

'Listen!' Elaine's attention had been caught by the television. An announcer was reading the regional news.

'... The dead girl is Debbie Joyce, a night club entertainer. A police spokesman said that she had been dead for several days when her body was found in the kitchen of her flat. The police are treating her death as murder.'

'Well, I'm damned!'

Valerie looked at her friend. 'That's the girl you went to school with, isn't it?'

'No.'

'But I remember you saying that night you went to the Cock—'

Elaine was suddenly irritable. 'You don't remember me saying I went to school with her because I didn't but I did know her when we were at school. We met playing hockey and we were friendly for a time.'

'Didn't you say Joyce wasn't her real name?'

'Whatever she's called now, her name when I knew her was Rosaline Parkin.'

'I wonder how she got herself murdered?'

'I would imagine that's easy enough if you carry on like she did at that club.' Elaine switched off the television. 'Now, for God's sake let's forget about it.'

Valerie shrugged. 'O.K. What are we going to eat?'

James Rendell locked the door of the shop, tried it twice, then stood on the edge of the pavement in the drizzling rain, waiting for a lull in the traffic down Prince's Street. It came and he crossed to a traffic island, waited again, then finally made it to the other side. It was not far to the city centre which was a blaze of light after the dark tunnel of Prince's Street. A man was selling newspapers in a shop doorway. A scrawled news-bill read: 'City Solicitor on Fraud Charge'. News of the discovery of Debbie Joyce's body had come too late for the evening editions.

Each working day for a week Rendell had forced himself to carry on normally, never leaving the shop between nine

49

in the morning and half-past five in the afternoon. Each evening as he walked up Prince's Street to the city centre, he steeled himself for the moment when he would come in sight of the newsvendor and be able to read the legend on the news-bill. He would deliberately avert his eyes until he was within a couple of yards, then . . .

He could think of no circumstances in which the body could have remained undiscovered for a whole week. He told himself again and again that she was dead, there could be no doubt of that, no possible doubt. He had seen . . . but he would not think about what he had seen.

On the Wednesday evening, two days after, he had gone to the Golden Cockerel with no clear object in mind. He had certainly not intended to go in but it came as a shock when from the end of Judson Street, he saw that the club was in darkness, the sign unlit. He hurried down the street, his heart thumping wildly. There was a little notice on one of the glass doors which he had difficulty in reading because of the dim light. By bringing his eyes close to the square of cardboard he could make out the words : 'The Management regrets that the club will remain closed for ten days during which time the premises will be redecorated and modernised to give patrons a better service in the future.'

For a while he was almost prepared to believe that this was part of a plan to deceive him, to lead him to some incriminating act. Was it possible that the police, for their own reasons, would hush up the fact that a crime had been committed? The thought scared him although he would not have been able to explain why.

Later that same evening he had gone to a side street from which it was possible to see the upper floors of Grenville House and for more than an hour he had stood there watching the windows which he knew belonged to her flat. They were in darkness. On the Friday in desperation he had almost telephoned the police to lay anonymous information.

The weekend had been purgatory. How could he go on

without knowing what was happening? Now it was Monday again. A whole week.

'Goodnight, guv.' The old man with the newspapers had got to know him although he never bought a paper.

He walked on. It was not far to the *Guardian* building where he lived with his sister and brother-in-law. The couple had a flat on the top floor of the office block of which they were caretakers. He took the lift and came out into a tiny vestibule on the eighth floor.

'Is that you, Jim?'

He went into his bedroom, washed, and changed his jacket for a woolly cardigan then he went through into the living room where they would soon be sitting down to their evening meal. His sister, Alice, was in the kitchen but he could talk to her through the open hatch.

'Where's Albert?'

'They got trouble with the radiators on the third. He's down there with the maintenance man. He said not to wait. Had a good day?'

'All right.'

'You don't look very well, Jim, and that's a fact.'

'I'm all right.'

He had been a fool to come to live with his sister and her husband; it would have been better if he had stayed on in his own house, alone. Now he had to keep up this constant pretence and, worse, endure their sympathy and professed understanding when they understood nothing—nothing!

The television was on as usual. The regional news. '. . . Debbie Joyce, a night club entertainer. A police spokesman said that she had been dead several days when her body was found in the kitchen of her flat. The police are treating her death as murder.'

He had been waiting so long, yet now that it had come it was like an unexpected blow. His legs would not support him and he sat down heavily.

'What was that, Jim—about a girl being murdered?'

He did not answer, he could not trust his voice.

51

'Weren't you listening?'

'What?'

Alice was irritated. 'It doesn't matter, forget it.'

He was recovering and experiencing a great flood of relief. His spirits rose, he began to feel almost gay.

By the time Alice had served the meal he was so excited that he could scarcely eat his food. She noticed the change in him and, as usual, misinterpreted the signs.

'What you need is a complete change, Jim. Why don't you take a few days off—go up to London and poke around the museums and art galleries? You used to love doing that.'

'I don't need a change, I'm perfectly all right.' He spoke between his teeth, he was so irritated by her chatter. Why couldn't she shut up and leave him alone?

'Old Probert would keep the shop going—do him good, he'd miss you.'

'I said I'm all right, Alice. For God's sake stop telling me what to do!'

It was so unusual for him to raise his voice that Alice was upset.

'There's no need to rave at me, Jim. I'm only trying to help. You want me to mind my own business, all right, I will.'

'I'm sorry.' He realised that he had gone too far. 'Really.'

But he was trembling and as soon as he could he left the table.

'Are you going out?'

'I thought I would.'

He went into his bedroom and put on his mackintosh and cap. He felt in the right-hand pocket of his mackintosh and was reassured. His nerves became steadier and his hands ceased to tremble. Before leaving he looked in the living room.

'You mustn't mind me, Alice, it's very good of you and Albert to have me here. Maybe you're right, perhaps I will have a few days but I'll wait for the better weather.'

*　　*　　*

Wycliffe telephoned Franks but the pathologist was unimpressed by the news that Debbie Joyce had been epileptic.

'Anything else? Otherwise I'll get on . . .'

Wycliffe was unusually diffident. 'Not about the girl, at least, not directly. I wanted to ask you, do you know Matthew Norman, the senior surgeon at Millfield?'

'As we work almost under the same roof, I'd have a job not to.'

'What sort of man is he?'

Even close friendship fails to compete with the Masonic solidarity of the medical profession. 'He's a good surgeon, one of the best.'

'I don't doubt it, but what sort of man is he?'

'Rather severe. He sets high standards for himself and for the people who work with him. He sometimes appears patronising but I don't think that he means to be so.'

'Married?'

Wycliffe could sense the pathologist's hesitation.

'I understand that he is separated from his wife though I know very little of his private life.'

'Any gossip about women?'

'Definitely not!' It was amusing to hear the emphatic almost shocked denial from Franks whose own affairs were notorious.

'Or the other thing?'

'Nor that.'

'All right, thanks.'

But now Franks' curiosity was aroused. 'Is he supposed to be mixed up in this affair?'

'That's what I'm going to ask him.'

'Be careful. He comes from a legal family, his father was Recorder of the city and his grandfather was a high court judge.'

'I'll remember.'

It was Franks who was now reluctant to end the conversation. 'From what I've heard, he lives for his work and his pots.'

'His pots?'

'Chinese blue-and-white porcelain. He's an authority.'

Wycliffe put down the receiver with a smile on his face.

Conniston Gardens was a crescent of large, Edwardian houses on the edge of Conniston Park. Giant elms, now bare, gave the place an air of slightly decaying elegance and it would have been no surprise to hear the clip-clop of horse's hooves as the brougham drew up, bringing the master from the station.

Wycliffe was received by the housekeeper and taken to a back room where Norman waited. He was very tall, slim but slightly pot-bellied. His head was abnormally large but his features were small and close together, a ready-made caricature. No need to look further for Debbie's well-dressed visitor.

'Good of you to come, chief superintendent. Sherry?'

There were enough books to call the room a library; the bookshelves reached to within a yard of the high ceiling and blue-and-white vases and jars were disposed along the tops of the bookcases. Glass-fronted cabinets on either side of the chimney breast housed smaller pieces. A large gas fire burned cosily in a fireplace framed by a huge white-marble mantelpiece. Above the fireplace there was a portrait in oils of a man in legal gown and wig. A severe, distinguished face whose features resembled Norman's but were more fittingly proportioned and disposed.

Wycliffe watched the surgeon with bland, expressionless eyes. Norman was finding it difficult to begin, he was the sort of man who would abhor any discussion of his intimate life.

'I heard on the television news that a young woman by the name of Joyce had been found dead in her flat. It was said that she had been murdered.'

'That is so.'

'I hoped that you would be prepared to give me more information.'

54

Wycliffe was cool. 'If I am satisfied that you are entitled to it.'

'She was my wife.'

'I see.'

Norman had got over the first hurdle and his manner became noticeably less tense. 'We were married a year ago but we separated after three months.'

'How long since you last saw your wife, Mr Norman?'

'A little over a week.'

'You visited her regularly?'

'Fairly regularly?'

'Why?'

A flicker of annoyance. 'She was my wife, the fact that we were separated did not mean that I was indifferent to her welfare.'

'Or she to yours?'

He ignored the question.

Wycliffe's manner was brusque, almost rude. Norman moved in a world where his word was law. Doctors, nurses and patients, patients in particular, held him almost in reverence. Daily, life and death lay, literally, in his hands. In those circumstances a man is bound to develop an armour of self esteem. To get him to talk freely about himself it was essential to break through.

'You have always lived in this house?'

'I was born here, my father was Recorder of the city.' He glanced up at the portrait over the mantelpiece.

'You live alone?'

A mild show of well-bred irritation. 'My housekeeper and her husband have a flat upstairs.'

Wycliffe was trying to picture the dead girl in these surroundings, sharing them with this man. If, as her neighbour had suggested, she enjoyed hurting people she had a ready-made victim in her shy, sensitive husband.

'Why did you marry her?'

Norman's anger flared. 'I really do not see . . .'

55

'Your wife has been murdered and such questions will have to be answered.'

He pursed his lips and seemed to consider. 'I suppose that you are right. It would be foolish to hamper the investigations in any way.'

Thank God for the objectivity of a trained mind.

'You were a man in your late forties, a bachelor, living in the house where you were born—'

It was Norman's turn to interrupt. 'Because a man is a bachelor, it does not necessarily follow that he wishes to be so.'

'But a girl in her twenties with a totally alien background. . . .'

Outside it was quite dark but the curtains had not been drawn. Norman stood up, went to the window and swept them together in a single vigorous movement.

'A man comes to terms with circumstances. Perhaps he solves his problems by pretending that they do not exist then something happens and pretence is no longer possible.'

Wycliffe looked instinctively at the shelves of books, the valuable porcelain, the desk and the well-worn swivel chair. His glance did not escape Norman who smiled, wryly.

'It wasn't enough.'

'How did you meet her?'

'By the most improbable chance. From time to time the staff at the hospital organise a dance and the consultants are expected to look in. A gesture. On this occasion Debbie was there, she had been invited by one of my juniors.' He broke off. 'Perhaps I should tell you that although she insisted on being called Debbie, it was not her real name. She was Rosaline Parkin, and she adopted the name Debbie Joyce for professional reasons. Anyway, she was there and it happened that I was standing by the buffet when she was choosing what she would have. She made it her business to draw me into conversation. At first I was a little distant but before long I found myself talking freely. Someone had told her of my interest in Chinese blue-and-white and she asked me several intelligent questions. It was clear that she knew nothing about the subject but her interest seemed genuine. To my own astonishment I found myself asking her to come and see my collection.' He gestured helplessly. 'She came and we went on from there.'

The sound of a table being laid came from an adjoining room, the rattle of crockery and cutlery.

Wycliffe was asking himself whether the interview could have gone quite in this way if Norman had murdered his wife. He had to admit that he had no data to go on. The Normans of this world are not often involved with the police and so in dealing with them there are few precedents.

But the surgeon's manner had changed. He was much more relaxed. Wycliffe suspected that this introspective and essentially solitary man was finding a certain relief in unburdening himself in a strictly professional context.

'For the first time in my life I fell in love. The phrase is an apt one, it precisely describes what happened to me—I fell, as helpless to control or influence my fate as a man who steps off a cliff.' He paused. 'It was a devastating experience. Do you find that absurd, superintendent?'

'If I found human nature absurd I should not be doing this job.'

Norman looked at him appreciatively. 'No, I suppose not; nor I mine.'

He pointed to the decanter. 'Are you sure that you won't?'

'Very well, thank you.'

They were silent while he poured the sherry with that economy of movement and precision which is only found in people who daily rely on the skill of their hands.

'Somebody said that a fool at forty must be a fool indeed. Of course, I asked her to marry me and she agreed. I did not question my fortune any more than one questions waking on a spring morning. Little things might have warned me but I was in no mood to be warned. We were married.'

A long pause during which he sipped his sherry and stared at the fire.

'It was like having a chair snatched from under you when you are about to sit down. Overnight she seemed to become a different person. You asked me why I married her, the question for me is, why did she marry me? I asked myself that question many times during each day and night that we were together and I still do not know the answer. It is true that I am comfortably off but she was not interested in my money. I have some status but she did not care about that either. She married me yet she seems to have hated me—why?'

Why, indeed?

'When she left me my first feeling was one of relief.' He gestured weakly with his long, white hands. 'But you cannot live with a girl like her, even as we lived, without missing her when she goes.'

'You tried to persuade her to come back?'

He nodded without speaking.

Wycliffe looked up at the Recorder's portrait and wondered what genetic cookery had produced this chancy blend of sophistication and naivety, of priggishness and sensuality, of pedantry and quirkish humour.

'Did you visit your wife last Monday?'

'Last Monday? Is that when . . .'

Wycliffe said nothing.

'No, I did not see her on Monday, I was at the hospital all day, at least, until half-past six or seven in the evening.'

'Just one more thing. Can you tell me anything of her background, her relatives, where she went to school and who her friends were?'

Norman shook his head. 'I must confess that I knew very little about her and the fact worried me. One's wife . . . But she was secretive. She told me once that she had lost her parents when she was a baby and that she had been brought up by a maiden aunt. That was all.'

'Did she leave any of her personal things here—letters, documents, that sort of thing?'

'She took everything with her, not that she had much.

When she left her belongings went into two suitcases.' He looked at Wycliffe then at his room, stored with possessions. 'That moved me deeply.'

'Is that why you set her up in the flat and paid her bills?'

Resentment flickered again then died. He nodded. 'I made her an allowance and I bought the flat in her name. It was the least I could do.'

Another silence, so profound that they could hear the faint hissing of the gas fire.

'How did she die?'

'She was strangled after being knocked unconscious by a blow to the head.'

'Have you any idea who might have killed her?'

'None.'

'The club where she worked has an unsavoury reputation.'

'All the possibilities are being investigated.'

'Of course.' Norman came with him to the gate. 'Thank you for coming.'

'You realise that you may be the subject of further investigation?'

'Yes.'

The rain had almost stopped and a pale radiance in the sky betrayed the position of the moon above the clouds.

He drove home slowly. The move which had cost him his office in a Queen Anne crescent had enabled him to become the proud owner of the Watch House, an old coastguard house built on the slopes overlooking the narrows through which all the shipping entering and leaving the port had to pass. A half acre of ground went with the house and, altogether, it was a great consolation to him on days when he threatened himself with an early retirement.

Ever since their marriage their home had been a place where he could relax. He took it for granted, scarcely realising that it was a rare talent of his wife's which made it so. In more than twenty years, even through the twins' most difficult periods, there had been few crises and none which threatened their marriage.

'Back to normal?'

'A girl strangled in one of the new flats in the city centre.'

'Is Jimmy Gill back?'

'No, but he will be as soon as he hears about this.'

He bathed, had his meal, helped to wash up then they sat together in front of the fire, reading and listening to records.

At nine o'clock he switched on the television for the news. The finding of Debbie Joyce's body was mentioned again. 'The police are treating it as a case of murder.'

Just after ten the telephone rang. It was Gill.

'I'm at the office. I heard about the girl so I looked in to see what was going on. I'd no sooner arrived than another report came through, an attack on a girl in the Godolphin Road area. She's been taken to Millfield. I gather that she made the 999 call herself so she can't be all that bad but I thought you'd better know.'

CHAPTER THREE

Valerie came back into the sitting room dressed for the street. 'Three aspirins, a glass of hot milk and bed for you. And don't forget to use disinfectant when you wash up.'

Elaine smiled weakly. 'Thanks, Val.'

Valerie opened the street door and banged it shut behind her. The air was moist and chilly but the rain had stopped. A thin mist drifted tenuously between the houses and haloed the street lamps. She hurried up the Close to a point where a convenient footpath cut through to Godolphin Road saving a quarter of a mile of walking. It led through allotments between ragged privet hedges. As she turned into the path it started to rain again, sweeping across the open ground. She was not a nervous girl but she did not care for this walk at night. The street lamps in Godolphin Road seemed a long way off. But who would be out on a night like this unless they had to be? She focused her thoughts on the winter coat she had bought in the sales and plodded on through the darkness.

She was half way through the allotments when a sudden movement, very close, startled her. She did not cry out and when she would have done it was too late, all she could manage was a choking gurgle. Her face was pressed hard against the material of a man's raincoat and there was something round her neck which made it almost impossible to breathe. She knew that he was trying to strangle her but she could not really believe it. The cord, or whatever it was, cut into the back of her neck but in front her coat collar had caught in it. All the same... She struggled and her waterproof hat fell off. Her head felt as though it would burst but she had not lost consciousness. Then the pressure was suddenly released and a man's voice said, 'Oh, God! Oh, God!' He moved away from her and she slipped to the ground in a sitting position, her head fell back into the privet bush and the twigs scratched her face and ears. She heard the man pounding off in the direction of the Close.

The odd thing was that she did not feel very frightened but she could not muster the strength to shout or move. After a little while she was able to drag herself to her feet. She had been sitting in mud which stuck to her clothing and she muttered to herself, 'Christ! I'm in a mess.' The thing was to get to a telephone.

She could not bring herself to go in the direction which her attacker had gone so she made for Godolphin Road. She remembered that there was a call-box where the footpath joined the main road. She felt weak and sick and giddy and her throat was painful but she made it. Godolphin Road was utterly deserted and she had difficulty in opening the door of the call-box but she got inside, lifted the receiver and dialled 999.

'Which service do you require?' The voice, cool and detached.

'Police.'

She managed to answer their questions then collapsed on the floor of the box leaving the receiver dangling on its cord. She did not lose consciousness, only the ability to move. She heard the police car arrive and she was afraid they would not see her but she could not call or get up. However there was no need; a constable bent over her and a little later she heard the ambulance.

In the end they put her to bed in the accident ward of her own hospital. She sat up, not displeased with the attention she was getting and rather glad that the scratches on her face and neck and the bruises on her throat made her look worse than she felt. But she was enough of a nurse to know that it would be a different story in the morning.

A plain-clothes policeman came in and sat by her bed. A

nurse drew the curtains round her bed to give some privacy. The policeman told her that he was Detective Chief Superintendent Wycliffe but he looked an amiable and kindly man.

'What about telling your parents where you are?'

She was not a local girl, her parents lived in Bristol and she said that the ward sister had arranged for them to be told.

'Now, if it doesn't upset you too much I want you to tell me what happened in as much detail as you can remember.'

She did so and her story was coherent and told with remarkable self-possession.

'That's fine, now two or three questions and I'll leave you in peace.' He smiled encouragement. 'Did you see his face? ... Was he much taller than you? ... You say that you had your face pressed against his coat ....'

She tried to explain that, in fact, she had seen nothing. The man must have been a good deal taller than she was but that meant little for she was only five feet two.

'You said just now that your hat fell off.'

'Oh, yes it did. My waterproof hat, a sort of sou'-wester.'

'I know, one of our chaps picked it up. Was it immediately after your hat fell off that he let you go?'

She considered, her forehead wrinkled under blonde hair. 'Yes, I think it was—it must have been.'

'He let you go, you slipped to the ground and you heard him say, "Oh, God!"—twice, then he ran off. Is that it?'

'Yes.'

Wycliffe wished that he might smoke. 'I would like you to think about my next question very carefully before you answer. Did you get any impression—any impression at all—as to why he released you?'

Again the puzzled frown. 'I've thought about it, of course.'

'It wasn't that you succeeded in breaking free from him?'

'Oh, no, he could have done it if he'd wanted to.' She shuddered without affectation. 'I can't say for certain but it seemed to me that he could have been shocked and frightened by what he was doing. Does that sound silly?'

'Not a bit! You mean that he could have been someone

subject to fits of violence and that, fortunately, he came out of this particular fit and was horrified by what he found himself doing?'

'Yes, does it seem likely?'

Wycliffe did not say but he thought not. Certainly there are psychopathic killers who appear to be quite normal and to have little or no recollection of their crimes between attacks, but Dr Jekyll does not supplant Mr Hyde *in the act.*

'You don't think that he mistook you for someone else and that when your hat fell off he realised his mistake?'

He saw from her expression that he had hit the mark.

'It was Elaine he was after! He must have stopped when my hat fell off because he saw my fair hair—Elaine is dark.'

'Elaine?'

'The girl I share a flat with. She should have been going through the allotments at that time, not me.' She explained.

'I'll be back.' He pushed through the curtain and looked up and down the ward for the sister. He met her in the passage and she must have been impressed by his gravity of manner for when he snapped, 'Telephone!' she led him to her office without a word and left.

He was put through to headquarters and to Gill. 'This attack, Jimmy, it looks as though he went for the wrong girl, he was after her flat mate, Elaine Bennett . . .'

'They've just found her.'

'Found her?'

'I sent a crime car to Edgcumbe Close to break the news —to tell this Bennett girl that her pal was in hospital. Constable Allen couldn't get any answer although there were lights on in the flat. When he pushed the door he found that it was unlatched and there she was, lying in the hall, strangled.'

'How long since?'

'Allen's message was timed at 22.31. I got the circus on the road and I was just going to phone you when your call came through.'

'Are you going there?'

'I'm on my way.'

Wycliffe was shaken. The cold resolution behind the killing dismayed him. A mistake, rectified as soon as possible. Logic. But what logic!

He went back to the ward, his every move watched by the other patients.

'I've just thought of something else,' Valerie said. 'A funny smell . . . it was when my face was against his raincoat.'

'What sort of smell?'

It was not the first time he had faced the problem of getting a witness to describe a smell. What an opportunity for some ingenious boffin to contrive an odour identikit!

'It could have been paint or varnish, or even the polish they sometimes use on floors.'

'You mean wax polish?'

'Yes, I suppose I do.'

A moment of silence while she looked at him with worried eyes.

'Why did he want to kill Elaine?'

'I don't know.'

'Have you told her?'

'One of our cars called round some time ago.'

'She would have been in bed. You know she's got the 'flu?'

'You told me.'

Before leaving the hospital he talked with the sister. Under her professional gloss she seemed perturbed. 'No, I agree, it would be most unwise to tell her tonight; she's had enough, poor girl!' But Wycliffe had the impression that her thoughts were elsewhere. In the end it came. 'I think that I have probably been foolish . . .'

He waited.

'A few minutes ago a man telephoned to enquire after Valerie. He knew her name, he spoke of her as "Valerie Hughes, the girl who was attacked on the allotments".'

'What did he want?'

'Just to know how she was, he seemed concerned.'

It might be significant. Valerie had dragged herself to a

call-box in Godolphin Road and dialled 999. A patrol car
and ambulance had been sent but there had been few people
about to see. Not many could know of the attack even now
and who would know the identity of the girl?

'You told him that she was in no danger?'

'I am afraid I did.'

'What was his reaction?'

'He seemed relieved.'

'The call came through the switchboard?'

'Of course!'

The switchboard operator remembered the call. 'He
wanted to know if the girl who had been attacked on the
allotments had been admitted. He sounded genuinely worried
and I saw no harm in putting him through to the ward
sister.'

'Call-box or private subscriber?'

The operator reflected. 'Private, I'm sure of that. I mean,
I didn't have to wait for the call-box routine.'

'Can you place the time of the call?'

'It was a few minutes after eleven.'

The girl's 999 call had been logged at 21.43 which meant
that the attack had probably taken place at 21.30 or there-
about. If the call to the hospital had been made from the man's
home—and from where else could such a call have been
made?—it meant that he had gone to the house in Edgcumbe
Close, committed the second crime and reached home in an
hour and a half. Not much to go on, especially as there was
nothing to show whether he had a car, used public transport
or merely walked. But that was the kind of evidence the police
were good at getting. Even on a dark, misty night it was
unlikely that he could have moved about much without
being seen by somebody. There was a chance.

He was inclined to believe that the call to the hospital
had come from the killer and that it was made out of concern for the girl he had mistakenly attacked. But other in-
terpretations were possible and to guard against a second

attack on Valerie Hughes he arranged for a round-the-clock police guard at the hospital.

Edgcumbe Close was near the hospital, a quiet cul-de-sac of small, detached villas, several of them converted into flats to attract hospital staff. Number fourteen had been properly converted with separate access to the top flat by an outside staircase at the back. The close was crowded with police vehicles, a van which looked like a black maria, waiting for the body, a Range Rover and three patrol cars. A uniformed policeman at the gate saluted Wycliffe. The mist was turning to rain again.

'They're using the window, sir.'

To avoid the hall where the body was, Wycliffe climbed in. The front room seemed to be full of men and he could hear Smith, the photographer, cursing in the hall. 'Not enough bloody room to stand sideways ... you need a sodding sky-hook in this place!'

Franks was there and came over to Wycliffe. 'We seem to be back in business with a vengeance. Not much I can tell you. She was strangled, no doubt of that, but no blow to the head this time. Death occurred between, say, half-past nine and ten. I arrived here about five minutes to eleven.'

Wycliffe nodded and turned to Scales who looked pale and weary. 'Go home, get some rest. Where's Mr Gill?'

'Mr Gill is upstairs talking to the girls in the upper flat. They are both nurses and they were on the two-till-ten shift. They arrived home about tweny minutes past ten but there's a separate entrance to their flat and they had no idea that anything was amiss.'

Smith was packing up his photographic gear. Wycliffe went out into the hall. Elaine's body was lying where it had fallen, one leg doubled under her, her back against the wall. She was wearing a green dressing gown over a baby-doll nightie. She must have been going to bed or already in bed when her murderer arrived. From where he stood the mop of black curls almost covered her face. Despite his years in the force he always found it hard to come to terms with violent death, especially of the young and this was the second body he had seen in a single day.

Gill's voice came through from the front room and Wycliffe went to join him.

'Nobody seems to have heard a thing. There was nobody upstairs when it happened and the neighbours are blind and deaf. These bloody suburbs, nobody cares a fart whether you live or die.' Gill too, was moved by the senseless killing.

Wycliffe went through into the room behind the sitting room to which there was a communicating door. A bedroom with twin beds. Bright and chintzy but almost squalid in its untidiness. Powder spilled on the carpet, clothes all over the place. One of the beds had the clothes thrown back. There was a second door into a bathroom and loo for midgets. He had to go out into the hall again to reach the kitchen which had the things kitchens usually have and a sink-full of dirty dishes. What is it which turns bachelor girls into house-proud mums?

The front door was open, rain blew into the hall. They were moving the body.

'There's nothing for us here.'

'Nothing.'

James Rendell sat on the stairs in the front hall of a suburban house. The front door and the door leading into the sitting room were both shut and there was just room for a hall-stand and a telephone table. The hall lantern was fitted with ruby glass but the man's features were grey, scarcely warmed by the reddish glow. He wore a wet mackintosh and he held his hands tightly clasped between his knees to stop them trembling. For a long time he had been staring at the black and white tiles on the floor which seemed to change their pattern as he watched, then when it seemed, at last, that he was sufficiently composed he reached for the telephone and dialled a number. He listened while the instrument went through its repertoire of clicks and burrs.

'Millfield Hospital.'

He made a tremendous effort to keep his voice steady. 'I wanted to enquire about Valerie Hughes—the girl who was attacked on the allotments.'

'Hold on, please.'

An interval of silence then a woman's voice. 'Ward sister speaking. Are you a relative?'

He hesitated. 'A friend—a friend of the family.'

'Miss Hughes is suffering from shock.'

'She'll be all right?'

'Oh, yes. She needs rest and quiet.'

'Thanks—thank you.'

'Who shall I say—'

He dropped the receiver. He was shivering now, his hands once more clasped between his knees, his body doubled up, contracted as though he would shrink into himself.

The minutes passed. A car stopped nearby, he heard voices, doors slamming then silence once more. He was becoming calmer but the dampness seemed to be seeping through to his bones.

He reached for the telephone again and dialled.

'474655.' A woman's voice.

He did not answer at once for, suddenly, his voice had let him down. The number was repeated on a rising note of impatience.

'Is that you, Alice?'

'Who'd you think it is, the Queen of Sheba?'

'It's Jim.'

'You don't say!'

'I think I'll stay here for the night, I don't feel like coming back just now.'

The woman sighed. 'You're being silly, Jim. What good can it do? You'll just brood over there on your own and make yourself worse. The last bus hasn't gone yet, you could still make it . . .'

'No, I think I'll stay, just for tonight.'

'All right, if you must. Make sure you have a hot drink

before you go to bed. And what about breakfast? Have you got any eggs?'

'I've got everything I need thanks.'

'Well, all right. What else can I say?'

'Nothing. See you tomorrow evening after work.'

'Yes. All right. Good-night, Jim.'

'Good-night, Alice.'

'And Jim . . .'

'What is it?'

'You won't do anything silly, will you?'

'Of course not.'

Wycliffe drove slowly through the wet, all but deserted streets, to his headquarters.

In the darkened building the C.I.D. floor was a brilliant band of light. Wycliffe went through the duty room and up the stairs to his office. It was rarely that he used the lift. Another protest against something indefinable, part of his resentment of this crude, new, impersonal building in which he had to work; in which, perhaps, he saw some threat to his identity.

Gill joined him in his office.

'Elaine Bennett, twenty-five, free-lance nurse, at present nursing an old woman out at Kemsley Rise. She's been on that job for the past three weeks and each night she's taken the route through the allotments to pick up a bus in Godolphin Road. I got this from the girls upstairs. They also told me that her parents ran a bakery business in the city until a couple of years ago, now they've retired and they've got a little bungalow at Paignton.'

'Have they been told?'

'I passed it to the Paignton nick, they'll see to it.' He took out a cheroot and lit it, flicking the match on the carpet.

Wycliffe filled his pipe. Two girls murdered and a third attacked, apparently in error. A week separated the two killings. Were they linked? There was nothing to suggest it

70

except the improbability that there were two killers loose in the city and the fact that both girls had been strangled.

'The girls upstairs also told me that Elaine had a boyfriend, a chap called Nigel something, they can't remember what but they think it's Sears or Swears. They don't know where he lives or where he works but they gave me a passable description and he's got a red Mini.

'They're naturally a bit coy about speaking their minds now but it's obvious they didn't like her. She was a staff nurse at Millfield and chucked up her job to go into private nursing. The girls obviously feel that the hospital wasn't good enough for her.'

The telephone rang.

'Wycliffe.'

It was D.C. Dixon. Wycliffe had forgotten all about him, spending the night in Debbie Joyce's flat.

'He walked in ten minutes ago, sir, opened the door with his own key.'

'Who walked in?'

'Debbie's boyfriend, sir, the man she's been sleeping with. He's with me now and he's had quite a shock.'

'I'll send a car, you can pack up at the flat and bring him in.'

No sooner had Wycliffe passed on the news to Gill than they were interrupted again, this time by the press and Wycliffe had to go out to give them a statement.

It was one o'clock when Dixon arrived with the young man who had been Debbie's sleeping partner. Wycliffe saw Dixon in his office, alone, before tackling him.

'He took it badly, sir. I'd say he'd had the shock of his life. He's called Frisby, Donald Frisby, and he's been spending most of his nights at the flat for the past four months. He's an assistant projectionist at the Ritz cinema and he shares a flat with three other chaps; a real bachelor pad if you ask me.'

All these young people belonged to the same age group as Dixon yet his attitude towards them was that of an older man,

71

censorious and a little patronising. It was the policeman talking. Was he the same off duty?

'He knew that she should be back today?'

'Yes, sir. He says she told him that she would be in London for a week and that she would be back in the flat tonight.'

The doctor's description had been accurate. The dark brown eyes and blond, curly hair were in striking contrast. His build was slight and there was something vaguely feminine about him. He wore the same clothes as the doctor had described: blue jeans, checked shirt and leather jacket. He looked pale and confused, no more than a boy.

Wycliffe had had tea sent up and offered him a cup. He drank it down greedily.

'I can't think why anybody wanted to kill her.' His lip was trembling.

'You know that she was married?'

'Married? Debbie? I can't believe that!'

'But it's true, I was talking to her husband earlier this evening. Her husband bought the flat and paid the expenses but they lived separately.'

The rather vacant face darkened. 'Was it him?'

Wycliffe answered obliquely. 'I don't think he knew of your existence.'

Frisby looked at the chief superintendent, his eyes troubled. 'I don't know what to say. She went to London to look for a job in one of the clubs. If she got one she was going to move up there and I was going to join her later on. We were going to set up together.'

'Where did you meet?'

'At a party, one Sunday. You know how it is, there was a swop round of partners and I found myself with Debbie. I don't usually get that sort of luck.'

'When was this party?'

He looked vague. 'I can't remember exactly. September some time, I think.'

'She gave you a key to her flat?'

'After a bit. You see, she works till two in the morning and

I'm not through at the cinema till half-eleven so I took up to go round to the Cock to pick her up. The trouble with that was that it cost money; Riccy, that's her boss, don't like to see people just sitting, you got to be spending money one way or another. Anyway, Debbie said if I had a key I could go straight to the flat and that's what I've been doing.' He brought out a packet of cigarettes then thought better of it and put them away again.

'Smoke if you want to.'

'Thanks.'

'What time did you leave the flat each morning?'

'Between ten and eleven as a rule.'

'It's odd that Debbie's neighbour doesn't seem to know about you.'

He smiled, sheepishly. 'You mean the old dear in 604? Debbie made sure of that, she used to keep cavy for me every morning. Just out of devilment to keep the old so and so guessing, she said.'

'Do you know a girl called Elaine Bennett? She's a nurse.'

'Can't say I do. I don't know any nurses.'

'You didn't sleep at the flat while Debbie was away?'

'No, she wouldn't have liked that.'

'Why not?'

It was too much for him but he tried, 'Well, I know it sounds a bit odd, specially seeing she's . . . what I'm trying to say is, she liked to run things. I mean, you had to remember . . .'

'To remember what?'

He shifted uncomfortably in his chair. 'It's hard to say.'

'You had to remember that she was boss, is that it?'

'I suppose so.' He studied the end of his cigarette for a moment. 'She wasn't exactly bossy but she liked to set the pace, if you understand me.'

'How old are you. Twenty?'

'Nineteen.'

Wycliffe questioned him for the better part of an hour then let him go. He learned very little.

Poor sap. ' "She liked to set the pace",' Wycliffe muttered, 'I'll bet she did. In every way.'

Donald Frisby, 19, Assistant Projectionist at the Ritz Cinema.

Matthew Norman, 48, Senior Consultant Surgeon at Millfield General.

An object lesson in the irony of sex but there was more to it than that.

A middle-aged man, inhibited and shy; a not very bright youngster of nineteen who could scarcely be regarded as a type specimen of male virility. Lady Bountiful distributes her largesse. The message was clear. No male chauvinist pigs need apply.

Wycliffe sat alone in his office with only the green-shaded desk lamp lighting the big room. It was utterly quiet, the world could have died around him.

When he heard of Elaine's death, while he was still at Valerie Hughes' bedside, his first reaction had been disbelief followed by dismay. It was the cold resolution of the killing which had dismayed him—like an execution.

The killer must have rung the doorbell more than once. Elaine had gone to bed and it would have taken her a while to get up, put on a dressing gown and answer the door. Meanwhile he had stood waiting in the rain. What had he said to her? He must have been intensely excited. Had he managed to disguise his feelings? At least sufficiently for her to admit him without creating a major scene on the doorstep. The fact that he had used Valerie's name in ringing the hospital meant that he knew the girls and probably the set-up at the flat.

'I wanted to let you know that Valerie has had an accident.'

'An accident? You'd better come in.'

And then in the little hall, she, totally unsuspecting . . .

No need of a preliminary blow to prevent a struggle or to stop her from screaming. Before she could scream it was too late.

And what about the other case? The murder of Debbie Joyce or Rosaline Norman née Parkin. Here too the killer had been admitted to the girl's flat. She was, it seemed, making him a cup of tea. Did this mean that she knew him? Not necessarily, but if not he must have told a convincing story. But here the circumstances were very different from the murderer's point of view. He was on the sixth floor of a large building with people coming and going all the time. There were probably people in the flats above and below and on the other side of the thin partitioning walls. There must be no struggle, no possibility that she would scream. At a suitable moment, when she was stooping getting milk from the refrigerator, he struck. Again, in the cold, calculating efficiency of the crime there was the suggestion of an execution.

Wycliffe smiled sourly. He had at least talked himself round to the conviction that both crimes were the work of the same hand.

He drove home through empty streets. The rain had stopped and it was turning colder. As he got clear of the city he could see the moon riding high through a rift in the clouds and when he turned off the road into his own, private lane the Watch House lay below him, white in the moon-light and the navigation lights in the estuary were pale and insignificant.

He undressed in the bathroom and posted himself between the sheets but Helen woke.

'What time is it?'

'Half-past two.'

'Sure you wouldn't like something?'

'Yes, six hours sleep.'

She kissed him lightly and turned over. Within minutes her regular breathing told him that she was asleep.

He was not so lucky. How long was it since he had stood by his window, watching the traffic and complaining of futility? Less than twelve hours. But during that time the body of a murdered girl had been discovered, another girl had been brutally attacked and a third had been murdered. During that time . . . as often when he tried to reconstruct events in a coherent and orderly fashion his mind was invaded by a series of pictures, like slides put into a projector at random, out of sequence. Phrases came back to him, often meaningless, always out of context.

Debbie Joyce lying on the tiled floor, her black hair almost hiding the unspeakable things which had happened to her face.

'Debbie liked to set the pace—'

'You got the impression sometimes that she took a delight in hurting people.'

'Why did she marry me? I asked myself that question many times during each day and night that we were together and I still do not know the answer.'

Elaine Bennett. Her body too was crumpled up on a tiled floor. She too, had dark hair.

Both girls were twenty-five years old.

One thing seemed certain, the killer was not a homicidal maniac killing at random.

Sleep came at last, it must have done, for the next thing he knew was being awakened by Helen with a cup of coffee.

'It's eight o'clock.'

CHAPTER FOUR

THE INFORMATION WYCLIFFE had given to the press was necessarily scanty and it made headline news only in the local paper. The London dailies gave it a paragraph in the stop press. But this was the lull before the storm. Once the reporters had had time to dig around, the 'City of Fear' or something like it would be on every front page. Two killings and an abortive attack were more than enough to resurrect Jack the Ripper.

Mr Bellings, the deputy chief, always sensitive to publicity of any kind, looked in on Wycliffe to say that they must be careful not to foster a mood of hysteria on the strength of two killings. Wycliffe suggested that he might like to issue a statement but Mr Bellings was too astute to be caught that way. 'I have every confidence in your discretion, Charles.'

Meanwhile routine work went ahead. An industrial chemist was preparing a number of pieces of material very lightly impregnated with various solvents and resins for Valerie to smell. The area where the attack on her had been made, fenced off and guarded through the night, was now being thoroughly studied and searched. Through the night also the flat in Edgcumbe Close had been explored in meticulous detail. The detectives' reports were on Wycliffe's desk, so were reports from the pathologist and from forensic. They amounted to very little, no new information. The killer had left no identifiable trademark and, what was equally important, Elaine Bennett, like Debbie Joyce, seemed to have lived only from day to day. No letters, no mementoes to shed light on her twenty-five years of life. Debbie, at least had her professional photographs. Wycliffe could only marvel at the way these young people lived their complex lives out of a suitcase when his continuing sense of individuality seemed to depend on a lorry load of books, papers, photographs, notebooks, ornaments and pictures. But Mr and Mrs Bennett had come over from Paignton during the night and he was hopeful that they might fill some of the gaps.

W.P.C. Saxton came in with another batch of reports. Her blue uniform, a faultless fit, looked as though it had just come off a Hartnell peg; her ash-blonde hair was like 'after' in the shampoo advertisements and her skin, even in this winter weather, was lightly tanned. Sometimes he almost wished her on Bellings who coped with a middle-aged dragon. He was unintentionally brusque.

'Do you live at home?'

'No, sir, I live in lodgings during the week but I go home most weekends.'

'Have you kept a lot of things from your childhood and schooldays—books, school reports, photographs—that sort of thing?'

She showed no surprise. 'No, sir, that's what mothers do, isn't it? My mother has a hoard of such stuff from my first pair of shoes onwards.' She hovered. 'If you're thinking of Elaine Bennett, sir, I doubt if you've found much in her flat but I wouldn't mind betting that her mother will have a real store of this sort of thing.' She smiled.

W.P.C. Burden had been given the job of visiting the hospital and breaking the news to Valerie Hughes. Sue Burden was the same age as the girls, pleasant, homely and, by nature, sympathetic.

'You mean that after he left me he went to the flat and . . .' Valerie's brow wrinkled in an effort of comprehension. 'I can't believe it, truly, I can't.' She sat, propped up by pillows, staring at the foot of the bed.

'I mean, why Elaine?'

'That's what we've got to find out.'

'This other girl, Debbie Joyce, I mean, girls like that ask for it, don't they?'

'How well did you know Elaine?'

A shrewd look from the blue eyes. 'We've shared a flat for over a year.'

'What sort of girl was she?'

'We got on.'

'Did she have a regular boyfriend?'

A small smile which quickly faded. 'There was a boy called Nigel Sears but he was just one in a long line. It wasn't serious.'

'Doing the rounds?'

'She had a regular boy a few months back. I thought she was going to settle down but something went wrong.' A thoughtful pause. 'Elaine hated the idea of being tied to anything or anybody. I mean, that's why she gave up the hospital. And it was the same with boys.'

'Sleeping around?'

'A bit.'

'Names?'

'What do you take me for?'

'We've got to know about her if there's to be any chance of finding the chap who killed her.'

A solemn nod. 'I suppose so. In any case it makes no difference now.'

But what she knew amounted to very little, a few Christian names, the makes of one or two cars owned by Elaine's boyfriends.

'Elaine knew that Debbie had been murdered?'

'We heard it on the telly last night at six o'clock.'

'Did she say anything which suggested that she knew the girl?'

'Oh, she knew her all right, they were quite friendly when they were at school.'

'You mean that they went to school together?'

'No, I don't know the details but they didn't go to the same school, I think they met playing inter-schools hockey.'

'But in that case Elaine would have known her as Rosaline Parkin, and that name wasn't mentioned yesterday.'

'No, but she'd seen her since, at the Golden Cockerel, and recognised her.'

'Was Elaine a regular at the Golden Cockerel?'

'I don't know about a regular but I think she went there fairly often.'

'Did she seem very surprised or shocked when she heard about the murder?'

Valerie frowned, trying hard to be objective. 'No, I don't think so. She said something about it being no wonder she got murdered, considering the way she carried on at the club.'

'What did she mean by that?'

'I don't know. I doubt if she meant very much, Elaine liked to appear as though she had inside information about anything that happened.'

'Did you have the impression that she herself felt threatened?'

Valerie shook her head decisively, then regretted it because of the pain it caused. 'No, I don't think the idea entered her mind; I'm quite sure it didn't.'

They were silent for a time while Valerie sipped an orange drink.

'She didn't talk about herself much and rarely mentioned the past. Her father and mother were a bit of a drag, kind and all that, thought the world of her but over-protective, if you know what I mean. Not like mine—"Get out and get on with it, girl!" She had quite a good education, she took "A"-levels and she was an S.R.N., I'm only state enrolled. She'd have been a sister by now if she'd stayed with the hospital.' She shivered. 'God, I can't take it in that she's gone.'

Sue Burden reported to Chief Inspector Gill who told her that she was to take charge of Elaine Bennett's parents. 'Go back with them to Paignton or wherever it is they come from, find out what you can.'

'The trouble is, sir, I haven't a clue what it is I'm supposed to do.'

Gill put on his baby-frightening smile. 'Simple! Find out why she got herself strangled and who did it. If her mother is like most, she'll talk, all you've got to do is pin your ears back and ask the right questions. You'll also go through the girl's belongings and all the stuff her mother keeps.'

The W.P.C. frowned. 'But I don't see where it's likely to get us, sir. Surely it's obvious the man's a nutter, he wouldn't have had a *reason* for killing her, not a real motive.'

Gill grinned. 'No thinking in the ranks. Run along now and get on with it.'

She met the Bennetts and got them into a police car. He was tall and thin and pale; she was dumpy, not to say fat, and normally, one would think, cheerful. Now her cheeks were stained with tears and she had an unhealthy flush.

'She was such a good girl. Why would anybody want to. . .?'

They accepted the young policewoman without seeming to notice her. When they reached their bungalow in Paignton, which had a view of the sea, they let her make them a cup of tea and, later, they were persuaded to eat a little of the omelette she made from cheese and eggs. Mr Bennett hovered over her as she worked in the kitchen.

'Mother's taken it very hard.' But, if anything, he was more distraught than his wife.

Unable to stay at his desk for long, Wycliffe drove out to the allotments. He approached from Godolphin Road, a fairly wide, straight road lined with semi-detached villas built between the wars. Most of them had lapwood fencing and a few shrubs in the gardens. There was a bus stop every three hundred yards or so and a telephone kiosk on a patch of waste ground where the path across the allotments joined the road. It was not an arterial road but carried a fair amount of traffic between the city and large housing developments in its eastern suburbs.

The allotments presented a bleak prospect, a biting wind swept across the almost bare soil, rattling the corrugated iron sheeting of the ugly little sheds. Policemen stood about, waiting to be of use to the experts, stamping their feet and flailing their arms to keep warm. Sergeant Smith, the sour photographer, stalked about with his cameras and cursed steadily. Gill was sitting in a patrol car by the constable on radio watch. Wycliffe got into the back seat.

'Anything?'

Gill twisted round in his seat. 'It's obvious where he stood waiting, a gap in the privet hedge. The ground is well trodden but there are no identifiable footprints. He must take a size nine or ten in shoes which means that he's no midget. Of course, we've collected an assortment of litter but there's only one item which might be useful.' He reached into the glove tray of the car and produced a transparent polythene envelope containing a smaller manilla envelope which had a little window near the top. 'It was found where he was standing. As you see, it was crumpled and it's possible that he pulled it out of his pocket with his handkerchief. Of course, it may be nothing to do with him . . .'

'What is it—a wages packet?'

'I think so. The pay card fits in so that the man's name shows through the window. If it did come from his pocket it might help.'

'I'll take this.'

'It hasn't been checked for dabs.'

'I know.'

Gill grinned. 'In any case it's a job for a D.C.'

'I know that, too. They get the best of it, don't they?' That, to a point, was genuine. As rank had separated him more and more from the spadework—and footwork—of detection, he had felt increasingly frustrated. It would have been absurd to pretend that he did not welcome the chance to direct investigations instead of accepting direction from others but he still envied the men who worked at the level where it all happened. Occasionally, as now, he broke out.

He drove to a firm of wholesale stationers who had their offices in the city centre and was taken to the manager.

The manager only glanced at the envelope. 'No, Mr Wycliffe, we don't supply them, I wish we did.' He reached down a catalogue and flicked through the pages. 'Here we are, they're made by Deacon and Hall, part of a wages system which they supply. As far as I know there are three firms in the city using the system. The biggest is Pneumax, they make compressors and compressed air equipment. They must be the largest employers in the city; then there is Magnelec, the radio and television people, with about a thousand or fifteen hundred on their pay-roll and, finally, Goosens who assemble Italian typewriters and business machines under licence, they employ three or four hundred. The envelopes are supplied in the flat. Wages clerks lay the computer print-out on the envelope with the correct number of notes and the machine folds and seals them.'

'What about coin?'

'They don't pay coin. They have an agreement with the unions to pay to the nearest pound and carry forward balances.'

He was tempted to continue playing truant and to visit the three firms but his conscience got the better of him and he returned to his office and set a detective constable to work.

There were two reports in his tray amounting to new evidence. Valerie Hughes had sniffed the chemist's array of lightly impregnated fabrics and picked out turpentine as the perfume of the month. Wycliffe had little faith in the outcome but he gave instructions for the three firms using the Deacon and Hall wages system to be questioned about the use of turpentine in any of their technical processes. The other item seemed more promising. In response to an appeal on the local radio a woman had come forward who had been in Marshfield Road shortly after the time at which Elaine Bennett must have been murdered. Marshfield Road is the alternative, longer route from Edgcumbe Close to Godolphin Road.

'I was taking the dog for a little walk, poor thing, he'd been cooped up all day. Just to the main road and back. As I was coming back down the road, not far from my house, I saw this man. He was hurrying along, half running and I thought to myself he must be wanting to catch a bus in Godolphin Road. In the evenings they're few and far between.'

'Did you get a good look at him?'

'Not a good look. For one thing he was on the other side of the road but he passed under a street lamp and I could see him plain enough.'

'What did he look like?'

'Well, it's hard to say. I mean, he was just ordinary looking.'

'Tall or short, thin or fat?'

'Oh, tall and not fat. He had this long mackintosh which looked as though it was wet through and through. It was clinging about his legs.'

'Was he wearing a hat?'

'Yes, I think he had some sort of hat. I think it was a cap but I'm not sure.'

'Old or young?'

'Well, I don't know but I got the impression he wasn't a youngster. It went through my mind that he must be pretty fit hurrying like that and I wouldn't have thought that if he'd been a young man, would I?'

'Glasses?'

'I don't think so. I'd have noticed if he had.'

'You saw his face?'

'Well, I must have done but I can't tell you what he looked like.'

'Were there any cars parked along Marshfield Road at this time?'

'There are always cars parked there and especially at night, people are too lazy to put their cars away and they leave them in the street.'

'Could this man you saw have been running towards a parked car and not to a bus stop in Godolphin Road?'

She hesitated. 'I suppose so, but what would have been the point of running? He was wet enough already.'

'Did you hear a car start after he passed you?'

'I might have done, I can't really say one way or the other.'

Not much but decidedly something. The bus stop where Marshfield Road joined Godolphin Road was the one before the allotments and it might be possible to get something from a conductor or driver on the route.

Whenever Wycliffe was working at headquarters he lunched at Teague's, an old-fashioned eating house, narrow, little more than a broad passage between a supermarket and a bank. Two lines of high-backed booths separated by a matted walk, a set meal each day, well prepared. There was an atmosphere of calm, almost of reverence, and people conversed in low voices as though in church. There were groups of two, three or four people, regulars, who always sat in the same booth and though each group must have been well known to all the others they rarely exchanged more than a brief nod in passing. It had taken some time to convert Gill to Teague's, and even longer for him to moderate his voice and manner to the prevailing standards.

They did not have to give an order; the waitress brought Wycliffe a lager, Gill a draught beer then the soup of the day followed by the main course.

'I've put Sue Burden on dealing with the Bennett parents,' Gill said. 'She's been with them most of the morning and now she's gone back to Paignton with them.'

'She knows what she's looking for?'

Gill shrugged. 'A motive? Links between the two girls? Her guess is as good as mine. She won't find anything, the chap is a nutter and short of a fluke we shan't get him until he gets careless and starts to show off.'

Wycliffe sipped his lager. 'He's rational to the extent that he chooses his victims; any girl won't do. He was obviously concerned about Valerie Hughes, so concerned that he seems to have telephoned the hospital for news of her.'

Gill shook his head. 'It comes to the same thing in the end. They may start by rationalising what they do but finally it comes down to what it is, the lust to kill. In any case, on what criteria does he choose his victims? As likely as not it's the colour of their hair or the way they wriggle their

85

backsides when they walk.' He grimaced and startled a passing waitress. 'The fact is that no girl will be safe until the bastard is locked up.'

There was sense in what Gill said, sense based on experience but Wycliffe did not agree with him.

As they were returning to the office after lunch the afternoon edition of *The News* was already on the streets and the placards asked a succinct question:

MADMAN ON THE LOOSE?

Wycliffe and Gill were making their way among the crowds of people returning to work; everybody was in a hurry, shoulders hunched against the biting wind. There was little opportunity for talk but Gill was like a dog with a bone.

'Night patrols and decoy girls, that's the only answer to this kind of thing.'

Wycliffe was placatory. 'We may come to that, Jimmy, but we don't want to exhaust our resources just waiting for something to happen.'

The bus station enquiry was productive. At 10.05 the previous evening a conductor on a 622 bus out of the city had noticed a man near the bus stop at the junction of Marshfield and Godolphin Roads. For what it was worth the conductor's description tallied with the woman's. Tall, middle-aged to oldish, wearing a mackintosh and cap, he was hurrying in the same direction as the bus was travelling.

'We passed him before the stop and at the stop I waited for him to catch up thinking he wanted to get on.'

'But he didn't?'

'He just went by as though the bus wasn't there. I don't think he noticed.'

'What did he look like?'

'I can't tell you more than I have. The only light came from the bus and when you're standing in the light you can't see much of anything beyond it.'

A middle-aged man, fairly tall, taking size nine in shoes and active for his age. He worked for one of the three firms who used the Deacon and Hall wages system and he had recently been in contact with turpentine.

Wycliffe smiled to himself. If only it were that simple. Such a summary assumed that witnesses were accurate, that all the facts referred to the same man and that that man was a killer. Going long with the idea however, Wycliffe would have added to the list of attributes one which he regarded as important, the man had a conscience.

Nigel Sears, Elaine Bennett's current boyfriend, had been found; he was an electrician working for a firm of contractors and Gill had him picked up.

He was stocky, bullet-headed, upset and scared.

'You've heard?'

'One of my mates showed it me in the paper.' He sat, fidgeting, not knowing what to do with his hands.

'She was your girl friend; was it serious?'

'Not exactly serious; we didn't aim to get married or anything like that.'

'Why not?'

The boy shifted uncomfortably. 'Well, it wasn't like that. For one thing, Elaine had other boyfriends. I mean, I wasn't the only one.'

'Like that, was she?'

He flushed. 'She wasn't like anything, she just hadn't settled down to one bloke yet.'

'All right, don't shout at me, lad. Did you go to bed with her?'

'Once or twice.'

'And the others—did they?'

'I don't know, do I? I wasn't the first.'

'You've got a Mini, haven't you?'

'Yes, why?'

'Clapped out?'

'She's six years old, but—'

'You'd have done better with Elaine if you'd had a Jag, is that it?'

He reddened again. 'I don't see what you're getting at.'

'She liked a good time?'

'Is there anything wrong with that?'

'Ever heard of Debbie Joyce?'

'I heard that she had been found dead in her flat.'

'But before that?'

'I knew that she was a singer at the Cock.'

'So you're one of that lot, are you?'

Sears was resentful. 'I'm not one of any lot, I've been to the Cock twice.'

'With Elaine?'

'Yes, she wanted to go there but it isn't my sort of place. Too pricey for one thing.'

'Did Elaine know Debbie—apart from seeing her at the club?'

His forehead wrinkled. 'I think she might have done.'

'Think?'

'I'm pretty sure. After her act Debbie would change then come and join the customers—you know the routine. The first night I was there I thought she was coming to our table but she changed her mind and sheered off. Elaine said, "She knows better than come here", but she wouldn't tell me what she meant.'

Gill glared in silence at the young man for some time, then he said, 'O.K. That'll do for now but don't go swanning off to Majorca without saying good-bye.'

Gill caught Wycliffe in a reflective mood. He was standing by the big window in his office, apparently mesmerised by the endless flow of traffic.

'Two lads in their twenties, Debbie Joyce's sleeping partner and the latest of Elaine Bennett's boyfriends, neither of them killers, psychopathic or otherwise. These crimes are the work of a mature man.'

Gill tapped ash on to the carpet. 'I'm inclined to agree, and, on the menu so far we have Papa Bourg and Mr Matthew Norman. From what you say, Norman seems well qualified by background, temperament and experience to be a nutter and Bourg might do anything in the way of business.'

Wycliffe laughed despite himself. 'Neither of them has a weekly wage packet and Bourg certainly isn't tall and thin. All the same, I agree that they should be checked out.'

'I'll have a word with Norman this afternoon.'

'Leave it to Scales.'

Gill grinned amiably. 'You think I might create a diplomatic incident?' He knew his limitations and accepted them.

'Could be. Seriously, I can see the possibility that Norman might have killed his wife but there is no evidence of any connection between him and Elaine Bennett.'

'She used to be a nurse at Millfield.'

'So did hundreds of others.'

Reports were trickling in all the time.

Scales had established that the maiden aunt who had brought up Debbie Joyce or Rosaline Parkin, was dead. She had died of a heart attack two years before. Rosaline and her aunt had lived in a dreary little terraced house near the docks where the lorries rumbled past day and night. The neighbours were full of praise for the way in which the aunt had struggled to bring up her niece.

'And what thanks did she get, poor soul? As soon as she could keep herself young madam was off and never come near the place again in five years. Not but what that could have been a blessing in disguise for even when she was at school she was always in trouble. But she was back quick enough when the old lady died, selling up her bits and pieces.'

Another neighbour had a similar view.

'So she'd changed her name, had she. I read about a Debbie Joyce in the paper but I didn't know it was her. Well, I don't wish nobody any harm but you can't help feeling sometimes that there's a sort of justice in these things. She was always out for number one and she was that rude! I remember once when . . .'

Detection commonly proceeds by laborious and exceedingly tedious processes of elimination which mean that, at the end of an investigation, it is usually possible to look back through the reams of paper and to show that most of the work was wasted. Yet there is no other systematic approach. An inspired guess may sometimes save days of slogging but guesses are only inspired when they turn out to be right.

So the three firms who used the Deacon and Hall wages system were persuaded to provide lists of the names, addresses and ages of all weekly paid male employees. When these lists were to hand detectives would go through them picking out the middle-aged and those who lived in the eastern suburbs. With these new, much shorter lists, they would attempt some further elimination, say, all those men under five feet eight in height which would mean seeing the men concerned. Almost certainly all of it would prove a waste of time. They would narrow the field to two or three perfectly harm-less, middle-aged men whose wildest excess was a couple of pints at the local on a Saturday night.

CHAPTER FIVE

Four or five days of almost continuous rain while the city sprawls under leaden clouds, its roofs and streets gleaming in the steely January light. Another two months of winter ahead. Then, without warning, comes a golden day, the sun shines from a blue sky, the air seems to be filled with a luminous, golden haze, the buildings and streets have been washed clean and people smile at total strangers. A taste of spring and hope is reborn.

Wednesday was such a day and Wycliffe caught himself whistling as he waited patiently at a junction to join the main stream of traffic city bound. A long-haired youth in a Mini held back to let him in and he was so surprised that he missed his gear.

Sun streamed through his office window and W.P.C. Saxton had put a little cut-glass vase of snowdrops on his desk beside the daily papers. He glanced at the headlines with detachment as one does on holiday.

'Killer Terrorises City'; 'The Dangerous Age?'—a reference to the fact that the three girls attacked were twenty-five years old. 'M.P. Demands Vigilante Patrols'.

If Wycliffe was still in doubt about the kind of man he was looking for the crime reporters were not; a madman, a compulsive killer, a psychopath. One reporter claimed to have been reliably informed that young police women, in plain clothes, were acting as bait in police traps, risking their lives each night in unfrequented streets and alleys. 'Despite the risks Chief Superintendent Wycliffe has more volunteers for the work than he can use.'

All to give the great British public a warm feeling inside to go with their cornflakes.

Against all this (and Jimmy Gill) Wycliffe's reasons for believing that he was dealing with a rational man and not a homicidal lunatic began to look thin. His only evidence was the killer's failure to finish what he had started with Valerie Hughes and the strong possibility that he had telephoned the hospital in some anxiety to find out how she was. If Wycliffe was right, the man had killed Debbie Joyce and Elaine Bennett either because they had done him some injury or because they threatened him in some way. What kind of injury? What kind of threat? Good questions. It came back to possible links between the two girls. They had not been to the same school. Debbie had passed her eleven-plus and gone to Cholsey Grammar while the Bennetts' bakery had been sufficiently prosperous to send Elaine to Bishop Fuller's, a rather plush day-school for girls. But they had known each other as schoolgirls and been friendly for a time.

There was little prospect of identifying the killer on present evidence. Neither Mrs Burton, the witness in Marshfield Road, nor the conductor of the 622 bus could remember enough of the man they saw to make an identikit picture of any value. Medium height or tall, middle-aged or old, not fat, wearing a fawn or grey mackintosh and a cap. Added to that he probably took size nine in shoes and it was possible that he worked at one of the three concerns that used the Deacon and Hall wages system. That was all they had and no amount of suggestion or persuasion could make it more. All the same, detectives were touting this meagre description round the neighbourhood of Godolphin Road and a radio appeal had gone out for anyone who had seen such a man on Monday evening.

Wycliffe, still in search of his common denominator, had decided to begin with the two schools.

Cholsey Grammar had become Cholsey Comprehensive and they had moved into new buildings since Rosaline Parkin's day. A trim heap of glass-sided packing cases standing out like a very sore thumb in the semi-rural landscape on the northern outskirts of the city.

The headmaster had been reorganised with his school, but reluctantly, and Wycliffe could see in his office signs of reactionary nostalgia. Team photographs on the walls, an M.A. hood and gown behind the door and the Wadham crest on a wooden shield above the bookcase.

'I read in the newspaper what had happened to the poor girl. I remember her very well. She was dark and sallow, rather striking. Academically she was good but her background didn't help—no tradition of academic work. Of course, nowadays, we no longer expect it.' A profound sigh.

Wycliffe asked obvious questions and got obvious answers. The central heating made the room uncomfortably warm and with the sun shining on well-tended playing fields it could have been a summer's day. A teacher's voice droned monotonously in the next room and Wycliffe could imagine rows of children drowsing over their books.

'We are looking for a possible link between Rosaline and the other girl who was killed—-Elaine Bennett. Elaine did not go to this school, she was a pupil at Bishop Fuller's.

The headmaster ran a thin hand over his balding skull. 'I don't know her, of course.'

'Were there any organised contacts between the two schools —games, excursions, that sort of thing?'

'There used to be, certainly. The girls played them at hockey and, now I come to think of it, Rosaline was a good little hockey player, a winger, very fast. And that reminds me of another thing, she had fits.'

'Fits?'

'She was epileptic and she had a fit once on the hockey field. We felt that she should give up games but the school doctor said that she must be allowed to carry on a normal life.'

It is difficult to frame questions when you have no idea of what it is you are trying to find out.

'What sort of girl was she—rebellious? Conformist?'

The headmaster scratched his chin. 'It was a good many years ago, remember, but as far as I can recall she was neither one nor the other. Some children, not necessarily the most worthwhile, fit into school like a hand into a glove. Rosaline was not one of those but I don't recall her as a trouble maker either.'

He frowned in an affort of recollection then reached for his internal telephone.

'I'll ask my deputy to join us, her memory is more dependable than mine.'

Miss Finch came in and was introduced. She was aptly named, her movements were quick and darting like those of a small, slightly pugnacious bird. She was plump and fiftyish with the clear skin which is sometimes the prize of life-long celibacy.

'Rosaline Parkin? Yes, I remember her very well. I saw in this morning's paper that it was she who was killed in those new flats.'

'I was saying to the superintendent that she was an intelligent girl and not, as I remember, the sort to be in trouble.'

Miss Finch smiled. 'Not the sort to be found out certainly. In my experience she was dangerous, a very bad influence in the school and usually clever enough to escape the consequences of her actions.'

The headmaster looked crestfallen. 'Indeed? I am surprised.'

'Surely you remember the trouble she caused on one of those vacation trips that Miss Russell organised?'

'What sort of trouble?' Mildly, from Wycliffe.

Miss Finch frowned. 'It was before my appointment as deputy head but I was here on the staff. A Miss Russell was deputy and she organised a lot of out-of-school activities. On this occasion she took a party of girls, drawn from several schools, to a hostel in Dorset for three weeks during the summer vacation. They were to experience the advantages of communal living of which, as day-school pupils, they had been deprived.' Miss Finch's lip curled.

'What happened?'

'I did not hear all the details. Miss Russell dealt with the matter herself but I do know that the parents of a girl from another school complained that their daughter had been harassed and bullied by a group of girls of whom Rosaline Parkin was the ringleader. There was a good deal of very unpleasant gossip.' Miss Finch paused and smoothed the skirt of her Jaegar two-piece. 'I'm afraid it emerged that the whole trip had been something of a disaster and Miss Russell could not entirely escape responsibility.'

'What happened to the girl—to Rosaline?'

Miss Finch pursed her lips. 'Nothing happened to her. She was not punished in any way.'

The headmaster was embarrassed. 'Now you mention it I do remember there was a complaint from a parent which I passed to Miss Russell. I had no idea that it had turned out to be as serious as you say.'

Miss Finch shrugged. 'That *is* interesting. I had supposed that Miss Russell would keep you informed.'

'Do you remember the name of the parents who complained?'

'No, I do not, nor the school from which the child came. Like most things in school it was a nine-day wonder.'

'Perhaps some other member of your staff?'

'I think it very unlikely, there are only two or three of us left from the old days.'

'This Miss Russell, did she leave to take up another appointment?'

The headmaster nodded. 'Oh, yes, a school somewhere near Cambridge. I could look it up if it is of any interest to you.'

Miss Finch intervened. 'No need. She went as deputy head to Lady Margaret's near Huntingdon. She was very fortunate to get such an appointment, very fortunate indeed.'

Wycliffe stood up. 'Perhaps you will have a word with other members of staff who were here when Rosaline was a pupil and telephone me if there is anything further you can tell me.'

The headmaster escorted him to the main entrance through hordes of children swarming the corridors during a change of lessons.

The atmosphere at Bishop Fuller's was different. Miss Buckley, the headmistress, had her office in the Georgian mansion which formed the nucleus of the school. A shabbily elegant room with panelled walls, glass-fronted bookcases and tall windows.

'Elaine Bennett—when you telephoned I got out her file.' She fingered a blue folder on her desk. 'Of course I heard what had happened to her and I imagine that is why you are here.'

A few minutes introductory fencing.

'She was not a particularly able girl—five Ordinary level passes but she failed her Advanced levels.'

'What about her as a person?'

A miniscule shrug. 'She was not a popular girl either with her contemporaries or with the staff. Over-indulgent parents. Elaine behaved as though she had a prescriptive right to special treatment, needless to say, she didn't get it here.' No false sentiment with Miss Buckley.

'Did she play hockey?'

He received the what-have-I-missed-here look and Miss Buckley put on her library spectacles to refer to the file. 'Yes, she did, she was a member of our first team.'

'Would she have been likely to have played in matches against Cholsey Grammar?'

Another inquisitive glance. 'Presumably, since that was one of the schools on our fixture list at that time.'

'Can you tell me if she took part in any joint excursions or school visits with girls from Cholsey?'

Miss Buckley did not conceal her impatience. 'Really, superintendent, we are dealing with events which occurred nine or ten years ago. It is quite likely that she would have taken part in joint school activities, we did a great deal of that sort of thing.'

'But you have no records?'

'Good heavens, no! I suppose it's just possible that something of the sort might have been mentioned in her testimonial.'

Again a reference to the file.

'Yes, as it happens there is something here. Her house-mistress says that she took part in our German exchange programme, if that is of any interest.'

'Nothing else?'

'Nothing here.'

'Does the name Rosaline Parkin mean anything to you?'

She frowned. 'Wasn't that the real name of the girl who was murdered in the Grenville House flats? I think I saw it in the paper this morning.'

'Apart from that?'

'She was not a pupil here.' For Miss Buckley that closed the subject.

A bell rang and he became aware of a rising tide of movement through the building and beyond.

'Rosaline was a pupil at Cholsey while Elaine was here.'

Miss Buckley was unimpressed. 'I think I see your drift, superintendent, but surely it is unlikely that events so far back should have any significance now.'

Wycliffe ignored that one. 'Presumably there are members of your staff who were here in Elaine's day?'

'Of course, most of them. We are a very stable institution.'

Of course. That was what middle-grade executives and prosperous trades people paid for and skimped to do it. Stability and tradition.

'Then perhaps you would ask them if they remember any occasion when, in joint activities with Cholsey, something notable occurred involving Elaine?' It sounded thin, thin as railway soup.

'Notable? In what way?'

Wycliffe sympathised with pupils of Miss Buckley's faced with her uncompromising specificity.

'I've no idea, probably something unpleasant, perhaps

97

something which might have given rise to a deeply felt grievance.'

Miss Buckley closed Elaine's file. 'I doubt if they will be able to help but I will do as you ask.'

Wycliffe drove back to his headquarters through streets transformed by the winter sunshine. People strolled along the pavements and there were gossiping groups at the street corners. The women were dressed more colourfully and the whole population seemed to be a little high, mildly intoxicated by the warmth and the golden light.

On his desk a report summarised the conclusions of the detectives who had worked on the lists provided by the three firms using the Deacon and Hall wages system.

1. The three firms between them employ 3,600 persons.
2. 2,928 are paid weekly and of these 1,974 are men.
3. 953 of the men are over forty years of age and 521 are over 45.
4. The individuals in the second category of 3 are being further investigated.

Wycliffe turned to W.P.C. Saxton who was waiting to deal with the post. 'When I was at school it was all about filling a bath from two taps with the plug out.'

'Sir?'

'Never mind.'

Five hundred and twenty-one men. If one of them took size nine in shoes, was tall, thin and active and smelt of turpentine, then God help him.

Lies, damned lies and statistics. Wycliffe's sentiments exactly.

Despite the euphoric effect of the weather he was not optimistic about the case. Unless the killer made some further move . . .

He got a copy of an Educational Year Book and looked up Lady Margaret's School which the knowledgeable Miss Finch had said was near Huntingdon. He found it. Lady Margaret's School for Girls, Lynfield House, near

Huntingdon. 650 girls. Boarding with some day pupils. Headmistress: Miss D. M. Lester-Brown, M.A., B.Lit., Oxon.

He telephoned and after some brief negotiation spoke with Miss Lester-Brown.

'Miss Russell? Miss Dorothy Russell? Yes, I remember her very well.' The headmistress was suave, courteous and guarded. Even over the telephone he could sense that Miss Lester-Brown was marshalling her defences. 'No, she is not with us now, unfortunately she stayed with us for only one year.... She resigned.... No, as far as I know she did not leave to take up another teaching post.... No, I have no idea what she did.... In her letter of resignation she mentioned personal reasons.... No, I am afraid that I do not have her present address.'

'Thank *you*,' Wycliffe muttered as he put down the receiver.

Perhaps after all there was light ahead.

He picked up the telephone again and asked to be put through to the headmaster of Cholsey Comprehensive.

'Wycliffe again. I'm sorry. This Miss Russell who was once your deputy, when she was appointed you must have had a good deal of information about her—her background, where she came from, that sort of thing...'

The headmaster muttered something about confidentiality. Wycliffe was as bland as milk.

'I quite understand but all I want is to get in touch with her.... No, she is not still at Huntingdon and they have no idea what has happened to her. It is, or could be, very important indeed. If you could tell me her home town it might help—where she went to school.'

Reluctant assent. 'It will take me some time to find the papers, after all it was several years ago.'

'You will ring me back?'

'As soon as I can.'

'One more thing, don't teachers have service numbers?'

'They do, indeed.'

'Then perhaps you would let me have hers.'

Bread upon the waters.

He made one more telephone call, to Huntingdon C.I.D., asking them to make discreet enquiries concerning Miss Russell's stay at Lady Margaret's.

He lunched at Teague's and returned to deal with some of the accumulated paper-work. His industry earned the approval of W.P.C. Saxton who worried about it more than he did.

The headmaster of Cholsey Comprehensive telephoned with the information he had requested. Miss Russell had been appointed in 1960 and she had left in 1966. Before coming to Cholsey she had held appointments in Surrey and Bristol.

'Where was she at school, herself?'

'The Celia Ayrton Grammar School for Girls, near Lincoln. She left in 1944 to go up to Cambridge.'

'And her service number?'

The headmaster gave it.

Wycliffe telephoned the Department of Education asking for news of Miss Russell and spoke to a gloomy official who took a poor view of his enquiry and told him that it could only be considered if it came through the Home Office. Finally he put through a call to Lincoln C.I.D. for any information they could give him about Miss Russell and her family.

By the time W.P.C. Saxton left at half-past five, the mound of paper had been reduced to manageable proportions. He lit a pipe and stood by his window watching the home-going traffic. It was dark and the sky had remained clear so there was frost in the air. Everything sparkled, the car lights seemed brighter, more intense, the scene was vivid, cheerful, purposeful; these people were going home to wives, families, sweethearts, after a day's work. No longer did he murmur as he watched them, 'Futile!'

He was about to leave himself when the telephone rang.

'The editor of *The News* for you, sir.'

'Put him through.'

They were old acquaintances and both understood the rules of the game.

'I've a note here which purports to come from the killer, chief superintendent. I shall print it, of course but, as always, I want to co-operate. It's too late tonight but it will appear in our morning editions. I thought you might like to see it first.'

'I'll be over.'

The last edition was going out on the streets and the building was almost deserted. In the editor's office he was offered sherry.

'When we saw what it was we didn't maul it.'

The note lay in a polythene cover on the editor's desk and the envelope, crumpled and evidently rescued from the waste-paper basket, was beside it. The note and the address on the envelope had been written in block capitals using a soft pencil and the paper of the note was thick and of coarse texture like duplicating paper. The writing was neat and the message clear and concise:

I DO NOT WANT TO TERRORISE PEOPLE. THEY SAY THAT I AM A PSYCHOPATHIC KILLER BUT THIS IS NOT TRUE. IF I HAD BEEN I WOULD HAVE KILLED THE WRONG GIRL ON MONDAY NIGHT. THE WOMEN WHO DIED ARE TWO OF THE GUILTY ONES. PEOPLE CANNOT DESTROY THE LIVES OF OTHERS WITHOUT BEING PUNISHED.

The editor looked at Wycliffe with the air of one who, having delivered the goods, expects to see the colour of the other chap's money.

'What's all this about the wrong girl?'

'Presumably he made a mistake in attacking Valerie Hughes and when he discovered his mistake he let her go.'

'You knew this?'

'It was a possibility.'

'And Elaine Bennett was the right girl?'

'Presumably.'

'Why?'

'I've no idea.'

The editor was chagrined or pretended to be. 'If you would rather have your chaps followed round by reporters . . .'

Wycliffe said nothing.

'It looks as though this fellow is working off some sort of vendetta.'

'Perhaps. When did you get this?'

'It was delivered by hand to our street office before they closed at five-thirty this evening.'

'You mean that it was handed over the counter?'

'No, it was pushed through the letter box. One of the girls noticed it in the little wire cage when she was locking up. I've had a photostat done so you can take the original.'

Wycliffe nodded. 'This is obviously a reply to what you and others printed this morning.'

'Are you prepared to comment on what he has to say?'

'No, but thanks for the letter and the sherry.'

'They were both investments,' the editor said.

Back in his office Wycliffe treated the note very seriously. The note and the envelope were photographed then sent at once to forensic where they would be minutely examined and made to yield every scrap of information which they held. But he did not expect much. Here was a man who realised that block capitals give very little away. It is a waste of time to cut letters out of newspapers. A man with that much sense would be unlikely to give himself away through elementary carelessness.

Wycliffe sat at his desk with only the green-shaded desk lamp alight. He had not drawn the curtains over the big window behind him and the headlights of passing cars made wild patterns on the ceiling and walls. The subdued light fell on his blotter and on a photostat of the killer's declaration.

THE WOMEN WHO DIED ARE TWO OF THE GUILTY ONES.

Specific, unambiguous. You had to take this man seriously,

to believe him, to believe at least that he meant what he wrote at the time of writing it.

They were not dealing with an indiscriminate killer, that much was confirmed.

THE WOMEN WHO DIED . . .

Debbie Joyce and Elaine Bennett were both twenty-five years old. How had they harmed a middle-aged man? Wycliffe was more than ever convinced that he was middle-aged or older; these were not the crimes of youth.

PEOPLE CANNOT DESTROY THE LIVES OF OTHERS WITH-OUT BEING PUNISHED.

Perhaps it was not the killer himself who had been harmed but someone he loved. He saw himself as meteing out justice.

He was right about a common denominator but had he been right in going back to the girls' schooldays? At least they knew each other at school. It was imperative now to follow that lead both through the schools and in the later lives of the girls.

TWO OF THE GUILTY ONES . . .

The implication was that there were others.

Finally, I AM NOT A PSYCHOPATHIC KILLER.

The need to defend himself drove him to the risky business of writing to *The News*. He could not bear to be misjudged even in anonymity.

As he stared at the note Wycliffe began to see a vague picture through the eye of his mind. Tall, lean, fastidious, gentle. . . . Gentle! Yes, in spite of everything. A man to whom something had happened so devastating that he is completely thrown off balance, knocked off the rails. He has to rationalise his tragedy and, justly or unjustly, apportion the blame. It is in this process that he becomes obsessed.

For the past six months he had lodged with his sister and her husband in their little flat at the top of the *Guardian* building which Albert, his brother-in-law, called their penthouse.

He went up in the lift, took off his mackintosh and put it on a hanger in the hall cupboard.

'Is that you, Jim?'

His sister. Always the same welcome.

He went into his bedroom to wash and change his jacket.

Although he had lived there only half a year his room had acquired a distinctive character. There was a neat row of his books on the chest of drawers and two photographs in silver frames, one of a rather plain girl with short, straight hair and the other of a middle-aged woman with large, sad eyes. On the walls were reproductions of famous paintings, Vermeer, Canaletto, Hobbema.

He went into the living room which had a tiny dining alcove where the table was laid for the evening meal and Albert was already in his place. The television was on and the news had just started. The economic situation, a row in the U.N., a strike, the divorce of a famous actress.

Alice pushed two plates of pie through the hatch. 'You two get started, I'll be there in a minute.'

Albert was a stocky little man with black, curly hair and features which seemed to have been made of lumps of plasticene. He always looked very serious and solemn but he had a puckish sense of humour and Alice said that he ought to have been a clown.

'How's gaffer Jim?'

'All right.' He could never accustom himself to Albert's familiarity. He was a formal person and though he did not resent his brother-in-law's manner it embarrassed him because he could not reply in kind.

Alice came in with her plate. The general news had ended and the regional news began.

'. . . tension is mounting in the city. A spokesman at police headquarters said today that the possibility of further attacks could not be excluded. While there was no cause for panic it was hoped that young women in particular would behave sensibly and not go about alone or in unfrequented parts of the city after dark.'

'Terrible!' Alice said. 'Makes you afraid to put your face outside the door.'

Albert chuckled. 'You don't have to worry, old girl, he's after tender meat.'

The meal came to an end and Alice went to make coffee. Albert became serious.

'You thought any more about what I said to you?'

'Not really.'

'Of course it's your business but there's no sense in leaving a house like that and nobody living in it—costing you money and nothing coming in.'

'I'll have to think about it.'

'Eighteen thousand, perhaps more, Freddie Miller reckoned you'd get, easy as falling off a log. Eighteen thousand at seven per cent free of tax would be over a thousand a year—a nice bit of extra. Or you could use your capital to expand the business.'

Jim said nothing and after a little while Albert tried again.

'If you're really determined not to sell you could let. I mean there must be some good tenants and you could pick and choose. I mean, it's not as though you was thinking of getting married again . . .'

'I've got to live somewhere.' He gestured vaguely. 'I mean, given time, when I've got used to the idea I might go back.'

'On your own in a house that size? And there's the rates—going up all the time.'

'Yes, the rates are high.'

'There you are! I mean, it doesn't make sense, does it?'

'I'll think about it.'

Alice came in with the coffee.

'I was just saying to Jim about the house—'

Alice frowned. 'Oh, leave it, Albert. It's Jim's business after all.' She picked up the newspaper. 'What's on the telly?'

Looking back Wycliffe could point to a moment in each of his major cases when he had experienced an abrupt change of outlook, achieved a fresh point of view, and a new *gestalt*. It was the moment when he ceased to be a detached investigator and became involved, seeing the case from the inside. Helen, his wife, and his close colleagues never failed to observe the change in him even if they did not understand its cause. He became reserved, taciturn, brusque, he rarely went home for meals and he walked a great deal hardly ever taking his car from the park except to go home at night.

In the present case the change came while he was sitting at his desk that evening, staring at the photostat of the killer's message to the press.

He picked up the telephone and asked for his home number.

'Is that you? I ought to have rung you before, I'm afraid I shan't be home for a meal.'

'Now he tells me!'

'Sorry.'

'When shall I see you?'

'Probably lateish. Don't wait up.'

He put back the receiver with a feeling of release. It was odd but it was not new.

He glanced up at the clock. Five minutes to seven. He got his overcoat, opened the case file and extracted a couple of photographs which he put in his pocket then he switched off the desk lamp and left. He went down the stairs, through the duty room and out through the swing doors. The duty officer called 'Good-night, sir', but received no answer.

It was certainly frosty, he pulled up the collar of his overcoat and walked quickly in the direction of the city centre. As he approached the centre he turned off up Middle Street which ran behind a block of department stores. It was a remnant of the pre-war city and on the corner at the far end there was a pub which he had visited once or twice before. The frontage was faced with ornate green and buff tiles and the windows were frosted with elaborate scroll patterns. The Market Arms. During the day it was popular with people from the pannier market but at night there was a select clientele made up of shop-keepers and tradesmen who still lived in the district.

Wycliffe unbuttoned his overcoat and took his beer and

sandwiches to a little tile-topped table near the stove. Close by four men were playing whist for penny points. They took it in turn to examine Wycliffe with sidelong glances. Men in their forties and fifties who made enough to live in reasonable comfort and security without being affluent.

The fat man with a red face and an enormous signet ring was dealing. He seemed to obliterate the cards with his short fat fingers and he kept the tip of his tongue between his lips while he concentrated on the deal, like a child taking his first steps in drawing or writing. His partner was lean, colourless, with thinning grey hair and a straggly moustache stained with nicotine.

'Amy tells me your Joan is getting herself married.'

The fat man halted the deal. 'Saturday week at St Paul's. Chap who works in Finley's. He's only twenty-four but he's a buyer for their food hall. Done well for himself.'

'Might do a bit for you on the side.' The sally came from the third man, a bald, lugubrious individual who would have made a good undertaker. 'The odd box of oranges, a few trays of peaches off the back of the lorry.'

The fat man's face darkened. 'None of that, Sam, I run an honest business and always have.'

'No offence. Only a joke.'

'I hope so.'

They picked up their cards, counted them and found there had been a misdeal. They threw in, the fat man shuffled, baldy cut and the deal was restarted.

The fourth man who had not spoken so far, small, dark with curly black hair, said, 'There was hell up at my place before I left this evening. The wife wouldn't let Tessa go out. Afraid she'd be picked up by the lunatic.'

'Quite right too,' the fat man said. 'It's a disgrace the way the police let these bloody perverts run loose. What are they paid for? As far as I can see all they bloody do is go to football on Saturday afternoons.'

'Can I get you another, superintendent?'

The landlord had come, diplomatically, to put coke on the

stove. The message was not lost on the fat man who looked sheepishly at Wycliffe and received a bland stare in return.

There were three or four other tables occupied. One couple played draughts, the others sat, mostly in silence, drinking from time to time.

Why had he come here? He wanted a drink and a bite to eat, but why here? He asked himself the question and got only a vague answer. In fact he had formed a clearer picture of the man he wanted than he was prepared to admit. A solitary man, marked off from his fellows by events, but needing the reassurance of their presence. Where better than in a quiet pub like this one? He would not be among the card players but sitting alone, watching. If he was approached he would make some excuse.... . But Wycliffe was the only one sitting alone in this bar. He shrugged with self impatience. What a nonsensical way to go on!

When he had finished his sandwiches he got up, buttoned his overcoat, said good-night to the landlord and left. Conversation would break out as soon as he closed the door.

He cut through one of the narrow, communicating lanes to the city centre, crossed over and walked up Judson Street with the yellow glare from the Golden Cockerel ahead of him. Riccy Bourg was having his grand reopening.

The club entrance was squeezed between a male boutique and a music shop which had a window full of guitars and electronic gadgetry. The doorman, a pug in a monkey suit which was too small for him, met him just inside the door.

'Are you a member, sir?'

Wycliffe showed his warrant card and followed it with a photograph of Elaine Bennett. 'Have you seen this girl at the club?'

The pug held the photograph at arm's length.

'I seen her a few times.'

'When and who with?'

'She's been coming here off and on for months, a couple of times she was with a young man but most often she's with a party, several men and girls together. That sort turn up lateish, to finish the night off like.'

'There must be scores of girls who come in and out of this place in the run of a week.'

'Hundreds.'

'Then how do you remember this one?'

The pug looked knowing. 'Well she caused trouble, didn't she, and Mr Pirelli, the floor manager, pointed her out to me.'

'What sort of trouble?'

'Well I wasn't there, was I? I mean, I'm down here, but I heard she was drunk and made a scene with Debbie Joyce.'

'Is Mr Bourg in the club?'

The man made a move to the stairs. 'I'll see if he's there, sir.'

'You stay where you are.'

Wycliffe went upstairs and through the swing doors into a foyer where the smell of fresh paint struggled with a drench of commercial perfume. A girl in red, skin-tight pants and the sketch of a bra' asked for his membership number but settled for his warrant card and his coat. As she turned to hang up the coat he saw that she had a golden cockerel embroidered across her bottom; very fetching. What price women's lib?

Another set of swing doors and he was in the main room of the club. Plush lined booths round the walls, a dance floor in the middle and a band on a raised dais at the far end. Subdued lighting and a decor in red and gold. The night was young and there seemed to be more girls in red pants than customers. A young man in a red dinner jacket with a frilly shirt and a hairdo and beard like Disraeli's showed him to a booth and offered him a menu and wine list the size of a newspaper.

'Drinks are served at the tables, meals are available from ten until one. Our hostesses are delighted to partner un-accompanied gentlemen and the cabaret starts at ten. Games of chance in our salon through the curtained doorway by the dais.'

Wycliffe lit his pipe. One of the hostesses, a tall brunette with a sulky expression, came over to him.

'Care to buy me a drink?'

'Sit down.'

He showed her his warrant card. 'Police.'

'Just my luck.'

She was pretty under her make-up but her skin must have been very pale for the lighting only succeeded in making her look pink and naked.

'What's your name?'

'Della—Della Patterson.'

'How long have you worked here?'

'Just over a year.'

'So you knew Debbie Joyce pretty well.'

'I knew her all right.'

'How did you get on with her?'

'She was a bitch. The fact that she's dead won't alter that.'

'Is that your opinion or do the others share it?'

'Nobody liked her, she would do the dirt on anybody.'

'Like the pianist?'

She looked at him, surprised. 'So you've heard about that. He was in good company. I could write a book about her dirty tricks.'

'She seems to have got on with the boss.'

The girl nodded. 'He thought she was special. According to him she was what the customers came to see.'

'And was she?'

'We shall soon find out, shan't we?'

'Did she sleep with Bourg?'

The question really surprised her. 'With Bourg? You must be joking! He never looks at anybody but his wife. As far as he's concerned we're just part of the furniture. Hey up! Here he is.'

Riccy Bourg had come through the curtains by the dais

and was crossing the floor towards Wycliffe all smiles. He signed to the girl and she got up and went.

'Mr Wycliffe!'

'Your people must be slipping, I've been here ten minutes.'

'They jest tell me. I am much pleased to see you but we talk better in my office.'

'We talk better or, at least quicker, here.'

Riccy sighed and took his considerable weight off his feet.

'It is about poor Debbie. Why you come to me I don't know, I tell your young man—'

'It's about this girl, Elaine Bennett.' Wycliffe put Elaine's photograph on the table in front of him. Bourg looked at it with distaste.

'Who is this? She is not working for me.'

'Have you seen her in the club?'

He spread his hands. 'You ask me? Hundreds of girls come through that door. You expect that I remember?'

'This one, yes. Your muscle man remembers her very well.'

'Pouf! He is only bone above the neck that one but I will put on my glasses and look again.'

He produced a spectacle case and took from it a pair of spectacles with the thickest horn rims Wycliffe had ever seen.

'Now, I look.'

But at that moment a party of six or eight came into the room. The glasses came off, the band seemed to be rejuvenated, Bourg signalled frantically to the young Disraeli and it was some time before his thoughts returned to the photograph.

'Yes, she has been here. Half a dozen times, maybe more.'

Things were beginning to warm up. Two men came through the swing doors, laughing, saw Wycliffe and went out again.

'There, you see? You are bad for my business sitting there, Mr Wycliffe.'

'So the sooner you tell me what I want to know . . .'

'But I do tell you.'

'Not enough. What was the connection between her and Debbie?'

'Connection? What is this?'

'Something happened between them—here.'

Bourg looked at Wycliffe then at another group which had just arrived. 'It was nothing.'

'Tell me about it.'

Bourg looked at the ceiling. 'She was drunk, the girl in the picture. Six months ago, maybe more. She is in big party, you understand, three, four tables. Much laughing and a little fooling. No harm. There is cabaret and Debbie is singing. When she is finished singing, Debbie visit the tables, talk to the customers, have a little drink with them. They like that and it is good for business. Well, this night she join the table where your girl is with her friends and after a short time there is commotion and I go over to see. Your girl is more drunk than I think so I am very smoothing and I ask her what is wrong. She is very excited and she tell me that Debbie is under false pretences. She is not Debbie but is called Rosaline something.' He smiled broadly. 'Well, this is not news to me. This I know. Debbie Joyce is professional name but I cannot make the drunk girl understand this and so I ask her friends to take her home. There is no more trouble.

'Afterwards Debbie say she knew the girl when they was at school.'

'The girl has been back several times since.'

'Of course. Why not? No more trouble. When you are drunk you sometimes get very fixed idea that something is important then, when you are not drunk—pouf! All forgot.'

'You know that this girl has been murdered also?'

A calculating look from the brown eyes. 'I see it in the paper.' He shifted uncomfortably. 'I'm sorry but it has not to do with me.'

'This is a case of double murder, Mr Bourg, it would be very unwise to play games.'

But Wycliffe knew better than to see Bourg's attitude as necessarily sinister. His reflex response to the police was defensive and he was likely to appear most guilty when he had least to hide.

His chat with Bourg seemed to confirm that the only significant contact between the two girls had been while they were at school. But how did they become 'two of the guilty ones' nine years later?

'My men will have to question your staff about what you have told me.'

Bourg shrugged. 'But not tonight, eh? Tonight I get back some of the money I spend on making the place look so good.'

The club was filling and the cabaret started as Wycliffe was leaving. A stand-up comic with an Irish accent and a florid complexion told blue jokes one after the other.

Outside Wycliffe looked round for a bar, he wanted to get the feel and taste of the place out of his system. Tolerant of most things, he had difficulty in finding any common ground with the habitué of places like the Golden Cockerel. Vice in a cellophane wrapper with a red ribbon made him sick.

CHAPTER SIX

T HURSDAY WAS ANOTHER fine day but the wind had gone round to the north-east and strengthened, a bitter wind, dry and searching, probing every crack and crevice, stirring the dust in the streets and whipping up white horses in the estuary.

The News on Wycliffe's desk bleated triumphantly:

DRAMATIC DEVELOPMENT IN CITY MURDERS
EXCLUSIVE!
'I AM NOT A PSYCHOPATH!'

A photograph of the note was given a three-column spread in the middle of the front page.

More encouraging, W.P.C. Burden had returned from Paignton with a snapshot she had found amongst the mountain of stuff which Elaine's mother had treasured. Three girls of fifteen or sixteen, dressed in jeans and T-shirts, sprawled on a grassy slope in front of a disused hut that was half ruin. In the background, rocky outcrops and a moorland scene.

The girl with the mop of dark curls had been identified by her mother as Elaine, the second was Debbie Joyce, he could not think of her as Rosaline Parkin, less still as Rosaline Norman. The broad, high cheek-bones and the pointed chin were unmistakable. The third girl, fair, plump and smiling, was a stranger and somebody must have taken the snap.

Mrs Bennett was unhelpful. 'We never knew any of Elaine's friends. She never confided in us. I don't understand it really . . . we did all we could.'

Mrs Bennett did, however, remember Elaine spending a holiday after her 'O' levels at a hostel in Dorset, but she had not heard of any trouble there.

Wycliffe gave instructions for enlargements of the photograph to be made and for one to be sent to *The News*, others to the regional TV stations.

WHO IS THE THIRD GIRL?
NUMBER THREE—DO YOU KNOW THIS GIRL?
DID *you* TAKE THIS SNAP?

Ready-made headlines and almost certainly the quickest way to get answers.

He telephoned the editor of *The News*.

'Exclusive?'

'Not this time.' All the same it was from the local press that he expected results.

'You are taking over my front page.' Editors feel compelled to grumble even when good copy falls like manna from the skies.

Two girls had been murdered and in the mind of their killer they had been killed as a punishment—*two of the guilty ones*. Presumably there were others. Wycliffe had started from the assumption of a link between the two girls and it seemed logical to suppose that a similar link must exist between the dead girls and others marked down by the killer. If the nature of the link could be firmly established, if the real common denominator could be found then it should be possible to anticipate the killer, to know his intended victims and to protect them. So far it had been shown that Debbie Joyce and Elaine Bennett had known each other when they were schoolgirls and they had since met at Bourg's club. But Wycliffe was not entirely satisfied with Bourg's account of the clash between the two girls. Without some deeper cause of enmity it was unlikely that Rosaline Parkin, merely by changing her name, would provoke such a demonstration from Elaine drunk or sober. He sent for Dixon.

'Della Patterson is a hostess at the Golden Cockerel. I've no idea where she lives but you can find out either from the club or from Bourg. Find her and ask her for her version of

115

why Elaine Bennett and Debbie Joyce were at daggers drawn.'

'You think she'll know, sir?'

'I'll be surprised if she doesn't, she's been at that club for more than a year and I'll bet there isn't much she doesn't know.'

Dixon was on his way out when Wycliffe called him back. 'Are we keeping you busy, Dixon?'

Dixon studied the floor. 'I seem to have plenty to do, sir.'

'Don't you think that might mean that we find you useful?'

Dixon flushed to the roots of his blond curls. 'I hope so, sir. Thank you very much.'

Wycliffe thought of his own apprenticeship when any hint of approval from his superiors would have been interpreted by him and his contemporaries as softening of the brain. Times change.

Gill came in wearing a new suit which would soon acquire the slept-in look which distinguished all his clothes.

'I've had Lincoln C.I.D. on the phone; a chap called Evans—a Taff—says he worked with you when Noah wore rubber drawers.'

'Has he got anything for us?'

Gill sat down. 'Little enough. The Russells have lived in Saxby, near Lincoln, for generations. Dolly's father and mother kept an hotel. She was an only child. They retired some years ago and went to live on the coast but they're both dead now. There are still relatives about but they have no knowledge of or interest in our Dolly. I gather that she was unpopular—stuck up.' Gill paused to light a cheroot which he had been waving about in his hand. 'One of the relatives, a maiden aunt, says she had a letter from Dolly some time ago. It was an odd sort of letter and she ignored it.'

'How do you mean, odd?'

'I gather that it was about money but the old lady can't remember the details. She's going to try to find it but Evans says her house is like the bloody British Museum without a catalogue.'

The connections between the two murdered girls seemed slender enough but Wycliffe felt that it was the line to follow, and if he was right, the school teacher might turn out to be an important source of information. It was certainly more promising than a massive deployment of manpower to offer the public the illusion of security. Such exercises cannot be maintained and they are notoriously ineffective in catching criminals.

All the same he realised that he would have to make some move in that direction and with the co-operation of the uniformed branch and by drafting in men and cars from divisions outside the city he was able to muster a substantial force of mobiles which would patrol the city at night without exhausting his resources too rapidly. The administrative arrangements took him most of the morning and he handed over the operational planning to Gill.

Among the reports which came in was one from Scales. He had interviewed the surgeon, Matthew Norman, who appeared to have been thoroughly co-operative. Norman stated that he had been on an emergency case in the theatre at Millfield from half-past eight until gone eleven on the night Elaine Bennett was murdered. Enquiries at the hospital confirmed that Norman had successfully operated on the victim of a car crash who had suffered extensive abdominal injuries. He had been in the theatre for nearly three hours.

Exit Norman as a suspect in the Elaine Bennett case but Wycliffe had never taken the possibility of his guilt very seriously.

He was completely immersed in the case now, so much so that he was irritated by the intrusion of anything not strictly relevant. Usually he followed the national and international news with closest attention, eight in the morning on the radio, nine at night on the telly, these were sacred hours. But he had not heard a news bulletin for more than twenty-four hours. His responses to the world about him were automatic and disinterested except as they concerned or might concern his case.

Mr Bellings, the deputy chief, telephoned. 'You are an elusive fellow, Charles!'

Wycliffe, never communicative, was almost mute with Bellings.

'I think we can expect trouble from the press, Charles.'

'I don't doubt it.'

'So far they are being kind to you but it won't last . . .'

Bellings did not finish his thought. He had a stock of unfinished sentences which enabled him to make various points without actually saying anything quotable. He was saying now that another killing was almost inevitable and that it would do Wycliffe's reputation a lot of harm and not only in the press. If you listened to Bellings for long you would begin to believe that every time a dip snatched an old-aged pensioner's purse there were political repercussions. Bellings had a complex mind, he and Machiavelli would have understood each other.

'Apart from the preventive measures about which I received your memo, what other steps had you in mind?'

'I thought of writing him a letter.'

'A letter? Through the press?'

'It will have to be, I don't know his address.' He thought that he had gone too far and added, 'Call it an appeal, if you like.'

'But my dear Charles, you might as well appeal to a mad dog not to bite!'

'Perhaps, but it might be worth trying. We need time.'

Bellings took it hard. 'With three separate incidents there must be some leads.'

'There are but they haven't led anywhere. You've seen my reports?'

Why did he do it? Gratuitous provocation? Not really. His approach to his job was personal and immediate, Bellings saw everything in terms of press reaction, political and administrative repercussions, statistics and reports. There was little common ground, no hope of mutual understanding. They rubbed each other the wrong way at every contact but Bellings was able to conceal his feelings more effectively because he had the instincts of a diplomat.

'I think you should put the idea to the chief before you carry it any further.'

'I shall do, if I decide that it's worth doing.'

Was he serious about writing an open letter to the killer? Almost. The idea was growing on him. The man was sensitive to public opinion and it was just possible that such a move might put him off his stroke for a day or two, perhaps long enough to pull him in. It was worth a try. He picked up the telephone to speak to the chief constable but the chief was out of town until lunch time on Friday.

He mooned about his office most of the afternoon. He had arranged for detectives to visit the secondary schools in the city in an effort to discover the name of the girl whose parents had complained about her treatment at Miss Russell's community holiday. A trivial incident nearly ten years old. Was it likely that anyone would remember? His best hope was to find the school teacher herself and he had made it known to the press that the police would be glad to interview her.

Somewhere in the city there was a man who had killed twice and intended to kill again.

Intended was probably not the right word. *Would* kill again, he couldn't stop himself.

Wycliffe knew that there must be times when the man was tortured by doubts; hours or even days when he almost closed his mind to the knowledge of what he had done and so dulled the agony of remorse. Then came resolution, he would stop now. He would never kill again. He would give himself up. If they put him in prison he would be safe. But slowly, inevitably, his resolve was undermined, his conscience spoke to him with a different voice. If he stopped now he would be running away, betraying his trust. Reluctantly he would come to see that he must go on, it was his duty, part of the burden he carried. And so the way was made smooth for his next act.

The mechanics of the crime, planning the where, when and how were exciting. He became intoxicated by his capacity for clear, incisive thought and for prompt, decisive action. The tension grew from hour to hour, the rhythm quickened and the climax came.

It was a cycle.

D.C. Dixon reported directly to Wycliffe on his visit to the night club hostess, Della Patterson.

'She has a bed-sitter in a house in Bear Street, sir, down by the old harbour. I got there round one and she'd just got up—'

'Did she tell you anything?'

'In the end. At first she was a bit coy, said she'd already told you all she knew about Debbie Joyce.'

'Well?'

Dixon, obviously pleased with himself, wanted to make the best of his tale.

'It seems that the real trouble between Elaine Bennett and Debbie was over the floor manager, a chap called Pirelli.'

'Mr Disraeli.'

'Sir?'

'Never mind. What about him?'

'Apparently Elaine fell for him in a big way and for several weeks there was quite a thing going between them. Even some talk of marriage.'

'But Debbie put a stop to it?'

Dixon nodded. 'True to form, according to Della Patterson. She made a dead set at Pirelli and when she'd cut out Elaine she dropped him. There was no love lost between Debbie and the other girls, apparently she'd done the same thing before.'

'It's a wicked world, Dixon.'

'Yes, sir.' He lingered. 'A good many people must have felt like killing that girl, sir.'

'Fortunately there's a big gap between feeling like killing and doing it. And who felt like killing Elaine Bennett?'

'That's a more difficult one, sir.'

The telephone rang.

'Huntingdon C.I.D. on the phone for you, sir.'

After the usual preamble he asked, 'Any joy?'

'At first it didn't look very promising. Lady Margaret's is run like a nunnery, all the staff are resident and it's virtually impossible to do any unofficial snooping, but we had a stroke of luck. It turned out that our super has a friend whose daughter was involved in the Russell affair. It was largely from what she and one or two other girls told their parents that Miss Russell was asked to resign. Of course, she did and it was all smoothed over with no nasty scandal.'

'She was a lesbian?'

'So it seems. Is that what you were after?'

'I wanted to know why she resigned.'

Wycliffe asked one or two more questions but learned nothing new.

If this girl had received unwelcome attentions from Miss Russell and told her parents. . . . But it all happened nearly ten years ago. He kept coming back to that.

It was dark and once more he sat at his desk with only the green-shaded desk lamp to light the big room.

In the end he went home because he could think of nothing else to do.

He drove slowly out of the city and as he got clear of the suburbs he could feel the car being buffeted by the wind.

The living room of their new home had been made by knocking two rooms into one. There was a dining area at one end and they could sit down to a meal while they watched the ceaseless flow of traffic through the narrows at the entrance to the port. Even at night, unless the weather was bad, they often left the curtains undrawn so that they could see the pattern of light-buoys and the slow procession of ships up and down the channel, marked only by the lights they carried.

'Where are they?'

The twins, both of whom were doing post-graduate courses at university, were still on Christmas vacation.

121

'There's a film on at the Arts they wanted to see.'

'So long as they're together.'

'You're worried about Ruth?'

'I'd just as soon she was with her brother in the evenings until they go back or until we catch this joker.'

'Any prospect of that?'

'Not so's you'd notice.'

'I'll serve. It's fresh prawns with mushrooms and a curried sauce.'

They ate in silence. Wycliffe usually made the coffee but he did not stir and she went instead. When she came back he was sitting in his armchair staring at nothing.

'Coffee?'

He took the cup mechanically. Helen washed up without his help and when she came back he was still sitting. She settled down with a book—*Coastal Gardening*.

'Got a pencil?'

Helen looked up from her book. 'There's a ball-point in the magazine rack.'

'I know, how long since you've used a pencil?'

Helen closed her book on her finger. 'I can't remember, I usually use a ball-point or nylon tip. I think I saw a few pencils in one of the drawers of the cabinet.'

'In other words you don't use pencils and neither do I.'

'Is that something for the *Guinness Book of Records* or does it lead somewhere?'

'Our chap wrote his note to the paper in pencil—very soft —probably 5B.'

'Perhaps he sketches or draws or something.'

'I'd just got round to that.' He got out his pipe and started to fill it. 'Valerie what's-her-name, the girl who was attacked on the allotments, said that he smelt of turpentine.'

'So he paints as well.'

Wycliffe shrugged. 'It's a thought.'

CHAPTER SEVEN

S HEILA BARKER NÉE Jukes was getting breakfast for her husband and two children. Clive, aged one year, squatted disconsolately in his play-pen, beating the bars with a plastic toy; Denise, two and a half, lying on the floor, was scraping a crayon over a black and white picture of the Magic Roundabout.

Sheila, who had changed only predictably in nine years, was fatter, her breasts sagged more heavily and her mouth was a little harder and meaner.

Her husband called down the stairs, 'There's no socks in my drawer, Sheila.'

'They're still in the airing cupboard.'

A radio on the side board churned out pop music interspersed with inanities from the duty D.J.

She went into the kitchen and returned with an egg on a spoon which she plopped into an egg cup in her husband's place. 'Your egg's ready.'

The letter box rattled and she went out into the passage, returning with the morning paper. A picture on the front page and the headline above it caught her eye: DID YOU TAKE THIS PHOTOGRAPH? DO YOU KNOW THE THIRD GIRL?

When her husband came down she was still looking at the paper, spread out on the table.

'Look at this.'

Barker was swarthy, small and bony, already thinning on top though he was still under thirty.

He glanced at the picture and the headlines. 'They're still at it, then.'

She pointed with a fat, pink forefinger, 'That's Rosaline,

that's Elaine Bennett and the fair girl is Joan Simmonds. I wonder what they're after.'

Her husband sat in his place and sliced the top off his egg. 'You'd better tell 'em.'

'Why should I get mixed up in it?'

'No, I wasn't serious. It's got nothing to do with us.'

Sheila folded the paper and put it on the sideboard. 'Funny though.'

'What is?'

'Those two being killed like that. What are they supposed to have done?'

'Done?'

'In that note he wrote to the paper he said that they were the guilty ones.'

Barker laughed shortly. 'You don't want to take any notice of that nonsense. He's kinky—mad as a hatter.' He spoke with his mouth full of bread and egg. 'Just don't go gallivanting round the streets at night.'

'Fat chance I've got of doing that. When will I see you again?'

'Not tonight. There's a briefing session on the new promotion this afternoon and that means I shall have to stay in Bristol overnight. With luck I should be back lunch time tomorrow.'

Miss Russell and her partner were at breakfast in their high, narrow kitchen on the first floor. Originally it had been part of a bedroom which had now been partitioned to give a kitchen and bathroom. They ate a Swiss cereal breakfast with milk but no sugar and drank black coffee.

Miss Russell, now forty-eight, had changed little except that her hair was grey and tiny bristles sprouted on her upper lip.

'There's the paper-boy, Janet.'

Miss Carter, dumpy and cheerful, waddled downstairs to collect the paper off the mat. She came back up slowly, reading the front page.

124

'Look at that.'

She dropped the paper by Miss Russell's plate.

DID YOU TAKE THIS PHOTOGRAPH? DO YOU KNOW THE THIRD GIRL?

Miss Russell glanced at the headlines and at the photograph.

'What will they dig up next?'

'*Do* you know the other girl?'

'Yes, that's Joan Simmonds, they won't find her in a hurry, she's married and living in Malta.'

'Perhaps you should tell the police.'

Miss Russell regarded her companion with scorn. 'Why should I put myself out? It's all nonsense anyway, a newspaper gimmick I shouldn't wonder.'

'Those two girls have been murdered.'

'Probably because they asked for it. That Rosaline Parkin had all the makings of a tart and, from what I saw of her, Elaine Bennett wasn't much better.'

'You saw what the killer wrote to the paper yesterday— about punishing the guilty. He must have meant something.'

'Rubbish! It probably wasn't the killer who wrote it any-way. In any case, what's it got to do with me? I happened to have taught one of the girls, that's all.'

Miss Carter, as always, was bludgeoned into agreement by her companion. 'I suppose you're right. There must be plenty of people who will recognise the girl without you being involved.'

Miss Russell glanced at her watch. 'It's time I went down, the parents will be arriving.'

Friday was a day of frustration. Although Wycliffe was be-ginning to feel that he was on the right track and a number of leads were being followed, results were slow to come in. He feared that the third victim would be attacked over the weekend or shortly afterwards and, so far, he was helpless to prevent it.

The photograph of the three girls appeared in the morning paper:

DID YOU TAKE THIS PHOTOGRAPH?
DO YOU KNOW THE THIRD GIRL?

How long would it be before he got answers to these questions? Surely, with two girls already dead the third and whoever took the snap would lose no time in contacting the police. But Wycliffe knew from experience that many people have a surprising capacity for convincing themselves that whatever misfortunes befall others, nothing can happen to them.

But all publicity generates some response and by mid-day several women had been to their local police stations claiming to know the third girl; three, including a matron of fifty, claimed to be the girl and two remembered taking the photograph. All were regulars, ready to oblige with a confession or an identification at the drop of a hat.

The Department of Education, prompted by the Home Office, came through with the information that Dorothy Russell, when she resigned from St Margaret's, had cashed her pension contributions and ceased to be a registered teacher.

After lunch Wycliffe saw the chief constable and, despite an objection from Bellings, obtained permission to publish his own letter to the killer. He spent a good deal of the afternoon drafting the letter and, when it had been typed, he sent a copy to the editor of *The News*.

In the early evening he drove idly round the city. It was not that he wanted to check on Gill's dispositions, he did not, in any case, expect that they would serve any useful purpose except to reassure the public. He drove through the streets to keep contact, because he could not work from the abstractions which other people put on paper for his benefit. He passed through the city centre and down Prince's Street. There were few people about and not a lot of traffic. The wind played tricks with the the litter in the gutters.

The street lighting was poor and none of the shops was lit. That girl in the light-coloured coat, hurrying along the pavement, her body slanted to the wind, she probably felt safe in one of the main thoroughfares of the city but a resolute killer might do his work and be away before anybody realised what was happening. There would be no safety until he was taken. A police car cruised slowly down the middle traffic lane.

He reached the dock gates and turned off into a maze of streets where terraces of mean little houses alternated with the blank walls of warehouses. As he made his way northward semi-detached villas with front gardens took the place of terraced houses and there were no warehouses. Before the Second World War these had been the outskirts of the city, now the urban sprawl had engulfed former villages in all directions.

The killer was a man of the suburbs, Wycliffe felt sure of that. Once he had been at home in a neatly patterned sub-topia where each tiny garden had its forsythia, its flowering cherry, floribunda roses and bedding plants in season. He did not belong to the world of fish-and-chips and betting shops. There were thousands like him but he was different because he was a killer.

The crime cars and pandas were geometrically spaced, weaving complex, interlacing patterns through the streets.

The killer was vastly outnumbered but he had the choice of time and place. He could say to himself at any time when the odds seemed weighted against him, 'Not tonight'.

Or could he?

Was it not more likely that each time the resolution to kill needed time to grow, time to mature and that when it had he would be driven irresistibly to act.

Wycliffe sighed. A family man without a family. The phrase came to him out of the blue and he savoured it. It expressed two paradoxical ideas which had been in his mind for some time. The killer, a family man who knew what it was to have ties and obligations, responsibilities and compelling

127

loyalties—'People cannot destroy lives without being punished'. And the killer, a lonely man, haunted by ghosts.

But the paradox went deeper than that. From the beginning he had insisted that the man was rational to the extent that he did not kill at random; his victims were 'the guilty ones'. This had practical importance, it offered some prospect of discovering the killer through establishing his motives which was the reason for laying such emphasis on links between the victims. On the other hand Wycliffe, without splitting psychiatric hairs, was prepared to maintain that any multiple killer is mad, in particular that a multiple strangler cannot be sane. But, in his view, there was no necessary contradiction in attributing rationality to a mad man.

If he was right the crunch might come later, when the killer had run out of victims; that is to say when he had killed 'the guilty ones'. Then his madness might become irrational or, at least, require a further process of rationalisation.

At nine o'clock he made for home. The wind brought with it occasional flurries of sleet which clogged the screen-wipers. Helen saw that he was tired and dispirited and asked no questions. He allowed himself to be fussed over, dry sherry in front of the fire followed by a light meal. Fillets of sole poached in white wine with shrimps.

'*Sole dieppoise*,' Helen explained. 'I couldn't get any mussels so I used shrimps instead.'

Helen's cooking was much influenced by their last trip abroad. One year he had endured *sauerkraut* and sausages.

On the ten o'clock news they screened the picture of the three girls with the police appeal for information.

At eleven they went to bed but lay awake until after midnight listening for the twins to come in.

Prince's Street was the only one of the city's main throughfares to have escaped both the blitz and the developers. It was still a street of small shops interspersed with pubs, and many of the proprietors still lived in the rooms over their shops. The street had remained unchanged for long enough to attract the attention of conservationists and it was becoming increasingly the vogue to speak of it as 'interesting' rather than seedy.

One shop which was both interesting and seedy had changed little in fifty years. The signboard read : Probert and Rendell. Artists' Colourmen. Picture Framers and Restorers. In the shop window there was a large, gilt-framed oil-painting. It depicted a sea scene with fishing boats in the middle distance and a crowded jetty in the foreground. Exactly one half of the picture was encrusted with dirt and varnish so that the design was scarcely discernible while the other half was so clear and bright that the colours might have been just applied. Apart from the painting there were two display racks in the window showing a range of mouldings and a card which stated : Estimates Free.

Jim Rendell worked in what had once been a conservatory, built on to the back of the house. His partner and former employer, now seventy-five, looked after the shop but left most of the mounting and framing and all the restoration work to him. Anyone who judged their prosperity by the number of customers coming to the shop would have been misled for they were regularly employed by collectors, galleries and even museums throughout the south.

The glass walls of the conservatory had been replaced by brick but the sloping glass roof remained. The room had been divided by a partition and in one half Rendell did the restoration and mounting while in the other he had his picture framer's bench, his tools and stocks of mouldings. A cast-iron stove with a rusty smoke-pipe heated the whole place more or less effectively except in the coldest weather. The smells of turpentine, paint and glue were blended with the slightly sickly odour of linseed oil. An alarm clock, ticking away on top of a roll-topped desk, showed half-past five.

Rendell set about making a parcel of six small watercolours which he had mounted and framed in Hogarth moulding. He worked as he always did, systematically and without haste, completely absorbed in his task. As he was tying the string

Alfred Probert came and stood in the doorway. He was short and on the stout side. Long white hair and a moustache gave him a superficial resemblance to Lloyd George which he had cultivated, believing that there had never been a real statesman since the little Welsh wizard. He took a silver watch from his waistcoat pocket and compared it with the alarm clock.

'You off then, lad?'

'I'm off.'

'Are those Mr Walton's watercolours?'

'Yes, I'll leave them in the shop, he's calling for them in the morning.'

'What's up then, won't you be here in the morning?'

'It's Saturday.'

For fifteen years Rendell had not come to work on Saturdays but each week the old man pretended to be surprised.

'Well, I'll go upstairs to my tea. Mrs Probert doesn't like to be kept waiting. You'll shut the shop? Turn the lights out and lock up?'

'Yes. Good-night.'

'Good-night, lad.'

The same ritual every night, almost the same words but he never felt impatient, he would not have had it otherwise. He had worked with Probert for thirty-nine years, first as his apprentice, then as an employee, and for the past fifteen years as a partner.

He took off the long grey overall which he wore over his suit, hung it on a nail by the door and put on his mackintosh and cap. A quick look round the two rooms and he switched the lights out. Light came through faintly from the shop. A short passage and he was behind the counter in the shop where there was nothing displayed for sale. He switched out the light, let himself out through the shop door and locked it behind him, trying the door twice before he was satisfied.

A cutting wind blew down Prince's Street and he turned up the collar of his mackintosh. The shops were poorly lit, the street lamps were meagre and lorries thundered down the broad thoroughfare on their way to and from the docks. He waited his chance, then crossed in two spurts. It was not far to the *Guardian* building.

As usual, in the city centre, he waited until he was within a few feet of the newspaper seller before he allowed himself to read the placard.

Mystery of the Third Girl

He had seen the paper that morning so he knew what they were talking about. The photograph had had a strange effect on him. He had not known of its existence, there was no reason why he should have done, but the fact that the police had found and published it made him feel insecure. It was like an attack from behind, it made him realise that things were going on of which he had no knowledge.

He bought a paper.

The newspaper man said, 'Joining the big spenders, guv?'

He walked slowly past one of the big stores, reading in the light from the windows.

The photograph appeared for the second time under the caption: THE MYSTERY GIRL and the text went on to say that up to the time of going to press no one had come forward to identify the third girl in the picture nor had the police heard from whoever took the photograph.

If you recognise the girl or if you know anything of the circumstances in which this photograph was taken you are urged to telephone police headquarters, Telephone 323232, or get in touch with any police station.

Long-standing Vendetta?

The importance attached to this photograph by the police suggests that they take seriously the note which the killer addressed to this newspaper and which appeared in our columns yesterday . . .

His hands trembled so much that he could not continue to

read. He folded the newspaper and walked on slowly, breathing deeply to restore his calm.

'Is that you, Jim?'

He changed his jacket and came slowly into the living room. Albert was there.

'What you buy a paper for? You know we always get one.'

'Don't go running off, Jim, I'm just dishing up.'

If only they would leave him alone!

In the morning, by the time they had finished breakfast, the estuary was lit by the almost level rays of the sun, emphasising the contours of the landscape through highlights and deep shadows. A Norwegian vessel, her decks stacked with timber, crept up channel against the tide; a tug, towing a train of barges made out to sea. Wycliffe stood in the window of the living room and smoked his first pipe of the day. Soon now the killer would be opening his newspaper and he would read the famous letter. But would he telephone?

'I expect that I shall be in the office all day.'

'What about tomorrow?'

'I don't know. It depends. I could have incoming calls on the special number transferred here.'

His son, David, had left the old banger which he shared with his sister across the garage entrance. It was going to be one of those days.

He drove into the city and parked his car in the space which had his name painted on it. MR WYCLIFFE. Next to him was MR BELLINGS and next again, MR OLDROYD, the chief constable. Two other spaces were labelled; the hoi-polloi below the rank of chief superintendent had to fend for themselves. Bellings' E-type Jag was in his space but the chief's Rover was not. The chief believed that one of the privileges of rank should be a free weekend.

Wycliffe was morose, not because anything had gone wrong, not even because the case was bogged down but because he felt ineffectual and useless. All he could do was sit at the end of a telephone and wait.

At eleven o'clock he received a call purporting to come from the strangler. 'About your letter . . .'

There followed a description of what the caller proposed to do with his remaining victims. The details were obscene as well as impracticable. Telephone engineers and police were monitoring all calls to the special number and within a very short time, after dropping the receiver, a call came through on another line.

'A call-box in East Street, sir. There were two cars within easy reach so they should have him by now. What do you want done with him?'

Wycliffe considered. With these chaps, fortunately, it was all in the mind. 'Tell him if we catch him again we'll do him and let him go.'

Gill came in looking as though he hadn't slept. 'We seem to be getting nowhere fast.'

They had lunch of a sort sent up from the canteen.

At a quarter to two, after three more calls from kinks who claimed to be the strangler and while they were drinking a second cup of coffee, a call came through from St Thomas's Road Police Station.

'Inspector Rigg, sir. There's a young lady here who says she's got information about the photograph published in yesterday's papers.'

'Genuine?'

The inspector was careful. 'I think so, sir. She's certainly about the right age to have been at school with the girls. She seems a sensible sort . . .'

'I'll send a car to pick her up.' He signalled to Gill who had been listening on the second earpiece. Gill gave instructions over the intercom. Within twenty minutes she was in Wycliffe's office.

'Barlow—Pamela Barlow née O'Brien.'

Red-gold hair to the shoulders, green eyes and, of course, freckles. A broad forehead and a firm chin. She wore a yellow raincoat and neat little square-toed shoes with wedge heels.

Good legs. A dish—an Irish dish. She certainly earned Gill's approval.

'I live at twenty-three Water Lane, not far from St Thomas's Station.'

She had a copy of *The News* of the previous day on her lap with her handbag.

'They say you want to know about the third girl and who took the snap.'

Wycliffe nodded. 'That's right.'

'Well, I took the snap and the third girl was called Joan Simmonds.' She smiled. 'At least that was her name before she was married, she's called Roberts now; her husband is in the R.A.F. and they're stationed in Malta.'

'You're sure of that?'

'Of course. I had a letter from her Thursday.'

'Where was the photograph taken?'

'On the moor. It was a Saturday and the four of us were on some sort of charity walk. I can't remember the details.' She pulled her skirt over her knees. 'I know we stopped in front of that disused army hut to have our lunch.'

'Charity walks don't sound to me like Rosaline Parkin's cup of tea.' Gill was being frighteningly amiable.

She laughed. 'Well, she didn't finish the course. When we reached the road she hitched a lift back.'

'She was a friend of yours?'

'Not really. She was Elaine's friend. I went about with Joan Simmonds and Joan was friendly with Elaine. That's how it came about. In fact we went about quite a bit together at that time.' She fiddled with her handbag. 'Actually Rosaline and to a lesser extent, Elaine, had a reputation for being a bit wild and good girls were supposed to keep away.'

'And you were a good girl?'

'Mother thought so.'

Wycliffe intervened. 'Joan, Rosaline and you were all at the same school—at Cholsey Grammar, is that right?'

'Yes. Elaine was a cut above us, she went to Bishop Fuller's. She and Rosaline and Joan Simmonds met playing hockey.

I was no hockey player but all four of us used to meet some weekends.'

Gill stared at the girl. Wycliffe stared at his blotter. Winter sunshine streamed in through the window. Traffic was building up on the road outside. A fine Saturday afternoon and half the population wanted to get out of the city.

'We shan't keep you long, Mrs Barlow.'

'Don't mind me, my husband is glued to the telly on Saturday afternoons.'

'Being at Cholsey Grammar, you would remember Miss Russell?'

'Oh, yes, I remember her well enough.'

'I understand that she used to organise various vacation trips. Did you go on any of these?'

She looked surprised. 'I went on two, one was a camping holiday, the other we spent three weeks in a hostel.' She smiled again. 'An exercise in communal living, she called it. It was that all right.'

'Elaine Bennett and Rosaline Parkin went on both?'

'No, neither of them were on the camping trip.' She looked at Wycliffe with a puzzled frown. 'What is all this?'

Wycliffe ignored her question. 'How many girls altogether were at the hostel?'

She thought. 'Twenty-four or five, I suppose. Most of them were from Cholsey Grammar but several other schools were represented.'

'And Miss Russell was in charge?'

'Oh, yes. She was the only teacher. She organised it.'

'Did anything happen during those three weeks—anything you might think of as disturbing or even alarming?'

She pursed her lips and frowned. 'I think I know what you're after but why, I can't imagine.'

'What are we after?'

'The fuss there was about that girl.'

'What girl?'

'I can't even remember her name, she wasn't one of ours.'

'You mean that she came from another school?'

135

'She must have done but I can't remember which. She wasn't in the same dormitory as Joan and me, she was in with Rosaline and Elaine.'

'Tell us what happened.'

For the first time she hesitated. 'I wish I knew what this is in aid of. All the same, if you want the gory details. . . . It wouldn't mean anything unless you know that Miss Russell was a les. At least . . .'

'At least what?'

'Well, it's difficult. I mean, she liked to paw some of the girls, I don't think anything very bad happened.'

'Were you one of the girls?'

Curse of red hair and freckles, she blushed. 'Yes, I didn't like it but there wasn't much you could do. I mean, she made out she was being specially nice to you. Perhaps she was in her own way.'

'Rosaline too?'

'Rosaline especially. She got really browned off with the treatment.'

'What happened?'

She was reluctant. 'It really was quite nasty when you come to look back at it. I only heard the details when it was over. Of course, Rosaline was behind it.'

The two men waited.

'This girl that all the trouble was about was a real innocent and in the dormitory with that lot she had a good deal to put up with. One of her fads was that she didn't like taking a shower with the other girls so she used to get up early before the others were about. Of course, Rosaline got hold of this. She and Elaine and a girl called Sheila Jukes worked it all out. While this girl was in the shower they pinched her dressing gown and pyjamas so that all the poor kid had was a towel. She stuck it out in the showers for a while but in the end she had to come out. She made for the dormitory but they'd locked the door. Then, along comes Rosaline and pretends to be sorry for playing the joke on her. She said,

"Your things are in Miss Russell's room, all you've got to do is go in and get them."

'By this time the kid was nearly in tears and she said she couldn't go into Miss Russell's room with no clothes on but Rosaline told her not to be a fool. How did she think they'd got the stuff in there if the Russell was still in bed? She'd gone to the staff bathroom and everybody knew she took ages.

'Of course it was all lies but the kid believed her and opened the door of Miss Russell's room. As she did so Rosaline called to her, she turned to answer and Rosaline took a photo—a flash photo.'

Gill grinned with unusual ferocity. 'What a pleasant little crowd! What happened?'

'Not much at first, then, a few days later, prints of Rosaline's photo appeared on the notice boards and all over the place. There was this girl with nothing on coming out of Miss Russell's room. The door, by the way, had Miss Russell's name on it.' She stopped speaking, fished in her bag and came out with a packet of cigarettes. 'Do you mind if I smoke?'

Gill lit her cigarette.

'After that I'm not entirely sure what happened. I do know that the poor kid who was the victim of it all was sent home in disgrace. Joan Simmonds and I had to go with her in a taxi to the station to make sure she got on the train. She was in a terrible state.' She drew deeply on her cigarette and exhaled with obvious pleasure. 'Nothing happened to Rosaline and the other two as far as I know. The rumour went round that Rosaline had warned Miss Russell that if she made any fuss the headmaster would get to hear one or two things. Anyway, it all seemed to die a natural death and it wasn't long afterwards that Miss Russell left to go to another school.'

Wycliffe had made one or two cryptic notes in the convolutions of an elaborate doodle.

'This Sheila Jukes you mentioned. Was she from Cholsey Grammar?'

'Oh, yes, she was another of Rosaline's cronies.'

137

'You haven't kept in touch with her?'

She leaned forward to tap off the ash from her cigarette. 'No, we never had much to do with each other and I haven't heard of her since she left. She left in the lower sixth and I went on to "A" levels.' She sat back in her chair with a half smile on her lips. 'Now, do you mind telling me why you wanted to hear all this?'

Wycliffe still offered no explanation. 'We are anxious to get in touch with Miss Russell.'

'Well, that shouldn't be difficult. I saw her last week.'

'Here—in town?'

'In the central market. I spoke to her but she pretended not to see me—she was always good at not seeing people if she didn't want to.'

'You're sure it was her?'

'Positive—and she knew me, I could tell. She turned away that bit too quickly and became absorbed in a baby-wear stall.'

Wycliffe was looking at her with expressionless eyes. 'Didn't it strike you as odd that both victims of the killer should have been girls who were involved in this rather sick joke?'

She frowned. 'No, I can't say that it did, it only struck me how horrible it was that they should be two girls I knew.' She hesitated, then went on, 'You can't really think that there is any connection, surely? I mean, it would be too ridiculous, wouldn't it? After nine years!'

Wycliffe's face was still blank and his manner unusually pedantic. 'We are on the look-out for any links between the two murdered girls and you have told us of one such link, there may be others.'

'I see.' She looked doubtful and a little worried.

'Now, about this Sheila Jukes . . .'

But Pamela Barlow had told them all she knew. As she was leaving she turned to Wycliffe, the green eyes full of concern. 'You don't think it's possible . . . I mean, if he's mad . . . after all, I did come here, didn't I?'

Wycliffe was reassuring. 'I am sure you have no cause for worry, Mrs Barlow, but I will see that your house is kept under observation especially at night.'

When she had gone, Gill slumped back in his chair and lit a cheroot. 'I agree with her, it's bloody silly. All this for some damn fool kid's prank which happened nearly ten years ago.'

Wycliffe looked at him without speaking. Gill had never seen him so sombre. His manner was almost menacing. 'At least you know what you have to do.'

A little later he stood by while Gill briefed his men for the search. 'Dorothy Russell, aged 48, and Sheila Jukes, aged 25...'

When Gill had finished he turned to Wycliffe out of courtesy, 'Anything you'd like to add, sir?'

Wycliffe looked startled, as though his thoughts had been elsewhere. He snapped, 'Just find them while they're still alive.'

For the next couple of hours he haunted the control room where radio links with all the cars were maintained. From time to time the officer on duty was prompted to speak to him, to make some casual remark but Wycliffe behaved as though he had not heard.

Scales was the first to report back. 'Sheila Jukes used to live at fourteen Stokes Road, Cholsey. It's a council housing estate. Her father was—is for all I know, a welder. I got that from the headmaster at Cholsey Comprehensive and I'm on my way there now. Sergeant Ellis is gone to Harcourt Mansions, a block of flats where Miss Russell lived when she was at the school. It's our only starting point.'

Stokes Road was a long, depressing string of semi-detached council houses built between the wars. Each had its little front garden bounded by concrete posts and wire mesh. There was a light in number fourteen and Scales could hear the television. A teenaged girl answered the door and looked him up and down with interest. 'Jukes? There's nobody here called that. Mam! There's a man here asking for somebody called

Jukes.' She was joined by a thin, middle-aged woman with permed and dyed hair, eye-shadow and a cigarette which seemed glued to her bottom lip so that it bobbed up and down as she spoke.

'Jukes? They been gone ages, love. Emigrated. We moved in here when they went.' She considered. 'Five year ago last August.'

'Emigrated?'

She eyed him speculatively. 'Australia, I think it was. He was a welder; good trade for emigrating, they say. You a relative?'

'Police.' He produced his warrant card. 'We wanted to get in touch with their daughter, Sheila.'

'Oh, Sheila—that's different. She didn't go.' She massaged her bare arms against the cold. 'She married some fella just before they left and she stayed behind.'

'Do you happen to remember her married name?'

'No, dear, sorry. We wasn't what you might call friends. It was just when we first come to see about curtains and things they was getting ready for this wedding.'

'Was it a church affair?'

'Oh, yes, with all the trimmings. St Andrews, over across the railway.'

Scales thanked her and raised his hat.

'She's done something?'

'Oh, no. Just a routine enquiry.'

St Andrews was the parish church of what had once been the village of Cholsey. It had retained its graveyard intact with its avenue of yews and the vicarage had kept its garden but housing development pressed in on all sides. Scales reported in on his car radio.

The short drive up to the vicarage was muddy and unlit. A lighted window to the right of the front door was the only sign of life and his ring was answered by the vicar himself, a tall, spare man with fringes of grey hair, bald on top.

'Do come in!' He was taken into the room in which he had seen the light. A large room with a dusty decorated ceiling and oak panelling half way up the walls. There elegance ended and gave place to tattiness. A threadbare carpet, deal bookshelves, a cheap plastic shade where there should have been a chandelier, an ancient gas fire standing in a grate made for logs. The vicar's desk was littered with books and papers. 'I was working. You must forgive the muddle. A detective, you say, I would have taken you for a bank manager or a solicitor.' The vicar meant to be complimentary.

'You were asking about the marriage of someone called Jukes?'

'The bride was Sheila Jukes, the marriage took place about five and a half years ago and we want to know her married name.'

The vicar dangled a pair of heavy library glasses and regarded Scales with a knowing smile, 'Barker—she is now Mrs Sheila Barker'.

'You have a good memory, sir.'

'On the contrary, I have a very bad memory. It happens that you are the second person to come to me with that question.'

Scales felt his spine tingling.

'Three weeks, perhaps a month ago—certainly before Christmas, a gentleman came with the same enquiry. He said that he was an old friend of the family and that he had lost touch. He had been told that they had emigrated but that Sheila had married and was living in the city. Like you, he wanted to know her married name so that he could find her.' The vicar paused, reasonably, for breath. 'I searched the Registers and, of course, there it was—Jukes/Barker.' A benign smile.

'This man, could you describe him?'

'My visitor?'

Scales nodded.

'Oh, dear, this does sound ominous! I saw little enough of him. He arrived, like you, out of the night one might say. It was bitter cold and raining; he was muffled up with an overcoat and scarf. He refused to come into the house so we went straight to the vestry where our parish records are kept in a safe. A very few minutes while I searched and he was off again. To do him justice, he donated two pounds to church funds.'

'Old or young?'

'A subjective question, Mr Scales. He was grey and though he was not so thin on top as I, it seemed to me that we were much of an age—fifty to fifty-five.'

'Tall? Short? Thin? Fat?'

'About my build.'

'How did he strike you? Educated? Well off?'

'Oh, dear! These are difficult questions! I would say that he could have been a superior type of workman, a tradesman with his own business, perhaps.' Momentarily the vicar saw himself in 222B Baker Street, he was pleased with himself.

'Think, if you will, sir—was there anything about him—his manner, his dress, his speech, his appearance which struck you?'

The vicar reflected. 'No, I can't say that there was. He seemed to me to be a pleasant man in a little too much of a hurry to be quite as polite as he would otherwise have been. He might, even, have been nervous.'

They went to the vestry by a muddy path still littered with rotting beech leaves. Their way was lit by the vicar's flashlight. The vestry was damp and badly lit. It was a feat of strength to open the door of the massive old safe. The records showed that Sheila June Jukes had married William Edward Barker on the 3rd July.

Wycliffe's restless prowling brought him to the radio room just as Scales' second report was coming in. He was cheered, it was progress. With any luck it would be simple to locate Sheila Jukes and they had another witness who had almost certainly seen and talked with the strangler. It might be possible to get out some sort of identikit picture but Wycliffe had little faith in that prospect. Most people do not have the kind of visual memory which is necessary.

Wycliffe went through the Voters' List. There were three

William Edward Barkers and one of them was listed with Sheila June Barker at 3 Parkes Road, Maudsley. Maudsley was the nearest of the eastern suburbs, only a short distance beyond Godolphin Road. He looked them up and found them in the telephone directory.

He dialled the number. A man's voice answered.

'Mr Barker...? The husband of Mrs Sheila Barker?' Agreement tinged with nervousness and suspicion. 'Detective Chief Superintendent Wycliffe. I would like to talk to you and your wife.... This evening.... Thank you. In fifteen minutes.'

He drove out to Maudsley, along Godolphin Road, past the allotments. Although it was a fine evening there were few people about. Maudsley is a maze of roads which happened between the wars, some of them are still unsurfaced and unadopted and peter out unexpectedly into waste ground. Parkes Road was a crescent of semi-detached villas, the road lined with cars. His ring at number three was answered at once. A young man, swarthy, dark, already balding, the sort one expects to sell something. He received Wycliffe with a blend of nervousness and aggression. The sitting room was littered with children's toys. Barker waved him to a seat.

'The wife will be down in a minute. What's it all about?'

Wycliffe refused to be drawn until she arrived. She was blonde, pink and plump, running to loose fat, her eyes protruded slightly and she had a small, rather mean mouth. She looked at Wycliffe, 'Well? What are we supposed to have done?'

Wycliffe was bland. 'Nothing! Nothing at all. I want to ask you one or two questions and from what you tell me I shall know whether you need our help or not.'

She frowned. 'Why should we need your help?' And her husband demanded, 'What's all this about? We've got a right to know.'

'Did you, Mrs Barker, once know a girl called Rosaline Parkin?'

She nodded. 'I went to school with her.'

'And Elaine Bennett?'

'I didn't go to school with her.'

'But you knew her?'

'What if I did?'

'You will know that they have both been murdered.'

She looked at her husband and back to Wycliffe. 'What's that got to do with us?'

'Have you had anything to do with either of these girls since you left school, Mrs Barker?'

'No, I haven't, and anybody who says different is a liar!'

'Nobody does. The point is that we want to find out the link between the two girls—the reason why the killer chose them; then, knowing the link we might be able to make a shrewd guess at his next victim.'

They spoke together. 'Are you saying....?'

'Just that we have found only one real link between the two girls and that you were involved in that link.'

Barker got out his cigarettes and offered one to Wycliffe who refused. His wife's manner had undergone a complete change. 'Are you suggesting that I...?'

Wycliffe would not let her finish. 'I've no idea but we can't afford to take risks.'

'But the man is mad, he kills anybody...'

'We think not.'

Barker blew out a thin ribbon of smoke. 'You mean that Sheila and these two girls...but it's bloody fantastic! You heard her say yourself she hasn't had anything to do with them since she left school.'

'It's just possible that these crimes have their origin in events which took place then.'

Barker looked incredulous but his wife was worried. 'Give us a fag, Ted.' Her husband gave her a cigarette and lit it for her.

Wycliffe went on. 'You will remember a holiday with a party of girls in a youth hostel. You, Elaine Bennett and Rosaline Parkin played a cruel prank on one of the party...'

'I don't know about cruel, the kid was a creep, still wet behind the ears.'

'So you remember the incident?'

She smiled a little nervously. 'Yes, I remember it all right, it was a bit of a giggle.'

'I want to know the name of the girl who was your victim.'

'Look here, if my wife is in danger we want protection.'

Wycliffe was chilling. 'Your wife will be best protected if we catch the killer. Now, Mrs Barker, about this girl . . .'

She shook her head. 'I don't know her name. I don't think I ever heard it. We used to call her Buttercup which got shortened to Butters. She wasn't one of our lot.'

'What school did she come from?'

Mrs Barker looked surprised by the question. 'How should I know? She wasn't from Cholsey, I know that.'

'What was she like?'

'I told you, a died-in-the-wool little creep.'

'In appearance?'

'Oh, mousey—straight hair, cut fairly short; plain with freckles. Not very tall and thin—skinny.'

'Did she have any friends?'

'I shouldn't think so.' She paused. 'Wait a minute, there was a girl, another of the same sort—Buttercup and Daisy we used to call them. I haven't a clue what she was really called either.'

'Or the school she came from?'

'No, I'm sorry.' It was the first polite word she had spoken.

Try as he would he could get no further and he turned, reluctantly to the question of protection.

'Are you at home each night, Mr Barker?'

'No, I'm away two or three nights a week, I'm a rep for E.C.A. detergents.'

He arranged for a police officer to be in the house day and night and for Mrs Barker to be accompanied whenever she went out.

'No, I don't go out much. The chance would be a fine

thing. With two kids under school age and no car when Ted is away . . .'

Barker came to the gate with him. 'You seem to think this is pretty serious.'

Wycliffe was cool. 'Two girls have been murdered.'

'I hope there won't be any balls-up over this. If anything happens to my wife . . .'

'If anything happens to your wife, Mr Barker, I shall be most disturbed.'

He had telephoned instructions over the Barkers' phone and he waited by his car until he saw a patrol car turn into Parkes Road, then he drove back to headquarters.

The streets were quiet, the crime cars and pandas conspicuous.

Three girls had played a sadistic prank on a fourth nine years ago. A school teacher, for reasons of her own, had seemed to connive in their cruelty. Two of the girls had been murdered, one was now under police protection, that left the teacher.

Nothing new at headquarters. He decided to go home.

CHAPTER EIGHT

On SATURDAY MORNING he took his bed linen and his underclothes to the launderette. Alice would have washed them for him, gladly, but he would not allow that degree of intimacy. He bought a paper and looked with trepidation at the headlines. He received another shock :

AN OPEN LETTER TO THE KILLER
Detective Chief Superintendent Wycliffe, Head of Area C.I.D., writes to the killer of Debbie Joyce and Elaine Bennett through the columns of *The News* . . .

He could scarcely believe his eyes. He stepped into a goods entrance, out of the press of Saturday morning shoppers, so that he could read without being jostled.

Detective Chief Superintendent Wycliffe, Head of Area Crime Squad, writes to the killer of Debbie Joyce and of Elaine Bennett through the columns of *The News* :
'I read your letter to the newspaper and I accept your word that you are not an indiscriminate killer. I believe you when you say that you do not want to terrorise innocent people. But that is what you are doing. Each night thousands of girls and women are afraid to stir out of doors because of you. Two girls have died at your hand and another has suffered injury and shock because, you say, you made a mistake. You seemed to have been upset by your mistake for you telephoned the hospital to ask about her. But how does it feel to have taken the two other lives? How will it feel if and when you murder others? You say that they are guilty, but who are you to judge? Guilt is

147

decided by the processes of law. Are you so arrogant as to believe yourself above the law? If you are not indeed a monster you must have doubts about what you have done and even graver doubts about what you intend to do. Think again. Talk to someone. If you wish to talk to me you can do so by telephoning, day or night, 323232.

Charles Wycliffe,
Detective Chief Superintendent.'

What were they doing to him? On top of the photographs of the three girls this was too much.

'You all right, mate?'

He was standing there, staring at the newspaper, while a vanman carrying a huge cardboard box tried to get past. He slipped the newspaper into the bag with his washing and rejoined the endless stream of shoppers.

After he had washed and rough dried his clothes he went to the market and bought flowers. In the afternoon he would catch a bus to Colebrook cemetery and put his flowers on the grave. All this had become routine over the past few months, his Saturday routine. Until tea time he could pass the day well enough going about the tasks he had set himself with a sense of purpose. But this letter. . . . He thrust it resolutely to the back of his mind; it would be evening before he had to face its real challenge. Most evenings Albert and Alice were busy about their offices and he had the flat to himself. He read. An avid and undiscriminating reader, he went to the library twice a week and read whatever he happened to pick up there. But on Saturday evenings Albert was free and there was no place in the flat where he could read in peace. Even if he retreated into his bedroom it was not long before Albert would open the door—'Mind if I come in? I was thinking . . .'

So, after his first Saturday night in the flat he had gone out. He had wandered aimlessly around the city streets with the feeling that he was excluded from every human activity. In his wanderings he chanced on a little bar in Chester Street, between a Chinese restaurant and a bookmaker's. It was quiet there, he could sit in a corner and watch the regulars. In particular he watched four men who were there every Saturday playing solo. By listening to their conversation and without exchanging a word he had come to know a lot about them, their work and their families. It would have been the easiest thing in the world to have become involved and the possibility frightened him though he could not have said why. Whenever one or other of the card players caught his eye he frowned and looked away.

On this particular Saturday evening, between hands, they chatted about the strangler and speculated as to whether he would try again and if he did whether he would be caught.

The manager of the shoe shop, a little pot-bellied man, was dogmatic. 'It's obvious, he's a nutter. He'll go on until they catch him. That sort won't be put off. I mean, you or I would reason out our chances...'

The builder who, except when he was in the act of drinking, had a pipe between his teeth, shook his head knowingly. 'They never caught Jack the Ripper, did they?' He waited to let his point sink in. 'I mean, I agree with you, he's a mad man—he must be, but that doesn't mean he's stupid. They're cunning. I've got a cousin who used to work in Broadmoor and the things he told me you wouldn't believe! Like I said—cunning.'

He was not disturbed by their conversation. He listened avidly and was strongly tempted to join in. It gave him a feeling of confidence and superiority to hear their absurd comments. But he wanted to say, 'It isn't like that! You haven't the least idea...'

The giant with a red face who was a wholesale grocer was dealing another hand and the conversation petered out as they picked up their cards.

'What's trumps?' The fourth man looked like a prize-fighter but he was a foreman for the council.

'Clubs.'

'I'll try a solo.'

'Abundance on hearts,' from the builder.

'Pass.'

The manager of the shoe shop studied his cards. 'I'll try a mizzy.'

They played in silence and the manager made his call.

'If I had my way I'd bring back hanging. Mad or sane, they think twice if they know they're going to get the same as they dish out.'

The grocer blew out his flushed cheeks and belched. 'Hanging's too good for the likes of this one. I mean, it's obvious, they don't actually say so in the papers but you can read between the lines, he's after only one thing and he's ready to kill for it. Bastard ought to be castrated!' He laughed. 'Make the punishment fit the crime, that's what they say, isn't it?' He turned toward the solitary stranger who had sat watching their play for several Saturdays. 'I can see that you agree with me, sir. Castrate the bugger!'

He felt himself trembling. 'The girls were not raped!' He spoke the words in a voice scarcely above a whisper but he saw the attention of the four men suddenly focused on him. He got up, leaving more than half his beer in the glass, and walked out.

In the street he was still trembling and his heart was racing. He walked quickly as though he were trying to shake off all connection with the episode, as though he could leave it behind. His thoughts raced with his heart but they made little sense. He found himself muttering over and over again, 'You're a fool! You're a fool!' It was a fine evening and there were plenty of people about, twice he collided with someone and walked on with no apology.

By the time he was once more aware of his surroundings he had reached Prince's Street. Prince's Street, dimly lit, most of the shops shuttered and dark and despite the heavy traffic the pavements were like shadowy lanes except where the pubs made an orange splash of light. Now that he could think more clearly, he was afraid, afraid of the consequences of what he had done but more of the lack of control which made it possible for him to do it. What had he said? 'The girls were not raped!' And despite what the grocer had said several papers had stated that there had been no sexual assault. It was not so much what he had said as the way he had said it. And as though to dramatise the thing, to underline it, he had walked out.

'Hullo, darling.'

He stopped, confused, too absorbed in himself to realise at once what was happening.

'Hullo, darling. Want to come home?'

She was standing in a passage by the newsagent's, her thin, pale features lit by a street lamp. Then he understood and walked on. He heard her bored, indifferent voice, 'Suit yourself!'

He was tempted to turn back. Why not? He needed something to relieve the tension which had built up until it threatened his safety. It was tension—not wholly fear—but half-pleasurable excitement which kept the nerve endings tingling and seemed to cut him off from his surroundings. It was dangerous, if he had had any doubt of that this evening's episode had dispelled it. He turned, but she was already talking to another man.

Just as well.

He decided that he would go back to the flat. He would have his supper and by that time he could reasonably go to bed.

Albert was watching Match of the Day with a plate of sandwiches and a glass of beer on the table beside him. Alice was ironing.

'You're back early.'

'I thought I'd have an early night.'

'Good idea. There's some sandwiches; shall I get you a can of beer from the fridge?'

'No thanks, I'll just have a sandwich.'

He went to bed but it was a very long time before he got to sleep. He had kept the morning paper and he re-read the letter. He had been hurt and angered by what the newspapers had written about him and he had tried to explain. He had written to *them*, the anonymous thousands who read the newspapers and believe what they read. He wanted to put the record straight and he genuinely wanted to reassure people who were unnecessarily afraid. The last thing he had expected was a reply. Now it seemed almost as though he had addressed his letter to one man. He could not explain how he felt, even to himself, but this stranger, this policeman, had taken advantage to steal into his private world and to question what was already settled.

He turned off the bedside lamp and lay, staring at the ceiling. It was never dark in this room; at whatever time of night he woke he could see across it, the handbasin, the mirror gleaming, and his green-handled toothbrush. It was never silent either. Although the street below was usually quiet after midnight the main road through to the docks was less than a quarter of a mile away and the distant rumble of traffic seemed endless.

For a long time he turned and tossed in his bed. Once he got out and remade it. At all costs he had to avoid thinking about the future. Afterwards. Through most of his life he had taken a childish pleasure in looking forward to things, small things. An outing, doing a special job about the house or garden, holidays. . . . Several times, especially during the past day or two, he had had to struggle to extinguish the doubts which troubled him, but he had been able to fight it down.

Now. . . .

He felt that he was on the verge of being cheated, perhaps of cheating himself. After all the labour he had put into his plan. It had not been easy, he had traced four people who had been involved in an event which had occurred nine years ago. Four women, three of whom had since changed their names. He had gone about the task with patience and dogged persistence and he had succeeded. Now, half his plan was accomplished.

He told himself that it was too late for doubts, he had cut himself off with no place in the world of any other person. When Rosaline Parkin died he had ended the possibility of life for himself. 'There is no going back!' He found himself saying the words aloud through clenched teeth. Strange! At the start it had all seemed so straightforward and necessary.

He heard the church clock of St George's strike three on its cracked bell. Even after that it seemed that he did not entirely lose consciousness.

On Sunday morning he woke well before it was light, as on any other morning. Rather than disturb the others by moving round he read in bed until he heard Albert stirring. Albert for sure, Alice liked her bed, especially in the mornings. He joined Albert in the kitchen and they made coffee. It was the one time of day when his brother-in-law was taciturn so he did not have to talk. The day dawned fine and cold with clear skies. From the flat he could look out over the city and glimpse the sea, remote, pure and sparkling in the morning light. At nine Alice came in wearing her dressing gown with her hair in curlers. She made breakfast.

Although she was his sister, Alice irritated and repelled him. She was fourteen years younger so that they had not shared their childhood. She was blonde, plump and pink skinned; secretly he thought her gross. And she offended his sense of decency when, as now, she went round the flat wearing only her dressing gown which often failed to hide her heavy breasts. He compared her with his Rose who had been slim and dark and pale.

'What's the matter, Jim? You look peaky. Doesn't he, Albert?'

'I'm all right.'

'I don't suppose you'll be in for lunch?'

'No, I think I'll go over to the house.'

'Why not stay and have a decent meal for once?'

'No, I think I'll go over, there are several things I want to do.'

She shrugged. 'It's no use arguing with you but you don't look well.'

It had been the same with small variations on each of the Sundays he had been at the flat. Each Sunday he had reached the city centre in time to catch the 622 bus at ten o'clock. He was building a new habit pattern which would soon be as inflexible and necessary to him as the one it had replaced. But how long could it last?

The streets were almost deserted and they looked shabby and unkempt in the sunlight with the litter of Saturday still lying about in the gutters and on the pavements. He went up to the top deck of the bus.

He avoided looking out of the window while the bus was in Godolphin Road. After Godolphin Road the suburban sprawl thinned for a time then congealed again into a spider's web pattern of semi-detached houses and bungalows centred on the one-time village of Maudsley. Beyond Maudsley a dreary industrial estate, then Crowley; more urbanised countryside with the mushrooming university buildings, then Rhynton. Twenty-seven years ago when he bought his house in Rhynton it had been cheap, now there was competition to live that far out of the city.

He got off the bus by the pub and turned up Oakshott Avenue. Most of the houses in the avenue had garages and several of the men were out washing their cars on the concrete aprons. They greeted him with what seemed excessive friendliness as though they were anxious to make up for something.

Number thirty-seven was a corner house on the junction between Holland Drive and the avenue. The wooden palings were neat and well soaked with creosote and the privet hedge above them had been geometrically clipped. The windows shone and the curtains were drawn by just the right amount proclaiming that there was nothing to hide but no desire to display. He went to the front door, inserted his key, opened the door and passed inside. 'It's only me!' The house was silent but the shining black and white tiles in the hall, the well hoovered carpet on the stairs and the gleaming white paintwork all spoke of a well-cared-for home from which the housewife had popped out to the shops or, perhaps, to church.

He picked up a couple of circulars from the mat and went

through to the kitchen, opened the back door and collected a pint of milk from the step. He was experiencing an odd sense of detachment, an unreal calm. He seemed to be wholly absorbed in what he was doing, leaving no room for other thoughts, yet on the very fringe of his consciousness he was dimly aware of emotional conflict, of tension and turmoil. But it seemed at the moment to have little or nothing to do with him.

He got dusters and a vacuum cleaner from the cupboard under the stairs and went upstairs to the back bedroom. He opened the casement window and let in the cold, fresh air. Then he started to dust.

It was a single room with a divan bed. The bed was covered with a blue, linen bedspread and lying on it was a pyjama case in the shape of a dog with 'Jane' embroidered across it. There was a bedside cupboard, a built-in dressing table, a chest of drawers and bookshelves, all painted white with gilt fittings. He had made them all himself in those long summer evenings and during weekends which now seemed dream-like in recollection. Everywhere he looked he was reminded of years which had been the happiest of his life. One of the walls was almost covered with pictures of Jane, beginning with her as a baby and ending with the same photograph as he had on his chest of drawers in the flat, the girl with short, straight hair. She looked sixteen or seventeen.

'The three of us'—that had been the phrase constantly on their lips. From the beginning Jane had been a participating member of the trio, loved, protected and involved. His daily work had been no more than a necessary interruption of their lives at home. He worked hard because he wanted to secure the best for the three of them. Since his marriage to Rose no voice had ever been raised in anger in their house.

But he and Rose had seen the dangers of over-protectiveness too late.

He finished his dusting and started to vacuum the carpet. It was then that he seemed to reach a decision. He switched off the machine and went downstairs to the telephone in the hall. He did not need to look up the number. He picked up the receiver and started to dial then he remembered that telephone calls can be traced or he thought they could, he wasn't sure. Almost certainly the policeman who had written that letter would have his calls monitored—that was the word. He hesitated, then decided to go to a call-box. He noticed that his heart was thumping and he was trembling a little which must mean that he was excited though he didn't feel it. He put on his jacket which he had taken off to do his housework and let himself out by the front door.

There was a kiosk at the end of Holland Drive but it was too public so he cut through by a footpath to the post office which had one in a sort of yard at the back. Being Sunday, the place was deserted. He dialled 323232. He had no idea what he would say. The ringing tone, the double burr-burr repeated itself four times then there was a click as someone lifted the receiver.

'Mr Wycliffe speaking.'

A pleasant voice, kindly, he thought. His mind was racing but he could think of nothing to say. The silence lengthened and he would have dropped the receiver but the man spoke again.

'I think you must be the man who wrote to the newspaper.'

'Yes.'

'You have something you want to say to me?'

'I think so.'

'Perhaps you would like to come and see me?'

'Yes. When shall I come?'

'When you like, now if you wish.'

'This afternoon. Where?'

'At my headquarters in Morton Road, or anywhere else you prefer.'

'Out of doors. Edgcumbe Park, by the fountain.'

'When?'

'Two clock.'

'You will come?'

'I think so.'

The policeman was beginning to say something else but he dropped the receiver.

As he walked back to the house he still felt detached. It was difficult to believe that what he had just done or what he might do could really affect him.

When he arrived back at the house the boy had delivered his Sunday newspaper. It was lying on the mat. The same paper that he had taken for twenty-five years. In the beginning it had been sober, middle-of-the-road, but over the years circulation chasing had turned it into a careful blend of sex, sensationalism and sentimentality.

LETTER TO A MURDERER!
POLICE CHIEF WRITES TO STRANGLER!

In an unprecedented and highly controversial letter, published in a local newspaper, Detective Chief Superintendent Wycliffe, Head of C.I.D., invites the killer to come and talk things over!

The letter was reproduced in small type and followed by another explosion of king-size black print:

WHAT WE THINK.

We have grown accustomed to do-gooders, egg-heads and kinks who want us to believe that violence can be met by cosy chats on the trick-cyclist's couch but this is the first time we have come across a policeman who agrees with them!

Here we have a killer, a sadistic murderer who is guilty of two vicious killings and who *plans more*. What does our chief of police have to say to this man? We quote:

'I BELIEVE YOU WHEN YOU SAY THAT YOU DO NOT WANT TO TERRORISE INNOCENT PEOPLE...'

Laughable? But will you laugh if it is your wife or your daughter who is number three? Not so funny, is it?

WHAT WE SAY...

157

The scorn, the indignation and the moralising occupied the whole of the front page and spilled over into the nearest thing the paper had to an editorial.

He stood just inside the door, reading, then he climbed the stairs and made for the smaller of the two front bedrooms, the one over the hall. His 'glory hole' they used to call it. A table, a couple of chairs, an easel and a Victorian couch. On the table a jam-jar full of brushes and a box of oil-colours. On the walls, several paintings, views of the city in flat colour. In between the paintings there were framed reproductions of drawings by Michelangelo, Dürer and Leonardo. And there were shelves jammed with books.

He sat on the couch, staring at the floor between his feet. He could no longer understand his own changes of mood and they worried him. There were periods when his feelings seemed to be anaesthetised and for long spells he could go calmly about his affairs unaware, or at least insensitive to the mental conflicts and tensions which sometimes loomed so large that they threatened to overwhelm him. There were other times, brief intervals, when he was elated, when he had no doubts and his whole being was stirred to a strange excitement. Finally there were the dark times when he was weighed down by depression and doubt, when he seemed to have lost any context for his life, when there seemed to be no standards left against which he could measure his conduct or his desires. Lately these moods had succeeded each other more rapidly and with less apparent reason. But he refused to ask himself the question which lingered obstinately in the recesses of his mind.

He was vaguely aware of someone ringing the doorbell downstairs but he did nothing about it and eventually they went away.

He took his wallet from his pocket and from it he extracted a postcard photograph of a score or more girls on a beach, an older woman in the middle. Two of the girls had been ringed. A girl in the middle of the front row carried a card with 'Weymouth—1965' on it. He looked at the photograph for a long time then he got up and crossed the room to the window. The room was cold. Outside the sun shone with a brittle, frosty brilliance. Couples with children were setting out on their Sunday walks; through the centre of Rhynton and down the avenue to the river. On any fine Sunday afternoon in winter the path by the river was like a parade, prams, children, dogs.

There were shelduck, mallard and curlews out on the mudflats and solemn, tweedy men and women watched them through binoculars. He seemed to feel again a little warm hand in his.

He must have stayed in the room for a long time but when it was getting dusk he went down to the hall and dialled a number.

'Miss Coleman? Miss Dorothy Coleman?. . . I'm sorry to trouble you on a Sunday evening but I understand that you run a nursery school—a school for little girls. . . . Yes, that is what I was told. It is for my grandchild, she is four. . . . My daughter is a widow and she is coming to live in the city. . . . She has asked me to make the arrangements. . . . There are certain things I would rather not discuss on the telephone. . . . I'm afraid that I'm working all day. . . . If you could see me this evening. . . . At seven-thirty. . . . Yes, I understand. . . . My name? Oh, yes, of course—Grant—Douglas Grant.'

His hands were trembling as he replaced the receiver.

CHAPTER NINE

W YCLIFFE WAS UP early for a Sunday, before it was light. He made coffee and took it into the living room to stand by the window and watch the daybreak. The contours of the hills across the estuary slowly defined themselves, the navigation lights in the channel seemed to fade. A cold, steely grey light imperceptibly and slowly changed into a radiance which flooded the landscape with colour. He could not see the actual sunrise because his house faced south-west.

He lit his first pipe for the day.

From his early days in the force, on night duty, he had enjoyed the dawn. He liked to think of people waking from sleep, returning to the world, re-establishing their identities; remembering. But each day for some there would be a sad, perhaps a terrible awakening. You have to take up where you left off. No good fairy comes in the night to spin straw into gold or dreams into reality.

Somewhere in the city the murderer must wake this Sunday morning. Would he know a few moments of innocence before memory came flooding back?

Four schoolgirls and a wicked, perverted joke seemed to have started a train of events which had cost the lives of two of them almost ten years later. Was it possible?

The evidence seemed now to point that way and, intuitively, he was convinced but it was difficult to rationalise the idea. There were three questions: What was the connection between the killer and the schoolgirls? Why did he feel justified in murder? And why nearly ten years late?

There was no doubt in Wycliffe's mind that the killer was a middle-aged man. A husband? More likely a father. He remembered that there had been a complaint from the girl's

160

parents. But why wait ten years? It was easy to say that the man was deranged but there had to be some powerful and continuing stimulus to keep the hatred alive for that length of time and then to kill because of it.

A man with a sixteen year old daughter, an only child, doted upon, over-protected. (Perhaps a little private school—a thought there.) Then, too late, she is encouraged to 'mix'—it happens often enough. The girl does her best to adapt, tries too hard and grows more depressed with every failure. Culminating in the traumatic experience of the wretched Parkin girl's sick joke. Could this have brought about or precipitated a mental collapse? Unlikely.

But even if it did, why wait ten years to do something about it? Perhaps a slow disintegration, the man forced to watch his child gradually losing her identity in a relentless process of decline. He might feel compelled to blame someone for such a blow of fate. Rightly or wrongly (truth seldom counts in such matters) he might trace the origin of his grief back to some single incident, clearly, explicitly defined.

As an idea it was thin, but it was possible. He decided to do two things, he would get a list of the girls of the right age who had died in the city during the past year and he would get another list prepared of girls who had been admitted to mental institutions in the same period.

Taffy Evans, now Superintendent Evans, chose to telephone Wycliffe at his home rather than talk to headquarters. After recalling incidents which Wycliffe had forgotten and in the face of unrelenting taciturnity, he came to the point.

'I spoke to your man, Gill. . . . Oh, so he told you—you're lucky, boyo, my blokes tell me nothing. . . . About the Russell woman, her aunt found the letter, bless her woolly vest! She was asking her aunt to put up money for a scheme to start a prep school for girls. She had a premises in view, a country house outside Hereford. She said that she had the capital her parents left her but that she needed another seven or eight thousand. Auntie didn't want to know so she didn't bother to reply.'

Wycliffe asked if the letter was dated and from what address it had been written.

'It's ancient history, boyo, 28th December 1970 and it's on hotel notepaper—Brock's Private Hotel, Market Lane, Hereford. I don't suppose she's still there but it's the best I can do for you.'

Wycliffe detested being addressed as 'boyo' and his manner was rather more curt than the circumstances merited.

But the information was of little use.

Although a police appeal had gone out on the radio and on television there had been no response from Miss Russell. If Pamela Barlow really had seen her in the city market her silence must surely be deliberate. It was understandable that if she had re-established herself in the city she might want to avoid opening old wounds but it was just possible that the killer had reached her already. A woman living alone might not be missed for some time.

He heard the door open. His daughter, Ruth, in her dressing gown. Ruth was getting to grips with herself as a woman, leaving behind the gaucherie of adolescence.

'What's the matter? Uneasy conscience?'

She grinned. 'I smelt coffee.'

They sat on either side of the electric fire, drinking coffee in cosy silence.

Afterwards he telephoned his headquarters to get them moving on his two lists—registrations of deaths and admissions to mental homes. Not that they were likely to get far on a Sunday.

The newspapers arrived and he leafed through them. On the whole, a restrained and sympathetic press. One had chosen him as this week's burnt offering. But he was too hard bitten to be bothered by it. Bellings would be agitated.

At half-past eleven the telephone rang. He was in the living room alone. Helen and Ruth were in the kitchen getting lunch, David was still in bed.

'Mr Wycliffe speaking.'

162

The silence told him that this was the call he had waited for.

'I think you must be the man who wrote to the newspaper.' Mustn't try to hurry him, on the other hand don't give him too long for second thoughts.

'Yes.'

'You have something you want to say to me?'

Hesitation, painful and prolonged. 'I think so.'

'Perhaps you would like to come to see me?'

The door of the living room opened and David came in, wearing his dressing gown, dishevelled from bed. Wycliffe held up a warning finger.

'Sorry!'

'Yes. When shall I come?' The voice had increasing assurance.

'Whenever you like—now if you wish.'

'This afternoon—where?'

'At my headquarters in Morton Road, or anywhere else you prefer.'

More hesitation. 'Out of doors. Edgcumbe Park, by the fountain. Two o'clock.'

'You will come?'

'I think so.'

'You . . .' The receiver clicked back on to its rest and Wycliffe's phone buzzed. He replaced his receiver. A brief interval then another ring.

'Wycliffe.'

'He was calling from Rhynton, sir; a box behind the post office. A call has gone out to all mobiles in the area.'

Rhynton. Subtopia with a vengeance. The tall, thin man would now be hurrying home through the suburban roads, back to his semi-detached. A fine Sunday morning, people who knew him were bound to see him but they would never suspect. A solid citizen.

At noon headquarters called to say that they had missed him. The first mobile had arrived at the post office within three minutes of the message from the monitors but too late.

It came as no surprise to Wycliffe, he had not counted on such an easy win.

'Who is in this morning?'

'Mr Gill is in his office, sir.'

'Put me through. . . . Jimmy?'

Gill was sour. 'So they've balled it up.'

'You heard what he said to me?'

'I got them to play me the tape. Do you want me to put men in the park?'

Wycliffe hesitated. 'One good man who knows how to keep out of where he's not wanted.' He stopped to light his pipe with the receiver wedged against his shoulder. 'We shall have to do a house-to-house in Rhynton. Get it organised, Jimmy.'

'You think he'll come?'

'I wouldn't bet on it.'

They sat down to lunch at half-past twelve. A light meal. Helen was inflexibly opposed to the traditional Sunday lunch which lays out its victims until three. The sun was shining on the water and streaming into their living room. But for the skeletal elms on the hill opposite it could have been summer.

'I thought I might work in the garden for an hour,' Helen said. 'Are you going out?'

He nodded. With the university term looming the twins had decided to stay in and work.

Edgcumbe Park is a typical urban green space, shut off from the encircling roads by a thin belt of trees. Swings and slides for the kids, a pond with a fountain, slatted seats, wire litter baskets and lavatories tucked away behind rustic trellis next to the potting sheds.

Wycliffe arrived shortly before half-past two and sat on a seat by the pond. Even in the sun it was chilly. There were few people about, two or three children playing listlessly on the swings and half a dozen dog-walkers. There was no sign of a policeman, which was as it should be. He neither expected the killer nor did he not expect him. The man would have seen the letter the previous morning. He had taken twenty-four hours to mull it over, to have second thoughts and second

second-thoughts. Small things would influence his final decision one way or another and the fact that he had screwed himself up to the point of telephoning did not mean that he would keep the appointment. He seemed to realise that himself—'I think so' was the best he could manage and Wycliffe believed that he was being entirely honest.

A distinguished looking man in a well-cut overcoat and wearing an Enoch Powell hat advanced purposefully across the turf. A military bearing and a thick, greying moustache. Momentarily Wycliffe thought that the man was making for him but then a middle-aged lady tacked into his field of view, a lady in furs and wearing a floral toque. An assignation. They met on the gravelled path two or three yards from where Wycliffe was seated and without words but by gentle smiles and muted bird-like cooing noises showed their pleasure in the meeting.

Wycliffe waited for an hour then gave up. He found Gill's detective, told him to stay around for a little longer and to radio in if he saw anyone who might be the killer. Wycliffe walked the half mile back to his headquarters through streets which were in the firm grip of Sunday afternoon melancholy. He went to his office and was joined by Gill. Already the light was failing and he switched on his desk lamp.

'No luck, sir?' The grin on Gill's face was unmistakable.

'No, and you?'

'Not so's you'd notice. What's all this about registrations of deaths and admissions to mental hospitals?'

Wycliffe told him.

At four o'clock one of his lists arrived, sent by some clerk to the Hospital Management Committee who had given up part of his Sunday to make it. Three girls between 24 and 26 years old had been admitted to the city's mental hospital during the previous year. Only one was still there and it was expected that she would be discharged soon. Wycliffe telephoned the medical superintendent at his home and after a sticky five minutes satisfied himself that none of the girls was of interest to him.

A little later he had a call from the superintendent registrar. They had met at a civic dinner and the registrar, whose favourite reading was detective fiction, was falling over himself to be helpful. Four girls of about the right age had died during the year. One had been killed in a car smash, one had died in childbirth. The third girl, who had died of leukaemia was a newcomer to the city. Only the fourth girl looked at all promising from Wycliffe's point of view; she had died of an inoperable brain tumour. She was unmarried. Wycliffe telephoned the police station nearest her parents' home and asked them to get particulars, discreetly.

He sat, doodling on his blotter. This girl, the girl who seemed to have been the unwitting cause of all the trouble, must have had a mother but so far he had thought only of the father. Was it likely that the man who committed these crimes returned home afterwards to a wife? A family man without a family—his own words. So what had happened to the wife? He had postulated some traumatic experience which had turned the man's mind and he had assumed that it had been connected with his daughter's mental breakdown or death but the final blow might equally have been a tragedy affecting the wife.

His office oppressed him, he was deadened by it, muffled. He walked along the corridor to a room at the back of the building where Sergeant Bourne, surrounded by paper and filing cabinets, looked after reports and collation for the squad. Wycliffe picked up a file labelled 'Rhynton—House to House' and leafed through it.

'The file is incomplete, sir. They are still at it. The queries are starred in the top right corner.' Bourne was only twenty-five, up and coming. He believed in team work and the divinity of the computer so there was nothing to stop him.

The starred queries referred to houses where the men had not been able to talk to anyone or where the information given was regarded as either unsatisfactory or in some other way significant.

R6 '25 Horton Drive. Householder : George Bray. 35/40.
No reply. Neighbour states that the family visit relatives
on Sundays.

R21 '14 Coulston Road. Householder : John Harris.
25/30. No reply. Neighbour states that Mrs Harris is in
hospital having a baby. Husband is staying with parents
for the time being.

R29 '9 Stacey's Road. Householder : James Higgins.
45/50. No reply. Neighbour states that the family always
go out in their car on fine Sundays . . .'

A desperate lot of criminals there.

Wycliffe went back to his desk, lit a pipe and started to go
through the reports, starred and unstarred alike. Occasionally
he put one aside and ended up with four, all of them starred :

R58 '32 Hyde Avenue. Householder : Simon Kent. 50/55.
Widower. Lives with unmarried daughter who is now
in London staying with friends. States that he spent
whole morning in greenhouse.

R79 '6 Farley Close. Householder : Arnold Pearce. 40/45.
Married but lives alone. Guarded when questioned
about his wife. States that he spent the morning doing
his chores and did not go out.

R104 '37 Oakshott Avenue. Householder : James Rendell.
50/55. No reply. Neighbour states that Rendell recently
lost his wife and is living temporarily with relatives.

R146 '14 Holland Drive. Householder : Fredrick Polski.
50/55. Widower. Married daughter and her husband
share house. Polski states that he went for a long walk
between ten and lunchtime. Daughter confirms that this
is his habit. Married couple spent morning about the
house.'

Three widowers and one man who seems reluctant to
account for his wife.

Wycliffe looked at his clock, its gilded pointers stuck out

from the panelling, sweeping their silent orbits over gilded cyphers. He liked a clock which ticked, with Roman numerals and fretted hands. Seven o'clock. He telephoned his wife not to expect him.

He was depressed and uneasy.

It was a fortnight since the first murder, almost a week since the second. He felt that the next, if there was to be a next, was due—perhaps overdue. Rosaline Parkin and Elaine Bennett were dead; Sheila Barker was under the strictest surveillance which might mean that they had reached stalemate unless the school teacher was on the killer's list. If she was she must be in imminent danger. After having second thoughts about giving himself up the killer might feel a compulsive need to assert himself once more, perhaps even to atone for his moment of weakness.

Wycliffe rang through to Sergeant Bourne. 'Any further reports?'

'D.C. James has just come in with another batch, sir, and two checks on previous interviews.'

'Which?'

A moment's delay. 'R79 and R104, sir, Pearce and Rendell. Pearce was cagey about his wife and the reason seems to be that she's recently left him. She was twenty years younger and she's gone off with another man. Rendell's wife died six months ago and he is now living with his married sister, a Mrs Martin. She and her husband are caretakers of the *Guardian* building in the city centre; they have a flat on the top floor.'

'Has he been contacted there?'

'No, sir, he was out when D.C. James telephoned.'

'What did his wife die of?'

Hesitation. 'The report doesn't say, sir, if it's important I'll find . . .'

'Don't bother.'

He lit his pipe and wandered over to the windows. The curtains had not been drawn and he could see the brightly-lit main road with its endless stream of traffic. The windows were misted over by fine rain which refracted the light and distorted the view. He felt helpless.

If the school teacher had been living in the city for six months she should be in the Voters' List but she was not there under her own name. He returned to his desk and picked up the exchange telephone. 'I want to speak to Mr or Mrs Martin, they are caretakers of the *Guardian* building and they live on the premises.'

An interval. 'You're through, sir.'

A woman's voice.

'Mrs Martin?' He was amiable, casual. 'Is your brother there?'

'You've just missed him; he came in and went out again.'

'Never mind. As you know, we are making a routine check on all the occupiers of houses in the Rhynton district of the city . . .'

She sounded helpful, unflustered.

'I understand that your brother has made his home with you temporarily—since the death of his wife. . . . Yes, I'm sure it would be. How long has he been with you? . . . Since the beginning of July. Did she have a long illness?'

'She took her own life.'

'I'm sorry.'

'It was very sad.' She sounded a nice woman, genuinely upset. 'Tragic really, they lost their only child, a girl, a few years back and she never got over it. Never the same afterwards.'

'Have you any idea where your brother might be or when he's likely to be back?'

'He went out for a drink, he said he was meeting a friend.'

'Which pub does he use?'

'He doesn't have a regular pub, he's not much of a drinker.'

'It doesn't matter.'

'Shall I tell him to ring you when he gets back?'

'No, don't bother, it doesn't matter.' He thanked her and rang off.

This was it. No dramatic revelations, no blinding intuitive

169

flash, no brilliant deductive reasoning, just the result of plodding routine enquiries. The great detective has it handed to him on a plate by a small army of foot-sloggers who go about ringing doorbells like soap salesmen. Of course, he could still be wrong but he knew that he wasn't.

He telephoned Gill and arranged for a man to be put in the flat and for the house in Oakshott Avenue to be watched. 'The sister will have to be told and we shall want a full description for circulation, photograph if possible.'

Back to the school teacher. It was disturbing that she had not been found and it seemed fairly certain that she could not be living in the city under her own name. If her professional career had ended under a cloud she might well want the past forgotten. In his experience women were singularly unimaginative in the use of an alias. A married woman usually went back to her maiden name, a single woman would as often as not chose her mother's. It was worth a try. Without much enthusiasm he put through a call to Superintendent Evans at his home number and sat smoking while he waited for it to come through.

'Her mother's name? I don't have to find out, boyo, I know. Her mother was a Coleman, well known local family, farmers in a big way of business.'

And there she was in the telephone directory, or so he told himself. Miss Dorothy Coleman, The Nursery School, 6 Poulton Avenue. A woman running a nursery school would probably be obsessively concerned to avoid any breath of scandal.

He rang the duty room and told them to send a car to the school, to obtain admission if possible and to wait until he arrived. Then he collected his car from the park and drove to Poulton Avenue. It was a quarter past eight. Fine, misty rain cut down visibility and there were few people about.

Poulton Avenue consisted of large, semi-detached houses built before the first war. A neat little sign on the gate of number six showed up in the light of a street lamp: Poulton Avenue Nursery School.

A police car was parked a little way down the road, the house was in darkness and as Wycliffe drew into the curb a constable came towards him.

'Nobody home, sir. At least, I can get no answer.'

'I'll stay here, you go round the back and see if there's any sign of life there.'

Wycliffe sat in the car. The rain was so fine that it was little more than mist. The street lamps were blurred and the branches of trees overhanging from the gardens formed vague silhouettes, more like shadows.

Footsteps sounded clearly on the flagstones of the pavement and a woman, small and dumpy, stopped by the gate of number six. She looked at the car uncertainly then opened the gate. Wycliffe got out.

'Miss Coleman?'

'Is there something wrong? Who are you?'

Wycliffe introduced himself and she seemed irritated rather than surprised or concerned.

'Why are you here?'

'Perhaps we could talk inside.'

The constable returned and Wycliffe told him to wait. The woman unlocked the front door with a Yale key and switched on the hall light.

'I'm not Miss Coleman, my name is Carter—Miss Carter, I share the house and help with the school.'

The hall was bare and institutional but the stairs were carpeted and she led the way up.

'We live on the first floor.'

'Miss Coleman is not at home?'

'No, as you see, I've just come in myself but Miss Coleman usually goes out for her stroll at about this time.'

'In the rain?'

She smiled. 'It would take more than a drop of rain to put her off.'

He was taken into the front room on the first floor. It was a large room, sitting room and office combined. Old-fashioned chairs with worn upholstery, glass-fronted book-cases, a roll-topped desk with a telephone on it and gilt-framed oil paintings on the walls. Wycliffe was uneasy, partly because he was unsure of his ground. He had only flimsy reasons for supposing that Dorothy Coleman was Dorothy Russell.

'Is Miss Coleman likely to be long?'

'I shouldn't think so, she usually walks round a couple of blocks.'

She waved him to one of the easy chairs and perched herself on the edge of another, showing a lot of fat thigh above her stockings.

'How long have you known Miss Coleman?'

'Several years.'

'More than ten years?'

'Probably. Why do you ask?' Her manner was aggressive.

'Did you know her when she was Dorothy Russell?'

She dug in. 'Until you tell me why you are asking these questions I don't propose to answer any more.'

Wycliffe was bland. 'That's reasonable, I'll explain. I think that the woman who was Dorothy Russell may be in very great danger.'

She looked at him as though trying to read his mind. 'You really mean that?'

'I do.'

She seemed to relax her guard. 'I told her but she wouldn't take any notice. She's very obstinate.' She went to a side table and took a cigarette from a box. 'Smoke?'

But Wycliffe had crossed to the desk and picked up the telephone. He dialled and was answered almost at once. 'Wycliffe. I want all mobiles in Number 4 District to patrol roads within a half mile radius of Poulton Avenue. They are to look out for Miss Dorothy Coleman. Late forties...' He turned to Miss Carter. 'Height?'

'Five feet five.'

'Build?'

'Very thin.'

172

'Dressed?'

A moment of hesitation. 'Brown mackintosh with gilt buttons over a maroon trouser suit. She would be carrying an umbrella.'

He repeated the information into the telephone. 'She is to be brought here, to her home at 6 Poulton Avenue. Keep me informed at this number—347489.'

Miss Carter's aggression had disappeared, now she looked scared. 'You really think. . .?'

'Frankly, I've no idea but we mustn't take chances.'

Taffy Evans had said that the Russell parents had kept an hotel and the furniture here looked as though it had been rescued from the auctioneer's hammer when they sold up. A grandfather clock with a brass face, which must have come from the foyer, showed half-past eight.

'Miss Coleman knew that the police wanted to get in touch with her?'

'Oh yes, she saw it in the newspaper.'

'But she did nothing about it.'

'No, she thought it was all rather foolish.'

'The deaths of two young women?'

Miss Carter was anything but aggressive now; she flushed. 'I didn't mean that! Dot—Miss Coleman thought it was foolish to imagine that what happened to the girls had anything to do with her or with when they were schoolgirls.'

'She didn't want to get involved.'

'No, I suppose not. She can be very obstinate, as I said.' She ground out a half-smoked cigarette in the ashtray.

'What time did you go out this evening?'

'Just before six. I always go to see my mother on Sunday evenings.'

'Is everything as usual?'

She looked puzzled. 'I think so. Dot is often out when I get back.' Her expression changed suddenly. 'I've just remembered something! She had an appointment—not that it makes any difference.'

'An appointment?'

'A man phoned while we were having tea, he wanted to see the school and arrange for his granddaughter to come.' She went over to the desk and turned the pages of a desk diary. 'Here you are, Dot made a note of it—Mr Douglas Grant, seven-thirty.'

CHAPTER TEN

H E H A D N O T eaten since breakfast and he was hungry and cold. He must force himself to behave normally or he would do something stupid as he had last night in the pub. Above all he must occupy his mind so that he would not think about what lay before him. This was a trick he had learned in childhood. When a school examination or a visit to the dentist was imminent he would lose himself in a book and when the moment of crisis came it would take him almost by surprise.

While he was upstairs he shut the windows which he had opened to air the house, then he went downstairs, locked the back door, put on his overcoat and let himself out at the front. He walked down Oakshott Avenue with an easy stride, he looked calm and collected, he *was* calm. There were lights in most of the sitting rooms in the avenue and some had left their curtains undrawn so that he had glimpses of families gathered round television sets. He went to the bus stop in the centre of Rhynton. Another man was waiting there.

'Evening, Mr Rendell.'

'Good evening, Mr Oates.' He thought that his voice sounded quite normal. Oates had lived in Holland Drive for almost as long as he had lived in Oakshott Avenue and the two men had been acquainted for twenty-five years.

'Been taking a look at the house?'

'Got to keep an eye on things.'

'I suppose you'll be thinking to sell.'

'I haven't thought anything yet.'

He must have sounded brusque for Oates was quick to apologise.

'None of my business, of course!'

An awkward silence before Oates added, changing the subject, 'I suppose you've had the police?'

'The police?' He felt suddenly cold inside.

'Haven't they been to you? They've been going around asking questions. Something to do with the strangler; they seem to think he might live out here.'

'Out here?' He was at a loss what to say.

The bus arrived and they got on together. Oates took a ticket to the city centre and he did the same. It carried him beyond his true destination but he could walk back.

'Shocking business, killing young women.'

'Shocking.'

'Too lax in the courts, that's more than half the trouble. They've got to take a strong line on violence. You look at some of the sentences—you'd think they wanted to encourage it.'

He peered through the window into the darkness.

'I haven't seen you to speak to since your wife.... Very sad, terrible for you. I was saying to Marge only this morning, you've had more than your share ... more than your share.' Oates looked away, vaguely embarrassed by his own words.

He continued to stare at the dimly reflective window. Nothing was required of him but his mind was a ferment.

'I suppose you're still with your sister?'

'For the moment—for the moment.'

They arrived at the city centre and got off together.

'Like a drink before you go in?'

'Thanks all the same but they will be expecting me.'

'Another time.'

'Yes.' He watched Oates as they separated and saw him turn into a bar then he walked in the opposite direction. The police. Why should they think of Rhynton? The telephone call, it must have been a trap. He was shocked, partly because he had nearly made the call from his home, partly because he felt that it was unfair. The feeling of insecurity was almost overwhelming.

His appointment was for seven-thirty but it was now scarcely six o'clock. He felt a little weak and faint, partly because he had not eaten, partly because he had been upset by what Oates had told him. It was odd, he had hardly considered the risk that he might be tracked down and caught, he had feared only that he might give himself away. He had seen the extra police patrols, the crime cars and the pandas and he knew that all this organisation was for him but he had not once felt threatened. Why should he? All his life he had been on the side of the law and he found it impossible to accept that this had fundamentally changed. But Oates' news had shaken him. He remembered the ring at the doorbell which he had ignored. What would have happened if he had gone down—totally unprepared?

He decided that he would go to the flat, get something to eat and go out again. It was a short distance away.

As he came out of the lift on the top floor he could hear a television newsreader—something about a pay claim for engineering workers. Alice was sitting on the settee, knitting.

'Hullo! You're early. Albert's gone down to set the time switch.' She turned to look at him. 'What's the matter, Jim? Still feeling seedy?'

'I'm all right.'

Her kindly, rather stupid face, expressed concern. 'You don't look it, you . . .'

The newsreader went on, 'This afternoon police made house-to-house enquiries in the Rhynton district of the city. A spokesman said that an un-named man had telephoned Detective Chief Superintendent Wycliffe from a call-box in that neighbourhood this morning.'

'They rang you here.'

'What?'

'The police rang you here, they said there was no answer at the house and a neighbour told them you were living here. . . . What's the matter?'

He made a tremendous effort of control. 'You should have told me.'

'You didn't give me a chance. Anyway, it's not important. They said it was just routine enquiry, just to find out where everybody was. You really do look poorly, Jim.'

His legs had all but given way and he had dropped into one of the easy chairs. 'I must admit I don't feel so good, I didn't bother with getting any lunch.'

This was a problem Alice could cope with. She bustled through into the kitchen and called to him through the hatch. 'You must have been out.'

'What?'

'When the police called at the house.'

'Yes, I went for a walk. What did they want to know when they telephoned?'

'Nothing much, just whether you were living with us and where you were.'

'What did you say?'

'That you'd gone over to the house as you did every Sunday to give it an airing and they must have missed you.'

'That was all?'

'Yes.'

He felt a little better. If anything it might tend to put them off. Looked at from their point of view it would seem normal —it *was* normal.

Alice brought him a plate of cold meat, some crusty bread and a glass of beer. It put new life into him.

'You're not going out again?'

'I told Jack Oates I would meet him for a drink.'

'But you're not fit, Jim!'

She was genuinely concerned, she was his sister but she meant nothing to him. All the love and affection of which he was capable had been focused on his wife and his daughter. The three of us. No need for anyone else.

He put on his overcoat once more and felt in the right-hand pocket.

The weather had undergone an abrupt change. Instead of the clear, cold frosty night which had promised it had suddenly softened. The air seemed mild and a thin mist diffused through the streets. He walked brisky away from the city centre.

There were few people about and as he got clear of the city centre he had the impression that police patrols were more numerous and obtrusive than on previous nights. He felt that he was being watched. Now and then a patrol car cruised slowly past and twice he came upon police cars parked at intersections. He was climbing a steepish hill out of the city with residential roads off on either side, semi-detached properties with tiny front gardens and narrow strips of sour soil at the back. Rather dreary Edwardian houses which had been the homes of prosperous shop-keepers and tradesmen before the first war; families able to support a couple of maids.

Dorothy Coleman lived in Poulton Avenue which was one of these roads near the top of the hill. As he turned off a police car passed him at little more than walking speed. But nothing now would put him off, he was committed. It was almost as though he had surrendered his will to external compulsion. Twice before he had known the feeling. After spells of torturing doubt his resolution seemed to form and harden of itself.

On the third or fourth gate along the road he could read by the light of a street lamp, a white painted sign:

Poulton Avenue Nursery School
Proprietors: Misses D. Coleman and J. Carter

There was a light in an upstairs room but none on the ground floor. The little front garden had been paved over. He rang the doorbell and after a moment a light flicked on behind the coloured panes of the front door which was then opened.

She was small and thin—thinner than he remembered, with close-cropped brown hair which made her face look smaller and sharper than it was.

'Miss Coleman?'

She looked up at him through thick lenses. 'Yes, and you

179

must be Mr Grant. Please come in.' She had a rather harsh, metallic voice which must have carried without effort across many classrooms.

He refused her offer to take his coat.

'The school is here on the ground floor, I have a flat upstairs.'

The hall was bare and there was a faint smell of disinfectant but the stairs were carpeted. 'If you would like to come up to the flat we can discuss arrangements and you shall see the school afterwards if you wish.'

He followed her up to a landing and in to the front room. It was a cross between a sitting room and an office; a chesterfield and easies, an old fashioned roll-top desk. There were photographs everywhere, college groups, school groups and half a dozen large paintings in gilt frames—seascapes.

'Won't you sit down?'

He smiled vaguely but remained standing.

'About your grandchild . . .'

'Linda—yes. She is three and a half.' He was well rehearsed. 'My daughter divorced her husband . . .' He told a credible story, his voice was steady, normal. She made sympathetic noises.

'I know how difficult it is for a mother who has to work to keep herself and her child but our fees are not high. Will your daughter want Linda to come for the whole day or only part of it?'

He was still standing, showing some interest in the pictures. She seemed vaguely uneasy perhaps because of his refusal to sit down. His hand in the right-hand pocket of his raincoat felt the smooth wooden toggles which he had carved himself.

He made remarks about the pictures expecting that she would join him to point out their merits but she kept her distance. 'They were painted by my father; he made quite a reputation for himself at one time.'

He was patient. No false moves. But they were running out of conversation.

'I expect you would like to see the school?'

'If I may.'

She led the way downstairs and into a room off the hall. A large room, the original dining and drawing rooms knocked into one. Little tables and chairs, an elaborate climbing frame, a magnificent rocking-horse and open shelves all round stacked with books and toys. Lively murals on the walls.

'Our rest room is through here.' A smaller room with mattresses on low wooden frames.

'In the garden we have a toddler's adventure playground.'

He murmured approval and watched her every move. 'Very nice, very suitable. I'm sure my daughter will be delighted.' They were back in the main room and it seemed that his chance would never come but he must not take any risk. Then she darted in front of him and stooped to pick up a plastic cup from the floor which some child had dropped there. In an instant he had the cord out of his pocket. No fumbling. As she straightened, with her back to him, he twisted the nylon cord round her neck and pulled on the toggles with all his strength. She let out a scream which was cut off in a fraction of a second. He had heard a similar scream once before, the girl Bennett had screamed but the first one had made no sound.

She struggled weakly, briefly, then went limp. He held the tension until his forehead was beaded with sweat then he released her. She slipped to the floor and lay sprawled and twisted, her head resting on a rocker of the big toy horse.

His heart thumped unbearably and he could feel a powerful pulse in his neck, his head swam and he was afraid that he might collapse on the floor beside her but the faintness passed.

He stooped to recover the cord and was forced to look at her face. Her eyes were wide open and staring; she looked astonished and, perhaps because her jaw sagged, rather stupid. Her glasses had fallen off. He remembered her expression nine years ago when she had said, 'The trouble with Jane is that she has been spoiled, she is a self-indulgent child and it is high time that she grew up!'

He felt no pity.

As he recovered himself a little he looked round the room to see if he had left any trace of his visit and only then did he realise that the curtains had not been drawn. He was standing in the middle of a lighted room and all that had happened might have been seen by a passer by or even by someone in the houses opposite. At this moment they might be telephoning the police. He walked to the door and switched off the light, the hall light too; then he sat on the stairs in the darkness, he needed a little more time. At last he felt calm enough to leave. He made himself move slowly and deliberately. He let himself out by the front door and shut it behind him. He stood for a moment, listening for footsteps or the sound of a car but there was nothing and he walked to the gate; he closed and latched the gate behind him. Only once more. He would not allow himself to think about that. It was of no importance anyway. He had subordinated himself, forced himself to become an instrument, a tool, and when a tool has served its purpose . . .

Wycliffe felt cold inside.

'I think that we should search the house.'

She looked vague then frightened.

'What's on the top floor?'

'What? Oh, only two attics—lumber rooms, we never go up there.'

'We'll leave those for the moment.' By talking he hoped to get her co-operation without any panic. 'This floor first, you show me.'

The first floor was a self-contained flat, kitchen, bathroom, two bedrooms and the room they had just left. Nothing remarkable except that it was obvious neither of the women had much idea about housekeeping. All the rooms were untidy and looked as though they could do with a good clean.

'Downstairs?'

'All the rooms downstairs and the garden are given over to the school.'

Wycliffe led the way downstairs and opened a door on the left of the hall.

'That's the main schoolroom.'

The room was in darkness and he fumbled for the light switch. When he found it yellow light from a small bulb lit up a large, rather bare room with toddlers' tables and chairs and toys scattered about.

It was a moment before he saw her body. She was lying on the floor, her head resting on the blue-painted rocker of a magnificent rocking-horse. Miss Carter saw her at almost the same instant; she let out a gasp but made no other sound. She made no move to enter the room but stood in the doorway, staring, her fist thrust between her teeth like a little girl.

Wycliffe bent over the body but it was obvious that nothing could be done; the strangler was thorough.

Wycliffe went out into the hall and closed the door of the schoolroom behind him.

'Are you all right?'

Miss Carter nodded but she did not remove her hand from her mouth. Wycliffe piloted her gently up the stairs to the sitting room and persuaded her to sit down.

'Would you like something? Tea?'

She shook her head and he went to the telephone. He was put through to Gill.

'I've found her. You'd better get the lads out here and let Franks know. 6 Poulton Avenue—the nursery school. . . . No, I shall stay here for the moment. I've got another job for you. Did you get a description from the sister . . . and a photograph? Good! All your mobiles—I want every pub in the city visited beginning with the city centre. They won't have a photograph but they will have the description. Get them moving, Jimmy.'

At first, as he walked, he looked nervously about him but soon he seemed to regain confidence and his whole bearing changed, he stepped out briskly and looked neither to the right nor the left. It was raining, a thin misty drizzle and though from the hill there was a view right across the city he could see only a suffused, angry glow in the sky.

By the time he reached the city centre his mood was buoyant, he felt pleased with himself. For the third time he had not flinched from a dangerous, difficult and horrifying task. He had made a plan and he had carried it through—to the letter. He had been *competent*—that was the word.

He tried never to think of the girl on the allotments, the girl he had nearly killed by mistake. He wanted to blot out that memory because of the guilt he felt, the sense of guilt which had made him so quick to defend himself in the newspaper. A psychopathic killer they had called him. The accusation had frightened him because it was not only, or even mainly, his mistaken attack on an innocent girl which made him feel guilty, it was the fact that he had wanted to go on, to finish what he had begun. When the girl's hat had fallen off and he had seen the blonde hair it had taken every scrap of will power he possessed to release her. He had known the urge, almost the compulsion to kill. And he had scurried off to the flat and strangled his real victim in a frightening explosion of lust without any plan and at terrible risk.

But in his good times, as now, he could believe that what he had done had been deliberate, a rational and sensible change of plan made necessary by circumstances outside his control.

Once more and it would be over.

He was tempted to finish the thing tonight but he knew that he must resist that kind of prompting. To be competent you had to be calm, that was his secret, and he realised that he was not calm now. He was excited, pleasurably but dangerously so.

But there was no question of going back to the flat—not yet. He walked on through the city centre. A wet Sunday evening and hardly anybody about. Without consciously directing his steps he found himself in Prince's Street. He liked Prince's Street after dark, it seemed to have a teeming life of its own which went on just below the surface. A life which was no more than hinted at by the furtive figures in doorways or by the girls who accosted any unaccompanied male. Now and then between the shops there was an open door into a dimly lit passage and a mysterious stairway.

He walked along the pavement with a seemingly purposive stride but in fact he was looking hopefully into every doorway. At the Joiners he went in for a drink. The bar was crowded, full of noise and tobacco smoke and he had to elbow his way to the counter. But, as usual, he seemed to be invisible to the bar-girls until someone said, 'This chap was before me'. Then he ordered a whisky though he rarely drank spirits. He retreated with his drink through the crowd to a clearer space by the windows where there were marble-topped tables. It was there that he saw her, sitting with a gin glass in front of her, showing a great deal of thigh. Her pallor was striking and the great dark eyes in her thin face seemed to have a monopoly of all her vitality. She sat, staring at the blank window, apparently unaware of her surroundings. Then she looked up and caught him watching her. Automatically and with scarcely any change of expression she put out her invitation and with equal inevitability he accepted. They were separated by several yards and neither had spoken. The encounter suited his mood, he could play with fire without getting burnt.

He went over to her table. 'Can I get you another drink?'

She glanced back at the crowd round the bar and shook her head. 'It's not worth it.' She stood up, adjusted her shoulder bag and said quietly, 'Just round the corner. Number nine. Open the door and go straight up the stairs.'

He was tremulous with excitement. 'Can't I walk with you?'

She looked at him in surprise. 'No skin off my nose, love, but what if your wife gets to hear of it?'

'I haven't a wife.'

She shrugged. 'Suit yourself.'

She walked quickly with small steps, her heels tapping on the paving stones. He held her arm, thin and rigid through the material of her coat sleeve. He had difficulty in adjusting his pace. It was the first time he had walked out with a woman since. . . .

He was silent because he could not trust himself to speak. He had never been with another woman, only with Rose. When he married her at 25 he was a virgin, as she was. Before he married, during the war, he had had the same temptations, the same opportunities as other men but fastidiousness and fear had combined to restrain him. Now for years he had lived like a monk while he watched Rose sink deeper and deeper into depression. But suddenly he was free, unshackled, there was no longer the slightest reason for restraint. He had nothing to fear and nothing to lose.

They turned into number nine. She pushed open the front door and as they entered the little hall she saw him eyeing the door of the bottom flat which was closed.

'What's the matter?'

'Is there another girl in there?'

She laughed. 'Why? Isn't one enough for you?'

She started up the stairs and he followed. 'Aren't you nervous, going with strange men?'

'No good to be, is it?'

She led him into a bedroom where a gas fire was burning. The room looked homely and cheerful, her dressing gown was on the bed and her make-up and toilet things were spread out on the dressing table.

She had taken off her coat and was hanging it in the wardrobe. 'Four pounds, love.'

He took the notes from his wallet and handed them to her. He stammered. 'I'll give you more if . . .'

She gave him a hard look. 'If what? You're not kinky, are you?'

'No, of course not! I meant if you are . . .' He hesitated, then added, 'if you are nice to me.'

She looked doubtful but she smiled. 'We'll see.' She had put the money in a drawer and taken off her dress. Her skin was white as paper. He watched her, fascinated by her very indifference.

'Aren't you going to undress?' How many times had she said those words?

He started to do so. It had not occurred to him that his attraction to this girl sprang from her resemblance to Rose. Rose as she was twenty years ago when Jane was still a little girl. His approaches to Rose had always been tentative, hesitant, her gentle smiling submissiveness disarmed lust and filled him with tenderness. This prostitute, lying naked on her bed, her legs separated waiting for him, had the same effect. She saw the change in him.

'What's the matter? Can't you do it? Come here, I'll help you.'

'No.'

He came to her nevertheless and covered her body with his. He stared down into her eyes and his gaze troubled her for it expressed none of the emotions she was accustomed to read in the faces of men. He looked puzzled as though he had suddenly found something which it was very difficult to explain or understand.

'What's the matter?'

He was caressing her pale face with his hands. His thumbs ran gently down the line of her jaw on either side. It was something remembered from long ago. His thumbs moved down the throat to where he could feel the gentle pulsing of her blood.

'Oh, Rose!'

'What are you talking about? I aren't called Rose, my name is Brenda.' She saw a change in his expression and was frightened. 'Here! What are you doing? Lay off that!' Then she screamed.

There were heavy footsteps racing up the stairs and a policeman burst into the room.

'All right, dad, we've been looking for you.'

He made no protest but started to dress without a word.

'You all right, love?'

She was sitting on the foot of the bed staring at the man and, suddenly, she started to tremble. The constable put her dressing gown round her shoulders. 'Go into the other room, love, and make yourself a hot drink. He didn't hurt you, did he?'

She shook her head. 'No.' Then she added, 'How did you know?'

'We've been looking for him and they told me in the Joiners you'd picked him up.'

In a very few minutes they were gone and she was left alone.

CHAPTER ELEVEN

Wycliffe talked to him in an interview room at headquarters. A little room with pale green walls, brown linoleum on the floor and furnished with a table and two chairs. Wycliffe sat on one side of the table and Rendell on the other; a constable stood by the door.

'Do you smoke?'

'No, thank you.'

'Do you want to make a statement?'

'I don't know. I would rather you asked me questions.'

'In any case I must caution you.' He repeated the formula. 'How long since you had any food?'

'I don't know but I couldn't eat anything.'

'A cup of tea?'

'No, thank you.'

Rendell was 53 but he looked 60. His hair, thin on top, was uniformly grey, his features were deeply lined and he had a whitish stubble on his chin. His skin looked grey and bloodless. His eyes stared unfocused at the table top and his hands rested palms down.

'Would I have killed her?' He asked the question apologetically.

'At any rate, you didn't, you did her no harm other than shock.'

'But would I have killed her if—?'

'Perhaps.'

He smoothed the table top with his palms. 'It's been like a nightmare, haunting me. I could never be sure.'

'Of what?'

He glanced up quickly, surprised by the question.

'It's still Sunday, isn't it?'

'A quarter to eleven on Sunday evening.'

He nodded. 'It doesn't seem possible.'

Wycliffe took out his pipe and lit it.

'The newspapers said that I was a psychopathic killer.'

'And you said, "It is not true. If I had been I would have killed the wrong girl on Monday night".'

He stopped moving his hands and focused his eyes on them as though seeing them for the first time. They were well-formed hands, broad and powerful with blunt fingers. Fine brownish-grey hairs glistened in the light.

'But I nearly did kill her.'

'You stopped when her hat fell off and you saw that she had fair hair instead of dark. You realised that she was the wrong girl.'

He nodded several times and was silent for a while. 'Yes, I did stop, didn't I?' He clenched his hands. 'But I wanted to kill her, I don't know how I found the strength to stop. I wanted to kill her even after I knew.'

Wycliffe said nothing, he sat immobile, smoking his pipe in very gentle puffs.

'I didn't understand, you see.'

'What didn't you understand?'

'That it's like sex.'

There was a clock on the wall and every half-minute it made a loud click when the large hand leapt forward a little way. It seemed to distract Rendell, almost to frighten him and he moved his chair so that the clock was no longer in his line of vision.

'It was all so clear in the beginning. I had to punish the ones who killed my child and my wife. It was my duty.' He stopped, dissatisfied with what he had just said. 'No, it was more than that, I can't explain. It was something I *had* to do, I couldn't help myself.' He looked up at Wycliffe's face to see if he had made himself understood and met the bland impassive stare. 'I'm not trying to excuse myself, I *wanted* to do it, I knew it was right.'

'How did they kill your child and your wife?'

He seemed to think about the question for some time before answering. 'There never was a closer family than we were. We did everything together, the three of us. Of course, I had my work and Jane went to school but what I mean is, our lives centred on each other and on our home.'

'Where did Jane go to school?'

'It was a Catholic school but they took non-Catholics. It's closed now, The School of the Sacred Heart. We wanted her to be with girls who had had a good upbringing.

'It all started when she went away to that hostel with a lot of girls from other schools. We thought we ought to let her mix more. I find it difficult to tell you how they treated her there.' His voice faltered.

'I know about that.'

'She was never the same. A year later she was in a mental hospital. They said she had mental illness which sometimes affects young people.'

An eavesdropper could have imagined that he was outside a confessional. The subdued, continuing murmur of one voice, the occasional interjections from the priest.

'She came out after six months but she wasn't cured. She was on drugs and she wasn't our Jane any longer. Sometimes she treated us as though we were strangers, she would talk to us but a lot of it was nonsense, she would get her words wrong and her ideas all mixed up.

'She didn't get better, she got worse and they wanted to have her back in hospital but we wouldn't agree. I can't explain what she was like, she seemed to be cut off, we couldn't reach her. It went on for four years, she was twenty-one but we couldn't let her out of our sight, somebody had to be with her almost all the time. Not that we minded . . .'

He placed his palms together, carefully matching the fingers. 'She seemed to just fade away, physically and mentally, regression I think they called it.

'And then, one afternoon while I was at work, Rose slipped out to the corner shop to buy something for tea and Jane must have followed her. She walked straight out of the house in front of a van, never looked to right or left.'

'And your wife blamed herself?'

'Yes. Nothing would convince her that she was not responsible.'

He looked round the room vaguely as though not quite sure where he was.

'I can't understand it.'

'What can't you understand?'

He shook his head. 'I'm not a violent man but the girl on the allotments and the woman tonight. . . . After I came away from the nursery school I was worried by the way I felt. I had to prove that they were wrong.'

'Who were wrong?'

'The newspapers.'

'What happened to your wife?' The question jolted him out of his line of thought.

'Rose killed herself. They gave her tablets to make her sleep, she was always taking tablets. Then one morning after I'd gone to work she took all she had. I found her when I came home in the evening.'

'That was last July?'

'Yes.' He passed his hand over his thinning hair as though trying to brush away some irritation. 'That evening, after they had taken her away, I saw it all clearly for the first time. Ever since Jane had become ill I'd been asking myself, "Why? Why should it happen?" And there it was all the time; Jane had told me—she told me everything.'

'What had she told you?' The priest would have said, 'Continue, my son.'

'About the three girls and that woman, how they persecuted her. Suddenly it was clear as daylight and I knew what I had to do.'

'You set about finding these people?'

He nodded. 'It took me six months but I did it.' There was a note of pride in his voice.

In the silence which followed the clock jerked forward

three more times, the clicks seemed to get louder. The constable at the door cleared his throat and Rendell turned as though surprised to see him there. The silence continued and two or three times Rendell turned to look at the policeman. Finally he said, 'Does he have to be there?'

Wycliffe made a sign and the constable went out closing the door behind him.

Rendell became increasingly restless, twice he put his hand into his inside breast-pocket and withdrew it again.

'You want to show me something?'

Rendell's hand darted with bird-like swiftness and came out with his wallet. He laid it on the table, opened it and extracted a page torn from a small notebook which he placed in front of Wycliffe. The page was dog-eared and creased from constant handling and it contained three lines of meticulous writing:

A succession of frustrations or sometimes a single, severe frustration leads to a massive withdrawal from reality and sweeping regression.

The words *single, severe frustration* had been doubly underlined.

'You see? That proves it, doesn't it? I copied that out of an encyclopaedia. Regression, they say there, that's what the doctor said about Jane.'

Wycliffe passed the paper back and Rendell restored it to his wallet with great care as though it were a precious document, but he did not put his wallet away.

He looked Wycliffe straight in the eyes. 'That's true, isn't it?'

'If you took it from a reliable encyclopaedia I suppose it must be.'

He was excited, trembling, so that his fingers fumbled as he searched his wallet a second time. He came up with a piece of paper similar to the first which he handed over.

'I copied that from a book I got out of the library.'

This piece was not dog-eared or creased, it was obviously more recent than the other.

The schizophrenic reaction is probably not inherent in all human beings. Many authorities believe that it cannot occur in the absence of certain hereditary factors.

Rendell was watching him with extraordinary intensity as he read.

'Well?'

'There are many different kinds of mental illness.'

'Schizophrenia, that's what they said it was. I read it in the letter they gave me to give to our doctor. Hebephrenic schizophrenia.'

Wycliffe's placidity was beginning to irritate him. 'Can't you see what it means?'

Wycliffe was treading warily. 'I think I understand what it means but I'm not sure what interpretation you are putting on it.'

Rendell was rocking on his chair with impatience. 'If it's true that it's hereditary then I'm to blame.'

'For what?'

'For everything! I kill for the sake of killing, I'm a mad-man like the papers said and I fathered a child who through no fault of her own . . .'

'Rubbish!'

The word and the manner in which it was spoken stopped him like a blow. He quietened down.

'Why did you want to kill the prostitute?'

The abrupt change caught him off balance as Wycliffe intended that it should.

'Why? I don't know.'

'You always have a reason for what you do.'

He thought about that. 'Yes, I do. You are right.' His brow furrowed in an effort of concentration. 'She was dark and thin and pale—like Rose.'

'Did you want to kill Rose?'

194

A spasm of anger quickly evaporated. 'No! For God's sake, why should I want to kill my wife?'

Wycliffe waited, knowing that the explanation—the rationalisation—would come.

'She lay there waiting for me—resigned. Ready to give me what I had paid for.'

'Well?'

He hesitated for some time then he said in a low voice. 'Rose submitted because she was my wife. She never uttered a word of complaint but . . .

'Each time I vowed I would never make any more demands on her. I felt like a beast. But it's something you can't always control, the situation is there and before you know where you are . . .' After a moment he added, 'Now they will lock me up and I shan't be able to kill anybody again.' He said the words as though they contained inestimable comfort.

Wycliffe went up to his office and stood by the window in the darkness. He was trying to come to terms with himself. Why had he subjected this man to an interrogation which served no recognised professional end? Out of curiosity? If that meant that he needed to understand. Surely that was more important than knowing about the electrostatic detection of footprints or the latest methods of recording and analysing the statistics of crime.

The telephone rang and he groped for it briefly. 'Wycliffe.' It was Gill. 'So it's all over?'

'They will say that he's unfit to plead.'

'I told you; he's a nutter. They're all the same.'

WYCLIFFE
AND THE DEAD FLAUTIST

The events described in this book take place on the River Fal, near Truro, in Cornwall. Many people will be able to identify the approximate locality but they will not find the Duloe Estate, nor will they find the Bottrells, the Landers, or the Biddicks, for all the people in this story are imaginary, and so are the events in which they become willingly, or unwillingly involved.

Chapter One

A Sunday in August, almost midnight; the night was soft and still, moonless but starlit. On a broad promontory between two creeks of the River Fal, the Duloe Estate spread out in a pattern of light and shade; the sweep of the park and the random patches of woodland disguised contours, creating here and there pools of deep shadow. Duloe House, home of the Bottrells, square and stark, commanded the landscape as it had done for two hundred years. Outbuildings formed two court-yards behind the house and, at some distance, nearer the upper creek, there was a second house, neither as old nor as large as Duloe, a building of low eaves, steep gables, and tall chimneys — Treave, home of the Landers. Inland from the estate, a half-mile from the river, a village of fifty or sixty houses, clustered and straggled about its church and pub.

There were two or three lighted windows in the village, an isolated cottage on the estate showed a single light, an upper window at Treave glowed plum-red through its velvet drape, but Duloe House was in total darkness. Everywhere there was stillness and it seemed there could be no living creature abroad. But in the shadow of a shrubbery, under the lighted window at Treave, Paul Bottrell, a boy of sixteen, waited.

He did not know how long he had been there and he had all but given up hope when he heard a faint sound, a sound repeated close at hand, a movement of the air, and a whispered: 'Hi!'

'I was afraid you wouldn't come.'

'Sh! That's mother's room and I don't think she's in bed yet.'

He felt her hand in his, warm and confident. They moved off, keeping to the grass border of the drive.

A few yards, and they turned off the drive along a footpath through the shrubbery; the shrubs gave place to trees and the trees made strange patterns against the sky. Although there was no moon outlines were clear.

'Listen!'

Someone was playing a flute, a melody, plaintive and melancholy. Paul put his arm around her. 'Jean!'

She said: 'Doesn't Tony ever go to bed?'

They could see the light from the cottage. The sound of the flute grew louder and the tune changed; the melancholy air gave place to the lilting rhythm of a reel which quickened the pulse. The light was in a downstairs room, the front door was shut, and a blind covered the window. On the blind the shadow of the flute player was enlarged and grotesque.

Paul said: 'He's a strange man.'

'Don't you like him?' Jean wanted definition.

Paul, always wary of committing himself, hesitated, then: 'I don't know; sometimes when he looks at me he makes me feel odd.'

They emerged from the woodland into the park. Duloe House brooded on its eminence, blind and silent. They walked, hand in hand down the slope to the river, through a belt of trees, and came upon a wharf largely overgrown by brambles and gorse. Beyond, the river ran smooth and luminous between shadowy banks.

Paul said: 'The skiff?'

'All right.'

On that other occasion, exactly a week ago, similar words had been spoken and already it was as though they were adhering to an established ritual. They followed a path through the undergrowth along the wharf and came to a boathouse. It rose in front of them, low to the eaves, but with a great expanse of roof. Paul opened a door in the side of the building and Jean followed him in. The house was open at one end to the river but it was eerie in the near darkness. Soft, liquid sounds came from movements of the water below the staging on which they stood.

The wet dock was occupied by a white launch which loomed large in the dim light and confined space. They passed around the bow of the launch to the other side of the dock where a cranky little river skiff was moored beside the launch. They got in, cast off, and Paul propelled the boat out of the house by working hand over hand along the staging. Once in the open river he unshipped the oars.

'Lower Creek?'

'No, let's do the same as last week.' Then they had followed the Upper Creek and almost reached the village.

'We shan't get far, the tide's too low.'

'Never mind.'

The little boat slid along, the water chuckling beneath the bow. Paul rowed cleanly, without splash. Now that they were on the water it seemed lighter and they could see each other clearly.

Paul said: 'I can't believe this.'

'What?'

'Well, all our lives we've lived next door to each other and, until I went away to school, we saw each other nearly every day . . . Even after that there were holidays . . . Now it's as though I've never known you.'

'And this holiday is nearly over.'

He stopped rowing. 'Don't, Jean!' He shipped the oars and came to sit beside her in the stern, leaving the boat to drift. She let him draw her to him and kiss her on the lips. He kissed her hair, her ears, and her neck and fondled her breasts.

Then there was a shot. It was not particularly loud; it sounded muffled, but it reverberated briefly between the banks.

Jean broke away. 'What was that?'

'A shot.'

'I know that, idiot! But who goes shooting in the middle of the night?'

'Somebody after a fox, or it could be poachers after old Roskilly's deer. They've tried it before.'

201

Jean got up and moved, cautiously, to the centre thwart. 'I'll row for a bit.'

'Are you angry with me?'

'Should I be?'

She gave the shore a wide berth and entered the creek, following the channel. Here the creek was broad but it narrowed quickly so that half a mile away, in the village, it was no more than a stream. The church tower rose out of the trees in silhouette against the night sky and the water was dark and shining. Once they were startled by a sudden quacking from the shore as something disturbed a family of roosting ducks.

Rounding a small promontory on their left they came in sight of an old cottage from which there had once been a ferry, now Treave property.

Paul said: 'There's a light in the cottage. Your father must be there again.'

The girl said nothing.

'Does he often spend the night there? I thought he only used it for his photography.'

'He sleeps there at weekends sometimes.' Her manner was distant, dismissive.

She continued rowing as the creek narrowed until finally the keel ploughed into soft mud. It was of no consequence on a rising tide.

Jean said: 'Anyway, it's time I was getting back.'

'Already?'

Somehow the magic of the night had deserted them.

She back-paddled clear of the mud until the channel broadened and she was able to head the boat downstream. As they passed the cottage a light was still burning in an upper window but nothing was said.

They reached the boathouse in silence, berthed the skiff, and retraced their steps across the wharf. Paul put his arm around her. 'What's wrong, Jean?'

'Nothing. Don't be silly.'

They walked up through the park and as they entered the wood she said: 'Tony is still up.'

The way ahead seemed brightly lit and as they drew near the flute player's cottage they saw that the light came not only from the window but also through the open door.

Paul said: 'That seems odd. Perhaps we ought to find out if he's all right.'

'I don't want to be seen. He might tell my parents.'

'All right; you wait here.' The boy went ahead; she saw him standing in the doorway and she heard him call, softly: 'Tony? Are you there?' Then he went inside and a moment later she saw his shadow on the blind.

The door opened directly into the living-room. Paul knew the place well and everything looked as usual but there was a smell — acrid, and vaguely familiar, though he could not identify it. Then he rounded the draught screen and he could see the rest of the room.

Tony Miller was sitting in his usual chair by the window, his flute on the table at his elbow. He had a shotgun between his thighs, the butt resting on the floor, the muzzle pointed at his throat. Paul knew about shotguns but he had never before seen the consequence of a full charge entering a living creature at close range. The lower part of Tony's face had gone, leaving only a mess of blood and tissue. Blood had spattered the wall and the plastic covering of the table; even the gleaming flute was spotted and streaked with blood.

Paul felt faint. He turned away and steadied himself with one hand gripping the edge of the table.

Jean had heard nothing since he disappeared inside and it seemed a long time. The light, streaming across the clearing, intensified the shadows where it failed to reach. The silence was total and she began to feel uneasy. Then she heard soft footsteps, they sounded stealthy and seemed to come from somewhere close to the cottage. Peering against the light, she made out a vague figure standing by the corner of the building. It seemed that he (she was sure that it was a man) must have come round from the back. She had a momentary glimpse of the pale blur of his face then, immediately, he withdrew. Had he spotted her? She must have been easily visible in the stream of light from the cottage.

She decided to join Paul and ran across the clearing. He met her at the door and spoke in a horrified whisper. 'He's dead! He's been shot!'

'*Shot*?'

'I think he's killed himself.'

Chapter Two

The day before — Saturday — the Wycliffes had returned from a three-week holiday in the Dordogne. They had been there before — twice, and he had secretly entertained the notion that he might settle there on his retirement and take up fishing. There were difficulties: his French was not very good, he found the summers too hot, he had never fished in his life, and he did not particularly like Frenchmen. Added to that he guessed that if he broached the idea to Helen she would say: 'Over my dead body!'

As it was he had spent three weeks half-dazed by heat, sunshine, and white wine. He had vague recollections of delicious meals and convivial evenings at a restaurant just a few yards (metres) down the road from their cottage. (The cottage was rented from a countess who personally checked the cutlery, crockery, and linen, before they left.) He remembered the cathedral at Périgueux with its five great domes, the caves at les Eyzies, and a street scene in Sarlat where they were dress-rehearsing an outdoor performance of Henry V.

It was all very pleasant in a dreamlike way but secretly, towards the end, he missed the unpredictable showers, the smell of moist earth in the garden, even those murky days when everything drips. But as luck would have it they returned home to a heatwave, the garden was parched and within hours of their arrival Helen had produced an alarming list of plant casualties.

'I'll bet,' Wycliffe said, 'there's a hosepipe ban.'

On Monday morning he was on his way to the office, stuck in a queue for the ferry, breathing the usual cocktail of lethal gases from other people's exhaust. Oddly, when he got there, the sight of the police building, for all its naked ugliness, lifted his spirit. His parking space, labelled with his name and rank, and a welcoming grin from the desk sergeant, completed his home-coming.

He spent half an hour with the chief chatting about police and office politics, and an hour or so with his own deputy, John Scales, being briefed on progress or lack of it in cases on hand. Through the files he renewed old acquaintances and met new ones.

At half-past eleven Wycliffe had his office to himself, a chance to ease his way back into the burrow, but it did not last. Diane's voice came through on the intercom: 'Mr Kersey wants to see you.'

'Ask him to come in.'

Detective Inspector Doug Kersey, colleague of nearly twenty years.

Coming back after three weeks' absence can be like wearing new spectacles; one sees familiar faces with a keener perception. Wycliffe thought Kersey looked older. Certainly the grey hairs were taking over, spreading upwards from the temples; and his face, always deeply lined, now seemed furrowed. Wycliffe sighed.

'Good holiday, sir?'

'Fine! How are Joan and the girls?'

The civilities over, Kersey hooked up a chair and sat down. 'I reckon they've been saving this one for you. I've had Tom Reed on the line and he thinks he's got a homicide dressed up as suicide . . . Mind if I smoke?'

The question was rhetorical, but today there was a difference: Kersey came out with a pouch of tobacco, a little machine, and papers. 'I thought the chore of making 'em plus the lousy taste might put me off.'

'Where, and who?'

'The Duloe Estate, on the river, four or five miles south of Truro.'

'Isn't that the Bottrell place?'

Kersey referred to his notes. 'Let's get it right: Hugh Cuthbert Grylls Bottrell, Ninth Baron Bottrell.'

'Is it the noble lord himself?'

'No, the estate foreman: Anthony Charles Miller, bachelor, mid-thirties. He lives — lived — in a cottage on the estate. A girl, out dog-walking, found him. To be accurate, her dog did. He'd been shot with a 12-bore at very close range making a nasty mess of his face and neck.'

'So where does the notion of suicide come from?'

Wycliffe had to wait while Kersey concentrated on inserting a cigarette paper into his little machine.

'When he was found Miller was sitting in his chair —'

'He was indoors?'

'Yes. Didn't I say?'

'I wish you'd get that thing going then concentrate on what you're supposed to be telling me.'

Kersey grinned. 'Sorry! I expect I'll get better at it; I had an uncle who could roll these things with one hand. Anyway, Miller was in his living-room, sitting in his chair, the gun between his thighs, butt resting on the floor, muzzle pointing at his neck. There was a bit of string tied to the trigger — typical of a suicide with a long-barrelled shotgun. But Tom Reed is no fool and he says it's one for us.'

'I'll have a word with the chief.'

'Before you do there's something else you should know. The girl who found him is Simon Lander's daughter.'

'Lander, the lawyer?'

'And member of the Police Authority as ever was. The Landers are neighbours of the Bottrells. According to Reed, their house, Treave, was built on estate land. What's more, the Landers have been lawyers to the Bottrells since they wrote with a goose quill on parchment. Anyway, I gather Lander is already on Tom's back, convinced that Miller committed suicide and that Tom is stirring things unnecessarily.'

'You'd better contact Franks; we must have a path report before the body is moved, and with a question between suicide and murder we shall need ballistics evidence. Get Melville down. As far as our people are concerned: scenes-of-crime there as soon as possible, Lucy Lane with a couple of DCs first thing in the morning and, if we're still in business, you can follow when you've off-loaded whatever you're on at the moment. Ask Truro to arrange accommodation — they can book me in at the village pub from tonight — if there is one and if they've got a room.'

It was one of his idiosyncracies to stay at places most likely to offer local contacts. In his lectures to cadets he was fond of saying: 'In any murder investigation if you shut yourself off from the locals you are working with one hand tied behind your back.'

Kersey said: 'If you start getting organized now, it will still be evening before you get there.'

'So what? The evenings are light and I shall have a chance to talk to Reed on the ground.'

He did not say that a day or two by the Fal might help dispel any lingering withdrawal symptoms from the Dordogne.

Kersey fingered fragments of tobacco from his lips and grinned. 'As I said, perhaps they laid this one on as a welcome home.'

'I'm going out to lunch — coming?'

'No, I promised Joan . . .'

He went to his usual restaurant, run by a fat woman whose husband, a Czech, was the chef. The place was old-fashioned, the food was plain and good; there was a regular clientele, very little conversation, and no — definitely no — muzak.

'Good holiday? Nice to see you back, Mr Wycliffe. Salad today: ham-off-the-bone or chicken.'

'I'll take the ham, Annie.'

In a world that was changing too fast for him Wycliffe clung to those things which survived as a drowning man clings to a plank.

He was glad to be alone. In a few hours he would be at the start of an intimate involvement with people he had never met who, for reasons often unconnected with any crime, would feel the need to lie. As usual, much of his investigation would be concerned with pinning down the innocent.

When he returned from lunch the internal telephone was

ringing. It was Freda, the grey dragon who guarded the chief. 'Oh, Mr Wycliffe, if you are free, Mr Oldroyd would like a word, in his office.'

A trip along the corridor and through the padded door. Freda was amiable; she had her likes and dislikes which she made plain regardless of rank but Wycliffe was among her elect.

'Please go in, Mr Wycliffe.'

'Do sit down, Charles! I almost said "light up" — I can't get used to you without your pipe.'

Something tricky. Bertram Oldroyd was not given to beating about bushes. He sat in his swivel chair studying his finger nails then, abruptly: 'I suppose you've heard from Reed?'

'Just before lunch; I'm going down there shortly.'

'And I suppose you know Simon Lander?'

'The lawyer? . . . I've met him a few times on committees.' Wycliffe guessed what was coming but decided to let his chief sweat it out.

'Yes, well, Simon's got his long fingers in quite a few pies. Among others, as you must know, he's a member of the Police Authority. And they listen to him.'

Oldroyd looked over his glasses. 'He lives next door to the Bottrells on land that once belonged to the estate and the two families have been mixed up for generations. Anway, Simon is worried, he's convinced that this Miller fellow committed suicide — says he's a strange sort of chap and that he's been very morose lately. Tom Reed has other ideas and he isn't being very communicative.'

'Should he be?'

Oldroyd smiled. 'Don't get testy, Charles! If there's been a crime Lander will want to get it sorted. Just form your own opinion and if you decide there's a case, tell him so.'

'But tactfully.'

Oldroyd looked at him with slightly narrowed eyes. 'Isn't that second nature to you, Charles?'

The message was clear: 'Watch your rear and don't rock the boat more than you have to.'

*

It was half-past five when Wycliffe arrived in the village, an uneasy mix of old cottages and modern bungalows with a pub and a church. A lane beside the pub was signposted: 'Duloe and Treave only. No throughway.' Duloe is Cornish for 'two inlets' and the estate is situated on a wooded promontory between two creeks of the River Fal.

Wycliffe drove along a poorly surfaced, narrow lane with no passing places. Fortunately, after three or four hundred yards it ended in a large circular space all but enclosed by a high stone wall backed by trees. Imposing granite pillars, green with moss and each surmounted by the effigy of a sleeping cat, marked the entrance to the estate, while nearby, in a more modest setting, a white-painted gate was labelled Treave.

Wycliffe passed between the pillars with their cats and down a long, rutted drive encroached upon by rhododendron and laurel. Once or twice, through the trees, he glimpsed the lower creek. Then, abruptly, he emerged from the gloom of the shrubbery into early evening sunshine, and there was the house. It was small as country houses go, a single rectangular block: two storeys of Georgian severity, the front relieved by a pillared portico and a balustraded terrace, probably added later. He parked on weedy gravel beside a patrol car and a police van. The house fronted on parkland grazed by sheep and studded with trees. The ground sloped easily to the river — a green channel between wooded banks.

Evening comes early to these river valleys and the light was already golden. A large motor launch loaded with trippers cruised upstream while a disembodied voice echoed between the slopes: 'On our left we have Duloe Estate, home of the Bottrell family since 1660. The present house was built at the beginning of the last century after a disastrous fire . . .'

The launch passed out of sight around the next bend and the voice was cut off as though by a switch. After that there was no sign of life anywhere, human or animal. The house stared with blind eyes across the valley and in this controlled and domesticated landscape Wycliffe experienced a strange sense of desolation. Then a uniformed copper came crunching towards him over the gravel.

'Mr Reed is at the cottage, sir . . . I'll show you.'

The constable escorted him around the front of the house, past some outbuildings, and into a patch of woodland. In a clearing they came upon a typical Cornish cottage, stone-built and slate roofed. Ordinary enough, but transformed by its setting into a woodman's cottage out of Grimms' tales. The constable said: 'In the old days it belonged to the gamekeeper.'

Reed was alone in the living-room with the body. As senior CID officer for the sub-division he and Wycliffe were in frequent contact and it was not long since they had been involved together in a major case. Reed was a large man (stooping now to avoid the low beams), bald, except for a fringe of auburn hair; he had a fresh complexion and clear blue eyes of peculiar innocence.

Miller's body was there, sprawled in an armchair by the fireplace. A shotgun discharged at close range makes a mess; much of the man's neck and lower jaw were missing; only torn tissues and congealed blood remained, and this had spattered and dripped and dried on his clothing and on every adjacent surface.

'Whose gun is it?'

'His, sir.' Reed went on: 'I've moved nothing; our scenes-of-crime chap took his pictures without disturbing anything and the surgeon was careful.'

'What did the surgeon say about time of death?'

'He thought late yesterday evening or early morning, say between ten and two.' Reed rarely looked at the person to whom he was talking; one had the impression that his eyes were focused on some far horizon.

Because of the barrel length (and this one was unusually long) it is difficult to commit suicide with a shotgun. The problem is sometimes solved by attaching a piece of string to the trigger. In this instance the string had been passed under the victim's right instep so that the pull was in the right direction.

'What makes you suspect murder?'

Reed's eyes focused briefly on Wycliffe. 'Two things. First the string is too short; he couldn't have reached the string any more than he could have reached the trigger.'

It was true. Wycliffe stooped, picked up the end of the string, and drew it taut; it came inches short of the probable reach of the dead man's fingers.

'You said there were two things.'

A smile appeared on Reed's lips. 'I discovered that Miller was left-handed but the trigger string passes under his right instep — obviously for a right-handed person.'

'So the killer was trying to cover his tracks by rigging a suicide but he wasn't very good at it.'

Reed nodded. 'It looks to me like an unpremeditated crime and the killer was in a panic when he tried to improvise.'

Wycliffe was noncommittal. 'I gather Lander still thinks he killed himself.'

'Yes. It seems Miller arrived back from a holiday on Friday — sooner than expected, and very depressed. Lander thinks something must have happened while he was away.'

'What sort of chap was he? Do we know anything about him?'

'Not a lot. He seems to have been an unusual type for an estate foreman. He came here four or five years ago in answer to an advertisement in *The Countryman*, and that's about it, so far.'

'He lived here alone?'

'For the most part but, looking around upstairs, I get the impression he might have had company from time to time.'

'Are there any relatives?'

'Lander knows of none.'

Wycliffe brooded on the young man, now horribly disfigured in death. In life he must have been presentable: he was fair, his features fine and sensitive — what could be seen of them. His eyes were disturbing — naturally, because they were open and staring, but Wycliffe thought that even in life they might have caused a tremor of disquiet. A good figure with no spare flesh, five-ten or eleven. What had persuaded him to bury himself in this place while still a young man?

On the table, within his easy reach, was a gleaming flute, now spattered with dried blood. The case was open beside it.

'It seems he played a lot — mainly to himself.'

Wycliffe said: 'The pathologist should be here soon and I've got a ballistics man coming to take a look at him before he's shifted.'

The living-room seemed to confirm the image already forming in his mind: the furniture had probably changed little since the gamekeeper's day but there were improvised shelves stacked with books, mainly paperbacks, ranging from classical and modern fiction to works on history, philosophy and psychology. There were framed contemporary prints on the walls, and a sophisticated audio box of tricks with racks of tapes and compact discs.

Indeed an unusual estate foreman.

Reed said: 'Do you want what little I've got in the way of background, sir? So far I've talked to Lander and his daughter, and I've had a brief word with his lordship. Apart from the girl's statement about finding the body there have been no formal interviews.'

'I'll take a look round before getting too involved.'

Wycliffe went through to the kitchen: a bottled-gas stove, running hot-and-cold water, and a fridge — the essentials but no frills. Under the sink there was a wine rack half-full of bottles. One end of the kitchen was screened off and fitted with a hand-basin and a shower cabinet. The whole place had an air of positive neatness and cleanliness, more to be expected of a rather fussy spinster than a youngish bachelor.

He went back to the living-room and up the narrow, creaking stairs. Two doors opened off a tiny landing. The first led into a small bedroom, little more than a cell. There was a single bed, a chest of drawers, a shelf of books, and a curtained-off corner for hanging clothes. On the chest there was a clock-radio. As in the downstairs rooms it was adequate — no more.

The other bedroom was larger, with a double bed, wardrobe, tallboy, and washstand — more relics of the gamekeeper's day. The room was apparently unused though the bed was made up.

He returned downstairs and joined Reed, standing outside in the filtered sunshine. Reed said: 'Odd, isn't it? Looks as though he kept that room for when he had company.' He added: 'I think we're about to have company ourselves, sir; I heard a car.'

'That will be Fox.'

Wycliffe's scenes-of-crime officer was lean and long-legged, with a receding chin, an obtrusive nose, and a certain hesitancy in his walk — like a discriminating stork. He arrived with his assistant, loaded with gear from his van which could not be brought close to the cottage. Fox had the job of putting the scene of crime on record through scale drawings, photographs and inventories. This he would do superbly well — missing nothing, but, as Wycliffe once remarked, 'Only Fox could be surrounded by trees without knowing that he was in a wood.'

At this stage Wycliffe liked to spend time familiarizing himself with the location and with the people, without taking aboard too much detail. Leaving the cottage to Reed and to Fox he walked back towards the big house. Even by Cornish standards for country houses Duloe was not large; it was pleasantly situated in a few acres of park and woodland with adjoining farms. There were no formal gardens, no Grecian temples; no fountains and no nymphs. It had never been one of the 'great houses'; now it had the appearance of a small estate slipping gently into decay.

He reached the house and climbed the broad steps to the terrace where weeds sprouted between the paving slabs. Looking up at the pediment he saw again the effigy of a sleeping cat — this time carved in relief and with an inscription, just legible: 'Innocens et Necesse'.

'Harmless and necessary.' A voice from behind him. 'Filched from *The Merchant of Venice* — Shylock and his "harmless and necessary cat".'

Wycliffe turned to face the speaker.

'Commending my ancestor for a barony, in 1795, Pitt said that he had made himself "harmless and necessary to government for thirty years". The first Baron Bottrell promptly adopted the phrase as his motto and the cat as his emblem.'

'A sleeping cat?'

A quick smile. 'Simply with closed eyes. Isn't that essential to being harmless? You, I take it, are Charles Wycliffe . . . Hugh Bottrell. I'm so glad you've been able to come down and look into this terrible affair.'

The Ninth Baron was suave, polished, and probably in his early fifties, but athletic, slender and supple; he had a good crop of dark hair turning grey and even his jeans and cotton tunic were worn with distinction.

'Would it trouble you to give me a few minutes of your time, Mr Wycliffe? . . . Come inside.'

Wycliffe followed him through an empty entrance hall, down a dimly lit corridor, to a room at the back of the house. By contrast with what he had seen so far this room was light, cheerful and welcoming. French windows opened to a paved courtyard and, in the courtyard, a weeping ash filtered the evening sunshine. Chintzes, in which greens and mauves predominated, helped to merge indoors with out.

'My wife, Cynthia . . . Chief Superintendent Wycliffe.'

Cynthia Bottrell was younger than her husband, probably still under forty; an elegant woman, sleek and blonde, who knew how to dress to give herself the height she lacked.

A restrained smile and the touch of a cool hand: 'Do sit down.'

The only possible dog for Lady Bottrell — an English setter — spread its elegance over the carpet in a pool of sunshine by the window. It turned a brown unwinking eye on Wycliffe but otherwise did not disturb itself.

Bottrell seated himself in a corner of a large settee, one arm spread along the back, legs crossed. 'I thought we might help to put you in the picture.'

Wycliffe said nothing and Bottrell continued: 'Tony Miller was employed as an estate foreman but he was altogether a superior person, well read, fond of music . . .'

'Then why — '

'Why come here to a more or less menial job?' Bottrell interrupted, smooth as whipped cream. 'I suppose because he wanted to

215

live in the country, because it suited him to have a house to himself, and because like many young men today he shirked responsibility. He came here five years ago on a two-way trial; he liked us and we liked him, so he stayed.'

'Did he have any particular friends?'

'As far as I know he had no enemies. Reed's notion that he was murdered seems to me fantastic.'

Lady Bottrell, serene and decorative in a bergère chair, intervened for the first time. 'But that is not an answer to the question, Hugh. Tony had friends, Mr Wycliffe, if one cares to call them that. He was gay, and inclined to be promiscuous.' Her manner was oddly incisive, perhaps spiteful.

Bottrell snapped: 'You exaggerate, Cynthia!' But immediately modified his tone. 'I'm sorry, my dear, but Tony is dead and one is reluctant to speak ill of him.'

Wycliffe was realizing that almost everything in the room had seen better days: the carpet was threadbare in places, the wallpaper faded, the upholstery worn. The pictures on the walls were all modern prints except for a single gilt-framed portrait in oils of an elderly man in full regalia.

'My grandfather,' Bottrell said, 'in his coronation robes.'

And on a pier table below the picture, silver framed, was a photograph of the young queen signed: 'Elizabeth R'.

They were interrupted by a new arrival, unmistakably another Bottrell male. The man came in from the courtyard and stood just inside the room, looking about him. 'I thought I left a book here . . . I was sitting where you are, Hugh. It could have slipped between the cushions . . .'

Bottrell got up. 'My brother, James, Dr Bottrell . . . Mr Wycliffe . . . Superintendent Wycliffe is here to look into the circumstances of Tony's death.'

James Bottrell carried more weight than his brother, his features were heavier, his body slacker, his manner more sombre and deliberate. He wore a khaki shirt and crumpled corded trousers. He was lame, dragging his left leg and holding it stiff as though from a knee injury.

Routing among the cushions of the settee he acknowledged his brother's introduction with a casual glance in Wycliffe's direction. 'Really? I wish you joy.' Then, to his sister-in-law: 'You haven't seen my book, Cynthia? — Hurwitz and Christiansen — I'm sure I left it here . . .' And after an unproductive pause: 'Damn it, it's big enough!'

Lord Bottrell looked at Wycliffe in mild embarrassment but his wife was untroubled. 'You need a secretary, James — or a nursemaid.'

Defeated, Dr Bottrell left by the way he had come.

Cynthia turned to Wycliffe with a smile. 'James is my husband's twin; but he had the luck — good or bad — to be second on the scene. He's a psychologist and not long ago he resigned a consultancy to come here and write a book on the criminal mind or something of the sort.' Lady Bottrell's manner was amused and tolerant. 'He has a sort of lair in the old stables where he lives, only emerging in search of meals, lost books, or spectacles.'

Lord Bottrell said: 'James has the brains of the family.'

Wycliffe, though pleased with these insights into family life, felt the need at this stage to be single minded: 'Getting back to Miller, I understand that he had only recently returned from holiday.'

'That's right. He came back on Friday though he wasn't due until Sunday. Something quite serious must have happened to upset him; he wasn't at all himself.'

'Do you know where he spent his holiday?'

'He didn't say; he was rather a secretive sort of chap.'

The telephone rang and Lady Bottrell reached for the receiver without moving from her chair. 'Duloe House. Cynthia Bottrell speaking . . .' She turned to Wycliffe. 'It's for you.'

It was Reed, speaking from the cottage. 'Dr Franks is here, sir.'

Reluctantly, Wycliffe left. Lord Bottrell followed him on to the terrace. 'Come at any time . . .' And then with a certain diffidence: 'First impressions can be deceptive.'

A thought occurred to Wycliffe: 'I shall have to talk to Lander and to his daughter; can you put me in the picture about the Lander household?'

Did his lordship resent the question? There was a significant pause before he said: 'I can tell you something, I suppose. Simon's father is still alive and lives with them. Then there is Jean — she is sixteen and, of course, her mother, Beth.'

Wycliffe thanked him and walked off towards the cottage, brooding. He was puzzled; he had a feeling that he had been treated to a piece of theatre. The Bottrells were acting, though not to an agreed script. But he knew better than to conclude that this had any neccessary connection with the crime. Lift any stone . . .

Shortly after leaving the house he met a young man — a boy, coming up from the direction of the river. The boy wore swimming trunks and flip-flop sandals, and his hair was wet. Another Bottrell? No doubt, the future Tenth Baron. For a moment it looked as though the boy might stop and speak but he did not.

When Lord Bottrell returned to his wife's sitting-room she was out in the courtyard watering her potted plants. As he joined her she said, without turning round: 'You're on thin ice, darling.'

'You think so? He seems a decent sort; not looking for trouble, I'd say. But you weren't exactly helpful.'

She went to a tap to refill her watering can. 'One had to give him something. You don't think you could have stopped them finding out that Tony was gay? Everybody in the village knows and when the press gets hold of it so will a few million others.'

'I don't see much in this for the press.'

She turned to look at him. 'With a peer involved? Don't be so naive, Hugh!'

For a while Cynthia went on with her watering and Bottrell stood watching, half hoping, half afraid that she had not said all she intended.

It came at last. 'I wish you weren't so mixed up with Lander.'

'Lander? But he's our solicitor. How can I avoid, as you say, being "mixed up with him"?'

Cynthia turned to look at her husband. 'Don't treat me like a fool, Hugh! I don't know what all this is about; I'm not sure if you do. In any case I don't want to know. But the police are asking who killed Miller, and why? They'll keep on asking until they find out. Sooner or later they'll get on to the Biddick girl. They may or may not be interested in what she has to tell but the press certainly will be and Lizzie Biddick is not a girl to turn down a good offer.'

'I don't know why you bring her into it.'

'Don't you? I wonder.'

Wycliffe found Franks waiting for him, sunning himself at the cottage door. The two had worked together on almost every homicide in the region for twenty years. Their temperaments were decidedly incompatible; Franks opposed a cheerful cynicism to Wycliffe's rather gloomy fatalism. That they got on as well as they did was largely due to the pathologist's good humour and tolerance.

'This is awkward, Charles; I know these people.'

'Which people?'

'The Bottrells, damn it! I occasionally go sailing with Hugh.'

'What's that got to do with it? Your job is to give an opinion on how this poor devil died, not to sit in judgement on anybody.'

Franks looked at him with speculative eyes. 'Sometimes I wonder about you, Charles.'

'It's mutual.'

They went inside. Reed and Fox could be heard moving about upstairs. Franks bent over the body in the chair.

'I don't want him shifted yet; I've got Melville coming down to give an opinion on the possibility or otherwise of suicide from the ballistics point of view.'

Franks turned to him. 'You still have doubts?'

'Let's say I don't want any arguments from the lawyers if and when this comes to court.'

'Well, if I can't shift him what do you want me to tell you — that he's dead?'

'Melville should be here at any minute; I was expecting him before you.'

Franks looked at his watch and sighed.

A man stood in the doorway; he was small, sharp-featured with tiny eyes bright and restless as a squirrel's. 'Gentlemen!' His eyes took in the room, then he went over to stand by the dead man. 'So nothing's been moved. I take it I'm free to examine the weapon?'

'DS Fox, the scenes-of-crime officer, is upstairs; I would like you to work with him.'

Fox came down and Wycliffe joined Franks outside.

Franks said: 'Old Melville is a fusspot. I hope he won't be all night.'

'What's your opinion of Lord Bottrell?'

'As somebody to go sailing with he's a very pleasant companion. He's not one of the world's brains, but no fool either.'

'You've met his wife?'

'Naturally; a very attractive woman.'

'But?'

Franks grinned. 'Too much the dominant female for my taste. I fancy she's more mother than mistress to our Hugh. But she fits in at Duloe, the perfect chatelaine; you'd think she was born to it.'

'And wasn't she?'

'Her father has a smallholding down the river. I've been told that most Wednesdays you can find him in Truro market hanging about waiting for somebody to buy him a drink.'

'What about the brother — Bottrell's brother?'

'I've never met him but we've corresponded.'

'About what?'

Franks drew a quick breath. 'You are a wonder, Charles! Why the hell should I tell you all this about people who are friends of mine?'

'No reason at all, but you will.'

'He's asked my professional opinion a couple of times on cases he wants to discuss in a book he's writing on criminal psychology.'

'I gather there's a son and heir.'

'Yes, Paul; he's sixteen; a nice lad — quiet, studious, doesn't give much of himself away.'

'Thanks; that puts me in the picture.'

220

'Don't you want to know about the Frog?'

'The Frog?'

'Lander — that's what everybody calls him.'

Wycliffe recalled that Lander's thin-lipped mouth seemed to stretch almost from ear to ear.

'Does he go sailing with his lordship?'

'Only when his lordship can't shake him off politely. Lander has all the compelling charm of toothache on a wet Sunday. Apart from that I only know that he's supposed to be a good estate lawyer. Certainly Hugh won't turn around without asking him first. Sometimes I get the inpression that Lander works him by strings.'

'The place doesn't look exactly prosperous.'

'You can say that again! Hugh has Marks and Spencer, ICI, and a few others, to thank for still being here. His grandfather made some shrewd investments back in the twenties and early thirties. Without them Duloe would now be a theme park or something equally bloody.'

They chatted for a while before Melville joined them.

'I would like to take the weapon back with me. If you will have it tagged and logged I'll give you a receipt.' The little man was a model of crisp efficiency.

Reed who had remained in the background through all this did what was necessary.

Wycliffe said: 'You've formed some opinion?'

Melville pursed his lips. 'It's obvious to anybody that the charge was bunched, indicating that the weapon was fired at close range.'

'But how close? Consistent with it being held between the thighs with the muzzle in contact with the neck or under the chin?'

'Almost certainly the muzzle was in contact with the neck — the neck rather than the chin . . .' Melville paused, his expression full of doubt and caution. 'I can't be definite but my impression is that the weapon at the time of discharge was not in a more or less vertical position as it would have been if gripped between the man's thighs with the butt on the floor.'

'So can you suggest any scenario that would account for the injuries as you see them?'

221

Melville stood first on one leg, then on the other. 'I don't want to commit myself. Deceased was certainly sitting or sprawled in his chair when the gun was discharged. Beyond that . . .'

Experts tend to be cocooned in their expertise and anything beyond bald fact has to be prized out of them. Wycliffe was brusque.

'Unless you are prepared to go further than that, you have told us no more than is obvious.'

The brown eyes flicked from Wycliffe to Franks and back again. 'Well, if I have to be more specific I would say that the deceased could have been threatened while on his feet; he could have retreated and fallen or slumped into the chair, then his assailant might have brought the muzzle of the shotgun into contact with his neck, forcing the head back, and fired . . .'

'So you would discount the idea of suicide?'

'What I have seen is, I believe, inconsistent with suicide.'

The little man was thanked and sent on his way with the shotgun in a polythene wrapper.

Wycliffe said: 'I can imagine what counsel would do to him.'

Franks began his examination of the body while Fox made a photographic record of every stage.

While they were at it two men arrived with a stretcher-trolley to take the body away.

Franks glanced at his watch. 'God! It's half-seven. Well, that's it, then! I'm hoping to get dinner in Truro; what are you doing?'

'I don't know; they've arranged something. But what have you got to tell me?'

Franks looked from Wycliffe to the body. 'About him? What do you expect? You know that he's dead, you know that he was shot, and you know when. The rest is in your province. Anyway I'll give you a ring when I've had a chance to look at him on the table . . . Sure you won't come with me for a meal?'

Under Reed's supervision the men removed Tony Miller's body, carrying it to their van parked on the outskirts of the little wood.

Chapter Three

When the body had been taken away Wycliffe said: 'It's getting late, we'll pack up for the night and carry on in the morning.'

Fox looked at him in injured protest. 'But we've just started, sir!'

Wycliffe was indifferent. 'It's up to you.' He turned to Reed. 'I shall want a man here to keep an eye on the place overnight.' And then: 'You probably haven't had more than a snack since breakfast; what about coming along to the pub with me? Incidentally, did they book me in there?'

'Yes, sir. I only hope you'll be comfortable.'

They went to the village in Reed's car and an hour later they came out of the pub dining-room into the warm darkness. People were sitting at tables outside, talking in low voices.

Wycliffe said: 'See you in the morning; I think I'll go for a walk.'

Without consciously making any decision he set off down the lane towards Duloe. The silence was absolute until an owl hooted and a pale form passed soundlessly within a few feet of his head. Away to his left he could see the glare in the sky from the lights of Truro. It was the darkness of a moonless summer night when only detail and colours are missing.

He was in a strange mood — detached, irresponsible; he could not take seriously this case in which he had so readily involved himself; perhaps it had been no more than an excuse to avoid the routine of the office for a day or two longer. And yet, so it seemed, a man had been murdered.

As he approached the entrance to the estate he noticed a small

223

house away to his right, well back from the lane. He could see its shadowy outline against the sky, box-like and stark. There was a light in a downstairs room and the sound of pop music reached him, muffled and throbbing.

He arrived in the broad open space at the end of the lane. The white gate of Treave stood out, and beyond he could see the lights of the house. The pillars at the entrance to Duloe loomed but the drive itself was soon swallowed up in darkness. Somewhere a fox barked, briefly imperative.

Perhaps it was the setting. But there was something of unreality about the people too: the Ninth Baron, trying a little too hard to be all things to all men; his wife, elegant in her once charming sitting-room, seated in her bergère chair, while her father cadged drinks at the weekly cattle market; his lordship's brother, apparently obsessed by his study of the criminal mind and, finally, the young Apollo, the heir presumptive.

Outside the family, the dead man, the superior estate foreman who was supposed to have shot himself. 'A promiscuous gay,' said her ladyship. Bitterness there. And the lawyer — Lander, whom Franks had nominated as his lordship's puppet-master.

Wycliffe brought his watch close to his eyes: half-past nine. Why not? His call would be unexpected, probably resented, and that could be an advantage.

He pushed open the white gate. He could see the house in silhouette, low, with interesting roof profiles, tall chimneys, and gables. He crunched down the gravelled drive and started a dog barking in the house. The front door was set in a broad, arched alcove; he pressed the bell. There was light in the room to the left of the front door. Another came on over his head and he was conscious of being inspected through a small glass panel in the door. The door opened.

A frosty, 'Yes?'

It was Lander himself, lean and gaunt and petulant. The dog, a black and white collie, was held by its collar.

'Chief Superintendent Wycliffe. I know that this is an unreasonable time to call but in the circumstances . . .'

From the hall, Wycliffe could hear a television in the lighted room, and the door was ajar. He realized that he was about to be shunted elsewhere for a tête-à-tête with the lawyer which had probably been rehearsed. This was not what he had in mind and with that effrontery which good policemen can carry off to order he pushed the door wide and left Lander no alternative but to follow him in.

'I'm very sorry to disturb you . . .'

The television was showing a play; two people had been watching; a woman and a young girl. Lander made the best of the situation.

Now that he could see the man clearly Wycliffe realized that, if not actually drunk, he was affected by drink; his eyes had a glazed look, his movements were too deliberate and his speech unduly precise.

'Chief Superintendent Wycliffe . . . My wife, Beth, my daughter, Jean . . .'

The television was switched off. Lander saw Wycliffe seated and returned to the chair he had recently left. On a small table at his elbow there was a whisky glass, one-third full.

A 'period' room belonging to no period; a white ceiling with exposed beams; a high wainscot, then a shelf with an array of willow-patterned plates and dishes; it was reminiscent of certain hotel dining-rooms where it all comes with the carpet.

'A whisky, Mr Wycliffe?'

Wycliffe declined. 'There are just one or two points I would like to deal with informally and at first hand.'

'What a strange time to call!' Beth Lander, acid, deprived of her play. She was auburn-haired with pale, freckled skin; her hair was scraped back into an absurd pony-tail, drawing attention to her rather pinched features and to her slightly protruding eyes.

Lander coughed and sipped his whisky.

The girl, Jean, her long legs cased in tight jeans, her feet bare, remained curled up in an armchair. Her father glared at her but she seemed not to notice. She was attractive; pale like her mother, but she had a mop of red hair, and incisive features, well composed; a Rossetti girl. Wycliffe noticed that her eyes were slightly swollen; tears had been shed not so long ago. Sixteen, Bottrell had said.

There was a brittle silence while they waited for him to begin. He turned to Lander: 'Apart from the conditions in which he was found, Mr Lander, what makes you so sure that Miller killed himself?'

Lander, like a man emerging from anaesthesia, coming to grips, mustered some slight aggression: 'The circumstances . . . Surely if you find a man with a shotgun between his thighs and the muzzle at his neck — '

Wycliffe interrupted: 'I said, apart from those circumstances. I gather from Mr Reed that you were not greatly surprised.'

'Of course I was surprised!' Lander spluttered in his agitation. 'Is Reed saying that I expected the man to kill himself? . . . What I said was that he came back from his holiday before time, very depressed. Lord Bottrell remarked on it . . . Something must have happened . . .' His voice trailed off, the thread of his argument apparently lost.

Watching Lander talk at any time must have been a distracting experience; whenever he opened his mouth his face seemed almost to split in two.

Wycliffe said: 'I'm afraid the indications are that Miller was murdered, and that makes his early return and his depression even more important. Have you any idea where he spent his holiday?'

Lander took a sip of whisky and put the glass down. 'You're sure you won't join me? . . . No? . . . I've no idea where he went.'

'And he gave you no indication of what had upset him?'

This was too much for Lander; he snapped: 'My dear Wycliffe, I was not in the man's confidence!'

'I'm told that he was homosexual and inclined to be promiscuous.'

Lander suppressed a too hasty retort and said, simply: 'I know nothing of his private life.'

226

Before the cock crows twice? . . . At any rate Lander's protests were unconvincingly vehement.

'To your knowledge, did he have people to stay at his cottage?'

'I don't know about people staying there but he had visitors. I've no knowledge of who they were or what his relationships with them might have been.'

Beth Lander had been following the exchange, her eyes on one speaker, then the other; now she asked: 'So you are quite certain that Miller was murdered?'

'That is where the evidence points, Mrs Lander.'

'Is it the case that gays who are unfaithful to their partners run a greater risk of jealous revenge than people who are sexually normal?'

It was Wycliffe's turn to be taken off balance. 'I'm afraid I've no data on which to judge.'

'That is what I have read, but Dr Bottrell says there is no evidence to support it.'

Lander, more than ever ill at ease, and trying hard to follow the exchange, said: 'Lord Bottrell's brother is an authority on the psychology of crime.' He made it sound like wife beating.

A straw in the wind? Mixing the metaphor, human motives are so complex that a poor copper, searching desperately for a lead, is accustomed to finding himself up the proverbial creek. All the same, he was intrigued by the woman's question.

He wanted to involve the daughter, who had not yet opened her mouth. Try something banal: 'You had a very distressing experience this morning, Miss Lander.'

She looked startled, and shifted her feet off the chair to sit normally. For her, the situation had become formal.

'You were taking the dog for a walk, I believe?'

'Jean has made a full statement, Superintendent,' Lander said.

'I know, but I haven't had a chance to read it. What time was it, approximately?'

'Half-past eight? I don't know exactly — it was quite early.'

'Your walk took you through the spinney, past Miller's cottage?'

227

'It's a short cut from our garden through to the estate.'

'And you wanted to walk in the estate.'

Lander said: 'We wander at will, Superintendent. Without referring to a map I doubt if any of us could say where our land ends and Duloe land begins.'

Wycliffe ignored him. 'You often go that way?'

'Sometimes.'

She was tense, but her answers came almost casually, like a well-learned lesson. Was it the questions she anticipated which troubled her?

'The door of the cottage was open?'

'Yes.'

'Your dog ran in and you followed — is that correct?'

'Yes.'

The girl was lying. Years of experience had nurtured a sixth sense in these matters and he was probing close to the nerve. She was leaning forward, looking at him as though mesmerized and gripping her knees with her fingers.

Deliberately he offered her an escape route: 'You knew Tony Miller pretty well?'

The tension relaxed; a dangerous corner negotiated; she almost sighed with relief. 'Yes, I suppose so.'

'What did you think of him?'

She looked surprised. 'I don't know. He was a bit odd. I can't say I thought about him much.'

That was candid; he believed true; but there was something very wrong. He was puzzled; he could understand the girl being distressed, but not afraid. He would have to take it further but not now with Lander breathing down his neck.

As though on cue somebody opened the door; a thin, elderly man stood in the doorway. 'Ah! I didn't know you had someone here.'

Lander said: 'This is Chief Superintendent Wycliffe . . . Meet my father, Mr Wycliffe . . .'

The old man shook hands more at ease than his son. They had the same build and similar features, but a white, straggling moustache helped to hide in the father the wide mouth so conspicuous in his son.

Wycliffe, having stood up, remained standing.

'You are here about young Miller?'

'Yes, sir. We've come to the conclusion that he was murdered.'

A slow nod. 'So I understand.' He seemed about to add something but changed his mind and finished: 'You've got a problem on your hands, Mr Wycliffe.'

Beth Lander got up from her chair. 'I'll make your cocoa, Father.'

The mantel clock chimed: a quarter past ten. Wycliffe apologized for intruding. 'I must be getting along to my hotel.'

Simon Lander asked: 'Are you staying overnight?'

'I'm booked in at the village pub.'

Lander looked disapproving. 'At the pub? You'll find it's pretty basic.'

'I expect I shall survive.'

Wycliffe let himself out by the white gate with a sense of relief, almost of having escaped. A certain tension was to be expected but in all his dealings with families he had rarely experienced such an awareness of separate individuals between whom there was no common ground, no accord; only suspicion and hostility. Grandfather, father, mother, and daughter were continuing to live together in the same house long after all but the most conventional bonds had disappeared. It was not what they had said or done, it was a matter of attitude, of atmosphere . . .

As Lander returned to the drawing-room his daughter brushed past him without a word and he heard her going upstairs. The room was empty. He was about to switch on the television but changed his mind; what he did and said when Beth returned from making his father's bed-time drink would be critical. At all costs he must maintain the status quo; no sharp words, no clever repartee; he must be calm, kind, and reasonable; eminently reasonable. He finished his whisky but did not sit down. He was going to pour himself another but decided not to. That bloody man! He hadn't come to ask questions, he'd come to stir the pot. And he'd chosen his time!

He heard heavy steps on the stairs: his father going up to bed, then Beth in the hall. She came in. 'Where's Jean?'

'Gone up to her room.'

Beth busied herself gathering up newspapers and magazines and returning them to the rack. Without looking at him she demanded: 'What was all that about?'

'They think Miller was murdered.'

'I understood that; I'm not stupid. What puzzles me is why you pretended to think differently.'

'I — '

'It doesn't matter. What was wrong with Jean?'

'Naturally she was upset, being questioned by Wycliffe. It was quite disgraceful — coming here at night and subjecting the girl — '

'Have you finished with this?' In her tidying she had picked up his empty whisky glass.

He was still confused and she was deliberately harassing him; he would have liked to slap her, but he swallowed hard. 'Yes . . . Yes, I — '

His wife went on: 'You had her crying in your study earlier. What was that about?'

She was looking at him now, her head thrust forward, her hair scraped back, forehead and cheek bones shining, eyes staring . . . He thought: My God. Why did I ever . . . ? But he forced himself to speak calmly. 'I knew that she was lying . . . I know lies when I hear them.'

'Oh, you're an expert on lies; I'll give you that. But what was she lying about?' She raised her voice. 'What about?'

Lander went to stand by the fireplace, his back to the room. Perhaps because he did not want to see his wife he spoke over his shoulder. 'You don't know what your daughter has been up to. On Sunday night, when you thought she was in bed, she was out with young Paul. She was out at one in the morning — one in the

230

morning, mind you! She went out after we thought she'd gone to bed . . . That's what she was lying about.'

'And you made her tell you that. How very clever of you! And you made her cry into the bargain. You are a natural bully, Simon!' She spat it out. 'You're also drunk. Do you think Wycliffe didn't see it?'

'I still haven't told you . . .'

'What haven't you told me?'

'It doesn't matter.' He was feeling slightly more sure of himself, on safer ground; she had, he thought, been diverted from the Miller theme.

He was wrong. In a calmer voice she said: 'What is this Miller business about, Simon? Does that girl come into it?'

'What girl?' He sounded hoarse.

'Don't treat me like a fool! What happened to her?'

He made an effort to compose himself. 'If you are talking about the Biddick girl, she left. You must know that.'

'Sudden, wasn't it?'

'I don't know about that. She gave in her notice, and went. You can ask Cynthia.'

His wife was silent for so long that he turned to face her. She was looking at him, her eyes so coldly speculative that he was disturbed. She said in a level, unemotional voice: 'Up to now I've never troubled about your little games but if you're mixed up in this then you had better watch out.'

He was alarmed; he had never known her either so bitter or so self-confident, usually she took refuge in hysterical weeping. 'I don't know what you're talking about, Beth. What am I supposed to have done? Unless you tell me — '

She cut him short. 'No, Simon! It is you who will start telling me if we are to talk at all.'

'But what do I tell? You know what there is to know!'

He stood there, staring at her, the great gape of his mouth exposing too many teeth and she turned away. 'It doesn't matter. We shall see.'

*

That night Wycliffe lay long awake pondering on the people he had met for the first time that evening. The Bottrells. On the face of it they were a family like any other but in truth they were very different, survivors of a threatened species, like his countess in the Dordogne. For three centuries Bottrells had lived at Duloe, managing the same land, handing on their privileges and obligations from father to son, with a vested interest in continuity, resisting and wrestling with change.

Wycliffe told himself: 'My father was a small-time farmer, I'm a policeman, my son is a scientist working for the UN in Kenya, but Paul Bottrell, by the grace of God and the stock market, will one day take up the family struggle as the Tenth Baron.'

And the Landers had much in common with the Bottrells: for six or seven generations they had practised law in the county town; for the whole of that time they had acted as estate lawyers for the Bottrells, and for ninety years they had lived in a house, built on land once part of the estate.

Wycliffe tossed and tumbled in his bed trying to grasp what such continuity meant, how it affected the attitudes and responses of the two families to the fluid society in which they now found themselves; dinosaurs who have outlived their strange forests and mighty swamps.

At last he fell asleep, a small smile on his lips, muttering: 'How long is a piece of string?'

Chapter Four

He awoke in daylight, not knowing where he was. For a moment it seemed that he had gone back in time; the sloping ceiling with exposed beams and the dormer window reminded him of the farmhouse bedroom which had been his in childhood. Then he noticed the faint smell of beer which pervades every corner in any pub and he was fully awake. He got out of bed and crossed to the window. The church was only yards away, the width of the pub car park. Beyond that he could see the roofs of a few houses, then fields and trees with just a glimpse of the river in the middle distance. He put on a dressing gown and went in search of the bathroom.

Lander had warned him that facilities would be basic. It wasn't four-star but there was a shower with plenty of hot water. Back in his bedroom, he dressed. He was fussy about his clothes, especially during a murder inquiry; he had no wish to look like an undertaker or even a manager for Marks and Spencer, but he believed that relatives of the deceased were entitled to a certain restraint. Years ago he had settled for a lightweight grey check, very subdued, though Helen still claimed that he looked like a bookie. With this suit he wore a matching fisherman's hat. The outfit was renewed as required and Helen hoped in vain that the pattern would be discontinued.

At half-past seven he went downstairs. The door of the bar was open to the street and the landlord, in singlet, trousers and slippers, was smoking his first cigarette of the day and taking the morning air. The bar cat performed the intimate contortions of her toilet on the step beside him. In the dining area the kitchen door was open and Wycliffe could see the landlady at her stove; bacon sizzled in the pan and the smell made his mouth water.

She turned towards him. 'Egg and bacon — is that all right?'

'Fine.' Helen would not have approved of that either.

'A sausage?'

'Why not?'

She was fiftyish, plump, and wrapped around in a spotless white overall.

'I've only got you and a young couple in at the moment. We've cut down on what we used to do — taking it a bit easier now we're getting older. Bert — that's my husband, tells me you're here to look into things down at the House.'

It was one way of putting it.

'Come in and pour yourself some coffee if you want to. The pot's there on the hotplate and there's cups in the rack. This won't be long now.'

Wycliffe poured himself a cup of coffee.

'Jill Christophers, the housekeeper at Duloe, is my half-sister. She's quite a bit younger than me . . . A funny business. O'course Jill never talks about the family but you can tell. And that Miller — I know he's dead and one shouldn't speak ill of the dead but he was a strange one — never had much to say, but it was the way he looked — his eyes!' She glanced through the doorway into the dining area where there was movement. 'Oh, they're down, I wasn't expecting them just yet . . .'

Wycliffe retreated. The young couple were already seated at table and they looked at him with sufficient interest to show that they had been told who he was.

One of them had switched on the television. Breakfast TV was one of his pet hates — all that plastic *bonhomie* to go with the cornflakes. Now they were presenting a species of news. The Magellan space craft was probing the clouded secrets of the planet Venus, the ultimate in global warming; there was trouble in the Gulf; and the drug barons in Colombia had shot a member of their government. Set all that against the murder of an estate foreman. Simple, ordinary murder no longer shocked, so it was

234

no longer news. Sometimes he wondered if it was becoming respectable.

But despite the television he enjoyed his breakfast and by eight-thirty he was at the cottage where Fox had arrived ahead of him.

The living-room looked as though the removal men were expected at any minute. Fox, with his half-glasses well down his nose, and his head held back to see through them, was seated at the desk going through its contents.

'Anything to tell me?'

Fox stood up, removed his glasses, and switched to his lecture mode: 'Judging by the prints I have so far recorded, sir, I would say that there have been two men, other than Miller, in the cottage fairly recently. One of them at least was a frequent visitor; his prints are scattered about and they seem to cover a considerable span of time.'

'How recent is fairly? Yesterday?'

'No, sir. Apart from the dead man's I've found none that seem to me as recent as that. Of course I have the upstairs rooms still to do.'

'Any more?'

'Yes; there is a fair sprinkling belonging to a woman who seems to have been a regular visitor also, but none of them are fresh. At a guess I'd say she hasn't been in the cottage for some days at least.'

Various items were laid out on the desk top. There was a ledger-type book with columns in which Miller listed jobs to be done, the date of completion, receipt of invoice and so on. There was a duplicate order book and a file for invoices labelled 'To Office'.

'Nothing of a personal nature?'

Fox opened one of the drawers with the flourish of a magician opening his magic box. He lifted out a wad of bank statements and a cheque book. The statements were unexciting; they told the hackneyed tale of a man living just within his income; Mr Micawber's recipe for happiness.

'Any letters?'

'None, sir. Nothing to indicate any connections he might have had away from this place except this.' Fox produced a recent hotel bill from the Crown Hotel, Dorchester, covering a four-night stay with certain meals.

So that was where he had spent his foreshortened holiday.

It was early days but Wycliffe was impressed by the man's anonymity, the apparent absence of roots. 'Send his dabs to CRO, with a description and, if you can find one, a photograph. If not, follow up with one of yours of the body.'

'You think he's got form, sir?'

'I don't think anything; it's routine.'

It was clear that Fox had not said all that was in his mind and it came out just as Wycliffe was about to leave: 'I don't quite know how to put this, sir; there's no evidence I can put my finger on — it's just a hunch, but I think somebody has been here before me.'

Fox having hunches was a welcome change. Usually he suffered from a sad deficiency of ingredient X. But Wycliffe knew what he was talking about: anybody accustomed to making systematic searches acquires a sixth sense about coming second on the scene. It may be an unnatural tidiness or the absence of personal idiosyncracies in the way things are stowed, supplemented, in this case, by the fact that so little of a truly personal nature was found.

It was worth bearing in mind.

On the way out he met Lucy Lane, newly arrived with DCs Curnow and Potter.

Detective Sergeant Lucy Lane, thirtyish, now an experienced member of the squad, had surmounted the hazards of being both female and attractive in a hand-picked brotherhood. A caustic and ready wit had been more than equal to the Romeo element, but the male chauvinists had proved more refractory.

'Mr Kersey expects to come down this afternoon or first thing in the morning unless you tell him to the contrary.'

'Good! I want you, Lucy, to concentrate on finding out about Miller's friends and associates; who he mixed with, either on the estate or in the village. Did he have people staying here? Find out what the village thought of him. Get your DCs taking the routine statements from the principals and muster what help Reed can give for a clip-board exercise. We want gossip. I'm going to quiz his lordship on Miller's background.'

It was classic procedure: first get to know the victim; once you do, the chances are that you will discover why he became one. You might even find out who made him one.

He was less conscious of location now, more absorbed in the routine of a murder inquiry which is much the same anywhere. He arranged for an Incident Van to be positioned in the open space near the estate entrance.

As he was passing in front of the big house he encountered the vanguard of the press — two of them, not conspicuously fired by a great sense of mission. There had been a brief press release from headquarters the previous afternoon, scarcely noticed by the media: 'A thirty-seven-year-old man, Mr Anthony Miller, was found shot dead in his cottage on the Duloe Estate this morning. When found, the dead man was seated in a chair with his shotgun between his knees. Mr Miller was employed as foreman on the estate and he lived alone. The circumstances of his death are being investigated.'

As a news item it had all the drama of the classic: 'Small earthquake in Chile; few casualties.'

Now interest was building; no doubt spies had reported a take-over by crime squad.

'Is this a murder investigation, Mr Wycliffe?'

'So it seems.'

'Dressed up as suicide?'

'The situation was as described in the press release.'

'Do you have any idea of why Miller was shot or who was responsible?'

'At the moment I have no idea.'

The questions continued but the answers were no more profitable and at length Wycliffe escaped to go in search of Lord Bottrell. Instead of going up to the front door he went around to the back, acting on the principle that the back of a building is usually more informative than the front. It is where they keep the plumbing.

He passed under a broad granite arch into a large paved yard with the house forming one side and outbuildings the other three. A section of the yard had been walled off to form the court with its ash tree. Everywhere there were signs of neglect and decay. Grass grew between the cobbles and there were places where the cobbles had been dug up and not replaced. The back of the house itself was in fairly good trim, but for the outbuildings the story was one of peeling paintwork, crumbling mortar, and loose or missing slates.

Much of the former coach house was now no more than an open shed housing several motor vehicles, but the remainder had been turned into an estate office. There was a sign saying so: 'Duloe Estate Office. All enquiries'. As well start there as anywhere; he was, after all, on what Perry Mason used to call a 'fishing trip'.

A young woman, hammering away at a typewriter, paused to ask him his business, then: 'Lord Bottrell is in his office — through there.'

Informality was clearly the order of the day.

He was received with something very like warmth and wondered how long it would last.

'I don't employ an agent — can't afford one — so I have to do the work myself. Lander does the clever bits, he's got the know-how and the staff. He has a large practice in Truro but he always finds time for our troubles.'

The office was plain, sparsely furnished, but business-like: a desk, filing cabinets, a set of drawers for plans, bookshelves with books on the law and estate management and, on one wall, a large-scale map showed the estate lands outlined in red. Hung in a place of honour, over the fireplace, was a rather romanticized watercolour of the house seen from the river.

Bottrell said: 'John Varley in the eighteen-thirties. Not especially valuable but I'm very fond of it . . .'

Wycliffe was more interested in the map. The house and its outbuildings were shown in considerable detail and, at some distance, nearer to the upper of the two creeks than he had

238

supposed, was Treave. Midway between the two houses Miller's cottage was shown close to a footpath through the wood. Wycliffe noticed a second isolated little building, on the creekside, below Treave.

'Is that a house?'

Bottrell came to stand beside him. 'Tytreth — Cornish for ferry house because there was once a ferry across the creek there. It's on Treave property, not mine. Until a couple of years ago an old couple lived there but they moved into sheltered accommodation in Truro and since then Lander has fitted it out for his photography. He's a photography buff — quite well known; he writes articles and things . . . Anyway, I don't suppose that is what you came to talk about.'

'No. I want to get as complete a picture as possible of the dead man, the kind of life he led, and the people with whom he was most closely associated.' Wycliffe added, with apparent casualness: 'All we have at the moment is a few fingerprints.'

Bottrell was quick to respond: 'Mine amongst them, I expect.'

'Perhaps; it would help if we could make a comparison — for elimination purposes.'

'Of course! Send along your chap with his little inky pad any time.'

'Thank you. Now, returning to Miller, what can you tell me about his family, his background, his life before he came here?'

'Very little; he was not very communicative. I know hardly more now than I did five years ago when he took the job.'

'Presumably there was a written application and references?'

Bottrell went to one of the filing cabinets and returned with a file containing only three or four sheets of paper. 'This is it.' He spread the papers on his desk. 'Born and educated at Church Stretton, Shropshire . . . Did pretty well at school — O-levels, A-levels . . . And after all that, a job in a local garage . . . Maintenance man at a horticultural college . . . Ditto at a country park in Lancashire . . .'

'Gaps?'

Bottrell glanced through the papers. 'There could have been, I suppose; this isn't overloaded with dates.'

'References?'

'Copies of testimonials from his employers enclosed with the application.'

'You didn't take up references?'

'The money wasn't attractive; there were six applications of which his was the only one remotely suitable so I had him down, liked what I saw, and appointed him.'

'Perhaps I could borrow that file. What other employees have you, sir?'

A wry smile. 'Very few. Outside, apart from Tony, only Harry Biddick, the gardener; he lives close by, on the road to the village. Then there's Delia, my secretary; she's from the village.'

'You run this place with two men?'

'I wish I could. No, I employ casual labour and contractors as I need them — it's cheaper. Tony's job was to keep an eye on that side — mostly the farms; they are let to tenants but I'm responsible for repairs.'

'And in the house?'

'No retinue of servants there either, I'm afraid; a man and his wife — Ralph and Jill Christophers — living in, and a couple of girls from the village, part-time. For a while we had a girl living in but she left and I don't think we shall replace her.'

'So, actually living on the estate, apart from you, Lady Bottrell, and your son, there are three people: Dr James Bottrell, and the Christophers, man and wife. Your gardener, your secretary, and two maids, live out. You realize that we may have to interview these people?'

'Of course.'

The smooth tanned features were composed. He waited for any further questions, tolerant and relaxed. In their previous encounter his wife had been a disturbing influence.

'It seems that he had homosexual companions; do you know who they were?'

240

A vague gesture. 'He was a free agent, the house was his to do as he liked as long as he worked here.'

'It seems there was also a woman who was at least a frequent visitor.'

'Really? Isn't it the case that some men are bisexual?' A quick smile. 'You should talk to James about it, he's an expert on abnormal psychology.'

'You've no idea who this woman might have been?'

'None.'

'I understand from Lander that he had visitors at the cottage from time to time.'

'Lander would probably know.'

'You were there fairly often — would you say every day?'

A sharp look, prompted by this first direct, personal question, but Wycliffe's manner was bland, his expression mild, anything but threatening.

'I suppose I called in at the cottage most days.'

'But you saw no one there other than Miller?'

'Of course he was not always alone.'

'Did you ever see a woman there?'

Bottrell was becoming slightly flustered. 'Once or twice, I think. I didn't take a lot of notice.' He gathered his wits. 'You must understand, Mr Wycliffe, that when I arrived any visitor would realize I wanted to talk business with Miller and generally they would leave us to get on with it.'

'I see.' Perhaps the most non-committal phrase in the language and enough to leave Bottrell with a vague disquiet.

'When was the last time you saw him alive?'

A frown. 'Saturday evening — the day after he returned from his holiday.'

'Can you put a time to your visit?'

'It wasn't a visit; I happened to meet him in South Wood when I was out for a stroll, about seven it must have been. Tony was often out around that time — usually with his gun; he liked to shoot the odd rabbit or a brace of pigeons for the pot — he was a good cook.'

241

'Did he have his gun on that occasion?'

'No.'

'Did he seem his usual self?'

Bottrell hesitated. 'As I told you he came back early from his holiday. It was obvious that something was preying on his mind but I've no idea what. When I met him on Saturday evening he was withdrawn, inclined to be sullen . . .'

'Do you do any shooting, Lord Bottrell?'

'No. It doesn't appeal to me. My brother does a bit — he occasionally borrows Tony's gun, but as a family we don't live up to the country tradition, I'm afraid.'

'It seems that he spent at least part of his holiday in Dorchester; does that mean anything to you?'

'Dorchester? No, not a thing.'

Wycliffe got up from his chair. 'Well, thank you, sir. I shan't trouble you any more for the moment.'

He was escorted through the outer office to the yard where Bottrell made conversation for a minute or two, then: 'You must come in for drinks one evening. Cynthia would like that.'

On the point of leaving, Wycliffe turned back. 'Just one more thing, sir. I wonder if you can tell me who owns the vehicles in the garage over there?'

'But of course! The Rover is mine and the Mini belongs to Cynthia. James lays claim to the old Vauxhall, and the Escort hatchback was Tony's. The Land Rover is a general workhorse for the estate.'

'Did Miller take his car on holiday?'

'He certainly took it but he could have left it in the station car park at Truro and carried on by train. That is what I do whenever I go anywhere at a distance.'

'When did he leave?'

Bottrell considered. 'Monday — a week ago yesterday. He must have set out early — before eight; he was already gone when I made my rounds as I do every morning before break-fast.'

Wycliffe thanked him again and left. Despite his apparent

candour his lordship was hiding something — quite a lot, Wycliffe thought. The question was whether he was hiding anything relevant. In any case no point in a frontal assault now, better to wait for the ammunition train.

Half-past twelve; Wycliffe went to lunch at the pub where he was staying, pleased to slip into a new routine. Whenever he was forced to break a regular habit he was uncomfortable until he had formed a new one.

There were several men around the bar and one of them, a wizened little fellow wearing a black peaked cap, was holding forth oratorically. He broke off as he caught sight of Wycliffe. There were free tables in the adjoining dining area and Wycliffe went through. The blackboard read: 'Dish of the day: Home-made Cottage Pie'.

He chose a table in an alcove. Helen had once accused him of living in a psychological alcove, wanting to see without being seen. It was true that he hated being up front, on view.

'A menu, sir?' A plump girl who had been serving in the bar the night before.

'No, I'll take the dish of the day . . . and a glass of dry white wine.'

The waitress brought his wine and he sipped it while waiting. He was trying to make some sort of pattern out of what he had learned since arriving at Duloe. The central character was the dead man; a homosexual living alone in a remote cottage. Witnesses agreed that he had been depressed when he returned from his holiday and it seemed that the killer had tried to take advantage of this by rigging a fake suicide.

So far his thoughts were clear, but beyond that point logical reasoning failed him as it often did. He was left with a rag-bag of phrases and images which cropped up in his mind unbidden and in no particular sequence.

'At least with closed eyes — isn't that essential to being harmless?' Lord Bottrell on the family totem.

'. . . gay and inclined to be promiscuous.' Lady Bottrell.

'I fancy she's more mother than mistress to our Hugh.' Dr

243

Franks. And Franks again: 'Sometimes I get the impression that Lander works him by strings.'

'. . . gays who are unfaithful to their lovers run a greater risk of a jealous revenge . . .' Beth Lander.

'You should talk to James, he's an expert on abnormal psychology.' Lord Bottrell.

His pie arrived, an individual one in its own dish. With his fork he probed the nicely browned potato topping and found plenty of meat in a rich gravy underneath.

'Mind if I join you, sir?' It was the little man in the black cap — which he kept on.

Wycliffe did mind, there were other tables, but he had been well brought up, taught to wash behind his ears, not to pick his nose, and to be polite to strangers: 'Not at all.'

'I could do you a bit of good.'

Wycliffe began eating and said nothing.

'I'm Bottrell's father-in-law.'

Still no response.

'What's that you're drinking?'

'White wine.'

'I'd rather have a whisky.'

'You've just come from the bar.'

'What I've got to tell you, Mister, is worth more than a bloody whisky. For starters, my daughter's husband — his lordship, is a poof.'

'What is your name?'

'Me? I'm Ernie Sims; like I told you my daughter is married to — '

'Well, Mr Sims, if you have anything to tell the police in connection with the death of Anthony Miller you should go to the Incident Van at the entrance to Duloe and make a statement.'

'Like hell! The reporters will listen to me.'

'I expect they will but I doubt if they'll pay because they won't be stupid enough to print what you tell them.' Wycliffe wished that were true. 'Now, perhaps you will let me get on with my meal. If you do not attend at the Incident Van I may send an officer to interview you at your home.'

'Are you threatening me?'

'If you choose to think so.'

The little man got up, muttered something, and went back to the bar.

Wycliffe was intrigued. He wondered what manner of woman who, with this unpromising assistance, had contrived to produce Lady Bottrell. There was more to it than the luck of the genetic bran tub, there was upbringing. No wonder the poor woman, after marrying off her daughter, had given up the unequal struggle, and died.

As he was leaving, three men came in. Wycliffe recognized two of them as agency reporters. They saw him and grinned with amiable cameraderie. Lord Bottrell's father-in-law was set fair to get drunk.

Chapter Five

The Incident Van — a king-sized caravan — was in position near the entrance to the estate. Under the blind eyes of the recumbent cats a uniformed policeman patrolled, ready to repel boarders or at least to check visitors. The van would provide a local base and communications centre for officers on the case. There were a couple of typewriters with VDU screens for their use though the bulk of the recording would still be done at sub-division. DS Shaw, Wycliffe's administrative assistant, was organizing that end.

Lucy Lane was already installed in the van. DCs Curnow and Potter were taking statements from the principals, while Reed's men were on house-to-house enquiries: 'How well did you know the dead man? . . . When did you last see him? . . . Can you tell us anything about his way of life, his friends, or anything else that might assist our enquiries? Where were you on Sunday night? . . . Did you, at any time, hear a shot?'

The mills of God were trundling into action.

The van was new and Wycliffe wandered through the compartments looking at this and that. At one end there was a little cubbyhole for the officer in charge. He came back to stand by Lucy's chair and said, musing: 'He must have done something.'

'Sir?'

'Miller — must have done something to get himself killed.'

It was not a very profound statement, coming from the head of CID, yet it expressed quite simply his belief that in most murder cases the victim is an active participant in his own death. There is something he has done, or heard, or seen, or known . . .

'I want this fingerprint business sorted out, Lucy. Lord Bottrell has volunteered. Send somebody with a bit of tact; I don't want Fox upsetting the customers. As cover, if for no other reason, we shall need to do his brother and Lander also. Send Curnow, he knows how to keep his big feet out of things.'

He was staring out of the window and thinking that of all the places where he had worked from a van this was probably the strangest. The high, almost circular wall, forming a sort of amphitheatre, the stone pillars with their emblematic cats, the trees — these things together with that sense of isolation, created an impression of some archaeological site which had remained undisturbed for centuries.

'And another thing, Lucy: get in touch with Dorset CID. Miller stayed at the Crown in Dorchester for the four nights of his holiday. We shall be grateful for anything they can get; in particular whether he arrived by car, whether he had a companion, how he spent his time . . . It's only a few days ago. We could be lucky.'

So Lord Bottrell was homosexual. That was no surprise; he had suspected as much on sight, and her ladyship had dropped hints. So what? Homosexuality was not invented by Wolfenden, nor was it ever confined to communities of one sex. Look at the chronicles of Bloomsbury.

What mattered was that everything pointed to Bottrell having been involved with the dead man, and if Bottrell and Miller were lovers . . . With her talk of homosexual jealousy Beth Lander had deliberately seeded an idea she had wanted him to have. Why?

Well, Bottrell would have to come clean and Wycliffe suspected that he would make a virtue out of necessity. But there was much more to it than that; he was a long way from any hint of a pattern.

He had reached the door of the van when Lucy called to him. 'Where will you be if . . . ?'

'Out.'

He walked down the drive, past the house and on down the sloping parkland towards the river. The sheep eyed him without interrupting their grazing. He passed through the screen of trees and found himself on a quay largely overgrown with brambles and gorse with a few spindly sycamores. It was about half-tide; the river was smooth, bottle-green near the shore, catching the sun further out. The numerous bends shut out any distant prospect, creating the illusion of a landlocked water. Not a soul anywhere. Then an eldritch screech echoed across the valley, a heron taking off from the opposite bank. It flew low across the water and landed not far away to merge at once with the background. And he was in this place to investigate a murder.

A little to his right, he caught sight of a low roof almost hidden by shrubs. He walked towards it along a well worn path. It was a boathouse with walls of hand-sawn planks, grey-green with lichen, and a roof of rough-hewn slate. Some of the planks were rotten and there were slates missing from the roof. Old buildings are like old people, they can be ripe and mellow or ignoble and depressing. The boathouse had reached that point when one wished that it could be frozen in time. A door in the side was open and he went in.

A fine old place; a wet dock surrounded on three sides by a wooden platform, all under cover. In the dock there were two craft; a rowing skiff and a rather splendid launch with plenty of varnished wood and brasswork, now tarnished. She had a cabin amidships and *MV Jezebel* on her transom.

Despite the end open to the river, wooded banks and dark water combined to produce a church-like gloom in the boathouse and slight movements of the water outside caused a rhythmic chuckling under the duck boards.

As his eyes became accustomed to the dim light he saw that there was another door in the far end. It was partly open and he could see into some sort of storeroom. He decided to take a closer look but as he approached, the door opened wide and Jean Lander came out.

'I thought I heard somebody,' she said. A slight figure, her burnished red hair was about her shoulders and by contrast her face seemed unnaturally pale. She was dressed as he had last seen her, in the uniform of the young: T-shirt and jeans, now with trainers added. She stood, expectant, on the edge of defiance.

248

He tried to disarm her. 'Isn't this a splendid boathouse!'

She looked about her without interest. 'Yes, I suppose it is. I think it's the only one left on the river.'

'Do you go boating with the Bottrells?'

'I used to but they don't take Jezebel out now. Lord Bottrell prefers sailing and he keeps a boat down river at Restronguet.'

She remained tense, prepared to make polite conversation but waiting for what she knew must come.

He said: 'You lied to me last night, Jean, and that means you lied in your statement.'

'Yes.'

'I don't know why or how you lied, only that you are not very good at it.'

Her eyes were dark-ringed. For a while she said nothing. He wondered what she had been doing in the boathouse. He could see into the room from which she had come: all sorts of gear was stored against the walls and on the floor: oars, coiled ropes, a couple of kedge anchors, an outboard motor, oil drums . . . It all looked as though it had remained undisturbed for a long time.

'Are you going to tell me about it?'

When she spoke her tone was flat, matter-of-fact: 'What I said about finding Tony Miller was untrue. It was during the night that we found him.'

'We?'

'Paul was with me — Paul Bottrell.' She took a deep breath. 'On Sunday night we went out after my parents thought I was in bed.' She added after a pause, defensive: 'We don't do that sort of thing often; Sunday was only the second time.'

'When was the first?'

'The Sunday before.'

'Any particular reason for choosing Sundays?'

She flushed. 'It's just that my father usually spends the night at his studio on Sundays — where he does his photography.'

'You came here?'

'Yes, we took the skiff and went for a row.'

'Couldn't you do that in the day?' It sounded like the silly question it was.

She frowned. 'It was more fun to meet at night. In any case my father doesn't like me being with Paul; he doesn't like me having boyfriends.'

'So what happened on Sunday night?'

She brushed her hair back from her eyes with a girlish gesture, a trick which owed all to genes and nothing to guile but Wycliffe was moved. Sex had entered the equation. Policemen and judges are not neutered; perhaps they should be.

She said: 'Well, when we came back and we'd put the skiff away Paul was taking me home by the short cut through the spinney — '

'What time was this?'

'About half-past one in the morning, perhaps a bit later. There was a light in Tony's living-room and his front door was wide open. Earlier, just before twelve, when we passed the cottage his door was shut and he was playing the flute. That was nothing unusual; Tony was known for staying up half the night, but when we came back a lot later and found his door open . . . Anyway, Paul went in to see if he was all right.

'Of course, he was dead.' She let the words fall with bleak finality.

'And you told no one.'

'We knew that he was dead, we thought he had killed himself, and there was nothing anybody could do.'

'Did you see him?'

She nodded and turned away.

'You realize that you and Paul between you may well have made the catching of a killer more difficult. You not only withheld information but you made a false statement to the police.'

She flushed and her lips were trembling so that he thought she might burst into tears, but after an interval she spoke in a low voice: 'It was my fault; I know it was a terrible thing to do but I was scared of my father. I thought somebody was bound to find

250

Tony in the morning and that a few hours couldn't make any difference.'

'But despite all that you pretended to find him yourself.'

She nodded. 'I couldn't sleep and when it was morning, with people moving about again and still no news, I couldn't stand it any longer; I had to do something . . .'

'Did you tell Paul?'

'Yes, she did, but afterwards.'

They had not heard him approach. Paul was standing in the doorway, a lean silhouette, his manner, even his posture was nervous, tentative, yet aggressive.

Wycliffe ignored him. 'What about your father? What does he know about all this?'

She said: 'He knew that I was out with Paul Sunday night. I don't know how he found out. He didn't say anything that morning but in the evening, before you came, he had me in his room.'

'He was angry?'

She nodded.

'Does he know that you found Miller's body while you were out?'

'I don't think so.'

'You don't know?'

She made a curious little movement as though defending herself. 'I can't tell with Father . . . He saves things up.'

The boy said: 'You've no idea what it's like. He hits her.'

'Stop it, Paul!'

Wycliffe turned to the boy. 'It was definitely you who discovered the body? You may have to swear to it in court.'

He was surly. 'Yes, Jean stayed outside at first.'

'When you passed the cottage earlier, and heard the flute, did you form any impression that Miller had company?'

'No.'

Jean said: 'He only played when he was alone.'

'Let him answer. Between then and when you returned to find him dead, did you hear anything else?'

251

'You mean the shot?'

'You heard a shot?'

'Yes, but we didn't take much notice. You occasionally do hear a shot at night; somebody after a fox or somebody trying to poach old Roskilly's deer — he rears them for venison and poachers have had one or two goes.'

'How long was it after you heard the shot before you got back to the cottage?'

'We were in the boat when we heard it; it must have been a good hour.'

'Where, exactly, were you?'

'On the river, about a couple of hundred yards upstream from here.'

'Can you show me from the shore?'

The girl said: 'I suppose so.'

They led the way back to the overgrown quay, crossed it, and followed a narrow path along the river bank, walking in single file.

Paul said: 'This path runs along the shore of the creek, more or less; in fact you can get to the village this way if you don't mind a bit of mud.'

'Past Mr Lander's studio?'

The girl turned her head to look back at him. 'Yes, it does, but that's a good way on.' Her manner was curt. 'Anyway you can see where we were from here.'

They were on a beach. Shrubs and a few trees, their roots largely exposed in the crumbling bank, fringed a stretch of muddy shingle which was probably covered at the top of the tide.

Jean pointed. 'We were there, just at the entrance to the creek, in the channel.'

'And, according to you, it must have been about half-past twelve.'

It was Paul who answered: 'That's as near as I can get.'

Wycliffe said: 'All this happened the night before last but you've kept it to yourselves until now.'

252

They were silent. Wycliffe saw someone standing, watching them from up the slope, among the trees; a young man, stockily built, dressed in jeans and a bomber jacket. 'Who's that?'

Paul followed his gaze. 'Matt Biddick; his father works on the estate. He's dotty about birds and all kinds of wild life. He's always around when he isn't working.'

'What does he do?'

'Pretty well anything. Whenever anybody is short handed they send for Matt.'

'Going back to Sunday night; is there anything else you haven't chosen to tell me?'

They were silent for a while then Jean said: 'There is something. While Paul was in the cottage I saw somebody.'

'Go on.'

'I was waiting at the edge of the clearing and I saw somebody at the side of the cottage — to the left when you face the front. He was only there for a moment. I think he saw me in the light from the front door and drew back. I've no idea who it was.'

'But it was a man?'

'I thought so. There was just once when I caught sight of his face but it was only a sort of blur.'

'What did you do?'

'Well, I was a bit scared and I ran across to the cottage. That was when I went in . . .' Her voice trailed off.

The boy said: 'When we came out Jean told me about the man and we looked, but we couldn't find anybody.'

Wycliffe let out a deep sigh: 'Of course you will both have to make full statements setting out all this. Neither of you comes out of it with any credit.'

A motor boat with a family party aboard putt-putted downstream and for a minute or two the odd little group on the shingle was the centre of their attention.

When they had disappeared round the next bend the boy said, 'There's something I wanted to ask . . .' His grey eyes sought Wycliffe's in concern. 'Is it true that when the police came there was a string tied to the trigger of the shotgun?'

'Yes.'

'Well, I don't think there was when I saw it. I know I was upset but I remember wondering how he could have reached the trigger . . .'

Wycliffe stooped, picked up one of the flat stones and tried to send it skimming across the water. It bounced once, and sank. He said: 'I'm no good at it.'

Not surprisingly, the pair looked at him, uncomprehending.

When they had left, Wycliffe set out along the path which led eventually to the village. Probably at almost any other time he would have had to pick his way through squelchy mud but three weeks of drought and sunshine had baked the surface of the path to a brick-like hardness.

He reached the creek; it was broad at first but narrowed to vanishing point in the middle distance where the tower of the village church rose out of the trees. Opposite him, on the other bank, there were fields of corn ready for cutting, there were houses strung out along the shore, and a jetty with a veritable flotilla of small craft moored off. But on his side he could see nothing but thinly wooded slopes and the path pursuing a sinuous course along the edge of the tidal mud. Lander's studio must be tucked away, around a corner.

He had learned something from the two youngsters: the shot which killed Miller had been fired at 12.30; a nice round fact to put on paper. But he had learned too of complications: the Lander girl had seen a man at the side of the cottage an hour later. It would make sense to suppose that he had been inside when young Bottrell went to investigate, that he was the killer, and that he had escaped by the back door only to find his escape temporarily blocked by the girl.

He strolled comfortably, missing only the consolation of his pipe; a year or so of voluntary deprivation had not altogether quelled the pangs of addiction. Thoughts drifted across his mind, inconsequential and tenuous. How often had he wished that he could think as he supposed others did? A is to B as C is to D so XYZ must follow. But did anybody really think like that?

Back to the man Jean Lander had seen: what was he doing, lurking around the cottage an hour after the killing? Faking the suicide? It was possible. Why had it taken so long? And there was the boy's story of the string, and Fox's suspicion about an earlier search. Had the man returned?

He thought of the young couple: an odd pair thrown together as refugees from their parents. They had withheld information and the girl had made a false statement; he should have breathed fire but he hadn't — and wouldn't.

The path rounded a promontory at the entrance to the upper creek. Here the foreshore was rocky, and above the tide mark, there were indications of former industry: a roofless stone building, its walls covered with ivy; vestiges of a slipway; and baulks of timber, blackened by age, set upright in the ground. Here and there channels had been cut into the rock for some purpose now obscure.

Nestling in the angle of the promontory was Tytreth — Lander's studio, a grim little building of slatey stone with granite coigns and a slate roof. It was built into the slope of the hill well clear of the tide and backed by trees. A paved slipway of weedy granite setts ran down to the water.

A convoy of mute swans cruised past in formation, now and then dipping their necks to scavenge the bottom mud; otherwise there was no movement anywhere, and no sound. Despite the picture-postcard houses across the creek, the moored boats, and the church tower upstream, it was easy to imagine that this was a countryside recently evacuated in the face of some sudden and mysterious scourge. The cottage helped the illusion: the windows were shuttered on the inside, the door was an affair of massive planks secured by a hefty padlock, and above the door was a little grey box bearing the words: 'Securex Alarm System'.

Looking up through the trees, above and behind the cottage, Wycliffe could make out a gable and a window belonging to Treave House. Was Lander defending this outpost against raiders by sea?

He opened a narrow, iron gate labelled 'Private' and climbed some steps beside the cottage. They brought him to a well-kept but steep path through the trees and a minute or two later he was in Lander's drive, not far from the white gate. Instead of letting himself out by the gate he took the path through the spinney which would take him past Miller's cottage.

It troubled him sometimes that his actions seemed almost as inconsequential as his thoughts. What had prompted this meandering exploration which had taken up a good deal of his afternoon? What would he do now? No one could accuse him of being hamstrung by some preconceived idea or plan. Sometimes he felt like a small boy with a jigsaw puzzle, picking out the bits which attracted him because of their pretty colours or interesting shapes. If someone had pressed him to justify his whimsical procedures he would probably have muttered: 'I don't know if I can; I call it field work.'

It was as he emerged from the trees in front of the big house that he decided he was on his way to talk to his lordship's brother, the psychologist.

'He has a sort of lair in the old stables . . .' Lady Bottrell, on her brother-in-law.

The stable yard opened off the main yard. Smaller, and cobbled like the other, some attempt had been made to preserve it; the cobbles were free of weeds, the walls had been freshly pointed, and the stone drinking trough in the middle was now an ornamental feature. Much of the former stable building had been demolished, leaving only the foundations, but the end with a loft had been converted into an attractive little house, startling in its incongruity.

The varnished door was not quite shut and from inside he could hear the rattle of a typewriter. There was no bell or knocker so he rapped with his knuckles.

'Come in!' A peremptory command.

After the sunlight the room seemed to be in darkness but as his eyes accommodated he saw James Bottrell, seated at a long table, doing a rapid two-finger exercise on an old Remington. The table was littered from end to end with books, pocket files, and heaps of loose papers. The wall spaces were taken up with bookshelves and row upon row of box files.

It was a strange room, long and narrow and high, like the nave of a church. At one end a spiral iron staircase led up to a gallery from which other rooms opened off. Daylight came from a skylight over the gallery and from a high window at the other end.

'So you've found me; now find yourself a seat.' Bottrell typed to the end of a page, ripped out paper and carbons from the machine and separated them. 'Be with you in a minute . . . There!'

Wycliffe had found a seat. Bottrell removed his spectacles and regarded him across the table. 'I suppose this is about Miller.'

'How well did you know him?'

'I knew him; it was through me that he got the job here.'

'Really? Your brother didn't mention that.'

'He doesn't know. He was advertising for a foreman; it was the sort of job Miller wanted at the time so I suggested he should apply. If Hugh had known I had a hand in it Miller wouldn't have stood a chance.' The grey eyes were steady, as though challenging a response.

'How did you — '

Bottrell cut him short. 'It must have been early in '84. At that time I was a consultant in the North Midlands and Miller was referred to me.'

'What was his problem?'

Bottrell shrugged. 'He was sexually insecure. A man with strong homosexual compulsions accompanied by guilt. His GP sensibly decided that a stitch in time might save him from your lot and the barred windows.'

'He had committed an offence?'

'Perhaps, but if he had, nobody had preferred charges. Anyway, I thought a course of rural quietude the best prescription, so I put him in the way of applying for Hugh's job.'

He paused to take a cigarette from a box, and light it. He pushed the box across the table to Wycliffe. 'Smoke?'

'No, thanks.'

'Given it up.' It was a statement, not a question.

'I used to smoke a pipe.'

The grey eyes regarded him, thoughtful and unblinking, so that he felt like a specimen. Finally, Bottrell said: 'One of those who prefers the world he knows to oblivion or a dubious alternative.'

Wycliffe felt the need to assert himself. 'You saw a good deal of Miller?'

'He came here to play chess once or twice a week. He was good.'

'Did you go to his cottage?'

'Hardly ever.'

'I've been told that Miller was promiscuous.'

Bottrell let the ash from his cigarette drop on to his shirt and brushed it away with an irritable movement. 'My sister-in-law wanted to believe it, at least to convince Hugh that it was so.'

'Why would she wish to do that?'

Bottrell looked at him for a moment then said: 'You don't need me to spell it out.'

Wycliffe was scanning the labels on one shelf of box files: Community Factors, Social Group, Genetic Factors, Family Background, Political Allegiance, Race . . .

Bottrell said: 'Clumsy, isn't it? I should have started with a computer; now it would be too much of a bind, transferring all that on to disc or tape. But it's frustrating, working near the end of the century with equipment appropriate to the thirties.' He waved his cigarette in a broad gesture. 'Do you realize, Wycliffe, that we've arrived at another *fin de siècle*? And the last one was the prelude to 1914. The issues are different but the menace is greater: this "disease called man" has now reached epidemic proportions.' His lips twisted in an odd little grin. 'Yet you've given up smoking so, presumably, you want to stay on to see the fun.'

258

Wycliffe was trying to find a footing with this man who looked like a slow witted bear but had a quick-silver mind.

'When did you last see Miller?'

'Sunday evening.'

'Any idea of the time?'

Bottrell inhaled on his cigarette and blew out a cloud of grey smoke. 'Between nine and ten. I was here working when he walked in.'

'You may well have been the last person to see him alive other than his killer. Did he seem distressed, excited, depressed?'

'You're asking me did I see him as a man likely to commit suicide or get himself murdered within the next couple of hours. The answer is no, he wasn't much different to usual, a bit more taciturn perhaps.'

'What did he want?'

An amused glance. 'What do people want from the chap next door? If they're not borrowing the lawn mower or come to complain about the dog, it's human contact, and not necessarily to talk. I asked him if he'd like a game of chess but he refused. He sat where you are for about fifteen minutes; he didn't say much — a few banal remarks. I had the impression he was trying to make up his mind whether he wanted to talk or not.'

'He was troubled?'

'He had something on his mind but I've no idea what.'

'Something which happened while he was away, perhaps?'

'Perhaps.'

'Whoever killed him played up the idea of depression in rigging an apparent suicide.'

'Then he or she was a poor psychologist. If there is such a thing as a suicidal type, Miller was not one. What's more, the fact that your chap spotted the fake so readily suggests that the killer wasn't very bright.'

'A poor psychologist and not very bright. You haven't greatly narrowed my field.'

Bottrell grinned. 'Pity! Most cops I come across are bastards but you don't seem a bad sort.'

'One more thing: we think there was a woman at the cottage, either as a frequent visitor or perhaps living there for a time.'

'That wouldn't surprise me.'

'Despite his homosexuality?'

A wry smile. 'Kinsey should be required reading for coppers, Mr Wycliffe. There are all degrees of homosexuality; attitudes and behaviour patterns are as varied as with heterosexuals. Even the committed male homosexual may be painfully aware of his deviance from the accepted norm. He may feel that by establishing a relationship with a woman he will be able to resist his homosexual drive and perhaps overcome it. It rarely works.'

'Have you any idea who this woman at the cottage could have been?'

Bottrell seemed to hesitate. 'The only woman who's been around and isn't now is Lizzie Biddick. She was a maid at the house — living in.'

'What happened to her?'

'She left. I can't say exactly when but it was very recent. You could ask Cynthia.'

'A local girl?'

'Her father, Harry Biddick, is Hugh's gardener.'

'And Matt Biddick, the birdwatcher, is her brother?'

Bottrell grinned. 'You're learning. There's a whole tribe of them; they live just up the road, towards the village.'

There was an interval while Wycliffe tried to bring about an awkward silence — one which the other party feels driven to break. It didn't work with Bottrell; he sat relaxed, complacent, and waited. A little battery clock on the table clicked away more than a minute and it was Wycliffe who spoke first.

'I've just come from Lander's studio.'

'Really? An escorted visit?'

'No. I walked round by the shore out of curiosity. The place is like Fort Knox.'

'Lander's photographic hide-out. He keeps his collection there and a lot of expensive equipment.'

'His collection?'

'Photographs of historical interest. You should get him to show you; I believe they're quite valuable.'

'Do you see much of the Landers?'

'Not more than I can help. Lander is a solemn ass and his wife is a harridan. She pretends to be a victim of marriage but it's Lander who's the victim and he's too big a fool to see it. I think you've met their girl — Jean; she drops in here occasionally.'

'For?'

'God knows! She drifts in here, looks things over with that detached insolence of the young girl learning to be a woman. She asks odd questions about anything that happens to be on her mind at the moment, then drifts out again. Still, I prefer them at that age to what they become later.'

'You don't like women, Dr Bottrell?'

Bottrell laughed. 'God's second mistake, Nietzsche called them; but I find them necessary, and sometimes amusing.'

Wycliffe was running out of questions but, like a dog worrying a bone, he was reluctant to give up.

'After Miller left you on Sunday evening, what did you do?'

Bottrell frowned. 'As far as I remember I read for a while then went to bed.'

'You were alone?'

'Unfortunately, I usually am.'

'You did not hear a shot?'

'When I sleep, I sleep.'

Wycliffe stood up. 'Thanks; I've no doubt we shall meet again.'

Bottrell limped after him to the door. 'Do you play chess?'

'Not on duty.'

'Pity! With Miller gone I'm reduced to intellectual masturbation.'

'Damn the man!' Wycliffe was back in the big yard behind the house, sore with himself rather than Bottrell. He felt outclassed; he had allowed Bottrell to make the running and all because he had ignored the first commandment in the holy writ of interviewing technique: 'Always assume that the other party is at least as intelligent and quick witted as you are.' All the same he had learned something, though, he suspected, only those things which Bottrell had wanted him to know. In fact there had been an element of forced feeding.

He decided to look for a quicker way to the cottage than trotting around three sides of the house. He found it in a small arched entrance to a kitchen yard where there were dustbins and a clothes hoist. A second arch opened on the east side and through it he could see the spinney within a hundred yards. As he passed under the first arch a woman came to stand in the doorway of what, presumably, was the kitchen.

'Can I help you, sir?'

'You are Mrs Christophers?'

She smiled. 'And you must be the police gentleman.'

A contradiction in terms? He hoped not. She was younger than he had expected — thirty-five? On the plump side though not fat, a mass of brown hair, a clear skin, and dark brown eyes — no Celt, but Cornish through and through. Why the real Cornish pretend to be Celts nobody will ever know; or the Bretons, or the Welsh, or the Irish. Why not leave it to the brawny, bony, sandy-haired Scots in whom Julius Caesar would certainly recognize his old enemies.

'Lord Bottrell told us about you.'

'I would like a word . . . Chief Superintendent Wycliffe.'

'You best come in, then.' She held out a soft hand. 'Jill Christophers. Pleased to meet you, I'm sure.'

The kitchen was large with plenty of unused space because modern appliances and utensils take up so little room. The floor was carpeted and every working surface shone.

'I was just making a pot of tea, if you'd like a cup, Mr Wycliffe. My Ralph will be here any minute; that man can smell the teapot a mile off.' She laughed.

And she was right; almost at once her husband arrived with an assortment of vegetables in a basket. 'Harry says there's no runner beans worth picking today, they'll have to have carrots as

262

a second veg tonight.' He caught sight of the intruder. 'Oh, I didn't know . . . Mr Wycliffe, is that right? . . . Ralph Christophers.'

'You like it strong? . . . Do sit down for goodness sake!'

'Strongish,' Wycliffe said. 'A little milk but no sugar, please.'

'Might almost be a Cornishman. Now then, Ralph, Mr Wycliffe wants to ask us a few questions.'

Ralph Christophers was small and spare, about the same age as his wife but without her ebullient cheerfulness. He sat in what was obviously 'his place' and looked at Wycliffe with a sombre air. 'I don't want you to misunderstand me, Mr Wycliffe, but Jill and me work here — we're employed, and it begins and ends there. That seems to us the best way.'

'And that wasn't true of Tony Miller?'

Christophers sipped his tea and looked at Wycliffe over the cup. 'Well he was employed too but he was a different class and he was on terms with his lordship that you might call friendly.'

Jill nodded. 'That's right.'

'So?'

'So nothing. It means we didn't see much of Tony Miller and we can't tell you much about him. I'm sorry.'

'But it must have been different with Lizzie Biddick; she worked in the house and presumably came directly under you, Mrs Christophers.'

Jill concentrated on shifting her cup and saucer and the teapot into slightly different positions but said nothing. It was her husband who spoke, slowly and after due thought: 'I don't know where Lizzie comes into this, Mr Wycliffe; all I can say of the girl is that she did her work, what Jill told her to do. What else she did was her business.'

'Ralph means,' Jill said, 'there were nights when she didn't sleep in her room.'

There was a black look from husband to wife but Jill seemed not to notice.

'Isn't she the gardener's daughter?'

'Harry Biddick's daughter — yes.'

263

'And the Biddicks' house is just up the road, so why did the girl live in?'

It was Jill who answered. 'They're a big family, Mr Wycliffe. Lizzie is one of seven children. Her ladyship offered the girl living-in as much to help out Harry and his wife as anything else. I mean, with three bedrooms to sleep nine.'

'Is Lizzie the eldest?'

'Second. Her brother, Matt, is the eldest; he must be twenty-one or two.'

'Why did she leave?'

Christophers shrugged. 'I've no idea.'

Delicately, as though treading on tin-tacks, Wycliffe said: 'You've no idea who it was she spent those nights with?'

They both shook their heads but said nothing.

'When did she finish here?'

It was the woman who answered: 'Sunday — a week ago last Sunday. She was away early Monday morning.'

'What do you mean — "away" — isn't she back with her parents?'

Jill Christophers looked at him in astonishment. 'Back there? Not Lizzie! She was off to London. Leastwise, that's what she told everybody. All I know is she was gone from here when we got up that morning.'

Wycliffe said: 'Presumably her parents know where she is.'

The housekeeper again adjusted the position of her cup and saucer with concentrated attention. 'They know no more than anybody else. Lizzie is a very wilful girl — always been the same.'

Wycliffe tried again: 'Miller left early that same morning at the start of his holiday.'

She looked at him and the look said, as plainly as words, 'So you've got there at last!'

Early in any police investigation almost everyone concerned holds back something — secrets little or large, relevant or not. Usually the pressure of events squeezes out the truth and seemingly untellable things are eventually told, rarely with any great distress. No point then in the earnest copper getting himself into a twist and forcing the pace early on. Wycliffe drank his tea, thanked the couple, and left.

So, on the face of it, the girl had been having an affair with Miller and it certainly looked as though they had gone off together. But four days later Miller had returned. And the girl? Two days after his return Miller was murdered with an unconvincing attempt to make it look like suicide . . .

A long way to go.

It was clouding over. An end to the drought? Not according to the experts, but a weak front that might or might not produce a spitting of rain.

Chapter Six

In the police caravan Lucy Lane was going through the statements and the first of the house-to-house reports, a red felt pen poised to draw the attention of the big chief to relevant items. Daughter of a Methodist parson and a graduate in English Literature, she had made her unlikely choice of career believing that society was sick and that she must weigh in with her pennyworth on the side of healing. No sentimentalist, and a firm believer in a stick-and-carrot philosophy, the police had seemed a rational choice. Disillusionment there had been, sometimes in massive doses, but she soldiered on.

As usual the reports were thin on facts but there was enough background material to justify the exercise. The shopkeeper said: 'No good asking us about Miller, we never saw him in the village!' The publican: 'In five years he never set foot inside my bar once . . .' The vicar: 'There's a lot goes on in this village apart from the church — we've our own cricket team, there's a tennis club, a music society, a painting group . . . But the young man preferred to keep himself to himself . . .'

And there were more barbed comments: 'Ask Lord Bottrell how Miller spent his spare time,' and 'If you ask me there was something very odd about that young man . . .'

Only one person, an old maid, claimed to have heard the shot and she had no idea of the time.

Chapter and verse are rare commodities in police work. Lucy numbered, logged, and bunched the reports for filing.

She heard the duty officer in conversation with someone in the next cubicle. They had a visitor. A head peered round her door: 'Lord Bottrell, sarge.'

His lordship came in looking self-conscious.

'I'm afraid Mr Wycliffe is not here, sir, but if I can be of any help . . .'

Bottrell stood awkwardly in the doorway of the little cubicle as though making up his mind, and then: 'May I sit down?'

There were bench seats and they faced each other across a narrow table.

'You are . . . ?'

'Detective Sergeant Lane, sir.'

'Yes, well, I've been visited by a very large young man like something out of a rugby scrum who took my fingerprints.'

'Which, Lord Bottrell, you volunteered to give.'

'Oh, I'm not complaining. It's what follows that is difficult — when you've matched my prints against others found all over the cottage — upstairs and down.'

'You were a frequent visitor?'

A flicker of irritation. 'You know damn well that I was — and why. I thought I'd better tell somebody the facts myself and not leave it all to gossip.'

His lordship was staring out of the window where the most conspicuous object was a gate pillar surmounted by one of his oh-so-discreet cats.

Lucy Lane studied her fingernails, determined not to make the next move.

'How long have you been in the force, young lady?'

'Several years.'

'So you are no stranger to the vagaries of human conduct. You may even grasp that it is possible for two men to share a deep affection each for the other which is by no means wholly sexual.' He placed a hand over his eyes as though shielding them and, after a pause, he went on in a different voice: 'In these days love is an unfashionable word but it's what I felt for Tony and, I thought, he returned.'

Then he was silent and when Lucy looked up the vaguely

patronizing mask had wholly disappeared; his features were crumpled as with a child about to burst into tears.

She gave him time and when he spoke again he had to some extent regained control though he spoke slowly and with hesitation: 'It is very hard to pretend to no more than ordinary concern and a merely formal grief when most of what has seemed worthwhile in one's life is suddenly taken away . . . One is allowed to weep for a wife, even for a mistress, but not . . .' He choked over his words and broke off with a gesture of frustration. 'There is not even an acceptable word for the relationship!'

The atmosphere was becoming claustrophobic; misty rain had clouded the windows creating a sense of isolation, even of intimacy.

Lucy Lane said: 'Your words were: "I thought he returned."'

He gave her a sharp look. 'You are very perceptive and, of course, you are right. In recent weeks I've had reason to suspect that our relationship might be one-sided.'

'Reason for jealousy?'

'Yes, reason for jealousy and, by God, I was jealous!'

Lucy spoke quietly: 'So you will understand why all this is relevant to the inquiry — why what you have told me must go on record.'

He was drumming with his fingers on the table top. 'Oh, I understand . . . I understand! Why don't you caution me? "Anything you say . . ." No, that is unfair, uncalled for. I'm sorry.'

For a time they sat in silence then Bottrell said: 'There is more. I told Wycliffe that on Saturday evening I met Tony when I was out walking in South Wood.'

'That is in your statement.'

'Yes, but we had one hell of a row, and that is not in my statement.' He made an irritable movement. 'You know, I suppose, that lovers' quarrels can be among the most vicious? . . . We shouted at each other, making the wildest accusations. At one point I thought he might attack me and I hoped that he would . . .'

'Why are you telling me this?'

He looked at her. 'I don't know. Perhaps I'm trying to cover myself, on the grounds that it's better you should hear it from me than from another. You would think that on an estate like this there must be some privacy somewhere. There isn't! You are always seen by somebody; you are always overheard.'

'And were you seen or overheard on Saturday evening?'

'What? Oh, I don't know. I'm getting paranoid.'

'Of whom were you jealous?'

Bottrell hesitated. 'I'm not prepared to say; I don't want to involve another person.'

'Another man?'

'Yes.'

'It may be necessary to return to that later.'

'We shall see. I'll tell you one thing, young lady, you should have been a priest — a woman priest. You have the art of inducing confession.'

'Just one more question, sir. Does Lady Bottrell know of your association with Miller?'

A small smile. 'I think Lady Bottrell is omniscient.'

'Are you willing to make a statement embodying what you have told me?'

'Would I have come here if I wasn't?'

Wycliffe made for Miller's cottage and found Fox in the living-room, writing up his notes.

'They've been ringing around, sir, trying to get you. It's DS Shaw at sub-division.'

He put through a call and spoke to Shaw.

'Your request to CRO, sir; we've had a fax. It reads: "Subject unknown under attributed name but prints and description relate to Donald Anthony Ross convicted at Dorchester Crown Court October 1976 of assault occasioning actual bodily harm. The victim was his wife, Sharon Patricia Ross, aged 39. Ross, then 23, was sentenced to two years and released with full remission in February 1978. Request documentation if required." That's the message, sir. Puts a different complexion on things, don't you think?'

'We may need the file for the record so you'd better put in an application, but for practical purposes I can probably do better through the bush telegraph. That is Billy Norton's territory and I fancy he was already there in the seventies when this happened.'

He dropped the telephone on its cradle, given as Hercule Poirot would have said, 'furiously to think'. But Wycliffe had less confidence in his little grey cells than the Belgian.

So Miller — as Ross, had already served a sentence for assaulting his wife when he consulted Dr Bottrell after the unspecified incident in 1984. Did Bottrell know that at the time? Did he know it now? Did anyone within the Duloe orbit know? Good questions. More to the point, had Lizzie Biddick gone off with him?

And Dorchester was where Miller — he would have to stay Miller and not Ross — had spent his short holiday. There was a pattern emerging. But had the dead man been murdered as Miller or Ross?

Fox was demanding attention. 'I'm almost through here, sir. Now I've got my report to prepare.'

'Anything fresh upstairs?'

Fox considered. 'As to prints, in the small bedroom, only the dead man's; in the other room, his, along with those of two other men.'

'None of the woman's?'

'No, sir.'

'I see. Is that all?'

'For the moment, sir.'

'Well, there's one more thing from me: I want you to check the woman's prints against those of Lizzie Biddick, a girl who, until recently, worked in the house, living in. You should find plenty of material in her room.'

Wycliffe walked back to the Incident Van. It was overcast and raining — not real rain but a fine intermittent drizzle. Probably the sun would break through again before it set. Wycliffe yearned for a real Cornish downpour; so did the jaded, parched countryside.

So Miller had a record — nothing spectacular, but it was for violence against a woman. So where did the Biddick girl fit?

In the Incident Van he found Lucy Lane, obviously anxious to tell him something, but he gave her no opportunity. He telephoned Detective Superintendent Billy Norton at Dorchester.

The usual Arab tea-party, exchanging greetings. When did we last meet? Keeping well? And Helen? . . . How is Mildred? He remembered the name in the nick of time.

'Donald Anthony Ross — mean anything to you?'

'Ross? Not off the cuff. Tell me.'

'Convicted of occasioning actual bodily harm to his wife in '76 — got two years. There's no reason why you should remember — '

'But I do! It comes back. I remember feeling a bit sorry for the boy. Not that I condone wife beating but that woman was a cow. She was God knows how much older, and if ever I saw a case of kidnapping . . . I was DI at the time; I don't recall the details but I can turn 'em up. Anyway, what's he done now?'

'Got himself murdered, apparently under an alias — Tony Miller.'

'That figures; he was a loser. Had any detail from CRO yet?'

'Not yet.'

'No, they'll probably wait for leap year or something. Anyway, I'll dig out the file, summarize the main points, and I'll fax 'em to you. By the way I heard that a DS of yours was making inquiries about a chap staying at the Crown here. Any connection?'

'That chap was our Miller — your Ross.'

'Well, I'm damned! By the way, what was he doing in your part of the world?'

'Estate foreman for Lord Bottrell.'

'That fits; I remember he was in the Parks Department here — hadn't long come down from somewhere up north.'

'Who needs files with you around?'

'We aim to please. Leave it to me.'

Wycliffe put the phone down. Lucy Lane was ostentatiously occupied. 'You gathered what that was about?'

'Not really, sir.'

Wycliffe explained and she was mollified. 'So Miller had form, and for battering a woman.'

'Yes but it doesn't make him a murderer. Anyway, there's more to it than that.' He told her about the girl, Lizzie Biddick. 'It's an interesting thought that if that damned trigger string had been a few inches longer we might well be saying now that Miller had committed suicide in remorse and that we should be looking for the girl's body.'

'It's still possible that he killed her.'

'Oh, it's possible, and I want you to get Lady Bottrell's account of the girl; exactly what the arrangement was, what was said when she talked about leaving. Does she know of any association between the girl and Miller — or anybody else for that matter?' Wycliffe grinned. 'Woman talk, Lucy! Draw the lady out.

'Now let's have your news.'

'A couple of things, sir. There was a message from Mr Kersey to say that he's been held up but that he'll be down in the morning.'

'And?'

'Lord Bottrell has been here, baring his soul. He admits to having had a jealous quarrel with Miller when they met that Saturday evening.'

'You'd better tell me about it.'

When she had finished Wycliffe said: 'Did he give you any indication of the cause of his jealousy?'

'No, sir, he refused. I told him we might have to come back to it.'

'Perhaps this is leading us back to the Biddick girl.'

'No, he admitted that it was a man.'

'He's willing to put all this into a statement?'

'He's already done so.'

'Good! On the Miller killing, Jean Lander and the Bottrell boy are coming in to make statements. It seems the girl actually saw someone outside the cottage while young Bottrell was inside.'

By early evening the rain, such as it was, had gone, the sky was clear and the sun shone. There is something about the Fal valley on a fine summer evening reminiscent of landscapes in biblical pictures: Adam and Eve in the garden; the lion lying down with the lamb; Ruth amid the alien corn — a timelessness, a sweet sadness. On his way back to the pub for his evening meal, Wycliffe stopped at the Biddicks' place. The land between the house and the road amounted to a small field and it was meticulously cultivated with regimented rows of broccoli, savoys, potatoes, onions, beans, carrots . . .

The voice of a male pop singer wailed in the house. A brawny, black-haired man, wearing a bib-and-brace overall and smoking a short-stemmed pipe, was hoeing between lettuces.

'Mr Biddick?'

'That's me.'

'Superintendent Wycliffe.'

Biddick spoke through his teeth, while still gripping his pipe, and went on with the hoeing. 'What can I do for you, then?'

'I want to talk to you about your daughter, Lizzie.'

Biddick paused and took the pipe from his mouth. 'Talk to the missus then, the girls is her business.' He looked at Wycliffe with dark eyes in which there was a hint of amusement. 'You'll find her in the house but I warn you, she might not be best pleased. She's cooking supper.'

The green front door, which had two little glass panes at eye level, was opened by a stockily built young man with spiky black hair and a ruddy complexion — the birdwatcher. Wycliffe had seen him down by the creek.

'You are Lizzie's brother — Matt Biddick, isn't it? . . . Superintendent Wycliffe.'

'I know who you are; I suppose you want to see Mother.' The dark eyes made it clear that soft talk was wasted. 'You best come in and I'll fetch her.'

273

In the living-room there was a good smell of cooking but the pop music from a vintage portable radio was raucous and deafening. Matt went through into the adjoining kitchen and before the door closed behind him Wycliffe had a glimpse of a woman's arm as she stirred something on a stove. He was not left alone, a dark girl of about sixteen was setting places on a long, narrow table. She had the bold beauty and early ripeness of a gypsy girl. If Lizzie was anything like her . . .

At one end of the table, where the cloth did not reach, a boy of nine or ten, with great concentration, was copying plant names from seed packets on to wooden labels, using a felt pen.

Wycliffe was reminded of Victorian morality prints: 'The Fruits of Industry and Thrift'. In keeping, the room was sparsely furnished but both tidy and clean. If the size of the family had led him to expect squalor and chaos he had misjudged the Biddicks.

Neither the girl nor the boy seemed to notice his presence. After an interval the door from the kitchen opened again and Mrs Biddick came in, leading a little girl by the hand and trailed by her son. 'Turn that thing off, so we can hear ourselves speak!'

It was easy to see where the good looks came from. Mrs Biddick was the sixteen year old girl, thirty years on, her figure thickened by childbearing. She said to Wycliffe: 'You can sit down.' She herself sat on a kitchen chair by the table and lifted the little girl on to her lap. Her son remained standing behind her chair.

The older girl had finished laying the table and her mother said: 'Go and keep an eye on the stew, Chris.' Then she turned to the boy with his labels. 'Leave that, Tommy. Go and help father with his weeding.'

When the two had gone, Wycliffe said: 'I'm anxious to get in touch with your daughter, Lizzie, Mrs Biddick.'

'So am I, but I don't see what either of us can do about it.'

'You've no idea where she is?'

'London; that's where she said she was going.'

'Does she know anybody in London? Does she have some place to go?'

A slight lift of the shoulders. 'If she does, she never told me.'

She reached out a hand and straightened the knife and fork at the place where she was sitting. 'It all started when she got to know Miller; she got restless — said she wanted "to better herself" and "get out of this place" — that kind of talk. She was working part-time over at the house then but her ladyship offered her full-time, living-in. It seemed a good idea; she'd have the chance to be a bit more private like — more than she could here anyway — live her own life.'

Mrs Biddick was parting her little daughter's black hair with her fingers as she spoke. 'But Lizzie was determined to break away an' that's all there is to it. She knows there's a home for her here when she wants one an' that's all I can say.'

Wycliffe was impressed by the woman's serenity, she was imperturbable as a rock, yet she seemed possessed of a broad tolerance and understanding.

The little girl on her lap was staring at Wycliffe with dark, unblinking eyes. Her mother said: 'It's rude to stare at the gentleman, Nessa!' She went on: 'Lizzie needs a man — God knows that's natural enough at her age — but there's right ways and there's wrong ways to go about it.'

Her son, standing behind her, seemed about to speak but changed his mind.

A door banged somewhere at the back of the house and yet another boy, this one about seven or eight years old, came in through the kitchen. He stood, looking from his mother to the visitor, black-eyed.

'Where's your sister?'

'She found a frog an' she's showing it to Father.'

'Go and wash your hands; supper's nearly ready.'

Wycliffe said: 'I don't want to pry into your family's affairs if they don't concern my inquiry but I must ask if you know what kind of relationship your daughter had with Mr Miller. We know that she spent time at his cottage.'

Mrs Biddick pouted. 'I wish I knew. I never really trusted that man, he was twisted, an' I don't say that because he went with men.'

'If we could find your daughter she might be able to help us with our inquiry into his death. I'm told that she left a week ago last Monday; the housekeeper and her husband say she was already gone when they got up. At the moment we know that Miller went off on his holiday early that same morning and we have to look into the possibility that she went with him.'

Matt was gripping the back of his mother's chair, tense and hostile. 'If anything's happened to Lizzie it wasn't Tony! I saw him after he came back and I asked him if he'd given her a lift. He said he hadn't seen Lizzie that morning, and I believed him.'

This spirited defence of Miller took Wycliffe by surprise, it was the very reverse of what he had expected. Even the boy's mother turned to look up at him. She said: 'Who's saying anything's happened to Lizzie, Matt? Don't get yourself worked up, boy!'

Wycliffe realized that if he was going to learn anything from the Biddicks it would be from the boy rather than the mother. He got to his feet. 'We've no reason to think that any harm has come to your daughter, Mrs Biddick, but we do need to contact her. Perhaps you could let me have a recent photograph if there is one. It would be copied and returned to you almost at once.'

Her eyes were full of suspicion. 'I don't want Lizzie's photo in all the papers and on the TV. We can do without that.'

'I promise you that we will use it with discretion.'

She lifted the little girl off her lap and crossed the room to a dresser. After searching in a drawer for a moment or two she came back with a polyfoto which she handed over.

'It's not much of a photo — one of them you take yourself: she came home with several of 'em a few months back.'

In the photograph a young woman with a mass of dark hair was smiling rather self-consciously at the camera.

Mrs Biddick saw him off at the door; her husband was nowhere to be seen; presumably he had taken refuge at the back.

Wycliffe had not gone far along the road when he heard heavy feet pounding after him and he was overtaken by Matt Biddick, breathing hard — Wycliffe suspected more from excitement than exertion.

'There's things I couldn't say in front of Mother.' He fell into step beside Wycliffe and they covered some distance before he spoke again. Then: 'You don't understand . . . I mean, Father works for Lord Bottrell — like the Christophers, like Tony, and like I do sometimes . . . Then there's his tenants and they that work on the farms . . .' He paused, finding difficulty in making his point. 'I mean, people got to think of their living. It isn't like working in a factory . . . Like I say, you don't understand.'

Wycliffe said: 'I might, I was brought up in the country and my father was a tenant farmer. Our landlord was "The Colonel".'

The young man turned to him in disbelief but said nothing.

'What were you going to tell me?'

Still he hesitated. 'First they try to say Tony killed himself. Now, if anything's happened to Liz it'll be Tony who done it. He's dead, he can't defend himself, so he's fair game, and it'll let them out.'

They were interrupted by the sound of a car approaching from the village and they stood aside to let it pass: a white Mini being driven at a fair speed. Wycliffe had a glimpse of a woman at the wheel.

'Her ladyship,' the boy said. 'Now they've got something to make 'em think — her seeing me with you.'

'You were saying?'

'I was saying there's things people won't talk about; leastways not to people like you.'

'Such as?'

He plucked up courage and it came in a burst: 'Lord Bottrell was crackers about Tony — couldn't keep away. I mean, he's years older — nearly an old man, and Tony had to put up with it . . .' He broke off, confused. 'Anyway, now you know.'

The truth dawned on Wycliffe. 'But Tony preferred you; is that what you are saying?'

'And what if I am? I'm not ashamed of it. What's more, Bottrell was jealous as hell.' He added, after a pause: 'We was trying to get out.'

'To get out?'

'To start up on our own. Tony was educated, he could do all the paperwork *and* he was well up in all the horticultural stuff. Me — I can turn my hand to most anything that's practical. With a bit of capital we meant to set up in business, laying out and maintaining people's gardens. We decided to try to raise enough money to buy a van and equipment and, o'course, we would've needed somewhere to live . . .'

'You spent quite a bit of time at the cottage with Tony?'

'You could say. I used to drop in there when I was out at night — spend part of the night there.'

'So you must have known him and the cottage pretty well. I want you to go there with DS Fox and check Tony's belongings — see if you can spot anything that should be there and isn't.'

He looked doubtful. 'I don't know if I can do much, but I'll try.'

They walked a little way in silence then Wycliffe said: 'Is that all you wanted to tell me? I thought it was about your sister.'

He was getting flustered again. 'Yes, it was, but I don't know how to put it so that you take it serious. Liz was always telling me things.'

'What things?'

He clenched his fists in frustration. 'She was in with all of them . . . She knew about their goings on — things they wouldn't want talked about. I mean, Lander collects dirty pictures in that studio of his, and the doctor is having it off with — ' He stopped, suddenly cautious. 'Well, she had stories about all of 'em.'

'Is it possible that she made up these stories?'

He was not angry; he turned to look at Wycliffe and his expression was almost pleading. 'I knew you'd say that and it could be true, but there was something. Liz was getting money.'

'Money?'

'More than she was earning at her job anyway — a good bit more. I've seen her with a little bundle of tens and fivers more'n once. She offered me some and when I refused she said: "There's more where that came from." O'course she was showing off but there must've bin something in it.'

'You're talking about blackmail?'

278

'I wouldn't be talking at all if I didn't think things needed looking into.'

'She didn't give any hint about where the money came from?'

'No, but this last few days I got to thinking . . . Well, it's possible . . . I mean, something's happened to Liz and it could be any of 'em.'

'You really think something has happened to your sister?'

'She's been gone more'n a week and she said she'd write to me as soon as she got there . . . But there's more to it than that.' He made a helpless gesture. 'I can't draw a picture! I'll tell you this: you should be trying to find her.'

They were approaching the village and they came to a halt just short of the first of the houses.

The boy said: 'I wonder sometimes if she left here at all, that's the truth of it.'

Wycliffe felt sorry for him. 'Just one question; you're a birdwatcher, a naturalist; are you out much by night?'

'Depends on the weather, three, sometimes four nights a week, I'm out for a bit. On them nights I usually finish up at Tony's — I mean I used to. There's a badger sett down in South Wood I bin watching lately; I made a bit of a hide there, but I move around . . .'

'Were you out the night Miller was killed?'

'No.'

'Do you ever meet anybody out at night?'

An amiable grin. 'I don't meet 'em because I see 'em first — not very often though. I've seen Lander a few times.'

'Doing what?'

'Nothing, just like he was out for a walk.'

'And the doctor?'

'I never see him at night — evenings he's out an' about, sometimes with a gun. He likes to pot at the pigeons.'

Wycliffe had run out of questions. 'Well, all I can promise is that we will do everything possible to find your sister.'

Wycliffe had his meal and then sat outside in the dusk, nursing a pint. Before going to bed he telephoned Helen on the guests' phone at the bottom of the bedroom stairs.

'It's me.'

'I thought it might be.'

A ritual exchange they had used on countless occasions over the years.

'Settled in all right?' Helen never asked questions requiring detailed answers over the telephone.

'I'm staying at a pub close to Duloe — just above Trelissick and the ferry — remember?'

'Of course I remember.'

They had spent a holiday in Roseland on the other side of the river. 'How's the garden?'

'Praying for rain — like me. You've only been gone about thirty-six hours so it can't have changed much.'

It was strange; when he took over an 'away' case he seemed to lose contact, to live in a different time scale. 'Of course, I'm being stupid.'

'I'm used to it. Any idea of when you'll be back?'

'Not before the weekend unless something blows up at the office.'

That night in bed he brooded for a long time before going to sleep. However he chose to put it, Lizzie Biddick had disappeared in suspicious circumstances and she had been associated with Miller, a man with a record for violence against a woman. If he had been called upon to investigate the disappearance of Lizzie Biddick with Miller still around, Miller would have been his prime suspect; the man would have been subjected to intensive questioning, every detail of his holiday would have been ferreted out and he, Wycliffe, would have had in the back of his mind the thought that it was an open and shut case.

Did the fact that Miller was dead alter this situation?

Chapter Seven

Wednesday morning, at a little after eight o'clock. As on every other morning for three weeks past the sun was shining and there was no hint of a breeze but, due to the proximity of the river and the not too distant sea, the air was moist. As the church clock chimed the quarter Wycliffe was buying his newspaper at the village shop. The landlord and the cat were at their posts. In the little square several people waited for the Truro bus: housewives with their shopping bags, young men and women — some with briefcases, on their way to work. A little way up the road sheep were being herded into a truck from a farm gate: market day in town.

As Wycliffe came out into the sunshine he felt a lift of the spirit. This was how things should be; the scale was right. He turned down the lane which led to Duloe, looking over his newspaper as he walked. At the bottom of the front page a couple of paragraphs were headed: 'Cornish Estate Murder'. The text amounted to no more than a recapitulation of the details of the crime; no mention of Lizzie Biddick, but that would come. He arrived at the Incident Van to find Kersey waiting for him.

'You must have set out at crack-of-dawn.'

'Almost; it's called being keen, sir. Anyway, somebody has sent you a naughty picture. It came by yesterday afternoon's post in an envelope addressed to "The Head of CID". I got the lab to make copies and I've brought them with me just in case. But this is the original. It's been checked for dabs and it's clean.'

The photograph was in black and white, achieving those soft half-tones which were, in part, a consequence of the long

281

exposures necessary for indoor work before the days of fast film. The condition of the print was good though the margins were slightly foxed and there was a stain on the back. Also on the back was a number and the word, Nadar.

Kersey said: 'The lab puts the date somewhere in the eighteen-seventies. It seems this chap, Nadar, who made it, died in 1910. They think the number is a catalogue number and that it came from somebody's collection.'

The subject was a busty young girl, nude, lying on a bed or divan. At the time it was taken the photograph would have passed for art or pornography according to the eye of the beholder and the hands in which it was found. Opinion would have been slanted by the presence of pubic hair, clearly defined.

In itself the photograph was unremarkable but it had been elaborately tampered with, using colours and a very fine brush. Marks had been made in the neighbourhood of the larynx suggesting the bruising left by the thumbs after throttling, the lips had been skilfully redrawn to allow of the insertion of a protruding tongue, and the region around the eyes stippled in imitation of petechial haemorrhages. To complete the picture, areas of the face and chest had been tinted to suggest cyanosis.

Wycliffe picked up one of the copies of the photograph and slipped it into his wallet. 'Was this all there was? No message?'

'Nothing.'

'Well, whoever did this knew something about post mortem appearances after throttling, but it's hard to see why he took all that trouble simply to send it to us. Obviously he isn't stupid enough to think we would accept it as material evidence of a crime, so what was the point? . . . Incidentally, when was it posted?'

Kersey said: 'The envelope was postmarked Monday, the day after Miller's death, but there is no collection over the weekend after Saturday midday, so it could have been posted at any time between then and first collection Monday morning.'

'Where?'

'I'll give you one guess.'

'Don't fool about.'

'The postmark says Truro. Odd, isn't it? Of course I'm not suggesting there's any connection with the Miller business.'

Wycliffe turned a mental somersault. 'No? But I'm not so sure. You don't know it, but Miller had form. Under his real name, Ross, he was convicted in '76 of occasioning actual bodily harm to his wife and sentenced to two years. Billy Norton, who handled the case, was sympathetic but it doesn't alter the fact that Miller had a conviction for violence against a woman.'

Kersey was rolling one of his cigarettes. 'So somebody with a devious mind is trying to tip us off about his record. Is that it?'

'It could be but would this photo mean anything at all to us if we didn't already know his record?'

'That's a point.' Kersey put a match to his cigarette which flared and crackled like burning straw. Wycliffe gave him a look of condescending pity.

The telephone rang and Wycliffe answered it.

'DS Fox for you, sir.'

Fox was speaking from sub-division. 'I obtained prints from the room at Duloe formerly occupied by the girl, Lizzie Biddick . . .' There was no way of stopping Fox talking as though he were in court.

'Did they match?'

'With the quantity of material in her room and in the cottage I was able to make a very thorough comparison. There is no doubt in my mind that the girl who occupied that room is the one who frequented the cottage.'

'Good! Did she leave any personal belongings in her room?'

'I didn't make a search, sir, but I saw that there were odd items of food in one of the cupboards.'

'Did Lady Bottrell or anyone else make any difficulty about you going to her room?'

'No, sir. I only saw the housekeeper; she told me where to go but she didn't come with me, nor did she ask what I wanted to do.'

As Wycliffe put the phone down Lucy Lane arrived with a tray, three mugs of coffee and a few digestive biscuits; the triumvirate was in session. Over the years they had learned to avoid each other's spines and to work together without friction or too much attention to rank. Wycliffe had never needed to trouble himself about rank; none of his people was in any doubt that he could bite as well as purr.

Outside, from time to time, villagers drifted along to stare at the cluster of police vehicles, at the van, and at Cerberus guarding the portal. But they soon got bored, and left. Fortunately the new van was fitted with one-way glass so that the inmates could see without being seen.

Wycliffe pushed the photograph to Lucy Lane with a brief explanation. She examined it for some time before passing it back. 'How very odd! Do you think there's a connection with the case?'

'That's the question; but speaking of photographs, I've got one of Lizzie Biddick; her mother gave it me and I want copies made.' He fished in his wallet and came out with the polyfoto. 'It's time we started serious inquiries; we must find out what's happened to that girl. Apart from anything else, Fox has just confirmed that prints left in her room match those found all over the place in Miller's cottage.' He passed the little photograph to Lucy Lane. 'That's her — or she, if you prefer it.'

'Will somebody tell me who we are talking about? Who is this Biddick girl?' From Kersey.

Wycliffe explained.

Lucy Lane examined the polyfoto in detail then reached for the fake. 'The two girls are very much alike. Do we have a hand lens?'

Rather shamefacedly, Wycliffe produced one from his pocket and Lucy applied herself to a fresh examination of both photographs. After a while she said: 'Both girls in these photographs are wearing pendants — '

Kersey laughed. 'Big deal! Who could ask for more?'

Unruffled, Lucy went on: 'I was going to say that the pendants are similar, though the one in the fake has been drawn in.'

'Let me see.' Wycliffe took the photographs and looked at them together. The girls were certainly alike. He went to work with his lens. In the polyfoto the pendant was plain to see: a medallion, about the size of a two-pence piece, suspended around the girl's neck by a fine chain. In the fake, a similar disc and chain had been carefully drawn in pencil. But what seemed to clinch its significance was that it carried an identical design to the one in the photograph. 'It looks,' Wycliffe said, 'like a nine and a six arranged in some sort of monogram. Of course they could be two nines or two sixes, depending on which way up you look at them . . .' He passed the photographs to Kersey. 'See for yourself.'

Kersey looked, and agreed that it was so.

Lucy Lane said: 'They're not numbers, sir. That is the zodiacal sign for Cancer — the crab. I've seen birth-sign pendants just like this one. On the other side there would be a crab. I suppose Lizzie must have been born between June 22nd and July 22nd.'

Kersey muttered. 'Somebody is trying to tell us something but not very hard.'

Wycliffe turned to Lucy Lane: 'Did you get anywhere with Lady Bottrell over the Biddick girl?'

Lucy went on: 'I saw her last evening and received a lesson in the art of answering questions politely without saying much. At any rate I've got her version of the facts about the girl.

'It seems that Lizzie was already working in the house part-time when Lady B offered her full-time work and the chance to live in. It was intended to relieve the population pressure in the cottage where there were seven Biddicks between the ages of three and twenty-two, plus mum and dad. Added to the accommodation problem the Biddick household was being disrupted by Lizzie who was feeling her feet as a young woman and causing friction.

'The arrangement seems to have worked and there was a good prospect that the girl would settle down, but a fortnight ago, out of the blue, she announced that she was leaving and that she wanted to go almost at once. She said that she now had a chance to make a life for herself. She was grateful to the Bottrells for their help but unforthcoming about where she was going or why. Lady B talked to her mother but Mrs Biddick had had enough. "Lizzie wants to go her own way — so let her — that's what I say."'

Lucy sipped her coffee. 'Then, a week ago last Saturday, Lizzie told Lady Bottrell she would be leaving on the Monday, catching the 10.30 London train from Truro. On Sunday, Lady Bottrell gave her her wages, her fare, and a cash leaving present. She also offered to drive her to the station next morning and Lizzie accepted but, in the morning when it was time for them to be leaving, Lady B went in search of her and found that she'd already gone.'

Wycliffe asked: 'But nobody actually saw her leave?'

'No, sir. They simply assumed she must have gone because she wasn't around.'

'And Miller left that same morning. According to Lord Bottrell he must have been away, in his car, before eight o'clock. The obvious conclusion, though not necessarily the right one, is that they went off together.'

Wycliffe recounted his interviews with the Christophers and with Lizzie's family. 'The housekeeper says there were nights when Lizzie didn't sleep in her room and she obviously thought the girl spent those nights with Miller. But the point is, if she went off with Miller, she didn't come back with him.'

Kersey had been unusually silent, trying to come to terms with a case of which he was hearing the detail for the first time. Now he drained his coffee mug and reached for another biscuit. He tapped the photograph with the edge of his biscuit. 'With Miller's record this could be what happened to the poor little fool and some oddball is trying to tell us about it in his own way. It seems to me we need to know more about Lizzie's last days in Duloe and whether they were her last days anywhere.'

Wycliffe agreed. 'We need to know whether she caught a London train or any other. If Miller was involved, did he merely drop her off at Truro station? Did he leave his car in the park

286

there and travel on by rail either with her, or alone? As things stand we've no conclusive evidence that the girl left here at all.'

'But if she's still here . . .'

'Don't let's get carried away . . .' Wycliffe broke off and his expression changed. 'Having in mind what her brother told me, it seems to me unlikely that she was having an affair with Miller and it's just occurred to me that Fox found no trace of her in the upstairs rooms. It's difficult to understand why, if they were having an affair, they confined their activities to the living-room and the kitchen when there were two good beds upstairs.'

Lucy Lane said: 'It doesn't make sense.'

'No, it doesn't. We are not there yet. For the moment let's remember that we have a dead man who was shot but we don't have a dead girl who was throttled; all we have is a much doctored photograph of a young woman who lived a century ago.'

He turned to Lucy Lane. 'For a start, I want you, Lucy, to take a good look at her room at Duloe. Find out if she left anything behind and see what you can get from Jill Christophers; she'll be more likely to talk when her husband is not there . . . And you, Doug — I want you to get somebody to pick up the girl's trail between here and Truro, that Monday morning. If she made the trip she must have been seen. I know ten days is a long time but we've got to try. Also see if the railway people can tell us anything. Another thing: arrange for Miller's car — it's in the old coach house — to be gone over by Fox. You'd better have it transferred to a garage at sub-division.'

Most cases have a distinguishing feature or perhaps an atmosphere which long afterwards comes vividly to mind whenever the case is mentioned. He was beginning to think that in this instance it would be a sense of stillness and of isolation. He was always aware of the river and the creeks on three sides. Although the village was close at hand it was all too easy to imagine that the estate and the lawyer's house were cut off; self-contained, autonomous. It affected his thinking, inclining him to restrict his search for explanations to the Bottrells, the Landers, and their appendages, as though they existed in a closed community.

Now he was in search of another Lander — Lander père — the old man he had met briefly during his visit on that first evening. His spies in the Incident Van had reported Simon leaving for the office as usual and, half an hour later, his wife, Beth, had driven off in her little Fiat. So there was a chance of catching the old man alone.

He walked down the gravelled drive and rang the door bell but his only achievement was to set the dog barking. Then he heard the whine of an electric motor not far away and he set off around the house. The sound came from a large brick-built shed in the kitchen yard. The door was open so he coughed loudly to announce himself and went in.

Lander senior was seated on a stool at a bench fitted with a variety of power tools for small-scale work in wood. At the moment he was turning a slender shaft on a tiny lathe. On the windowsill at the back of the bench, plastic boxes in rows were labelled: Detached shafts, Column bases, Capitals, Arch mouldings . . .

He stood for a full minute with no acknowledgement of his presence and was beginning to think that he was invisible when Lander removed the shaft from the lathe chuck and dropped it into the appropriate box. His bony fingers, despite enlarged joints, were nimble and precise. He turned on his stool to face Wycliffe. 'Now, sir!'

His grey overall was powdered with wood dust which had also become trapped in his moustache and even speckled his cheeks and the lenses of his spectacles. But the grey eyes were alive.

'Interested?'

'Intrigued.'

'Then take a look through that door.'

The door led into another section of the shed, the floor of which was largely taken up with the model of a church or, more likely, a cathedral, under construction. The outer walls reached only to window level but the nave arcade was complete on the north side and in process of erection along the south aisle.

288

'I'm building a cathedral on a scale of one thirty-second. When I was a boy I wanted to be an architect but family tradition made me a lawyer. In any case they wouldn't have let me loose on cathedrals. Now I can please myself . . . You see, I shall virtually complete the interior before I get far with the exterior walls . . . I shall make the roof removable in sections so that one can see all the goodies inside . . . Of course there will be a tower at the crossing . . . I machine those parts which lend themselves to it but the mouldings, capitals, bosses, corbels, etcetera involve carving which is a trial for old fingers and old eyes . . .'

The old man's voice was thin and rather high-pitched; words came tumbling out as dammed up enthusiasm found its vent. Wycliffe recognized the danger and began to draw away from further involvement. It took time but he managed it and they returned to the workshop where Wycliffe was given a stool.

'I'm surprised that you found me here; I suppose you wanted Simon?'

'No, I assumed that he would be at his office.'

Wycliffe was sizing him up: an elderly, retired professional man, absorbed in his hobby, inclined to be garrulous, and reaching an age when even the most dramatic and tragic events were losing their emotional impact, their cutting edge — the 'I've seen it all before' syndrome.

But he saved Wycliffe from having to bring the subject around to the crime. He removed his spectacles and began to clean them with a grubby handkerchief and while he was watching Wycliffe with unfocused eyes he said: 'Do you really believe, Mr Wycliffe, that Miller was murdered?'

'There is very little room for doubt, I'm afraid.'

Lander put his spectacles back on and turned his gaze on Wycliffe. 'It seems from the little I know that there are only two pieces of evidence pointing to murder: first, that the string to the trigger was too short for him to reach; second, that he was left-handed whilst the set-up suggested a right-handed person.' He broke off. 'Of course you will have access to facts not available to me . . .' The grey eyes were innocent and inquiring.

Wycliffe was cautious. 'You don't find the facts you have mentioned convincing?'

He did not answer directly. 'Well, it's true that Tony had a tendency to left-handedness but, in fact, he was ambidextrous. He sometimes helped me with delicate little jobs in assembly which are getting too much for my old fingers and his either-handedness was invaluable. I don't think he would have troubled too much about which hand he used to pull the trigger.'

'You saw a good deal of him?'

'He looked in fairly often. He was interested in what I am doing.'

'But what about the short string? Do you have any explanation of that?'

The old man seemed to smile under the luxuriance of his moustache. 'You don't think, Mr Wycliffe, that in this case you may have an unusual factor at work — a mischievous person with no other motive than to complicate matters and make trouble?' Lander senior was garrulous but he was not a fool.

'Are you suggesting that someone found the dead man and deliberately cut the string to mislead any investigation?'

'You are quick to grasp the implication, sir. You think, perhaps, that it is a possibility to be considered?'

'If I said yes, would this "imp of the perverse" have a name?'

Lander laughed outright. 'My dear sir, I can name you no names! I merely offer an idea, a suggestion — an alternative to the rather frightening possibility that we have a murderer in our midst.'

Wycliffe was uncomfortable; the sun streamed through the windows of the workshop and he was sweating though Lander remained, to all appearances, serenely cool. At the same time Wycliffe felt mentally adrift; he sensed that there was something to be gained by talking to this man but only if he could interpret what was said and discern some motive behind it. All he could do was to play the game and guess at the rules.

'Perhaps there is another point which favours murder: Dr Bottrell knew Miller both as a man and a patient and he is strongly of the opinion that Miller was an unlikely suicide.'

Lander nodded. 'That doesn't surprise me — I mean the fact that James said so doesn't surprise me.'

'I see.'

Another nod, this time emphatic. 'Yes, I really think you do.' He sat, waiting, looking Wycliffe straight in the eyes. It was almost a challenge, as if he would say: 'If you want me to tell you something you must find the right questions.'

Wycliffe tried a fresh approach. 'I, of course, am a stranger. Until a few days ago I knew nothing of the people I am now meeting. It would be a great help if you would tell me something of the two families — the Bottrells and your own.'

'With pleasure.' He seemed to mean it. 'We have acted for the family since we set up a law practice in Truro in the 1830s.' A brief smile. 'Before Victoria came to the throne. It was nearly seventy years later, at the turn of the century, that my grand-father bought a piece of land from the estate and built this house. Since then we have been neighbours.'

An observation seemed to be required. 'Your son and the present Lord Bottrell seem to get on remarkably well.' It sounded weak but it curtailed the history lesson and produced a broad smile.

'That's easily explained; they are the same age, they went to the same schools, they did their National Service and then went up to Oxford together. In other words they are, and always have been, good friends.'

'And I suppose that Lord Bottrell's twin brother, James, made up the trio?'

A tremor of uncertainty; a sensitive spot? But the old man's response when it came was smooth enough: 'Poor James was unlucky. While still very young he developed a tubercular lesion in the joint of his left knee — you must have noticed that he is markedly lame. However, on the credit side, he had the good fortune to be among the first to benefit from the then wonder drug — streptomycin. It worked, and further progress of the disease was halted.'

The old man brushed sawdust from the sleeve of his overall.

'But he had suffered a serious setback to his education and development. His illness forced him to drop out of his age group — no boarding school, no games, no National Service, and only a very belated entry to university. But, as you know, he caught up and certainly outdistanced the others academically.'

Wycliffe, anxious to pick some plums out of this pie, risked a question or two. 'When did he give up his consultancy and come here to live?'

'When his Aunt Cecile died and her money made it possible. That was two years ago.'

'Wasn't it a little odd? Coming back here to live in his brother's backyard so to speak?'

The old man grinned. 'Not if you remember that, as an unmarried man, he had no other real home. Although Hugh inherited the estate it was still the place where James was born and brought up.'

Something in the old man's manner seemed to indicate a readiness for other questions.

'When did the present Lord Bottrell inherit?'

'Nine — no, ten years ago.'

'Was his mother still alive?'

'Very much so! She died only a couple of years back — within weeks, actually, of her sister-in-law, Aunt Cecile.' A ruminative chuckle. 'I doubt if James would have come back had his mother been still around.'

'They didn't get on?'

The old man waved a thin hand. 'Families, Mr Wycliffe! Her ladyship was possessed of a very dominant personality and I'm afraid that she discriminated most blatantly between her two sons. Hugh could do no wrong — he was something of a mother's boy — while poor James . . . Ah, well!'

The sigh was unconvincing and Wycliffe was sure that he had been deliberately fed with certain facts under the guise of indiscretions from a garrulous old man.

Wycliffe tried one more throw: 'There is just one other question, Mr Lander, then I will leave you to get on with your

292

work. I shall be interested in anything you can tell me about the girl, Lizzie Biddick.'

The old man looked at him in surprise, genuine or simulated. 'Biddick? You are talking about the gardener's eldest girl. She worked in the house — I believe she lived in for a few months — one of Cynthia's protégées, I think. Anyway she left quite recently — went to London, so they tell me. Why? Is she concerned in this Miller affair?'

Wycliffe left it at that.

He walked back to the Incident Van brooding. Although there was little that was specific he felt that he had come away with something more than the conviction that Lander père was a wily customer. He mulled over what he had been told, trying to extract the meat. Some source of friction between James, on the one hand, and his brother and Lander on the other? In the end he settled for a muttered: 'They're an odd lot!' And a few paces farther on he added: 'Very odd!'

Jill Christophers said: 'This part was altered by Lord Bottrell's grandfather when there were still two or three housemaids living in. The only way into the family's rooms from here is through that door and Ralph has to make sure that's locked at night.'

She and Lucy Lane were standing in a little hall beside the kitchen.

'Upstairs on the next landing is our flat, then there's another flight, and on that floor there's a bathroom and three more rooms; Lizzie had one of them.'

'And the other two?'

Jill shrugged. 'Store rooms, junk really.'

The housekeeper asked no questions; in fact, throughout the inquiry so far, Lucy had been asked very few questions. People answered more or less readily what they were asked, then waited as though anxious for a minimum of involvement. A pity, for as Wycliffe frequently reminded her, questions are sometimes more informative than answers.

'Lizzie had a key?'

'To the little door beside the kitchen. That reminds me, if you're going up you'd better have her room key. I locked it until we know what's to be done with the things she left behind.'

Lucy went upstairs. On the first landing there was a single door to the Christophers' flat, then the stairs continued to the next landing where there were four doors, one of them locked, and that was the girl's room. One thing was clear; Lizzie could have come and gone as she wished, day or night, disturbing no one.

The room was furnished with heavy pieces, evidently brought from other and larger rooms elsewhere in the house: a mahogany wardrobe, an ornate walnut dressing-table, a chest of drawers, and a bed with brass rails. But there was a basin with hot and cold water, an electric fire, and a gadget for making coffee. Lucy recalled the cheerless, draughty attic which had been hers at university (no washing facilities; lavatory and bathroom two flights down) and thought Lizzie had done pretty well for herself.

Lucy made a start on the wall cupboard next to the washbasin: some oddments of china and cutlery, a can-opener, a box of shredded wheat, a jar of instant coffee, a packet of sugar, a bottle of milk half-full and curdled . . .

She turned to the wardrobe which was empty except for a little pile of books tied about with string. Lucy slid them out and looked at the titles: a mixed bag — Thomas Hardy's *Jude the Obscure*, Lawrence's *Sons and Lovers*, John Updike's *The Witches of Eastwick*, and Yukio Mishima's *Forbidden Colours*. Each of them had Miller's name on the flyleaf. Lucy wondered what Lizzie Biddick had made of that lot; a remedy for innocence in four not-so-easy lessons.

The dressing-table was clear but the glass top was smeared with lipstick and face cream. A wastepaper basket contained used tissues, a drinks can and some sweet papers. On the face of it the room had been vacated by a girl who cared nothing for the impression she left behind. But there was another interpretation:

294

that when Lizzie last left her room she did so with every expectation that she would be back to complete her packing, perhaps to tidy up, perhaps to return the borrowed books.

In which case . . .

Lucy sat on the bed, looking about her, wondering if she had missed anything. People put things on the tops of wardrobes. She stood on a chair, reached in over the fretted rail and came out with a large shoulder bag, almost new. It was limp and apparently empty. She zipped it open on the bed — nothing, but in one of the side pockets she found a wallet-purse and a building society passbook.

The building society account had been opened about a year earlier and followed by small deposits of a few pounds at a time, but more recently larger sums had been credited so that the balance now stood at well over a thousand pounds.

Lucy muttered to herself: 'Not on her wages!'

The purse held a hundred and twenty pounds in fives, tens and twenties, a single, standard-class ticket to London, and a seat reservation for the 10.30 train on the day she was supposed to have left.

It was enough.

Lucy was not so hardened that she felt no sympathy with or distress for this silly girl. She went downstairs and found Jill Christophers in the kitchen working fruit into a cake mixture in a large, stainless steel bowl. 'His lordship is very fond of fruit cake but he can't abide the shop stuff.'

'Lizzie left some of her belongings in her room.'

'Really? Your policeman said there were books in the wardrobe; I haven't looked. I just locked the door until her ladyship tells me what she wants done. I've been here long enough to know better than take anything on myself.'

'When did you last see her, Mrs Christophers?'

Jill paused in her mixing. 'I've got to think . . . It was Sunday evening; I went up to her room to ask her to square up for some batteries Ralph bought for her radio.'

'Did she seem her usual self?'

Pursed lips. 'As far as I could see. She was packing. There was a big hold-all on the floor, bulging with stuff and another she was working on. I said to her: "You won't get much more in that."'

'What sort of hold-alls were they?'

'Those blue canvas things with leather straps.'

'And that was the last time you saw her?'

She hesitated. 'No, it wasn't. It's just come back to me. I saw her later in the evening — about half-nine it must've bin. Ralph was watching the telly and I had one or two things to do down here. As I was coming out of our flat I met her on the landing.'

'Did you speak to her?'

'Just what you'd expect. She said she was going out for a bit of fresh air.'

'Can you recall how she was dressed?'

A shrug. 'Casual. Not for going anywhere special: dark-blue slacks and an orange blouse. It was a warm evening but she wasn't going far like that.'

'Was she carrying anything?'

'I think she had her handbag but I couldn't swear to it.'

'You didn't see her again, but did you hear her?'

'Yes, I did: her room is right over our bedroom and I heard her moving about up there. I thought she was finishing her packing.'

'Any idea of the time?'

She frowned. 'I do, as a matter of fact. I'd had my first sleep and I looked at the clock; it was five minutes past one . . . Be a dear an' roll up my sleeve, it's slipping into the mix.'

Lucy did as she was asked. 'Just one more question, Mrs Christophers, does Lizzie wear a pendant with her birth sign?'

'Always; it's one of her things; she's daft about the stars and all that; her horoscope is the first thing she looks at in the paper.'

'Do you know her birthday?'

A quick smile. 'July 4th — Independence Day — she seemed to think that made her something special — silly girl!'

When there were no guests the Bottrells had their meals in the breakfast-room which was conveniently close to the kitchen. It was a shabby little room but it overlooked the park with glimpses of the river and it caught the morning sun. As usual, at midday the table was set for four and the food was laid out under covers. There was a heated trolley for hot dishes and the family arrived as it suited them.

At 12.30 Lord and Lady Bottrell had the room to themselves. Lord Bottrell helped himself to soup from the trolley while Lady Bottrell, already at table, sprinkled hers with Parmesan cheese.

Lady Bottrell said: 'Have you seen the papers this morning?'

'I glanced through the *Telegraph* — nothing about Tony.'

'You should have tried the tabloids. "Our correspondent understands that Lord Bottrell is deeply distressed by the crime. It seems that the two men were close friends so that their relationship was more intimate than is usual between employer and employed . . ." That's a quote and just a sample.'

'You know where that came from: your father has been talking.'

Lady Bottrell broke off a morsel of bread and put it into her mouth. 'They don't need him. Anybody in the village would do as well. I warned you, Hugh.'

'You warned . . .!' He had started angrily but broke off. 'I'm sorry, Cynthia, but this is a nightmare.' He brought his soup to the table and sat staring at it as though mesmerized.

'You know that Jean lied to the police and that Paul is involved?'

'Yes. I suppose Paul told you; I had to hear it from Lander.'

Lady Bottrell spooned up a little soup and raised it to her lips where it vanished soundlessly. She patted her lips with a napkin, then: 'Hugh, was Lander giving Lizzie money?'

Bottrell had picked up his spoon, now he put it down again. 'For God's sake, Cynthia, how would I know?'

The door opened and James Bottrell came in. 'What is it today?' He lifted one of the covers. 'Ham like soggy blotting paper. Why can't we have ham off the bone, Cynthia?'

Lady Bottrell was chilling. 'We can if you like to pay for it and, perhaps, cook it, James.'

James helped himself to soup and sat down. 'So now young Paul has got himself tangled in the Lander net.'

Chapter Eight

Kersey said: 'Lizzie Biddick found out that Miller was an ex-con and blackmailed him. She went to see him that Sunday night to collect, perhaps, a final instalment before she went away, but instead of paying he throttled her and disposed of the body. The following day he set off on his holiday but came back early, scared and conscience stricken. On the Sunday night, exactly a week after murdering the girl, he shot himself. How's that?'

Wycliffe looked at him. 'Did you think that up all by yourself? For one thing, how did he manage to shoot himself?'

Kersey made a broad gesture. 'You can make too much of that bit of string. Maybe it was too short for him to reach with his hand but he might have caught it round his foot. I reckon I could do it.'

'Perhaps you should try rolling your cigarettes that way.'

Lucy Lane had long since learned to recognize Kersey's excursions into fantasy as Aunt Sallys, designed to set going an argument. They were having lunch at the pub, at the table in the alcove which Wycliffe had made his own. They were served with the dish-of-the-day, a prawn salad with fresh prawns which Kersey could not peel. 'Damn it! Joan always does it for me.'

Lucy reached for his plate. 'Give them to me!'

Wycliffe said: 'How much of that nonsense you talked just now do you believe?'

Kersey grinned. 'Well, perhaps not all, but I reckon there's a core of truth.'

Lucy sipped her apple juice. 'Anyway, the pendant Lizzie wore makes it pretty certain that whoever sent the doctored photograph intended to suggest a connection.'

Kersey agreed. 'It also means that he knew more than was good for him. So are we looking for the girl or her body?'

Wycliffe hesitated. 'We mustn't forget that Miller could have sent the photograph himself; we know that it could have been posted at any time after midday on Saturday. As to whether we are looking for the girl or her body: for public consumption we are investigating a suspicious disappearance but we shan't be able to keep that up. The time has come to get a team together and search for her body. I want you to organize it, Doug. Of course you'll need men from sub-division and a dog handler. Arrange it through Reed.'

Kersey said: 'We've had one positive response so far on the Biddick trail — a clerk in the travel centre at Truro Station remembers her buying her ticket and reserving a seat on the Friday before she was due to travel on the Monday. He was struck by the fact that it all seemed new to her; she seemed quite flustered about making a trip for which most people wouldn't bother to make a forward booking.'

Wycliffe left the pub and walked back to the Incident Van, glad of the fresh air to minimize the soporific effect of a couple of glasses of Chablis. Dixon, the duty officer, handed him an official envelope. 'The pathologist's report, sir, by messenger. And Dorchester CID phoned: Superintendent Norton will be out for most of the rest of the day and could you ring him before he leaves.'

'Get him for me, please.'

The pathologist's report was mainly important as documentation. Unless a pathologist is bloody minded (and Franks was not), anything worth knowing has been passed on by phone before the report is in type. He skimmed the technical jargon and put the report aside for filing. After all, from a pathological angle there is little new that can be said of an otherwise healthy man who has been blasted by a shotgun discharged at short range.

Norton came on: 'I've put through the promised fax to your sub-division — just a précis of the main points from the file. I've also had a report from our chap who's been looking into the

Ross/Miller visit. They remember him at the Crown. He arrived, alone, on the Monday morning and left his car in the hotel car park. Apart from breakfast he had only one meal in the hotel during his stay: that was on Tuesday evening when he dined there with a woman of about his own age. The staff remember her as sophisticated and well turned out, not quite his style.'

Norton paused for breath. 'The file reminded me that he had a sister in Dorchester at the time of his trial — Olivia Ross, and this could have been her. We haven't traced her yet but we'll keep trying. By the way, was he still playing the flute?'

'Yes, why?'

'Only that counsel for the defence — still wet behind the ears — made a lot of that. Finally, the judge — old Itchy — you remember Itchy? — looked over his half-glasses and said: 'Am I to understand that counsel is advancing this accomplishment of the defendant as testimony to his rectitude and good conduct?'

Wycliffe felt broody, in need of time to ponder but, as in Elizabethan drama, it was time for the clowns; the TV team had arrived and he was required to stand outside the van, squinting in the sunshine.

He said that the inquiry was continuing, that there was no immediate prospect of an arrest but that a number of leads were now being followed. He added, tongue-in-cheek, that he had been impressed by the co-operation of the public.

Then the interviewer sprang his question. 'Is it true that you are trying to contact Miss Lizzie Biddick who formerly worked at Duloe?'

'Yes, we would like to talk to Miss Biddick.'

'Would you say that she has disappeared?'

'In the sense that we don't know where she is. She left her employment after giving proper notice but she did not leave a forwarding address.'

'You have no reason to think that anything has happened to her?'

'I have no evidence that she is not alive and well if that is what you mean.'

'Do you think that there may be a connection between her leaving and the murder of Tony Miller?'

'Our reason for wanting to talk to her is that she knew Mr Miller very well and might, therefore, be a helpful witness.'

And with that the media dragon was temporarily appeased.

Wycliffe was disturbed. Tony Miller had been found dead in circumstances which suggested suicide. A closer look had caused the investigating officer to revise that first impression. For suicide it was necessary to read probable homicide. At that stage he, Wycliffe, had taken over; a straightforward killing complicated only by the rigged suicide. So two questions had needed answers: Why was Miller killed? And by whom?

Then a dotty picture, among other things, had brought Lizzie Biddick into the case. Lizzie, it seemed, was a footloose girl, sexually attractive, searching for something without knowing what, and possibly engaged in a spot of blackmail. But she had disappeared from the scene days before Miller's death. Now, instead of that death, Wycliffe found himself concentrating on the girl's disappearance. He was confused; there was a risk of proceeding to run around in ever decreasing circles, perhaps with the classic consequence. He must clear his mind and lay down definitive lines on which to proceed.

On the principle that onlookers see most of the game he decided on another talk with James Bottrell. But was James a mere onlooker? Whether he was or not he was a shrewd observer and even his biased and distorted observations could be instructive.

Once more he rapped on the varnished plank door of the little house in the old stable yard but this time there was no reply and the door was shut. After a second and a third attempt he heard footsteps inside, the door opened and Bottrell was standing there looking vaguely dishevelled and off balance. 'Ah! It's you . . . You'd better come in.'

Wycliffe followed him into the hall-like room; it was much as he had seen it before except that the cover was on the typewriter and there was no sign of work in progress.

'I usually take a nap after lunch; I suppose it's a sign of approaching old age.'

'I'm sorry to have disturbed you.'

They sat as before, facing each other across the table. A slight sound caused Wycliffe to look up at the gallery. A woman was standing in the doorway of one of the rooms, almost in silhouette, but the light shone on her blonde hair and caught the silky folds of the bedroomy thing she wore. It lasted only for an instant, then the door closed, but Wycliffe was in no doubt that the woman was Cynthia Bottrell.

Bottrell glanced up but he was too late. 'Well, what can I do for you?' He had recovered his poise.

Without comment Wycliffe handed over the photograph of the nude girl with its imaginative additions.

Bottrell studied the photograph in detail. 'Where did you get this?'

'It's a copy of one sent to me anonymously, through the post.'

'It's kinky.'

'Is that a professional opinion?'

Bottrell chuckled. 'You realize the original was probably taken in the last century?'

'I've been told so, but it is the additions which interest me; the pendant which has been sketched in is similar to one worn by Lizzie Biddick — it has her birth sign on it.'

Bottrell re-examined the photograph with care. 'Odd! This girl is vaguely like Lizzie. Anyway, whoever made the amendments knew what he was about, medically speaking if not artistically.' He looked up. 'Have you shown this to Lander?'

'Should I have done?'

'As I told you, Lander is a photographic buff and he's interested in the history of photography. At least he collects old photographs — originals when he can afford them, copies when he can't. I'm sure he would be interested in the original of this.'

Wycliffe could see that the door which had closed behind Lady Bottrell was once more open — just a crack. She was listening, and Bottrell must have known that she would be.

302

Bottrell looked quizzical: 'You have some reason, other than this photograph, to be interested in the Biddick girl?'

'We found a considerable sum of money and other things in her room which she would not willingly have left behind; also, and significantly, her rail ticket.'

'So you are wondering if this photograph was intended as a message.'

'Yes.'

Bottrell lit a cigarette and dribbled smoke into the air. 'You think something has happened to the girl?'

'It seems likely.'

'When did you get this?'

'It was posted in this district during last weekend.'

Bottrell seemed thoughtful. 'You suspect Miller?'

'Should I?'

A movement of slight impatience. 'I've no data on which to form an opinion.'

Wycliffe said, as though the remark was a casual one: 'I thought you might have more data than most.'

Bottrell's expression hardened. 'Will you explain that?'

'Instead I will ask you another question: Did you know Tony Ross?'

There was a longish pause, then Bottrell spoke, picking his words with care: 'I know that Miller changed his name from Ross.'

'How do you know?'

'He told me.'

'When?'

'When he first came to consult me.'

'Did he tell you why?'

Bottrell fiddled with papers on the table in front of him. 'He didn't need to. It's a phenomenon every psychologist comes across in his work, a desire on the part of someone who has endured a traumatic crisis to change his or her name, to escape, symbolically, from an identity which has been imposed and has become distasteful.'

303

'Or inconvenient.'

A faint smile. 'You choose to be cynical but this distaste is real enough. The image of ourselves that we present to the world is not of our own choosing or wholly of our own making and it usually differs dramatically from our self-image — '

Wycliffe cut in without ceremony: 'Miller, as Ross, had a criminal record. Did he tell you that he had served a gaol sentence for assaulting his wife?'

Bottrell paused in the act of raising his cigarette to his lips. 'He did not.'

Wycliffe wondered what Cynthia Bottrell was making of this conversation. He stole a glance up at the gallery. A line of light showed that the door was still open. Bottrell seemed oblivious or indifferent.

Wycliffe decided to change the subject. 'Lizzie Biddick was getting money from somebody.'

'Blackmail?'

'If Miller killed himself we would have a credible interpretation of the sequence of events: Lizzie is extracting money from Miller under threat of disclosing his true identity; he kills her and later, out of fear or remorse or both, he kills himself.'

'But Miller didn't kill himself.'

'The only material evidence against it is that the trigger string was too short.'

'So?'

'It has been suggested that someone discovered the body and cut the string before, or even after, young Paul entered the cottage that night.'

'Surely that is absurd! What possible motive could there have been?'

'I admit that with a motive the idea might be more credible, but the facts are that the shot which killed Miller was fired at approximately 12.30. It was after 1.30 that Paul went into the cottage and saw the body. While he was in there, Jean Lander, waiting outside, saw a man lurking close to the cottage. If that man was the killer, what was he doing there an hour after the shot? If he was not the killer, what was he doing there anyway? I would give a good deal to know who that man was.'

They looked at each other across the table. Bottrell said: 'I'm afraid I can't help you there.'

'And yet the list of possible candidates must be a very short one.'

Bottrell stubbed out his cigarette. 'You think so? All sorts of people wander around this place at night. God knows why.'

Wycliffe changed the subject. 'I talked to Lander senior this morning.'

'And he showed you his cathedral?'

'He did. He also told me about your unfortunate illness as a child.'

Bottrell's face lost all expression. 'Did he! Well, that was a long time ago.'

Something there. Wycliffe sat back in his chair, missing his pipe. These moments came at longer and longer intervals but when they did the sense of deprivation was still acute.

Bottrell was watching him. 'May I ask if this is the end of a round or the end of the contest?'

Wycliffe ignored the question. 'Did Lizzie Biddick come here?'

Bottrell lit another cigarette. 'Ah! Merely an interval! I was wondering if we might get to that. Yes, she did.'

'Often?'

'Several times, anyway. Lizzie was — is, for all I know — desperately anxious to be noticed. It's not uncommon, especially amongst women; many of them construct some private mythology through which they come to terms with their insignificance; others need an external prop. When Lizzie discovered that, as well as being a psychologist, I had a medical degree, I became an irresistible target.'

'What did it amount to?'

Bottrell grinned. 'A need to talk, a need to impress. The confessional is a great institution for straightening out psychological kinks. A good priest is worth his weight in gold because he gives his people time, and he listens. His penitents come away convinced that their sins, at least, are important.'

'Getting back to the girl . . .'

'Yes, well, she turned up here one evening, latish, saying she was worried about a pain in her left breast and that she hated going to her GP. I didn't intend to fall for that one — not so early in our acquaintance anyway — so I fetched the gin bottle and we talked. Or she talked. As I say, she came back several times, presumably for more of both.'

'Did you ever get around to her pain?' Wycliffe allowed his curiosity to get the better of him.

A thin smile. 'She forgot about it.'

Up in the gallery the line of light was still visible, marking the open door.

'When did you last see her?'

'The Sunday evening before she left — or intended to leave. She came to say goodbye.'

'At what time was this?'

'It must have been coming up for ten.'

Wycliffe was looking at him with an expressionless stare, neither penetrating nor aggressive, but bland.

Bottrell said: 'All right, I've just realized it myself! I was the last person to admit having seen Miller alive, and now . . .' He smiled a whimsical smile. 'I suppose it must mean something. It's up to you to decide what.'

'Who was she getting money from?'

'I've no idea. Certainly not from me.' He raised his arms, braced his shoulders, and suppressed a yawn. 'I've said that Lizzie talked, but she didn't tell me anything. Most of it was pure fantasy — how her school teachers begged her mother to let her stay on at school. "They said I'd be sure to get to Oxford." Another time it was how, at fifteen, she'd been raped by a famous TV star, down here on holiday, and her parents had been paid to hush it up. Another version was that the TV chap had offered her a part in one of his shows to hold her tongue but she'd turned it down . . . The stories were different each time but

306

variations on a theme: people notice me, therefore I'm real. An amendment to Descartes.'

'Did she tell you that she was going to London?'

'Oh, yes. I pointed out that it was a big place and asked her if she knew anybody there. She said that she did and that "he" would be her protector, so there was no need to worry.'

'She told you nothing about her life at Duloe, and about her relations with Miller?'

'Nothing, and I didn't ask. The girl needed to unwind and that is what she did. That, with a glass or two of gin to make her slightly tipsy, was her therapy.'

Wycliffe stood up. 'I am beginning to envy your patients, Dr Bottrell, and I'm sure that I shall need to hear more of this one.'

'You know where to find me.'

He saw Wycliffe to the door then returned to his seat at the table.

A moment later Cynthia Bottrell looked over the gallery rail. She came down slowly — Woman Descending a Staircase — but it was lost on Bottrell who did not look up. Her dressing gown was of blue silk, she had not a hair out of place, and she moved with languid elegance like a romantic actress approaching her big scene.

'Do you think he saw me?'

'I've no idea.'

'If he did, will he tell Hugh?'

'Why should he?'

She said without aggression: 'You don't care a damn, do you?' She ran her fingers through his hair. The dressing gown had slipped open exposing her breasts. 'All you want from me is a good lay.'

'And you need to be laid. So what? You don't want a husband, you've already got one, and it would be a pity to give up being a ladyship — you do it so well.' He looked up at her. 'In any case we are both a bit long in the tooth for romance.'

His manner was playful rather than overtly cruel but a deep flush spread upwards over her fair skin. She pulled her dressing

307

gown about her and looped the sash. 'You are a real bastard, James!'

She fiddled with an untidy heap of papers on the table, boxing them together. 'Does Wycliffe really believe that Tony Miller committed suicide?'

'Of course he doesn't!'

'That photograph he showed you . . . Where did it come from?'

'Why ask me? In any case it's not difficult to guess.'

She was silent for a while, then she asked: 'What about Lander, James?'

Bottrell reached for his cigarettes. 'What about him? At the moment Simon is not a happy man and I doubt if his prospects will improve.'

Another pause, and then she said: 'I'm scared, James. There are so many questions I'm afraid to ask.'

'Then don't ask them.'

'Tell me one thing: is the Biddick girl dead?'

'How should I know? Wycliffe evidently thinks so.'

She ran a finger up the nape of his neck, lifting his hair. 'Did you screw her?'

'I can't remember.'

'Pig!' She looked at her watch. 'It's only a quarter past three and Hugh won't be home before six; we could go upstairs again.'

He looked at her with a small satisfied smile. 'Is that all you think about?'

'I'm afraid to think of much else.'

Lucy Lane was in the van. 'I've had young Bottrell and the Lander girl here to make their statements, sir. They're like babes in a wood.'

Wycliffe was in no mood for sentiment. 'I'm glad there are some innocents in this case even if they are also liars. That Bottrell brother is as slippery as an eel.'

He called to the duty officer. 'See if you can get Dr Franks on the line, Dixon.' He went through to his own cubicle and waited, brooding on all the things he should have said to the psychologist and didn't, but would, by God! next time. Underneath, he was well aware that if thumbscrews were out, there was no way to force a man like Bottrell to talk except by flattering his vanity or knowing enough to lever out the truth.

The telephone bleeped. 'Franks? . . . Yes, it's me.'

'About my report?'

'No, about your friends, in particular about Dr James Bottrell.'

'I told you; I've never met the man.'

'But you know of him and you've corresponded. In any case it wouldn't matter if you'd never heard of him. I understand that he has a medical degree as well as a doctorate in psychology. In 1984 he was a consultant at the North Midlands Hospital — '

'Charles!' Franks interrupted. 'I wonder what your response would be if I asked you to get the dirt on the head of CID at Middleton-in-the-Marsh?'

'I doubt if Middleton-in-the-Marsh would have a CID officer on the strength. In any case I'm not asking you for dirt, just about his professional standing and the appointments he's held.'

'Yes, and why he left them. No dirt, and you won't be interested. Anyway, I'll see what I can do but you'll owe me a good dinner if I come up with something.'

Wycliffe was thinking of Lizzie Biddick; her activities seemed confined to Duloe: her parents' home, her room in the big house, visits to Miller's cottage, and to James Bottrell's maisonette. Were these the true limits of her territory? Even the railway booking clerk had been struck by her naivety; conscious of her sense of adventure when she was merely buying a ticket for London. And what of Miller, and the quirky James? Whatever the breadth of their past experience it seemed that both had settled for life virtually within the confines of the estate. And Lander, and the Bottrells — did they venture far from their little promontory on the river?

He was reverting to his first impression of Duloe as a psychological island. But where, if anywhere, did it get him?

The Biddick girl. He couldn't get her out of his mind: culture from Miller, gin and sympathy from James Bottrell. And sex?

James had said something about her anxiety to be noticed, that she was busy constructing some private mythology through which she might come to terms with her insignificance.

But specialists specialize in half-truths. Wycliffe remembered his own youth: the feeling of being adrift, groping after those vague limits within which he must learn to live. He had been lucky, perhaps naturally cautious; too many are trapped in their own audacity. He hoped without much conviction that Lizzie hadn't paid with her life.

The clock above his table said, digitally, 16.15. That damned 24-hour clock! Another of the grudges he held, justly or unjustly, against the French.

There was a commotion in reception — DC Dixon expostulating, and Matt Biddick's voice, mumbling in sullen protest.

'Let him come in!'

The young man stood in the doorway of Wycliffe's cubicle, abashed now that he had attained his object.

'Sit down.'

Biddick perched himself on the edge of a bench seat. He reminded Wycliffe of a sturdy mongrel dog, ready to be friendly, but not to fawn. Wycliffe said: 'You went to the cottage with Mr Fox this morning? I haven't had his report yet.'

The boy shrugged. 'I couldn't help much. Only a couple of things. I remember the bottom drawer of his desk was full of stuff, now it's empty.'

'What did he keep there?'

'There was scores of letters — all in their envelopes like, but slit open. He must've saved 'em up for years.'

'You said there were two things.'

'Yes, his diary — a big thick exercise book, it was always in the top drawer. Whenever he couldn't remember something he would look it up in his diary. He used to say: "It's all here, Mattie, boy!" He used to call me that.'

The boy was blinking rapidly and there were tears between his lids. He pulled himself together. 'But that wasn't what I come about. I think I might've found something.'

'Tell me.'

'You know Lander's studio? . . . There's a well on the rising ground behind there. The old couple who lived in the house used to get their water from it before Lander put the pipes in.'

'So?'

'Somebody's bin messing about with the cover. They've had it off and put it back. They've tried to make it look like it's never bin off but you can tell . . . It's a wood cover an' before it was all covered with grass and suchlike.'

Wycliffe got up from his chair. 'Let's take a look.'

In the adjoining cubicle DC Curnow was typing a report. Wycliffe recruited him. Curnow was blond, six feet-two and big with it, throwing doubt on his claim to unalloyed Cornish descent. His other distinguishing attribute was an insatiable thirst for knowledge. Folklore had it that he spent his spare time working through the *Encylopaedia Britannica* and it was said that he had reached Volume Five: 'Conifer-Ear diseases.'

They passed through the white gate and crossed Lander's drive, apparently unobserved.

If Lizzie Biddick had met her death anywhere on the estate then her body would almost certainly be found in the immediate neighbourhood unless it had been removed by boat. Presumably that was possible, though the only available boat seemed to be the skiff in the boathouse.

They trooped down the narrow path through the trees and came in sight of the creek with the roof of the little house just below them. Biddick pointed to the left of the path, to somewhere in the featureless growth of nettles and brambles which covered the rising ground behind the house. 'In there.'

They followed him along a trail, recently trampled, and came to a small clearing. Grass and twigs had been strewn over a hinged wooden cover about thirty inches square. They were ten yards or so from the little house and level with the shuttered windows of the upper floor. A barely discernible path led to rough granite steps which descended to the backyard.

'All right, let's have the cover up.'

The debris was easily swept aside. It was obvious that the cover had been recently disturbed, the edges were free and rust had flaked from the hinges. Curnow lifted it with ease and laid it back.

The well was circular, lined with stone, and parged with clay below about five feet. The water level was ten feet or so lower than that. Just below its dark gleaming surface Wycliffe could see what looked like the twin handles of a bag of some sort.

Biddick was staring down into the well, tense and silent.

Wycliffe spoke to break the spell: 'Have you any idea how deep it is?'

He was shaken but he made an effort. 'No. I remember it used to run dry in a drought — like now.' He added, after a pause: 'If we can rig a pulley and a rope sling I'll go down.'

Wycliffe laid a hand on his arm. 'Better not; leave it to us.'

That evening a small group gathered around the well: Wycliffe, Kersey, Fox with his camera, and a little man in overalls, a police technician who would do the work. The light had turned golden, the waters of the creek had a coppery hue, and the birds were silent. On these summer evenings by the river, the light, the stillness and the silence combine to engender a sense of foreboding, even of menace.

A uniformed policeman was stationed in Lander's drive to stop anyone coming down the path. Lander had been told of what was going on and his only comment had been: 'I'd forgotten there was a well.'

An aluminium ladder, assembled in sections, had been lowered into the well and secured by crooks at the top. Its lowest rung just reached the surface of the water.

Wycliffe said: 'Carry on.' The little man in overalls got his feet on the ladder and started to descend. He carried a short pole with a crook on the end, like a boat-hook. Though he was small and the ladder was placed vertically against the wall of the well, there was little room for manoeuvre. Standing on the bottom rung he fished with his hook and caught the handles at his first try. It was a bag, and heavy; he had to climb the ladder, dragging the bag after him. When he reached the top Kersey took it from him.

It was a large, blue canvas hold-all, filled so that it must have been difficult to run the zip. Tied to one handle was a label, sodden but still readable: 'Miss Lizzie Biddick, Passenger to Paddington'.

Kersey was moved; his own daughters were close to Lizzie's age. 'Poor little sod! You'd think she was off to Lapland but she went nowhere.'

He was stooping over the bag and he looked up at Wycliffe. 'Shall I open it?'

'Just to make sure.'

Fox was taking photographs for the record.

With difficulty Kersey drew the zip. The bag was stuffed with wet clothing. Kersey felt around inside and muttered: 'Just what it seems.'

Both men had been troubled by the image of a dismembered corpse.

The man in overalls said: 'Do you want me to have another go?'

He went down again, this time using his pole to feel around in the water. After a moment or two his voice came, echoing up the well: 'Something here, guv!'

'Careful.'

'I'm touching bottom, there's not much water . . . More mud than anything . . . I've got it!'

The hook came up with a second hold-all, similar to the first. It was dragged up the ladder and handed over to Kersey. Like the other, it contained nothing obviously sinister.

The little man was definite: 'There's nothing else down there of any size; that's for sure.'

Kersey said: 'You weren't expecting to find her down there.'

Wycliffe merely shook his head.

They had arrived too late for the evening meal. The landlady had offered to cook them something but they had settled for sand-

313

wiches and beer at one of the tables outside. Kersey was accepted as a boarder. 'If you're no more trouble than your boss I shan't complain.'

There were people at every table, mainly couples, some with children. It was dusk, there were gnats, and now and then a bat flitted silently forth and back above their heads, quartering the air.

Kersey said: 'So the search is on tomorrow.'

'You've fixed it?' Wycliffe's question seemed to arise more from politeness than interest.

'They've been very helpful — Reed's lot and division. We shall muster a team of eighteen or twenty, plus two dogs and their handlers. Reed is having sketch maps prepared and division are providing a couple of frogmen to look at the deep water around the quay and the boathouse.'

Wycliffe's thoughts were running on other lines; he said: 'The housekeeper thought she heard the girl returning to her room late at night — '

Kersey interrupted: 'But it was our joker, collecting her baggage, is that it?'

'It looks that way. He won't have left any traces but we'd better get Fox to look over the place first thing in the morning. Just to keep the record straight.'

Kersey yawned. 'Another?'

'No, I've had enough to make me sleep.'

'What's the programme for tomorrow?'

'I want you to supervise the search; I intend to spend some time with Lander, and I want Lucy available in the van.'

Lady Bottrell was watching television, one of those all-in wrestling contests between politicians which masquerade as informed discussion. It was evening, the french windows were still open, the courtyard was filled with golden light, and no breath of air stirred the leaves of the ash tree. The door opened and Lord Bottrell came in, agitated but hesitant, and stood looking at his wife.

'Are you watching that?'

She waved her electronic wand and the screen went blank. 'Obviously I'm not going to. What is it?'

'I've been talking to Harry Biddick. It seems they've opened the old well behind Tytreth and found Lizzie's bags — the things she was supposed to have taken with her.'

'Who opened the well?'

'The police — who do you think?'

Lady Bottrell looked pained. 'There is no need to lose your temper, Hugh. Have you spoken to Lander?'

He knew that his worries were about to be elucidated by a simple process of logic which would leave him feeling frustrated and inadequate.

'I tried, but Beth said he's shut himself up in his study and switched off his phone. She asked him but he wouldn't speak to me. It looks bad.'

'You think the Biddick girl is dead?'

'Evidently the police think so and so does poor Biddick. What else can anyone think? This, on top of Tony . . .' He was near to tears.

Lady Bottrell's smooth brow wrinkled into a frown. 'Tell me truthfully, Hugh, how far are you implicated in all this?'

He slumped on to the settee. 'I am not "implicated" as you call it! I am upset and worried.' He spread his hands in appeal. 'Who wouldn't be?'

'You had a row with Tony Miller on the night before he died — '

He was shaken. 'Who told you that?'

'What were you quarrelling about? Was it the girl?'

He had picked up a newspaper to keep himself in countenance, now he dropped it again. 'Why, for God's sake, should we quarrel about her?'

'Perhaps you were jealous because he was spending time with her.'

'But that is nonsense! Tony had no interest in women — not in that way.'

'So what was the quarrel about — who was it about?'

'It had nothing to do with anything that has happened — nothing!'

'Who?'

'The boy Biddick — Matthew.'

For the first time Lady Bottrell was taken by surprise and she was incredulous. 'You are telling me that Tony was having an affair with that young lout and that you demeaned yourself — ' She broke off, unable to continue. 'Really, Hugh, you should write this up for the tabloids and pay off our debts.'

The door opened and James Bottrell came in. 'Am I interrupting something?'

In a perfectly normal voice she said: 'Of course not! Don't be foolish, James.'

Chapter Nine

Next morning there was more activity at the entrance to Duloe than the cats had slept through since 1815 when Major General Lord Bottrell, Second Baron, returned home to a hero's welcome after Waterloo. The Incident Van was hemmed in by a police personnel carrier, a Land Rover, and a clutch of patrol and crime cars. A score of men and women, searchers to be, wearing working uniforms and wellington boots, milled about waiting for the briefing. Two German shepherd dogs sniffed and wagged and, very occasionally, yelped in the excitement of the moment. From the steps of the Incident Van Kersey called forth order out of chaos while Wycliffe remained inside, unseen.

'You all know what you are looking for. We want a thorough search, with a minimum of disturbance or damage. A young woman is missing and she must be found. We don't know what has happened to her but there are circumstances which suggest that she did not leave the area last Monday week as she intended to do.

'Sergeant Jarvis is in charge of the search; he will be stationed in his command vehicle in front of the big house and you will report to and take instructions from him.

'I am handing you over to Sergeant Jarvis.'

The searchers were paired off, instructions given, maps and beating sticks issued, emphasis was laid on co-ordination through radio and visual contact, and at 08.20 hours the searchers moved off. Already police frogmen were at work in and around the boathouse where there was a depth of water at all states of the tide.

Back in the van Kersey said to Wycliffe, 'I'll see the circus on the road then I'll be back.'

As Kersey was leaving the telephone bleeped. 'Wycliffe.'

'Dr Franks for you, sir.'

'About James Bottrell: you're in for a disappointment — no dirt to speak of. It seems he was a late starter academically; his limp is due to a tubercular knee-joint which blighted his childhood and messed up his education. Anyway, he eventually did his pre-clinical at Oxford and then went on to King's. After his hospital stint he joined a general practice in Nottingham — I'm short on dates but you'll have to put up with that. All I've got is that in '72 or '73 he was back at university for a post-graduate course in psychology, followed by a consultancy at the North Midland. Later he joined the Prison Department as a psychologist and packed it in when his aunt left him money. I wish I had a rich aunt.'

'What about him as a man?'

'You mean, what about the dirt. There isn't any. He has a reputation as a cold fish — very. Acquaintances, but no friends — he fended off colleagues when they wanted to be sociable. His treatments were sometimes unconventional but never over the line. As to sex, he seems to have had it off with any discreetly available female.' Franks ended: 'Is that worth a dinner?'

'No, but maybe I'll stretch a point.'

It was hot; the searchers were in for a gruelling day. The weathermen had predicted inland temperatures in the mid-eighties. Even at Duloe, on the river and within a mile or two of the open sea, there was no hint of a breeze. At ten o'clock Lucy Lane was in the van catching up on paper work — word processing, chasing her fingers over the keyboard like a frenetic virtuoso playing Scarlatti.

In his own cubicle, Wycliffe, in shirt sleeves, flicked a ball-point in and out, staring out of the window at a squirrel half-way up a tree. The squirrel seemed to return his gaze so that he was persuaded the creature could see him despite the one-way glass.

The boisterous arrival of a gunmetal BMW, sleek and stylish, startled them both.

The driver was a woman: late-thirties, blonde; wearing tailored mauve trousers with a matching, patterned, silk blouse. Her figure was slim, her hair sculptured to her head; she had jade earrings, and an air of elegance. The car door slammed and, almost at once, she was confronting Potter, the duty officer. 'Chief Superintendent Wycliffe, please.'

Potter would have prevaricated but she cut him short. 'Tell him I am Tony Miller's sister.'

Wycliffe put on his jacket and went to meet her; she held out her hand. It was cool, his was sweaty.

'Olivia Sanders, née Ross.'

She put down her suede handbag and took a seat across the table from Wycliffe, at ease with all sorts and conditions of men.

For some reason a conventional expression of sympathy seemed out of place so he did not attempt one. 'I assume you have been to the police station?' (If she had and he hadn't been told there would be trouble.)

'No. I spent the night in Truro, made a few inquiries, and learned that I should probably find you here.' She smiled. 'I wanted to be sure of reaching the top.'

Wycliffe was annoyed that the woman made him feel he had something to live up to. 'I expect you know that your brother died on Sunday night but you may not have known at first that he had changed his name.'

'I did know, as a matter of fact. That is partly what I've come to tell you, but before I do you should know something of the family. Tony and I were the only children and I am the elder by two years. Our father was a drunk — amiable to outsiders, less so at home.'

She had prepared her little speech, succinct and convincing; now she was delivering it with as little emotion as if it concerned people with whom she had only a professional connection.

'Fortunately mother made sure that we had a reasonable education. I became a nurse and as soon as it was practicable I left home and never went back. I qualified, and eventually came south to

work in Dorchester General. I kept in touch with my brother —
birthdays, Christmas — that sort of thing, then, one day, to my
astonishment, he turned up in Dorchester, married, with a job in
the Parks Department. His wife was sixteen years older, and a
bitch.'

She paused and looked straight at Wycliffe. 'I expect you know
the upshot of that little romance. Tony went to prison, we lost
contact, and I heard no more of him until just over a fortnight ago
when he telephoned me from the Crown and I had a meal with
him there. It was then that he told me he had changed his name.'

Wycliffe was gazing out of the window at the BMW and her
eyes followed his. 'You are wondering how the BMW fits in with
Health Service nursing. It doesn't. For me things have
changed. I'm now a partner in, and matron of, a private nursing
home.' Another smile. 'But in any case that is my husband's car
— you see, in a traditional hospital romance, I married the
surgical consultant. He's a neurologist.'

Wycliffe decided to be bored; he turned to look at her with
mild, dreamy eyes. 'I still don't understand why it has taken you
four days to make any contact.'

She rested her hands on the table, fingering the bracelet of her
watch. 'I admit it must seem a little strange. The fact is that my
husband has rather rigid ideas about certain things.'

'He doesn't want you to become involved, is that it?'

'He doesn't even know that I met Tony and I certainly don't
want him to know that I have contacted you now. As far as he is
concerned I have no longer any connection with my family. That
is what I came to tell you.'

'And the car?'

'Bernard — my husband — is away, attending a symposium in
London. He always travels any distance by train and the BMW is
a great improvement on my workhorse Escort . . .'

'Why did your brother want to renew contact?'

'I'm not sure; I think he wanted me to lend him money. He
didn't ask outright but he went into some detail about a scheme
he had for starting a business — landscape gardening, that sort of

thing. He even talked about the amount of capital he would need.'

'So you had the definite impression that he intended to leave his job here?'

'Oh, he made no bones about that! He said the situation was becoming intolerable.'

'In what way?'

She made a helpless gesture. 'Tony's emotional life has always tended towards the dramatic. This time it was some homosexual entanglement from which he wanted to extricate himself but the other party wouldn't let go. It seems things had reached crisis point with recriminations and threats making life very uncomfortable.'

'Did he name the other party?'

'No.'

'Hasn't it occurred to you that this relationship might have provided the motive for his murder?'

She looked at him, her hard, blue eyes incredulous. 'You think that's possible? I'm afraid I didn't take it very seriously and I can't really believe — '

'Did you lead him to think that you might help him financially?'

'I did not. I suggested that he talked to his bank. I owe a great deal to my husband and however unwarranted his prejudice may be, I would do nothing to seriously displease him.'

'You are referring to his attitude towards homosexuality?'

'Of course!'

'Isn't such a prejudice unusual in a medical man and a neurologist at that?'

'Perhaps you are confusing neurology with psychology.'

Wycliffe felt snubbed, an unusual experience which was probably good for him.

'Are you the next of kin?'

'No; father is still alive. You didn't know?'

'We found nothing in your brother's possession to indicate any relative.'

321

'I'll give you his address.' She took a professional card from her handbag and wrote on the back. 'When I last heard, he was still more or less compos mentis . . . He's in some kind of sheltered accommodation for the elderly.'

What she had told him was helpful; he now had a reasonable explanation of Miller's visit to Dorchester and of his depression. More important, he had a hint of another side to the quarrel with Lord Bottrell on the night before the murder.

Wycliffe found it possible to be moderately pleased with the woman; he even thanked her for coming.

'If my name can be kept out . . .'

But that was pushing her luck. 'I can promise nothing at this stage.'

She picked up her handbag. 'If I could see where Tony lived . . . ?'

She had every right. He called Lucy Lane and introduced the two women, fascinated by the ensuing mutual appraisal. As they walked away from the van he heard the woman say: 'So you are a detective sergeant . . .'

He had disliked her. Of course she had put on an act, everybody does, but hers had offended him because it was blatant. An act, to be acceptable, must be so well practised that it fits like a glove. But is it then any longer an act?

There was a tap on his door and Potter, the duty officer, came in. 'Radio message from PC Fuller, sir. Subject has just gone down the path to Tytreth.'

On the pretext of fending off sightseers and the press Wycliffe had stationed a man in Lander's drive with instructions to report the lawyer's movements. Although it was past ten o'clock his car was still parked in front of the house; he had not gone to his office. Wycliffe had hoped that for one reason or another he would be drawn to his little house by the creek so that the inevitable interview — confrontation? — could take place there. He liked to meet any important witness at least once in their preferred habitat; talking to anybody in a police interview room is like studying animal behaviour in a laboratory.

322

He said to Potter: 'Tell Mr Kersey I shall be at Tytreth.'

Walking down the path through the trees he saw none of the searchers but he heard an occasional shout and once a dog barked. As he came in sight of the back of the house he saw that the shutters of one of the upstairs windows had been opened and, dimly, through the small window panes, he could see into the room. Lander was there, his gangling figure bent over something which he seemed to be polishing with some vigour.

He went down the steps and around to the front door. The padlock had been removed but the door was shut and there was no knocker or bell. To save his knuckles he rapped on the door with a coin. Almost at once he heard footsteps on the stairs, a bolt was drawn and the door opened. Lander was in his shirt sleeves, wearing a grey apron and, in a rubber-gloved hand, he held a piece of rag. Wycliffe noticed a faint smell of turpentine.

Lander seemed startled. 'Wycliffe!' He immediately controlled himself. 'You took me by surprise; no one ever comes here.'

'May I come in?'

The door opened into a tiny lobby and Wycliffe followed Lander through a second door into a room lit only by artificial light. It must have been the former kitchen-cum-living-room but now it was a photographic laboratory though, even to Wycliffe, it looked old fashioned. There was a sink set in a bench with an impressive array of bottles and jars on shelves above it. There was some chemical glassware, and a stack of white enamel trays of different sizes. The only item which struck Wycliffe as typical of a modern darkroom was an enlarger, draped under polythene in one corner. Stairs led to the upper floor. Overall there was that faintly acrid smell associated with any stock of chemicals.

Lander was manifestly uneasy and inclined to aggression. He peeled off the glove he was wearing and tossed it, with the rag, into the sink. 'I suppose you know that photography is my hobby.' He added: 'You'd better come through.'

They moved into the adjoining room which, until Lander opened the shutters, was in almost total darkness. The transformation from darkness to brilliant sunshine from the creek was dramatic. The room, formerly the parlour, was large and Lander had made it his studio. One wall was taken up by a nest of metal drawers of various sizes, presumably for his collection of photographs and, above them, were bookshelves. In the middle of the room a massive camera stood on a tripod, all teak and gleaming brass. For the rest there were numerous lamps on telescopic stands, various screens and a low bench with padded drapes which could have served as a model's throne.

'Please sit down.'

Lander, himself, sat in one of the two armchairs and placed the tips of his bony fingers together, rigid and expectant. The previous evening he had been flushed by whisky; now he looked grey, either a sick or a very worried man.

Wycliffe was relaxed and conversational, anxious not to raise the tension too soon. 'This is a very pleasant room. Do you spend much time here?'

'All the time I can spare.' There was a brief pause while the lawyer sought for something to match the mood: 'Somebody said: "If you're going to have a past you need a house to keep it in."'

'And this is your past?'

A faint smile. 'Also, I hope, my future.'

'Devoted to photography.'

'To historical aspects of photography. The modern obsession, clicking away with a contrivance of high-tech gadgetry, has no appeal.'

'Judging from the equipment next door you do all your own processing.'

Lander was responding to Wycliffe's approach. He leaned forward in his chair, crossed his legs, and clasped his long fingers about his knees. 'You probably wonder what goes on out there. I admit that it's more like an alchemist's kitchen than a photographer's darkroom. Actually I try to repeat the techniques of the early photographers using their materials. I've tried my hand at daguerreotypes, calotypes, wet and dry plate work . . . As a youngster I wanted to be a chemist, just as my father before me had wanted to be an architect, but tradition was too strong.'

He was talking too much.

Wycliffe turned to the museum-piece camera, bringing the subject back to photography. 'Do you use this monster or is it merely an interesting fossil?'

'I use it constantly. I call it my Old Faithful.'

It was strange to see a reflex softening of those bizarre features at the mere mention of the camera. Despite long experience of the masks people wear Wycliffe could still be surprised by a chameleon-like change triggered by an object or a phrase.

'It was about a photograph that I came to see you.'

From his wallet Wycliffe produced the defaced print of the nude girl and handed it over. It was obvious that Lander had braced himself for whatever might come and the mask was once more in place, but as he held the photograph his hand trembled.

After an interval he said in a controlled, formal voice: 'This is a Nadar print — that is to say it was made by the Frenchman, Gaspard-Felix Tournochon, who adopted "Nadar" as his pseudonym. He did a number of nude studies — daring for their time — in the sixties and seventies of the last century. May I ask how you came by it?'

'It was sent to me anonymously through the mail.'

'And you are obviously taking it seriously. Couldn't it be a sick joke?'

Wycliffe was patient. 'I am taking it seriously because it was posted in the Truro district during the weekend in which Miller was killed and the pendant which has been drawn around the girl's neck is identical with a birth-sign pendant worn by Lizzie Biddick.'

Lander handed back the photograph. He was cautious, vetting his every word, but his hand was unsteady. 'I see! As far as I knew, until last night, she had left for London more than a week ago.'

'And it is more than a week ago — the evening of last Sunday week — that she was seen by Mrs Christophers, leaving the house, and by Dr Bottrell whom she called on to say good-bye. No one admits to having seen her since. Her rail ticket, her money, and other personal things have been found in her room; her bags, already packed, have been retrieved from your well, and we are now searching the neighbourhood for her body.'

The lawyer was grave. 'I can understand your concern, but the photograph — '

Wycliffe cut in: 'I am anxious to trace the source of the photograph. I suppose Nadar prints are not easily come by?'

'No, but any serious collector might have some; I have two or three in my collection.'

'But not one of this particular print?'

Lander subjected him to his sombre gaze before replying: 'No, I have never seen that particular print or another like it.'

There was a pause, as though a certain stage had been reached at which their relative positions were defined.

Twice, the lawyer's thin lips parted as though he would speak but he remained silent. Wycliffe appeared to brood over the print then, abruptly, he held it up. 'Would you agree that this was intended to draw my attention to Lizzie Biddick's disappearance?'

Lander considered the point. 'If the pendant is taken to identify the girl then I suppose that must have been the intention.'

'And to suggest that she had been murdered?'

'That seems to follow.'

'One would have thought it simpler to send an anonymous letter but if a photograph was used, why not a modern one? Why deface a print which had some value and must have been difficult to come by?'

Lander made a dismissive gesture. 'Your correspondent — if one may call him that — must be a very devious individual.'

He sat in his chair, doing his best to appear impassive, his great jaw set, his brown eyes fixed on Wycliffe in an unblinking stare.

By contrast Wycliffe's eyes were vague, his expression dreamy, and his manner tentative. 'Hasn't it occurred to you that this may have been a deliberate attempt to implicate you? The print was posted locally and you are well known as a photographer and collector of historic photographs. As I see it my attention is being directed to a possible link between you and the missing girl.'

Lander was showing signs of increasing uneasiness, the long bony fingers of his right hand began to beat out a tattoo on the arm of his chair. He said, with emphasis: 'Mr Wycliffe, I know that girl only as the daughter of Lord Bottrell's gardener and as a house-maid at Duloe.'

'She has never been inside this house?'

'Not, at least, since it has been occupied by me.'

Looking past the lawyer, out of the window, Wycliffe could see the still waters of the creek, the moored boats, and the toy-town houses on the other side. He had one of those moments of self-doubt, of incredulity; finding it surprising that he, Charlie Wycliffe, should be here in this strange room, interrogating a man he scarcely knew, trying to extract an admission which might make that man a murder suspect.

Lander was looking at him with a curious expression; he appeared to be waiting. With an effort Wycliffe recovered his role and his voice became official: 'I think, sir, that you should be clear about the situation: this is likely to become a murder inquiry in the near future and I must point out that reticence, understandable in ordinary circumstances, could be misconstrued now.'

The lawyer was shaken. 'Are you threatening me, Chief Super-intendent?'

'I am asking you to bear in mind that there are people in whom Lizzie Biddick confided. I have been told of certain photographs which she claimed you have here. I am not suggesting that their possession in any way infringes the law, merely making the point that the girl seems to have been familiar with this place. Add to that the fact that her baggage has been found in a well behind the house and I have reasonable grounds for a more detailed investi-gation.'

The point went home but Lander fought back. His manner was mildly contemptuous: 'I hardly think I need take seriously a statement about the contents of this house which must have reached you at second-hand. It is no more than gossip. As to the discovery of the girl's baggage, it is obvious that the well was a convenient place to dump things, the possession of which would have been incriminating. That the well happens to be on my land is irrelevant.'

Wycliffe was unruffled. 'You may be right, but in a case which looks more and more like murder I must follow every lead however slender.'

Lander was agitated, he placed the tips of his fingers together and it seemed to steady him. 'How do you propose to follow this "lead" as you call it?'

'I was about to ask you to allow my men to make a search of these premises as a matter of routine.'

Lander contrived to look astonished. 'With what object?'

'To confirm your statement that Lizzie Biddick did not come here.'

'And if I refuse?'

'I am sure that you will not be uncooperative, but a refusal would force me to apply for a warrant.'

'You mean you would go to a magistrate?'

'Certainly.'

Lander made no response but there was a faint visible pulse in his left temple.

Wycliffe said nothing and for a time there was silence in the sunlit room. Distantly the clock in the village church chimed and struck twelve; it seemed to take for ever. The tide had uncovered the muddy margins of the shore and several of the smaller craft across the creek were aground.

Abruptly, Lander broke the silence. 'I have nothing to hide as far as the law is concerned and I want it clearly understood that I know nothing of the girl's whereabouts nor of what happened to her. As far as I knew she had left for London as she intended.'

Wycliffe, speaking softly, said: 'But she did come here from time to time?'

Lander nodded. 'Yes.'

'A regular visitor?'

328

'Most Sundays. I was probably foolish to deny it in the first place but one tries to avoid domestic friction.'

'You agree to your premises being searched?'

He reacted angrily: 'Do you think I want you applying for a warrant? Even if you didn't get it the application and the fact that I had refused permission would discredit me professionally — as you well know.'

'You will let me have the keys of this place until a search can be arranged?'

'Do I have a choice?'

Wycliffe retained his official manner. 'You realize that I must also ask you to make a formal statement concerning your association with the girl? You have not been officially interrogated, there has been no witness to our conversation and nothing has been recorded. You may come to the Incident Van or, if you prefer, to Truro police station.'

'I will come to your van. I want you to understand that I am most concerned to avoid publicity which could damage me professionally and in my family life.'

Wycliffe was left with a sense of wonder at the spectacle of a man like Lander, a lawyer, putting his reputation into the hands of a young girl; making himself dependent on her goodwill and her discretion, or on his ability to buy both. The sergeant under whom Wycliffe had served his green years had once remarked: 'There is commonsense, there is professional caution, there is decency, and there is the marriage tie, but there is also Sex.'

On the face of it Lizzie's demands had been modest, but perhaps not, and thereby a tale might hang.

On his way to lunch Wycliffe called in at the Incident Van. There were two reports. The first was brief, on the examination of Miller's car. Nothing had been found to suggest that the missing girl had been a passenger in it, voluntarily or otherwise. The second report included an inventory of the contents of Lizzie Biddick's two hold-alls, recovered from the well. Clothing accessories and toilet articles accounted for the great bulk of

329

items but among the rest there were several paperbacks, a couple of magazines and one item that was starred:

'Item 28: A4 envelope containing 14 photographs; various subjects and sizes.' A footnote read: 'These photographs are included with this inventory as they may have interest.'

Somebody showing a bit of initiative. Wycliffe tipped out the photographs. Despite immersion the envelope itself was only slightly damp and the photographs were untouched. He recognized several snapshots of members of the Biddick family, they were labelled on the back with first name diminutives, or 'Mum' and 'Dad'. Of the others there was one of Miller, seated in front of his cottage.

One photograph stood out from the rest; it was larger, and an obvious quality product. It showed Lizzie herself, quite naked, in a pose identical with that of the girl in the Nadar print. On the back was written: 'Guess who?'

Thoughtful, Wycliffe walked to the pub to share the table in the alcove (now carrying a 'Reserved' card) with Lucy Lane. Tourists crowded the dining-room and clustered around the bar. There was an extra waitress on duty but the landlady herself came over.

She spoke in a low voice: 'I've got a bit of fresh salmon, if you fancy it — with a nice salad; and for a sweet there's a bread pudding in the oven — my own recipe. Don't worry! It won't lie heavy on your stomach, 'tis light as a feather.'

'With a half-bottle of something light and fruity it sounds wonderful.'

Lucy said: 'Mr Kersey not coming?'

Wycliffe explained. 'How did it go with Olivia Sanders née Ross?'

Lucy took her time. 'At least she's the sort of woman I can get on with — a realist. What she had to say about her brother was interesting. She thinks he should have been a creative artist of some sort but he was too mentally lazy to discipline himself. While he was still at school he had poems published and he played in the regional Youth Orchestra, but when it came to

330

further education it was easier to drift into the local garage. Of course his father didn't help.'

The salmon arrived with a salad which was a good deal more imaginative than the usual tomato, limp lettuce leaf, and onion ring which masquerade as salad in most pubs. And the half-bottle was a hock, not at all bad.

'According to his sister, Miller had a real guilt complex about his homosexuality and the woman he married made the most of it.'

Wycliffe poured the wine. 'Lander is coming in to make a formal statement about his relations with Lizzie and I'm turning Fox loose in his studio.'

Lucy dissected her salmon, speared a little of the salad on her fork, and popped it into her mouth. Wycliffe always felt loutish when eating in her company. Having cleared her mouth, she sipped her wine and patted her lips. 'You think he killed her?'

'It's possible, I suppose.' He was casual.

'And Miller was killed because he knew too much.'

Wycliffe sipped his wine and said nothing for a while, then: 'All crimes of violence are distressing but here, it seems to me, there is a chilling element, calculating . . . passionless.'

Lucy Lane looked at him in surprise. 'You think so?'

He had picked up his knife and fork but dropped them again. 'What I think is that we need to get a fresh hold.' He was looking at her with his most solemn and stolid expression.

Chapter Ten

'They've found her, sir!' Potter, the duty officer, with a rare display of animation.

'Where?'

'Block twenty-five on the grid, sir.'

Pinned to the display board was a copy of the map supplied to the searchers. It had been divided into a grid of fifty-metre squares. Wycliffe studied the map. Block twenty-five covered part of the shore of the upper creek adjacent to Lander's studio.

'Mr Kersey was here when word came through and he arranged for scenes-of-crime and the doc to attend. He's down there now, himself.'

'Then I'll join him.'

The suspicion of a grin flickered across Potter's thick lips betraying his thought: 'No show without Punch'. Chief supers are not expected to be where the action is except in times of dire emergency.

The path from Lander's drive, down through the trees to the Upper Creek, was now familiar ground. He scarcely noticed his surroundings and had no eyes for the view. When he reached the strand the house was as he had first seen it, blind and deserted; Fox had not yet started work on the lawyer's hide-away. Wycliffe was surprised to find no one about, then he heard voices not far away and a constable appeared on the path which led in the direction of the boathouse and the quay.

'This way, sir.' Potter had lost no time in warning his comrades.

Kersey and three or four of the searchers were close by,

screened from the house by a scrub of elder, blackthorn, gorse and bramble. They were on the little promontory where he had seen signs of a former industry; that industry, he had discovered since, was boatbuilding in the early years of the century.

Kersey was brooding over a ditch — a channel less than eighteen inches wide and about the same in depth, cut for some purpose now unknown.

The girl was lying face upwards in the ditch and she was naked, even her birth-sign pendant had been removed. Her body was bloated and discoloured; she had been dead for several days.

And there were the tell-tale signs of a particular kind of violence: bruises on either side of and slightly below the larynx, more bruising around the neck; petechiae about the face, neck and chest; cyanosis . . . She had been throttled.

Kersey said: 'We saw the dotty picture; now we've got the real thing. Poor little bastard! . . . One of the dogs found her; you can't see this ditch until you're nearly in it.' He pointed to a couple of rotting planks lying nearby. 'They were on top of her, weighed down by stones.'

'To keep the gulls off.'

'I suppose so; they would soon have given the game away with their squawking.'

Even now three or four herring gulls planed and swooped overhead as though waiting their chance. The girl was lying on a bed of black estuarine mud and her flesh, although protected by the planks from the gulls, had been ravaged by the more surreptitious attentions of crustaceans.

Kersey had briefed himself from local knowledge. 'They tell me there's more than a foot of water in this channel at an average high tide — enough to submerge the body.'

'But not to move it.'

'No, the weighted planks made sure she stayed where she was put.'

When Wycliffe was able to turn his attention to the surroundings he was surprised to find that they were not overlooked. The scrub bushes and trees which shielded them from the house also cut them off from the creek and the river. A very private place for murder. But had the girl been killed on the spot? Or had her body been dragged or carried from elsewhere? The ground, stony in any case, was now parched and hard so that whatever had been done it was unlikely that any traces would be found.

Fox arrived to take photographs and to plot the exact position of the body on the map. He was followed by the local doctor, a young man, somewhat awed by the task which had been thrust upon him. He introduced himself: 'Dr Prentiss . . .' and broke off as he caught sight of the body. 'Good God! How long has she been there?'

'Up to eleven days. No one admits to having seen her in that time — a week last Sunday.'

Prentiss was thoughtful. 'So that, alternately, she must have been lying in salt water, or left high, if not dry, according to the state of the tide. The ambient temperature will have fluctuated wildly between the extremes when she was submerged at night and exposed to full sun at low tide by day — with every possible variation in between.'

The doctor was setting his mental house in order to good effect. He ran a hand through his mop of blond curls. 'What exactly are you expecting me to tell you?'

Wycliffe was understanding. 'To be frank, not much. In the circumstances I doubt if the pathologist will be very informative before he's done the autopsy.'

Confidence restored, the young man went on: 'She obviously didn't drown, she was strangled — or throttled. There are no other obvious signs of ill-treatment but it may be a different story when she's out of there and one is able to take a good look. I assume she's the missing girl?'

Kersey said: 'We are assuming that too, but even her mother would have difficulty in recognizing her.'

Her mother — Wycliffe thought of the vigorous and resolute little matriarch and her brood. Abruptly, the thing in the ditch became the girl who, searching for a way of escape, had blundered against the glass walls of her cage like a frenetic

334

bumblebee. Wycliffe felt anger rise within him; it was unprofessional and unproductive but healthy, even in a policeman.

To Kersey he said: 'You'd better notify the coroner and Dr Franks.' He looked up and was shaken to see Matt Biddick coming along the path from the direction of the quay.

He hurried to meet him. There was no need to say anything; the boy said it for him: 'You've found her.'

'Yes.'

'How did she . . . ?'

'I don't know yet. As soon as I do . . .'

'Can I see her?'

'Better not.'

A momentary show of temper, quickly followed by resignation.

Wycliffe said: 'I'm going to tell your mother now.'

The boy put out his hand. 'No! I'll tell mother.'

They were waiting for the mortuary van — rather for the men who manned it; the van could get no closer than the Landers' drive.

Wycliffe looked about him: nothing had changed. Why should it? Nature was taking its course, part of the recycling process. Humans made such a fuss; and there were far too many of them anyway. That was the logic of life. But compassion and fear blend with human perversity to defy all logic, and Wycliffe was moved by a sense of strangeness, of alienation, as well as by the pathos of it all.

Two attendants from the mortuary arrived, piloted by a uniformed man. They brought a stretcher and a polythene envelope in which the body would be placed.

Straps were manoeuvred under the girl, she was lifted out of the ditch, and, within minutes, all that remained of Lizzie Biddick had been carried away.

Suddenly Wycliffe felt very tired; there was a sense of anticlimax — strange in the circumstances — but he had experienced it before. They trooped back to the Incident Van, the searchers were recalled and sent on their way; the two

335

frogmen had packed their gear and departed long since. Wycliffe made a brief statement to the press who had monitored the search after their own fashion.

Now the congestion outside the gates of Duloe was reduced to the Incident Van and a couple of crime cars.

Wycliffe, slumped in his chair, said: 'We still haven't found the clothes she was wearing when she set out that Sunday night.'

They were in luck with the post mortem. Dr Franks was available and, by six o'clock, less than four hours after the finding of the body, he was on the telephone to Wycliffe.

'For your ears only. I've made no internal examination so this is provisional, but it's pretty obvious that she was throttled. I can find no evidence of sexual intercourse having taken place at or around the time of her death but I wouldn't expect to when she's been lying in a ditch, washed by the tide, for God knows how long. So, on the face of it, a common-or-garden sex crime.'

Wycliffe said: 'We worked that out for ourselves.'

'Then you were wrong. Admittedly it could still be a sex crime but with an unusual variation. Somebody coshed her first. Nothing fancy, just a good old fashioned swipe with a sock full of sand or similar.'

'Enough to kill outright?'

'Obviously not, because it wasn't what she died of. But enough to put her out and endanger life. There may well be a fracture of the occiput and possibly contrecoup lesions, but I shan't know yet. More on that in our next. But going back to the throttling: the killer seems to have made deliberate use of some necklace thing she was wearing to render the pressure of his thumbs more effective. The nature of the bruising makes that pretty certain. I suppose he removed whatever it was, scared of possible prints.'

'So that's it then?'

'For the moment anyway. If I find later that she's been injected with Bulgarian umbrella poison I'll let you know.'

Wycliffe thanked him, and meant it. Not all pathologists are willing to raise their heads above their stainless steel sluices until they've prepared the ground with a barrage of typescript.

Wycliffe contacted headquarters, heading off some of the inevitable pressure from the media by arranging that future statements would be issued through a press officer at sub-division. He, himself, would attend a briefing following any significant development. The media was asked to avoid the vicinity of the estate. It wouldn't work altogether, but it might help.

When told of the pathologist's report, even Kersey admitted to some mystification. 'Odd! I suppose he coshed her because she struggled.'

'Having come provided with a suitable weapon.' Wycliffe was sarcastic. 'I think Franks, by talking about a sand-filled sock, means a weapon with a certain resilience which can do a lot of damage without spilling blood and brains all over the place. These things don't lie around, waiting to come in handy.'

Kersey's rubbery features achieved one of his famous grimaces indicative of thought. 'I suppose he could have topped her because she threatened him, then tried to make it look like a sex crime.'

'Who, in this scenario, is he?'

'Lander, of course. Who else?'

'And what was she threatening Lander with?' Wycliffe's manner was irritatingly pedantic, usually a sign that he was groping after some idea of his own and was being confused by discussion. He went on: 'I admit that her passbook shows she was getting money from somebody — perhaps from Lander. Conceivably she was blackmailing him with the threat that she would make their association public; in which case, keeping her quiet might have been worth a few hundreds. But murder . . . ?'

For once Lucy aligned herself with Kersey. 'But we don't know, sir, what else she may have had on Lander. We've heard about dirty pictures but there could have been something really serious.'

337

Wycliffe nodded. 'All right, so let's assume that Lander thought he had reason to fear her — reason enough to kill her, would he have done it on his own doorstep? Would he have taken the trouble to collect her baggage, only to hide it down his own well?'

Kersey said: 'A sudden outburst of violence followed by blind panic. We've seen it often enough before.'

'An outburst of violence, with a cosh at the ready — which is where we came in. Let's leave it at that until Lander has said his piece; he's due to make a statement anyway. And first thing in the morning Fox can get back to the studio and find out what that has to tell us.'

Wycliffe leaned back in his chair and yawned. 'Meantime we've got a few — a very few, facts: the housekeeper says she saw Lizzie leaving the house at about half-past nine on the night she disappeared. James Bottrell says she was with him, "coming up for ten". Lander says he was expecting her at ten but that she didn't turn up. After that — nothing.'

Wycliffe suppressed another yawn. 'Nothing, that is, until now — an interval of eleven days. And during those eleven days Miller was murdered. It would be incredible if the two crimes were unconnected, yet there was a week between them. Of course, Miller was away for some of that time . . .'

'She came most Sundays, after she had helped with the meal at the house.'

'When did these visits start?'

'About a year ago.'

Lander was sitting opposite Wycliffe in the Incident Van with only the bench-like table and a cassette recorder between them. A uniformed constable stood by the door. Lander seemed distrait, he looked about him uncertainly as though not quite sure where he was, his eyes and his hands were never still.

'How did it start?'

'What? Oh, I met her when I was out walking the dog. She told me she was interested in photography . . .' His voice trailed off.

338

'What happened then?'

He looked at Wycliffe as though startled by the question then recollected himself. 'She asked me if I would recommend a reliable camera which wasn't too expensive. I was short with her at first but she seemed genuinely interested.'

'Did you suggest that she might come to the studio and talk it over?'

He frowned. 'I suppose I did; I don't know. Anyhow, she came. And now she's dead!' His eyes sought Wycliffe's, their expression haunted and oddly disturbing.

Wycliffe said: 'Mr Lander, you are making a statement in connection with two very serious crimes; you have been offered the chance to defer your statement until the morning when you may be more composed. I advise you, once more, to do that.'

The lawyer became very tense, the muscles of his great jaw tightened and colour showed in his pale cheeks. Speaking slowly, and enunciating each word with exaggerated clarity, he said: 'And I want this over — tonight!'

A moment later he added in a more normal voice: 'I will try to be more restrained but there is something you must understand: I needed Lizzie — I never in my life had a truly intimate relationship with any woman . . .' His voice let him down; his hands were trembling and he clasped them together. 'I would have done anything for Lizzie!'

Like a boy with his first girl, even the repetition of her name seemed to give him pleasure.

'The idea that I would have harmed her is . . . is preposterous! . . . Of course, you are sneering; any normal man would. I don't hold it against you.'

'I am not sneering, Mr Lander, far from it. I am trying to establish a sequence of events. Now, did Lizzie, at any time, ask you for money?'

'No, but after I'd known her a little while I made her a present.'

'How much?'

'Two hundred pounds, and I gave her other presents at intervals.' He was quieter, his outburst seemed to have calmed him.

'How much, over the year?'

'I don't know, perhaps a thousand.'

'Did she ever threaten you or demand anything else?'

'Never!'

There was a longish pause during which the tape could have picked up only background sounds from the police radio in the next compartment. Then, Wycliffe asked: 'When was the last time you saw her?'

In a voice that was barely audible he said: 'I saw her when I called on the Bottrells on Saturday evening — just briefly — in the corridor . . . She smiled at me.'

'You did not see her on the Sunday?'

'I didn't; I expected that she would come at about ten, but she did not.'

'You had an appointment?'

'An arrangement — like other Sundays, except that she wouldn't be staying the night.'

'You knew that she was off to London the following day?'

'I knew that was what she intended to do.'

'So this would have been a farewell visit.'

There was another lengthy silence, then, looking down at his hands, and speaking very quietly, he said: 'I was going to try to persuade her to stay.'

'How?'

Wycliffe could scarcely catch the words of his reply. 'I would have given her a choice.'

'A choice?'

'If she agreed to stay I would have given her a large sum of money.'

'Or?'

Without raising his eyes, he said: 'I would divorce my wife and marry her.' He leaned forward and clasped his hands tightly together on the table.

'The following day, when you heard that she had gone, you must have been very distressed.'

'I couldn't believe that she would do that to me!' And after a

340

pause, he added with curiously naive satisfaction: 'And she didn't; did she?'

'But you made no inquiries?'

His look was accusing. 'How could I? I hoped and expected that she would write, or telephone.'

The clock on the wall showed 20.25. The sun, close to setting, was screened by the trees and dusk had already settled over the little enclave of the cats.

The policeman by the door, shuffled his feet and coughed. Lander turned sharply; startled.

Wycliffe's manner became more official; his voice hardened: 'But we know now what happened to her, and her body was found in a ditch less than a hundred yards from your studio; her baggage was hidden in your well.'

Lander looked at him like a man under torture; but suffering roused him. He raised his voice: 'How *can* I say anything, when I know nothing?'

Wycliffe sat back in his chair. 'I have only one more question to ask you at this stage; then I am going to adjourn this interview: Did the photograph you saw — the Nadar print — come from your collection?'

Lander drummed his fingers on the table top then, abruptly, he said: 'I gave it to Lizzie.'

'Why?'

There was a far away look in his eyes. 'Lizzie spent a lot of time going through my collection. The photographs seemed to fascinate her — that one in particular. She said the girl was like her and she asked me to take one of her in the same pose.'

'And did you?'

He nodded.

'Please answer for the tape.'

'I did.'

'This interview ends at 20.35.' Wycliffe switched off the tape and turned again to Lander who sat, as though mesmerized. 'I may have further questions and it would be convenient if you did not go to your office in the morning.'

'Is that an instruction?'

'As you well know, Mr Lander, it is a request.'

That evening when Wycliffe called on the Biddicks to express his sympathy the whole family was gathered in the living-room to hear what he had to say. Lizzie's mother, dry-eyed but very pale, when asked if she really wanted the younger ones to hear how Lizzie died, was unequivocal: 'Lizzie was their sister; they've got the right.'

And her husband, like a well trained chorus, murmured: 'We're a family, Mr Wycliffe . . . A family . . .'

Wycliffe told them briefly what he had learned so far, and ended: 'One thing is certain; Lizzie didn't suffer. The blow would have meant immediate loss of consciousness.'

It was a strange experience; he was the centre of solemn and dignified attention from eight pairs of brown eyes, from the little girl on her mother's lap to Harry Biddick who sat, his unlit pipe clenched between his teeth.

The boy, Matt, was the first to speak. 'Did it happen where she was found?'

'I can't say at the moment. I hope that we shall know more later and I can promise that you will be told everything.'

Matt would have been more pressing but his mother cut in: 'No more, now, Matt! I reckon Mr Wycliffe has been straight with us and he's not going to be asked a lot of questions he can't answer.'

Wycliffe came away, deeply impressed, knowing that this experience would remain with him as one of the most moving of his professional life.

Before going to bed he telephoned his wife.

'It's me . . .' The usual ritual.

'Are you coming home?'

'Not yet.' He hesitated, not having formulated in his mind the question he most wanted answered. 'No news at your end?'

'Nothing in particular. Ruth telephoned earlier.'

'Is she all right?'

'Fine. You sound worried. Is something bothering you?'

'No, I just happened to be thinking about her.' In fact, he had been thinking of the naked body of the girl in the ditch. 'Look after yourself.'

'And you . . .'

Chapter Eleven

Cynthia Bottrell sat at table eating toast thinly spread with low-fat margarine. Opposite her, across the table, her brother-in-law, James, decapitated a boiled egg. They were alone. The morning sun flooded the breakfast-room, merciless to already faded wallpaper and fabrics, searching out dusty ledges and cobwebbed corners. James reached for a slice of toast, broke off a piece and dipped it into his egg.

Cynthia said: 'You'll get salmonella poisoning, eating runny eggs.'

'I'm neither pregnant nor aged; in any case doctors have a professional immunity.'

The black marble clock on the mantelpiece had stopped but a little battery clock beside it showed fifteen minutes past eight.

Cynthia said: 'Are they going to arrest Lander?'

'I suppose so. I can't see what else they can do. They'll be searching his studio today for corroborative evidence. Poor old Simon is really up shit creek.'

'Don't be vulgar, James! I don't like it.'

'No, of course! I tend to forget you're not the woman I sometimes go to bed with in the afternoons. Interesting woman she is. You should meet her. At certain times her vocabulary seems to consist almost exclusively of four-letter words.'

Lady Bottrell flushed. 'You are a mean beast, James! Anyway, do you think Lander killed her?'

James looked up from his egg. 'How should I know?'

'I asked what you thought.'

'Then I think he did.'

Cynthia poured coffee and added a dash of milk. 'What about Tony Miller?'

For a while James went on eating as though he had not heard then, abruptly, he looked up: 'You know Miller came to see me on the night he was killed?'

'You told me; what about it?'

James was in no hurry; he reached for a fresh piece of toast and buttered it. 'We were talking about Lizzie Biddick and he said he didn't believe she'd gone to London or anywhere else. I asked him what he knew and he said he wasn't prepared to come out in the open with an accusation but that he'd dropped a strong hint in the right quarter.'

Cynthia was watching him, her cup half-way to her lips. 'The photograph sent to the police?'

'I suppose so. What else? He must have sent it, it would be too much of a coincidence otherwise.'

'And he got shot with his own gun. Have you said anything about this to Wycliffe?'

'No. I should be in trouble for not speaking sooner. In any case, he's got there without my help.'

Cynthia, whose hearing was acute, said: 'That's Hugh.' And she added in a low voice: 'This afternoon?'

'That's up to you. You know where I live.'

'Pig!'

Lord Bottrell came in, looking harassed. 'Where's Paul?'

'He went out early and he's not back yet.'

Bottrell, at the serving trolley, tipped muesli into a bowl and added milk. 'I'm worried about Lander; the police seem to have made up their minds and it can't be right. I don't believe it!'

Lady Bottrell said: 'You always were a trusting soul, Hugh.'

Kersey said: 'It's a classic case: eminently respectable professional man, middle-aged, repressed — no sexual experience to speak of and not much in prospect — suddenly finds himself with an attractive young girl on offer. He goes overboard, gets himself into a mess, is faced with blackmail — only one way out.'

He was breakfasting with Wycliffe in the alcove. A few empty tables separated them from the young couple whose attention was divided between the two policemen and the television news which had just carried an account of the finding of Lizzie Biddick's body.

'The naked body of a young woman, discovered yesterday by police searchers on the Duloe Estate in Cornwall, has been identified as that of Elizabeth "Lizzie" Biddick, absent from her home for several days. The dead girl, who was employed by Lord and Lady Bottrell, had recently announced her intention of going to work in London.

'Detective Chief Superintendent Wycliffe said last night that the death was being treated as a case of murder, the second on the estate in a few days. In the small hours of Monday morning Anthony Miller, the estate foreman, was shot dead in his cottage. The police are searching for a possible connection between the two crimes.'

The item was accompanied by stills showing the frontage of Duloe House, a view of King Harry ferry, and a long shot which could have been of the little promontory where the girl was found.

Wycliffe finished his bacon and reached for the marmalade. He said: 'You must listen to the tape. Lander's statement is oddly naive — especially coming from a lawyer. Once he was launched he sounded more like a boy of fifteen talking about his first girl, the nearest thing to calf-love I've come across in a long time.'

Kersey poured himself a second cup of coffee. 'He's boxing clever. With Fox about to turn over his nest there wouldn't be much point in denying anything so he turns on the Mills and Boon. All roses and stardust until some nasty man drops out of a tree, throttles the girl, and dumps her body and baggage on his doorstep.'

'And Miller?'

'Oh, Miller comes back from his holiday, starts asking awkward questions and poking around — getting dangerous.'

Wycliffe bit into his toast. 'And, of course, it was Miller who sent us the photographic tip-off just before getting himself shot. Doug! You have a Lewis Carroll talent for making nonsense sound like logic. And I suppose Lander is "the type"?'

Kersey believed — or said he did — in the theory of criminal types. Now he grinned. 'Of course! All sexually repressed lawyers over forty-five should be locked up as a preventive measure.'

Wycliffe walked slowly down the path towards Lander's studio. He could not have explained even to himself why he was on his way there. Fox would miss nothing and it would all appear in his report, but Wycliffe felt the need to renew his sense of place; he could not visualize a sequence of events out of their physical context.

It was half-past ten and the tide was an hour into the ebb. The mud was no more than a fringe between the water's edge and the rocky shale of the beach. A flotilla of swans cruised close inshore. Across the creek, the only other living creature in sight, a man, performed one of those arcane rites peculiar to the brotherhood of the boat: standing in the stern of his craft he appeared to explore the bottom of the creek with a long pole.

Lizzie Biddick, then Tony Miller. Two murders which must be fitted into a pattern of interactive behaviour that was credible for the people concerned. 'Credible for the people concerned.' He spoke the words aloud.

Perhaps Lizzie had kept her appointment with Lander on that Sunday night: 'I was going to try to persuade her to stay — not to go away.' And if that persuasion had failed? Perhaps frustration and lust had erupted into an act of passion which is a euphemism for a sex killing. And the girl's body had been found naked in the ditch.

But she had been coshed before being throttled.

He arrived at the promontory where Lizzie's body had been found. The exact position, shielded from distant view by the scrub, was marked by pegs driven into the banks of the ditch.

Otherwise there was nothing to tell of the drama which had so recently occurred. The gorse was bursting out in a late flowering and its scent lingered, while the bees made the most of it. Had Lander carried or dragged the girl's body from the house to the ditch? Fox had found no trace but that was not surprising having in mind the condition of the ground. It would be much more significant if, in the house, he found nothing to suggest that a crime had been committed there.

The house itself looked different, it no longer had that blind and deserted look; not only were the shutters open, but the windows too.

His presence had been observed. Fox met him at the door. With no preamble he launched into an account of his doings. 'I've finished upstairs, sir, and I'm now working in the studio itself.' With Fox it was always 'I', his assistant was rarely mentioned.

'Where is . . . ?' Wycliffe had to think what the young man was called. 'Where is Collis?'

'In the back yard. He's looking at an old shed where they used to keep coal and part of it was an earth privy.'

They were in the darkroom, no longer dark now that the shutters had been thrown back, and looking less mysterious though more tatty in the light of day.

'Anything upstairs?'

Fox looked aggrieved. 'A waste of time, sir. His prints and hers; a dressing gown and some casual clothes of his in the wardrobe, and that's it. He had a go at cleaning off prints but he wasn't very good at it. The bed sheets have been used but there's nothing to suggest any violence.'

Wycliffe said: 'You carry on. I'll take a look around.'

He climbed the narrow stairs. From a tiny landing at the top three rooms opened off: in one, a shower cabinet and WC; another was empty, and the third was the bedroom. If he had expected anything resembling a love nest he was disappointed; the furnishing was basic: a four-foot bed with a couple of pillows and a duvet; a wardrobe, a table, and an armchair. The whole lot could have been picked up in a saleroom at a knock-down price, and a bedroom in a back-street hotel could hardly have offered a less stimulating setting for illicit or any other kind of love.

There was a table beside the bed and, along with the alarm clock, there were copies of a highly technical photographic magazine.

What had the girl wanted from these men— from Lander, from James Bottrell, and from Tony Miller? And what had she got, apart from modest sums of money from Lander?

Wycliffe's thoughts drifted, vague and inconsequential, though underneath he was aware of a growing dissatisfaction with what he called Kersey logic: A kills B, C finds out, so A kills C. Put like that it sounded reasonable, but less so when one began to know the people involved and tried to link them with the details of what they were supposed to have done.

He was staring out of the bedroom window, at the creek, the swans, the boats, and the houses opposite. Suddenly it was as though time had been suspended and he experienced one of those moments which he had known since childhood when he looked about him and found everything strange and unfamiliar as though he had just arrived from some other place.

His mother had used to say: 'Why aren't you playing, Charles?' His teachers: 'Day dreaming again, Wycliffe!' From Helen it was: 'Penny for them.' Oddly, in his adult life at least, such experiences had seemed to anticipate some critical decision, or a decisive phase in whatever case he happened to be engaged. At least he went downstairs feeling, quite irrationally, that something had been achieved.

Fox was going through the metal drawers where Lander kept his collection of photographs. Of necessity it was a cursory examination as the drawers must have contained many hundreds, if not thousands.

Fox slipped easily into his lecture mode: 'Each photograph has its own envelope with details recorded on it and a catalogue number. The catalogue is cross-indexed so that any print can be traced under the name of the photographer, the year it was made, or the nature of the subject. Subjects are classified into — '

Wycliffe cut him short: 'But do they tell us anything relevant to the case?'

Fox removed his half-glasses and polished them. 'Perhaps not directly, sir, except that the envelope which contained the Nadar print is still there — empty. So it definitely came from here — '

'Anything else?'

'I believe the dead girl told her brother that Lander collected what she called "dirty pictures".'

'Well?'

Fox spread out a score or more postcard-size photographs which had been removed from their envelopes; they were mainly sepia prints, some of them slightly faded. 'Catalogued as "Parisian Brothel Scenes, 1880-1920", sir.'

Obviously the notorious 'French Postcards' produced for the tourist trade and covertly circulated well into the forties. Wycliffe supposed they were as much a part of the history of photography, at least of its social role, as most of the other specimens contained in the metal drawers.

Collis, Fox's assistant, arrived and stood, diffident, in the doorway.

Wycliffe was firmly convinced that dogs and their owners grow to look alike and was beginning to wonder if the same applied to scenes-of-crime officers and their assistants. Collis, who had started as a quite ordinary youth, seemed to grow daily more lean and lanky, his nose was becoming beaked, and he had the permanent air of an entomologist examining a specimen, or of a bird wondering whether a certain grub was good to eat.

'What is it, Collis?' Fox, abrasive.

Collis said: 'I think I've found her clothes.'

Wycliffe took over. 'Show me.'

In the yard, which was cut back into the hillside, there was a shed divided into two unequal parts; the larger part had been a fuel store; the smaller, an earth closet. The closet retained its bench-like seat with a hole in the top. What was not immediately obvious was that the seat was removable. Collis lifted it off, and in the cavity, on a floor of black soil, there was a small heap of clothing.

Fox said: 'Bags, Collis!'

Collis went out and returned with a pack of tagged polythene bags. Each item was placed in a separate bag: the orange blouse, the dark-blue trousers, the bra and briefs but no footwear. At the bottom of the little heap they found a plastic handbag.

As the items were being bagged it was obvious that dried leaves and even tiny twigs had become caught up in the folds or hitched in the weave of the materials. No botanist was needed to tell them that this detritus had been picked up in the neighbourhood of the ditch where the body was found. In other words, it was out there that the girl had undressed, or been stripped.

Fox said: 'Not very good at covering his tracks, was he?'

When Wycliffe returned to the Incident Van, Potter, the duty officer, was surreptitiously brushing crumbs from his shirt front like a schoolboy caught eating in class. Potter's paunch was of concern to Wycliffe and the hierarchy because it raised a question about his fitness for the job and had twice blocked his promotion.

'Not again, Potter!'

'I'm going without lunch today, sir.'

'Anything for me?'

'Dr Franks would like you to ring him before lunch, and Lady Bottrell has been, asking if you would call on her at your convenience. She was here about twenty minutes ago.'

'She was alone?'

'Yes, sir.'

'Agitated?'

Potter considered. 'More broody, I'd say.'

Wycliffe telephoned Franks, who said: 'I've completed the PM — nothing to report except that she was four months pregnant. I'm in a bit of a rush but I thought you would like to know.'

Something to think about. He dropped the telephone and turned to Potter: 'I shall be at the house.'

As he climbed the broad granite steps to the terrace he was suddenly a boy again, with his father and mother, all in their best clothes, attending the annual dinner provided by 'The Colonel' for his tenants. The Colonel would be standing at the top of the steps to greet his guests: 'Ah, Wycliffe! I hear you got yourself a couple of good heifers in last week's market . . . Mrs Wycliffe, always a pleasure . . . And this is young Charles . . .'

To the boy, Wycliffe, it had seemed that the family in the big house must lead very special lives, far removed from the rough and tumble of ordinary mortals. Even now he experienced a sense of let-down whenever he discovered that they, like the rest, may have their feet of clay.

His wife sometimes accused him: 'At heart, you're a snob, Charles!'

The door stood open to the bare hall; he pulled at the lever-like handle which operated the bell and heard it jangle in some remoteness. A moment or two later Lady Bottrell came to greet him.

'So good of you to come.' She lowered her voice. 'Hugh has had to take old Mr Lander into Truro. When he discovered that Simon was wanted here, nothing would satisfy him but that he should go to the office himself.'

Wycliffe was taken to the room overlooking the courtyard and they were about to sit down when her ladyship caught sight of Harry Biddick weeding the borders. 'On second thoughts we might be better in the library.'

The library was high, long, and narrow; bookcases reached half-way up the walls though their shelves were largely empty. Above the bookcases family portraits in massive gilt frames hid their faces behind layers of varnish and the accumulated dirt of years. A large Gothic window, with heraldic panels of stained glass, took up most of the end wall.

Wycliffe and her ladyship sat opposite each other at a huge oak table on which documents and leather-bound books were arranged in orderly heaps.

'Hugh spends his spare time sorting this stuff. Some of it, he thinks, could be valuable to historians.'

Lady Bottrell was, for once, off balance and talking too much. Her smooth forehead wrinkled: 'This is rather difficult. I find it hard to cope with the fact that you, until a few days ago a total stranger, are now acquainted with the more intimate details of our lives.' She looked at him with a tentative smile: 'I am not complaining; perhaps in a way it helps . . .'

Wycliffe, wearing what Helen called his 'cow look', said nothing.

Uncharacteristically restive as well as talkative, Cynthia fiddled with the pink tape which secured a sheaf of documents. 'I assume that what you have seen and heard this morning satisfies you that Lander was responsible for the terrible things that have happened here in the past fortnight.' Her blue eyes sought his — not, as novelists say, in mute appeal, but searchingly inquisitive.

His response was chilly: 'You have something to tell me, Lady Bottrell?'

Tacitly, she accepted that she was not going to be met half-way. 'I suppose I have. James has confided in me something which he should have told you at the start.'

Wycliffe waited.

'On the night he was murdered Tony Miller called on James and, in the course of conversation, he said that he was sure that Lizzie Biddick had not gone to London or anywhere else. Tony implied that he knew what had happened to her and who was responsible. He did not want to come out into the open with what he knew but he said that he had dropped a broad hint in the right quarter.'

When Wycliffe still remained silent she went on: 'It seems obvious that he was referring to the old photograph which he must have sent to you knowing that you would trace it to Lander's collection.'

'When did Dr Bottrell tell you this?'

'This morning, at breakfast.'

'Did he suggest that you should pass it on to me?'

353

'On the contrary, he said that you were getting there without his help.'

She was looking away from him, staring at the great window, patterned with its coats of arms. The sunlight, passing through the stained glass, made patches of colour on the dusty surfaces of the table and books.

'But you thought it right to tell me.'

She turned to face him with resolute candour. 'I wanted you to feel quite sure — not to have any doubts.'

It must have been obvious to her that something more was needed and she went on: 'I don't think you understand, Mr Wycliffe, all that lies behind the relationship between my husband's family and the Landers.' Again the faint smile. 'The Bottrell emblem is apt; they are very like cats; they appear to see nothing; in fact, they miss very little. But also like cats, they rarely trouble themselves to do much about what they see — or hear. James's attitude to what he heard from Tony Miller is typical.'

'Are you suggesting that Lander has taken unfair advantage of the family?'

An ironic laugh. 'That is an understatement, Mr Wycliffe! I am not, myself, in a position to point to anything specifically illegal but I know that the brothers could have made trouble for Lander over the administration of the estate and, in particular, over the handling of the late Lady Bottrell's personal affairs. She had substantial private means and both brothers were beneficiaries under her will.'

'Why, then, did they do nothing?'

Her reply was instant and she was flushed with indignation. 'Partly because they both share in the Bottrell malaise and, in any case, Hugh is blindly loyal to his friends — an expensive attribute where the Landers are concerned.'

Perhaps she had spoken with more warmth than she had intended, at any rate she felt the need to elaborate. 'They are greedy people, Mr Wycliffe, and Simon is an unpleasant person in other ways. James, for one, has good cause to know that.'

Wycliffe was watching her, dreamy-eyed, wondering how far he was being indoctrinated. He said: 'Having gone so far, Lady Bottrell, I think you must go a little further.'

She seemed to be studying the pattern of coloured lights which had just reached her hand as it rested on the table. 'It happened a long time ago, when they were children. The three boys: Hugh, James, and Simon were up in a tree-house they had in South Wood. Simon was an ungainly boy and it seems James made some derogatory remark about him, as boys will. Simon then, quite deliberately, reached out with his foot and pushed James off the little platform on which he was sitting.'

'He was injured?'

'A fractured tibia and a dislocated knee-joint. Of course it could not be proved, but it was thought that the injury to the knee was responsible for the subsequent tubercular condition which threatened his life and ruined his youth.'

'I suppose this created ill-feeling between the two families?'

Lady Bottrell made a helpless little gesture. 'Not in the least. If it had been Hugh the story would have been different, but the then Lady Bottrell had no use for her second son and the whole incident was treated as just one of the hazards of childhood.'

'And what was — what *is* James's attitude?'

She spread her hands. 'I don't know; I have never heard him refer to it. All I know I have learned from Hugh.'

A clock somewhere in the house chimed the three-quarters, a quarter to one. Wycliffe stood up and uttered the time honoured formula: 'Thank you for giving me your time, Lady Bottrell.'

'I hope that I haven't been indiscreet.'

Wycliffe felt sure that any indiscretion had been carefully calculated.

Chapter Twelve

'This case begins to look more like a detective story.'

Kersey was spooning clotted cream over his apple strudel. 'I wouldn't know, I never read 'em.'

Wycliffe said: 'You never read anything but the crime sheets, Doug.'

They were at lunch; the dining area was crowded and there was a buzz of conversation so that, for once, they felt reasonably secure in anonymity.

Lucy Lane said: 'In what way like a detective story?'

'It's over-complicated. The story writer creates a theoretical framework for a crime and by devising alibis and false trails he turns it into a test of wits. The real-life criminal, if he's going to get away with it, keeps it simple and, if we catch him, it's as much by luck as by cunning.'

Kersey, preoccupied, said: 'No more cream, Lucy? You won't taste that!' And turning to Wycliffe: 'Is there a moral in this, sir?'

Wycliffe, who had picked up his spoon, put it down again. 'Just that we seem to be dealing with artificially contrived situations, lacking spontaneity. The approach is theoretical; one has the impression that it's all in some script.'

It was unusual for Wycliffe to do his thinking aloud and he had captured Kersey's attention.

'I'm not sure that I follow.'

Wycliffe poured himself more wine and drank a little. 'It's as though the criminal, like an author contriving his plot, set out to decide how somebody would behave in a series of hypothetical situations. Having decided, he tried to make it appear that this person did, in fact, behave in that way.'

'You are saying that much of the evidence we have could have been rigged.'

'Most of it, I think.'

'With the deliberate intention of involving somebody else.'

'Yes. I was finally convinced by the finding of the girl's clothing in Lander's earth closet. But it began — for us — with Miller's rigged suicide; the short string, intended to draw attention to the phoney nature of the suicide, perhaps to hint that the killer was liable to panic.'

Lucy Lane, frowning, asked: 'In your opinion then, is there anything in the way of direct evidence?'

Wycliffe was thoughtful. 'Yes, I think there is — the fact that Lizzie was coshed. That was something the killer was forced to do as a matter of expediency. He foresaw the necessity and provided for it, but I'm quite sure that he recognized it as a flaw in his plot. In my view, that is where we make contact with the killer instead of with his Frankenstein.'

'Does this let Lander off the hook?' From Kersey.

Wycliffe had not touched his sweet, now he pushed it aside. 'I've had growing doubts as to whether Lander would have been fool enough to incriminate himself in the wholesale fashion he seems to have done — panic or no panic. Of course it's possible that he's working a double bluff. We shall see.'

Wycliffe returned to the Incident Van shadowed, despite the appeal to the media, by a detachment of journalists. For once he was able to satisfy them with a blend of fact and platitude so that they were soon on their way back to the pub.

It was hot, and although the windows of the van were open the air inside seemed turgid and sticky. To add to his discomfort his lunch, whatever it had been, lay heavily on his stomach and, whenever he looked out of the window, he was confronted by a Bottrell cat.

It was all very well fantasizing about creative criminals but the only evidence which counted in the courts was of the sort which would have satisfied St Thomas: it must be capable of being seen and touched or, at least, photographed.

Above all he needed to keep in the forefront of his mind that the girl was the primary victim. If the case was to make any sense at all, Miller's death followed from that. So the question was: why had Lizzie Biddick been murdered? And it had seemed reasonable to assume that she had raised unruly passions in the breast of a repressed, middle-aged lawyer.

According to the housekeeper Lizzie had left her room at about nine-thirty, presumably to say good-bye to James Bottrell and to keep her regular Sunday date at the studio. But that would be a special visit — her last. She was leaving for London in the morning. The encounter, *if* it took place, must have been highly emotional — at least for Lander, and it was not impossible that frustration and passion had got the better of him and that he had attacked and killed the girl.

A credible scenario — until one tried to fill in the detail. In the first place it was odd that the girl should have been coshed before being throttled, but setting that aside — along with the nature of the cosh itself, where would such a crime have taken place? Surely in the house. But Fox, an experienced scenes-of-crime officer, had found no trace of any struggle — a fact which, though not conclusive, was highly suggestive.

Lizzie's body had been found naked in a ditch at some distance from the house and it would have made sense to carry it there in the hope of delaying discovery. But her clothing (except her shoes), bearing unmistakable signs of having been removed in the neighbourhood of the ditch, was found in a disused earth closet behind the house.

Wycliffe jabbed his ball-point into the scrap pad and pushed them both away. If Lander had killed the girl and disposed of her clothes, he must then have gone to her room, collected her more obvious baggage, and brought it back to hide in his well.

Rational behaviour? True, that killers are by no means always rational. Even so . . .

*

Wycliffe went in search of the Ninth Baron and found him in the main courtyard behind the house, washing his car. When he caught sight of Wycliffe he turned off the hose and wound it back on the reel.

There would be early photographs in the family albums showing the coach house and stables as they had been, with grooms and stable boys, perhaps an early motor car, sedate and strange on the cobbles, being polished by a chauffeur in striped apron, waistcoat, knickerbockers and leggings. Wycliffe wondered how it must feel to be the central character in a slow and tedious drama of decline.

'You wanted me?' Resigned.

'If you will spare a few minutes, sir.'

Bottrell looked pale and weary, his eyes dark, as though he had lost sleep. 'My office? Or in the house?' He glanced at his watch. 'Better be the office.'

His secretary was tapping at her pre-war machine.

'Don't put through any calls, Delia.'

When they were seated Wycliffe said: 'I suppose you remember very clearly the incident in the tree?'

A quick look of surprise. 'The tree?'

'When your twin brother was injured.'

Bottrell studied his fingers. 'So that's it! My wife has been talking.'

Wycliffe said: 'In a murder case one looks for sources of enmity.'

'A quarrel between children forty-odd years ago — do you see that as a source of enmity today? I'm afraid I don't follow your line of thought.' His lordship being haughty.

'All the same, I shall be grateful if you will tell me what you remember of the tree-house incident.'

Bottrell hesitated, but decided on co-operation as the only practicable option. He opened the bottom drawer of his desk and brought out a stack of the sort of things people keep in bottom drawers. From it he sorted out a mounted photograph which he handed to Wycliffe.

The photograph was faded and looked as though it had once been framed. In fact there was a row of framed photographs above the bookcase and this might, at one time, have been one of them.

It showed three young boys in shorts, sitting on a platform built round a sturdy-looking tree-house. One of the boys wore a horn on a cord slung about his bare shoulders, the others had bows, and each had a wooden dagger at his waistband.

They were only eight or nine years old but there was no difficulty in identifying the young Lander. He was very thin, hollow-chested, and big-boned, but even then it was his thin lips and wide gape which gave him away.

Bottrell said: 'That was in the days when little boys pretended violence instead of watching it on the box.'

'You're the one with the horn?'

'Yes.'

'Is that where it happened?'

'Yes, in the same summer that was taken. James was sitting with his legs dangling over the edge as he is in the picture. Simon was behind him. James made some jibe at him about bed-wetting — he was always good at jabbing in the needle and, next minute, he was over the edge.'

'Pushed over.'

'I suppose so.' Bottrell became irritated. 'It's all so damned silly! If James hadn't been unlucky enough to injure himself nobody would have thought another thing about it. The drop was only a few feet.'

'But his injuries are supposed to have caused the tubercular lesion which resulted in his lameness.'

Bottrell pouted. 'That has been said, but I gather that independent medical opinion wouldn't necessarily agree.'

'However, since that incident, there has been ill-will between them?'

'I suppose that is true, James and Lander have never been on good terms, but I really cannot see the relevance of this to the . . . to the tragedies which you are investigating.'

His lordship had become flushed. 'Tony and the girl — what possible connection could their brutal murders have with a childhood quarrel between James and Lander?'

'That, sir, is what I am trying to find out, but I won't take up any more of your time.'

Bottrell followed him through the secretary's office to the outer door. 'I hope you won't think that I am being obstructive . . .'

'Not at all, Lord Bottrell. If it becomes necessary to return to the subject I will make sure that you have a reasoned explanation of my interest.'

Bottrell stood watching him as he crossed the courtyard to the arched entrance.

They were in the Incident Van; Kersey was smoking one of his home-mades, the windows were wide open but Lucy's whole being seemed to be concentrated in mute protest.

Wycliffe's thoughts were elsewhere. He turned to Lucy Lane first: 'I want you to pass instructions to Fox at the studio. He is to discontinue work there, put things back as nearly as possible as he found them and bring the key to me.'

'You mean, after he's finished?'

'I mean now.'

Kersey said: 'So you've made up your mind.'

Wycliffe ignored the remark and went on: 'I want you, Doug, to arrange for a round-the-clock watch on Lander — discreet. Choose men who know how to keep their heads down.'

'Is he free to come and go where and when he likes?'

'That is what I shall tell him directly.'

'Is he to be followed if he leaves the estate?'

'No; I'm only interested in his movements on the estate. Any contacts he makes while under observation are to be reported at once.'

Kersey's rubbery features creased in a grin. 'I think I've got the message.'

*

Jean answered his ring. The girl looked at him with expression-less eyes and did not speak.

'Is there somewhere we can talk?'

Without a word she pushed open the door of the drawing-room. In a cold, distant voice she said: 'Will you sit down?'

'No, this won't take long. I want you to cast your mind back to that Sunday, nearly a fortnight ago, when you and Paul went out at night together for the first time.'

She looked at him, and waited.

'Will you tell me what you did that night?'

'The same as last Sunday, we went out in the skiff.'

'Where did you go?'

'The Upper Creek, but because the tide was high we were able to go farther up; that first night we nearly reached the village.'

'So you passed your father's studio both going and coming, knowing that he was there, and you did more or less the same thing the following week?'

'Yes.'

'You were spying on him.'

She flushed. 'Not spying on him . . . It's just that he'd made the cottage into a sort of mystery place and — '

'All right; we won't play with words, Jean. Now, when you were out there last Sunday you saw a light in an upper room; did you see anything that earlier time?'

Her expression became wooden and she said nothing.

'You think I am trying to trap you but I can promise that what you tell me is unlikely to harm your father and might help him.'

She still hesitated but, in the end, in a dull monotone, she said: 'There was a light in the downstairs room when we went up.'

'And when you came back?'

'I hope you were telling the truth when you said it couldn't harm him.'

It was not what he had said but he let it pass. 'Well?'

'When we came back father was standing in the doorway of the cottage and he seemed to be staring out across the creek.'

'He didn't see you?'

'Because of the light from the doorway we saw him before he could see us. I told Paul to stop rowing and we waited until he went in.'

'How long?'

'About ten minutes.'

'Have you any idea of the time when this happened?'

'It was a quarter past one.'

'How do you know?'

'I happened to look at my watch while we were waiting.'

'Good!' And he meant it. The housekeeper claimed to have heard someone in Lizzie's room at five past one. It was a slender thread but it was enough. He said: 'I think you have helped your father. Now, perhaps you will tell him that I would like to see him.'

A moment or two later Lander came into the room. Wycliffe was shocked to see the change in him in so short a time; he seemed to have shrunk — a cliché, but somehow descriptive of a certain aspect of the effect of shock and despair. He was unshaven and his face was grey.

No greeting, he simply said: 'Do you want me to come with you?'

'No, I would like a talk.'

A look of mild surprise. 'I expected you, or somebody, earlier. I suppose this is all part of the technique. Anyhow you'd better come to my room.'

He led the way to a room at the end of a long passage. It was dominated by a Victorian bookcase and a massive table with an inset leather top. The table was littered with little heaps of pocket files secured by tape.

Lander pointed to an upright armchair and sat himself at the table where his spectacles rested on an open file. He sat motionless, waiting, as though he had surrendered all initiative.

Wycliffe took a key from his pocket and handed it across the table. 'We have finished at the studio. I hope that there has been no unnecessary disturbance. You are free to return there whenever you wish.'

Lander held the key in the palm of his hand for a moment, staring at it, then slipped it into his pocket.

Wycliffe waited for him to speak, but he did not. After a pause, Wycliffe said: 'As things are I think there is nothing to be gained from further questions or from interference with your movements or your property.'

Lander was turning over the papers in his file, apparently unaware of what he was doing. 'So you've decided that I didn't . . .' He paused, and seemed to choke over his words, 'that I didn't kill her.'

'As I interpret the evidence there is no case against you. I'm sorry that you have been subjected to all the strain and inconvenience but you brought it on yourself.'

Lander shook his head in a helpless gesture. 'What does it matter? . . . She's gone; Miller killed her. He was a pervert. Then he killed himself . . . There's no point in talking.'

Wycliffe said: 'Doesn't it seem to you strange that such an effort was made to incriminate you?'

'No, it does not. Miller knew that I was doing my utmost to get him off the estate.'

'Why the antagonism?'

A flash of anger. 'Because, as I've said, he was a pervert and he had corrupted Lord Bottrell.'

'That was how you saw it.'

'That is how it was!' There was a pause before Lander asked in a curiously humble voice: 'You will be leaving me alone now?'

It was a plain question, asked without obvious rancour, and Wycliffe, though doubtful of what was implied, said: 'Yes.'

He stood up, but the lawyer did not move. 'I'll see myself out.'

As he left the house Wycliffe asked himself why he had not mentioned Lizzie's pregnancy and the only answer he could find disturbed him, because it was unprofessional.

Chapter Thirteen

When Wycliffe awoke he was aware of a change; the light was grey, no sunlight filtered through the flowered curtains, and the air felt different — still warm, but humid. When he parted the curtains it was to see the whole sky a canopy of cloud, leaden grey with a faintly coppery hue.

It was exactly a week since he and Helen had returned from the Dordogne.

Downstairs, at the alcove table, Kersey said: 'Weather's on the change.' If there had been a barometer Kersey would have tapped it. The young couple had switched on the television and the medicine man from the Met was expounding the threatening nature of his animated maps: 'Thunderstorms over France and the channel are expected to move northwards during the day and there will be outbreaks of heavy rain accompanied by thunder in much of south-west Britain . . .'

As usual, the landlord, in singlet and trousers, stood in the doorway smoking a cigarette, while the cat, on the step at his side, attended to her toilet. But the atmosphere had changed; now the stillness seemed charged and menacing. Wycliffe wondered if it was really the weather or his inner trepidation. He was worried. Satisfied that he had arrived at some understanding of the case, he knew that he had no evidence on which to proceed. He could wait for something more to happen and pray that it wouldn't be another tragedy. (He thought that he had taken reasonable precautions.) Or he could precipitate a crisis and risk finding himself in free fall without a parachute.

In company with Kersey he was at the Incident Van shortly

after eight-thirty. The overnight surveillance report on Lander was unexciting. Just before dark the lawyer had left the house and made for his studio; there he had opened the shutters of the studio room. For an hour, he could be seen at his desk, writing; then he had pulled down the blind, but the light had remained on all night.

Wycliffe asked Dixon, the duty officer: 'Nothing since?'

'Nothing, sir.'

Almost as they spoke the radio came alive: '105 to Zero Oscar . . .' There was urgency in the voice.

'Go ahead.'

'I couldn't make contact; I must have been in a dead spot. Lander's got visitors. Within the past couple of minutes Lord Bottrell and his brother James arrived and went inside.'

Wycliffe reached for the head-set. 'Wycliffe here. Go in after them. Any pretext, but don't be put off. I'll be right down.' He turned to Dixon: 'Who is it down there?'

'PC Watts, sir, a young chap from the local nick. Supposed to be one of the new whizz kids — just passing through.'

'You come with me.' To Kersey.

The tide was at flood, the highest he had yet seen it; the creek was a broad silvery sheet under a lowering sky; almost every scrap of colour had disappeared from the landscape. As they reached the little building on the strand Wycliffe felt two large, warm raindrops on his forehead and thought he heard a grumbling of thunder in the distance.

The door was open and they found the Bottrell brothers in the darkroom. PC Watts, in a track suit, was standing in the doorway of the studio.

'Mr Lander is dead, sir. These two gentlemen found him. I asked them to stay in this room until you arrived.'

Lord Bottrell was about to speak but Wycliffe stopped him. 'Just one moment . . .'

Wycliffe and Kersey went through into the studio, followed by the young policeman. The shutters were folded back but the blind was no longer down although the electric light was still on.

Lander was lying on the floor as though he had slipped out of his chair; his body was rigid, and his head twisted to one side. There was foam about his lips and the jaws appeared to be tightly clenched; his eyes were open and staring. His skin, which had been strikingly pale, now had a pinkish hue. On the floor near the body were two or three gelatine capsules of the sort used for the oral administration of unpalatable drugs.

In a low voice Wycliffe spoke to Watts. 'Where were they when you joined them?'

'In here, sir. Dr Bottrell was on his knees by the body; I fancy he was sniffing at the dead man's lips.'

'Did they offer any explanation of how they came to be here?'

'Lord Bottrell said that Mrs Lander had telephoned him, worried that her husband hadn't come home to breakfast, and because she got no answer when she telephoned here. It seems she never comes near the studio herself.' Watts added: 'I gather the lady is inclined to over-react.'

Kersey snapped: 'Well it looks as though she had something to react about. This blind was still down when you relieved the night man; who raised it?'

'One of the brothers, sir, before I got here.'

'How long did they have in here before you eventually got round to joining them?' Kersey disliked young coppers who fancied their chances in the fast lane.

Watts was as curt as he dared. 'The time it took me to make radio contact and receive instructions. Probably a little over two minutes.'

Wycliffe said to Kersey: 'You'd better get hold of the local GP — Prentiss, isn't it?'

Watts volunteered: 'Dr Bottrell phoned him, sir. It seemed the right thing to do so I didn't interfere.'

'All right; ask Dr Bottrell to come in.'

Bottrell came in, loose and large, his Viyella shirt open down the front, his trousers sagging from the belt. 'Hugh and I were having breakfast when Beth Lander phoned. One of her panics. Hugh said he would look in at the studio so I walked down with him. I suppose your constable told you that I've telephoned Prentiss. He was out on his rounds but they're contacting him.'

Lord Bottrell appeared in the doorway, harassed and diffident: 'Mrs Lander will be expecting to hear from me . . . I think I should telephone my wife and ask her to break the news . . .'

Wycliffe said: 'There's no reason why you shouldn't do it in person, if you wish, Lord Bottrell. There will be time enough for your statement later.'

When his lordship had gone Wycliffe turned to the brother. 'Poison, is that how you see it?'

James shrugged. 'What else? Probably cyanide. I caught a whiff when I bent over him just now. You know he dabbled in archaic photographic techniques in that witches' kitchen next door. Didn't they use cyanide of potassium or sodium as a reducing agent or something? Anyway, Prentiss will be here directly, do you want me to stay?'

Wycliffe, anxious for room to manoeuvre, said: 'No, I shall be asking you for a statement later and any professional observations you feel inclined to make can wait until then.'

Dr Bottrell limped away and Kersey watched him go as a cat watches an escaping bird. 'I don't like that bastard! I'm not suggesting that he killed Lander — suicide sticks out a mile — but there's something about that man . . .'

Wycliffe was gazing out of the window. Blue-black clouds lowered over the creek; the light was pale and limpid, but the little houses opposite stood out seeming strangely near. Raindrops trickled down the window panes as though the great sponge of cloud was being gently squeezed, but the threatened storm had not yet broken. In the studio the yellow light from the electric lamp struggled against the light of day.

The rain finally arrived as James Bottrell reached his own door. It was prefaced by a dramatic blue lightning flash, a searing sound as of material being ripped across, and a great thunderclap which echoed and rumbled through the shuddering air.

Instantly rain bounced off the cobbles forming spray which rose like a mist into the air; gutters were soon choked and water cascaded from the roofs so that within minutes the whole yard was awash. Another brilliant flash, a simultaneous thunder-clap, and the rain seemed to hesitate as the storm drew breath, only to resume seconds later with renewed ferocity.

Bottrell stood just inside his door, leaving it open. Anarchic nature suited his mood. He was excited, tense with anticipation. When he finally closed the door, the high, church-like room seemed to be in almost total darkness. Not troubling with the main lights, he crossed to the table and switched on a desk-lamp at the place where he usually worked. There, in the little island of light, before sitting down, he drew from his hip pocket an envelope, sealed, and inscribed: 'To Jean'. Sitting at the table, he slit it open and removed from it several sheets of thin paper which he unfolded and spread out to read.

The letter began: 'My dear Jean, I feel that it is to you that I owe an explanation of what has happened and of what I am about to do . . .'

The lawyer's handwriting, starting off bold and clear, degenerated almost to illegibility but James persevered to the end. It really was amusing, but what impressed him was the extent to which he seemed to be in the hands of a benevolent fate. By chance he had gone down with his brother in response to Beth Lander's appeal. By chance Hugh, with his usual timidity, had hung back, leaving him to investigate the premises alone and to find, not only Lander's body, but also this bizarre valediction. He had taken it thinking that Lander might have entertained some suspicion of him, or at least that his name would be mentioned . . .

He need not have troubled himself. He was being altogether too wary; he should trust in his karma.

He reached for a hard-covered manuscript book labelled in bold lettering on the front: *Case Book VI*.

There were similar books on a shelf among the box files but these were his notes on cases he had handled professionally. *Case Book VI* was special; it concerned himself. He opened the book;

369

most of the pages were blank but the earlier ones were covered in his surprisingly small and neat script. He selected a passage and read with total absorption, as though from some fascinating work of another hand:

'I wish that I could put on record my precise state of mind at the moment when I decided to kill her, and recount the processes of thought which led me to that decision. I cannot. There was no such moment and, as far as I am aware, there was no decision. I only know that the deed became compelling and inevitable.

'I do recall with remarkable clarity and vividness that night, a week earlier, when she told me that she was pregnant, but I cannot say whether or not that incident played any part in determining the course of events. I doubt it; I doubt it very much.

'It was a banal occasion. "You know that I am pregnant by you and that I am going away. I think you should give me some money." No threats. Indeed, she could have done nothing beyond complicating my life for a little while. She stood there — a peasant girl, with a certain prettiness that was already a little over-ripe. There was a dogged look in her brown eyes; her obstinate little mouth was daubed with lipstick, and tight trousers accentuated her thick thighs . . . Flesh without mind.

'I found her repulsive and could not believe that I had ever sought pleasure in her body. However, I told her that when she was settled in London I would regularly pay money into her account and, with this, she was not only satisfied, but cloying in her gratitude.

'As I have said, I do not think the incident changed anything. On the night before she was due to leave I waited for her at the creek-side where she would pass on her way to Lander's studio . . .'

Bottrell raised his eyes from the book to dwell on the images which these words had conjured out of the past and it was through his unaided memory that he now followed in exquisite detail the further events of that night to their climax.

Dr Prentiss arrived shortly after the storm had broken, his blond hair darkened and flattened by rain. He placed his bag on Lander's

370

desk and removed his waterproof which dripped to the floor. 'They caught me on my rounds.' The young man looked harassed, as well he might. 'Are you treating this as suicide?'

'Until we find evidence to the contrary.'

'But Dr Franks will be in on it?'

'In all the circumstances.'

Rain lashed against the window. At short intervals lightning forked over the creek in jagged streaks, followed instantly by the thunder-clap and great earth-shaking rumbles . . .

Prentiss stood for a while, staring down at the body, then he dropped to his knees and went through the limited routine permitted to him: sniffing, palpating the exposed flesh, and testing the flexure of the limbs. When he was once more on his feet, he said: 'Obviously a respiratory poison; I suppose it could be cyanide.' He stooped to examine the capsules on the floor then picked one up and held it in the palm of his hand.

The capsule was half red and half black with the word 'Penbritin' neatly printed in white letters on the black half.

Wycliffe asked: 'Can you tell me anything about them?'

'Penbritin is a trade name for a synthetic penicillin used to treat Gram negative bacterial infections — anything from 'flu to meningitis.'

Kersey demanded: 'Prescribed by you?'

Kersey received a cold stare. Prentiss was finding his dignity. 'No, I have never treated Mr Lander although he is on my list. It's possible that he got them from my predecessor. I shall check the records.'

He turned back to Wycliffe but had to wait before he could make himself heard against the rain and the reverberations of thunder. Then: 'More to the point now, these capsules separate very easily into two halves and can be put together again.'

Wycliffe said: 'You are saying that substitution of the contents would be easy.'

'Very.'

Kersey tried again: 'So you think he was murdered.'

'Do I? Perhaps you will explain.' Acid.

371

'Why would he go through all that rigmarole to poison himself?'

'I can think of one reason: I'm told that cyanide is decidedly unpalatable as well as distressing in its effects, but Lander could have swallowed any number of these before the first began to release its contents in the stomach making him wish he'd thought of something else.'

Wycliffe was brooding. 'Assuming that it was cyanide I suppose death would follow quickly upon ingestion.'

Prentiss ran a hand through his wet hair. 'I'm no toxicologist. All I can say is that the active agent is hydrocyanic acid and the effectiveness of any of the cyanide salts depends on the rate at which the acid is released in the stomach.'

'But minutes rather than hours.'

Prentiss put on his waterproof and picked up his bag. 'Probably. Now, if that is all I'll get back on my rounds. I'll let you have my report.'

Wycliffe thanked him. When the doctor had gone, Kersey grinned. 'That young man is learning! He must also be keen, to go to his patients in this.'

At that moment a double fork over the creek was followed by the loudest crack yet; the light flickered but recovered.

When they could once more hear themselves speak Kersey said: 'Don't you think it's odd that Lander didn't leave a kiss-me-good-bye note — even a confession?'

'Perhaps he posted it to the coroner.' Wycliffe was preoccupied, dismissive. 'But speaking of the coroner, it's time we notified him. Then get Fox down here — No, not Fox — get somebody from division; I shall want Fox. I've no doubt this is suicide but we have to have confirmation. So, formal statements from all concerned; these capsules must go for analysis; we need to know the source and exact nature of the poison . . . But delegate all this; I want you back at the van as soon as possible.'

Kersey was looking at him with a puzzled frown. 'Did you think that Lander might kill himself?'

'The short answer to that is, no. If I had . . .'

372

'Then you must have thought he was at risk from someone else, or that he was dangerous on the loose.'

Wycliffe was curt. 'I thought that he might be at risk, and I took precautions.'

Kersey persisted: 'Isn't the most likely explanation of his death that he killed himself because he was guilty, knew that we could get him, and couldn't face it?'

Wycliffe made an obvious effort: 'Think of it from his point of view, Doug; he's lost the only woman with whom he seemed able to establish an emotional relationship and he's faced with an inquest which is sure to bring out details of the affair for public gossip. He's lost both ways. And that's ignoring complications within his family. For anybody, a daunting prospect, but for a small-town, middle-aged lawyer . . .'

Kersey said: 'You speak of an inquest, not about proceedings in the criminal court.'

'Lander believed that Miller killed the girl, so with Miller dead there could be no criminal charge.'

Kersey looked at Wycliffe with an odd expression in which serious doubt mingled with an indulgent affection: 'And how do you see it, sir? Is there going to be a criminal charge at the end of this lot?'

Wycliffe looked at him, a deeply worried man. 'My God, I hope so!'

For a long time James sat, staring into space and when he eventually moved he was like a man emerging from the deepest sleep. He looked about him, at first with a certain wonder, then with increasing awareness as though taking aboard the trappings of his daily life and resuming contact.

The storm centre had moved away, an occasional lightning flash dispelled the gloom and thunder rumbled in the distance, but the rain continued unabated, battering on the roof which, like the roof of a church, was open to the rafters. He was still seated, irresolute, when someone banged on the door and kept up a steady pounding. He closed his book, got up from his chair and walked to the door. Before opening it he took time to compose his features and to recover his customary manner and poise.

It was Jean Lander, soaked to the skin and deeply distressed.

She walked past him into the room without a word and went to stand by the table, her back towards him. Her shoulder-length red hair hung like rats' tails, T-shirt and jeans clung dripping to her body, her sandals oozed and squelched.

She said: 'I walked out on mother; I couldn't stand it. I mean, with what had happened to father she couldn't say a good word about him. You would think he did it just to . . . to inconvenience her!' She spat out the words.

He was still so tense that he could scarcely speak but he achieved a banal question: 'You walked out in this weather?'

'It wasn't raining then; I got caught in South Wood.' She added, her eyes wide: 'I can't go back — not yet!'

He was growing calmer and thinking fast. 'You'd better change into something so that we can dry your things. In the wardrobe, in that room at the top of the stairs, you'll find a woman's dressing gown — you can wear that. And the slippers might fit . . . There are towels in the cupboard under the wash-basin. Is there anybody with your mother?'

'Uncle Hugh and Aunt Cynthia.'

He was pleased with himself; she seemed to have noticed nothing.

He watched her climb the spiral staircase, a dejected figure. He found a portable electric fire, plugged it in, and arranged a chair on which to hang her clothes.

A few minutes later she came down wearing Cynthia's blue dressing gown, and slippers. She had dried her hair and now her pale face was framed in a rufous halo. She carried her wet clothing which she gave him when he held out his hand. 'I tried to wring them out.'

He draped the chair with her jeans, her T-shirt and her briefs — all there was apart from her sandals which he placed near the fire.

374

'Thanks, James.' She sounded tired to the brink of exhaustion.

He noted with satisfaction that she called him by his first name, while Hugh and Cynthia were courtesy 'Uncle' and 'Aunt'.

'Get yourself warm; you mustn't catch a chill.' He placed another chair near the fire.

He was being solicitous and, as always when he did not understand the sources of his own behaviour, he was troubled. The girl did not interest him; even sexually he was not attracted; her occasional visits were no more than an entertaining diversion and, at the moment, she was intruding on his privacy.

Yet he could not take his eyes off her.

She sat, her red hair hanging free and covering her face; her legs were crossed at the knees under the skirt of the dressing gown, and she was bending over, massaging a bare foot.

It was as he continued to watch her that an idea came to him, an idea so intriguing yet so simple that he could scarcely contain his excitement.

He said, softly: 'Jean!'

She turned to face him.

'There is something I ought to give you. You know that it was I who found your father?'

'Yes.'

'On his desk there was a letter.'

'A letter? Uncle Hugh said that he had left nothing . . .'

'Hugh didn't see it; I was alone in the room. There was no envelope but I could see that it was for you and of such a personal nature that you wouldn't want the police or any stranger to read what he had written.'

She was incredulous. 'You mean he wrote to me?'

He crossed to the table and she followed him, he handed her the pages of her father's letter and she looked from them to him, uncertain.

'I should read it now; perhaps it will tell you something you want to know.'

He placed a chair for her but she remained standing, the letter in her hand.

His eyes never left her face as she read; he saw her expression change from incredulity to wonder, and from wonder to pain. He saw cheeks become flushed and tears form between her lashes.

Her neck was slender and long, and lightly freckled; she wore a silver filigree pendant set with a blue stone. He knew now why, and for what he had waited. This time he would not be staring into bland unconsciousness, he would watch the fleeting expressions of those features and those eyes as astonishment was succeeded by fear and fear by terror; terror which would become petrified in death.

There would be tremendous risk. But had he not shown that he could cope with any situation? He had been too timid, and timidity now would cost him precious and unimagined sensations.

The moment would come when she finished reading the letter and turned to him for support, sympathy, or whatever else her tedious little mind found necessary to restore its equilibrium.

Chapter Fourteen

Wycliffe's departure from the cottage was undignified as well as uncomfortable. He climbed the now slippery path to Lander's drive wearing a plastic bag over his head but he was rescued at the top by a crime car, stationed there to pick him up. Back in his cubicle, he drank strong coffee, troubled by disturbing thoughts and a sense of guilt. He could not rid himself of the memory of Lander in that last interview or of the pathos in the lawyer's question: 'You will be leaving me alone now?'

Next door, Lucy Lane drank her coffee while vetting and filing reports. In reception, Potter, mortally scared of thunderstorms, let his grow cold, and he would have fingered a rabbit's foot, had he possessed one.

The roof of the van resounded to the rain like a drum and the whole area around the Duloe entrance was a sea of thin mud. Wycliffe telephoned sub-division and spoke to DI Reed — Tom Reed — who had been in at the start. Wycliffe brought him up to date against a background of thunder-claps and crackles on the line which threatened the connection.

'Now I want you to get me a search warrant, Tom. I'll send a DC along and he'll give you the specifics. He's to bring it back here and I'll leave word what's to be done with it.'

Wycliffe was worried, well aware that he was banking heavily on his reading of a man's mind — and on bluff. The thunderstorm was moving away but the rain continued unabated for a while, then stopped as abruptly as it had begun. He was waiting for Kersey, but decided to wait no longer. He called Lucy Lane and they set off together, leaving word for Kersey to follow.

They went in a crime car, with Lucy driving; they passed between the granite pillars with their newly bathed cats and along the drive. Leaves, twigs, and even small branches had been battered from the trees, a legacy of the storm, but there was also a freshness in the air, sharp and exhilarating. They made for the back of the house and passed under the stone arch into the main yard. The place was deserted. Great puddles, amounting to pools, covered much of the yard. Lucy negotiated the narrow, angled entrance to the stable yard and pulled up outside the varnished door.

As on another occasion the door was not quite closed but this time, without knocking, Wycliffe pushed it wide. The sight which met his eyes would always remain in his memory. In the gloom, two figures, a man and a young girl, stood close. The girl, her red hair swept back, wore a blue dressing gown and in one hand she held a little sheaf of crumpled papers. The man stood over her, his arms raised as though arrested in some action or gesture. The light from the high window fell full on their faces. Bottrell's expression was concentrated — intense; while Jean, her cheeks blotched and tear-stained, looked up at him in astonishment and dawning terror.

There was a stillness in the scene, as in a photograph, but there was also menace.

Wycliffe was half-way towards the couple when Bottrell turned his head to look at him, uncomprehending. The man was abnormally pale, his eyes were vacant, and there was an interval before blankness gave place to unease. He was the first to speak: 'Jean was caught in the storm and she came here.' He sounded hoarse.

The girl, still clutching her papers, seemed paralysed. Lucy Lane went to her and murmured something.

Wycliffe, too, was striving to re-orientate himself; he felt like an actor who, having mastered his part, finds himself in the wrong play. He felt strangely short of breath and his words, when they came, seemed absurdly inadequate: 'Does Mrs Lander know that Jean is here?'

There was a perceptible pause before Bottrell answered, 'No.'

But Wycliffe spoke to the girl with great gentleness: 'Jean, will you let Miss Lane take you home? There's a car outside and you can take your wet clothes with you.'

She looked at him as though she too were making a slow return from some other realm of consciousness, then she nodded.

Lucy collected the clothing and followed the girl out. The letter went with her but Wycliffe could leave that to Lucy.

Bottrell watched and listened, but said nothing.

Wycliffe turned on him. 'Sit down!' It was an order.

Without a word, Bottrell went to his usual chair where a desk-lamp made a pool of yellow light on the table. In front of him was a hard-covered manuscript book labelled: *Case Book VI.*

Wycliffe sat in the chair opposite, across the table.

Bottrell, still vague and uncoordinated, muttered: 'I need a drink.' He got up and went to a small cupboard below the shelves of box files; he fumbled for a moment or two then returned with a gin bottle and a glass. He poured himself three fingers, drank it off in a couple of gulps, then poured the same again.

For Wycliffe it was a much needed respite.

In a very short time colour had returned to Bottrell's cheeks, his facial muscles seemed to recover their tone, his eyes were once more focused. With an expansive gesture he said: 'Shall I get you a glass?'

Wycliffe shook his head and Bottrell held up the bottle: 'Holland's gin! All down to a seventeenth century medico at Leyden — concocted from juniper berries as a medicine!'

In his anxiety to appear normal he was overdoing the act. He drank a little more gin, wiped his lips, and put his glass down.

'So it's over! . . . Not a very satisfactory case from your point of view, I suppose. The good news is that Lander has saved you a hell of a lot of paper work.'

As he sought for and almost found his usual wavelength Bottrell settled more comfortably in his chair. 'Incidentally I have to admit to an indiscretion. Lander left a sentimental letter addressed to Jean, and I pocketed it . . . Decided to give it to the girl myself instead of having your minions make a meal of it . . . You came in the middle of her reading the thing and now it's gone with her . . . No harm done.'

Wycliffe sat still, his gaze expressionless.

Bottrell looked at him, expectant, perhaps troubled by his total lack of response. He paused, long enough to light a cigarette. 'You see, Wycliffe, Lander was emotionally retarded . . . He'd never discovered what it was all about and how to handle it at the proper age, and so we have this romantic schoolboy act from a man of fifty. As to Lizzie . . . Lizzie was fluttering around, picking up this and that — a magpie for experience. She wasn't particularly interested in sex but like most women she delighted in contriving situations which made her the centre of attention. But Lizzie had no notion of a settled relationship, legitimate or otherwise . . .'

Bottrell waved his cigarette in a dismissive gesture. 'Of course, to a normal man, Lizzie was no more than an amusing diversion, but to Lander she was a match to the blue touch-paper — '

With total irrelevance Wycliffe cut across this chatter, which he had scarcely heard, and crystallized the only thoughts in his mind: 'Jean Lander was within moments of her death! You would have killed her!' In his agonizing attempt to confront the monstrous possibility that he might have arrived too late he could only repeat the accusation: 'You would have killed her, you bastard!'

The afternoon was clear and cool; great billowy white clouds floated in a blue sky — English weather — a staple product before the Met people discovered computers and invented global warming. Once more Wycliffe made for the stable yard and the varnished door.

The interior was transformed by lights, pendant from the roof beams; they must have been there all along but were now switched on. The effect was demeaning, exposing a dusty shabbiness and chasing mystery away. Fox and Collis were there. An area of the big table had been cleared and on it was a

380

collection of polythene bags, duly tagged. Wycliffe, feeling detached — remote — said: 'They are not our bags.'

'No, sir. This is just how I found the stuff, in a cupboard next to the one where he keeps his gin. You might say, they're exhibits from his private black museum. These things are all directly connected with the two killings.'

Wycliffe picked up the first of the bags to catch his eye: 'C.B. VI.1. E.B. Rubber truncheon (See also C.B. IV.14) now, with adherent hair.' Through the polythene, Wycliffe caught the gleam of a long, black hair adhering to the roughened surface of the rubber.

Fox said: 'The code refers to his case books and E.B. must be Elizabeth — Lizzie — Biddick, sir.'

'Thank you, Fox.'

A small bag, appropriately labelled, held Lizzie's pendant and chain; a large one, had its contents listed as: 'Miller's diary and selected letters.' A third, small but gruesome, held a hand-kerchief, heavily stained with what purported to be Miller's blood . . . Lizzie's sandals were in yet another bag — the missing items from her clothing found in the earth closet.

Fox, slipping for once into the vernacular, said: 'We've got a nutter, sir!'

Wycliffe picked up Bottrell's case book and turned the pages. It would prove a rich diet for the contending lawyers and their consultant psychologists and psychiatrists. Bottrell would be squabbled over by a flock of his professional peers and if ever the case came to court he would be the star of a drama in which Lizzie Biddick and Tony Miller — like Hamlet's father, would have only bit parts.

'Do you think we do a worthwhile job, Fox?'

'I try not to think about it, sir.'

'I look forward to the time when I shall have the leisure to analyse my motives in choosing Lander as the scapegoat.'

Bottrell sat back in his hard chair, blew a smoke ring and watched it rise. 'Of course he was the obvious choice — the man was making a fool of himself with the Biddick girl and if anything happened to her he was sure of top billing in the list of suspects.

'What you don't know is that I *contrived* that relationship — I put her up to it . . . Oddly enough, the stupid girl went soft on him but it was I who set it up. So, I ask myself, did I have it in my mind even then that I might one day kill her? You will see from my case book that I can't decide at what stage that act became inevitable. Was it before or after she confronted me with the news of her pregnancy? Was it, perhaps, long before that — when I first met her?'

The scene was an interview room at sub-division where any fly on the wall was living through a unique experience; certainly neither Wycliffe nor the middle-aged copper standing by the door, had ever known anything like it. Almost from the moment of Wycliffe's dramatic accusation Bottrell had seemed to accept, even to anticipate his fate; now in the dreary little interview room it was as though he relished the prospect before him.

'You'll find more than enough to put me away.'

He had refused a solicitor and declined to answer questions, but volunteered to 'discuss his case'. This was officially interpreted as agreeing to make a statement and that statement was now being recorded on tape.

He leaned forward to engage Wycliffe's attention more closely: 'You see, Wycliffe, the apparently rational processes of the conscious mind are often no more than surface manifestations of turmoil, deep in the unconscious. I wonder sometimes whether Lander was my target from the first, and the girl only a means to an end.'

He was frowning, speaking with great earnestness. 'But if that is so, how far did it arise from that episode, forty-odd years ago, when Lander pushed me out of a tree for saying he peed in his sleep?'

Suddenly Bottrell's features and his whole body relaxed; he grinned broadly: 'Absurd, isn't it? But no more so than most of our efforts to masquerade as rational beings.'

Once more Wycliffe was a captive audience, listening to the narcissistic outpourings of a disordered mind.

'I got a kick out of fixing Lander — calculating the extent to which his essential stupidity would off-set his cunning if ever he decided to kill. And then I contrived the thing as it seemed to me he would have tackled it — with that fatal blend of bravado and panic. My problem was that he was no killer — he lacked the moral courage — he was hard, but brittle — no fibre. It was an unconscious recognition of that fact which produced in you, Wycliffe, a gut reaction against his guilt.'

The window was high, but the sound of constant traffic on the roundabout outside, with the occasional squeal of brakes or screech of tyres, furnished a background for all that was said and done in the little room.

'Did you expect that Lander would kill himself?'

Bottrell blew out a cloud of grey smoke. 'It was on the cards but I didn't count on it.'

An hour later they were still there; a break had been called for refreshments and when they resumed, Bottrell took a cigarette from the pack on the table and lit it.

'This interview resumes at 12.28 hours.'

Bottrell said: 'Killing Miller was a simple necessity. He mentioned, quite casually, that the girl had told him she was pregnant by me. It meant nothing much to him then but it would have meant a great deal when her body was found and he realized that she had been murdered.

'It happened that I had borrowed his gun before he went on holiday so, on the Sunday night, I returned it, and rigged my little charade for your people — short string and all. It seemed to me the sort of stupidity which would have marred any attempt by Lander to lay a false trail.'

Bottrell tapped ash from his cigarette into the tin lid provided. For a moment or two his grey-green eyes were unfocused and he seemed lost in thought. It was quiet now, the traffic outside had dwindled to an occasional car as evening settled over the town.

'Then there was the photograph — the famous Nadar print.'

Bottrell smiled. 'Lizzie gave it me — she was always giving me things, trying to buy attention. It occurred to me that by amending it and sending it to you I could ensure that Lander was put squarely in the frame . . . And it worked, didn't it?'

Another silence, and Bottrell yawned, throwing back his arms. 'God, I'm tired! In any case I think I've said all I want to say except that you and I will be plagued by psychiatrists and psychologists. They will fight first over whether or not I am fit to stand trial and there will be some nice fat fees for the taking . . . I only hope that Meyrick — a former colleague — is in on the act; it would make it all worth while to lead the old windbag up the garden.'

Sunday morning; the church bells were ringing, the sky was clear blue but there was just a touch of autumn in the air. Now the investigation would wind down but, in offices far from the valley of the Fal, discussions would soon begin concerning a possible case: R. v Bottrell. A decision would have to be made — whether or not Bottrell was fit to plead. Those involved would know nothing of Duloe or Treave, and nothing of the people who lived and died there — except what they found in the files. As for Wycliffe, although his investigation was all but over, many months would go by before he heard the official last of the case.

He found Kersey in the Incident Van smoking a real cigarette and reading a transcript of the Bottrell interview. Kersey pushed the papers away, uncommonly subdued: 'It seems to me that we deal with two kinds of real criminal — the merely wicked, and the truly evil; those with some sense of guilt and those with none; they either have a conscience, or they don't.'

Wycliffe was standing, looking out of the window. 'Your terminology is old-fashioned, Doug; Bottrell diagnosed his own case as "arrested development of the super-ego as a consequence of parental indifference".'

Kersey said: 'I call that passing the buck.'

'So do I, but what of the sins of the fathers — and mothers?' Wycliffe was looking up at one of the gateposts for perhaps the last time. 'Anyway, I hope those bloody cats have nightmares!'

WYCLIFFE
AND THE LAST RITES

Chapter One

Wednesday

He came in from the bathroom, still naked, and reached for his briefs. Katherine, sitting up in bed, watched him dress. Geach was a big man – not tall, but powerfully built, rough hewn; his body surfaces seemed to consist of intersecting planes rather than curves. The tangle of hair on his chest was turning grey but his head was thatched with dark, tight little curls. He put on his shirt, socks and trousers and came to bend over her.

'All right?'

'I expect I'll live.'

He kissed her on the lips, then on her breasts. His features, like the rest of him, were on a generous scale; the skin of his face, free from any blemish, was coarse, lightly pitted like the skin of an orange. He was smiling, a little smile of self-content.

He went to the door, paused, and looked back. 'See you later!'

'I'll be down.'

'Don't bother; have a lie-in. Elsa will look after me.'

It was as though he had patted her on the head and said, 'You've done your bit.'

She remained in bed, motionless, staring at nothing. After sex with Abe she seemed to exist only by proxy, a reflection in a mirror. She was nothing, she felt nothing, she had nothing – not even a body that was hers.

Of course this was nonsense! Abe was no monster, and she was better off than most; she had a daughter; she had a home – an old house which she loved; a car for her own use . . . money, which she could spend without question . . . True, these things were contingent upon her being and remaining Mrs Abe Geach, but hadn't she settled for that?

'You don't know when you're well off!' Others would have told her, but there was no need. She told herself. But that was logic and she had never found much consolation in logic.

From the bed she could see herself in the mirror of the dressing table: one of Abe's contrived titillations. I am thirty-nine. Do I look it? Her hair was dark and lustrous; no sign of grey yet. Later she would go through that iron-grey phase which is supposed to make men look distinguished but delivers women to the sorcery of hairdressers. Well, she would have none of that. If it turned out that there was life after the menopause she had no intention of making herself ridiculous, fighting a rearguard action.

The pallor of her skin was accentuated by her dark hair and eyes. Johnny Glynn had said once, 'Your eyes are like minefields, Kathy – still, yet menacing.' Vintage Johnny Glynn, master of the slick phrase and the slicker lay. God! I mustn't start thinking of all that.

Watching herself in the mirror she ran her hands slowly through her hair, lifting its weight from her head and letting it slip back through her fingers.

Her twin sister, Jessica, had gone about things differently . . . She wondered about Jessica. Was she happier? Silly question. Was she content rather than resigned? Against all the odds it might be so. Two women, a man, and a teenage boy, trying to scrape a living out of a few acres with little real know-how between them.

In a sudden burst of restlessness Katherine got out of bed and drew back the curtains. There it was, the scene that had become part of her: the lawn and the shrubbery, then the low, crumbling bank, a stretch of muddy shingle, and the creek. There were primroses in the hedge which separated them from the church-yard. Across the creek the little boatyard, with its shed and thicket of masts, stood out against the rising ground of Trennick Wood. The rusty iron roof of the old shed glowed red and orange in the sunlight. It was half-tide and gulls padded about the muddy margins. Perhaps it was the house she had married.

She put on her dressing gown and slippers, spent a few minutes in the bathroom, then went downstairs to the kitchen. They always breakfasted in the big, old-fashioned kitchen. Abe was finishing his second egg and there was a yellow smear on his chin. He had eaten two soft-boiled eggs for breakfast every morning since the age of thirteen, when his mother decided that male adolescents required special nourishment. Now, at forty-one, regardless of hazards from cholesterol and listeria, he clung to his eggs as an addict to his regular shot.

The wall clock showed ten minutes to eight. Kathy said, 'Julie not down yet? She'll be late for school.'

Abe looked at her in mild reproach. 'It's Wednesday; from today she's off school for the Easter holidays. You did know, Kath.'

Black mark. She should have remembered.

Elsa came in from the yard. 'Oh, you're down, Kathy. There's plenty of coffee in the pot.'

Elsa's position in the family was ambivalent, a sort of cousin who was also a sort of housekeeper. She was three years younger than Kathy, unmarried and childless, yet, in Kathy's eyes, she was the real woman of the two. One could hardly look at Elsa without being conscious of her plump body, her pink skin, and her freckled fairness. Did Abe ever . . . ? Very likely; but Kathy had decided early on that there would be no friction on that score.

Kathy poured herself a cup of coffee; no sugar, but a dash of semi-skimmed.

Abe finished his second egg, drank his coffee, and said, 'I shall be in the site office for most of the day if you want me . . . '

Abe looked what he was, a prosperous builder, and he followed tradition in carrying on the family firm.

'Try to keep Julie away from the farm, and the Vinter boy.'

Kathy was irritated. 'I can't choose her friends for her and neither can you; she's seventeen.'

'You could try.'

As he spoke, Julie came in wearing a jade-green dressing gown over her nightdress. A slim, dark girl, her hair was tousled, her

389

eyes puffed with sleep. She yawned, bracing her shoulders and stretching her arms. 'Any coffee going?'

Abe, briefcase in hand, was ready to go. 'Ah, there you are!' He pecked at his daughter's cheek, ruffled her hair, and said, 'Bye, kid! Have a good day, and keep away from young Vinter, he's a poof!'

'He's not a poof, Dad.' Julie's protest was mild.

'Well, if he isn't he's in training to be one.'

Julie produced a handkerchief from the pocket of her dressing gown, moistened it with her saliva, and wiped the egg from his chin. 'You are a mucky pup, Dad!'

She went with him out into the yard, to his car.

Elsa said, 'They make a good pair. She knows how to handle him, which is more than can be said for her mother. I bet she'll come back with a nice crisp tenner tucked in the pocket of her dressing gown.'

They heard Abe's car drive out of the yard and a moment or two later Julie came in with a handful of mail which she dropped beside Kathy's plate.

'I met the postman.' She stood, hesitating, then, 'I think I'll go up and get dressed. Then I'm going out – is that all right?'

'It's your holiday.'

The two women sat on, nibbling cold toast and sipping coffee. Elsa lit a cigarette.

Although Abe built houses with designer-everything, finger-tip central heating and a proliferation of elegant plumbing, Trigg House itself was, in all these things, at least forty years behind the times. But that was how Kathy liked it. Above all there was this archaic kitchen with a great square table in the middle, reminding her of the farmhouse in which she had been brought up.

Julie came down dressed for the street: jeans and a T-shirt with an unreadable slogan. 'All right; I'm off. Don't worry if I'm not in for lunch . . . Bye!' She was gone.

Katherine's eyes followed her daughter. 'She's changed. I seem to be losing contact and it worries me sometimes.'

'She's growing up, Kath; she's a young woman.'

Katherine reached for another piece of toast, changed her mind, and pushed her plate away. 'Abe is right about young Vinter; I wish she would find somebody else.'

Elsa mumbled with her mouth full, 'You don't know when you're well off. At least he's safe. She's not going to turn up pregnant one day – not by him, anyway.'

Elsa cleared her mouth and reached for her coffee cup. 'By the way, I suppose you know that Jessica is working part-time for Arnold Paul?'

Kathy paused, her cup to her lips. 'What on earth is she doing there?'

'Housework, I suppose – what else? I gather things have got too much for the old housekeeper biddy now that Arnold has his brother there. I heard it in the shop yesterday but I thought you must know.'

Kathy put down her cup. 'I can't believe it!'

'I don't know why not; she's done the church cleaning for years.'

Kathy was tense. 'That's different. I wish to God she'd agree to sell the bloody farm. Abe's syndicate would pay through the nose and it's not as though she'll ever make a decent living from it.'

Elsa blew out a cloud of pale-grey smoke. 'Not with the hangers-on she's got there now, she won't. At least Jess is willing to work, I'll say that for her; I don't know how she fits it all in.'

Kathy was on her feet. 'I'm going upstairs to change. I shall have a word with Jessica.'

A quarter of an hour later Kathy came down, transformed; she wore a fine checked skirt, a silk blouse, suede jacket and shoes, all in matching shades of grey, set off by a jade necklace and earrings mounted in gold – Abe's Christmas present.

Elsa was appraising. 'You're taking the car?'

'No.'

'You're never walking along the river bank in those shoes?'

'I'm going round by the road.'

'I see. We want to bolster our courage. Anyway, don't blow your top when you get there; it won't do any good.'

*

The village square, junction of three roads, merged with the foreshore where boats were drawn up on the shingle. At spring tides, when the wind was right, there was sometimes flooding and none of the houses around the square was without its stock of sandbags, ready filled. Across from Trigg, the garage with its petrol pumps adjoined the boatyard, while pub, post office, general store, café and a few houses completed the square.

'Morning, Kathy!' Tommy Noall, at the garage, his head under the bonnet of a car. They had been at the village school together until the age of eleven. Henry Clemens, who kept the general store and post office, was washing down his shop front. 'Nice morning, Mrs Geach! Makes you think the good Lord has given us spring at last.' Henry was the churchwarden.

Kathy usually enjoyed walking through her village, knowing, and being known. She was still one of the Dobell twins but she was also Mrs Abe Geach, wife of the contractor who built quality housing, government offices and schools. At such moments it pleased her to be both, but the news about Jessica had put her off-balance.

She turned up Church Lane, which followed the Trigg boundary until it reached the churchyard. The trees, their leaves breaking out of bud, were misty green against the sky and, opposite the church, in the gardens of detached villas, there were camellias and magnolias in flower.

Another two or three hundred yards, and she was in open country, out of sight of the village. Only the church tower, with its four pinnacles and flag-pole, rose out of green fields to mark where the village lay. A ramshackle gate labelled 'Minions' gave on to a rutted track which ran through an area of scrub where tethered goats were browsing. The track dropped steeply between high hedges, to end at another gate and the farmyard where hens strutted and pecked over the cobbles. A house backed on the yard and there were outbuildings on two other sides. As always, the yard, the hens and the smells brought back her childhood with disturbing poignancy. Nothing had changed.

Minions had belonged to her parents, both killed in a coach crash in the early years of her marriage. Jessica had insisted on keeping the farm going, first with the help of paid labour, later with the doubtful assistance of a succession of lame ducks needing a roof over their heads. The latest and, so far, the most enduring of these, was a family of three: Laurence and Stephanie Vinter, and their son, Giles.

As Kathy unhooked the gate Jessica's collie came bounding out of the house, barking, but changed to tail wagging when he saw Kathy. The door led directly into the kitchen and Kathy went in without knocking. The boy, Giles, was seated at the kitchen table, his school books spread out in front of him. He was the same age as Julie and they were in the same form at school. Slim, and small and fair, with the delicate features and colouring of a girl, his eyes were an intense blue, accentuated by the powerful lenses of his spectacles.

'Oh, Mrs Geach!' His manner was precise and distant.

'Working in the holidays, Giles? I wish Julie would. What subjects are you doing for your A-levels? Physics, chemistry and biology – the same as Julie, isn't it?'

'I'm doing mathematics instead of biology.' Giles glanced down at his books and back again. 'You want to see Miss Jessica? I think she's mucking out the goat house.' The blue eyes blinked at her and she realised that she was being dismissed.

She found Jessica manhandling a bale of bedding-straw into the goat house.

'Kathy! Let me dump this and we'll go indoors.'

They were twins, but no more alike than most sisters. Jessica was more sturdily built; her hair and eyes were less dark, her skin was lightly tanned, and her expression more open. She had a ready smile. In her denim blouse and jeans, her hair caught back with a clip, she seemed to typify the modern working woman in a way that Kathy had no desire to emulate but envied all the same.

The bale disposed of, Jessica came out of the goat house brushing herself off. She surveyed her sister. 'You look like an advertisement in *Country Life*, Kath! Those shoes haven't been along the river bank. Where's the car?'

'I walked round by the road.' Katherine was terse.

'Oh, I see; giving the peasants a treat.'

In the kitchen Jessica spoke sharply to the boy, 'There's straw in the goat house that needs spreading, Giles. Don't use it all; there's enough for tomorrow as well.'

Giles got up without a word and went out into the yard. 'That boy would never get off his backside unless I chivvied him . . . Gets it from his mother. Come into the sitting room . . .'

Kathy said, 'I thought Julie might have been here.'

'She was, but it seems his highness wasn't in the mood for dalliance. They chatted for a few minutes then she was dismissed. Everybody to their taste but I don't know what she sees in him.'

The house fronted on an inlet from the river overhung by trees, and the tiny window of the sitting room let in a dim and sombre light. Little had changed here over the years except by wear and tear; the black leather sofa, the armchairs, his and hers, the coloured prints in gilded frames, the upright piano against one wall – all had been there when the girls were born in the room above. So had the roll-topped desk and the wooden filing box which successive Dobells had used for their farm records and accounts.

'Take the weight off your feet, Kath. Feel like a sherry? To be precise, do you feel like risking my fortified wine which I now buy in five-litre plastic containers? I serve it from a sherry bottle but it might taste better from an old boot.'

The two sisters sat, side-by-side on the sofa, sipping fortified wine. 'Where are Laurence and Stephanie?'

'Laurence is out digging potatoes. As for Stephanie, it's the first day of the curse so she won't put in an appearance till midmorning.' Jessica sighed. 'And lately she's taken to having afternoons off. Where she goes, God knows, but I notice she's having more baths than she used to.'

'But if they're no use, why do you put up with them, Jess?'

Jessica poured herself a little more wine. 'Top you up? . . . No? . . . Oh, I don't know! I can't get anybody else and though Laurence isn't God's gift as a farm labourer, he works hard at whatever you tell him to do.' Jessica grinned. 'And he's got other attributes – of a sort.'

Katherine looked at her sister. 'I hope you don't mean what I think you do.'

Jessica's laugh had in it a strain of bitterness. 'You're an old prude, Kath! Sometimes I think you've turned being a woman into a career – like you took a course or read it in a textbook.'

Katherine was piqued. 'And what have you done?'

Jessica emptied her glass. 'Me? I don't know – what comes naturally, I suppose.' She was suddenly serious. 'If I've done nothing else I've plucked the feathers from a few cockerels and put a stop to their crowing – and I'm not dependent on any one of the bastards.'

'And I am? You might as well say it. But don't let's get into an argument. If you agreed, we could sell this place to the syndicate. You'd get a good price for your share and you could insist on a stake in whatever they made of it. You'd be well off, and still your own woman.'

But Jessica was indignant. 'Not on your life! If you've come here to push Abe's barrow, you're wasting your precious time. If I give up here it won't be for what I can get. Billy Eva would like to add it to his holding; then, at least, it would stay as a farm. As it is, I sell all I can grow, there's a steady demand for the goats' milk, and Billy is going to rent Five-acre for his store cattle . . . All that, with what I get from the church, and now from Arnold Paul –'

'That's another thing, Jess – I've just heard about it.'

'So? It's only two afternoons a week and the money's good.'

'But it's charring, Jess!'

'So what? I've been keeping the church clean for years.'

'But that's different . . . '

'Why? Because people might be daft enough to think I do it for love? Really, Kath!'

As always, in her encounters with her sister, Kathy was outmanoeuvred and made to feel naive and snobbish. It was she who changed the subject.

'I was saying to Elsa, I'm a bit worried about Julie; she's been seeing a lot of Giles lately.'

Jessica's reaction was similar to Elsa's. 'At least she's safe with him – no drugs, and not much sex either if I'm any judge.'

'What do they do when she comes here?'

'Sometimes they go out bird-watching but mostly they stay up in his room. For God's sake, Kath; they're seventeen! All the same, I wouldn't be surprised if they spend the time doing their homework.'

Jessica broke off and became solemn again. It was as though she had waited for a chance to turn the conversation her way. 'Kath, did you see in the local rag that Mrs Ruse – Derek's mother, is dead?'

'Ruse? The mother of the boy killed in the hit-and-run – yes, I saw an account of her funeral. What about it?'

'She was only fifty-five and they say she never got over Derek's death. After sixteen years she was still grieving . . . '

'So?'

Jessica was silent for a while, then she said, 'I was going around with Johnny Glynn at that time.'

'Everybody thought you would marry him – me included.'

'It was all fixed, and it was what happened that night which put an end to it.'

'But Johnny satisfied the police he wasn't involved. Of course, not everybody believed him.'

'I know they didn't, but he was telling the truth.'

Katherine looked at her sister. 'If Johnny wasn't there, who was?' Her manner became more intense. 'Jess, were you with him, whoever he was?'

Jessica made a sudden movement. 'I'm being morbid, Kath. Forget it! Let's talk about you. I hear Abe's got the contract for the new school up Liskeard way . . . I hope he's going to live long enough to enjoy it all – not like his father.'

Good Friday

'Almighty God, we beseech thee graciously to behold this thy family, for which our Lord Jesus Christ was contented to be betrayed . . . '

The Reverend Michael Jordan, Vicar of Moresk, in his

396

high-pitched, boyish voice, recited the first collect for the day to a congregation that filled his church.

By some quirk of tradition the Good Friday morning service had acquired a significance for many villagers who were unlikely to be seen in church at any other time. The occasion was signalled, shortly before half past nine in the morning, by a stroke on the tenor bell to be repeated at one-minute intervals until the service began at ten. Each stroke marked a year in the thirty-three years of Christ's life on earth.

The morning was fine and sunlight streamed through a south window to fall dramatically on a larger-than-life statue of the Christ, set at the top of the chancel steps.

It was a family occasion; the Geaches were there, occupying a pew halfway down the central aisle. Abe, out of his element, was flushed, as though he had fortified himself beforehand. He fumbled the responses and was unsure when to sit or stand. Even Jessica, who rarely attended a service, sat next to Julie on the inside. Kathy, in a hat that she kept for funerals, looked about her and realised that hers was one of less than a score of hats in the congregation, and those were largely confined to women whom she regarded as church hens.

'We will sing the hymn, "O sacred head, sore wounded, Defiled and put to scorn . . . " Verses three and four will be taken as a solo.'

Arnold Paul, at the organ, reached his high point in a composition of his own: 'Chorale Prelude by Arnold Paul, in the manner of J S Bach'; a lengthy introduction to the hymn based on Hassler's melody.

Kathy was watching her daughter who seemed to have eyes only for Giles Vinter. The boy sat with his parents in the pew in front; he faced straight ahead, as though unaware of anyone else in the church, and followed precisely the requirements of the ritual. She asked herself again, what did Julie see in him? Surely it was natural for a young girl to be attracted by masculinity? But there was nothing macho about Giles. On the contrary he was half a head shorter than Julie, his appearance was effeminate, and his short-sightedness caused him to peer like a cartoon professor.

Of course he had more than his ration of brains, but when had brains stirred the hormones of youth?

Paul's prelude came to an end and a chord brought the congregation to its feet. For no obvious reason Kathy felt vaguely depressed and apprehensive. Her sensations were similar to those she often experienced at the approach of a thunderstorm, when the atmosphere itself seemed permeated by some undefined menace. She wondered if she might be on the brink of an illness.

To her surprise the solo was taken by Stephanie Vinter from her place in the congregation. Kathy was impressed. Stephanie's unaccompanied soprano had a bell-like sweetness, a magical quality which suspended normality and, when the organ brought in the congregation for the final verse, it was as though everyone drew breath again. During her solo Giles had watched his mother with total absorption and seemed to live with her through every moment of the experience.

The congregation knelt. 'Almighty and everlasting God, by whose Spirit the whole body of the Church is governed . . . '

Laurence Vinter, his head bowed low, studied the grain of the bookrest. For weeks he had lived with a growing sense of unease and tension. He could point to no significant change in the daily life of the farm, nor in their relationships, yet he was conscious of an impending crisis.

As each day passed it seemed that their words became overloaded with meaning, that their simplest actions might be fraught with sinister implications. At times he felt that he was picking his way along a crumbling traverse, and his concern was not lessened by his inability to decide whether the crisis was real or, as he often suspected, a creation of his own disordered mind.

Another hymn, and towards the end of it the vicar ascended the steps to his pulpit.

'My text is taken from Isaiah, chapter 53, verse 3: "He was despised, and we esteemed him not."'

On those occasions, as now, when Jessica attended a service, she felt a little like an actor on the wrong side of the footlights, detached and inclined to be cynical. It was she who had dusted the altar, polished the lectern, swept and hoovered, cleaned and tidied. It was she who, when the Eucharist was to be celebrated, prepared the elements. But, by one of those curious psychological quirks, she retained an almost superstitious regard for the statue of Christ which dominated the approach to the chancel. The statue was a loose 3-D rendering of Holman Hunt's excruciating painting, *The Light of the World*, differing mainly in that the statue held the lantern aloft.

Jessica always dusted the Christ figure with a feather duster, never allowing contact with her hands or her clothing and, in doing so, she avoided the eyes.

Now, while the vicar developed his theme, she found herself gazing at those eyes, though she could not see them distinctly, and she was disturbed; they seemed to be accusing, and she was filled with a sense of guilt.

'Now to God the Father, God the Son, and God the Holy Ghost . . . ' A final hymn, the benediction, and the service drew to its end. With the church clock striking eleven the congregation trooped out into the sunshine.

Kathy said: 'Will you be in for lunch?'

Abe glanced at his watch. 'Christ, no! I've got a site meeting in St Austell and I'm late already.'

'It's Good Friday.'

'So what? It's easier without a lot of blokes around pretending to work. I'll collect the car and be off.'

Julie was hanging back. 'Aren't you coming home, kid?'

'I want a word with Giles.'

Geach muttered, 'That young wimp! She's hooked on him.'

Kathy turned to her sister. 'Why not stay and take pot luck with us, Jess?'

Jessica looked across to the porch where Stephanie Vinter was the centre of a congratulatory group, while her husband and son waited on the fringe. 'Thanks all the same, Kath, but it doesn't look as though anybody else intends to do any work this morning, so I'd better.'

She set off up Church Lane.

The Vinters got away at last and started walking up the hill. Giles saw Julie waiting and joined her; his parents walked on.

Stephanie said, 'Are you ill, Laurence?'

'No.'

'There's something the matter with you.'

'Doesn't that apply to each of us?'

'Don't fence. You're cutting yourself off. Sometimes I wonder if . . .'

'What do you wonder?'

'Nothing. Here's Giles. What did Julie want?'

'She wanted me to go out with her this afternoon.'

'Are you going?'

'No.'

'What's the matter between you and Julie?'

'Nothing.'

Easter Saturday

On Saturday evening Jessica went as usual to do one of her stints at the church. She entered by the south door in her stockinged feet, having kicked off her half-wellies in the porch. No point in getting river mud on the nice carpet; she would only have to clean it up. It was overcast and raining and, though it was light enough outside, inside the light was dim; the lantern held aloft by the Christ figure glowed like a maleficent eye and she looked away. The altar and chancel were barely visible in the gloom.

Following an unconscious routine, she dropped the padlock on a little table next to the visitors' book and walked down the carpeted aisle. The chancel tiles were cold to her feet. After the severities of Lent there were flowers everywhere – lilies and tulips, ready for Sunday – Easter Sunday. The flower ladies had been and there would be a mess in the vestry toilet where they got their water. Cleaning up messes was work for the peasantry.

She was on her way to the vestry; the self-closing door from the chancel was wedged open – the ladies again. She tried to shut it but it wouldn't budge. In the vestry she removed her mac and hood, and put on an old pair of slippers which she kept in a cupboard with her cleaning gear.

First things first: the Lenten hangings which had been in place through Passion-tide had been taken down but they must be brushed and folded away with their mothballs.

Jessica worked with seemingly effortless ease, but her thoughts were elsewhere; she was thinking of her sister. Kathy has everything a woman could want; she doesn't have to do a hand's turn if she doesn't want to. And if she took the trouble to understand him, she could twist Abe around her little finger.

While I . . . What do I do? I work like a slave for little more than subsistence, and I play the whore for nothing. Yet we are twins, two peas from the same pod. Why do I do it? To stop myself thinking? . . . As a punishment? . . . And what about him? Does he have nights when he forces himself to lie awake for fear of nightmares? . . . Always the same: the boy's white face, and his eyes staring up through the spokes of the cycle wheel. As I move away, those eyes seem to follow me . . .

She had brushed and folded away the hangings; now she was dealing with the vestry door. The flower arrangers had forced the wooden wedge in too far and she couldn't shift it. A hammer: there were a few tools in a cupboard in the tower, a hammer amongst them. She went to fetch it and while she was there the church clock went through its groans, grunts and clatter, preparatory to striking seven. She found the hammer and returned with it to the wedged door. Stooping, she swung it very gently, nudging the wedge.

'Practising your croquet, Jessica, or is it golf?'

She was startled. It was Arnold Paul, the organist, for whom she now worked a couple of afternoons a week. Plump, amiable, and a trifle smug, he was standing in the aisle, watching her.

'It's jammed. One of the women on flowers this week doesn't know her own strength.'

'I came in to collect some music.' He crossed to the organ console and was hidden by the curtain.

The wedge was freed and the door to the vestry closed. The organ played softly, an odd little tune. Jessica had no ear for music. Next on her schedule: cleaning the vestry toilet. The floor was swimming with water mixed with leaves, flower stalks, and wrapping tissue; five or six unwanted vases had not been put away.

When she returned to the church the organ was silent and there was no sign of Arnold. Odd. He usually called out when he was going. Perhaps he had. She crossed to the console, there was no one there and the lid was down over the keys. She was being foolish, yet she was tempted to wedge the south door shut. But that would be too absurd.

Saturday evening routine dictated two more jobs: a whisk round with a feather duster on the altar and chancel, and a bit of elbow grease on the lectern to bring up the shine. It was while she was dusting that she thought she heard a movement somewhere in the body of the church.

'Is anyone there?'

She was unusually nervous. Why am I so jumpy? She followed the same routine in the depth of winter on nights when, without a torch, it would have been impossible to find her way through the churchyard. She called again with no reply and she went on with her work. Then there was someone – the vicar. She was polishing the lectern.

'Good evening, Jessica. I hope I didn't startle you? I came across to fetch my nice new service book.'

She was glad he had come.

Apart from anything else she liked the vicar, and it was not given to many to be liked by Jessica. She believed that he was a good man, and innocent; the sort who could touch filth without being soiled, perhaps without even knowing.

'I'm almost through.'

'It all looks splendid, Jessica, but then, it always does. I really don't know what we would do without you.'

Easter Sunday

The following morning at seven-fifteen, Michael Jordan, Vicar of Moresk, crossed the road from his vicarage to his church. At thirty-eight, he was unmarried, and his sister, Celia, several years older, kept house for him. It was a balmy spring morning but whatever the weather, in winter darkness or in the brash light of high summer, he took pleasure in so beginning his day. He felt part of the great Christian tradition which, probably on this very site, reached back to the missionary work of St Sulien, patron saint of his church, among the heathen Celts.

He passed through the sixteenth-century lich-gate, followed the gravelled walk among the gravestones, glimpsed the river between the trees, and arrived at the south porch. To his astonishment he heard the sound of the organ, a sustained chord of discordant notes. He had in his hand the key to a padlock by which the church was supposedly secured against latter-day Vandals but the padlock was missing and the heavy oaken door with its wrought-iron latch and ring stood open.

He experienced a tremor of disquiet; an awareness, as he interpreted it, of the proximity of Evil. Michael saw himself and the rest of mankind doing daily battle with Evil which, for him, was a positive and potent force. He pushed the door wide and was somewhat reassured to see the padlock on the table just inside the door, next to the visitors' book and offertory box. But the vibrant dissonance of the organ chord filled the church, setting his teeth and his nerves on edge. He looked across at the console but the curtain hid anyone who might have been there. Somebody playing the fool?

He entered the nave, genuflected towards the altar and, in the act, caught sight of a figure sprawled across the chancel steps. His fears intensified. Summoning his courage he walked down the aisle and approached the steps. Jessica Dobell lay on her back, diagonally across the steps, and she was certainly dead. Her head was turned slightly to the right and her skull had been smashed, just forward of the crown. Her hair around the injury was a mass of clotted blood, while something more viscous than blood had oozed on to the tiled step. Her blue denim shirt had been ripped open, exposing her breasts; and her jeans, unzipped, had been dragged part-way down her thighs along with her briefs.

Adding to his horror and sense of desecration, she was lying at the very feet of the statue of Christ; Christ with his lantern held aloft – *Lux Mundi* – *The Light of the World*.

Jessica's hair was spread out so that it reached, and partly covered, the bare feet of the statue, and Michael was irresistibly reminded of Mary Magdalene who anointed the feet of Jesus with her perfume and 'wiped them with her hair till the house was filled with the fragrance'. Always a little disturbed by the image which that passage conjured up, he was deeply distressed that his mind should seize upon it at such a moment. Instinctively he crossed himself and murmured an incoherent prayer.

Only last night . . . Had she been there ever since?

Although he was filled with revulsion he could not keep his eyes from her body. He was astonished to see that, away from her injury, her features were composed; she looked in death as she had been in life, a very attractive woman. If only her breasts and thighs were covered . . . He stooped, with the foolish intention of drawing her shirt-front together, but stopped himself in time. The police would take a poor view of such interference and there was no possible doubt that they must be involved.

The continuing, droning chord on the organ made it impossible to think. He could hear the muffled purr of the electric blower and, as he approached the console, he saw that five notes, apparently chosen at random in the 'great', were permanently depressed by little wedges of paper, folded to the appropriate thickness and inserted between the keys. Once more he was on the point of committing a blunder – by removing the wedges; instead, he switched off the blower and silence descended like a benediction.

What he had to do was clear: he must lock the church, go back to the vicarage and telephone the police. But he really could not persuade himself to leave the poor woman so obscenely exposed. He went to the vestry and returned with a surplice which, with great gentleness, he arranged to his satisfaction.

Then he prayed briefly, genuflected, and left.

Eight o'clock Holy Communion was celebrated at St Sulien's each Sunday but, on this special Sunday which commemorated the risen Lord, those who came would find their church locked against them.

Forty odd miles away, as crows are said to fly, on the estuary of the Tamar, Detective Chief Superintendent Charles Wycliffe was in his garden accompanied by the cat, Macavity. The pond had recently been cleaned and refurbished so that now, its ecological equanimity disturbed, it had produced inordinate quantities of blanket weed. Wycliffe, armed with a trident-like weapon, had lifted out a mass of the green, filamentous, slimy stuff and from it he now rescued trapped newts, tadpoles, young frogs, and nymphs of dragonflies, all to be returned to the pond.

But not snails. Helen was adamant. There were too many snails, so those that were found must be banished into the outer darkness. He disliked such a god-like decisive role but the task was otherwise agreeable; contemplative, and on balance constructive, ideally suited to his middle-aged psyche.

Macavity, more virile in his pursuits and aspirations, put on his mouse-hunting act. Watching some phantom rodent, whiskers a-tremble and tail rigid, he would stalk the imagined quarry and, insinuating his plump body through the herbiage with infinite care, the mighty hunter would crouch, ready for the spring – then pounce.

All this despite the fact that the sight of a can of Whiskas, preferably open, was necessary to induce in Macavity any sign of a salivary reflex.

The Wycliffes would never see fifty again; they were on the slope – definitely. For twenty years they had lived in the Watch House, a former coastguard station converted to a dwelling house, and their half-acre of garden sloped to the narrows where the estuary met the sea. Were they happy? Wycliffe told himself that happiness is a peak experience that comes in small doses – a few seconds at a time; at most a few hours. But they were content; content with each other and with their lot.

After rearing their two children they were mostly alone again. The boy, David, was married and more or less settled in Kenya with his wife and child; while their daughter, Ruth, lived with her former boss in a nebulous relationship so far unproductive of offspring.

Easter Sunday: the church bells of St Juliot, their nearest village, were pealing in celebration and their sound rose and fell, carried on a fitful breeze. The air was soft and warm. Wycliffe knew that it was going to be one of those idyllic days, always to be remembered. For a few hours at least the Watch House and its garden would become an exclusion zone within which he, Helen, and Macavity would pursue their separate illusions in blissful relaxation.

He was wrong.

Helen's voice came from the terrace. 'Telephone!' And, as he reached her, she said, 'It's Lucy Lane.'

Detective Sergeant Lucy Lane was the day's duty officer in CID. 'Sorry to disturb your Sunday, sir, but there's a report from C Division, logged at 09.33. At about 07.30 this morning, Jessica Dobell, a woman in her late thirties, was found dead in St Sulien's Church, in the village of Moresk, near Truro. She appears to have died from a depressed fracture of the skull caused by a powerful blow. DI Rowse from sub-division, attending, says it's murder.'

'You did say Moresk?'

'I did, sir.'

'That's only a few miles from the Duloe place.'*

'A bit nearer Truro, and on the other side of the river.'

'What on earth's happening down there?'

'I've no idea, sir; perhaps they get bored in the off season.' Lucy Lane had little time for rhetorical questions.

Wycliffe sighed as he replaced the telephone. A well established routine made detailed instructions unnecessary. DI Kersey, on call, would gather together a small headquarters team while the local inspector would call in the police surgeon, inform relatives, arrange formal identification, and notify the coroner. But Wycliffe must visit the scene and, according to what he saw and heard, decide whether or not to become personally involved.

Wycliffe and the Dead Flautist

'A murder, apparently, at Moresk, near Truro.'

'I'll make some coffee.'

Helen was by no means indifferent to tragedy but when crime and violence are woven into the fabric of daily life an extra skin is part of the survival kit.

'Are you likely to be home this evening?'

'Possibly, it's only fifty-odd miles.'

Helen grinned. 'Some of them very odd, as I remember. Anyhow, I'll put your weekend bag in the car. Go and make yourself respectable.'

So much for his Easter Sunday.

Helen was right; getting on to the spine road from the complex of creeks and streams which is the Tamar valley, and off it, to that not dissimilar complex which is the valley of the Fal, makes an interesting experience. Wycliffe was not a good driver; in fact he had no rapport with any mechanical device more complex than a can opener, and the journey took him longer than it should have done. 'Turn off left in Tresillian', he told himself. He did, then got lost in a bewildering maze of lanes, narrow and tortuous, and peopled by stolid men in large cars who simply stopped and waited with patronising patience for him to extricate himself from every impasse.

He finally arrived in the village as the church clock was striking twelve.

Chapter Two

Easter Sunday (continued)

Moresk village and a patch of woodland on the other side of Truro are almost all that survive to perpetuate the name of that great forest of Morrois where Tristan fled with Iseult, only to be discovered by King Mark. Although the village is quite close to Truro it was Wycliffe's first visit, and he was surprised to find such a populous little place tucked away in one of the creeks. He stopped in the square which, on one side, was bounded by the foreshore and the waters of the creek. Small boats were stranded on the shingle, lying at odd angles, and a pair of swans waddled around the garage forecourt among the petrol pumps. He decided at once that he liked the place.

He could see the church through trees away to his left but separated from the square by a substantial house in its own grounds. He left his car, found Church Lane, and a minute or two later arrived at the lich-gate where a small crowd had gathered under the eye of a uniformed policeman.

'DI Reed is in the church, sir.'

Wycliffe found the south porch and entered the church. Coming in out of the sunlight, the nave seemed to be in near darkness though the chancel and altar were floodlit like a stage set. Three men were in conversation near the chancel steps and one of them came to greet him. It was DI Reed.

Reed and Wycliffe had worked together several times. He was a large man with a high colour, fleshy features, and a neck which bulged over his collar. A fringe of red hair surrounded a bald patch. 'Welcome aboard, sir.'

Reed led him to the chancel steps. Tread boards were in place to protect whatever evidence there might be until scenes-of-crime had finished. The body was sprawled across the steps, at the very feet of a statue of Christ. The head to one side exposed a ghastly wound to the parietal region of the skull.

Wycliffe stood gazing down at this woman whose concerns in life had now, by reason of her death, become his. What shocked him most about violent death was the ease with which the thread is snapped; but here was something more, something bizarre, and he was troubled.

'She wasn't killed here, like that – the body has been arranged.' A banal observation but something was expected of him and it was all he could find to say.

Reed, at ease, comfortable, said, 'No, she was dragged from over by the pulpit. There's blood on the tiles there, and traces in between.'

Wycliffe could scarcely take his eyes from the body. Never before had he been confronted with a murder which made such a profound first impression; yet he found difficulty in putting that impression into words.

Ripping open the victim's blouse to expose the breasts is a common enough feature of sexual assault on a woman, but jeans and briefs had been pulled down just far enough to uncover the pubic triangle – and no further. Her body had been arranged in an abandoned pose across the chancel steps and her abundant hair, dark and lustrous, had been ordered so that it reached and spread over the sandalled feet of Christ.

What he was seeing was a set piece such as a surrealist sculptor might devise in order to shock, and so to make a point. But to prepare this set piece and make whatever point was intended, a woman had been murdered.

Belatedly he noticed that she was wearing bedroom slippers, an old pair that had seen better days.

Reed said, 'That's how she was found, sir; nothing has been disturbed except that a surplice, used by the vicar to cover her, was taken away. No sign of any footwear other than those slippers, and she didn't walk here in those.'

'Doesn't it strike you as . . . as grotesque?'

Reed puffed out his cheeks. 'Kinky is the word that comes to mind. If it was a sexual assault it didn't achieve a climax.' Reed smoothed his bald patch with an enormous, freckled paw. 'My guess is that it was never intended to, but what was intended, God only knows.'

'What was she doing in the church?'

'She was a sort of caretaker-cum-verger and she looked in on Saturday evenings to make sure everything was ready for Sunday.'

'Next of kin?'

'There's only a sister and she's been told. Deceased wasn't married. There's a smallholding just up-river from here which she ran with the help of a couple living in. They've been notified. The sister lives in Trigg House, adjoining the churchyard, and she's married to Abe Geach, the contractor.' A quick look. 'Does that mean anything to you, sir?'

'Should it?'

Reed shrugged. 'Money. He's got contracts all over the two counties and he's one of those who manages to keep warm and dry whatever the financial climate. I mention it because he carries quite a bit of weight around here.'

'She has no parents living?'

'Both killed in a coach crash several years back.'

DS Fox, Wycliffe's scenes-of-crime officer, had completed his first series of photographs of the body but more would be taken when the pathologist arrived and it could be disturbed. Now Fox turned his attention to the immediate setting.

Wycliffe, as always, was fascinated by Fox; it was an experience to see him go to work. He would arrive, unburdened, followed by his assistant, the long-suffering Collis, laden like a Spaniard's donkey. A room, a river bank, an alley, a night-club, or a church, it was all the same to Fox. He seemed to show not the slightest interest in his surroundings in general but concentrated on each item or aspect as it presented itself to him on some mental list. A wizard with molehills, he was apt to miss the occasional mountain.

Brooding, Wycliffe turned once more to the inspector. 'The weapon?'

410

Reed pointed. Lying at some distance from the body, near the pulpit, and barely visible in its shadow, was a long-handled hammer with a smallish head. 'It's an unusual sort, sir – like they used to use for wheel-tapping on the railway.'

Stooping, Wycliffe could see that the head was encrusted with dried blood and there was blood on the tiles.

Wycliffe returned to the chancel steps and the body. 'Presumably she's been here all night. What was the weather like yesterday evening?'

'Wet. It rained all the evening, sir; I checked.'

'So it's unlikely that she came here dressed like this.'

'She didn't; there's a heavy mac with a hood in the vestry but, as I said, no footwear. I understand she usually came to work along the river bank and that must have been pretty muddy. What she wore on her feet is a bit of a puzzle at the moment.'

Wycliffe was soaking up all the detail of which he was capable. His questions were curt and there were intervals during which he stood, staring down at the dead woman or watching Fox's antics with the camera.

'Who found her?'

'The vicar: the Reverend Michael Jordan. There he is . . . ' Reed indicated a youngish man in clerical garb, seated in one of the pews, head bent, eyes closed, as though in prayer.

Now that Wycliffe had become accustomed to the uneven lighting he could see that the church must have the support of dedicated and well-heeled parishioners. There was an impressive tapestry above the altar and the altar cloth was elaborately embroidered; the aisles and the pews were carpeted and many of the pews sported embroidered hassocks on which the knees of the devout might rest at ease. Flowers were everywhere and the air was heavy with their scent, blending with the lingering tangy odour of incense.

'What did the doctor have to say?'

'He's still here. That's him, talking to my sergeant – Dr Sparrow. I think he's loath to go; he's not often in the limelight and I suppose it's a change from sore throats and backaches.'

The doctor was in his early sixties, short, stocky and weather-beaten. Dressed in shabby tweeds he was almost a caricature of the traditional country doctor.

'You don't need me to tell you what she died of but you might want my view on when. My guess would be, sometime last evening, between eight or nine and midnight. I can't do better than that but I imagine you will have Franks to do the clever stuff.'

'And the sexual aspect?'

The doctor pouted. 'What about it? The chap obviously didn't really get around to it. I imagine the situation was a bit off-putting.'

'One more question, Dr Sparrow – not a professional one – are you acquainted with the vicar?'

'I know him, naturally, but I'm no churchgoer.'

'An unbiased view, then. What sort of man is he?'

Sparrow chuckled. 'So that's how you blokes go about it! Well, I'd say he was a sincere, hardworking chap; always on call – like me.' A sly grin.

'Popular?'

'I think so; he's pushed up church attendance, so they tell me, and despite his Holy-Joe appearance and manner, he's accepted by the young. They call him Michael, or even Mike. He didn't go down well with the diehards at first, but they seem to have come round. Why don't you have a chat with him?'

'I'm going to.' Wycliffe thanked the doctor.

Jordan got up from his seat as Wycliffe approached. His blond hair clipped short and his smooth, pink, unblemished skin gave him an unused look, reminiscent of a young baby. Wycliffe had the uncomfortable feeling that he might be dealing with a postulant for sainthood.

The preliminaries over, Jordan said, 'This morning I was due to celebrate Holy Communion at eight, and matins at eleven . . . Now, I suppose, it will be some time before I can conduct any services here at all . . . Apart from anything else there is the question of desecration. The bishop will have to decide what is to be done . . .' The blue eyes were troubled.

'How long have you been in Moresk, Vicar?'

'Four years at Michaelmas.'

'So you must know the people. This woman, Jessica Dobell . . . I understand she kept the church clean.'

'That is an understatement; Jessica saw to everything, from cleaning, to preparations for the different services. I don't know what we shall do without her.'

'You've seen the weapon?'

The vicar nodded. 'It comes from a cupboard in the tower where we keep all sorts of things which might be handy about the church – from flower vases to drawing pins. It's horrible to think . . . '

'I gather that the dead woman didn't live with any relative.'

'No, Jessica had certain views about marriage and family life . . . ' His eyes sought Wycliffe's and seemed to beg for understanding. 'You will hear rumours . . . gossip.'

Reed and the vicar between them were opening up vistas, giving Wycliffe his first glimpse of the people whose intimate lives would be his concern in the days or weeks ahead. It was his job to invite their confidence and probe their deceptions until a rather special kind of truth was established – that arcane variety which is recognised in the Courts.

As always, he felt a stirring of excitement at the prospect; an excitement tinged with the guilt of a voyeur.

'If I might suggest, Mr Wycliffe . . . ' The vicar was nervous but resolved to make his point. 'If I might suggest, it could be a mistake to approach this young woman with a prejudice. After all, a certain laxness in sexual matters does not necessarily mean that those concerned are not caring and hard-working people.'

Verily, a saint! But Wycliffe was mildly snubbing. 'I try not to prejudge anybody, Mr Jordan.

'Now, you must have noticed that the dead woman is wearing slippers – '

The vicar smiled. 'Jessica always wore slippers when she was working, and always the same old pair. She kept them in a cupboard in the vestry. You see, she walked to work by way of the river bank, which is always muddy, wearing short wellingtons which she left in the porch.'

'Show me.'

He was conducted to the south porch with its slatted seats and notice boards but there were no boots.

Jordan was puzzled. 'That is strange.'

Back in the church Wycliffe said, 'One more question, Mr Jordan, and I want you to think carefully before you answer. Apart from the south door being unlocked and the body on the chancel steps, was there anything else, however trivial, which struck you as unusual when you arrived this morning?'

The vicar put his hand to his forehead. 'Of course! The organ! It's hard to believe, but that went entirely from my mind . . . Anyway, I'll show you.'

Wycliffe followed him to the organ console.

'An instrument of this quality – it's a two-manual Willis – may strike you as a little out of place in a country church like ours, but Arnold Paul, our unpaid organist, rescued it from a disused London church, had it dismantled, renovated, and rebuilt here – all at his own expense.'

'What about it?'

'Yes, of course! I digress. If I switch on the blower you will understand.'

The vicar threw a switch and the church was once more filled with a nagging discordance.

'You see that certain notes in the "great" are wedged down with folded bits of paper and when I arrived this morning this rather distressing sound greeted me along with the rest.'

'Does it mean anything to you?'

The vicar looked blank. 'Nothing at all!'

'Anyway, switch it off.' Wycliffe waited until peace was restored, then: 'This organist . . . '

'Mr Arnold Paul – he lives almost opposite the church; a man of independent means, a keen and able musician. I would have expected him to be here but he was probably prevented by your man at the gate.'

'I'll send for him. Just one more question, Mr Jordan. Would you have expected to find Jessica here when you arrived this morning?'

'Oh, no. She was only concerned with the preparations, not with the actual services.'

'And yesterday evening?'

'Yes, she usually comes – came in on Saturday evenings. She liked to have everything spick and span for Sunday.'

Crossing over by the chancel steps Wycliffe asked Fox, 'Anything to tell me? What about the weapon – any prints?'

'The weapon has been wiped clean; in fact there are no significant prints anywhere that I've examined so far.'

'All right. When you've finished here, take a look at the organ console – you'll see why when you get there. I shall want photographs. Pay special attention to the paper or card used to wedge the keys but don't disturb anything until the organist has seen it.'

He left the church and walked in the churchyard. Unlike Fox, he felt a compelling need to fit the crime and the scene of the crime into a broader context.

The church was built on sloping ground between the creek and the river; a fringe of pines and a scattering of ash and lime trees offered shelter in winter and shade in summer. Through the trees he could see the grey roofs of a substantial old house, presumably Trigg, where the dead woman's sister lived with her affluent husband. Beyond the house he glimpsed the silvery waters of the creek.

The earliest tombstones he could find dated from the sixteen-nineties and there were not many later than the nineteen-sixties when, with the dead making increasing demands on the land of the living, cremation became necessary as well as fashionable. He was interested in the names: Angove, Geach, Carveth, Noall, Dobell . . .

One of the newer stones caught his eye: 'In loving memory of our dear parents, John and Katherine Dobell, killed in a coach accident, 23rd September 1975. This stone is erected by their twin daughters: Katherine and Jessica.'

The churchyard was well but not obsessively cared for so that primroses flourished and bluebells were sprouting.

'Nice place!'

It was Doug Kersey, his principal assistant and colleague for twenty years.

'So you've arrived.'

'I brought Shaw and Potter; Lucy Lane is following on with Dixon.'

'Have you been inside?'

'I had a look and a word with Reed. What is it? Some sort of ritual killing – or what?'

'Or what, I should think.'

'It's bloody queer, anyway.'

A relief not to have to spell everything out.

'There's a guy in there, says he's the organist and that you want to speak to him.'

'Have you heard anything of Franks?' Franks was the pathologist.

'They couldn't find him at first but they've run him to earth. He's down here, spending Easter with friends in St Mawes. He should be along at any minute but he won't be pleased, that's for sure.'

It would have been easy to write Kersey off as a hard-faced cop. He looked the part and, to some extent, it was the image he cultivated. But, early in their association, Wycliffe had discovered behind the mask a moral and compassionate man.

Wycliffe found the organist sitting in a pew at the back of the church. As it happened, the sun was striking down through a stained-glass window in the south wall suffusing the man's face with a rosy pink glow. Paul was in his late fifties but his hair was white; he was plump, smooth-skinned, meticulously groomed, and soberly dressed. Wycliffe recalled Mr Polly's 'portly capon' and smiled secretly.

Wycliffe held out his hand. 'Mr Paul? Have they shown you your organ?'

'I've been shown nothing. I was told to sit here and wait.'

Evidently a man not accustomed to being instructed, but he was not slow to thaw. He stood, looking down at the wedged keys. 'How very odd!'

'Do you make anything of it?'

Paul fingered his smooth chin. 'I hesitate to answer that because the notion seems so utterly absurd. On the other hand, those notes could hardly have been chosen by chance.'

'Tell me.'

'Doesn't that combination mean anything to you?'

'I'm afraid not.'

'Well, the depressed notes are A,B,E,G, and a second G, an octave higher: the notes used by Schumann in his Variations to flatter Meta von Abegg, his girlfriend of that time.'

Wycliffe, despite Helen's efforts, knew little about music but he thought he knew the keyboard. He said, with diffidence, 'But isn't the second note, the black one, B flat?'

The organist was impatient. 'Of course it is, in our notation; but the Germans call it B, which is what Schumann did. That fact, if nothing else, makes it certain that these notes were not chosen at random.'

'Can you suggest any reason why someone might want to draw attention to this piece of music in such dramatic circumstances?'

Paul looked at him with puzzled eyes. 'It means nothing to me. I can't understand it.'

'The dead woman was employed to clean the church so, presumably, you knew her?'

The abrupt change of subject was too much for Paul's precisely ordered mind but he made the effort. 'Knew her? Of course I knew her; and not only through her work here. A few weeks ago I persuaded her to work for me part-time in the house. She came two days a week – Tuesdays and Fridays – for three hours each afternoon. She was very good and, surprisingly, she hit it off with my old housekeeper who is not the easiest of women to get along with.'

'Was she interested in music?'

'Not as far as I am aware.'

'Would you say that anyone setting up this charade needed to be knowledgeable about music?'

Paul hesitated. 'It depends what you mean by knowledgeable. I am sure that a great many people who would not think of themselves as particularly musical would know of the Abegg Variations and of the differences between our notation and the German.'

'Just one more question, Mr Paul – one that will be asked of everyone in any way involved – where were you between, say, seven-thirty and midnight last night?'

'I was at home.'

'Anyone to substantiate that?'

Paul hesitated. 'My housekeeper, I suppose, but she is very deaf and, as we were not in the same room, her evidence may not be reliable.'

There would be more questions for the organist but now Wycliffe wanted to broaden his approach, to get some idea of the probable scope of his inquiry. And Dr Franks had arrived.

Wycliffe joined the pathologist as he stood, taking in the disturbing spectacle of the obscenely exposed body of a murdered woman sprawled at the feet of a holy statue.

Franks was short, not really fat, but a roly-poly of a man. He was cynical, as most pathologists are, but good humoured, as many are not. More to the point, Wycliffe respected his judgement.

Franks said, 'I suppose you realise you've spoilt my holiday?'

'It's a habit I have. What do you make of it?'

Franks, unusually sombre, admitted, 'I thought I'd lost the capacity for surprise, Charles. On the face of it I shan't be much use to you; the forensic aspects seems plain enough. But my guess is you'll be up to your neck in trick cyclists if it ever comes to court. Anyway, let's get on. If Fox is ready to take his pictures . . . '

When Franks had made his preliminary examination, he said, 'Well, it all seems consistent with a nasty knock on the head and I shall be surprised if I have much more to tell you after the autopsy.'

'Nothing on the relative positions of attacker and attacked?'

Franks shrugged. 'If you think it would help, I don't mind doing your job for you. The cranium was fractured in the region of the left parietal, not far from the sagittal suture – in other words, near the top of the head. My guess is that she was stooping or crouching at the time, that her attacker was to her left, and that she raised her head to look up at him as the blow fell. How's that?'

'The power behind the blow?'

Pause for thought. 'The long handle, with a good swing, would generate plenty of momentum without much muscle power behind it. The hammer head isn't very heavy but it didn't need to be.'

'So it could have been a man or a woman?'

Franks nodded. 'Yes, sex doesn't enter the picture from that angle but there seems to be plenty of it about otherwise.'

'Time of death?'

A chubby grimace. 'She seems to have been what the books call "a sound muscular subject" and she was doing moderately energetic things before she got clobbered. On the other hand the temperature in this place in the late evening and night can't be anything to write home about.' He was bending over the body once more, attempting to flex an arm. 'Now, as you see, rigor is on the way out . . . Taken with the body temperature . . . '

Wycliffe said, 'Well? Do I have to do my own sums?'

'I'd give it between seventeen and twenty hours. What is it now – about three? . . . Say between seven and ten last night. If I had to be more precise I'd go for mid-way between the two, but don't put much on that.'

Kathy was in the garden, standing by the steep bank which was almost a wall, the boundary separating Trigg from the church-yard. There were clumps of primroses and the hawthorn bushes which surmounted the bank were coming into leaf. Through the screen of twigs she could see the graves, and the church itself, mellow, lichen-encrusted stones which looked as old as time.

And Jessica was lying dead, just that little distance away. At some time during the evening or night Jessica, in some ways her yardstick, her touchstone, had been viciously murdered. She tried but failed to grasp what it would mean to her. The little policewoman in her trim uniform – a girl in her twenties – had

419

tried to cover her feeling of inadequacy with a professional gloss. 'Your sister would have known almost nothing, Mrs Geach. The doctor says death was instantaneous.'

She had never imagined life without Jessica and she could not now. It was strange, for in recent years they had not been close. Not since . . . Since when? . . . Her marriage to Abe? No, their intimacy had survived that. It dated from Jessica's break with Johnny Glynn. Something to do with the death of the Ruse boy? That seemed to be what Jess was hinting at on Wednesday at the farm. She had been on the point of confiding something, but had changed her mind. At any rate it was sixteen years since they had ceased being twins and had become merely sisters.

Now Katherine felt that she wanted to weep for Jessica, for herself, and for the might-have-been.

'I think you should come indoors; it's clouding over and getting chilly out here.' Abe had arrived, ponderously solicitous.

'I'm not cold.'

'Vinter has been on the phone.'

'What does he want?'

'Well, it's only natural he should want to make contact.'

She was venomous. 'All they're worrying about is being kicked out of the farm, but they've got some explaining to do.'

'Explaining? You don't think they had anything to do with it?'

'Why wasn't I told – why wasn't anybody told – that Jess didn't come home last night? It was the police who went to them, not the other way round.'

He put his arm around her. 'Come in and have a hot drink – a toddy is the thing for you, my girl!'

For some reason Katherine was incensed by his attention and broke away. 'Lay off, Abe, for God's sake! You think everything can be cured by sex or alcohol – or both.'

420

Chapter Three

Easter Sunday afternoon

The headquarters team mustered by Kersey had arrived: Detective Sergeants Lucy Lane and Shaw; and Detective Constables Dixon and Potter – known, because of their respective physiques, as Pole and Pot. With help from the local police, Sergeant Shaw, the squad's Pooh-Bah, wearing his administrative hat, was involved in arranging accommodation for the team and finding a hall or other building which could be used as an Incident Room. The two DCs, again with local support, would be concerned with interviews and inquiries under Kersey's direction.

All of which left Wycliffe free to assume his preferred role, a roving commission, getting to know everybody who was, or might be, involved – in particular, the victim. He considered whether to begin with the sister and brother-in-law at Trigg, but decided on the farm because that was where the victim had lived her life.

He conscripted Lucy Lane – Detective Sergeant Lucy Lane, in her thirties, dark, warm-skinned and eligible, but still single. 'I wouldn't inflict this world on a child of mine. I see too much of it.'

A sentiment which shocked Wycliffe to whom hope was an ultimate resource.

'Shall I get the car?'

'No, let's walk.'

It was characteristic that he should walk rather than drive or be driven; he refused to allow his days to become crowded with events in a frenetic succession of images like a television screen, lacking even commercial breaks to aid digestion.

The immediate countryside about Moresk is one of low,

rounded hills and gentle slopes, moist lanes and trickling water. Standing by the ramshackle gate which led to the farm they could follow the course of the river as it narrowed and was lost between the slopes. No more than a quarter of a mile away a rambling old house in a hotch-potch of styles, not unlike Trigg but larger, fronted on the river. It was backed by a plantation of larches and, on the rising ground behind, a tower dominated the Lilliputian landscape.

Wycliffe said, 'What is it? It looks like a lighthouse.'

It had the proportions of a factory chimney, but it had lancet windows and, at the top, a domed structure slightly greater in diameter than the tower.

Lucy, who had relatives in the county and knew about such things, said, 'I suppose it's a folly. Anyway, it belongs to the Carey family who live in the big house – what's left of them – and it.'

Wycliffe had a weakness for follies and promised himself closer acquaintance with the tower but he had no intimation then of the circumstances which would bring this about.

They passed through the farm gate, and between tethered goats, down the slope to the farmyard which vividly recalled Wycliffe's own childhood. In the yard a man in bib-and-brace overalls was scattering handfuls of grain for the chickens. It was like being in a time warp of fifty years.

'Mr Vinter?'

The man was very tall; thin, and bony, with that stoop which is sometimes habitual to the tall. He seemed to study Wycliffe for a while before speaking, his blue eyes expressionless, then, 'Laurence Vinter – yes. Are you a policeman?'

'Chief Superintendent Wycliffe. This is Detective Sergeant Lane.'

'You'd better come inside.'

They were taken into the sitting room where a woman sat by the window, reading. The light from the window with its tiny panes fell on one side of her face and form, leaving the rest in shadow. She was very fair, with an oval face and perfect features; her straight hair, with its meticulous central parting, precisely framed her face and was caught up in a coil at the back. She wore a blue pinafore frock over a print blouse.

'My wife, Stephanie; Chief Superintendent Wycliffe . . . Detective Sergeant Lane.'

Stephanie Vinter rested her book, still open, on the windowsill, and stood up, eyeing the policewoman. Her little blue eyes were hard.

On the face of it the Vinters were an oddly assorted couple, the woman, small, refined – exquisite; the man, ungainly, angular, and somehow unfinished. But they shared a certain deliberation in speech and manner as though they existed in a world where the pace of life was slower.

The preliminaries over, Wycliffe was seated in a wicker chair which creaked, while Lucy was given a hard kitchen chair which did not. Wycliffe began his questions. 'When did you last see Miss Dobell?'

The two looked at each other and, after a pause, it was the woman who answered, 'Last evening, at about seven. We have our meal at six . . . '

Laurence Vinter said, 'She always goes to the church on Saturday evening to make sure that everything is right for Sunday.'

'But last evening she didn't come back.'

'No.'

Wycliffe was impatient. 'Didn't you expect her back? Weren't you concerned?'

It seemed for a moment that they had no more to say, then Laurence spoke: 'You must understand that our position here is somewhat equivocal. I mean we are not family; we live here in return for helping out on the farm.'

It was Lucy's turn. 'But surely that doesn't mean that you were indifferent to her being out all night with no news?'

Another silence. Laurence Vinter studied his long bony fingers, his wife looked across at him, her gaze expressionless. Wycliffe would have liked to shake them both. 'Well?'

Finally Laurence raised his head. 'It wasn't unusual for Jessica to be away all night.'

'Without warning you?'

'Yes.'

'Have you any idea where she spent those nights?'

'No, and she wouldn't have welcomed any question or comment.'

'How often did this happen?'

Laurence shrugged. 'Three or four times a month? Probably about that.'

'Was it always a Saturday night?' From Lucy Lane.

'On the contrary, it was usually mid-week.'

'Was she ever away for more than one night?'

'A couple of times but then she warned us in advance.'

Wycliffe turned to the woman. 'Presumably, if she intended to be away, she took an overnight bag or something . . . '

'No. She left here the same, whatever her intentions, dressed for the weather as it happened to be.'

'She had a car?'

'No, there is a truck, but that is used only for farm work.'

'So she left here yesterday evening, just after seven, to walk to the church. Is that right?'

'After our meal, as my wife said. It was raining, and she put on her heavy mac with a hood, and the short wellingtons she wears about the farm.'

A collie dog padded into the room, looked and sniffed around, then went out disconsolate.

Wycliffe said, 'How long have you lived with Miss Dobell?'

'Three years last month.'

'Before that?'

Vinter, after the customary pause, said, 'I was a lecturer at Bristol; I had a breakdown and had to give it up.' He spoke slowly, as though his words were being dredged up from some deeper layer of consciousness. 'In the process we lost our home and it happened that we spent the winter of eighty-seven in temporary accommodation near here – a winter let. At the start of the holiday season we had to get out, and Jessica offered us accommodation on condition that Stephanie took on the house-work and I helped on the farm.'

Lucy Lane's verdict would be enlightening.

In a surprisingly short space of time he had arrived where the churchyard bordered the river and there was a kissing-gate. He could continue along the river bank to the village or he could go up through the churchyard. He decided to leave the path and look in at the church.

Lucy Lane found little of interest in the roll-top desk: invoices and receipts and a simple account book recording farming transactions, copies of returns sent to the Ministry, a few letters concerning the farm, nothing personal . . . There were the minimum records which, processed on the cheap by some shrewd, old-fashioned book-keeper, would serve to keep the tax dragon at bay and claim all the subsidies on offer.

In one of the pigeon-holes she came across a chunky, hard-covered, well-thumbed manuscript book labelled 'Farm Diary' and she leafed through it. Jessica had made systematic but telegraphic entries about seed-sowing, planting, spreading fertiliser and goat-kidding – there was not, as far as she could see, a single entry of a personal nature.

She turned to Vinter. 'Now I want to look at Miss Dobell's bedroom and I would like you or Mrs Vinter to come with me.'

Vinter was sullen. 'It's nothing to do with us.'

But Stephanie said, 'I'll come up with you.'

In the bedroom Lucy opened drawers and peered into the wardrobe. She was impressed, as Wycliffe had been, by the characterless nature of the room, and by the fact that in all probability it had been the same for fifty years at least. Stored away in the chest were unused sheets and blankets which must have been new in Jessica's grandmother's day, and when the drawers were opened the stench of mothballs filled the room. The window was small and tightly shut so that one seemed cut off from the river and the world outside.

Jessica's clothes were incidental: several pairs of jeans, a couple of skirts, two or three jumpers, a blouse or two and a random selection of underclothes.

It was depressing. Stephanie, watching from the doorway, was ironic. 'Clothes were hardly Jessica's main interest in life.'

'But didn't she have anything personal? What did interest her other than the farm?'

A faint smile. 'If she had another interest I never discovered it – unless it was men.'

'Didn't she receive any letters other than business ones?'

'I've no idea.'

Lucy was becoming irritated by the woman's smug detachment. 'But you must have seen whatever the postman brought.'

'No. There's a mailbox by the gate which she kept locked. She emptied it herself and handed over whatever concerned us.'

Finally Lucy looked under the bed and was rewarded by a metal deed box which she dragged out. 'Did you know about this?'

Stephanie raised her shoulders but said nothing.

The box was not locked and she spread its contents on the honeycomb quilt: a small, shaggy teddy bear with a squeak; a cheap camera at least twenty years old, a photograph album and a few items of jewellery, wrapped in tissue paper, presumably her mother's. Finally Lucy brought out a small number of envelopes held together by an elastic band.

The envelopes caught Lucy's attention; she sensed a find. There were three; they had been through the mail and carried recent post marks, the latest, no more than a week ago. They were cheap, business envelopes and were addressed in carefully distorted block capitals, the badge of those who, for some reason, wish to appear illiterate as well as anonymous.

Lucy slipped a single sheet of lined paper from one of them. In the middle of the otherwise blank page was a biblical quotation, written in the same block capitals as the address: 'Thou hast played the harlot with many lovers – Jeremiah: 3:1.'

Lucy was intrigued. It struck her as slightly mad. A daughter of the manse she was nevertheless a child of the sixties and, for her, anonymous admonishment by way of biblical texts belonged to the same epoch as the Salem witch trials. She was tempted, but restrained her curiosity about the other envelopes, knowing that Fox would not welcome her prints being added to any others there might be.

'Did you know she was getting anonymous letters?'

'I knew that she'd had one.'

'Did she tell you?'

'I was there when she opened it. It must have been about a fortnight ago. She had come in with the mail – three or four items, she glanced through them and held up one envelope addressed in pencil and in block capitals. She said, "See this? Somebody who doesn't like me." She slit open the envelope, removed a sheet of paper, glanced at it, showed it to me, and said, "Silly cow!" '

'Did you get the impression she knew who had sent it?'

'I got that impression – yes.'

'She gave you no hint?'

'No.'

Lucy said: 'I must take these – and the photograph album. I'll give you a receipt.'

Family photographs are a good source of background. Everything else went back into the box.

It was downstairs as Lucy was leaving that Stephanie thawed. At the last moment it seemed that she was reluctant to break off contact with another woman. 'You probably think that we are unfeeling, but if you had lived as we have for the past three years . . . You see, neither Laurence nor I had any experience of this kind of life . . . But it wasn't only that.' She paused, then added, 'Jessica was a hard woman. Of course we should never have come here.'

'What did you do before?'

'I was a librarian, I have a degree in English. Of course I made the mistake of giving it up when I married – and lost my independence. Laurence had visions of us doing some literary work together while he carried on with his job, but nothing came of it.' She blinked, and her blue eyes misted over. 'Recently, I've been spending some time at Trecara, helping to catalogue Carey's library . . . Are you married?'

'No.'

'Sensible woman . . . Ah, well, Giles is my future.'

Chapter Four

Easter Sunday evening

In the churchyard the rooks were cawing, coming home to roost. Wycliffe entered the church by the south porch. A uniformed policeman stood guard.

'No sightseers?'

'They got tired, sir. But the press have been – and gone. Mr Kersey dealt with them.'

Just inside, on the table where the visitors' book and offertory box were normally kept, Fox and his assistant were logging their treasure trove: little envelopes, each with its tag; the hammer, an ordinary hammer except for its long handle; rolls of film; a clutch of scale diagrams . . .

A grumbling noise from the tower warned that the clock was about to strike and Wycliffe counted the seven strokes almost in disbelief. Fox had taken away his floodlamps, the lighting was dim, the church was returning to normal. Evidence of its desecration had been removed, the flowers were as fragrant as ever, and the statue of Christ looked out across the chancel steps, lantern held high.

'Anything, Fox?'

Fox, excessively lean and lanky, brooded over and fiddled with his hoard like a fastidious stork arranging and rearranging its nest material. Asking him a question was like interrogating a computer, one had to get him into the right mode first. After the necessary lapse of time he said, 'Large numbers of prints, sir, but I've no way of knowing at the moment whose. The weapon was wiped clean, so were the organ keys and the blower switch.'

'You've got the bits of card used to wedge the keys?'

'Pieces of printed paper, sir, neatly cut and folded. They came from a magazine.'

'Any indication which?'

'A religious magazine, but there are several and I shall have to check them out.' Fox produced a block plan of the chancel and the adjacent area including the organ. 'I found a few flakes of mud, sir – river mud, I think, on the carpet of the south aisle. I've marked them with an M on the plan.'

The distribution of the flakes suggested that someone with muddy footwear had walked from the south porch towards the chancel. It was obviously possible that the mud had come from the feet of the killer and that he or she had reached the church by the river bank. The vicar had only to cross the road from his vicarage.

Fox went on, 'I found no actual footprint but one of the flakes carried an impression of the toe of what was probably a rubber boot. It was too fragile to take a cast but I've got photographs.'

'Good. Is Mr Kersey about?'

'I think he must be; I saw him a few minutes ago.'

Wycliffe found Kersey studying an inscribed tablet set in the wall of the chancel. Kersey read aloud: 'Thou shalt not kill, Thou shalt not commit adultery, Thou shalt not steal, Thou shalt not bear false witness . . . ' And he added, 'That little lot adds up to our meal ticket.'

Wycliffe grinned. 'I'd be quite willing to take early retirement. Anyway, what's new? I hear you've had the press.'

'A reporter from the Plymouth paper with his cameraman, another from the local, and an agency chap.'

'Did you let them in?'

'Yes. The body had gone and Fox was all but through. I kept 'em up the west end, away from the chancel area, but they got their pictures.'

'Any good news?'

'Shaw has found us a home, an old school building just off the square, only recently vacated. The Central Stores people are fitting it out. Lucy Lane has laid on a house-to-house: the last time anybody saw Jessica; whether anybody was spotted entering or leaving the churchyard last evening . . . Actually, anybody could get in or out almost anywhere along the boundary wall. There's even a footpath and a kissing-gate down by the waterside.'

'I know. What happens here when Fox has finished?'

'The vicar has agreed to us putting seals on the place for the time being. Incidentally, Tom Reed has gone back to his burrow but we know where to find him.'

'I didn't get any lunch; did you?'

'No, and I'm beginning to miss it. Let's look in at the pub, sir, they must do some sort of evening meal. Ted Shaw did a bit of prospecting there earlier and it's got the Shaw Seal of Approval.'

The Hopton Arms was in the square by the post office, on the corner of Church Lane. Its sign carried a colourful portrait of the old royalist general on one side, and his achievement of arms on the other. The windows were diamond paned, there was a bit of fake timbering, and a rustic board, inscribed in Gothic lettering, offered meals and accommodation.

Kersey said, 'It's a bit olde worlde and the food probably comes out of a microwave but if the beer is reasonable I can live with that.'

Inside, the bar was at one end of a long room, cluttered with the usual furniture, tables with plastic tops that looked like marble and shiny wooden chairs that looked like plastic. At the far end, above glass doors, was a sign with the word 'Restaurant' in blue neon light and, beyond the doors, guarded by a couple of rubber plants, tables with blue cloths were laid, ready for the evening meal. Apart from the landlord, and three or four regulars drinking at the bar, the place was empty.

'Chief Superintendent Wycliffe and Inspector Kersey; am I right?' The landlord came from behind the bar, holding out his hand. He was a big man with short, dark curly hair; he wore a Yacht Club jersey and blue denim trousers. 'Johnny Glynn, at your service. Everybody calls me Johnny. Your Mr Shaw, who was here earlier, made provisional bookings for both of you, and for a DS Lane.

Wycliffe growled and Kersey said, 'What's your draught bitter like?'

'You shall try it, gentlemen – on the house.'

The pints were drawn and the landlord stood watching while they were sampled. 'Well?'

Kersey said, 'It's good bitter, I'll give you that.'

The landlord glanced up at the clock. 'We serve meals from eight on Sundays; seven-thirty on other days; menus on the tables.'

Wycliffe inquired, 'Why Hopton?'

Johnny grinned. 'Royalist general in the Civil War, he met General Fairfax of the parliamentary lot on Tresillian Bridge, not far from here, to agree terms for ending the war in Cornwall. That was March 1646, and legend says he slept here.' Johnny shrugged. 'Could be true, and it might have been good for trade once; now if you said the Virgin Mary slept here they'd want to know "Who's she?" It's the new education.'

Wycliffe picked up his glass, Kersey had his refilled, and they moved away from the bar to seats at one of the little tables. It was dusk, and the lights were switched on.

Kersey said, 'That landlord is a bit of a pain but the place is all right.' Changing the subject, he went on, 'So you've been to the farm, sir . . . ?'

Wycliffe studied the bottom of his glass but refused a refill. 'The dead woman – Jessica . . . Imagine a girl in her very early twenties, her parents killed in a coach crash . . . She insists on keeping the family farm going and, for seventeen years, she succeeds more or less, sometimes going out to work to make ends meet . . . '

'A determined young woman.'

'You can say that again.'

Wycliffe was still struggling to come to grips with the personality of the victim; trying to assess what he had gleaned from his visit to the farm.

'That little house . . . It's spartan. Either she was indifferent to creature comforts or she had a pretty broad streak of self-denial. The family who lived with her had a bleak time, that's for sure.'

Kersey finished his beer. Knowing from experience what this was all about, he asked the right questions: 'What are they like?'

Wycliffe grimaced. 'The man was a lecturer – Bristol – modern languages, but had a breakdown. Academic . . . Well-intentioned, probably hard working, but there's something . . . A square peg doomed to find himself in round holes, and resenting it.'

'And the woman?'

'Ornamental, probably well educated . . . musical. I'd guess not much of a clue when it comes to things like earning a living or organising anything more complicated than tea and biscuits for the vicar.'

Wycliffe twisted his empty glass on a beer mat. 'Anyway, we should have the Lane version shortly. I left her there to snoop around and arrange for their statements. By the way, I want you to make inquiries about Vinter – why, precisely, did he give up his job? It shouldn't be difficult, it was only three or four years ago. And, while you're about it, you might check him out with CRO.'

Kersey lit a cigarette. 'You think he might have form?'

'How should I know? I'm simply trying to size him up; he made me feel uncomfortable.'

Kersey waited, but no more came. Time to prime the pump: 'And our Jessie got herself murdered, so there must have been emotional dynamite around somewhere.'

'Exactly. Presumably a man. Jessica was sometimes away all night; on two occasions, two nights running.'

'No explanation offered?'

'None.'

Kersey said, 'All the same, it's difficult to square the staging and the props with any kind of sex killing I've ever come across.'

Wycliffe nodded. 'It's hard to square any sort of killing, sexual or otherwise, with that theatrical set-up in the church. I've never met anything quite like it. Killing somebody against that background to the accompaniment of five notes which Schumann strung together to flatter his girlfriend – all played at once . . . There's a dangerous dottiness . . . '

People were drifting in, ordering drinks at the bar and taking them through the glass doors to the dining tables in the restaurant. They came mainly in couples but there was one party of five or six. 'You'll have to push the tables together tonight, Johnny; Gemma's got a birthday – her twenty-ninth.'

A wag called, 'Hey up, Gemma! You had that one last year.'

Lucy Lane arrived, an attractive, youngish woman on her own, and a stranger. She was watched, and there was obvious surprise when she joined the two middle-aged men at one of the bar tables. Only the better informed knew they were from the police.

Lucy, taken into the squad as a gesture to sexual equality, had quickly established herself in the hierarchy and she had side-stepped promotion because her next move would have taken her out of CID.

'I hope I did the right thing, sir? I suggested to Ted Shaw that it might be a good idea to make a provisional booking here.'

Wycliffe said, 'I'll tell you in the morning. Do you know what he's doing with the others?'

'They've been fixed up by sub-division: a small, private hotel in Truro; transport has been laid on.'

'I think we'd better find a table.'

But the landlord had already reserved one in a corner by the window.

'Will the hock suit you?'

'What's Chicken à la Marengo?'

'I'm not keen on mushrooms.'

'You'll have to put up with 'em if you have that.'

Meanwhile the party atmosphere was warming up. It seemed that everybody knew everybody else and apparently meaningless sallies raised gusts of laughter and fresh banter from around the tables.

The meal was served by two waitresses from a kitchen, seen through an open door, where a fat woman in a white coat did things with pans on a stove. No microwave in sight. Johnny, the landlord, moved from table to table.

'Everything to your liking, madam, and sirs?'

Wycliffe said, 'Is it always like this?'

'Not every night – this is about usual for Wednesdays and Sundays, they're our busy nights. Perhaps they're a bit more subdued than usual tonight because of Jessica.'

Kersey said, 'Nobody would notice.'

Wycliffe asked, 'Was the dead woman in on these occasions?'

'She didn't come here.'

'And the Geaches?'

The landlord's mobile features were suddenly expressionless. 'No.'

Gemma's health was drunk around the tables and they sang 'Happy Birthday to You', but with the arrival of the cheese-board and coffee, things began to quieten down.

'Well, what did you make of the farm, Lucy?'

Lucy Lane, as always, took time to consider. 'I don't know about the farm, but the house is a museum piece – as you saw. The dead woman intrigues me: all that scraping and saving and going out to work, just to keep going. Incidentally, she kept a farm diary but there's nothing in it of a personal nature that I can see. I brought it away with me just in case.'

After placing a fragment of cheese on a water biscuit and nibbling it, she went on: 'Jessica was getting anonymous letters – or notes, three in the past two months. I handed them over to Fox, still in their envelopes, but I looked at one. It accused her of being a harlot, in a quotation from the Bible. Fox has promised to have them processed, with copies, by the morning.'

Wycliffe said, 'That's all we need! Anyway, what was your impression of the Vinters?'

A wrinkled brow. 'I think I got her measure, sir, but I'm not so sure about him. Stephanie has a degree in English; she was a librarian before she married, and recently she's been spending two or three afternoons a week at Trecara Manor – that's the house with the folly – helping to catalogue Carey's library. I don't suppose she gets paid for that. She doesn't seem a bad sort and I may sound catty, but I doubt if Stephanie has ever felt under any obligation to earn a living.'

'And Vinter?'

'As I said; he's a different case. Not much of what goes on inside shows. Seven-tenths, or whatever, submerged.'

'A possible killer?'

Some hesitation, then, 'If I asked you that question, sir, I'd get short shrift.'

Wycliffe grinned. 'But?'

'I felt there was something, but I couldn't put my finger on it.'

Wycliffe turned to Kersey. 'We've already agreed, that's one for you, Doug: some background on Vinter. Lecturer to labourer in one jump calls for explanation. He mentioned a breakdown but we need to know what kind. It shouldn't be difficult.'

Kersey emptied his coffee cup and sat back. 'That was a good meal.'

Wycliffe refused more coffee and said, 'I think I'll take a walk.'

Predictable; that was his routine when away from home: after the evening meal, a solitary walk, a telephone call to Helen, then bed.

Outside it was chilly, and he fetched a coat from his car, still parked in the square. It occurred to him that he ought to look in at the newly established Incident Room before indulging his whim. DS Shaw would have worked the usual minor miracle and deserved at least a paternal pat.

He found the former school, tucked away behind the post office in the middle of its asphalt playground: traditional Cornish, circa 1900, a single-storied, twin-gabled building of grey stone with granite coigns. Although small, it had two doors, one with 'Girls and Infants', the other 'Boys' carved in the granite lintels. The girls' door was open, and lit. A board propped on the steps carried a poster: 'Police Incident Room', and a uniformed PC said, 'The room on the left, sir.'

The former classroom, separated from another by the usual glass screen, was clean, well-lit, and would probably be almost cosy when the two bottled-gas heaters were working. Furniture and equipment disgorged by Central Stores was being arranged and installed by police personnel, while British Telecom chalked up Sunday overtime. Boxes of stationery were stacked on the floor and a bevy of VDUs, lined against the wall, yearned blankly for partnership with their electronic keyboards. Shaw looked upon his work and saw that it was not so bad, and getting better.

'There's a lady here, sir – Mrs Geach – sister of the dead woman. She insisted on waiting to see you though I told her it was by no means certain you would be in. I put her in the interview room.'

The 'interview room' turned out to be a former store cupboard with a tiny window. It now had a table and two chairs but such is the power of a name that Wycliffe at once recognised and accepted its role. Even the smell seemed to be right. The woman stood up as Wycliffe came in.

'Katherine Geach – Jessica's sister. I thought you would have come to the house . . . ' Her manner was accusing.

'Superintendent Wycliffe.' He mumbled the introduction, sounding apologetic. God knows why except that the woman was strikingly good looking, with restless dark eyes. She was obviously distressed.

He tried sympathy but without effect. Her hands, clasped tightly together, rested on the table top. 'You know that my sister worked part-time for Arnold Paul – the organist at the church?'

'He told me.'

'So you've talked to him! You know that he has his brother living with him?'

'I understand that is fairly recent.'

'Yes.'

Suddenly she seemed to have run out of steam; she had been rehearsing what she would say for too long, now she had to stop and think. 'Yesterday morning – Saturday – my sister came to see me . . . '

'Is that unusual?' asked Wycliffe, recalling that he was a policeman.

She was pushed a little further off balance. 'Well, I suppose it is.' She made an irritable gesture. 'I don't know; the fact is that I usually go to see her rather than the other way round. Does it matter?'

'Probably not. So she came to see you?'

Hesitation. 'Well, she was in the village, shopping, and she just dropped in. She wanted to tell me about something odd which had happened at Arnold Paul's place on Friday afternoon.'

'She was worried?'

'I don't think she was worried, just intrigued.'

'Anyway, go on.' He was in the driving seat now. Mean, but necessary.

'She doesn't – didn't think that Philip – the man who came to live there – is Arnold's brother. She thought there was something crooked going on.'

'Can you enlarge on that?'

'Apparently she had heard them quarrelling more than once and sometimes Arnold called the other man "Timmy" instead of "Phil" as he usually did. Anyway, on Friday afternoon the quarrel was worse. The other man was threatening, and Arnold said, "All you'll achieve by that, my boy, is to put us both inside." There was more, but I can't remember it all.'

'They must have been very careless to let your sister overhear this.'

'They didn't know she was there; she was early, and Mabel Tripp, the old housekeeper, let her in.'

'But Mabel, herself – '

'Mabel is as deaf as a post.'

'You think this could have something to do with what happened to your sister?'

She looked down, fiddling with her handbag. 'I thought you should know, just in case.'

'Yes, you are quite right.' He suspected that there was something more, perhaps something that she found more difficult to talk about.

She looked up. 'I was wondering if I ought – '

There was a commotion outside and a man burst into the little room.

'Kathy! What the hell are you doing here? I've looked everywhere – ' He broke off, and turned on Wycliffe: 'What do you mean by keeping my wife – ?'

Wycliffe stood up. 'I assume that you are Mr Abe Geach. I am Detective Chief Superintendent Wycliffe. Your wife was waiting for me here when I arrived. She volunteered some information and I was about to ask her to make a formal statement. But that can wait until the morning when she has had time to think over what she has told me.'

He turned back to the woman: 'You were about to say . . . ?'

'Oh, nothing, it was of no importance.'

'In the morning, then. At the same time, Mr Geach, there are some questions I shall want to put to you, so I suggest that you are available then.'

Geach stood, rocking on the balls of his feet like a boxer. 'I've got my business to attend to in the morning.'

'No doubt, but this is a murder inquiry. I, or one of my officers, will be at Trigg sometime during the morning – unless you would prefer to come here?'

Wycliffe let his gaze rest on Geach until the silence was observable, then turned to the wife. 'Just one other matter while you are here, Mrs Geach, I understand that the farm belonged to you and your sister jointly – is there a formal agreement?'

'Yes, Jessica insisted on it. The agreement was drawn up by Harry Nicholls of Nicholls and Greet in Truro.'

'Do you know if your sister made a will?'

'We both did, leaving our interest in the farm to each other.'

'Well, thank you for coming along, Mrs Geach. I shall certainly look into what you have told me.'

Geach hesitated, then shrugged. 'Come on, Kathy; let's get out of here.'

Wycliffe was puzzled by Madam Geach. The story about Paul and his brother was probably true and might be significant but people, even the bereaved, do not usually come running to the police in such a hurry. Could Katherine really believe that her sister had been murdered in such an extraordinary way because she had overheard something incriminating from the Pauls? Or was she anxious to divert attention from nearer home?

Wycliffe returned to the square, determined not to be deprived of his walk. The square was reasonably well-lit with lights from the houses as well as a couple of street lamps, but as he walked towards the foreshore he seemed to be approaching a wall of darkness. It was only when he had left the square behind and could feel the shingle beneath his feet that he began to see the gleam of light on the water, to distinguish the shadowy banks of the creek, and the outlines of overhanging trees. Then, turning a little more to his left, he could make out the irregular roof of Trigg against the sky.

The organist, Arnold Paul, and his alleged brother: interesting. It was by no means impossible that a man who had made a good killing in some illicit deals and escaped the law should retire to a village like Moresk and find a respected place in the community. Few villains carry labels, many are neither brutish nor un-cultured. Wycliffe well remembered a drugs dealer who had a reputation as a poet, and an armed bank robber who translated philosophical works from the Russian . . . Nor was it unlikely that such a man would be sought out in retirement and latched on to by another crook in need of a hideaway.

Walking along the shore, crunching over the shingle, he came upon a footpath which seemed to follow the line of the shore and to mark the boundary of Trigg land; obviously the other end of the path from the farmhouse by which he had reached the kissing-gate and the churchyard. He ventured along the path for a few yards and was surprised to find that the trees gave out and that there was open ground, across a lawn, to the house. There were lights, both upstairs and down, and Wycliffe wondered what sort of inquest was taking place there. For some reason, which he preferred not to examine, overtly sexual men like Geach stimulated his aggression.

The organist thing nagged like a sore tooth. It could be a lead, but he was dubious. Even assuming that the dead woman had overheard something deeply incriminating, how had they found out and acted with such dramatic dispatch? And why the bizarre window dressing? Above all, why draw attention to the organ and, therefore, to the organist?

Wycliffe muttered to himself, out of temper, and gave up the idea of a walk. He returned to the square, collected his bag from the car, and re-entered the Hopton Arms. The tables in the restaurant were deserted and had been cleared. There were three or four people around the bar, a couple playing darts, and others scattered among the little tables nearby. Kersey was there, alone at one of them, nursing a glass of bitter.

'Lucy is having an early night. Feel like a nightcap?'

'No, I'm half asleep as it is.' He told Kersey of his interview with Katherine Geach, and of the arrival of her husband. 'One of us must go there in the morning. I shall be interested to see whether they choose to be interviewed separately or together.'

'Do you think there's anything in this business with the Paul brothers?'

'I've no idea; that's for tomorrow.' He stood up. 'Now I'm going to phone Helen, if I can find a phone in this place.'

The landlord had overheard: 'There's a pay-phone in the corridor outside the bedrooms, but if you want privacy, you can use the phone in the office.'

Wycliffe was chastened.

'It's me.'

'I thought it might be. So you're not coming home tonight.'

'No, this looks like being difficult. I'm at the Hopton Arms in Moresk Village – I'll give you the number.'

'Comfortable?'

'Seems so. The food is good.'

Just in time, he stopped himself from asking how the garden was looking, realising that he had been away only a few hours.

'Have you been for your walk?'

'A short one.'

'Look after yourself.'

'And you. Good night.'

He went to bed, determined to put the case out of his mind, and lay awake thinking about Jessica Dobell. Her character, if anything, would provide the key; he was sure of that. And what did that amount to? Jessica – work and sex. It was like the word-association game played by psychologists. Work and sex which she pursued aggressively, with almost frenzied dedication and no regard for her own comfort or anybody else's.

One looked for an aim – an end in view. Money? Security? There were easier ways. Wycliffe felt instinctively that there was no aim, no vision of a future. But what? Could it be an obsessive concern to obliterate something that was past?

He needed to know more about her.

There was nothing wrong with his bed but he tossed and turned. Once, when he got out to recover his duvet from the floor, he looked out of the window and discovered that it was raining, a soft spring rain which sometimes comes when the wind is southerly, bringing with it the tang of a not too distant sea.

His little clock said five minutes past one. He returned to bed and, resigned to sleeplessness, fell asleep almost at once. When he awoke it was broad daylight.

For the Geaches it was a troubled night. To avoid disturbing one another they separated. Abe slept in the spare room but, shortly after daybreak, he crept into their bedroom and found Katherine wide awake. Clumsily solicitous, he came to sit on the side of the bed and stroked her hair.

'We've got to talk, Kath.'

'What is there to say?'

'The police are coming this morning and they will go on until they find out who did it.'

'Isn't that what we want?' Listless.

'Of course, but we ought to be ready to tell them certain things. I mean, they're outsiders, they didn't even know her.'

'You've got something on your mind; why not say it?'

Abe ran a hand through his dark curls. 'I don't want to upset you but think of how she was found. I mean, you *know* how she was found – you insisted on knowing. What I'm trying to say is that there must have been something in her life which explains her death – and the way of her death. That's how the police will look at it.'

'There was what she found out about Arnold's brother – as I told Wycliffe.'

'That the brother wasn't who he said he was and that they seemed to be mixed up in some shady business. Do you think they would have killed her because she overheard something of that sort? The chances are they didn't even know they'd been

445

overheard, but even if they did, even if they decided to kill her, would they have laid on a bloody peep show to do it?'

She was silent for a while, her dark eyes staring at the ceiling.

Geach went on: 'She must have been killed by somebody who meant to kill her and who chose to do it in that way – making a show, what they call nowadays a statement.'

'Like: "Here is a whore!" That's what you mean, isn't it? You're saying that whoever did it was warped – perverted!'

Abe said quietly, 'All right. Did she know anybody like that? . . . Do we? Or somebody who might be?'

She turned to look at him and for the first time he thought that he had her whole attention. 'You still haven't said all you want to say, Abe.'

'No, I'll say it now. Have you thought of Lavin?'

'The houseboat man!' She sat up in her astonishment. 'But Jess had nothing to do with Lavin. His boat happened to be berthed on the foreshore belonging to the farm and the rent was their only contact. He's so badly disfigured that, apart from the lad who lives with him, he doesn't see anybody. Jess hardly ever mentioned him.'

Geach was solemn. 'What you say is true, up to a point; Lavin is a recluse and most of his contacts are through the boy, but you can take it from me, Kath, Jess knew Lavin very well and she spent a lot of time with him.'

'Are you saying they were having an affair?' Her voice was hard.

Geach held out a hand to rest it on her arm. 'I've no proof that they went to bed together, but Jess and he were pretty close. I know that, and I think I should tell the police.'

'Why?'

'Why?' Geach reasoned patiently, as though with a child. 'How old is he? Forty? Not much more, and from what I've heard it's about seven years since he had his accident. God knows what goes on in the mind of a man like that, living there with only the boy for company. Career gone, family gone, friends . . . I don't know the details, but it must be something

446

like that. Then along comes Jess – a very attractive woman, and she gives him friendship and whatever . . . '

Katherine was frowning. 'But everybody says the pair on the boat are gay.'

'Well, they would, wouldn't they? And they may be, but in Lavin's case it could well be Hobson's choice.'

Katherine tried to come to grips with this further insight into her sister's life. 'But even if what you say is true, why would he want to . . . I mean, why . . . ?' Her voice faltered.

Geach squeezed her arm. 'I know what you mean, kid. But what if, for some reason, Jess wanted to stop seeing him – to break off whatever they had between them? That's one possibility, but there's another. If there was a gay thing going between Lavin and his boyfriend there would be jealousy . . . '

'You mean it could have been the boy . . .'

'We just don't know, but we ought to put the police in the picture.'

After a long silence she looked up at him with sudden suspicion. 'How could you possibly know what you've just told me?'

He spoke quietly. 'Let's leave it that I do know it, Kath – just for now.' His manner was pleading.

She said in a toneless voice, 'All right. Just for now.'

'There's something else . . . '

'Go on.'

'About the farm. I know it's too early to talk about the long term but it's got to be kept going for the present, and without Jessica . . . '

'Well?'

'I've got a chap labouring on the Highertown site who rented a smallholding until last year when he went bust. Nothing would please him more than to get back to farming, even on a temporary basis. He could help out there.'

'Who's going to pay him?'

'He can stay on my pay roll until things – well, until we know where we stand over the other business.'

Katherine swept back her hair in a tired gesture. 'I don't feel right about the "other business" as you call it, Abe. If it goes ahead now it's like taking advantage of what happened to Jess.'

Geach put his hand on her shoulder. 'Yes, well, there's no hurry to do anything. Just see how you feel as time goes on.'

Katherine looked at her husband, and was thoughtful. 'I wish I knew what was behind all this, Abe. It can wait, but don't take me for a complete fool.'

Chapter Five

Easter Monday

Lucy Lane, first down, said, 'It was the usual bacon, egg and sausage thing, or kedgeree. Johnny was anxious to get on, because of the holiday, so I said kedgeree.'

Kersey, who carried on a more or less clandestine affair with saturated fats, grumbled, 'It's as bad as being home.'

Wycliffe, more Jesuitical, preferred such decisions to be made for him. 'Kedgeree suits me.'

There were only two other tables occupied, one by an elderly, studious-looking couple who were probably touring Cornish churches or looking for ley lines; the other, by two pin-striped salesmen types who must surely have strayed off the spine road and got pixilated.

At a little before half past eight the police party left the pub for the Incident Room around the corner. In the fine, misty rain every surface shone or glistened, and every ledge dripped. Kersey stopped at the post office. 'I want some cigarettes.'

'Get a couple of newspapers at the same time.'

Despite the rain there was activity in the square; a van was unloading at the post office, a couple of cars were filling with petrol at the garage, and a boat was being hauled up the slipway. The Truro bus was about to move off, though without its usual complement of workers and shoppers. Easter Monday was a holiday for most people.

In the Incident Room order had been extracted out of chaos. As yet it was on a small scale – just three fumble-fingered policemen tapping away on their machines. He was guided to his tiny office, leaving Kersey and Lucy Lane to sort out what was new.

Wycliffe's cubby hole had been carved out of a classroom as an office for a former headteacher. There was just room for a desk, a cupboard and a couple of chairs, and the original furniture was still there. In one of the desk drawers he found a little book recording visits by the school nurse and a pad of forms for reporting damage and dilapidations affecting buildings and equipment.

When Kersey joined him he was standing, staring out of the window at the gleaming wet asphalt of the playground and the boundary wall. He was recapturing that childhood experience of school – utterly cut off from the world, while a clock on the wall doled out some of the longest minutes and hours that he would ever know.

The two of them sat down. 'Mind if I smoke, sir?' A ritual question, but an acknowledgement of their hierarchic relationship which would probably last for the rest of the day. Kersey had the newspapers.

'Anything in them?'

Kersey pushed over the regional paper, the *Morning News*, folded back.

'They weren't in time for the national early editions we get down here, but this chap's done pretty well.'

There were two library pictures of the church: one of the exterior, the other a view of the chancel.

The headlines read: 'Murder in Church', 'Ritual Killing?'. And the text went on: 'When the Reverend Michael Jordan, Vicar of Moresk, arrived to celebrate Holy Communion at his church on the morning of Easter day he found the partly clothed body of Jessica Dobell, sprawled across the chancel steps, at the very feet of a statue of Christ. She had been brutally killed by a blow to the head, believed to have been inflicted by a hammer found close to her body.'

The wedged organ keys were said to provide: 'a distressing, nerve-jangling discord as an accompaniment to this scene of horror which confronted the vicar.

'It is difficult to see this crime as other than a bizarre and senseless ritual murder.'

Wycliffe said, 'That should bring 'em down by the car load. Anything more helpful in our own reports?'

'Nothing factual. Nobody was seen entering or leaving the church on Saturday evening or, if they were, it was so ordinary that the fact didn't register. Of course, we now have formal statements from the vicar and from the Vinters – including the boy.'

'What about gossip?'

'Jessica isn't getting quite the flattering obituary the victim can usually count on. There's some talk of her meanness, more of her sex life. No names, but it won't be difficult to ferret them out when the dust has settled a bit. It seems that the Women's Guild, under the presidency of the vicar's sister, resented Jessica having the church cleaning job – not that anybody else wanted it, but she was regarded as morally tainted.'

'The Vinters?'

Kersey brushed ash from his shirt front. 'Vinter is rarely seen in the village but he often goes to church with his wife on Sunday evenings. It seems he's interested in natural history – especially bats, and he's doing some sort of survey. Stephanie belongs to the Musical Society, run by the vicar and the organist. She's regarded as a kind of phenomenon, not quite real.'

Kersey's lined features contorted into one of his baby-frighteners, registering mirth. 'One woman said she didn't get taken down and dusted often enough. The boy, Giles, belonged to the Musical Society but gave up a month or two back, though he still goes to church with his parents. He's got the name for being a big-head. Seems he's something of a prodigy at school; a sound bet for the Oxbridge scholarship stakes.'

'Anything on the Geaches?'

'Another slice of family life. Geach's father died of a heart attack in his early sixties. Mother Geach is still around; she shares a harbour flat at Falmouth with another widow. Abe carries on where his father left off, a workaholic, and is expected to go the same way as his dad. He's also got a name as a womaniser. His contracts take him all over the two counties and he uses a rather plush motor-caravan as a mobile office and sleeping quarters. Useful for his women too.'

'Any suggestion of local women being involved?'

'One doorstep oracle hinted at Jessica – I suppose that was inevitable; but she backed down when pressed.'

'Paul and his brother?'

'Arnold Paul is well liked but so are most people who give away money. Nobody seems to have seen much of the brother.'

Wycliffe brooded. 'I think I'll see the Pauls while you have a go at the Geaches. Turn the screw a bit if you have to.'

Lucy Lane arrived with a handful of polythene envelopes and Jessica's photograph album. 'The originals of the anonymous notes, sir. The envelopes and the sheets have been kept separate. Fox has given them the treatment; plenty of prints on the envelopes but only the dead woman's on the sheets. Whoever sent them knew enough for that.'

Lucy laid them on the desk in front of Wycliffe. 'They are in order and the dates range over the past seven weeks.'

Wycliffe looked them over with a jaundiced eye, then began to read them aloud: 'The first one says: "Thou shalt not play the harlot – Hosea 3:3." The second: "Thou hast not played the harlot with many lovers – Jeremiah 3:1." And the last: "Thou hast played the harlot with them yet couldest not be satisfied – Ezekiel 16:28." A consistent theme.'

Kersey grinned. 'And spot on. I didn't realise the Bible was up to it.'

Lucy said, 'It's all there if you're prepared to look for it, but I can't imagine why anyone would go to the trouble of sending the things. What did they expect to achieve?'

Kersey shrugged. 'What do Jehovah's Witnesses expect to achieve when they come knocking on my door? Even the sight of me doesn't put 'em off. As to who sent these, I expect there are one or two members of the Women's Guild not averse to brooding on the sex life of an unenlightened sister. A spot of reforming propaganda might seem in order.'

Wycliffe agreed. 'Yes, propaganda is the word – these don't threaten. If the sender intended violence I would expect a more

452

aggressive follow-up to these. Surely anybody playing God would get a kick out of threatening the wrath to come before proceeding to execution.'

Lucy said, 'Perhaps, but the fact remains, Jessica is dead – murdered, and these messages were sent to her.'

There was no answer to that, so Wycliffe shuffled the plastic envelopes together and handed them back. 'All right, stir the pond, Lucy, and see what comes to the surface. Now, what's this photo album?'

He turned the pages: the Dobell girls, from nappies to school uniform, on to gangling adolescence and the first flush of maturity. In the earlier photographs parents were much in evidence, in the later ones, girlfriends and boyfriends took their place. At home Helen treasured a similar record of their own twins.

Lucy drew his attention to a snapshot taken on a beach, the sea in the background; the two girls skittish in bikinis, and two boys in trunks. They faced the camera, arms linked in pairs. 'Recognise the boys, sir?'

On close inspection he recognised the one with Katherine, a younger version of Abe Geach, the contractor, lusty, brawny and ready to go. 'I can't place the other.'

Kersey said, 'You should never have been a copper, sir. That's Johnny Glynn, our sneaky landlord. He looks a good deal thinner and a lot less smug.'

The sequence came to an abrupt end with several highly professional photographs of Katherine's wedding, a very up-market occasion. Then no more photographs. The wedding, or something else at about that time, seemed to mark the end of an era for the girls. The last two or three pages of the album had been used to paste in news clippings from the local paper.

Lucy said: 'The last is recent – just a few days ago.'

'Anything particular strike you about them?'

'They're a mixed bag. Of course the report of her sister's wedding is there and an account of the inquest on their parents and the coach crash.'

'Nothing significant? – Odd?'

453

Lucy was hesitant. 'Not odd exactly but it happens that three of the cuttings, including the most recent one, refer to a family called Ruse from Tresillian. In January seventy-six their fifteen-year-old son was killed in a hit-and-run while cycling home. There is a report of the accident, and of the inquest which recorded a verdict of unlawful killing against a person or persons unknown.'

'A bit unorthodox.'

'Yes. Anyway, the latest cutting is an account of the funeral, last week, of the boy's mother, aged fifty-five. I wondered why that family and the incident had such obvious interest for Jessica.'

Most of police time in any investigation is spent chasing shadows but the Yorkshire Ripper case reminded every CID chief of Sod's law – that it's the shadow you don't chase which turns out to be flesh and blood.

'Find out a bit about it – don't spend too much time. The original case will be in the files so have a word with Inspector Reed; he should be able to brief you.'

He turned to Kersey. 'Now, Doug, you're for the Geaches, and I'm for the Pauls.'

But, left alone, he continued to sit at his desk, assiduously manicuring his nails with a matchstick, a habit Helen deplored.

So. Anonymous messages had been added to the elaborate charade in the church. But he knew better than to be fooled by the decoration on the cake. Underneath he would find the usual drama of jealousy or hatred or greed, or any of them in combination; a drama with a scenario little different from many others. The difference in this case was that the theme had been so overlaid; so decorated and contrived that it was unrecognisable. A hint of madness? Perhaps; but madness allied to the logic of Alice's Wonderland.

He was on the point of leaving when Potter came in: 'The boy wants to see you, sir – the Vinter boy.'

'Send him in.'

Giles Vinter came in, looking about him with apparent interest, head held back because his glasses were halfway down his nose.

'Did you ever go to this school?'

'No. I was fourteen when my parents came here and I went straight to the senior school in Truro.' The blue eyes were solemn but there was no sign of unease as he took the seat Wycliffe offered.

'Can I help you? Or, perhaps, you can help me. I assume this is about Miss Dobell?'

But Giles needed none of the routine treatment for young witnesses. The glasses were pushed up with the middle finger of the left hand, an unconscious movement. 'I didn't like her. I am not upset about her death, but I don't want you to suspect the wrong person.'

'Can you help me to suspect the right one?'

'No, but I can tell you something I didn't tell you at first. On Saturday evening there was a telephone call for her after she left for the church.'

'Any idea of the time?'

He looked thoughtful. 'I was up in my room and my parents were downstairs talking. I think they were quarrelling, and I heard my father go out – he usually goes out between eight and half-past so it must have been about then. I was coming downstairs when the telephone rang; my mother wasn't in the living room so I answered it.'

'Go on.'

'It was a man's voice, he didn't give his name, he just asked to speak to Miss Dobell. I told him she was out and he asked if I knew where he might contact her. I told him she would be at the church. He thanked me and rang off. That was all.'

'You didn't recognise the voice?'

'No.

'Would you if you heard it again?'

'I don't think so; it was quite ordinary and we were always getting calls for her.'

'Did he give you the impression that he was worried or annoyed?'

'I don't think so.'

'I would like you to put what you have said into a fresh statement.'

455

'All right.'

'Before you do, just one or two more points: you said that you disliked Miss Dobell.'

'Yes; she was cruel, and she treated my mother very badly.'

'What about you and your father?'

'That too, but it was worse for my mother.'

The boy sat opposite Wycliffe, a slight figure, his blond hair cut short with a fringe, his head tilted back slightly to cope with his bifocals. He seemed self-contained and totally at ease. Wycliffe tried to draw him into talk: 'You used to belong to the church Musical Society but you gave it up . . . '

'They didn't want me.'

'I hear that you are working for your A-levels and an Oxbridge scholarship; do you think you'll make it?'

'If I decide to go ahead with it.'

'You think that you may not?'

'I don't know.'

'Do you play any games?'

'Only chess; no field games.'

'You play chess at home with your father?'

'He's no good at it. Mother plays with me sometimes, but it's not a woman's game.'

Wycliffe gave up. 'Well, thank you for coming. If you go into the next room someone will take your statement.'

Wycliffe felt deflated. But what the boy had told him might mean something. Had the killer telephoned to make sure that Jessica would be at the church? It was possible.

Before leaving for the Pauls' he studied the 1/2500 Ordnance map. Wycliffe's attitude to maps was ambivalent, even whimsical; they were a necessary evil but they diminished his world. Unless it was essential, he preferred not to know what was around the next corner or over the next hill. But here, on this single sheet of paper, all the secrets of the neighbourhood were laid b. e the village, Trigg, the church, the path along the river bank, even the reed bed and the tower . . . No wonder people climb mountains and go to Greenland.

*

A century ago Moresk had consisted of a few cottages, Trigg House, the church and Trecara. The growth of Truro, the desire of shopkeepers and professional people to move 'out of town', and the fashion for second homes, combined to produce an overgrown village, lacking much coherence, but still a pleasant place to live.

The more prestigious villas were in Church Lane, on the other side from the church, and it was in one of these, behind a tall dry-stone hedge topped with flowering shrubs, that Arnold Paul had settled in his retirement. Wycliffe arrived there at about ten; it was still raining but there was a pearly brightness in the sky with a promise of sun.

As he stood on the doorstep he could hear music – one of Wagner's blockbusters – he neither knew nor cared which. After some delay the doorbell was answered by Mabel, lean, angular, and no-nonsense. Because he shouted, or because she read his lips, she understood his purpose.

'You'd better come in.'

He was shown into a large room in which the senses were drowned under a welter of sound.

'You'll have to wait; he's still in the bathroom. You can sit down, but you mustn't touch things; he's fussy.'

Wycliffe traced the source of the music to a space-age, slim-line music centre in one section of which a compact disc spun smoothly, and in deceptive innocence, while feeding its coded barrage of sound to two columnar speakers, strategically placed in the room. Any means of volume control eluded him.

Having met the well-groomed, precise, and rotund organist, who looked like Trollope's Mr Harding, Wycliffe was surprised by the comfortably relaxed and untidy room. Shelves covering most of one wall were stacked with what seemed to be musical scores; shelves on another wall held a little library of books on musicology, wedged in anyhow. Framed portraits of composers found space where there were no shelves, and any convenient ledge supported its dusty plaster bust of some eminent musician.

The point was made that Arnold Paul was a musician.

Despite the ear-splitting noise Wycliffe had not had time to get bored before Paul came in looking more than ever like a well-heeled clergyman in mufti.

'Ah, Mr Wycliffe! The music is rather loud I'm afraid, but I like to hear it in my bath.' He picked up a remote control device and silence came with the impact of a negative thud.

'There! Now, how can I help you?' He sat in one of the several armchairs, crossed his short legs, and was all attention.

'I had hoped to see your brother also.'

'My brother?' A look of surprise. 'I'm sorry, but that isn't possible; he left early this morning.'

'Left? Where did he go?'

Paul seemed slightly put out by the abruptness of the question but he put a good face on it. 'He took the seven twenty-one train to London. I ran him into Truro while I was still only half awake.'

'A sudden decision?'

'Not really.' Paul uncrossed his legs and went on with exaggerated patience: 'My brother and I do not get on well together and recently there has been increased friction. Last week it reached something of a climax and we agreed that it would be better to revert to the old arrangement under which we lived apart.'

'So, where has he gone?'

Paul was brusque. 'If you are asking me for his address, I don't know it. Probably he has booked in at some hotel while he looks around for a place that will suit him.'

'Presumably he has some sort of business?'

The little man shifted irritably in his chair. 'I know nothing of my brother's business, Mr Wycliffe! And, quite frankly, I do not understand your interest.'

'Perhaps you will give me his former address.'

Paul spread his hands. 'I cannot do that. We were in touch only by telephone until he came here and it was always he who made contact. To be frank, when he wanted something.'

'His first name is Philip?'

Paul's little eyes were alert and guarded. 'Yes, but really – '

'But you sometimes addressed him as "Timmy".'

458

A slight start of surprise. 'You are well informed, Mr Wycliffe, Timmy was a sort of pet name he picked up as a child. I have no idea of its origin.'

Arnold Paul was not easily put off balance but there had been a significant delay before he offered his explanation. Not that what he said was improbable.

'Your brother is younger than you?'

'By two years.'

'You were overheard to say, during one of your disagreements: "All that would achieve is to put us both inside".'

A faint smile. 'Did I say that? That would have been in connection with his suggestion for a joint business venture – a rather bitter joke on my part, I'm afraid.'

'Your brother's business activities were on the wrong side of the law?'

Another smile, a little more nervous. 'Sometimes, perhaps in a grey area; in any case, not the kind of thing in which I would want to be involved.'

'What is, or was, your business, Mr Paul?'

'I was the financial director of the London and Midlands Credit and Investment Bank.' Distant.

'You retired early?'

'I was just fifty. Music has always been my real interest and I worked hard for thirty years so that I could make it my sole concern. I could, of course, have taken it up as a career, but I knew that my talent was insufficient to earn me, as a professional musician, the kind of money I needed to keep me in comfort and security.' A smile. 'You see, Mr Wycliffe, I have never been one for starving in an attic.'

'When did you last see Jessica Dobell?'

The sudden question brought him up short. He shifted uncomfortably in his chair. 'Oh, dear! I have been rather dreading that question. There is something I should have told you, or someone, earlier. I saw her in the church on Saturday evening. I store quite a lot of music in a cupboard behind the organ and I wanted – '

'You have a key to the church?'

'Certainly! I sometimes go across to play for my own amusement and, of course, there is the Musical – '

'Who else has a key, apart from the vicar?'

'Jessica had one, and Harry Clemens, the churchwarden – he owns the post office and general store in the square. Oh, and whoever is in charge of the flowers for the week.'

'What time was it when you saw Jessica?'

'About eight? At any rate between half-past seven and eight.'

'Someone telephoned the farm to speak to Jessica between eight and half-past. Was it you?'

'Why would I telephone her? I told you I have my own key.'

'What was she doing when you arrived?'

Paul hesitated as though the next bit would be even more difficult.

'There is a door off the chancel into the vestry which closes on a spring and a wooden wedge keeps it open when required. Someone had wedged it too securely and Jessica was trying to free it by knocking it gently with a hammer.'

'With a hammer.' Wycliffe's voice was bleak.

'I'm afraid so.'

'Who would need to wedge the door?'

'Oh, the women doing the flowers on Saturday afternoon. They get water from the toilet off the vestry. Almost certainly one of them wedged it open and couldn't free it.'

Paul was getting flustered. 'I realise that I have been very remiss in not telling you this before but you can see that it has no special significance.'

'That is for me to judge. You neither saw nor heard anyone in the church, or in the vicinity, when you were going and returning?'

'I saw no one.' He went on: 'I feel very guilty about this but, of course, I have never been in such a situation before. I was deeply shocked when I heard of Jessica's death and I suppose I was reluctant to involve myself.'

'The fact that your brother has now left, and that his whereabouts is unknown, has nothing to do with your belated decision to speak out?'

Paul's eyes widened. 'That is a most improper suggestion, Mr Wycliffe!'

'It was not a suggestion, it was a question, and when you withhold information from the police in a murder inquiry, it is the sort of question that is asked, and answers are sought. I would like to see the room which your brother occupied while he was here.'

'His room?' Paul seemed on the point of refusing but thought better of it. 'All right. If you will come with me . . .'

Wycliffe was taken to a large room at the back of the house on the first floor. It was a bedroom which had been turned into a bedsitter. Apart from the usual bedroom furniture, which included an unmade bed, there was a desk and, on the desk, a telephone and a rack of stationery. There was also a large ashtray holding a briar pipe. The lingering smell of pipe smoke rekindled a vague longing in Wycliffe.

Paul said: 'He's forgotten his pipe.'

'Nothing has been touched since he left this morning?'

'Everything is as he left it. As you see, even his bedding hasn't been removed.'

Wycliffe slid open the desk drawers; they were empty. On open shelves let into the alcove by the chimney breast there were several paperbacks. Wycliffe looked them over: the brainchildren of John le Carré, led by the inimitable Smiley.

'Are these his?'

'Yes, he has a taste for spy fiction.'

'I would like this room left as it is for the time being, Mr Paul. I'll send someone along to take a look at it.'

'Surely, Mr Wycliffe! . . . Are you implying that he might have a record?'

'You said yourself that his business activities were sometimes in a grey area of the law. From what the dead woman told her sister it is clear that she suspected him of some criminal involvement. She has been murdered, and I have to trace your brother if only to eliminate him from the inquiry.'

Paul was silenced.

'Just one more question, Mr Paul: when you saw her on Saturday evening, was she her usual self?'

The organist seemed dazed, but he made an effort. 'Entirely. She made some typical remark about flower arrangers who didn't know their own strength. I collected my music and when I left, she had already removed the wedge and she was polishing the tiles where it had scratched.'.

'Thank you. Now, I must ask you to make a written statement concerning what you have told me. I suggest that you come to the Incident Room in the old school building sometime this afternoon.'

Wycliffe left, thinking that it was one thing to take Arnold Paul down a peg or two, but quite another to imagine him or his elusive brother staging a melodramatic killing. But it was not impossible, and Philip or Timmy had made a quick and well-timed get-away.

Kersey crossed the square to the Trigg entrance. There was no gate, just two granite pillars with a much-weathered anonymous ornament on the top of each. Although it was not actually raining the air was saturated with moisture, and the moss, which grew on the gateposts and most of the stonework, was intensely green.

Three vehicles were parked on a freshly gravelled area near the house: a deluxe motor-caravan, a Rover saloon, and a Mini. The house had no particular shape, it seemed to have evolved at the whim of successive owners, all very long dead. The result was a pleasing jumble, mellowed by time, lichen, moss and ivy.

At any rate it pleased Kersey, who knew nothing of architecture but hated ostentation.

He had difficulty in finding the door, but when he did it was answered by a youngish woman, plump, pink, and freckled. 'Mrs Geach?'

'No. I suppose you're the policeman; you'd better go into the breakfast room.'

A room in which it was obvious that nobody ever had breakfast, it was a nondescript parking place for visitors who were not paying a social call.

Kersey sat for a couple of minutes gazing at gilt-framed

462

furnishing landscapes, and an enormous walnut sideboard with a marble top on which there stood a hideously ornate samovar. Geach must have made a habit of collecting the left-overs from country-house sales.

Geach joined him, loose limbed, shambling, ready for anything.

'Mr Geach? . . . Inspector Kersey.'

'I was expecting your boss.'

'We all have our little disappointments, sir.'

Geach gave him a doubtful look and sat himself in one of the armchairs. Kersey was perched on one of the high-backed dining chairs with a leather seat.

'All right. Fire away.'

Kersey said, 'I can see you're not a man to beat about the bush; neither am I, so I'll get down to it. How well did you know your sister-in-law?'

Geach screwed up his lips. 'How well do you know yours? Assuming you've got one. She had the farm to run; my wife and I have our own lives; we didn't live in each other's pockets.'

'I saw the motor-caravan. Nice job.'

Geach became wary. 'So?'

'Handy for site work; handy too, I imagine, for entertaining the odd visitor in private.'

Geach remained cool. 'If you intend to be offensive, I should warn you – '

Kersey cut in with practised skill. 'No, I should warn you, Mr Geach, that this is a murder inquiry and, whatever you think, a lot of dirty linen will be fished out of the clothes basket. Whether it's all washed in public will depend on the people concerned. You, for instance; you can talk to me, man-to-man, or you can put up with us ferreting around for days, weeks – months if necessary. You don't need me to tell you that there aren't any real secrets in a place like this. Then, of course, there are the lads who work on your sites . . . '

Geach took a packet of mini cigars from his pocket and lit one. 'Smoke if you want to. Have one of these?'

'No, thanks, I'll smoke my own.'

Geach was looking at him with something like amusement. 'You're an impudent bastard, but I think we might get on.'

'Good! So you entertain the occasional woman in your van.' Kersey put on his best conspiratorial leer. 'Nothing to do with me unless one of 'em happens to have been Jessica Dobell. Think before you say anything, we've already had a hint along those lines and it wouldn't take much for us to have the forensic boys turn over the van.'

Geach drew deeply on his cigar and blew out a cloud of smoke. 'I don't believe this! I've got a bloody good mind to boot you out and put in a complaint.'

'It's up to you, sir, but I think we each had our reasons for coming to this little chat alone.'

Geach thought about this.

Kersey knew that he was on thin ice but he felt that he understood the contractor. He also understood why Wycliffe had given him the job instead of doing it himself.

Geach squinted at him through the smoke. 'All right; I don't suppose it will do me any harm unless you are a bigger fool than I take you for. Jessica did see the inside of my van a couple of times.'

'She was away from the farm three or four nights a month – two nights running a couple of times.'

'Not with me, she wasn't. Twice, as I said.' He seemed about to continue, but hesitated. Kersey, apparently indifferent, was looking out of the window watching Katherine, hands thrust deeply into the pockets of her mac, walking by the river. Geach went on: 'My sister-in-law, sex-ways, was a woman and a half, Inspector; damn nearly a nympho. She couldn't get enough.'

'You are saying there were others? The chap who lives there – Vinter, perhaps?'

'That's for sure, but she wouldn't want to be away nights for that, would she? All in working hours, so to speak.' Geach brushed ash from his jumper. 'No, the man you should be talking to is Lavin – the houseboat man – that's where she spent those nights away – some of 'em anyway. I intended to tell you that much before we started.'

'How do you know?'

'She told me.' He fixed Kersey with a quiet stare. 'She got some of her kicks that way – talking about it.' He shrugged. 'She pretended that in her book, sex-ways, I didn't rate very high; five out of ten, if that.' A crooked smile, 'While Lavin, if half of what she said was true, should have a medal to show for it. But I reckon that was her ploy, she probably did the same with him.' Geach became thoughtful. 'Jessica was one of those women who hates to take anything from a man. When she did, she couldn't bring herself to admit it.'

'You know Lavin?'

'I've only seen him a few times but he's lived in that boat for a couple of years – he took it over from Shorty Boase, when they put the old man into a home. Anyway, Lavin's very badly disfigured – doesn't show himself much; some sort of accident a few years back. But it didn't put Jessica off. No way.'

'Does he live by himself?'

Geach relit his cigar and spoke between rekindling puffs. 'No, he's got a boy living with him – I say boy, but he could be in his twenties. They call him Jumbo because he's a big chap and a bit ponderous. There's something odd about him, but he's Lavin's lifeline to the outside.'

Kersey was almost affable. 'Now, sir, if you can tell me the last occasion when the deceased visited your van . . . '

'It must have been early March, I could probably work it out.'

'You do that; ready for your statement.'

'You still want a statement?'

Kersey was cheerfully ironic. 'You must be joking! You've been sleeping with the victim of a sex killing and you ask me if we want a statement. You're in the target area, my friend, and I think you know it.' Kersey broke off and stood up. 'So let's say, this afternoon, at the old school, sir.'

Geach, too, got to his feet. 'Will my wife have to know about Jessica?'

'Why should she? Unless it turns out you're the man we're looking for, then you'll have other things to worry about.'

'You're going to take a statement from her?'

'On the matter of what she was told by her sister about the situation between the Paul brothers. You don't have to worry. I'll send along a nice friendly DC and they can work it out between 'em here.'

As Geach followed him out into the hall a slim, dark girl flitted away down the passage.

'Your daughter?'

'Yes, damn it! Was that door shut?'

'Not quite.'

On the doorstep, Kersey said, 'What do you think of the Vinters?'

'Off the record?'

'Carried to the grave.'

'All right. Vinter's one of life's also-rans; two left feet. And Stephanie? She looks like a bit of Dresden china but there's a rumour Vinter isn't the boy's father.'

'What about the boy?'

Geach blew out his cheeks. 'He's supposed to be very bright but to my mind he's a poof in the making. Our Julie's got a thing about him and he's been to the house once or twice, but I told him to bugger off.'

Kersey left, pleased with himself; the contractor was no longer cocky.

Chapter Six

Easter Monday (continued)

'The dead woman's clothes, sir. Just returned from the path lab.'

Each item had been bagged and tagged separately: jeans, denim jacket, torn shirt, briefs, socks and slippers. Lucy Lane was laying them out on a trestle table in the Incident Room in case it became necessary to send them to Forensic.

Wycliffe was aware of a certain tension in her manner. 'What's the problem?'

'There's this; another anonymous.' She held out two polythene covers, one containing the envelope, the other the message.

'Another? Where did it come from?'

'It was found in the pocket of her jeans, sir. It's postmarked last Thursday, two days before she was killed.'

'Why wasn't it reported and dealt with last night?'

'It was missed when the body was stripped at the path lab. The clothes remained in the bins all night and the envelope was only found when they came to be bagged and logged this morning.'

Lucy waited for the obvious question: 'Who was attending?' But it didn't come. Wycliffe knew the virtue of the occasional blind eye. Somebody had boobed, but it wasn't the end of the world and nit-picking, to be effective, must be strictly rationed.

Lucy was still uneasy. 'Fox processed it this morning.'

Panic stations, obviously, and a closing of ranks. Lucy had been talked into being the sacrificial lamb; not in character. She went on, 'When it was found, the envelope hadn't been opened. It seems Jessica didn't attach much importance to these messages; she must have stuffed it into the pocket of her jeans and forgotten all about it.'

467

'What does it say?'

As with the others, the message was brief: 'These shall hate the whore and shall make her desolate and naked – Revelations 17: 16.'

'What do you make of it?'

'It's different – an obvious threat this time.'

'The missing link in the chain?'

Lucy looked vague. 'I suppose it could be, sir, but the writing seems different as well as the aptness of the quotation – as though someone tried to imitate the others, not very successfully. The paper and envelope are the same as the others but anybody can buy them.' She added, abruptly, 'I would like to talk to the vicar's sister about these.'

'You think she sent them?'

'With respect, sir, it's only that she probably knows more of what goes on amongst the women of the village than anybody else – I mean, those connected with the church.'

'And you think a woman wrote these things?'

'I would like the chance to find out.' Lucy had recovered her poise. Obviously she thought the storm cones had been lowered.

'All right; go ahead. Anything else?'

'I had a word with DI Reed about the Ruses . . . ' She added, to jog his memory: 'The cuttings in Jessica's photo album about the boy who was killed in the hit-and-run.'

'Well?'

'He remembers the case well. He was a sergeant in Traffic at the time and much involved. The lad was cycling home from Trispen at about half-six in the evening. It was winter, and dark, and he was hit by a motorist. His body and the bike were then pushed over the hedge, presumably to delay an inquiry, and not found until next morning. There were doubts as to whether the boy was dead when his body was pushed over, and local feeling was very strong.'

'The culprit was never found?'

'No. Johnny Glynn was a prime suspect but there was no evidence against him that would stand up in court. The inquiry went on for months and, in theory, the file is still open.'

Wycliffe had a vague recollection of reports concerning the investigation but he had not been directly involved. 'Ring DI Reed and say that I will look in on him tomorrow afternoon to discuss the case.

It was mid-morning when Lucy arrived at the vicarage; the rain had stopped but it was still wet underfoot. The doorbell was answered by Celia, in person. Lucy introduced herself and showed her warrant card.

'My brother is in Truro for a meeting with the bishop.' Uncompromising. Lucy almost expected the door to be shut in her face.

'It was you I came to see – if you can spare me a few minutes.'

Celia Jordan was grey, her hair, her eyes, her skin, and her frock – the frock reminded Lucy of a nun's habit. And Celia's manner was bleak.

She hesitated, sizing up her visitor. 'All right, I can give you a few minutes. Wipe your feet – I've just hoovered the passage.'

The vicarage was modern, built by the Church Commissioners when they sold off their legacy of old and over-large properties which catered for a more prosperous and fecund clergy. But the Jordans had contrived to give the place an appearance of being steeped in decades of ecclesiastical dreariness and gloom. There was an abundance of varnished woodwork, fawn and brown fabrics, and drab wallpapers relieved only by prints of holy pictures.

She was taken to a room at the back of the house, obviously the Vicar's study. There was a desk, a prie-dieu, and a great many shelves of religious works. It was dimly lit because the window was shielded by a conifer hedge grown close to the house. Celia occupied a swivel chair behind the desk and left Lucy with the choice of two kitchen chairs facing her. The reception of young people arranging weddings and christenings must have been equally grim.

Lucy presented the first three messages, arranging them on the desk. Her manner was ingratiating. 'You probably know the village and the villagers better than most. These are anonymous communications received by the dead woman in the weeks preceding her death and we are anxious to trace their source. I've really come to you for advice.'

Celia put on her spectacles which were secured by a silk cord about her neck. She studied the exhibits in silence. It was difficult to judge her age; her cheeks and forehead were smooth, but her mouth seemed slightly shrunken and her upper lip was corrugated with the finest wrinkles. Her examination of the exhibits was brief and when she looked up she seemed mildly impatient. 'You realise that these are quotations taken out of context? In their proper context they are largely metaphorical, even allegorical.'

Lucy was defensive. 'But they were copied out and sent to the dead woman so, presumably, they were intended to apply to her.'

She received a bleak look over the top of the spectacles. 'That much is obvious. What more do you expect me to say?'

It was going to be hard going.

'You will know, of course, that Jessica's conduct was the subject of criticism by some in the village?'

'By me, you mean, and by women of the Guild. I make no apology for that; a woman with her reputation was quite unsuited to employment in the church. In this matter I disagreed with my brother.'

'So that you are to some extent in sympathy with the sender of these notes.'

A frown. 'They seem harmless. There can be no crime – certainly no sin, in reminding the wrongdoer of her error.'

'As they stand, they seem rather pointless. What could they be expected to achieve?'

Celia removed her spectacles and chose to be sententious: 'One should never underestimate the power of the word.'

'But a threat might have made it more effective.'

'I see no threat in these at any rate.'

Lucy produced the fourth message and handed it over. 'This was sent two days before Jessica was murdered.'

The glasses were replaced and this time the examination took

470

longer. She brought out a Bible from one of the desk drawers and referred to it briefly.

The woman was obviously intelligent and she had a formidable presence. Lucy was reminded of a university tutor under whom she had suffered; a female dragon who commonly handed out the look she now received, usually with a barbed comment: 'Your essay displays a singular, one might say a perverted, talent for missing the obvious.'

Celia contented herself with: 'Surely you must see that this fourth specimen comes from a different source?'

'What makes you say so?'

'Whoever sent the first three, knew her Bible. She may have used a concordance, but she knew how to use it effectively.' Celia held up her hand when Lucy would have spoken. 'Yes, yes! All right! I said "her", and "she", and that is what I meant. These are the work of a woman; there can be no doubt of that.

'Anyway, my second point is that the first three quotations are both accurate and apt, whereas the fourth is neither. A sentence has been made by inserting a capital letter where there was none, and the context is not only allegorical but ludicrously inept.' She was contemptuous.

She went on, her manner accusing, 'I don't know if you have looked up the source paragraph?' And she quoted, giving Lucy no chance to reply: ' "And the ten horns which thou sawest on the beast, these shall hate the whore and shall make her desolate and naked." '

A faint smile. 'One would have to be very much at sea before making use of such a source when there are so many more apt ones to choose from.'

Lucy said, meekly, 'That thought had occurred to me.'

'Really.' Celia was not interested; she was shuffling the exhibits, comparing them. 'Apart from that it seems clear that the fourth envelope. and message were written by a different hand. However, that is not my concern.' She gathered the polythene wrappers together and handed them back. 'Now, if that is all . . . ?'

Lucy had only a vague idea of what she expected from her

471

interview with the vicar's sister but this was certainly not it. She felt more than ever like a first-year student being dismissed after a tutorial that had gone badly wrong. On the other hand, the woman had confirmed her own ideas about the fourth message, and she had an argument to put to Wycliffe.

Much of Wycliffe's time during any case was taken up with what he called 'fringe activites' – extended telephone conversations with the chief, and with his own deputy, back at headquarters; receiving and reacting to reports concerning other cases all over the two counties, in fact, with the CID management of the police area as a whole. He was fortunate in that his deputy preferred administration to work on the ground – a case of Jack Spratt would eat no fat and his wife would eat no lean. So it worked, and made it possible for him to commit himself to individual investigations of importance.

But, like any other, the present case had its share of administrative and public relations chores. Even on this Easter Monday morning, Bertram Oldroyd, his chief, wanted to know what was going on; and, more remarkable still, the media were turning up in force for a briefing.

Oldroyd was relaxed and teasing. 'You attract these headline-grabbing cases, Charles. Sometimes I think you work it with the media. Seriously, though, is this a piece of black magic ghoulishness or has it been dressed up to look like one?'

Wycliffe, as always on such occasions, aimed to be both brief and vague. 'I don't know . . . I doubt if it's a cult thing.'

'What, then?'

He resented being forced to condense his vaporous notions and impressions into words which, once spoken, condition one's later thoughts. 'I feel that there is hatred behind this thing, and not only against the murdered woman.'

'You think there could be other killings?'

He said, with a curtness and finality, hardly diplomatic in speaking to the chief, 'I've no idea.'

'If you think we are dealing with some kind of psychopath . . . '

'I don't have any view on that at the moment, sir.'

472

And the telephone was dropped at the other end, with Old-royd saying to himself, 'One of these days . . . '

In fact, Oldroyd's questions were little different from those he could expect from the reporters when they arrived.

The media is not easily roused from its weekend lethargy. Even in a normal week an investigation which starts on a Sunday stands some chance of escaping serious attention until halfway through Monday. Then their interest depends on certain 'newsworthy' features. As Wycliffe feared, this one had them all, and when the time arrived for the briefing he faced a whole gaggle of reporters and a couple of TV cameras. The murder of Jessica Dobell was news.

But they were good humoured. 'You don't need my help to embroider this one, it's ready made.' They knew him of old and there was an element of camaraderie. At least three of the older men had worked his patch for twenty years. To give them something he dropped a word about the anonymous notes.

'What did they say, these notes?'

'They were quotations from the Bible. I'm not prepared to quote them at the moment.'

'The Bible can be pretty gruesome. Were they abusive? Threatening?'

'Cautionary, I'd say.'

'Were they sent by the killer?'

'As I don't know the killer or who sent the notes that's a difficult question.'

After ten minutes or so they sheared off to the pub. A few drinks, a scout round the village, a spot of chatting-up the locals, and that would be that for a while.

Back in the office he was joined by Kersey, reporting on the Geach interview. Kersey summed up: 'Geach is no fool and he has his eye to the main chance. It's hard to say whether he would have the knowledge or the inclination to rig the set-up in the church, but if it served his purpose he might be capable of anything.'

Kersey yawned. 'It's obvious he thinks he's in the frame and I encouraged him to go on thinking that way. Incidentally, he's more amenable than he might be because he doesn't want his wife to know he'd been sleeping with her sister.'

Kersey yawned again, this time with total abandon. 'This place makes me sleepy – enervating they call it. Anyway, most of what Geach said is in his statement; what isn't, is in my report. Mainly he was anxious to divert attention from himself, and he chose the houseboat man – Lavin. According to him Lavin had been having it off with the girl on a regular basis.'

Wycliffe turned the pages of his copy of the file. 'Have we got anything on this Lavin, apart from Geach's story?'

Kersey said, 'He crops up in the reports. He bought the houseboat just over two years ago and went there to live with his friend – or whatever the boy is. It seems Lavin is a biochemist; he worked for one of the big drug firms until he was badly injured in a gas explosion. According to gossip he got hefty compensation.'

'Any idea how he spends his time now?'

'He's taken up natural history and he's supposed to be making a study of life in the creeks and streams about here. The boy goes off in a canoe, collecting samples and they say the boat is like a laboratory.'

'So we need to know more about him.' Wycliffe looked up at the clock. 'But it can wait until after lunch.'

They had a snack meal at one of the bar tables where there were too many near neighbours to talk shop, so there was little said. Wycliffe watched a couple at the next table, a man and a young girl who, between mouthfuls of cottage pie, jointly attacked *The Times'* crossword. The man's auburn hair, silvery at the ends, hung to his shoulders and his untrimmed beard reached to his chest. Yet his face, where it could be seen, had a youthful freshness. Wycliffe was reminded of storybook pictures of Rip Van Winkle. The girl, fair, with an English rose complexion, had that demure composure of a young lady from a Victorian drawing room.

Wycliffe was intrigued; they spoke little, there were murmurs and small gestures, and from time to time one of them would pick up the pencil and make an entry on the grid, all with an air of felicity and of total contentment in each other's company.

As he was leaving, Wycliffe had a quiet word with Johnny, the landlord.

Johnny said, 'Hector St John Carey and his niece, Alicia.'

'They come here often?'

'Almost every day.'

Wycliffe remembered the riverside house with a folly like a lighthouse. 'The house with the folly?'

'Trecara, the house with the folly.'

Wycliffe was puzzled by the abrupt change in the landlord's attitude whenever he was asked about someone living in the village. In his professional role he was amiable, even chatty; but a question about any of the villagers brought down the closed sign. His replies became taciturn, his manner suspicious.

When Wycliffe and Kersey returned to the Incident Room, each to his own report, Wycliffe was interrupted by a phone call from Franks, the pathologist.

'Nothing new, old chap! Healthy woman. Fit. Muscles like a navvy; I wouldn't care to have tangled with her except in a friendly.'

'Not pregnant by any chance?'

'Nor by any mischance, though you won't be surprised to learn that she was no virgin. She died, in case you're still interested, as a result of a massive depressed fracture of the skull involving the temporal bone of the left side.'

Wycliffe said, 'Don't tell me, I know: the blow was probably inflicted with a blunt instrument such as a hammer. Thanks.'

Franks chuckled. 'We do our best, but we can't solve all your cases for you, Charles.'

Wycliffe had no sooner dropped the telephone than Fox arrived with his report. Fox's reports were models of their kind: scale diagrams, meticulously drawn, and enlarged photographs, all interspersed with Fox's idiosyncratic prose in pristine type. The man worked like a mole and Wycliffe was expected, not unreasonably, to show appreciation. Having done so, he looked at the formidable wad of paper and asked, 'Anything for special attention?'

'There's the toeprint, sir.' He turned the pages to a blow-up, contrast-intensified, of the mud flake print found on the carpet in the aisle of the church. 'It's from the toe of a left rubber boot, sir. An acquaintance in the trade says it's almost certainly size nine or ten and it might just be possible to identify the boot if we find it.

'At any rate we know that the dead woman wore rubber boots and they are missing but they were fives.'

Wycliffe should have been interested, and tried to sound so. 'It's worth following up. Anything else?'

'The pieces of paper used to wedge the organ keys came from the *Church Quarterly* for September of last year. There are quite good prints on two of the pieces, unidentified at the moment. It's a theological publication and, according to the newsagent, it is ordered specially for the vicar.'

'Good! So that narrows the field. No luck with any of the other prints?'

'Not so far, sir.'

Wycliffe picked up his ballpoint and tried to look politely dismissive. Reluctantly, Fox took the hint and left.

The truth is that whatever the contributions from technical and forensic boffins, the hard core of police investigation still consists in what people can be persuaded to tell them. And persuasion becomes increasingly difficult as the champions of everybody's liberty but the victim's turn the thing into a chess game.

Wycliffe pushed Fox's papers away, sighed, and returned to his work. Ten minutes later when he was settling once more to the business of digesting facts and regurgitating them in the bland porridge of a report, he was interrupted again by a tap at the door: Dixon with a letter.

'Sent on by messenger from the Truro nick, sir.'

The envelope was addressed in a woman's hand, schoolgirl style, to: 'Superintendent Wycliffe, Truro Police Station.' The single sheet it contained was headed: 'Tilly's Cottage, Bell Hill, Moresk, Nr Truro.' The message was brief:

'Dear Mr Wycliffe,
I can't come to see you but if you come here I might be able to help you. I am at home after six o'clock each evening. It

476

is no good sending someone else and you must treat this as confidential.

Yours sincerely,

Grace Trevena (Miss)

Every case entices its ration of nutters out of the woodwork. They write letters, usually anonymous, make phone calls, often in funny voices, and even volunteer fictitious statements. This was probably a sample, but there was something about it, a certain basic simplicity, which struck him as unusual. And Trevena was a good Cornish name. He picked up his telephone.

'Is PC Trice there? . . . Send him in, please.'

Trice was the local Community Policeman, now seconded for duty with the squad. He came in, uneasily diffident. 'Sir?'

'Tilly's Cottage – know where it is?'

A look of relief. 'At the top of Bell Hill where it joins Church Lane, sir.'

'And Grace Trevena, who lives there?'

A slow smile. 'I know her; a youngish woman, probably middle-thirties, lives with her grandmother. She's hooked on astrology and fortune-telling . . . She runs a little shop in the market selling the gear and she writes bits for the local papers, "Your Stars this Week", sort of thing. There's also a society . . . Perhaps she's a bit loony but she's pleasant enough.'

'Thanks; that's what I wanted to know.'

As the door closed behind Trice he added to himself, 'Easier to buy a Ouija board.'

'Disraeli B. *Whigs and Whiggism. Political Writings.* Edited by W Hutcheon 1913.' Stephanie Vinter stood on the library steps against a section of shelves, the book in her hands. 'Hutcheon is spelt: H-U-T-C-H-E-O-N.'

Seated at the long table, Giles entered the book on a numbered, ruled sheet, while, on the other side of the room, Hector St John Carey stood on another set of steps and called down to his niece, Alicia: 'Halliway J O. *Rambles in Western Cornwall.* First edition 1861.'

The room, with its barrel roof, had some resemblance to the nave of a church, and there were mullioned Gothic windows at each end, but the walls were lined with bookcases which reached to the springing of the roof.

'I've brought you some tea.' A lean, grey-haired woman with a croaking voice arrived with a tray.

Carey descended the steps and took the tray from her. 'That is very kind of you, Winnie. So thoughtful . . . '

Perhaps books, even on shelves, have a civilising influence. What sort of deviant feels belligerent in a library?

The four of them gathered at the table. Stephanie poured; Carey passed the biscuits, murmuring pleasant nothings into his beard. They cooed at each other like doves. Then Carey said, 'It's good of you to help us, Giles; I hope that you are not bored. This paperwork is not very stimulating but they tell me that if you have a library, then you must have a catalogue. I don't know precisely why this is, but I am quite sure that your mother could tell you.'

Giles flushed, pushed up his glasses and smiled.

Stephanie thought, how long is it since I've seen him smile?

Alicia, wearing a grey overall, looked supremely beautiful.

Carey went on, 'What could be nicer than tea in the library with an intelligent young man and two women who are beautiful as well as intelligent?'

When second cups had been poured, Carey ventured, 'Are there any developments at the farm?'

Stephanie patted her lips with a handkerchief. 'Laurence is expecting to hear from their solicitor. That, I suppose, will be the end.'

Carey stroked the silkiness of his beard. 'You know that I meant what I said? Nothing would give me greater pleasure than to share this place with you—such as it is. You may wish to come for a time—until some other arrangements are made, or you may favour living with us permanently. Alicia and I lead a rather lonely existence, cut off as we are, and it would be good for both of us to have congenial companions. Is that not so, Alicia?'

'You know that I agree, Uncle.'

'There now!' He reached for another biscuit. 'These are good.

Winnie makes them herself . . . ' When he had bitten into the biscuit he went on: 'Do you know the meaning of Trecara in Cornish? It means the homestead of Cara and the word cara translates as friend.' He added, his eyes mischievous: 'Or even as love and, of course, Carey comes from the same root.'

Stephanie said, 'You are more than kind, Hector, but Laurence would find it difficult to accept such one-sided hospitality.'

Carey spread his hands. 'I do not see it as one-sided, but talk it over. I think that it would be a good arrangement for all of us.'

Giles looked at his mother. 'Is Mr Carey suggesting that we might come here to live?'

Carey said, 'Does the idea distress you, Giles?'

Giles flushed but did not reply.

On the houseboat not far away a man sat reading. The light fell upon the right side of his head and face, on his sandy hair and beard, in both of which there were streaks of grey. His features were lean and the prominent bone structure was hardly masked at all by the pointed beard. The gross disfigurement on the left side was softened by shadows but the pale scar tissue was evident even to the casual eye.

The boy sat at a bench, looking down a binocular microscope; the beam of the lamp was directed through the mirror on to a tiny watch-glass placed on the stage. The boy was massively built; he had a large head, dark hair, cut short, and a round face, amiable in its immaturity.

'The little beggar won't keep still.'

The man looked up from his book. 'Try adding a drop of glycerine.'

Incredibly, the great hand with its thick fingers performed the delicate operation of sucking up a little glycerine from a bottle into a pipette and adding one drop to the water in the watch-glass.

There was a smile on the smooth features. 'Ah, that's better; he's not so lively now. He looks like some sort of larva . . . '

'Is the body divided into segments?'

'Oh, yes.'

'Can you see a head?'

479

'Yes, he has a head – '

'And the rest of the body in two parts?'

'Yes – '

'Any legs?'

The boy peered down the microscope. 'Yes, he's got six legs on the middle – on the thorax.' He brought out the word with evident pleasure.

'So it's an . . . '

'An insect – I ought to have bin able to work that out, didn't I?'

'You need practice, that's all. Now let's see if you can decide whether it's a larva, a nymph, or an adult . . . '

The exchange continued to a resolution of the problem and the man returned to his reading. It was high tide and the houseboat was afloat so that there were creaks and chuckles to disturb the stillness. Once a duck squawked in fright and somewhere, distantly, a dog barked.

The boy said, 'Nice, isn't it?'

'What's nice?'

'Well, being on our own again. She's not going to come in and spoil it.'

'Shut up, Jumbo!'

The man's voice was peremptory, angry, and the boy's features seemed to crumple. 'I'm sorry, Brian . . . Really I didn't mean to . . . I just thought . . . '

'Yes, I know. Don't get upset. But you mustn't talk like that.' He added after a pause, 'Play me something, Jumbo.'

'Shall I?'

'Please.'

The boy fetched an accordion from under a bench seat and, after a preliminary trial, started to play. It was a strange melody which seemed always on the point of repetition, of finding a theme, then losing it in a fresh adventure. The man discarded his book and sat back in his chair, eyes closed; the boy's face became serious and intent. After a few minutes he stopped playing and put the accordion aside.

'Time for supper.'

The man said: 'You're right, Jumbo . . . It is nice.'

480

Chapter Seven

Easter Monday evening

The triumvirate assembled in Wycliffe's little office. Kersey lit a cigarette and, ostentatiously, Lucy Lane threw open the window to the dusk outside. Wycliffe looked from one to the other but made no comment.

'It's time to look at what we've got.'

Each of them had a file containing copies of the reports and statements so far. Idly, they turned the pages, searching for inspiration which failed to come. Wycliffe, at his most dry and succinct, gave an account of his interview with Arnold Paul.

'You've got a copy of his statement and you'll see it puts him in the crosswires as far as means and opportunity are concerned. As to motive, it could be that Jessica really did stumble on something that would have put him and/or his brother on the spot. CRO have nothing on either of them. So, if the brother is bent, he's been lucky, or he's worked under another name.'

Kersey said, 'Perhaps they're not brothers.'

Wycliffe agreed. 'Which would implicate Arnold. I had a word with Geoff Cox of the Met Fraud Squad. He'd never heard of Philip but he knew Arnold and his bank – nothing against either, but he promised to ask around and get what he can in the way of background. Meantime, I arranged for Fox to go over the man's room and he's sent off a set of prints to CRO just in case.'

He turned to Kersey. 'What about the other statements? I haven't read them.'

Kersey grimaced. 'As bland as milk. When you read them you begin to think that there never was a woman lying there in the church with her head bashed in.'

'I believe you've got a line on the Vinter breakdown.'

Kersey said: 'Yes, he's got no form but the word breakdown is a euphemism for getting the sack. He was suspended in eighty-five for sexually assaulting a girl student. I got this from a mate of mine in Bristol CID. He knew about it because there was a police investigation but no prosecution. It was more than a bit iffy and Vinter was allowed to resign. The girl was no Persil-white virgin and the feeling was that Vinter misread her signals or that she was working off a grudge.'

Lucy Lane, turning the pages of her file, said, 'He would be an expert at misreading signals where women are concerned.'

Kersey shrugged. 'You would know about that. At any rate, it cost the poor bastard his job.'

Wycliffe cut in: 'None of which disqualifies Vinter as a suspect, so we need to keep an eye on him. All right. We already know about Geach, so it's over to you, Lucy – your interview with the vicar's sister – Celia, isn't it?'

Wycliffe looked bored. He saw this as a routine exchange of information to save everybody having to wade through the reports. At these sessions he discouraged discussion. More than once he had been known to say, 'There are times when listening to other people's ideas only confuses my own.' An attitude which was more defensive than bigoted.

Lucy Lane summarised her visit to the vicarage. 'Celia is a very intelligent woman, but there's something odd about her.' She hesitated, then plunged. 'I think she sent the first three notes herself.'

'Did you put it to her?'

Lucy, to Wycliffe's surprise, flushed; an unusual phenomenon. 'No, sir. She is a very formidable woman. If it comes to a confrontation I would want to be better prepared. I wouldn't want to start something I couldn't finish.'

Kersey looked at her in mock amazement. 'This woman I must see!'

Wycliffe let it pass. 'So, at least, you don't think she was responsible for the fourth note?'

'No. That took her by surprise. And, as you know, I'm not

happy about that fourth note. I would like to have all four submitted for expert opinion.'

'Why not? We must also get something on the Jordans' background. Let's know who we are dealing with. Anything else?'

For a few minutes conversation drifted away from the case. Wycliffe and Kersey speculated, dismally, about the probable findings of the Criminal Justice Commission while Lucy continued to study her file.

Finally Wycliffe sat back in his chair, stretched, yawned, and looked at the clock. 'Well, nobody will listen to us; that's for sure. It's time for our meal . . . Lucy! Aren't you eating this evening?'

Lucy was still absorbed in her file. 'I was looking at his signature on my xerox of his statement.'

'Who are you talking about?'

'Geach.' Lucy pushed the open file across the desk and both men examined it. Wycliffe said, 'A bit florid.'

Kersey shrugged. 'Takes up a lot of paper, but so what? Chaps like Abe Geach boost their ego with a flashy signature.'

Lucy said: 'He signs himself Abe G Geach, but the last four letters are no more than a scrawl.'

Wycliffe was impatient. 'Come on, Lucy, if you've got anything, let's have it. My signature ends in a scrawl too.'

'No comment, sir. But just read aloud the letters that are legible.'

Wycliffe muttered as though to himself, 'ABEGG . . . Well, I'm damned!'

'It must be chance,' Kersey.

'It's certainly odd,' Wycliffe. 'But could there possibly be a connection?'

Lucy Lane said, 'I can't believe that it's chance.'

Wycliffe was studying the signature. 'Neither can I. Which means that whoever wedged the organ keys did it to draw attention to Geach.'

Kersey said, 'This is better thought about after a good meal.'

*

In contrast with the night before, several of the tables in the restaurant were empty and others were occupied by couples and threesomes there for a quiet meal. Wycliffe's table, in a corner by one of the windows, was a little removed from the others, a testimony to the discretion of the landlord.

The man himself came to take their order. 'Only one main dish tonight – Coq au vin. It's the real thing – none of your boiled chicken warmed up in a prepared sauce but, if you don't fancy it, I can do you ham-off-the-bone with a decent salad.'

Coq au vin was agreed.

'I can offer you a red burgundy which goes very well.'

Kersey said, 'I'm beginning to like this place.'

They had reached the dessert stage before the case was mentioned and it was Kersey who said, 'It strikes me as bloody silly whichever way you look at it. I mean, if Geach did the killing he'd hardly put his signature to it – musical or otherwise, and, surely, the same argument would stop anybody else with an ounce of common sense from trying to incriminate him in that way.'

Lucy Lane, meticulously dissecting a pear, said, 'I suppose the fact that the organ was used draws attention to Paul as the organist – '

Wycliffe cut in, 'Full marks, Lucy, for spotting the signature business but it adds one more bizarre feature to this case which bristles with them already. Instead of looking for runners in the means, motive and opportunity stakes, we might try to work out the kind of person who could lay on such an exhibition.' Wycliffe picked up his coffee cup and put it down again. 'Think of it: after the woman was killed by a blow to the head, her body was dragged to the statue of Christ so that her hair could be draped over the sandalled feet ... Either then, or before, she was undressed to the precise extent which would suggest obscenity without implying a sexual assault in the ordinary sense.'

Kersey was about to say something but Wycliffe stopped him. 'No, Doug, let me finish. After all that, he or she goes to the organ and wedges the appropriate keys, apparently to suggest Geach's involvement through his shared initials with the Schumann Variations, as well as a musical connection. Add to this that the bits of folded paper were carefully cut from a religious magazine, subscribed to by the vicar, and the whole seems to suggest a deliberate plan to involve, if not incriminate, several people.'

Wycliffe paused just long enough to sip his coffee, which had gone cold. 'Having laid on his charade, the killer then starts up the blower on the organ and simply walks away.'

He frowned in a final effort to give his ideas coherence. 'It's been my impression from the first that this tableau, or whatever one calls it, was intended to make a point beyond the death of Jessica Dobell. Now, of course, aside from all this, we have these anonymous notes which may or may not be the work of the killer but must be fitted into the pattern.'

He drank off the remainder of his coffee, made a wry face, and patted his lips with his table napkin. 'Let's think all this over and see if we can get some sort of notion of the kind of man or woman we are looking for – without trying to fit any particular individual into the frame.'

He looked at his watch. 'But not tonight. Tonight I'm having my walk.'

He set out to explore the village beyond the square and found himself in a pattern of three or four short streets made up, for the most part, of terraced houses with their front doors opening on to the pavement. There were shops, a Methodist chapel big enough to accommodate the whole population, and a pub. This was a fresh aspect of the village and it was where most of the villagers lived.

There was still light in the sky but curtains were drawn across many windows and fragments of TV programmes filtered through. From the pub came the murmur of voices and an occasional burst of laughter but over most of the village there was silence and the streets were deserted. It was half past eight.

These evening walks over the ground where he happened to be working were necessary to him, especially in small towns and rural communities. He had to get the 'feel' of the place, to have some idea of what it was like to live there. To start with he was an intruder, perhaps a threat. Sometimes he felt heir to the witch doctor, prowling at night among the huts of the villagers, peeking, prying and eavesdropping.

The notion appealed to him. Perhaps in the morning he should line up his suspects, place a dry pebble in the mouth of each, and woe betide the one whose pebble stayed dry. (Add that one to his training school lectures on Modern Investigatory Procedures.)

A steepish hill was lined with more little houses, but these were stepped against the slope. An enamelled blue and white sign on the corner house read 'Bell Hill'. He remembered that the woman who wrote to him, the fortune-teller, or whatever she was, lived at the top of Bell Hill, at the junction with Church Lane . . . Grace Trevena, that was it!

As he climbed the hill he found that he had decided to call on her. From witch doctors to fortune-tellers by easy stages. King Saul visited the Witch of Endor by night and modern police chiefs had been known to enlist diviners to find their missing bodies. Whimsical thoughts of the head of CID on his evening stroll. Did other apparently responsible and sage officials have such rag-bag minds? Sometimes it troubled him that the persona he presented to the world was such a fake.

Tilly's Cottage belonged neither to the rather dreary little terraced houses of Bell Hill, nor to the grander villas of Church Lane. Placed on a corner between the two it was a solid little house in its own garden, surrounded by pine trees. There was a light in one of the downstairs rooms.

Wycliffe opened the gate and walked down the crazy-paving path to the front door. His ring was answered by a female voice. 'Who is it, please?'

'Superintendent Wycliffe.'

He had envisaged a stringy female, close to forty, casting about for a tolerable route across the sterile plane of virginity. Instead he was confronted by a plump young woman with a mass of dark curls and a friendly grin.

'I'm Grace Trevena. So you've come. I've been wondering whether you would and thought you probably wouldn't.'

He was shown into a homely, comfortable living room turned

almost into a jungle by potted plants. An elderly woman sat knitting by an electric fire and, on the dining table, there was a portable typewriter, a few books with places marked, a box of paper and some carbons.

'This is my grandmother, who brought me up.'

The old lady acknowledged him with becoming formality.

Grace said: 'Will you have a drink? Sherry or gin – that's our limit, I'm afraid.'

He refused a drink but accepted a chair, and the girl resumed her seat at the table but turned to face him.

'I'm in the middle of my weekly article. I expect you've been told that I'm interested in the occult and that sort of thing. I've not got what it takes to do research but I learn from people who have and try to apply their methods. We have a society, and I run a little stall in Truro market where I sell the literature, cards, charts, and so on.'

She smiled as she spoke, so that one had the impression that it was all good fun. 'I'm telling you all this because it was how I came to meet Jessica in the first place.'

Wycliffe listened politely, the old lady's needles continued to click, and Grace never stopped talking.

'You don't look comfortable to me. Stretch out your legs and rest your head back. Make yourself at home. As I was saying, Jessica came to me for a Tarot reading and we ended up by doing a series.'

The plump girl's face was suddenly serious. 'It was worrying. I've never known such a series, so consistent, and so – well, threatening.'

'What was threatened?'

'Oh, her death – and death by violence. Of course I didn't let on to her. I mean, one can't. You do see that, don't you? I interpreted it as a crisis in her life but I was never in much doubt as to the nature of the crisis – if my reading was anything like right.'

'When did she first come to see you?'

'When was it, Gran? Seven – eight months ago?'

'It was last September, when we had the first decent weather of the year.'

She went on: 'I don't expect you to believe all this stuff about the Tarot and so on. I mean, you're not a convert, but I mention it because it led to us becoming quite friendly. Jessica confided in me. People do. When you take up this sort of work you get to be something like a priest – I mean, people rely on you to keep their secrets because it's your sort of profession . . . '

'Jessica told you things about her life?'

'Yes, she did, and I feel, now that she's gone, I'm free to talk if it would help to find out who killed her.'

'What did she tell you?'

'Oh, about the farm, about the Vinters, and about her affairs with men. She had quite a sense of humour when she got going. Of course, she was Aries – fairly typical – energetic, belligerent, and highly sexed . . . But not all that sure of herself underneath. I mean, she worried, and she had a sense of guilt which many Aries subjects don't . . . What are you, by the way? I'd put you down as a Leo.'

Wycliffe felt trapped, mesmerised. 'I was born on August the fifteenth.'

'There you are then! Fortunately you don't have the aggressiveness which sometimes goes with the Leo make-up. But as you get older, watch out for back trouble. Could be heart, but I don't think so.'

'You were telling me about Jessica.'

'Yes, I was. I can't keep to the point, can I? I'm a true Piscean – never know where I'm going until I'm coming back. Well, one evening last week she came here – Good Friday, it was, and I could see that she was worried and depressed. Even Arians have their fits of depression.'

Wycliffe, on the verge of losing patience, asked, 'What was she worried about?'

'Well, she started by asking if I'd seen in the local paper that Mrs Ruse, over to Tresillian, was dead. She reminded me that this was the mother . . . '

'Of the boy killed in a hit-and-run several years ago.'

She looked at him in surprise. 'So you know about that! Well, they never found out who did it and Jessica said that she knew

488

who was responsible and that she had been involved. She'd been trying to put it out of her mind ever since, but with the mother dying, and people saying the poor woman had never got over her grief – well, it brought it all back as bad as ever.'

'She said that she was actually involved in the accident?'

'That was how I understood her.'

'Did she say who was with her?'

Grace looked embarrassed. 'No. I asked her if it was Johnny Glynn – I shouldn't have done, I know, I was just being inquisitive. But with all the rumours . . . Anyway, she said it wasn't Johnny; that he'd told the truth. She asked me if I thought this was the crisis the Tarot predicted and I was weak; I said it might be.'

'And?'

The fat girl looked down at her hands. 'She seemed very upset and said she supposed she'd have to go to the police. Then there was a bit about not having played fair with her sister and not wanting to make it worse. I didn't quite understand that.' She looked at Wycliffe, soft eyed. 'I wasn't much help to her, was I? She left more worried than she came. Then, the very next night . . . '

Wycliffe said nothing and she went on, 'I didn't know whether to tell you all this. I mean, I don't really know anything and I could easily get somebody into trouble. I decided to leave it to fate; I usually find that's the best way.' She looked at him, earnestly searching for approval. 'I wrote to you and gave you the option. If you didn't come to see me, well that would be that. If you did, it wouldn't have been my decision.'

Wycliffe leaned forward in his chair. 'Miss Trevena . . . '

'Call me Grace, please. Everybody does.'

'All right, Grace – you do realise that Jessica was murdered and that her murderer has not been caught. He or she could kill again. What I am saying is that anything you can tell me of her life could be important. You spoke of the men with whom she had affairs. Who were they?'

The girl's voice was low. 'She mentioned Mr Geach – I suppose that's why she felt guilty about her sister; then there was the man on the houseboat, and Mr Vinter.'

'No one else?'

'No, I don't think so.'

Wycliffe became stern. 'Look at me, Grace!'

The brown eyes were solemn but not scared. The old lady's needles ceased to click.

'Think now, Grace! Was there anything else that Jessica told you about anyone – anyone at all, that reflected on them in a mean or discreditable way; anything they would not want to be known? If you tell me things that turn out to have no relevance then they will never be mentioned again, I can promise you that.'

The girl's brow wrinkled. 'I can't think of anything really . . . '

'But?'

'Well, it was quite a while ago now, just before Christmas. Jess was laughing about it.'

'About what?'

'Well, it seems so mean to tell you, but if I must . . . Jessica went to the church one morning, to get things ready for a christening in the afternoon, and when she opened the vestry door, the vicar was there with the Vinter boy. He was hugging the boy – fondling his hair. That was all . . . I mean, there was nothing dirty going on . . . But Jessica reckoned the vicar was a bit that way.'

'All the same, you were quite right to tell me.'

Unexpectedly, the old lady joined in. 'What Grace does with her cards and all that stuff is her business; it's nothing to do with me; I don't interfere. But I didn't like that Dobell woman in my house. There was something about her. I'm sorry she's been murdered but she's the sort of woman, in my opinion, who asked for it.'

A faint smile reappeared on the face of the fat girl. 'Now you know what Gran thinks.'

She saw him out, and he walked down Church Lane and back to the pub, thoughtful. The Hopton was quiet, the restaurant was closed and only a few regulars lingered about the bar.

'A nightcap, Mr Wycliffe?'

'No. No, thank you.' He was in no mood for Johnny. From

the telephone in the passage upstairs he said 'Good night' to Helen.

In bed, with the light out, he lay staring through the open window at a rectangle of starlit sky. He listened to the few late drinkers being seen off the premises, the muttered partings, the footsteps; then Johnny locking up. There must be a private part of the house, for he did not hear Johnny climbing the stairs. In fact the silence was so complete that he found himself listening to it as though to something positive.

A lot had happened in this first full day. It seemed a long time since Lucy's kedgeree. But were they any further forward? He had been right about Jessica; there was a history of trauma which could explain her frenzied life style. The Ruse boy: she had admitted to some part in his death. But through action or by association? Was it guilt or guilty knowledge? Either way, could it have any significance as a motive for her murder? Vendettas reaching out across the years are material for fiction, but they are rare in fact.

In the matter of suspects and evidence: no material progress; just a lucky dip. Were there any suspects with a credible motive? The Vinters? Certainly there was bitterness, possibly hatred. But murder? What did they gain? Geach – to divert attention from himself had brought in Lavin, the houseboat man. At most it was a banal little tale of sex which must be kept from the wife – for her own good, of course. Still, he must talk to Lavin.

Wycliffe sighed, and turned on his side. He thought of Arnold Paul and his precious brother. He felt in his bones that despite appearances they were a sideshow. And the vicar? It was possible that the vicar was homosexually inclined, and not impossible that Jessica had used the fact against him. But murder? And in his own church?

Wycliffe decided that he had had enough. He thumped his pillow, made a convulsive turn, and to his own surprise, felt suddenly relaxed.

Chapter Eight

Tuesday

At seven o'clock on Tuesday morning, almost forty-eight hours after Jessica Dobell was found dead on the chancel steps, Michael Jordan and his sister, Celia, were at breakfast. Even at breakfast Michael was already wearing his clerical collar and vest. Celia's grey eyes regarded her brother across the table with diagnostic rather than sympathetic concern.

'You are looking ill, Michael.'

The vicar paused, a spoonful of All-bran halfway to his lips. 'The last two days have been a strain. I suppose it shows.' His manner was defensive.

'I warned you about that woman, Michael. She was not a fit person to have in the church.'

The vicar parried with a professional response. 'The church is for sinners, Celia.'

'For sinners who repent. That woman was blatant in her sin and you allowed her to profit from the church.'

'She profited very little, poor soul; she worked hard for what she got.'

Celia continued to stare at her brother as though by concentration she might read his mind, and he flushed under her silent scrutiny. She said, at last, 'I don't think you've told me everything, Michael.'

'What more could there be to tell?'

Celia sipped her coffee without taking her eyes off him. 'I've been thinking: you went across to the church on Saturday evening – at around eight it must have been.'

'I went to fetch my new service book.'

'So you said. Was the Dobell woman there then?'

Michael's flush deepened. 'Yes.'

'You didn't mention it at the time.'

'Would you expect me to? You know quite well that Jessica was often there of an evening, especially if there was a service the following day.'

'Perhaps that is why you found these evening visits so necessary.'

'Celia! What are you suggesting?' She had sparked off his anger.

But Celia was unimpressed. 'No, I was forgetting; women do not interest you.'

On the point of an angry retort, Michael remained silent. There was a lull. Celia finished her coffee, patted her lips with her napkin, then spoke conversationally, 'You've finished your cereal, will you have some toast?'

'No, thank you.'

Once more the grey eyes were on him. 'Did you tell the police that you saw her at eight o'clock?'

'No.'

'Why not?'

His boyish face was scarlet once more. 'Well, they didn't ask me and it seemed, well . . . irrelevant.'

Celia shook her head. 'No, Michael! You wouldn't hold back information of that sort without good reason. It was obvious that the police would wish to establish when she was last seen alive.'

Michael looked down at his empty dish and fiddled with the spoon. 'Are you suggesting that I . . . That you think I might have . . . ' His voice trailed off.

'Killed the woman? No, I am quite sure that you would be incapable of killing anyone in any circumstances.'

'Well then, I don't see what you are getting at.' Sullen.

Celia poured herself another cup of coffee and added a dash of milk. She was cogitating and, once or twice, she looked across at her brother – thoughtful, speculative.

Michael was staring out of the window through which he could see the tower of his church rising above the trees.

493

Abruptly, as though the thought had just occurred to her, Celia demanded, 'Was there anyone else in the church at the time?'

'What? – No!'

After a long pause Celia said, 'I'm sorry, Michael, but you are prevaricating, if not actually lying. Either you saw or you have been told something which you are holding back from the police. That is foolish if not dangerous.'

There was a long silence and Michael was on the point of leaving the table when Celia spoke again, 'I had a policewoman here yesterday, while you were in Truro.'

'To see me?'

'No.'

Michael looked the question he was careful not to ask.

'She wanted to consult me about anonymous communications sent to the Dobell woman.'

Michael, already on his feet, sat down again. 'Anonymous communications? What did they say?'

'There were four of them, all quotations from the Bible and concerned with sexual depravity.'

Suddenly Michael had gone very pale. He said with great seriousness, 'The police must have heard something, Celia, otherwise why would they come to you?'

Her expression was smug. 'My work with the Women's Guild is supposed to put me in touch with the women of the village.'

'What did you tell the policewoman?'

'I told her that the fourth communication was not from the same hand as the other three.'

'How could you possibly know that?'

'It was obvious.'

Very carefully, Michael arranged his plate, cup, saucer and spoon. Without looking up he said, 'Recently, Celia, I have begun to feel that I am doing God's work here in Moresk. I thought you shared that feeling.'

'Well?'

'I hope we shan't be forced to move again.'

Celia stood up and began to clear the table. In a tight voice she said: 'Don't forget that it's Tuesday and I have my Fellow-ship meeting in Truro this morning. I shall catch the ten-twenty bus. Molly Symons has invited me back to her place afterwards so that I may not be home before you go to the Careys' this evening.'

Katherine Geach and Elsa were sitting at the kitchen table, drinking coffee. The old pendulum clock on the wall showed ten minutes past eight.

Katherine seemed to be studying the rings on her fingers. After a moment or two she said, 'I've been a fool, Elsa. Looking back, it's obvious that Abe had been seeing Jessica.'

Caution masked any expression there might have been on Elsa's freckled features. '*Seeing* her?'

Katherine snapped, 'You know exactly what I mean!'

Elsa shifted in her chair, pushed her cup and saucer away, and said, 'I've never heard anything of that sort and most gossip reaches me one way or another.'

But Katherine was not to be put off. 'Don't be difficult, Elsa! The only question in my mind is, when did it start?'

Elsa opened her mouth to reply when Julie came in, fully dressed. On holiday, it was unusual for her to be up before ten.

Katherine vented her annoyance. 'What's the matter with you? Can't you sleep?'

The girl ignored the question. 'Is there any coffee left?'

'In the pot, but you'll have to make your own toast if you want it.'

'I don't want any.'

Her mother's irritation subsided. 'Don't take any notice of me; I'm on edge.'

'I know. I'm going out, but I'll be back around lunchtime.' Julie drank a mug of coffee and a moment later she was gone.

Katherine called after her, 'You should take an anorak or something, it's going to rain.' But there was no response.

Elsa said, 'She looks all in. I didn't think this would have had such an effect on her. I heard her moving about in the night and once I thought she was crying.'

Katherine sighed. 'It's not what happened to Jess that's upsetting her, it's that bloody boy. I wish I knew what was going on there.' She added after a pause: 'I'm not much of a mother.'

Julie walked towards the foreshore and took the path along the river bank. The going was muddy but she picked her way. At the kissing-gate she gave a nervous glance up into the churchyard and hurried past. Her hands were tightly clenched so that her nails bit into the flesh. 'If only I can get him to talk!'

Since overhearing the conversation between her father and the policeman she had felt more than ever troubled and depressed. There were one or two girls at school who talked, glibly, perhaps for effect, of their fathers 'screwing around'. She was not, she told herself, old-fashioned about sex, but she had never thought of her father in that way. She had been naive; for that, apparently, was precisely what he did. And Aunt Jess had been one of his women. Did her mother know – or suspect?

But Aunt Jess had had other men – Giles' father, and the houseboat man, perhaps others. And now she was dead – murdered.

She could not take it in. She thought she had understood how things were at the farm. There was tension and bitterness, Giles had never made any secret of that, and it was obvious to anyone who spent any time at all there. It came about because her aunt seemed to take pleasure in humiliating the Vinters. And yet, despite that, it seemed that she and Giles' father were having sex.

No wonder the police . . . It was like something out of a tabloid newspaper. People would say – must be saying – 'Of course she asked for it!' And they would be speculating about which of her men . . .

But there was something else that troubled her even more deeply. It arose from a casual remark of her father's: 'Henry, down at the post office, says the bits of paper used to wedge the organ keys were cut from a religious magazine which he orders specially for the vicar.'

And it had come to Julie, irritatingly vague but compelling, a memory of having seen such a magazine, curiously mutilated. It was at the farm, but she could not recall exactly where, or in what circumstances.

As she drew level with the houseboat Jumbo came down the gangway with bags slung about his shoulders and carrying a battery of nets. He greeted her with his slow speech, seeming to listen carefully to his own words: 'Hello, Julie! I'm going out to collect spec-i-mens.'

Julie raised her hand but said nothing. She turned up to the farmhouse across the rough grass to the front door, and knocked.

It was opened by Giles. He pushed up his spectacles and regarded her with solemn attention but said nothing.

'I want to talk to you, Giles.'

The boy looked back into the house, hesitated, then closed the door. Still he did not speak.

Julie was at a loss, not at all sure what she wanted to say. In the end it came in the form of a bald question: 'Do you have any idea who killed Aunt Jessica, Giles?'

His blue eyes, enlarged by his spectacles, were cold, indifferent, and when he spoke his voice was toneless. 'What makes you ask me that?'

They were standing, looking towards the river where it was about half-tide. A band of mud separated the shingle from the water and gulls flat-footed around, searching for worms.

'I'm worried, Giles.'

The boy said nothing, he seemed to be staring across the river at the trees which overhung its banks.

Julie went on, 'Have you talked to Michael about it?'

'Why should I talk to Michael?' He sounded bored.

She felt as though she were trying to reach him through a barrier of cotton wool, and she floundered. 'Well, you seem to get on – I mean, it's obvious he likes you.'

Giles flushed and his manner became even more remote. 'I don't know what you mean. What would I have to say to him? Your aunt's death is nothing to do with us.' He added, after a pause, 'Anyway, I haven't seen Michael since before it happened.'

They were silent while Julie gathered her scattered wits to try again. 'Giles . . . Was Aunt Jess out all night sometimes?'

'Yes.'

'Do you know where she spent those nights?'

'It was no business of ours, and I've told the police all I know.'

'The police! Did they question you?'

'I went to them.'

'What did you tell them?'

'I told them something I thought they ought to know.'

Julie was getting nowhere but she was desperate to keep the contact going. 'They say the organ keys were wedged with pieces of paper cut from a religious magazine.'

He looked at her now but his expression did not change: 'So?'

Her courage failed her. She was utterly miserable. 'I don't know. I just wonder what will happen next.'

'That's simple. We shall have to go.' He was wilfully misunderstanding her. 'Your father has sent a man who used to be a farmer; he came yesterday and he's here again today. I expect he will take over.'

Julie was near to tears. 'I'm sorry, Giles. I hope it won't work out like that. I don't think mother . . . ' Her voice trailed off because she could not say what she wanted to say with any conviction.

Giles regarded her with a steady gaze and, without raising his voice, in the same monotone as before, he said, 'I don't want to talk about any of this, Julie, and I don't want to talk to you. I would rather you didn't come here any more.' He turned and went into the house, closing the door behind him.

Julie stood, looking at the closed door. In just a couple of days it seemed that her whole world had fallen apart.

Shortly after nine Wycliffe, with his briefcase, presented himself at the front door of Trigg, and was received by the housekeeper, fair and freckled; a youngish woman, plump, and running comfortably to seed.

'Superintendent Wycliffe. I would like a word with Mrs Geach.'

He was shown into the room with the Russian samovar on the sideboard where Kersey had interviewed the contractor. After several minutes, Katherine Geach came in, looking every inch the lady of the house in tailored pale-grey trousers and a matching silk top.

'We can't talk in here, it's like a morgue.'

He followed her along a corridor to a very large room at the side of the house with a bow window which looked out across a lawn to the river.

There were plenty of blue and mauve chintzes, a neutral carpet, sage-green walls with hunting prints, and a white frieze, but Wycliffe's immediate attention was claimed by a grand piano, very much at home in a corner of the room.

'Do sit down, Mr Wycliffe. Would you like something? Coffee? A drink?'

'Thank you, but no.'

She was very pale, doing her best to appear relaxed, but tension showed in the set of her jaw and in her restless hands.

'I'm sorry to return to a subject that must be painful to you but I am anxious to know more of your sister's life.'

She eased the set of her trousers. 'I want to help, but I think you're probably better informed on that subject than I am.' A hint of bitterness.

Wycliffe refused that gambit. 'I'm wondering if you can tell me anything about her association with Jonathan Glynn, and whether she confided in you concerning the accident in which a young boy called Ruse was killed.'

It was not what she had expected and she did not answer at once.

Wycliffe went on, 'I don't wish to probe unnecessarily into your sister's life, but in searching for a motive for what happened I have to look at all the possibilities.'

A quick, troubled look. 'And you think there could be a connection?'

'As I said, I'm merely looking at possibilities.' From his briefcase he brought out Jessica's album. 'If you can bring yourself to look at the last few pages . . . '

499

She took the album and turned the pages, lingering here and there. When she reached the news cuttings, Wycliffe said, 'Three of those cuttings are concerned with the Ruse family – two with the original hit-and-run, the third with the recent death of the boy's mother.'

She spent some time on the cuttings, then turned back to the photographs. When she finally closed the book and handed it back, her eyes were glistening with tears. She said, 'You obviously know more than you have told me.'

'I know that immediately before her death your sister was considering going to the police with information about the boy's death.'

'I see.' She was shocked. She accepted that the sixteen-year-old tragedy might have traumatically affected Jessica's life, but it had not occurred to her that it could have been the reason for her death.

After an interval, she asked, 'Are you suggesting that – '

Wycliffe cut in with decision. 'I am not suggesting anything; I am seeking information. You must understand that this is only one of many lines of investigation and implies no suspicion of any individual.'

She considered this piece of police doubletalk and tried again. 'After my marriage Jessica and Johnny Glynn became very close. We assumed that they would marry . . . Johnny had a reputation as a bit of a wild man.' Her eyes lost focus as she seemed to relive some incident from the past. 'He drove a farm-truck about the lanes at breakneck speed and everybody expected trouble. Jessica was often with him.'

'Did your sister drive at that time?'

'Jessica never learned to drive. I've often wondered why. At any rate, there was strong feeling against Johnny after the accident but there was no evidence to suggest that he was anywhere near. All I can say is that Jessica was not the same girl afterwards, though I had no idea what it was that might have changed her.'

'She said, in any case, that she was not with Glynn that night.'

'I know.'

'Could it be that she was with someone else?'

Katherine made a despairing gesture. 'How can I possibly know? She talked to me about it, briefly and for the first time, only a day or two before she died . . . I have to admit, she left me with the impression that she was involved.'

'But she said nothing of the person she was with?'

'No.'

Wycliffe returned the album to his briefcase. 'I am sorry to have caused you further distress. I hope that you will keep our conversation to yourself.'

On his feet, he looked across at the piano. 'Are you the pianist?'

A quick smile. 'No, that's Abe's little indulgence. He used to play a lot when he was younger. He's really quite musical.'

She saw him to the door; once more the lady of the house. She even remarked that the primroses were especially beautiful this spring.

Back in his makeshift office, Wycliffe was looking out of the window at a pair of jackdaws perched on a boundary wall. They had their backs to him and, like an old married couple with nothing new to say to each other, they watched the world go by. A herring-gull, yobbo of the strand, alighted a yard from them and the pair edged their way crabwise to a discreet distance but were not otherwise disturbed.

In the back of his mind he was thinking about the Ruse boy and who might have been involved with Jessica Dobell in that hit-and-run. Did it matter to this present case? Was it feasible that having escaped a possible manslaughter charge, all those years ago, the man would resort to murder to avoid exposure now? Of course, although the law might be lenient after such a lapse of time, public opinion would not.

But murder? And murder in such a sensational vein?

Anyway, he would be talking to Tom Reed.

A tap at the door, and Kersey came in. 'Anything from the Lady of the Manor, sir?'

Wycliffe told him, not forgetting the piano.

Kersey was thoughtful. 'Interesting! It could have been friend

Geach who took Jess for a ride that night. From the photographs the two couples seem to have been more of a foursome in those days.'

Wycliffe agreed. 'It's possible. It would explain what Jessica said to the Trevena girl; something about not having played fair with her sister and not wanting to cause further hurt – along those lines, anyway.'

Another tap at the door; this time the duty officer. 'The vicar would like a word, sir.'

'Ask him to wait a moment, please.'

Kersey said, 'Ah, the vicar! He's been keeping his head down; perhaps we should have made more use of him. If some of these parsons had their intelligence network computerised it would make Special Branch look like a bunch of amateurs.'

Wycliffe was thinking of Grace Trevena's rather pathetic story about the vicar and the Vinter boy. Put that way it sounded like a Victorian morality tale and perhaps that is what it was. He picked up his telephone. 'Ask Mr Jordan to come in, please.'

He was shocked by the change in the man. His baby face was pale and seemed to have lost its chubbiness. There was a darkness about the eyes and, above all, there was no sign of that smooth manner which seems to come with the collar and provides even the most timid clergyman with a measure of authority.

'Mr Jordan, this is Detective Inspector Kersey. Please sit down.'

The vicar looked at Kersey with obvious misgiving. 'I hope I'm not intruding, but I had to come . . . '

When he was seated he went on, 'It has been on my conscience though I cannot see how anyone can have suffered through my neglect. However, I mustn't try to condone it.' He had been looking down at his hands, now he met Wycliffe's eyes and said, abruptly, 'I was in the church on Saturday evening; I went there to collect my new service book.'

'At what time?'

'It must have been about eight o'clock. After eight, probably.'

Kersey snapped, 'You saw Jessica Dobell?'

'Yes, she was polishing the lectern.' He spoke in a low voice as though making confession.

'Presumably you spoke to her?'

'Something trivial – just a few words. I collected my book and left.'

'Did she seem as usual?' From Wycliffe.

'I think so. She made some remark about the weather – it rained all Saturday evening.'

'Was she alone?'

'I saw no one with her.'

Kersey spelt out the question emphasising each word. 'Did you see anyone either going to or coming from the church?'

Jordan hesitated, then, 'I saw no one.'

Wycliffe said, 'You realise that you were probably the last person to see Jessica Dobell alive – other than her killer?'

He nodded. 'The thought has kept me awake at night.'

'But failed to persuade you to do your obvious duty.' From Kersey.

Wycliffe followed up: 'I cannot understand, Mr Jordan, why you were so reluctant to come forward. You are quite sure that you are concealing nothing else?'

The poor man had never before been subjected to interrogation. His pallor had given way to a deep flush and he was on the verge of breakdown. Wycliffe did not pursue the question.

'I understand that the dead woman visited the church at odd times whenever she thought there might be something in need of attention?'

'Indeed she did. Jessica was most conscientious.'

'I'm thinking of a morning in late December when there was a christening in the afternoon.'

The fresh shock was obvious. There was an interval while Jordan contemplated his plump hands and, when he spoke, his words were barely audible.

'So you know about that?'

'I want your version.'

'It was innocent, but very foolish on my part.'

Wycliffe waited, the fingers of one hand beating a silent tattoo on the desk top. The mild tension he created was more than enough to loosen the vicar's tongue. It was like taking sweets from a child.

'You see, Mr Wycliffe, the boy Giles is not happy at home . . .
The situation is very difficult – a family unit living and working
with a woman whose background and aspirations are – were – so
different. I'm saying nothing against Jessica; she behaved as we
all do, according to our lights. But Giles is a complex and sensitive
boy, very easily hurt.'

Jordan looked up and was, perhaps, reassured by Wycliffe's
bland, attentive manner. 'In short, Giles sometimes came to me to
confide his difficulties. On the occasion you refer to he was
particularly upset and I was moved by his distress.' The vicar
shifted uncomfortably in his chair. 'Foolishly, I put my arm
around his shoulders, he rested his head against me and I
smoothed his hair. It was at this point that Jessica came in.'

'Are you homosexually inclined, Mr Jordan?'

Jordan looked at Kersey as though he had received a slap in the
face. He did not speak for some time but when he did he had
decided on a straight answer. 'I will tell you the truth. Since early
adolescence my sexual inclinations have been towards my own
sex but, with God's help, I have never, in any relationship,
allowed my impulses to carry me beyond a simple caress.'

'Did Jessica ever refer to the incident she had witnessed?'

'Not to me, but I heard from Giles that she sometimes taunted
him.' Jordan sighed. 'He was, understandably, deeply distressed
and bitter.'

Wycliffe was puzzled by the man. It was probable that he had
spoken the truth; certainly not the whole truth, but what was he
stretching his conscience to conceal?

Probe a little deeper. 'I understand that you subscribe to the
Church Quarterly.'

'I've done so since shortly after my ordination.'

'It seems that you are the only subscriber in this district.'

'Probably.'

'Are you aware that the folded paper used to wedge the organ
keys was cut from a copy of that periodical?'

'I was told so by your officer.'

'How do you dispose of your copies when you have finished
with them?'

'I don't dispose of them; I keep them for reference.'

'Will you check to see that you still have the issue for last September?'

The vicar made a little gesture of resignation. 'I have checked; that issue is missing.'

'Can you explain that?'

'I occasionally lend the odd copy to anyone who might be interested in a particular article.' He added, 'It doesn't bother me if they are not returned.'

Kersey interjected, 'You must have some idea who borrowed this particular copy.'

Jordan hesitated then, with obvious reluctance, he said, 'It was the issue which contained an article on the role of the Church in German reunification. Stephanie Vinter happened to see it and said she thought Laurence would like to read it. He is interested in the part played by the Church in the overthrow of Communism in Eastern Europe.'

Wycliffe was gazing at the vicar with disquieting intensity then abruptly, with a gesture of resignation, he relaxed. What was the point of keeping him on the rack?

But his manner was still brusque. 'I want you to make a further statement about your visit to the church on Saturday evening, and the loan of your magazine to Vinter. At the same time I must remind you that holding back information, however privileged, could delay our investigation and might be dangerous. Somebody who has killed once has broken through a psychological barrier and may well find it easier to kill a second time.'

Wycliffe got to his feet. 'Mr Kersey will show you to the interview room where you will be given the opportunity to make a fresh statement.'

Jordan looked at him, pale and solemn, but said nothing.

Left alone, Wycliffe was still worried by the man. Law enforcement has always had special problems with tender consciences but it is no longer approved procedure to put to the torture their troublesome possessors.

Chapter Nine

Tuesday morning (continued)

When Kersey had taken the vicar to make his statement, Wycliffe left for the houseboat. He went alone, counting more than he cared to admit on the interview with the former biochemist. It was not actually raining but a pearly mist softened outlines with the effect of a lens that is slightly out of focus. The surface of the water was greeny brown, still and shining; it was hard to believe that the tides reached so far. He passed the kissing-gate to the church and, arriving at the reed bed, encountered a troop of bird-watchers with their binoculars who charmed him with their twittered 'Good morning's.

As he approached the houseboat he could hear music – an orchestra; a radio or record player? Another musician? The orchestra gave way to a single female voice followed by an unaccompanied duet, and at the bottom of the gangway he stood still to listen. The sound seemed to fill the whole valley with trills and cadences which echoed back from the slopes and it was some time before he realised that the bearded Lavin was leaning on the rail looking down at him.

'You like it?'

An indeterminate grunt.

' "The Flower Duet" from *Lakme*. Heady stuff – an aural narcotic not to be taken by policemen.'

'Mr Lavin? Superintendent Wycliffe.'

'You'd better come up.'

On deck a short companionway led down to a saloon which was filled by the music. Lavin switched off the player.

The light, coming from a row of windows near the ceiling, had a

506

greenish hue. Below the windows were aquaria, lined end to end, and below them again, bookshelves and cupboards. There was a bench with an impressive binocular microscope, and another with a sink and rows of bottles.

Lavin stood so that his left side was shielded. He pushed forward a chair for Wycliffe and sat down himself. Certain movements seemed to involve a painful strain. 'What do you want?'

'I am inquiring about Jessica Dobell.'

'She's dead. Your interest has come too late to do much about it.'

Wycliffe was aware of the tension in the man; his whole frame seemed taut, and his manner was aggressive. 'What I can do is to find out who killed her and why. You were on intimate terms with her so you are an important witness.'

'Well?'

'She spent nights here?'

'Occasionally.'

'When did your relationship begin?'

'Our relationship as you call it began five or six months ago.'

'Was it affection, love, or just sex?'

A twisted smile. 'I could ask what the hell that has to do with you.'

'If you answer my questions, Mr Lavin, it will save us both time.'

'All right. I suppose you need to know these things. It was sex – just plain sex.' He seemed to hesitate, then, 'Jessica had no conception of a relationship based on anything other than what was useful or profitable to her. Sex was the area in which I happened to be useful and available. No commitment.'

He looked down at his left hand which was deformed and white with scar tissue. 'I'm not to every woman's taste, but she was titillated . . . ' He added at once, 'But I don't want you to think that the arrangement was one-sided. For a man as I am, sex at almost any price must be a plus.'

His head was turned away from Wycliffe so that it was hard to judge his expression.

He added after an interval, 'Poor old Vinter! His sphere of usefulness was on the farm, he didn't quite come up to scratch in bed. Stephanie was no good on the farm and not much use as a housekeeper. And the boy, Giles – the poor lad wasn't much use for anything in Jessica's terms.'

Lavin grimaced as though in sudden pain, and shifted himself in his chair. 'I suspect that there must have been others who passed – or, more likely, failed her tests.'

Wycliffe said, 'So you didn't even like her?'

A short laugh. 'No, I didn't even like her. But I didn't kill her though I'm not totally surprised that someone did.'

'Why do you say that?'

Lavin took time to think. 'There are crude expressions which would answer you precisely but, translated, I suppose one would say that she set out to stimulate a man to the limit of his sexual capacity then disparaged his achievement. Of course that would hardly square with the circumstances of her murder.'

'When did you last see her?'

'Ah!' For once he turned full face, his expression mocking. 'I saw her on Saturday evening when she was on her way to the church. I happened to be on deck as she passed.'

'Did she speak?'

'Casually. Of course, you have only my word for it that I didn't follow her.'

Wycliffe was trying to assimilate what he had been told; it shed fresh light on the dead woman and it also suggested that Lavin had been closer to the Vinters than he had supposed.

'Do the Vinters come here?'

'Laurence drops in for a chat quite often. He's an interesting chap, and knowledgeable; he's keen on natural history and the kind of work we are trying to do here.'

'Did I hear that he's interested in bats?'

'Yes, I believe he's doing a survey of the area for the county records.'

'What about Stephanie and the boy?'

A faint smile. 'Giles looks in occasionally to consult my bird books and he sometimes stays long enough to say "Thank you"

508

when he's found what he wants.' Lavin shrugged. 'He's a strange lad. Recently he's taken to going about with Jumbo on collecting trips. They make an odd pair but they seem to get on, though I suspect that's because of Jumbo's high level of tolerance.'

'And Stephanie?'

A wry look. 'I've never been to bed with Stephanie if that's what you're suggesting.'

'But she comes here?'

'Once in a while, to listen to a new CD if I've got one. Now what free time she has is spent at Trecara with old Carey and his books. The place is falling down about his ears but I gather he's got a good library and Stephanie is helping him to catalogue it.'

'The Vinters seem a very intelligent family; isn't it surprising that they find themselves reduced to the situation on the farm?'

Lavin nodded with emphasis. 'Stephanie's got a first class brain but she's totally unpractical. When it comes to the nitty-gritty of life she hasn't a clue, and Laurence isn't much better. There's no earthly reason why they should be shacked up here and treated like servants. With a bit of common sense added to their brains they could both land good jobs, whatever Laurence did or didn't do to his wretched student.'

'One more thing, Mr Lavin – the young man who lives here – I don't know his name or his status . . . ' Wycliffe was aware of the compulsions which drive policemen to speak with such pomposity but at a loss what to do about it.

A broad grin. 'His name is Mark Wheeler though he prefers Jumbo, and his status is that of a friend. If it wasn't for his reputation – I don't care a damn about mine – I wouldn't bother to tell you that I'm not homosexual. What Jumbo's predilections are I can't say, though I fancy he's a late developer.'

'You came here together?'

'Yes. I was a single man with a decent salary, living just outside Nottingham. I had a house, a boat on the Trent, and a cottage near Newark. Jumbo came to me at eighteen as a sort of odd-job man . . . At the time I thought I might marry and I was preparing the ground.'

509

A brief pause, then, 'Jumbo doesn't know who his parents were and he's spent most of his life in homes of various sorts. He's too gentle for this world . . . Anyway, I've no close relatives, so we have something in common. We suit each other and when I had my accident it seemed natural that we should stay together. He likes it here and the kind of life we lead; he's becoming quite a good naturalist, all he needs is a bit of theory and the essential jargon.'

'Where is he now?'

'Out with young Giles, actually, getting samples – from the marshy ground around the tower.'

'One more question, Mr Lavin – do you know Arnold Paul, the church organist?'

'I would probably recognise him if I met him but I have never spoken to him.'

Wycliffe was running out of questions; in any case he was only fishing. Before the investigation could take a firm direction he needed to know the victim better, to discover the sources of that hatred which was manifest in the staging of her death.

He thanked Lavin and left. As he reached the bottom of the gangway the music began again. He was impressed by Lavin, he even liked the man. Lavin was ready to admit that he suffered the frustrations of his disability, but he was not perverted by them. It seemed that his self-analysis was sufficiently detached to be objective.

On the other hand Wycliffe was sure that he had not been told more than Lavin wished him to know. A killer? You do not decide on the strength of fifteen minutes conversation whether or not a man is capable of murder. But would Lavin have staged such a tableau? Would, or could Geach have done so? Would Paul? Or, assuming that he had a motive, would or could the egregious Johnny Glynn? Significantly, perhaps, he stopped short of adding Vinter to his catalogue of interrogatives.

It was at this point that a fresh thought occurred to him. As Franks had said, the killer could have been a woman; even a woman of no particular strength. And setting aside, he hoped, any male chauvinist tendencies, he thought he now saw, in the

510

strangely logical yet freakish setting of the crime, more of female than of male psychology. Katherine Geach? Stephanie Vinter? There was no obvious reason why Katherine Geach would want to murder her sister, but the Vinter woman could be a different matter. The Vinters, man and wife, were credible suspects.

Lucy Lane drove to Truro and contrived to wedge her Escort into a tiny kerbside space somewhere near the offices of Nicholls and Greet in one of the Georgian houses in Lemon Street. Several of the houses in the street hid modern office blocks behind their deceptive façades but Nicholls and Greet practised no such deception; they fitted themselves into the domestic fabric of one of the houses with inconvenience and incongruity, but with consciences clear.

Harry Nicholls' office on the first floor retained its elaborate plaster cornice, its ceiling rose, its deep skirting boards, its multi-paned sash window and elegant panelled door. But, like its occupant, it showed every sign of running gently to seed. Harry Nicholls was fifty, a former scrum-half, now with thinning sandy hair, a high colour, a paunch, and an air of wistful bewilderment.

Lucy felt impelled to be brisk and bright. 'I think you know why I've come.'

The lawyer, concluding that any approach other than a strictly business one would be wasted on this attractive but severe young woman, said, 'The Dobell twins.'

'I understand there was an agreement between the sisters after their parents' death.'

Nicholls fingered a blue file but did not open it. 'Simple enough: ownership of the farm was shared equally between them under their father's will but it was agreed that Jessica should run the place, that Katherine would forgo any claim on the profits and would not be responsible for losses or debts incurred. Katherine's agreement was necessary to any change of use or the disposal of the property.'

'I believe that both sisters made wills at that time.'

'I'm not sure that I should discuss matters involving a living

511

client but, in the circumstances – murder and all that . . . Yes, they made wills each naming the other as sole beneficiary.'

'As far as their interests in the farm were concerned.'

'No, they both used the "all of which I die possessed" formula.'

'One wonders what Katherine's husband thought of that.'

Nicholls shifted around the files on his desk but said nothing.

'Those wills are still valid?'

'As far as I know.'

Lucy stood up. 'Well, thank you for being helpful, Mr Nicholls. I'm sure that what you have told me will be treated with discretion. I can't imagine that the wills are likely to figure in the case but . . . '

'No stone unturned. I know.' Nicholls got up to see her out. 'Do you play golf, Miss Lane?'

'No, why?'

'Or stay at four-star country hotels?'

'Not on my salary.'

'No, so you would hardly be interested in a development which offered such facilities . . . ' A bland smile. 'Just a thought.'

He had opened the door for her to pass through. 'Perhaps you will excuse me now, I have another appointment.'

When Lucy returned to her car and a hovering traffic warden, she was thinking that she might have underestimated Harry Nicholls.

Wycliffe continued to walk, feeling vaguely guilty because he was enjoying himself. He watched the ducks and the swans, he wondered what species of creature made that rippling arrow-like track on the water, swimming all but submerged, and whether the birds in disturbed flight over the opposite bank were jackdaws or rooks. He thought how pleasant it would be to retire into such a valley, sheltered, perpetually moist, and usually silent. He often imagined withdrawing into such peace and seclusion but rarely thought of what he might do there.

Helen would say, 'You'd be bored within a week; in any case the place is an infallible prescription for rheumatism.'

'Stop the world, I want to get off!' It was a feeling he had often enough, but at other times he was more or less resigned to staying aboard the roller-coaster, screaming with the rest.

But this was a good place. Perhaps a place to die in. Death, he imagined, might come easily, unnoticed, stealing like a mist up the river.

He could see Trecara ahead, a jumble of decaying walls, windows, gables, roofs and chimneys. A low, battlemented wall separated the grounds from the river bank and, as he rounded a bend in the path, he came in sight of an absurd Victorian Gothic gatehouse, now lacking a gate. A car was drawn up there and two men stood by it, talking. One was the whiskered Carey, the other, Abe Geach. Wycliffe was mildly surprised.

They were within a hundred yards of him; they shook hands, Carey turned back to the house and Geach to his car. Geach caught sight of Wycliffe, decided not to see him, then changed his mind and came across the weedy gravel to meet him.

'Good morning, Mr Wycliffe! Finding your way around? Will you let me give you a lift back to the village?'

'No, thanks. I think I'll walk.'

Geach seemed reluctant to leave it at that. 'I've been having a chat with Carey about his house. It's in a terrible state; parts of it could collapse at any time. Pity! It's a fine old place but upkeep is the problem. Trigg is bad enough but this is three times the size and it's been neglected.'

He was talking too much.

'Are you undertaking restoration?'

'Well, it's been talked about, but Carey couldn't run to it. To put that place in good shape would set him back forty grand. It's a difficult building – a rabbit warren.'

'And the rabbits?'

Geach chuckled. 'There's old Carey – though he's not as old as you might think. I'm forty-one and he could give me ten years – no more; then there's his niece, and the Pascoes. The Pascoes, man and wife, must be in their sixties. They started there as servants in Carey's father's time; what they are now, God knows. I doubt if they ever get paid.'

They had come to a halt beside the contractor's car.

'Do the Careys have any friends?'

Geach pouted. 'The vicar is a regular visitor, I believe; and recently Stephanie Vinter. That set a few tongues wagging. She's supposed to be helping him sort out his library so perhaps he's hoping to raise a bit of capital.'

He had his hand on the car door. 'Sure you won't change your mind?'

'Thanks all the same.'

Geach, still uneasy, drove off up the road which was little more than a track. Wycliffe followed him with his eyes, and wondered. Had Geach, newly married, already started to look back over the fence? If it was he who had been with Jessica on the night the Ruse boy was killed, and now, sixteen years later, Jessica had threatened or even hinted at exposure . . . Geach had a great deal to lose.

But the bizarre staging of the crime?

Wycliffe walked up the track, through the pillared order of the larchwood. In a few minutes the ground levelled off and he was clear of the trees. To his right, the folly rose, apparently out of a marsh in which thickets of reeds and rushes were interspersed with scrub willows.

He was tempted to take a closer look, but resisted.

Then, looming ahead, and coming towards him, he saw a bulky figure laden like a Christmas tree. When the two were within a few yards of each other Wycliffe said, 'You must be Jumbo.'

The broad face beamed. 'And you're the policeman. I've seen you pass the boat.'

Wycliffe looked at the nets and at the battery of collecting bottles draped around the lad's neck. 'Mr Lavin told me you were out collecting.'

'Yes, in the marsh. You see, this is a freshwater marsh and Brian thought we ought to compare it with the marshes by the river which are a bit salt – because of the tide. Some of the animals and plants you get up here wouldn't like that, and some you get

514

down there wouldn't like it up here.' His forehead creased in the effort of exposition. 'It's funny; some creatures and some plants are very fussy about how much salt there is but others don't mind much.'

Wycliffe said, 'I thought Giles Vinter was with you.'

Jumbo nodded. 'He was, but he didn't want to go home yet. I expect he's gone to the tower.'

'To the tower?'

'His dad is interested in bats and the tower is one of their roosting places. I think Giles is interested too.'

'Have you always been friendly with Giles?'

'No, only lately. He used to go around with Julie.'

Jumbo had very dark brown eyes and when he was speaking his expression was intent and serious. 'Brian – that's Mr Lavin, thinks that we might be able to write something about the valley and get it printed.'

Had anybody, so far, talked to Jumbo about the crime? He couldn't remember anything in the reports. 'Where were you, Jumbo, the evening Jessica Dobell was killed?'

'I was on the boat.'

'You didn't go out all that evening?'

'No.'

'So you couldn't have seen anybody – say, on the river bank?'

'Oh, I saw Jessica on her way to the church. Brian saw her too; he spoke to her – just said "Hullo" like.' His face clouded. 'That was the last time we saw her.'

'Mr Lavin told me that Jessica used to come to the houseboat sometimes.'

The boy's features went blank. He said: 'Yes.'

'Did you like that?'

A frown. 'I expect she was all right . . . But it wasn't the same when she was there. I don't think I liked her very much.' He added, after a pause. 'She spoilt things.'

Wycliffe went back to his earlier line. 'You saw no one else on the river bank that evening?'

'Well, I saw Mr Vinter, but that was afterwards.'

'After you saw Jessica – how long afterwards?'

'I don't know really. I was still on deck, just leaning on the rail; it was dark.' He lowered his voice. 'A bit before, Mr and Mrs Vinter was quarrelling. I could hear them. You can hear everything on the river when it's dark. Mr Vinter shouted a bit but Mrs Vinter didn't raise her voice, then I heard the door slam and he went past the boat, but he didn't see me. I think he was upset.'

'Did Mr Lavin see him?'

Jumbo shook his head. 'I don't think so; he was in the cabin, working.'

Wycliffe said, 'I'm keeping you; I expect you want to get home with your specimens.'

Stray ends from other people's lives. A man quarrels with his wife, he walks out and slams the door; it happens all the time. But through a coincidence of time and place this quarrel would occupy Wycliffe and his detectives. If Vinter was ever arrested and charged it would figure in countless documents and records and would appear in the press. In solemn tones, worthy of the Recording Angel, counsel for the prosecution would say, 'Mr Vinter, on that Saturday evening when Jessica Dobell was murdered, you quarrelled with your wife . . . '

Chapter Ten

Wycliffe returned to the Incident Room, thoughtful and morose. Kersey was there.

'Nice walk, sir?' Kersey was nursing a mug of coffee. 'Like some? Potter has set up a snack bar in what used to be the kids' cloakroom.'

A constable went to fetch the coffee and Wycliffe sat astride one of the chairs, resting his arms on the back. 'On Saturday evening, after Jessica left for the church, the Vinters had a quarrel and Vinter took an airing along the river bank in the direction of the church.'

'Where did you get that?'

'The boy who lives on the boat with Lavin; he overheard the quarrel and saw Vinter leave.'

'Reliable?'

'I think so; he's not so stupid as people make out; in fact I don't think he's stupid at all. Uncomplicated, I'd say. Of course, what he's told us doesn't amount to much evidentially, it merely means that Vinter joins the club – Paul and the vicar were both coy about admitting not only that they were out and about on Saturday evening but actually in the church. Geach is supposed to have been working in his mobile office, but who's to say he didn't take a little walk? There's nobody in this case with anything like a respectable alibi except, perhaps, Johnny Glynn who seems to have been at the bar as usual.'

Kersey agreed. 'But, for what it's worth, Fox thinks the wellington boot that made his precious toeprint belonged to Vinter. It's not a hundred per cent, but Fox has the boot and he's getting an expert opinion. Chances are he'll get no more than a probable but even a possible could be a useful lever.'

He put down his coffee cup and lit a cigarette. 'And there are other pointers to the Vinter household. Whoever wrote the fourth anonymous note must have had access to the others in order to imitate their style and content, and choose the same stationery. The notes were sent to the farm, and Stephanie admits having seen one of them. Add to this that the vicar loaned his *Church Quarterly* to Vinter – the one from which the wedges for the organ keys were cut. Things are beginning to gel.'

Wycliffe was less euphoric. 'It would be a pleasant change. Anyway, we'd better have Vinter in for further questioning, on the record. If nothing else, he lied in his statement. I'm seeing Tom Reed this afternoon; if you have Vinter in about four, I'll join you when I can. Anything else?'

'Not much. We've filled in a bit of Lavin's background. He was employed in the research division of British Drugs. He qualified as a medical doctor before taking a post-graduate degree in pharmacology. The firm wanted him to stay on after his accident but he opted to go with an out-of-court settlement of damages. Nothing known against him; he was regarded as something of a boffin and a loner. All sorts of more or less good-humoured jokes about him and his boyfriend.'

While they were talking Lucy Lane arrived.

Wycliffe said, 'Get yourself some coffee, Lucy. Potter has set up shop in the cloakroom.'

Lucy went out and came back with her coffee. 'I've talked to Nicholls, the lawyer. What we were told about the wills made by the two sisters is not quite right. According to Nicholls, if either of the two sisters died the other came into everything – not only the deceased's share in the farm.'

Kersey was unimpressed. 'So what? I don't see how it affects things. Of course Kathy gets Jessica's few belongings, whatever they are, but I don't imagine they would constitute a motive for snuffing her sister. Anything else?'

Lucy sipped her coffee. 'I don't know. As I was leaving, Nicholls asked me if I played golf or stayed at four-star hotels.'

Kersey laughed. 'He was winding you up.'

'I'm not so sure. It's occurred to me since that he could have been dropping a hint.'

'Of what?'

'There's been talk from time to time of business groups who want to cash in on Truro's prosperity with an up-market country park – hotel, golf course, swimming pool – that sort of thing. I believe that one or two schemes have already come to grief at the outline planning stage and I wondered if Nicholls was hinting at something of the sort affecting the future of the farm.'

Wycliffe was interested. 'I think you could have something. I happened to see Geach this morning, coming away from Trecara, being seen off by Carey. He seemed over-anxious to tell me that they had been talking about repairs to the house. It wouldn't surprise me if he had some deal in mind which could involve the farm and Carey's property.'

Kersey summed up: 'So the plot thickens as far as Geach is concerned. If he was involved in the RTA which killed the Ruse boy and our Jess was having qualms of conscience, plus the fact that she was being difficult about the farm . . . Well, you could say he was killing two birds with one stone.'

Wycliffe said, 'You have a talent, Doug, for making even your own brand of logic sound like fantasy. But Geach must be taken seriously. It's difficult to see him pursuing a double bluff with the Schumann thing but we know now that, musically, he was probably quite capable of setting it up.'

The three were beginning to loosen up; the atmosphere was coming right. Next door, telephones were bleeping; officers were tapping away at keyboards, nourishing the computer, scratching away in notebooks, or drinking coffee. Files were growing in number and bulk. They had settled in.

Wycliffe said, 'Before we get too bogged down, let's do what I suggested last night; let's try to work out some sort of specification for the criminal.' He turned to Lucy Lane. 'You have first go, Lucy.'

Lucy, taken by surprise, gathered her wits. 'Well, I don't think he's the sort to act on impulse. This crime was thought out in advance, planned, even to the cutting out and folding of the bits of paper to wedge the organ keys. Those bits of paper – so carefully cut, they bother me; the attention to detail for its own sake is obsessive.'

She paused, thoughtful, studying her finger nails. 'But the whole tableau seems to have been worked out beforehand and set up with almost loving care . . . Even the exact extent to which he would undress his victim was calculated. It's as though he got his kicks from brooding on every detail of what he would do. It seems to me that this adds up to a lot of hatred.'

Wycliffe was pleased. 'Good start! Hatred rather than lust?'

'I think so, yes.'

Kersey said, 'You talk about planning, but he didn't bring his own hammer.'

'No, but that makes another point – he knew the church well enough to know where he could find one, and he avoided using a weapon which might be traced to him. I think he's accustomed to being in the church so that nobody would think twice about seeing him there. He also knows the organ and must have at least an elementary knowledge of music.'

Wycliffe said, 'Right! Your turn, Doug.'

Kersey grimaced. 'This is worse than being in the witness box.' He fished in his pocket for cigarettes and lit one. 'I see him as a twisted bastard, sexually repressed. If he had it in for the woman he could have killed her straight off, no need to set up this charade in order to tell the world that she was a whore.'

He blew out smoke and Lucy fanned herself defensively. 'I'd be inclined to think that at one time he must have been bitten by the religious bug. The whole thing has a rather nasty flavour of self-righteousness: judgement and condemnation . . . Then there's the Mary Magdalene stuff. He knew his Bible; and how many do these days?'

'You don't think the motive for the crime was sexual?'

Kersey screwed up his lined features in uneasy doubt. 'I was afraid you'd ask me that. I mean, there's obviously a strong sexual element but somehow I can't see it as a bloke killing his

520

girlfriend just because she was having it off with somebody else. And yet . . .'

'Go on.'

'I was going to say that I still smell jealousy though somehow not of the woman . . .

Wycliffe was approving. 'I go along with you there. Is that it?'

Kersey grinned. 'I wouldn't want to upstage you, sir.'

Outside the mists had cleared and the sun was shining. Through the open window they heard the church clock dole out a single stroke.

Wycliffe said, 'One o'clock, we shall be late at the Hopton, but I'd better say my piece.

'You've left me with the difficult bit – the nature of the hatred which seems to underlie this crime. Unless the whole set-up is a deliberate con, this hatred isn't only directed against the victim. She is the focus, but it reaches out to others – to Geach, as shown by the wedged organ keys, to the organist, to the vicar whose church is defiled, and even to the Church itself.'

Wycliffe paused, sitting back in his chair. 'In essence, I agree with both of you, and in particular with Doug's emphasis on jealousy allied to hatred. I can't see this crime simply as murder; it looks to me more like a comprehensive act of revenge and defilement.'

He shuffled some papers on his desk; he was uneasy, and it served him right. He had trapped himself into making some sort of analysis of the vague notions that were in his mind. Ideas, once put into words, demand the gloss of logic and thereafter are set in concrete. But having started, he soldiered on.

'It seems to me that we are dealing with a strangely disturbed personality and, though both of you speak of "he", in my opinion there is more of feminine than masculine psychology behind this crime. It could be that we are looking for a woman. I don't suppose Lucy will agree with that.'

But Lucy did, with reservations. 'You may be right about the psychology, sir, but if you are I don't think it necessarily means that we are dealing with a woman.'

'Perhaps a man in drag,' from Kersey. 'But does all this help to pin down the killer? I mean, is he, she or it on our list?'

Wycliffe said, 'Our next question, obviously. If I had to answer it at this moment, I would say, "No".'

They crossed to the pub for lunch. Carey and his niece were well ahead with their meal, and today they shared their table with the vicar. From time to time Jordan glanced across at the police table, distinctly uneasy.

Kersey said, 'We're putting him off his lunch.'

By the time the police party had finished the others had already left and Wycliffe approached the landlord for enlightenment. As usual, Johnny was taciturn on the subject of personalities.

'His sister goes to Truro on Tuesdays and he lunches here.'

Stephanie Vinter spread a grubby blue tablecloth over one end of the kitchen table and laid three places with knives, forks and spoons. On the bottled-gas cooker a saucepan simmered, puffing out jets of steam. Stephanie's movements were listless, she was pale, her eyes were red and she had that curiously pinched look about the nostrils which goes with sleepless nights and distress of mind.

The backdoor opened and Vinter came in; he'd left his boots outside and was in his stockinged feet. Moving like a sleepwalker, he went to the sink and began to wash.

'How are you getting on out there?' Stephanie spoke as though she were inquiring about some distant undertaking of which she had only hearsay knowledge.

Vinter paused in the act of soaping his arms. 'All right.'

'The man that Geach sent – what's he like?'

'He's called Sandry. He seems a decent sort – doesn't talk much.'

'Did he give you any idea of what they intend to do?'

'He doesn't know any more than we do. He's still employed by Geach and, as far as he knows, he's just helping out on a temporary basis.'

'It can't last.'

'No. Where's Giles?'

'He went out but he'll be back for lunch.' Stephanie put plates to warm under the grill. 'Oh, there's a letter for you. It's on the dresser.'

Vinter finished washing, dried himself and went over to the dresser. With deliberation he slit open the envelope and unfolded the letter. 'It's from Jessica's lawyers.'

'Read it to me.'

'It says: "In connection with the estate of Miss Jessica Dobell, deceased, I shall be grateful if you will make an early appointment at this office to discuss with me matters arising which are of concern to you."'

'What does it mean?'

'Our marching orders, I suppose. What else?'

As he spoke, Giles came in. The boy stood inside the door, looking first at one parent, then at the other. 'Is something wrong?'

His mother said, 'No, I'm just going to serve out.'

They sat down to their stew in which the carrots were still hard. Stephanie said, 'We shall have to make up our minds; how much notice will they give us?'

Vinter, his fork halfway to his lips, put it down again. 'Let's leave it until I've seen the lawyer.'

Stephanie was about to protest but glanced across at her son and was silent.

Giles watched his parents but said nothing.

When the first course was almost over Vinter spoke to the boy. 'If, when we leave here, it meant you going to another school, how would you feel about it?'

Giles considered the question, then, 'When shall we go?'

'I don't know. We have no tenancy agreement so, as I was saying to your mother, it depends on the lawyers. But if it means another school we must make sure they use the same examining board.'

Stephanie got up from her chair. 'There's baked apple.'

She served the apple and they ate in silence. Suddenly Giles dropped his spoon with a clatter. There was a fourth chair at the table, unoccupied, and he was looking towards it with his expressionless gaze. He said, in a conversational manner: 'Don't you miss her?'

Wycliffe drove into Truro along the devious lane which is its principal link with points east. Just above the town it blossoms into a dual-carriageway and the descent offers a glimpse of the three spires of Pearson's Gothic revival cathedral. The police station, at the bottom of the slope, by a busy roundabout, escapes being a sixties horror, for which somebody should get a small medal.

Wycliffe parked his car and was received by the desk man. 'Mr Reed is in his office, sir. You know the way?'

Wycliffe did.

They were served with coffee in china cups – with saucers, and Reed said, 'I only get this kind of service during royal visits.'

His little office was separated from the CID room by a glass partition. He fiddled with a little wad of typescript. 'I made a few extracts from the Derek Ruse file and there are one or two photographs . . .

'The date was January 3rd 1976 and the boy was fifteen at the time. At about six-thirty in the evening he was cycling home from the village of Trispen, to Tresillian, after spending the afternoon with a school friend.'

Reed must have spent time he could ill spare getting together his dossier and Wycliffe felt a pang of guilt. But exploring blind alleys is a growth industry.

Reed said, 'Derek Ruse was a popular boy and the case aroused strong feelings – especially when the medical evidence suggested that he might not have been dead when his body was pushed over the hedge into an adjoining field.'

The sun, hidden all the morning, had broken through and was shining directly into the little office. With a massive forefinger Reed separated his collar from his neck. 'This damned office gets like an oven in the afternoons.'

He selected two photographs and passed them over. The first could have been taken in almost any of the minor lanes in the district; the second showed a field ditch by the side of a low hedge.

In the ditch, the boy's crumpled body lay under his bicycle which must have been pushed over on top of him. His glazed eyes seemed to be staring up through the wheel spokes.

Reed said, 'That lane wriggles across country between Trispen and Tresillian, up hill and down dale, and it's barely wide enough for a hearse.' He added, after a pause, 'You see how we found him – that was next morning, and it had deluged with rain all night, washing away any traces there might have been.'

Reed sat back in his chair. 'CID took over, but I was kept on the case. The experts reckoned the bike had been struck higher up than would have been the case with a car, so we concentrated on commercial and farm vehicles. We covered the area for miles around, and got nowhere. Of course we realised there might be no trace of the collision left on a sturdily built vehicle with a good fender.'

He paused and looked at Wycliffe. Reed's baby-blue eyes were possessed of a singular innocence. 'No need to bore you with the details, the point is, names began to be bandied about – one name in particular, Jonathan Selborne Glynn. Johnny may seem tame enough now but he had a name as a tearaway then. His father farmed near Trispen and Johnny used to drive around the lanes, hell-bent, in a clapped out pick-up, usually with his girlfriend – '

'Jessica Dobell.'

Reed nodded. 'You're ahead of me, sir. Anyway, we'd had complaints, so it was natural we should think of him. He admitted that he'd driven through the lane that evening – alone, he said, but he claimed it was more than an hour after the boy would have reached there on his bike. We might not have taken too much notice of his unsupported word but there were two reliable witnesses who saw him in the lane after half-seven that evening.'

Reed brought out a spotlessly white handkerchief to mop his forehead. 'Even the locals seemed satisfied, but I had my doubts. After the accident he could have driven back home and waited – there are plenty of farm gateways in which he could have turned the truck. All he had to do then was to drive along the lane an hour later and make sure he was seen. I put that to the DI, but of course he wanted evidence which I couldn't find.'

Reed spread his great hands. 'There were other suspects, but none that stood up.'

Wycliffe said, 'Well, all I can tell you is that shortly before her death Jessica Dobell confided in her sister, and in a friend, that she knew who was responsible for the hit-and-run and that she had been involved. She spoke of going to the police to tell what she knew.'

Reed stopped in the act of collecting his papers together. 'Did she mention Glynn?'

'In answer to a question, she said that it definitely wasn't Glynn and she added something else. She said that she wanted to go to the police but that she hadn't played fair with her sister and didn't want to make it worse for her.'

Reed looked at Wycliffe, incredulous. 'That adds up to Abe Geach. God, that would be a turn-up for the book! His name came up. Although he'd recently married her sister, it was rumoured that he'd been seen with Jessica in pubs far enough from home to feel safe. One story had it that he and Johnny had come to blows over the girl. Certainly Abe's Land Rover was putting on a lot of night mileage at the time but we couldn't get anywhere in that direction.'

Reed massaged his chin until it shone. 'Well, sir! Where do we go from here? Is there a chance of reopening the file? I don't like loose ends even when they're ancient history.'

Wycliffe got up from his chair and walked to the window. For a minute or two he stood looking down at the frenetic gyration of traffic at the roundabout. Panic in the ants' nest.

'At the moment I'm more concerned with Geach as a possible murder suspect.'

Reed nodded. 'I see that – if she threatened him.'

'I'm willing for you to tackle Johnny Glynn in general terms about the hit-and-run. Let him know that he's no longer under suspicion, hint that the case could be reopened, and see what comes of it. No mention of any possible link with the present case. And remember, the new evidence, such as it is, is hearsay. I don't need to tell you that it wouldn't stand up in court.'

Reed said, 'Fair enough. That's all I could expect.'

Chapter Eleven

Tuesday afternoon

When Wycliffe returned to the Incident Room, Vinter was just arriving in a police car. He looked pale and drawn like a man on the edge of collapse.

The little interview cubicle was crowded, with Kersey and Wycliffe on one side of the table and Vinter on the other. On the table between them was a tape recorder and, on the wall, a notice setting out the rights of those undergoing police interrogation. An electric clock clicked the seconds away.

Wycliffe felt sorry for the man and was mildly reassuring. 'This interview is to clear up matters which have come to light since you made your statement, Mr Vinter. You should attach no more and no less importance to it than that.'

Kersey switched on the tape. 'This interview begins at 16.04 hours. Present: Detective Chief Superintendent Wycliffe and Detective Inspector Kersey. If you wish, the interview may be postponed and take place in the presence of your solicitor.'

'I feel in no need of a solicitor.'

Through the window of the little room noises reached them from outside; the occasional sound of cars manoeuvring to pass each other in the narrow street, people exchanging greetings, and gulls in squawking flight.

Wycliffe left the initial questioning to Kersey.

'You didn't tell us in your earlier statement precisely how you came to leave your teaching post.'

There was a pause while Vinter looked from Kersey to Wycliffe and back again, then: 'But now you've found out for yourselves, as I knew you would.'

'You were dismissed following an involvement with a girl student.'

'Technically, I was not dismissed, I was allowed to resign and so preserve my pension rights.'

It was strange. This man was wearing the clothes he wore on the farm – bib-and-brace overalls and a khaki shirt – yet he spoke in a cultivated manner with the precision of an academic. He had been warned of the interview in ample time to change but he had chosen to come in his role as a farm worker.

'Would you say that you are, by nature, a man inclined to violence?'

'I would not. In that instance I was the victim of a rather unpleasant young woman. Of course I am bound to say that, am I not?'

Wycliffe intervened. 'It is your relations with Jessica Dobell which concern us now.'

Vinter was looking down at his bony hands, clasped together on the table top. 'I was employed by her.'

Kersey said, 'But you had sex with her.'

The clasped hands tightened. 'I am not proud of that.'

'Another case of a designing woman?'

Vinter shifted on his chair. 'No, Jessica was highly sexed and I am not a monk.'

'Was your wife aware of the relationship?'

'No.'

Kersey sounded relaxed, understanding. 'Difficult, wasn't it? All together in the same house?'

Vinter seemed to be struggling to explain a situation which he had never before put into words. 'These encounters were casual, spur of the moment affairs . . . They did not take place in the house, but while we were working together – in the fields, the barn – anywhere.'

Kersey said, 'Think carefully how you answer this, Mr Vinter. How did you feel about the woman? Were you fond of her? In love? Were you jealous of her having other men?'

Vinter looked at Kersey in astonishment. 'Why should I be jealous? I wished then, and I wish now, that I'd never seen her.

We used each other sexually, that's the simple truth. Most of the time I hated her.' He added, in a low voice, 'But I didn't kill her.'

Neither of the policemen spoke and, after an interval, Vinter went on, 'I put my family in the position in which we found ourselves. I was to blame. We were servants, and Jessica wasn't slow to make us understand that. It wasn't a question of being overworked – I've very little idea of what could reasonably have been expected of us; it was her attitude. She was contemptuous of us for the very reason that we had put ourselves in a position of dependence. She could not understand people who lacked the strength of purpose which she had and her instinct was to humiliate them.'

'You are acquainted with Lavin, the houseboat man?'

Vinter's surprise at the abrupt change of subject was obvious and he answered as though with relief, 'Yes. He's the sort of man I can get on with, but I don't see as much of him as I would like. He is the sort of man I can understand.'

'I believe you have a common interest in natural history.'

'I'm trying to do a little work on the bat population of this area.'

'This means going out early and late?'

'Yes, I visit their known roosting places and try to find others.'

'Is Mr Carey another of your acquaintances?'

Was there a momentary twinge of concern? 'I know him.'

'I believe your wife is a fairly regular visitor at Trecara.'

'She is helping Carey with cataloguing his books.' He added, as an afterthought, but giving it some importance, 'Since he's been on holiday Giles has been going with her.'

It was Wycliffe's turn: 'In your earlier statement, Mr Vinter, you said that you did not leave the farm on Saturday evening.'

Vinter sat forward on his chair and looked directly at Wycliffe. 'That was a lie.'

'So we have discovered. Perhaps we can now have the truth?'

'My wife and I had a row.' A small gesture. 'It doesn't happen often but tension has been growing. I mean, Stephanie wanted us to move in with the Careys – Carey knows how unhappy we have been and he offered us a home for an indefinite period, with no strings . . . This was some time ago . . . I suppose it was very kind of him but what would it make me?' A longish pause, and then: 'The long and short of it is that I can't take his charity. Stephanie says I could help out around the place – earn my keep, but that would be just a façade . . . Anyway, we quarrelled and I stalked out.'

'Where?'

He looked blank. 'I'm sorry, what are you asking?'

'Where did you go? A simple question.'

'Oh, I walked along the river bank to the village, through the village and back by the road. I cooled off.'

'You didn't go into the church?'

Vinter shook his head and spoke in a low voice, 'No, I didn't go into the church and I didn't see Jessica, but what is the good of me saying so?'

'At what time did you leave the house?'

'I'm not sure, but it would be about nine.'

'Did you see anyone, on the river bank, in the village, or on the road home?'

'There were one or two people about in the square but I didn't speak to anybody.'

'Anybody you recognised?'

'Tommy Noall was chatting to somebody on his garage forecourt but I doubt if he saw me . . .'

There was silence in the little room; only the electric clock, clicking the seconds away.

'Are you interested in music, Mr Vinter?'

Vinter's blue eyes met Wycliffe's. 'Why don't you ask me if I know enough to have set up the thing on the organ?'

'Do you?'

'Yes, but I didn't do it and I can't make any suggestion as to why anybody would want to.'

'When you left home on Saturday evening what boots or shoes were you wearing?'

Vinter hesitated for a long time and Wycliffe did nothing to hurry him. After one or two false starts, he said, 'I was wearing my wellingtons.'

'You have more than one pair?'

'No.'

'You know that one of those boots is being checked against evidence found in the church?'

'Yes.'

'You have no comment to make on that?'

'No, except that I wasn't there.'

'One more question. I understand that you borrowed a copy of the *Church Quarterly* from the vicar, in which there was an article that interested you. What happened to it?'

'I thought I had returned it.'

'Can you remember the circumstances?'

A long period of hesitation which puzzled Wycliffe, then, 'No, I'm afraid not.'

'It was with pieces of paper cut from that issue that the organ keys were wedged – can you explain that?'

'No, I cannot explain it.'

Wycliffe recited, 'This interview ends at 16.34. It has been recorded and will be transcribed. You will then be asked to read the transcription and to sign it if you agree that it is a correct record.' He switched off the tape.

'And then?'

'You will be free to go but I strongly advise you to think carefully about your walk on Saturday evening and about what happened to that issue of the *Church Quarterly*. Two of my officers will return home with you to make a thorough search of the house for the magazine. I can obtain a warrant, but if you have no objection that will not be necessary.'

'I have no objection.'

Wycliffe returned to his office. He felt confused and depressed. A few minutes later he was rejoined by Kersey.

'So you're letting him go.'

'Yes.'

Kersey blew out his cheeks. 'So what? This is only the third day after all. What can you expect?'

Wycliffe fiddled with the papers on his desk. 'I know all that,

Doug, but this woman wasn't found in some lay-by off the motorway; she was murdered in the heart of a small community of which she had been part for her whole life. Her associates are known, her life style is known, and the manner of the crime itself might be expected to point to the killer.'

Kersey said, 'I gather you weren't impressed by Vinter as a candidate.'

Wycliffe did not answer at once, then, 'Whatever I think there isn't enough evidence, material or circumstantial, to hold him, let alone charge him. Above all, there is no obvious motive. As far as I can see, Jessica Dobell's death did nothing to solve the Vinters' problems, it merely precipitated a crisis.'

Kersey persisted. 'So you don't think he's our man?'

'He still could be. For an innocent man, some of his answers were anything but spontaneous or convincing but, if he killed Jessica Dobell, there's a great deal more in all this than has so far surfaced . . . What was it Lucy said? Something to the effect that not much of what goes on inside Vinter shows – seven-tenths submerged. She could be right.'

Wycliffe sat back in his chair. 'When Franks said that we would be up to our necks in trick cyclists before we finished I didn't think it would start with me. But this case isn't going to be settled by studying bits of paper wedged between organ keys and toe marks on the bloody floor.'

It was unusual for Wycliffe to swear, and Kersey took note. 'So what's the agenda?'

'I want you to take Fox and Collis and search the farmhouse. Officially, you're looking for what's left of the vicar's magazine but that gives you an open brief. I've no idea what you might or might not find; that's why I want you there. Obviously if you find anything incriminating you'll act accordingly. Don't go until Vinter has signed his statement, then you can take him with you.'

Left alone, Wycliffe looked at the telephone, hoping that it would ring, and at the door, hoping that it would open. The investigation was losing its way; he had reached the stage of a punter picking winners with a pin. He needed a spot of luck. He trimmed his nails, emptied the little dish which Kersey had used as an ashtray, and tidied his files; placatory gestures to unknown gods.

And they seemed to work. At any rate there was a knock, the door opened and Dixon came in with a pink flimsy. 'Fax from CRO, sir. No record of prints from the Paul premises.'

Down the snake. But no sooner had Dixon returned to his post than the phone rang: 'DI Cox, sir. Met Fraud Squad.'

'Put him through . . . Geoff? This is Charles.' They had been at training school together but Cox had joined the Met and got stuck on the promotion ladder. It was from him that Wycliffe had sought information about the Pauls.

'When you phoned yesterday you mentioned that Arnold Paul, in an off moment, had called his alleged brother "Timmy". It rang a bell but I couldn't think why it should. Anyway it came back to me overnight. Arnold Paul was a witness for the defence in a case against a certain Timothy Raison a few years back. Raison was acquitted on charges of false accounting and misappropriation in a company of which he was managing director. That's history; more to the point, we've got a warrant out against him for jumping bail on fresh charges – perhaps a bit more serious this time. It sounds too much of a coincidence for there to be no connection so I'd like to send a chap down to talk to your friend.'

'Be my guest. But you don't see this Raison as a killer?'

Cox laughed. 'More of a twit. We meet a lot of his sort in our line, not very bright; they wade into trouble without noticing it and their success depends on others being bigger fools than they are. Of course, Raison is very small fry but intelligence isn't a conspicuous feature of the financial world – mostly it's cunning and greed.'

'He must have some sort of hold over Paul.'

'I'll keep you posted.'

The gods had failed him; he wasn't interested in crooked dealings which might or might not involve Arnold Paul.

It was almost six before Wycliffe heard from the searchers.

It was Kersey. 'I'm speaking on the car phone. The house

seems to be clean. We did a thorough search. Vinter showed not the slightest interest and refused to monitor what we were at. He went back to his work about the farm. Stephanie didn't turn a hair; she followed us around but made no complaint or comment. It was uncanny.'

'Was the boy, Giles, there?'

'Working at his books on the kitchen table. I gave him the chance to be in on the search of his room but he hardly looked up – just said, "No, thank you."'

'Tuesday is pasty night. Cornish pasties, me han'somes! How's that then? The real thing: plain pastry, chuck steak, sliced potato, turnip and onion; nothing minced, nothing diced.' Johnny, doing his Captain Birds Eye act, seemed his usual self. 'Of course, there's the cold table if you prefer it.'

'How big are your pasties?' from Lucy Lane.

'Two just fit on a ten-inch dinner plate – perfect. But nobody eats more than one, and young women worried about their figures are allowed to leave a bit.'

So pasties it was.

Wycliffe's mind was on Vinter. He was uneasy and all his cop instincts told him that he should have held the man for questioning. He told himself that he would have had to let him go again, but his professional conscience was not appeased. On the other hand . . .

The pasties arrived – golden brown, beautifully 'turned in', with a slot in the top to let the steam out.

Johnny was there. 'My wife makes 'em; that's mainly why I married her. You can use a knife and fork if you must, but the proper way is to pick 'em up and bite from the end – hold 'em in your table napkin but watch out for the gravy, it's hot.'

Kersey and Lucy Lane took Johnny's advice but Wycliffe, victim of his mother's aspiring gentility, used his knife and fork.

Lucy surrendered when only one-quarter of her pasty remained; the two men had cleared the crumbs. 'That was good!' – Kersey. 'Excellent!' – Wycliffe.

Johnny said, 'No dessert, no coffee, but a cup of tea with milk and sugar; then a walk. That's my recipe to aid digestion after a pasty, but if you don't like it, then there's sodium bi-carb on the house.'

Carey, with a gleeful flourish, laid down six of the seven tiles in his rack – 'H-R-A-T-R-Y. With your P, Jordan, that makes phratry.'

The vicar's smooth brow creased into a frown. 'Phratry?'

'Are you challenging?'

A self-conscious laugh. 'No – I know better than to do anything so rash. It's just that phratry is new to me.'

'It shouldn't be. The word has an excellent pedigree, going back to the Greeks; it means a religious or political division of the people – originally, I believe, based on kinship. Your turn, Alicia.'

Alicia studied her tiles and finally selected three:'I am adding I-S-E to journal, to make journalise – which will annoy uncle.'

Carey grinned. 'There should be an Officer of State – like the old Public Hangman who burned books – charged with the duty of formally banishing such words from the language.'

They were in one of the few rooms that remained habitable. It was small, with items of furniture too large for it brought from other parts of the house. Although the room was lit by electricity, the chill of an April evening was kept at bay by a paraffin stove, placed close to the table at which they were seated.

Tuesday evening Scrabble was a regular feature of life at Trecara, with the vicar as guest. For him, it was the social event of his week. The game ran its course with Alicia the winner.

'She has no compunction whatever in profiting from the dregs of the OED,' Carey said. 'Shall we have another game and try to teach her the elements of discrimination?'

Jordan smiled a dutiful smile but it was clear that his thoughts were elsewhere. There was no disguising the fact that he was preoccupied and distressed. He looked towards the window where the curtains remained undrawn against the darkness outside and rain trickled down the window panes. 'I really must get back or Celia will be worried.'

'Why don't you telephone? It's raining hard now but that probably won't last long. Tell her you'll be a bit late.'

The vicar hesitated. 'No, Celia likes to keep to a routine.'

Alicia said, 'I'll get the whisky.'

This too was part of the Tuesday ritual; just the one drink before Jordan left. Alicia went to get it.

Carey said, 'I can see that you are worried, and no wonder; it is a most distressing affair. And so inexplicable!'

Jordan fingered the tiles which he had collected together and boxed. 'I'm at my wit's end. I don't know what to do.'

Carey stroked his beard. 'If it would help to talk . . . ?'

Jordan shook his head. 'It is kind of you, Hector, but it's only with God's help that I shall see this thing through.'

Alicia returned with the drinks tray.

'Ah, Alicia, there you are!'

The two men drank their whisky; Alicia, her orange juice; then Jordan got up to go. He made an effort to sound normal. 'Another Tuesday gone by!'

Carey saw him off at the door. The rain had eased. Jordan said, 'Good night! And thank you, both.'

'Let me lend you a torch.'

'No – really, I don't need one.'

It was dark but in the country it is rarely so dark that one cannot see one's way. The weedy gravelled drive curved gently to the grandiose gatehouse. He felt a little relieved; the companionship, the whisky, and the mere admission of his distress had coloured his mood. Tonight he would pray, and tomorrow would be in God's hands.

The arch was ten or twelve feet wide – wide enough to add a certain dank clamminess to the air beneath it and to intensify the darkness. But he could see the dull gleam on the pool which always formed under the arch when it rained and he kept close to one side to avoid it. Then, suddenly, there was a movement close to him, perhaps he let out a startled cry. He experienced a crushing, pulverising pain in his head, and then – nothing.

*

That night Stephanie went early to bed; she was prepared against another bad night with tablets Dr Sparrow had given her. She read a few pages of *Mansfield Park*, her current bedside book. It was long since she had read it and she was surprised to discover that the intervening years had made it possible for her to envy poor Fanny Price. After a few pages she put down the book, swallowed a Mogadon washed down with water, switched off her light and snuggled under the bedclothes. Within a short time she was asleep.

Some time later she was awakened by a sudden breeze which blew a curtain of rain against her little window. Sleepily, she realised that Laurence had not yet returned from his bat-watching. Nothing unusual in that. Then she noticed the reflection of light coming from Giles' room and called to him, 'Don't stay up reading too late, Giles!'

'No, Mother.'

'Good night, dear.'

'Good night.'

Almost at once his light went out and Stephanie fell asleep once more. Her dreams were confused and several times they brought her to the edge of wakefulness, but she slept on. When she eventually woke it was from a mildly erotic dream, and her hand was between her thighs. She sighed, turned over, and realised that Laurence was still not beside her. It was light, with the pale-grey light of early dawn and it was still raining.

Chapter Twelve

Wednesday morning

Wycliffe awoke, feeling sure that he had been disturbed by some sound and, for a moment or two, unable to recall where he was. Then memory returned and so did the sound – a gentle tapping on his door. He sat up in bed and as he did so the door opened. It was Johnny, the landlord, in shirt and trousers.

'I'm sorry to wake you but Celia Jordan has been on the telephone. She wanted to speak to you personally but I insisted on taking a message . . .'

Celia Jordan? Wycliffe's brain was still clogged with sleep. The vicar's sister, of course. 'Well?'

'She says her brother is missing – that he didn't come home last night.' The landlord spoke with detachment, as though disclaiming all responsibility. 'She's a bit odd sometimes but I thought I'd better pass it on.'

Wycliffe, still coming round, looked at his travelling clock; it was a quarter past six. 'Perhaps you will knock on Mr Kersey's door, and on Miss Lane's, while I get dressed.'

Johnny withdrew. Wycliffe got out of bed and pulled back the curtains. At times in the night he had been aware of heavy rain, now it had given place to drizzle. His room overlooked the square and the creek where the usual pair of swans, padding about on the muddy shore, were the only sign of life.

In his dressing gown he used the pay-phone in the corridor to arrange for a patrol car to call at the vicarage. He was uneasy, apprehensive. He recalled his last words to the vicar: 'Somebody who has killed once has broken through a barrier and may well find it easier to kill a second time.' Pompous, but true. A pity he hadn't listened to himself with greater attention. He had hoped to induce Jordan to tell what he was holding back, but he had failed, and could now be facing the consequence.

Fifteen minutes later, with Kersey and Lucy Lane, he was sipping scalding coffee in Johnny's kitchen. Johnny was still inclined to backtrack. 'This could be a mare's nest. As I said, Celia's queer. I've heard talk that in his last parish – somewhere in Wiltshire – they had to put her away for a time.'

Lucy was sent to the Incident Room while Kersey and Wycliffe drove the short distance to the vicarage. A patrol car was parked outside and they were admitted by a uniformed copper. He reported in a low voice, 'My mate is with her in the sitting room, sir. She says she went to call her brother this morning and found that his bed hadn't been slept in. It seems he had a regular Tuesday evening date at Trecara – with the Careys – and he went last evening as usual. I phoned Carey just now and he says Jordan left there at about half-ten.'

'On foot?'

'Yes.'

'Do you know if he usually went by the road or by the river path?'

'His sister says he went by the road. The footpath doesn't save much between the vicarage and Trecara, and if it's wet or dark, it's difficult.'

Wycliffe said, 'I want you to stay here until relieved. If anything crops up get in touch with DS Lane at the Incident Room.'

Back in the car he and Kersey continued up Church Lane; they passed by the entrance to Jessica's farm, and a moment or two later they were at the top of the long track which led down to the manor house. At one time it must have been a well-maintained drive but now the surface was rutted and pot-holed – facts that were even more apparent in the car than they had been when Wycliffe walked it the day before. The mist was so thick that Kersey was deprived of his first close-up view of the tower, and as they jolted down through the larchwood even the tops of the trees were hidden.

They arrived in the open space before the gatehouse to find

Carey waiting for them. His silky hair and beard glistened with drops of moisture.

'He's here.' Carey was deeply distressed and found difficulty in being coherent. 'We found him. Alicia went back to the house to telephone but you must have already left . . .' He passed a hand over his face and beard and seemed surprised to find it wet. 'It doesn't seem possible; I saw him off at the door – watched him go down the drive . . . I can't understand how I didn't hear something . . .'

Wycliffe formally introduced himself and Kersey, then the two detectives moved under the arch where Carey had pointed. The vicar was there, lying in a crumpled heap on the ground. The body lay on its right side, half in and half out of a shallow pool formed by the overnight rain. The cause of death was apparent, a massive injury to the left side of the skull above the ear.

For some reason there was not much blood, but what there was had drained into the blond, fine hair, and trickled in rivulets over the cheeks. Away from the actual wound the undamaged skin was pale and seemed to have shrunk over the bones so that the brow-ridges, nose, and chin were more prominent. The vicar's appearance had aged in death.

Kersey said, 'No theatricals this time; no props.'

Wycliffe nodded. 'Simple panic, by the look of it.'

'He must have known more than was good for him.'

Wycliffe was solemn. 'He certainly knew what we should have known – or at least guessed. But here we are, still in the dark. We've missed something vital, Doug, and this poor devil has had to pay for it.'

Kersey said, 'As far as I'm concerned, there's now only one horse in the race. Jordan must have seen Vinter in or near the church on Saturday evening and – '

Wycliffe, irritable, cut him short. 'Get on the car phone; contact Lucy at the Incident Room, and tell her to notify the sister. Then, the coroner and so on. Franks is still at the address in St Mawes – he's going to moan about this – twice in four days, but that's his problem. I shall be at the house with Carey but let me know when the circus begins to arrive.'

Carey had been standing well away from the two men, indifferent to the drizzling rain, now Wycliffe joined him. 'Perhaps we can go up to the house.' He added, 'This must have been a great shock.'

Carey said, 'I shall be glad to get back; I'm worried about Alicia; she says very little but things affect her deeply.'

Seen at close quarters it was more than ever obvious that successive generations of Careys had altered and added to the original house, each in their own idiosyncratic style. The process had culminated in the Victorian gatehouse, after which, perhaps mercifully, money must have run out. Now Wycliffe was to see the inside.

It was depressing. Carey led him through a bare hall and down a long passage, all stone floored and uncarpeted, into a sitting room at the back of the house.

Carey was agitated. 'Perhaps you will excuse me for a moment; I must find Alicia.'

Wycliffe waited in the little over-furnished room where the light was so poor that it was hard to distinguish any detail in the pictures on the walls. The furniture consisted of large pieces from different periods, presumably collected from rooms that had fallen victim to the progressive decay. He noted the cast-iron grate with its surround of Delft tiles, and the stacked, sawn logs beside it, but there was an oil stove in the middle of the room.

Carey was gone for some time. When he returned he was accompanied by his niece and he had changed his jacket and trousers.

The girl was very pale but composed. She said, 'I've seen you at the Hopton, Mr Wycliffe. I'm sorry to have kept you waiting, it was my fault, I made uncle change into dry clothes.' She turned to her uncle. 'Now you will want to talk – I shall be in the kitchen with Winnie if you want me.' Her manner was that of an affectionate mother with her child.

When she had gone, Wycliffe said, 'Just a few questions, Mr Carey. Jordan was a regular visitor here on Tuesday evenings?'

'Yes. I think he enjoyed those evenings. I know we looked

542

forward to him coming.' He glanced at the table on which there was a Scrabble set. 'We usually played Scrabble.'

'So anyone who knew his habits could expect him to be leaving here at . . . at what time?'

'At about half past ten; that was his time, and that is when he left last night. I saw him to the door and watched him as he walked down the drive . . . It was dark, but a clear night.' Carey brushed his eyes with his hand; they glistened with tears. 'He was a good man, but not a happy one, tortured rather than comforted by his religion.'

'Presumably you neither saw nor heard anything unusual?'

'Nothing.'

'What was your impression of his state of mind?'

Carey frowned. 'Well, as you might expect, the poor man was terribly shocked and distressed by what had happened in his church – by the crime itself, and by its bizarre embellishments.'

Wycliffe waited, and when no more came he said, 'I think you were going to add something.'

Carey looked down at his hands. 'Yes, well, I suppose discretion would be out of place in the circumstances. Jordan had other troubles. Yesterday evening, after we had had our meal and while Alicia was in the kitchen helping Mrs Pascoe with the clearing up, he told me, in confidence, that he suspected his sister of having written the anonymous notes which were found in the dead woman's possession. It seems that she did something very similar in his previous parish with unpleasant though not tragic consequences.' After a momentary pause, Carey added, 'Not that he imagined for a moment that she had any part in the crime itself. There was no question of that.'

'I understand.'

Carey was uncharacteristically restless and troubled. Instead of staring at him Wycliffe chose to look at a portrait of a Carey ancestor which hung over the fireplace. It portrayed a strikingly beautiful young woman with a remarkable resemblance to Alicia.

Carey had followd his gaze. 'Elvira Carey. When she died in childbirth at the age of twenty-four, her husband built the tower to her memory.'

He had had time to recover his self-control though his manner was still uncertain and tentative. 'I have very little to go on, but I feel sure that Jordan's worries went even deeper. Looking back, I can't help wondering if he had some idea of the identity of the killer . . . There was something which he wanted to confide but could not bring himself to do. I feel now that if only I had seemed a little more receptive, if I had been a little more persuasive . . . Of course I had no idea that he was in any way threatened.'

Wycliffe was sympathetic. 'I understand how you feel. I had precisely the same impression – that he was holding something back, but I was reluctant to put pressure on him. Now, of course, I regret that I did not.'

'It distresses you?'

'Of course it does!'

Carey seemed surprised. It seemed a new idea that a policeman might have a conscience in such matters.

The rain had stopped and the skies were clearing. Watery sunshine brought fresh colour and life to the river and its banks, but under the arch of the Victorian gatehouse the preoccupation was with death. There a group of initiates began that sequence of rituals prescribed for the discovery of the dead victim of another's hand.

Dr Sparrow, manifestly grown in self-importance, was there to pronounce life extinct. DS Fox, attended by his acolytes, was there to record every minute aspect of the scene of the crime. Dr Franks, the pathologist, under direction from the coroner, had arrived to take charge of the body and supervise its removal to the mortuary, there to perform his peculiar rites. Screens had been erected to preserve all this from prying eyes, but there were none. Kersey, nominally in charge, was mainly concerned with how soon they would let him get back to the job.

Wycliffe arrived while Franks was still making his preliminary examination. The pathologist got up from his knees, brushing his trousers free of invisible dust – he invariably used a kneeling pad. 'Twice in four days of the only break I've had in months!

544

Do I, in some mysterious way, attract these diversions, Charles? Or do you arrange them for me?'

'Neither. I'm quite sure the poor chap got himself topped just to spoil your holiday. Now, what have you got for me?'

Franks became judicial. 'I could say that the medical evidence is consistent with him having died between ten and eleven last night –'

'Good! And I suppose you could also say that death probably resulted from a blow delivered to the left side of the skull –'

Franks finished for him, 'causing a depressed fracture at the junction of the parietal, sphenoid, and temporal bones.'

'In other words, you've nothing to say that might be useful.'

There was a doorway which gave access to what had once been the gatekeeper's room; now it was stacked with boxes, broken furniture, and old beer crates. From the standpoint of the killer it had been simple. Knowing that the pool would force his victim to walk on that side, all he had to do was to stand back in the doorway and wait.

Franks was stooping over the body, taking another look at the wound. 'Perhaps I could add that from the angle of the depression it seems likely that the assailant was significantly taller than his victim. If I was asked nicely, I'd say he must have been not far short of six feet.'

Kersey looked at Wycliffe. 'Interesting, don't you think, sir?'

Wycliffe pointed into the little room with its store of rubbish. 'Perhaps he stood on a box to give him more clout. He had plenty to choose from.'

Franks laughed. 'You see what he's like when you try to help.'

Fox, hovering now, asked if it was all right to go through the dead man's pockets.

Franks said, 'Enjoy yourself.'

Fox had provided himself with a selection of the regulation tagged plastic bags. He explored the pockets which were sodden down one side. The trouser pockets yielded three pounds eighty-four in coin and a grubby handkerchief. The jacket side pockets were empty except for a raffle ticket and a supermarket receipt, but the two inside-breast pockets were more productive: a wallet, a cheque book, a ball-point pen, and an engagement book. The wallet held fifteen pounds in notes, a cheque card, driving licence, and library card.

Wycliffe flipped through the pages of the engagement book then turned to Kersey. 'I want Vinter brought in for further questioning. And to keep the record straight we must organise the troops for another round of inquiries: where was everybody, why, and who saw what.

'Now, Fox: everything here is to be minutely examined. If we are to get any material evidence it must come from here. I'm serious about the possibility of one of those crates being used by the killer to stand on.'

Kersey said, 'Where will you be, sir?'

'Back at the Incident Room, keeping my head down.'

Lucy Lane had returned to the Incident Room after informing Celia of her brother's death and was bringing her notes up to date.

'How did she take it?'

Lucy swept back a stray lock of hair – the only sign that she had been turned out of bed and set to work in fifteen minutes flat. 'I find it hard to believe that she really "took it" at all, sir. That's the most charitable view. At first she said nothing. Then I suggested that it might help to talk and she said, "What about? You tell me that my brother is dead, that he was murdered; oughtn't you to be out with your colleagues looking for his killer? Instead of here, playing at being a social worker."

'As I was leaving, she said, "I must tell the bishop."'

Wycliffe said, 'Perhaps she really believes he's gone to a better place. I must admit it would be a comforting thought.'

He was still in his office, brooding, when his telephone rang. It was Kersey, speaking from the farm. 'I'm using the car phone. It seems that Vinter was out bat-watching last night.' Kersey contrived to make it sound like a perversion. 'And, according to Stephanie he hasn't been home since.'

'Wasn't she concerned?'

'Not so's you'd notice; he's often been away all night it seems.

But the point is I've just discovered that the farm-truck is missing. It looks as though he's been back and gone again, this time in the truck.'

'He didn't take it last night?'

'Not according to the boy; he says the truck was still parked in the lane when his father left. I've asked Stephanie to check, and find out whether he took anything else while he was about it. The long and short of it is, sir – he's done a runner.'

Wycliffe did not miss the note of criticism. 'All right; phone in what you've got on him and the truck and I'll have it circulated.'

It was necessary to report to the chief. Oldroyd resisted the temptation to say 'I told you so.' Instead, it was: 'You had to make a decision, Charles and, as it happened, you made the wrong one, but it's easy to be wise after the event. Any idea where Vinter might have gone?'

'It's by no means certain that he's gone anywhere.'

Oldroyd took a deep breath. The two men had worked together for many years and outside the office they were good friends. In the office there were frequent differences. 'You're holding back on this one, Charles. I take it you now know who you're after?'

Wycliffe was silent, and the chief prompted, 'Charles?'

'No, sir; I'm by no means sure.'

Oldroyd snapped, 'Then I hope you'll act as though you were.'

Wycliffe had scarcely replaced his phone when it rang again. It was Kersey. 'There's some money missing, sir; just a few pounds they kept for emergencies. Nothing else, according to her ladyship.'

'Cheque book? Credit card?'

'I asked her and she looked at me as though I was talking about the family silver.'

'How are they taking it – she and the boy?'

'Nobody could accuse them of dramatising the situation.'

'What was he wearing?'

'Overalls. It seems he didn't stop to change.'

'A man in overalls, driving a farm-truck, with only a few

pounds in his pocket, isn't likely to be making for sunny Spain. I'll pass you over to Lucy and you can give her the details for circulation. After that I want you back here to arrange a search of the vicar's belongings, in particular of his study and his personal papers . . . His sister? If she interferes she'll be obstructing the inquiry. Handle her tactfully, but no nonsense.'

When he put down the phone Wycliffe got up from his chair and stood, staring out of the window of his little office. Ahead, there was only the boundary wall, but overhead the sky was an intense blue and two seagulls, whiter than white, cruised and planed with effortless ease.

It was always his practice in a murder inquiry to concentrate on the victim, and Jessica's life, like anyone else's, was intimately woven into the pattern of the lives about her. To discover and trace all the threads was impossible; one must select, and he had selected those which seemed significant. They pointed to a limited range of possible suspects. The problem was to match the character of any one of these with the extraordinary circumstances of the crime. He had encouraged the drawing up of some sort of specification for the criminal but the plain fact was that none of the suspects had seemed to fit.

Now, overnight, the vicar had become a second victim and Laurence Vinter a fugitive.

Laurence Vinter . . . A man filled with hatred which could find no single target but nourished itself in the meticulous preparation of a tableau in which a brutal murder was no more than a centrepiece . . . A man who, threatened with exposure, had shown no hesitation in murdering a second time . . .

A tap at the door, which opened just as Wycliffe muttered to himself, 'Nonsense! It's not possible!'

Lucy Lane said, 'I've brought you some coffee, sir.'

And yet Vinter was on the run.

He turned away from the window and, for a moment, it was as though he hardly knew where he was.

'Are you all right, sir?'

He sat at his desk and seemed, suddenly, to relax. 'Yes, I'm fine, Lucy. I've just decided that I can't believe the impossible.'

'You're obviously not as good at it as the Red Queen. Perhaps you should practise more. Anyway, coffee.'

He was being mothered, indulged, and he rather liked it. Drinking his coffee, he said, 'I'm going to the farm amongst other places, Lucy, and I want you with me. Send a crime car with a DC to the farm to await our arrival. Mr Kersey is leaving a uniformed man there. Tell the DC to park in the farmyard for communications purposes.'

A few minutes later they were crossing the square together. News of the vicar's death must have got around but there were few people about. Two women outside the post office watched them go by, solemn faced and silent. There must be a sense of shock; probably a feeling of resentment against the police. Why did they let it happen? Despite all the publicity, fictional and documentary, violent crime, when it strikes home, still arouses an expectation of miracles. By the same token Wycliffe felt a responsibility for his failure to deliver.

The garage man had his head under the bonnet of a car and did not see them.

The tide was in, the creek and river were brimming. Swans and ducks cruised close inshore. Wycliffe and Lucy Lane walked along the river bank, past the kissing-gate to the churchyard, and on towards the houseboat.

Chapter Thirteen

Wednesday morning (continued)

Wycliffe said, 'Lucy, how many bats do you think there are likely to be within, say, a mile radius from here?'

'I've no idea: dozens, I suppose. Scores for all I know. Why?'

'I was just wondering.'

This was the beginning of a strange interlude in the continuing relationship between Wycliffe and his two closest associates. The next few hours would remain in the memories of Lucy Lane and Kersey as the period during which they had lost contact with him, when he neither heeded their opinions nor offered them encouragement or direction.

They were drawing level with the houseboat. No music this morning. The canoe floated astern. Jumbo, his arms resting on the rail, was looking down at them, his expression gloomy.

'Mr Lavin about?'

'He's in the cabin.'

'We'll drop in for a word.'

'You don't think we should be getting on to the farm, sir?'

'No hurry. I want to talk to Lavin about bats.'

Lucy followed Wycliffe up the gangway and Lavin came on deck to meet them.

'You'd better come below.'

In the cabin Lucy looked about her with interest. It was obvious that the routine of the boat had been disturbed. On a small trestle table at the foot of the companionway there was a coffee pot, a couple of used mugs, and eggy plates with crumbs of toast. A door stood open to a tiny cabin aft where there were two bunks with sleeping bags and a blanket or two.

Lavin, eyeing Lucy, was careful to present his uninjured profile. He closed the door on the bunks and found them seats.

Wycliffe said, 'You've heard about Jordan?'

'Yes.'

'May I ask how?'

'Rain or shine I go for a walk along the river bank in the early morning. This morning, as I was approaching Trecara, I met Vinter on his way home. He looked ghastly. I asked him what was up and he pointed back to Trecara, muttering something about the vicar, and hurried past.'

'What time was this?'

'Time? We don't take much count of time but I suppose it must have been between half-six and seven. He was in no state for a chat and he didn't want my company. I walked on and found the police at the gatehouse; they'd just arrived. Carey was there, looking like Marley's ghost, and he told me what had happened. But it was obvious enough; the poor devil was lying half in and half out of a pool of water with his head bashed in.'

'Have you seen Vinter since?'

'I haven't seen anybody. I had half a mind to look in at the farm but Stephanie isn't the sort to welcome visitors in moments of crisis.'

Wycliffe said, 'I came here to ask you about bats.'

'About bats?' Lavin's astonishment was obvious. 'What about them?'

'How many do you think there might be within the area that interests Vinter?'

Lavin shrugged. 'You should ask him. He concerns himself only with the immediate neighbourhood and, on the basis of figures he quoted to me, he's looking at a population of considerably less than a hundred. They seem to be spread over four species, mainly pipistrelles. About a third of them roost in the roof of the old tower, while the rest are scattered over a number of sites: house roofs, barns, an old adit . . . You name it. But what's all this about?'

'I've been wondering what Vinter did during those hours and

whole nights when his bats failed to keep him occupied — especially out of season.'

Wycliffe received a quick look from Lucy Lane with whom the coin had dropped.

Lavin too. 'Don't you think you should ask him?'

'I would if I could. Vinter is missing.'

'*Missing*?'

'After seeing you it seems he collected a few pounds cash they happened to have in the house and cleared off — in the farm-truck.'

Lavin was incredulous. 'But that's absurd! You're not suggesting that he had anything to do with what happened to the vicar? The man was upset — distressed.'

'I'm not suggesting anything, Mr Lavin, I'm telling you what happened.'

Lavin was fingering his beard. 'There's something damned odd going on!'

'I agree. I also think that your friendship with Vinter was closer than you or he have led me to believe. Did he often spend the whole or part of the night here?'

There was an interval while Lavin decided how to react. He didn't argue or protest but he chose his words with care. 'I think you should understand how things were at the farm while Jessica was alive. The Vinter family were in an intolerable position, and poor old Laurence could hardly deny that it was he who had got them into it. There was bound to be tension between him and his wife and there was no outlet. It was difficult for them to have a discussion, let alone a row, that wasn't monitored by Jessica. And, above all, however they felt about each other, they had to share a room and a bed . . .'

'So?'

A faint smile. 'You are quite right. Until comparatively recently, Laurence would often spend the whole or part of the night on the floor in this cabin. We kept a mattress, a pillow, and a few blankets always ready for him.'

'He never clashed with Jessica's visits?' It was the first time Lucy had spoken.

Lavin looked at her as though he had just been reminded of her presence. 'Obviously he knew when she was away.'

'But recently he has not come so often?'

'He has not come at all at night. I suspect that he made another arrangement. We never discuss the subject. Of course, he looks in of an evening and at weekends and he knows that he is always welcome when it suits him to come.'

Wycliffe stood up, his manner was brisk. 'Thank you, Mr Lavin, you've told me what I wanted to know.'

Lavin saw them off. At the gangway, he said, 'Vinter is a man with a conscience. As a policeman you must know what a liability that can be.'

The sun was shining, the tide was at flood, there were green reflections in the water and everywhere there was stillness.

As they turned up towards the farmhouse Lucy Lane said: 'Bat-watching as an alibi for spending nights out of his wife's bed . . . '

'What about it?'

'Just the cosy accommodations which are possible between men where women are concerned.'

'And not the other way round?'

'That's our weakness.'

A uniformed constable stood by the front door which was a little open.

'DC Curnow is parked in the yard, sir. I believe there's been a message for you.'

Wycliffe tapped on the door and a woman's voice called, 'Come in!'

Stephanie was in the living room. She stood up as he came in, a book in her hand, a finger marking her place. The book was *Madame Bovary*. 'Have you anything to tell me?'

'I'm afraid not, Mrs Vinter.'

She was pale but otherwise she looked as Wycliffe had first seen her: the straight blonde hair with its meticulous central parting, the blue pinafore frock, and the blouse with a pattern of tiny rosebuds. Her hard blue eyes studied her visitors.

'What will happen when you find him?'

Wycliffe was abrupt. 'That depends on the circumstances. Where is your son?'

'He's up in his room. Do we have to stay here?'

'You are a free agent as long as we know where to find you.'

'Hector Carey has invited us to stay at Trecara until this . . . '

'Until this has blown over?' Wycliffe's tone was like a slap in the face.

She had the grace to look embarrassed. 'It is easy for you to be censorious, Superintendent.' She turned to Lucy Lane. 'You see, don't you? The plucky little woman should stand by her husband in all things.'

Wycliffe looked at her, his grey eyes appraising but also puzzled. 'You believe your husband to be guilty of murder – of double murder, Mrs Vinter?'

She flushed. 'You have no right to ask me that question, Superintendent.'

Still watching her, his eyes grave, Wycliffe said: 'No right at all.'

In the yard, Lucy said, 'You were rough on her, sir.'

'You think so?'

DC Curnow, all six foot three of him, was standing beside his car. 'Mr Kersey wants you to ring him, sir.'

Hens were stalking about the yard, pecking at anything which showed between the cobbles. A man in overalls, presumably Geach's nominee, was brooming out the goat house.

Wycliffe got into the car and phoned Kersey who sounded mildly put out. 'I've had the press here, sir, wanting a statement.'

'What did you tell them?'

'I referred them to the Press Officer at HQ.'

'Good! Is that all?'

'No. Not long after we put out the fax on Vinter there was a call from the Transport police at Truro Station. The truck is in the station car park, standing out like a sore thumb among all the private cars.'

'Did they follow it up?'

'Yes. A man in overalls took a single standard class ticket for Plymouth shortly before the seven twenty-one was due to leave.'

'Any evidence that he boarded the train?'

'They're trying to contact the conductor who checked the tickets. I've been on to Charlie Harris at the Plymouth nick and he's going through the motions.'

'Anything from the vicarage?'

'They've hardly got going, sir. I sent Dixon with a WPC. I thought she might cope better with Celia.' Kersey added after a pause, 'You seem very laid back about the Vinter angle, sir. I mean, we've got a presumed double murderer on the run –'

'That I let slip through my fingers.' Wycliffe hesitated. 'I understand how you feel, Doug, and I don't want you to be too much involved with the Vinter saga. Then, if the sky falls, you'll be like Macavity.'

'What about him?'

'He wasn't there.'

Wycliffe got out of the car and stood, for a moment or two, looking about him, then he turned to DC Curnow. 'I want you to report back to Mr Kersey. Ask him to see that the constable here is relieved as necessary.'

Then to Lucy Lane. 'We are going to the tower.'

'Curnow could drop us off in the Trecara drive, sir.'

'No.'

They walked along the river bank. The screens were still in place around the gatehouse but there was no sign of activity. They continued up the slope, through the larchwood, and arrived on the marshy plateau without a word spoken. The tower loomed out of the scrub, looking more impressive because of the surrounding plain. They followed a raised, stony path which formed a causeway across the marsh to the door at the base of the tower. The lintel above the door was of slate and deeply incised with an inscription: 'Elvira 1833 – 1857. *Amor aeternus.*'

Lucy said, 'I wonder if he would have put up a monument if she'd died at forty-four instead of twenty-four.'

'You're a cynic, Lucy.'

'I'm a realist where men are concerned.'

The stout door, studded with hand-forged nails, was held fast by a crook in a staple. Wycliffe opened the door and they were faced with a spiral stair which wound upwards around a massive central pillar or giant newel post. As they climbed and made circuits of the pillar they came across small lancet windows through which they had fleeting glimpses over the countryside. Lucy counted sixty-eight steps before they came to another door, blocking their way.

Wycliffe muttered, 'Only a latch-lock.' And to Lucy's surprise he produced a length of stiff wire from his pocket, bent it into shape, and had the door open almost at once. 'My one parlour trick.'

The door opened into a circular room about nine feet in diameter. It was windowless except for a single slit in the circular wall into which someone had wedged a piece of transparent plastic, neatly cut to shape. Beneath the window there was a granite slab supported on pillars, like an altar. There was just enough light to see by.

Lucy said, 'It's a little chapel!'

The floor, swept clean, was tiled in slate and the wall had been decorated with murals but the paint had flaked off leaving only hints of what had once been there. Taking up most of the floor space was a camp bed, a wicker chair, a table with a lamp on it, a small bookcase with three or four shelves, and an oil stove of the old type with a fretted top.

Wycliffe said, as though to himself, 'This is where he does most of his bat-watching.'

Lucy sensed the relief in his voice. 'You expected this?'

'Something like it.'

There were army blankets folded neatly on the mattress, there was even a pillow of sorts. The shelves held several books as well as a tin kettle, a saucepan, a teapot, and a china mug.

Lucy watched while Wycliffe walked very slowly around, looking at everything, taking it in. He seemed to approve of what he saw, and finally he said, 'Do you ever feel you could settle for something like this, Lucy?'

She looked at him in astonishment. 'As a way of life? Starting from here I should end up with a cardboard box, under a bridge.'

Wycliffe nodded. 'You're probably right; it's a slippery slope.'

At last, with seeming reluctance, he said, 'We had no breakfast and if we don't go now, we shall get no lunch.'

'You are not going to search the place – or have it searched?'

'Later.'

They arrived at the Incident Room just as Kersey was leaving for the pub. He was subdued, almost sullen.

'The chief has been trying to contact you, sir. He seemed to be in a bit of a twist.'

'He'll be at lunch now.'

At the Hopton, Johnny Glynn was behind the bar as usual but Wycliffe thought the man gave him a strange look. No doubt Tom Reed had been talking to him.

The table usually occupied by the Careys was empty.

They ate in silence for a while but it wasn't in Kersey's nature either to sustain a grievance or to keep quiet for long. He said, 'Are you going to be around this afternoon, sir?'

'Yes.'

'No reports of any sightings from Plymouth. He must be lying low. In overalls and with hardly any money it can't be easy.'

Wycliffe said nothing and Kersey tried again. 'Fox found muddy footprints on one of the crates in the gatehouse. It looks as though somebody stood on it to get greater clout – as you said. He's taken it away to examine it for possible prints.'

'Good.'

The meal continued in silence and while they were still drinking their coffee Wycliffe got up to leave. 'I shall be in my office.'

Kersey turned to Lucy, half-accusing. 'Are you in on this, whatever it is?'

She told him what she knew.

'What did he mean about me being like Macavity – isn't that the name of his cat?'

557

Lucy grinned. 'Macavity was T.S. Eliot's Mystery Cat who, whatever feline crime had been committed, always had an alibi. He wasn't there.'

'What a thing it must be, to have an education.'

'You must have heard of the musical – *Cats*.'

'Perhaps. Anyway, it sounded a bit nasty to me.'

'I don't think he intended it that way; he's up to something and he's worried. He doesn't want anybody else involved.'

Kersey grinned. 'In case the sky falls.'

'I suppose so.'

In the afternoon there was a long session on the telephone with the chief. Acrimonious at the start, it ended in a resigned acceptance of a situation that couldn't be changed. 'Well, I hope you're right, Charles. If you're wrong, the media will roast us.' Oldroyd sighed. 'And in a year or two I was hoping to go out, peaceably, with my OBE. Clarice was looking forward to that.'

Oldroyd's prospective OBE was a perennial joke in the two families; so all was not lost.

As Wycliffe dropped the telephone the duty officer came in. 'Johnny Glynn from the Hopton wants a word, sir. He won't talk to anybody else.'

Johnny looked nervous, but determined. 'I could have said my say back at the pub but I don't want my wife involved.'

He sat down, looking about him with curiosity. 'I used to be in here pretty often as a boy, usually to get my backside tanned.'

'You wanted to tell me something, Mr Glynn?'

'Yes. Inspector Reed came to see me this morning. I'm sure you know what about. Anyway, I refused to talk to him.'

Wycliffe said nothing, and Johnny went on, 'I suffered quite a bit of aggro over this business the first time round. I told Reed and his boss at the time that I wasn't involved and that was the truth.'

'I think that is accepted.'

Johnny was flushed; little beads of sweat stood out on his forehead and his gestures were exaggerated. He was well primed. 'I was going to marry Jessica Dobell. It was understood.

But she couldn't settle for one man and it was the other man she was with that night . . . ' He shook his head. 'That finished me!'

Abruptly, he said, 'Do you mind if I smoke?' He brought out a pack of cigarettes, lit one, and leaned forward, confidentially: 'There's another thing I think you should know. It was Jessica who was driving that night.'

'I understood that she couldn't drive.'

Johnny spread his hands in a helpless gesture. 'The silly bugger was trying to teach her . . . In that lane, with a foot clearance when you're lucky!' He broke off. 'Well, you've got to remember, Mr Wycliffe, we were all a lot younger then – and a bit mad.'

Wycliffe said: 'The other man?'

Johnny sat back in his chair. 'No names, Mr Wycliffe. What I know came out in one hell of a row I had with Jessica at the time. I kept quiet then, when it would have helped me to speak out, and I shan't talk now. I've got my living to get in this village.'

He reached forward to tap ash into Kersey's little bowl. 'I came here because if you knew the facts you might ask yourself what was to be gained by stirring it all up. It was a bad business but there must be a limit. Anyway, this is a private chat – no witnesses, no statement.' He sat back, rather pleased with himself, and waited.

Wycliffe said, 'I've listened to what you have told me.'

Johnny waited a little longer, expecting more, but when no more came he stood up. 'Well, I must be getting back . . . '

At five o'clock Wycliffe went to the post office stores and bought a few things; at six he announced that he would not be in for the evening meal, and telephoned Helen; at six-thirty he set off with a borrowed rucksack slung over his shoulder.

He was in a strange mood, almost one of desperation. He *knew*, but in the absence of material evidence he could not act. And that fool, Vinter . . . One had to sympathise, perhaps admire, but it was wrong, and sure to prove tragically wrong in its consequences. Now he was virtually putting *his* job on the line in behaviour almost as quixotic.

He followed the path along the river bank which for him had acquired a symbolic significance, it was the link binding together the elements in his chain: Trecara with its folly, the farmhouse, the houseboat, the church, Trigg, and the old school which was his base.

In the valley it was already evening, the light had a golden hue and the birds were silent. The tide was running out and there were banks of mud being worked over by the gulls. A tidal creek or inlet is not a single landscape, but a cycle of landscapes following the changing patterns of time and tide.

Somewhere in the woods across the river there was a shot which put up a flight of flustered and flapping pigeons. Looking up into the churchyard, through the kissing-gate, he could see a woman on her knees, tending one of the graves.

There was no one to be seen on the houseboat but smoke came from the cowled chimney. The farmhouse looked deserted but there would be a uniformed man on duty there somewhere. It was the thing to do, in case Vinter returned to his home. Wycliffe was not in a mood to appreciate the irony of it.

Smoke drifted idly upwards from one of the Trecara chimneys and the screens were still in place at the gatehouse.

He followed the track up through the larchwood and on to the marshy plateau. The tower stood out against a dark, towering cloud mass in the southern sky.

The nearer he got to his goal the more absurd his project seemed. He crossed the causeway, let himself into the tower and climbed the spiral staircase to the locked door. A moment later he was inside, and he felt better. It was considerably darker than it had been in the morning and he could just make out the objects which he knew to be there. He took a torch from his rucksack and swept the room with its beam.

Nothing had changed.

He had planned what he would do. First he would light the lamp and the oil stove. He had assumed that there would be enough paraffin, and there was. Life on his father's farm had taught him something about paraffin and bottled gas. Vinter's lamp was a monster, with twin wicks and a pink glass bowl on a fretted brass stand. It spread a pale but sufficient radiance over the little room. The oil stove did not flare, flicker, or 'yellow' and was soon casting the shadow of its fretted top on the ceiling. The place was becoming cosy.

He emptied his rucksack on to the table: a couple of cans of beer, a piece of cheese, some bread rolls, a bar of chocolate, a bottle of water, and a portable telephone.

Half past seven. He peered through the slit window; the clouds now covered as much of the sky as he could see. Soon it would rain; and soon it would be quite dark. In the lamplight the paintings on the wall seemed to acquire increased definition; he could make out trees, a faun, a woman in a flowing gown. He noticed too that the boarded ceiling had been painted at one time but he could make nothing of the design.

There was a hatch which must give access to the dome and, presumably, to the bats. He wondered how Vinter got up there, then realised that the ceiling was low and that by standing on the table, a tall, active man could make it.

He was beginning to feel at home. Sometimes he felt not only that he understood, but that he had some kinship with those who deliberately narrowed their horizons, drew in their tentacles, and retreated from life.

He looked at Vinter's books: biographies, journals and diaries in French, German, and English, and recognised another bond; the attempt to live at second-hand.

He began his search of the room. It was no great task. He found what he was looking for, under the camp bed, in a shallow cardboard box without a lid. The box held Jessica's missing half-wellingtons in a plastic bag, a Bible, the mutilated remains of a *Church Quarterly* magazine, a few sheets of notepaper and some envelopes. He did not handle his finds but left them in the box in full view, on the floor.

He was just in time. There were footsteps on the stairs, slow, weary footsteps. Wycliffe turned down the lamp. It seemed an interminable time before there came a fumbling with the latch-lock and the door opened.

Wycliffe turned up the lamp. 'I was beginning to think you wouldn't come.'

Vinter stood just inside the door, holding on to it as though for support. 'Christ! I might have known.'

He came forward into the room, staggering with fatigue, and slumped into the wicker chair. He looked at the cardboard box with its contents.

'So you found them?'

'Of course; you knew they were there.'

'I put them there, didn't I?'

Wycliffe looked down at him and said, in a tone of mild rebuke, 'Don't play the bloody fool, Vinter, and don't treat me like one.'

Chapter Fourteen

Thursday morning

It was five in the morning, still dark and chilly, when a police car dropped Wycliffe off at the Hopton. He let himself in with the key Johnny had given him. In his room, he undressed, had a quick wash, and got into bed. He told himself that in the next few hours he must be in a position to show that his conclusions were inescapable. '*Inescapable*,' he muttered the word, drowsily – repeatedly, and its syllables seemed to acquire an hypnotic rhythm: in-es-cap-a-ble, so that he fell asleep.

The next thing he knew it was daylight and his little clock showed seven-thirty. He joined Kersey and Lucy Lane in the dining room for the tail end of the eight o'clock radio news.

'It has just been reported that during the night a man attended voluntarily at Truro Police Station in connection with the murders of Jessica Dobell and the Reverend Michael Jordan in the village of Moresk just outside the town. The man has not been named and a spokesman said that he had not been charged with any offence but was helping with inquiries.

'Yesterday, the police issued a description of Laurence Vinter, a farm worker, employed by the murdered woman, and wanted for questioning in connection with the crimes.'

There were several people at breakfast, more than on any day so far, and Kersey warned, 'Press, on the next table; ears flapping.'

Kersey and Lucy were subdued, conscious of the need to get back into step, but unable to speak of what was uppermost in their minds, so the three dissected their kippers in silence. Even

563

Johnny had his own reasons for keeping away, and it was a relief when Wycliffe said, 'Well, if we are ready . . . '

Outside it was a typical late-April morning with a moist softness in the air and the promise of a warm day.

Kersey went to buy cigarettes and newspapers at the post office and came back grumbling, 'They looked at me like I was Dracula.'

In his office Wycliffe's manner was still detached. 'Anything from the vicar's papers?'

Lucy said, 'I spent most of yesterday afternoon with Curnow and WPC Dash going through them. Apart from his professional records and correspondence, we found only sermon notes and little essays on knotty theological points. Student stuff. I've rarely seen anybody with fewer personal papers; certainly nothing in the nature of a diary.'

Wycliffe seemed resigned. 'It was too much to expect that he made a record of whatever he knew. Why should he?'

Kersey brought the conversation around to Vinter. 'So the official line is that he gave himself up.'

'He *did* give himself up.'

Lucy Lane asked, 'But what persuaded him to come back?'

'He wasn't going anywhere; there was nowhere for him to go. The Plymouth thing was a feint to get us off his back for a while. In fact he went no further than Truro, and spent yesterday skulking around, keeping out of sight as much as possible. He returned to the tower on foot, after dark, with a half-bottle of whisky and a supply of aspirin tablets. I suppose he hoped for the chance to do what he felt he must do, calmly and with a bit of dignity.' Wycliffe sounded oddly defensive.

Kersey looked at him in surprise. 'Suicide! You expected that?'

'Of course I didn't *expect* it!' Wycliffe sounded irritable. 'But after seeing his hideaway in the tower I felt sure that he would come back to it – that was all. I suppose it's what I might have done myself.' He made an apologetic gesture. 'At any rate, I was sure he wasn't stupid enough to go on the run.'

'But why suicide?' From Lucy Lane.

Wycliffe's eyelids were pricking and there was a heaviness at the base of his skull. He could have done with a couple of those aspirins.

'As Vinter saw it, our investigation, if it was allowed to go on, could lead to only one conclusion, and he felt that he couldn't live with the consequences of that.'

Wycliffe had been fiddling with the objects on his desk, arranging and rearranging them. (In stressful times he still missed his pipe.) He looked up. 'I don't know if Vinter loves his wife, he's certainly proud of her, yet it was he who brought on her the humiliations of life on the farm, and he can't forget that.'

Kersey was looking at Wycliffe, his lined features creased even more deeply by doubt. 'I don't know about Lucy, but I'm still at sea.'

'It's simple enough. Vinter intended to offer himself as a nice, tidy, uncomplaining scapegoat and, if he had succeeded, the evidence being what it is, we should have been forced to pack up and go home. You can't prosecute a dead man but you can saddle him with a load of guilt, and Vinter wanted to settle for that. It was my problem to persuade him otherwise. Even now he's biding his time in a police cell waiting to make some damn-fool confession.'

Lucy Lane said, 'But the circumstantial and some material evidence *is* against him.'

'Yes, and there's more in the tower. Fox is up there now, giving the place a thorough going over. In this case evidence likely to incriminate Vinter has been scattered about like confetti.'

He shifted uncomfortably in his chair. 'Although we worked out a specification for our criminal we made no use of it except to agree that it didn't fit any of our suspects. We laid stress on the planning, on the obsessive attention to detail, but we ignored the absence of any identifiable overall purpose. I said something about revenge and defilement but didn't follow it up. The crime was anarchic, not planned to achieve anything, only to disrupt.'

Lucy Lane agreed. 'A disturbed mind reacting to real or imagined frustration.'

Kersey fished in his pocket for cigarettes. 'Soon somebody is going to say "paranoia"; then I shall go.' He lit a cigarette. 'Back to Vinter, I've been reading the transcript, and I must admit there are times when you wonder if he wasn't deliberately landing himself in it, leaving himself open to suspicion. It took him a while to decide what he had on his feet when he walked by the river that night and he finally settled for wellingtons.'

Lucy Lane said, 'So he's shielding either his wife or his son.'

Wycliffe said nothing, and Lucy Lane looked at him with curiosity. 'What exactly happened last night, sir?'

He seemed put out by the question but after a brief hesitation he said, 'We ate some bread and cheese and drank a can of beer.' He gave Lucy a sidelong glance. 'We also talked, but not on the record, and there will be no report. It was two o'clock when I phoned Division, asking them to divert a patrol car.'

He sat back in his chair as though to signal that discussion was over, and turned to Kersey. 'I hope you realise, Doug, that I put myself out on a limb and it was no place for company.'

Kersey looked embarrassed. 'Being out on a limb has never bothered me unduly, sir, but I take your point. I understand.'

'Good. Now, I want you to look after things here and deal with Fox. Lucy and I will be at the farm. Keep me informed of any developments.

'Ready, Lucy?'

They were just leaving when the telephone rang and Wycliffe answered it.

Fox, pleased with himself. 'I've got two possibles, sir: an index finger and thumb of the right hand on one of the boots, and just a suggestion of a thumb on the magazine that needs enhancement. I'm pretty sure, but I'll do a full comparison check back at the nick.'

For once, Wycliffe's heart warmed toward his scenes-of-crime officer. It was not much, but it was something to put in the file.

The media people had lingered over breakfast but now they were gathered around the old school entrance. He pushed through them with a curt, 'No statement!'

Lucy made for his car, still parked in the square, and this time he made no objection. There were unusual numbers of people in the square, gathered in little groups as though they sensed that another act in the drama was about to be played.

As he got into the car he said, 'Of course, this case will never come to court.'

When they were driving out of the square, Lucy said, 'So you've made up your mind.'

'I should have seen it earlier. Instead I talked nonsense about female psychology. It was only on Tuesday evening that I came to terms with the idea. Of course Jordan knew, and I should have guessed as much from his attitude. But by Wednesday morning Jordan was dead, and it was too late.

'I even warned him, without being clear in my own mind what I was warning him about . . This case has been a shambles from the start, Lucy.'

They drove up Church Lane, past the church, and clear of the houses. Lucy pulled up at the farm entrance and Wycliffe got out to open the rickety gate. The goats were browsing as usual and, in the sunshine, Elvira's tower looked more like a misplaced lighthouse than ever.

Gingerly, Lucy drove down the rutted track to the farmyard entrance and stopped at the second gate. Wycliffe did not get out immediately and Lucy sensed his reluctance.

'How will you handle this one, sir?'

'As gently as possible. Vinter is in custody and we are asking his wife and son to make further statements. That must be our line for the moment. Of course any formal interrogation will be on the record with a lawyer and, perhaps, a psychologist or one of that ilk, sitting in. But I would like a chat beforehand.'

They were still in the car, watching the hens pecking over the cobbles. Vinter's stand-in was tinkering with an ancient tractor. He looked across at them, but showed no particular interest.

Wycliffe pushed open the car door. 'Let's get it over!'

The house door was shut; Wycliffe knocked, but there was no response.

The man with the tractor called to them, 'I haven't seen anybody this morning but you could try around the front.'

567

They walked around the house to the front door which was slightly open. Wycliffe knocked again with no result so he pushed the door wide and called out. The narrow passage hall was almost blocked by two large suitcases, and by books, tied in bundles and stacked against the wall.

Giles was standing at the far end of the passage looking vague. 'My mother isn't here.' He was not wearing his glasses and his face looked oddly naked and vulnerable.

'It seems you're moving out.'

The boy looked at the cases and the books. 'Yes. Mother is down at Trecara, getting our rooms ready.'

Lucy followed Wycliffe through into the sitting room and the three of them stood facing each other in semi-darkness. The curtains had not been drawn back.

Wycliffe said, 'Perhaps we could have some light.'

Lucy Lane drew back the curtains and the three of them sat down.

Wycliffe said, 'You're not wearing your glasses.'

'No, they fell off, and I stepped on them.'

'Haven't you got a spare pair?'

'Yes, upstairs.'

'Then why not go up and get them?'

The boy sat, hands on his thighs, massaging them in a curious stroking movement that rocked his body to and fro. He was very pale. He said nothing for a time, then, 'No, I'll get them later.'

The rocking movement continued and the blue, unfocused eyes seemed to shut him off from real contact.

Wycliffe said, 'You know that your father is in custody?'

A flicker of the eyelids. 'He is not my father.'

'Not your father?'

'My father died before I was born. He was a famous mathematician. That man is my stepfather.'

'Have you always known this?'

'I have always thought that he could not be my father. He is a stupid man.'

'Very well. Your stepfather wants to confess to the murders of Jessica Dobell and Michael Jordan.'

568

The rocking movement ceased, but there was no other response. He sat, motionless, his eyes unfocused.

'Do you think your stepfather is guilty of those crimes, Giles?'

The boy clasped his hands tightly together and there was a long silence before he said, 'He deserves to suffer; more than any of them.'

Lucy Lane asked, 'More than Jessica Dobell?'

The blue eyes were turned on her and a hint of a smile trembled on his lips. 'She's dead.'

Wycliffe wondered at the mental deterioration which appeared to have taken place in such a short time. 'Why did you dislike Jessica so much?'

The rocking movement was resumed and he spoke in a harsh voice: 'She was an animal! She tried once to get me to . . . '

Lucy Lane asked, 'What did she try to get you to do?'

'I don't know.'

Lucy tried again, 'Do you disapprove of all people who enjoy sex, Giles?'

The question disturbed him. Two or three times he looked from Lucy to Wycliffe and back again. Finally he shook his head and did not reply.

Wycliffe said, 'I thought you were fond of Julie Geach.'

For the first time Giles raised his voice. 'I don't want to talk about her!' He made oddly defensive movements with his arms as though warding off a blow. 'Her father called me a . . . No, I won't talk about it. I won't!'

Lucy Lane looked across at Wycliffe, a look which asked clearly enough, 'How far do we go with this?'

Lucy was right to sound a warning note, but for him there were other considerations than the Rules of Evidence. Almost holding his breath, Wycliffe asked, 'Why did you attack Michael Jordan?'

The boy trembled as though in an effort of self-control but he managed to speak calmly, 'I didn't want to hurt him.'

'So why did you?'

The rocking movement recommenced and for some time he did not speak. Then, very quietly and reasonably, he said, 'I set them a puzzle which I knew that nobody could solve . . I wanted to see

569

what they would do. I wanted to make them suffer and pay for everything . . . '

'And the vicar?'

'He saw me with that woman's boots in the churchyard. I didn't know, but he told me, and he said that I must tell them, that I must go to you.' His hand, resting on his thighs, were squeezing the flesh so tightly that he must have suffered pain. 'He threatened me. He shouldn't have done that . . . '

In the silence that followed, the telephone startled all three of them. Lucy went to answer it. There was a brief exchange, and she replaced the receiver.

'That was Mr Carey; he says that he was expecting your mother earlier this morning but that she hasn't arrived.'

For a while the boy gave no sign that he had heard, then, in a flat voice and looking straight ahead, he said, 'She's upstairs.'

Wycliffe signed to Lucy to stay and started up the stairs.

The door of the Vinters' room was wide open. The curtains were drawn across the little window, but there was enough light to see the form of a woman on the bed. At close quarters he could hear shallow, irregular breathing. He swept back the curtains, letting in the light.

Stephanie Vinter, wearing a dressing gown over her nightdress, was lying across the bed. A good deal of blood had seeped into the honeycomb quilt from a wound in her head, concealed by her hair. As he stood over her she opened her eyes but there was no sign of recognition. She moaned briefly and her eyes closed again.

Wycliffe went to the top of the stairs. 'Ambulance, Lucy! She has a head wound with some loss of blood but she's semi-conscious . . . '

Back in the room he saw on the floor an old-style desk lamp which he remembered as being on the bedside table. Its base was stained with blood. The boy's spectacles lay beside it where they had fallen and been trodden upon.

He turned to find Giles standing in the doorway. 'She isn't dead, is she? . . I couldn't sleep and when it was getting light I came in to talk to her . . We sat on the bed, and I told her . . . ' He had difficulty with his speech, choking on the words. 'She tried to

tell me that I should .. She said we would go together .. I
couldn't believe it! . . . I was angry and I picked up the lamp and
my glasses fell off . . . '

Thursday evening

It was ten-fifteen and the three were sitting at their table in the
restaurant after a late snack meal. The kitchen had closed long
ago and they were alone in the room. Through the glass doors
they could see the usual group of regulars clustered on stools
around the bar.

On their table was a bottle of burgundy; Kersey picked it up
and held it to the light. 'There's another drink in there. Shall we
split it?'

Lucy put a hand over her glass and Wycliffe shook his head.

'All right; mustn't let it go to waste.'

Wycliffe said, 'Vinter was at the hospital with his wife this
afternoon. It seems she's conscious. I wonder what will happen
there.'

Lucy said, 'I wonder more what will happen to the boy.'

'It won't be up to us, thank God! And I doubt if the lawyers
will have much say. He's spending the next two or three days
under observation in the psychiatric ward at the hospital and it's
from there that the magistrates will take their cue.'

Kersey finished off the wine. 'Was Vinter the boy's father, or
wasn't he?'

Wycliffe yawned behind his hand. 'Does it matter? The trick
cyclists will enjoy finding out. But, whether he was or not, the
boy's hatred was directed mainly against him.'

Lucy Lane said, 'I'm going to work on Johnny for some more
coffee.'

Kersey watched her go. 'She's coming on, that girl.' Which
from Kersey was praise indeed.

Wycliffe was twisting his wine glass by the stem, watching the
reflections in the bowl. 'It's been an eventful week: two murders,
a psychotic teenager in custody and his mother in hospital; the
Met investigating the dubious dealings of the church organist
and Abe Geach just one step nearer his four-star dream.'

'You sound bitter.'

'Do I?' Wycliffe sat back in his chair. 'Causes seem so disproportionate to their consequences. Just imagine that Vinter hadn't played the fool with his girl student, or that the Ruse boy had set out on his cycle ten minutes earlier, or that Giles Vinter had drawn a different number in the gene raffle, or that almost anything had been just that little bit different . . It's no wonder Jessica went to a fortune teller.'

Lucy came back. 'Johnny is bringing the coffee. He says there's to be a service of rededication in the church tomorrow morning and that Jessica's funeral will be on Monday afternoon.'

Katherine Geach was sitting up in bed. The clock radio on her bedside table showed a quarter to eleven. The curtains were not drawn and a top window was open to the darkness and the stillness outside. She had a magazine open on her lap but she was not reading, she was looking at herself in the dressing table mirror. Five nights ago her twin sister, Jessica, had been brutally murdered, but here nothing had changed. Had she? She looked in the mirror and felt guilty.

She could hear Abe splashing about in the bathroom. A minute or two later he came in, wearing his dressing gown. He slipped it off and got into bed beside her. After a minute or two his hand reached between her thighs. So far, since Jessica's death, she had refused him.

'Oh, all right.'

He put his arms round her and held her tightly for a while. 'That's my girl! Now let's get that bloody nightdress off.'

In the village of Moresk things were returning to normal.